"A GRAND COLLECTION." —*Booklist*

"A LITERARY SAMPLER, A BOOK WITHOUT PICTURES FOR LOVERS OF WORDS."
—*Houston Post*

"READING *PLAYBOY* WITHOUT THE PICTURES HAS NEVER BEEN MORE SATISFYING."
—*Roanoke Times & World News*

"That *Playboy* has always showcased first-rate mainstream fiction is evident from this superlative anthology of stories . . . constantly entertains and provokes."
—*Publishers Weekly*

ALICE K. TURNER has been *Playboy* fiction editor since 1980; she previously worked as an editor at *New York* magazine, Ballantine Books, *Publishers Weekly*, and *Holiday*. She lives in New York.

"A WORLD OF VARIEGATED BLISSES HERE."

—*Library Journal*

"FABULOUS . . . ONE OF THE TOP SELECTIONS OF SHORT FICTION ON THE MARKET TODAY."

—*Abilene Reporter News*

"Whatever your taste in fiction, there's a story for you here."

—*Wilmington News Journal*

“SATISFYING . . . REELS IN GREAT STORIES FROM DECADES PAST TO HELP MAKE THE MEAL.”

—*Houston Chronicle*

“HERE’S ONE *PLAYBOY* YOU REALLY WILL READ FOR THE STORIES. . . . A FINE ADDITION TO ANY BOOKSHELF.”

—*Albuquerque Journal*

“Burly, two-fisted story collection with high levels of testosterone.”

—*Seattle Times/Post Intelligencer*

Playboy Stories

The Best of Forty Years of Short Fiction

Edited and with an Introduction by
Alice K. Turner

PLUME
Published by the Penguin Group
Penguin Books USA Inc., 375 Hudson Street, New York, New York 10014, U.S.A.
Penguin Books Ltd, 27 Wrights Lane, London W8 5TZ, England
Penguin Books Australia Ltd, Ringwood, Victoria, Australia
Penguin Books Canada Ltd, 10 Alcorn Avenue, Toronto, Ontario, Canada M4V 3B2
Penguin Books (N.Z.) Ltd, 182–190 Wairau Road, Auckland 10, New Zealand

Penguin Books Ltd, Registered Offices: Harmondsworth, Middlesex, England

Published by Plume, an imprint of Dutton Signet,
a division of Penguin Books USA Inc.
Previously published in a Dutton edition.

First Plume Printing, June, 1995
10 9 8 7 6 5 4 3 2 1

Copyright © Playboy Enterprises, Inc., 1994
All rights reserved

REGISTERED TRADEMARK—MARCA REGISTRADA

The Library of Congress has catalogued the Dutton edition as follows:

Playboy stories: the best of forty years of short fiction /
edited and with an introduction by Alice K. Turner.
p. cm.
ISBN 0-525-93735-8 (hc.)
ISBN 0-452-27117-7 (pbk.)
1. Short stories, American. 2. American fiction—20th century.
I. Turner, Alice K.
PS648.S5P53 1993
831'.018054—dc20 93-28754
CIP

Printed in the United States of America
Original hardcover design by Steven N. Stathakis

PUBLISHER'S NOTE
These stories are works of fiction. Names, characters, places, and incidents either are the products of the authors' imagination or are used fictitiously, and any resemblance to actual persons, living or dead, events, or locales are entirely coincidental.

Without limiting the rights under copyright reserved above, no part of this publication may be reproduced, stored in or introduced into a retrieval system, or transmitted, in any form, or by any means (electronic, mechanical, photocopying, recording, or otherwise), without the prior written permission of both the copyright owner and the above publisher of this book.

BOOKS ARE AVAILABLE AT QUANTITY DISCOUNTS WHEN USED TO PROMOTE PRODUCTS OR SERVICES. FOR INFORMATION PLEASE WRITE TO PREMIUM MARKETING DIVISION, PENGUIN BOOKS USA INC., 375 HUDSON STREET, NEW YORK, NEW YORK 10014.

Contents

Preface

Forty years ago, the first issue of *Playboy* magazine appeared, the famous issue with the calendar pinup of Marilyn Monroe. Two short stories, one by Ambrose Bierce and a Sherlock Holmes adventure by Arthur Conan Doyle, were included in its table of contents. Both of these were reprints, of course (as was Marilyn's picture), for the fledgling magazine's shoestring budget did not extend to purchasing new work of the quality it aspired to.

That first issue sold 50,000 copies and made history. There appeared to be a considerable audience for a publication that, in Hugh M. Hefner's words, "would reflect a masculine (though not hairy-chested) zest for all of life" and would be "urban and urbane (not jaded or blasé), sophisticated (not effete), candidly frisky (not sniggering or risqué)." Good fiction was to be an important part of the package.

Cautiously, the editors continued to reprint material from tried-and-true authors (Erskine Caldwell, Somerset Maugham, John Collier, Ray Bradbury) until, in the ninth issue, they printed an original story, "Black Country," by Charles Beaumont (included as the first story in this collection). By the end of the second year, all the stories were new, and major writers like James Jones were already looking to a market that offered a kind of creative freedom largely absent from the "family" magazines that predominated in the 1950s.

Over the past forty years, *Playboy* has published hundreds of stories by the top writers of the second half of the twentieth century. This anthology reprints a selection of the best of them, one from each year since the beginning, a format which has a certain historical neatness. Juggling stories to include as many authors as possible, with no more than one story from each, was not easy, and there were some casualties and near-casualties. For instance, Vladimir Nabokov and Gabriel García Marquez each published quite a few stories, but it turned out that only one story by each writer was legally available—and both were from 1971. What to do?

In this one case we have chosen to include both. Nabokov was so much a part of the magazine in the 1960s and 1970s that he couldn't be left out. And "The Handsomest Drowned Man in the World" is a perfect miniature from Garcia Marquez. We made this exception just once—partly because both stories are short—but some fine writers were unfortunately squeezed out by the limitations of time and space.

Others were left out on purpose. For better or worse, this is largely (though not entirely) an anthology of stories in the "mainstream" literary tradition. *Playboy* has also been a congenial home for top-quality genre fiction, mostly in the crime and suspense field and in science fiction. We are, in fact, the only magazine that regularly and easily crosses the line from literary fiction to genre fiction and then heads back again. Dazzling collections could be compiled along genre lines, and, looking to the future, some fine stories have been saved against that day.

Nearly all of the authors collected here have famous names. Over the years, *Playboy* has found and published many new writers too, and continues to do so in the 1990s, but when the lode of treasure is as great as that found in forty years of these back issues, it is difficult to veer from the masters. They're hardly a like-minded crew. There is no "formula" to *Playboy* fiction—though we admit to a weakness for a good, strong story line—and we think you'll find a pleasing diversity to these stories.

Charles Beaumont

Black Country

September 1954

"Black Country" was the first piece of original fiction *Playboy* published. Its author, Charles Beaumont, who had previously written for the pulps, soon became a contributing editor for the new magazine and wrote many *Playboy* stories and articles before his death in 1967. He was also a screenwriter (*The Seven Faces of Dr. Lao,* among others) and one of the best and best-known scriptwriters for Rod Serling's popular television series, *The Twilight Zone.* "Black Country" could stand as a prototype for *Playboy*'s ideal story of the 1950s with its jazz background, its jazz-inspired tempo, its hint of the supernatural, and its satisfyingly macabre ending.

Charles Beaumont

Black Country

Spoof Collins blew his brains out, all right—right on out through the top of his head. But I don't mean with a gun. I mean with a horn. Every night: slow and easy, eight to one. And that's how he died. Climbing, with that horn, climbing up high. For what? *"Hey, man, Spoof—listen, you picked the tree, now come on down!"* But he couldn't come down, he didn't know how. He just kept climbing, higher and higher. And then he fell. Or jumped. Anyhow, *that's* the way he died.

The bullet didn't kill anything. I'm talking about the one that tore up the top of his mouth. It didn't kill anything that wasn't dead already. Spoof just put in an extra note, that's all.

We planted him out about four miles from town—home is where you drop: residential district, all wood construction. Rain? You know it. Bible type: sky like a month-old bedsheet, wind like a stepped-on cat, cold and dark, those Forty Days, those Forty Nights! But nice and quiet most of the time. Like Spoof: nice and quiet, with a lot underneath that you didn't like to think about.

We planted him and watched and put what was his down into the ground with him. His horn, battered, dented, nicked—right there in his hands, but not just there; I mean in position, so if he wanted to do some more climbing, all right, he could. And his music. We planted that too, because leaving it out would have been like leaving out Spoof's arms or his heart or his guts.

Lux started things off with a chord from his guitar, no particular notes, only a feeling, a sound. A Spoof Collins kind of sound. Jimmy Fritch picked it up with his stick and they talked awhile—Lux got a real piano out of that git-box. Then when Jimmy stopped talking and stood there, waiting, Sonny Holmes stepped up and wiped his mouth and took the melody on his shiny new trumpet. It wasn't Spoof, but it came close; and it was still *The Jimjam Man,* the way Spoof wrote it back when he used to write things down. Sonny got off with a high-squealing blast, and no eyes came up—we knew, we remembered. The kid always had it collared. He just never talked about it. And listen to him now! He stood there over Spoof's grave, giving it all back to The Ol' Massuh, giving it back right—*"Broom off, white child, you got four sides!" "I want to learn from you, Mr. Collins. I want to play jazz and you can teach me." "I got things to do, I can't waste no time on a half-hipped young'un." "Please, Mr. Collins." "You got to stop that, you got to stop callin' me 'Mr. Collins' hear?" "Yes sir, yes sir."*—He put out real sound, like he didn't remember a thing. Like he wasn't playing for that pile of dark-meat in the ground, not at all; but for the great Spoof Collins, for the man Who Knew and the man Who Did, who gave jazz spats and dressed up the blues, who did things with a trumpet that a trumpet couldn't do, and more; for the man who could blow down the walls or make a chicken cry, without half trying—for the mighty Spoof, who'd once walked in music like a boy in river mud, loving it, breathing it, living it.

Then Sonny quit. He wiped his mouth again and stepped back and Mr. 'T' took it on his trombone while I beat up the tubs.

Pretty soon we had *The Jimjam Man* rocking the way it used to rock. A little slow, maybe: it needed Bud Meunier on bass and a few trips on the piano. But it moved.

We went through *Take It from Me* and *Night in the Blues* and *Big Gig* and *Only Us Chickens* and *Forty G's*—Sonny's insides came out through the horn on that one, I could tell—and *Slice City Stomp*—you remember: sharp and clean, like sliding down a razor—and *What the Cats Dragged In*—the longs, the shorts, all the great Spoof Collins numbers. We wrapped them up and put them down there with him.

Then it got dark.

And it was time for the last one, the greatest one . . . Rose-Ann shivered and cleared her throat; the rest of us looked around, for the first time, at all those rows of split-wood grave markers, shining in the rain, and the trees and the coffin, dark, wet. Out by the fence, a couple of farmers stood watching. Just watching.

One—Rose-Ann opens her coat, puts hands on hips, wets her lips;

Two—Freddie gets the spit out of his stick, rolls his eyes;

Three—Sonny puts the trumpet to his mouth;

Four—

And we played Spoof's song, his last one, the one he wrote a long way ago, before the music dried out his head, before he turned mean and started climbing: *Black Country.* The song that said just a little of what Spoof wanted to say, and couldn't.

You remember. Spider-slow chords crawling down, soft, easy, and then bottom and silence and, suddenly, the cry of the horn, screaming in one note all the hate and sadness and loneliness, all the want and got-to-have; and then the note dying, quick, and Rose-Ann's voice, a whisper, a groan, a sigh . . .

Black Country is somewhere, Lord,
That I don't want to go.
Black Country is somewhere
That I never want to go.
Rain-water drippin'
On the bed and on the floor,
Rain-water drippin'
From the ground and through the door . . .

We all heard the piano, even though it wasn't there. Fingers moving down those minor chords, those black keys, that black country . . .

Well, in that old Black Country
If you ain't feelin' good,
They let you have an overcoat
That's carved right out of wood.
But 'way down there
It gets so dark
You never see a friend—
Black Country may not be the Most,
But, Lord! it's sure the End . . .

Bitter little laughing words, piling up, now mad, now sad; and then, an ugly blast from the horn and Rose-Ann's voice screaming, crying:

I never want to go there, Lord!
I never want to be,
I never want to lay down
In that Black Country! . . .

And quiet, quiet, just the rain, and the wind.

"Let's go, man," Freddie said.

So we turned around and left Spoof there under the ground.

Or, at least, that's what I thought we did.

▪ ▪ ▪

Sonny took over without saying a word. He didn't have to: just who was about to fuss? He was white, but he didn't play white, not these days; and he learned the hard way—by unlearning. Now he could play gut-bucket and he could play blues, stomp and slide, name it, Sonny could play it. Funny as hell to hear, too, because he looked like everything else but a musician. Short and skinny, glasses, nose like a melted candle, head clean as the one-ball, and white? Next to old Hushup, that cafe sunburn glowed like a flashlight.

"Man, who skinned you?"

"Who dropped you in the flour barrel?"

But he got closer to Spoof than any of the rest of us did. He knew what to do, and why. Just like a school teacher all the time: "That's good, Lux, that's awful good—now let's play some music." "Get off it, C. T.—what's Lenox Avenue doing in the middle of Lexington?" "Come on, boys, hang on to the sound, hang on to it!" Always using words like 'flavor' and 'authentic' and 'blood,' peering over those glasses, pounding his feet right through the floor: *STOMP! STOMP!* "That's it, we've got it now—oh, listen! It's true, it's clean!" *STOMP! STOMP!*

Not the easiest to dig him. Nobody broke all the way through.

"How come, boy? What for?"

And every time the same answer:

"I want to play jazz."

Like he'd joined the Church and didn't want to argue about it.

Spoof was still Spoof when Sonny started coming around. Not a lot of people with us then, but a few, enough—the longhairs and critics and connoisseurs—and some real ears too—enough to fill a club every night, and who needs more? It was COLLINS AND HIS CREW, tight and neat, never a performance, always a session. Lots of music, lots of fun. And a line-up that some won't forget: Jimmy Fritch on clarinet, Honker Reese on alto-sax, Charles di Lusso on tenor, Spoof on trumpet, Henry Walker on piano, Lux Anderson on banjo and myself—Hushup Paige—on drums. New mown hay, all right, I know—I remember, I've heard the records we cut—but, the Road was there.

Sonny used to hang around the old Continental Club on State Street in Chicago, every night, listening. Eight o'clock roll 'round, and there he'd be—a little different: younger, skinnier—listening hard, over in a corner all to himself, eyes closed like he was asleep. Once in a while he put in a request—*Darktown Strutter's Ball* was one he liked, and some of Jelly Roll's numbers—but mostly he just sat there, taking it all in. For real.

And it kept up like this for two or three weeks, regular as 2/4.

Now Spoof was mean in those days—don't think he wasn't—but not blood-mean. Even so, the white boy in the corner bugged Ol' Massuh after a while and he got to making dirty cracks with his horn: *WAAAAA! Git your ass out of here. WAAAAA! You only* think *you're with it! WAAAAA! There's a little white child sittin' in a chair there's a little white child losin' all his hair . . .*

It got to the kid, too, every bit of it. And that made Spoof even madder. But what can you do?

Came Honker's trip to Slice City along about then: our sax-man got a neck all full of the sharpest kind of steel. So we were out one horn. And you could tell: we played a little bit too rough, and the head-arrangements Collins and His Crew grew up to, they needed Honker's grease in the worst way. But we'd been together for five years or more, and a new man just didn't play somehow. We were this one solid thing, like a unit, and somebody had cut off a piece of us and we couldn't grow the piece back so we just tried to get along anyway, bleeding every night, bleeding from that wound.

Then one night it bust. We'd gone through some slow walking stuff, some tricky stuff and some loud stuff—still covering up—when this kid, this white boy, got up from his chair and ankled over and tapped Spoof on the shoulder. It was break-time and Spoof was brought down about Honker, about how bad we were sounding, sitting there sweating, those pounds of man, black as coal dust soaked in oil—he was the *blackest* man!—and those eyes, beady, white and small as agates.

"Excuse me, Mr. Collins, I wonder if I might have a word with you?" He wondered if he might have a word with Mr. Collins!

Spoof swiveled in his chair and clapped a look around the kid. "Hnff?"

"I notice that you don't have a sax man anymore."

"You don't mean to tell me?"

"Yes sir. I thought—I mean, I was wondering if—"

"Talk up, boy. I can't hear you."

The kid looked scared. Lord, he looked scared—and he was white to begin with.

"Well sir, I was just wondering if—if you needed a saxophone."

"You know somebody plays sax?"

"Yes sir, I do."

"And who might that be?"

"Me."

"You."

"Yes sir."

Spoof smiled a quick one. Then he shrugged. "Broom off, son," he said. "Broom 'way off."

The kid turned red. He all of a sudden didn't look scared anymore. Just mad. Mad as hell. But he didn't say anything. He went on back to his table and then it was end of the ten.

We swung into *Basin Street,* smooth as Charley's tenor could make it, with Lux Anderson talking it out: *Basin Street, man, it is the street, Where the elite, well, they gather 'round to eat a little* . . . And we fooled around with the slow stuff for a while. Then Spoof lifted his horn and climbed up two-and-a-half and let out his trademark, that short high screech that sounded like something dying that wasn't too happy about it. And we rocked some, Henry taking it, Jimmy kanoodling the great head-work that only Jimmy knows how to do, me slamming the skins—and it was nowhere. Without Honker to keep us all on the ground, we were just making noise. Good noise, all right, but not music. And Spoof knew it. He broke his mouth blowing—to prove it.

And we cussed the cat that sliced our man.

Then, right away—nobody could remember when it came in—suddenly we had us an alto-sax. Smooth and sure and snaky, that sound put a knot on each of us and said: Bust loose now, boys, I'll pull you back down. Like sweet-smelling glue, like oil in a machine, like—Honker.

We looked around and there was the kid, still sore, blowing like a madman, and making fine fine music.

Spoof didn't do much. Most of all, he didn't stop the number. He just let that horn play, listening—and when we slid over all the rough spots and found us backed up neat as could be, The Ol' Massuh let out a grin and a nod and a "Keep blowin', young'un!" and we knew that we were going to be all right.

After it was over, Spoof walked up to the kid. They looked at each other, sizing it up, taking it in.

Spoof says: "You did good."

And the kid—he was still burned—says: "You mean I did *damn* good."

And Spoof shakes his head. "No, that ain't what I mean."

And in a second one was laughing while the other one blushed. Spoof had known all along that the kid was faking, that he'd just been lucky enough to know our style on *Basin Street* up-down-and-across.

The Ol' Massuh waited for the kid to turn and start to slink off, then he said: "Boy, you want to go to work?"

Sonny learned so fast it scared you. Spoof never held back; he turned it all over, everything it had taken us our whole lives to find out.

And—we had some good years. Charley di Lusso dropped out, we took on Bud Meunier—the greatest bass man of them all—and Lux threw away his banjo for an AC–DC git-box and old C. T. Mr. 'T' Green and his trombone joined the Crew. And we kept growing and getting stronger—no million-copies platter sales or stands at the Paramount—too 'special'—but we never ate too far down on the hog, either.

In a few years Sonny Holmes was making that sax stand on its hind legs and jump through hoops that Honker never dreamed about. Spoof let him strictly alone. When he got mad it wasn't ever because Sonny had white skin—Spoof always was too busy to notice things like that—but only because The Ol' Massuh had to get T'ed off at each one of us every now and then. He figured it kept us on our toes.

In fact, except right at first, there never was any real blood between Spoof and Sonny until Rose-Ann came along.

Spoof didn't want a vocalist with the band. But the coonshouting days were gone alas, except for Satchmo and Calloway—who had style: none of us had style, man, we just hollered—so when push came to shove, we had to put out the net.

And chickens aplenty came to crow and plenty moved on fast and we were about to give up when a dusky doll of 20-ought stepped up and let loose a hunk of *That Man I Love* and that's all, brothers, end of the search.

Rose-Ann McHugh was a little like Sonny: where she came from, she didn't know a ball of cotton from a piece of popcorn. She'd studied piano for a flock of years with a Pennsylvania longhair, read music whipfast and had been pointed toward the Big Steinway and the O.M.'s, Chopin and Bach and all that jazz. And good!—I mean, she could pull some very fancy noise out of those keys. But it wasn't the Road. She'd heard a few records of Muggsy Spanier's, a couple of Jelly Roll's—*New Orleans Bump, Shreveport Stomp,* old *Wolverine Blues*—and she just got took hold of. Like it happens, all the time. She knew.

Spoof hired her after the first song. And we could see things in her eyes for The Ol' Massuh right away, fast. Bad to watch: I mean to say, she was chicken dinner, but what made it ugly was, you could tell she hadn't been in the oven very long.

Anyway, most of us could tell. Sonny, for instance.

But Spoof played tough to begin. He gave her the treatment, all the way. To see if she'd hold up. Because, above everything else, there was the Crew, the Unit, the group. It was right, it had to stay right.

"Gal, forget your hands—that's for the cats out front. Leave 'em alone. And pay attention to the music, hear?"

"You ain't got a 'voice,' you got an instrument. And you ain't even started *to learn how to play on it. Get some sound, bring it on out."*

"Stop that throat stuff—you' singin' with the Crew now. From the belly, gal, from the belly. That's *where music comes from, hear?"*

And she loved it, like Sonny did. She was with The Ol' Massuh, she knew what he was talking about.

Pretty soon she fit just fine. And when she did, and everybody knew she did, Spoof eased up and waited and watched the old machine click right along, one-two, one-two.

That's when he began to change. Right then, with the Crew growed up and in long pants at last. Like we didn't need him anymore to wash our face and comb our hair and switch our behinds for being bad.

Spoof began to change. He beat out time and blew his riffs, but things were different and there wasn't anybody who didn't know that for a fact.

In a hurry, all at once, he wrote down all his great arrangements, quick as he could. One right after the other. And we wondered why—we'd played them a million times.

Then he grabbed up Sonny. *"White boy, listen. You want to learn how to play trumpet?"*

And the blood started between them. Spoof rode on Sonny's back twenty-four hours, showing him lip, showing him breath. *"This ain't a saxophone, boy, it's a trumpet, a music-horn. Get it right—do it again—that's lousy—do it again—that was nowhere—do it again—do it again!"* All the time.

Sonny worked hard. Anybody else, they would have told Ol' Massuh where he could put that little old horn. But the kid knew something was being given to him—he didn't know why, nobody did, but for a reason—something that Spoof wouldn't have given anybody else. And he was grateful. So he worked. And he didn't ask any how-comes, either.

Pretty soon he started to handle things right. 'Way down the road from great, but coming along. The sax had given him a hard set of lips and he had plenty of wind; most of all, he had the spirit—the thing that you can beat up your chops about it for two weeks straight and never say what it is, but if it isn't there, buddy-ghee, you may get to be President but you'll never play music.

Lord, Lord, Spoof worked that boy like a two ton jockey on a ten ounce horse. *"Do it again—that ain't right—God damn it, do it again! Now one more time!"*

When Sonny knew enough to sit in with the horn on a few easy ones, Ol' Massuh would tense up and follow the kid with his eyes—I mean it got real crawly. What for? Why was he pushing it like that?

Then it quit. Spoof didn't say anything. He just grunted and quit all of a sudden, like he'd done with us, and Sonny went back on sax and that was that.

Which is when the real blood started.

▪ ▪ ▪

The Lord says every man has got to love something, sometime, somewhere. First choice is a chick, but there's other choices. Spoof's was a horn. He was married to a piece of brass, just as married as a man can get. Got up with it in the morning, talked with it all day long, loved it at night like no chick I ever heard of got loved. And I don't mean one-two-three: I mean the slow-building kind. He'd kiss it and hold it and watch out for it. Once a cat full of tea tried to put the snatch on Spoof's horn, for laughs: when Spoof caught up with him, that cat gave up laughing for life.

Sonny knew this. It's why he never blew his stack at all the riding. Spoof's teaching him to play trumpet—*the* trumpet—was like as if The Ol' Massuh had said: *"You want to take my wife for a few nights? You do? Then here, let me show you how to do it right. She likes it done right."*

For Rose-Ann, though, it was the worst. Every day she got that look deeper in, and in a while we turned around and, man! *Where* is little Rosie? She was gone. That young half-fried chicken had flew the roost. And in her place was a doll that wasn't dead, a big bunch of curves and skin like a brand new penny. Overnight, almost. Sonny noticed. Freddie and Lux and even old Mr. 'T' noticed. *I* had eyes in my head. But Spoof didn't notice. He was already in love, there wasn't any more room.

Rose-Ann kept snapping the whip, but Ol' Massuh, he wasn't *about* to make the trip. He'd started climbing then, and he didn't treat her any different than he treated us.

"Get away, gal, broom on off—can't you see I'm busy? Wiggle it elsewhere, hear? Elsewhere. Shoo!"

And she just loved him more for it. Every time he kicked her, she loved him more. Tried to find him and see him and, sometimes, when he'd stop for breath, she'd try to help, because she knew something had crawled inside Spoof, something that was eating from the inside out, that maybe he couldn't get rid of alone.

Finally, one night, at a two-weeker in Dallas, it tumbled.

We'd gone through *Georgia Brown* for the tourists and things were kind of dull, when Spoof started sweating. His eyes began to roll. And he stood up, like a great big animal—like an ape or a bear, big and powerful and mean-looking—and he gave us the two-finger signal.

Sky-High. 'Way before it was due, before either audience or any of us had got wound up.

Freddie frowned. "You think it's time, Top?"

"Listen," Spoof said, "God damn it, who says when it's time—you, or me?"

We went into it, cold, but things warmed up pretty fast. The dancers grumbled and moved off the floor and the place filled up with talk.

I took my solo and beat hell out of the skins. Then Spoof swiped at his mouth and let go with a blast and moved it up into that squeal and stopped and started playing. It was all head-work. All new to us.

New to anybody.

I saw Sonny get a look in his face, and we sat still and listened while Spoof made love to that horn.

Now like a scream, now like a laugh,—now we're swinging in the trees, now the white men are coming, now we're in the boat and chains are hanging from our ankles and we're rowing, rowing—*Spoof, what is it?*—now we're sawing wood and picking cotton and serving up those cool cool drinks to the Colonel in his chair—*Well, blow man!*—now we're free, and we're struttin' down Lenox Avenue and State & Madison and Pirate's Alley, laughing, crying—*Who said free?*—and we want to go back and we don't want to go back—*Play it, Spoof! God, God, tell us all about it! Talk to us!*—and we're sitting in a cellar with a comb wrapped up in paper, with a skin-barrel and a tinklebox—*Don't stop, Spoof! Oh Lord, please don't stop!*—and we're making something, something, what is it? Is it jazz? Why yes, Lord, it's jazz. Thank you, sir, and thank you, sir, we finally got it, something that is *ours,* something great that belongs to us and to us alone, that we made, and *that's* why it's important, and *that's* what it's all about and—*Spoof! Spoof, you can't stop now*—

But it was over, middle of the trip. And there was Spoof standing there facing us and tears streaming out of those eyes and down over that coal dust face, and his body shaking and shaking. It's the first we ever saw that. It's the first we ever heard him cough, too—like a shotgun going off every two seconds, big raking sounds that tore up from the bottom of his belly and spilled out wet and loud.

The way it tumbled was this. Rose-Ann went over to him and tried to get him to sit down "Spoof, honey, what's wrong? Come on and sit down. Honey, don't just stand there."

Spoof stopped coughing and jerked his head around. He looked at Rose-Ann for a while and whatever there was in his face, it didn't have a name. The whole room was just as quiet as it could be.

Rose-Ann took his arm. "Come on, honey, Mr. Collins—"

He let out one more cough, then, and drew back his hand—that black-topped, pink-palmed ham of a hand—and laid it, sharp, across the girl's cheek. It sent her staggering. "Get off my back, hear? Damn it, git off! Stay away from me!"

She got up crying. Then, you know what she did? She waltzed on back and took his arm and said: "Please."

Spoof was just a lot of crazy-mad on two legs. He shouted out some words and pulled back his hand again. "Can't you never learn? What I got to do, god damn little—"

Then—Sonny moved. All-the-time quiet and soft and gentle Sonny. He moved quick across the floor and stood in front of Spoof.

"Keep your black hands off her," he said.

Ol' Massuh pushed Rose-Ann aside and planted his legs, his breath rattling fast and loose, like a bull's. And he towered over the kid, Goliath and David, legs far apart on the boards and fingers curled up, bowling balls at the end of his sleeves.

"You talkin' to me, boy?"

Sonny's face was red, like I hadn't seen it since that first time at the Continental Club, years back. "You've got ears, Collins. Touch her again and I'll kill you."

I don't know exactly what we expected, but I know what we were afraid of. We were afraid Spoof would let go; and if he did . . . well, put another bed in the hospital, men. He stood there, breathing, and Sonny gave it right back—for hours, days and nights, for a month, toe to toe.

Then Spoof relaxed. He pulled back those fat lips, that didn't look like lips anymore, they were so tough and leathery, and showed a mouthful of white and gold, and grunted, and turned, and walked away.

We swung into *Twelfth Street Rag* in *such* a hurry!

And it got kicked under the sofa.

But we found out something, then, that nobody even suspected.

Sonny had it for Rose-Ann. He had it bad.

And that ain't good.

▪ ▪ ▪

Spoof fell to pieces after that. He played day and night, when we were working, when we weren't working. Climbing. Trying to get it said, all of it.

"Listen, you can't hit Heaven with a slingshot, Daddy-O!"

"What you want to do, man—blow Judgment?"

He never let up. If he ate anything, you tell me when. Sometimes he tied on, straight stuff quick, medicine type of drinking. But only after he'd been climbing and started to blow flat and ended up in those coughing fits.

And it got worse. Nothing helped either: foam or booze or tea or even Indoor Sports, and he tried them all. And got worse.

"Get fixed up, Mr. C, you hear? See a bone-man; you in bad shape . . ."

"Get away from me, get on away!" Hawk! and a big red spot on the handkerchief. *"Broom off! Shoo!"*

And gradually the old horn went sour, ugly and bitter sounding, like Spoof himself. Hoo Lord, the way he rode Sonny then: *"How you like the dark stuff, boy? You like it pretty good? Hey there, don't hold back. Rosie's fine talent—I know. Want me to tell you about it, pave the way, show you how? I taught you everything else, didn't I?"* And Sonny always clamming up, his eyes doing the talking: *"You were a great musician, Collins, and you still are, but that doesn't mean I've got to like you—you won't let me. And you're damn right I'm in love with Rose-Ann! That's the biggest reason why I'm still here—just to be close to her. Otherwise, you wouldn't see me for the dust. But you're too dumb to realize she's in love with you, too dumb and stupid and mean and wrapped up with that lousy horn!"*

What *Sonny* was too dumb to know was, Rose-Ann had cut Spoof out. She was now Public Domain.

Anyway, Spoof got to be the meanest, dirtiest, craziest, low-talkinest man in the world. And nobody could come in: he had signs out all the time . . .

The night that he couldn't even get a squeak out of his trumpet and went back to the hotel—alone, always alone—and put the gun in his mouth and pulled the trigger, we found something out.

We found out what it was that had been eating at The Ol' Massuh.

Cancer.

▪ ▪ ▪

Rose-Ann took it the hardest. She had the dry-weeps for a long time, saying it over and over: "Why didn't he let us know? Why didn't he tell us?"

But, you get over things. Even women do, especially when they've got something to take its place.

We reorganized a little. Sonny cut out the sax—saxes were getting cornball anyway—and took over on trumpet. And we decided against keeping Spoof's name. It was now SONNY HOLMES AND HIS CREW.

And we kept on eating high up. Nobody seemed to miss Spoof—not the cats in front, at least—because Sonny blew as great a horn as anybody could want, smooth and sure, full of excitement and clean as a gnat's behind.

We played across the States and back, and they loved us—thanks to the kid. Called us an 'institution' and the disk jockeys began to pick up our stuff. We were 'real,' they said—the only authentic jazz left, and who am I to push it? Maybe they were right.

Sonny kept things in low. And then, when he was sure—damn that slow way;

it had been a cinch since back when—he started to pay attention to Rose-Ann. She played it cool, the way she knew he wanted it, and let it build up right. Of course, who didn't know she would've married him this minute, now, just say the word? But Sonny was a very conscientious cat indeed.

We did a few stands in France about that time—Listen to them holler! and a couple in England and Sweden—getting better, too—and after a breather, we cut out across the States again.

It didn't happen fast, but it happened sure. Something was sounding flat all of a sudden like—wrong, in a way:

During an engagement in El Paso we had *What the Cats Dragged In* lined up. You all know *Cats*—the rhythm section still, with the horns yelling for a hundred bars, then that fast and solid beat, that high trip and trumpet solo? Sonny had the ups on a wild riff and was coming on down, when he stopped. Stood still, with the horn to his lips; and we waited.

"Come on, wrap it up—you want a drum now? What's the story, Sonny?"

Then he started to blow. The notes came out the same almost, but not quite the same. They danced out of the horn strop-razor sharp and sliced up high and blasted low and the cats all fell out. "Do it! Go, man! Oooo, I'm out of the boat, don't pull me back! Sing out, man!"

The solo lasted almost seven minutes. When it was time for us to wind it up, we just about forgot.

The crowd went wild. They stomped and screamed and whistled. But they couldn't get Sonny to play anymore. He pulled the horn away from his mouth—I mean that's the way it looked, as if he was yanking it away with all his strength—and for a second he looked surprised, like he'd been goosed. Then his lips pulled back into a smile.

It was the *damndest* smile!

Freddie went over to him at the break. "Man, that was the craziest. How many tongues you got?"

But Sonny didn't answer him.

▪ ▪ ▪

Things went along all right for a little. We played a few dances in the cities, some radio stuff, cut a few platters. Easy walking style.

Sonny played Sonny—plenty great enough. And we forgot about what happened in El Paso. So what? So he cuts loose once—can't a man do that if he feels the urge? Every jazz man brings that kind of light at least once.

We worked through the sticks and were finally set for a New York opening when Sonny came in and gave us the news.

It was a gasser. Lux got sore. Mr. 'T' shook his head.

"Why? How come, Top?"

He had us booked for the cornbelt. The old-time route, exactly, even the old places, back when we were playing razzmatazz and feeling our way.

"You trust me?" Sonny asked. "You trust my judgment?"

"Come off it, Top; you know we do. Just tell us how come. Man, New York's what we been working for—"

"That's just it," Sonny said. "We aren't ready."

That brought us down. How did *we* know—we hadn't even thought about it.

"We need to get back to the real material. When we play in New York it's not anything anybody's liable to forget in a hurry. And that's why I think we ought to take a refresher course. About five weeks. All right?"

Well, we fussed some and fumed some, but not much, and in the end we agreed to it. Sonny knew his stuff, that's what we figured.

"Then it's settled."

And we lit out.

Played mostly the old stuff dressed up—*Big Gig, Only Us Chickens* and the rest—or head-arrangements with a lot of trumpet. Illinois, Indiana, Kentucky . . .

When we hit Louisiana for a two-nighter at the Tropics, the same thing happened that did back in Texas. Sonny blew wild for an eight minute solo that broke the glasses and cracked the ceiling and cleared the dance floor like a tornado. Nothing off the stem, either—but like it was practice, sort of, or exercise. A solo out of nothing that didn't even try to hang on to a shred of the melody.

"Man, it's great, but let us know when it's gonna happen, hear!"

About then Sonny turned down the flame on Rose-Ann. He was polite enough and a stranger wouldn't have noticed, but we did, and Rose-Ann did—and it was tough for her to keep it all down under, hidden. All those questions, all those memories and fears.

He stopped going out and took to hanging around his rooms a lot. Once in a while he'd start playing: one time we listened to that horn all night.

Finally—it was still somewhere in Louisiana—when Sonny was reaching with his trumpet so high he didn't get any more sound out of it than a dog-whistle, and the front cats were laughing up a storm, I went over and put it to him flat-footed.

His eyes were big and he looked like he was trying to say something and couldn't. He looked scared.

"Sonny . . . Look, boy, what are you after? Tell a friend, man, don't lock it up."

But he didn't answer me. He couldn't.

He was coughing too hard.

Here's the way we doped it: Sonny had worshipped Spoof, like a god or something. Now some Spoof was rubbing off, and he didn't know it.

Freddie was elected. Freddie talks pretty good most of the time.

"Get off the train, Jack. Ol' Massuh's gone now, dead and buried. Mean, what he was after ain't to be had. Mean, he wanted it all and then some—and all is all, there isn't anymore. You play the greatest, Sonny—go on, ask anybody. Just fine. So get off the train . . ."

And Sonny laughed, and agreed, and promised. I mean in words. His eyes played another number, though.

Sometimes he snapped out of it, it looked like, and he was fine then—tired and hungry, but with it. And we'd think he's okay. Then it would happen all over again—only worse. Every time, worse.

And it got so Sonny even talked like Spoof half the time: "Broom off, man, leave me alone, will you? Can't you see I'm busy, got things to do? Get away!" And walked like Spoof—that slow walk-in-your-sleep shuffle. And did little things—like scratching his belly and leaving his shoes unlaced and rehearsing in his undershirt.

He started to smoke weeds in Alabama.

In Tennessee he took the first drink anybody ever saw him take.

And always with that horn—cussing it, yelling at it, getting sore because it wouldn't do what he wanted it to.

We had to leave him, alone, finally. "I'll handle it . . . I—understand, I think . . . Just go away, it'll be all right . . ."

Nobody could help him. Nobody at all.

Especially not Rose-Ann.

. . .

End of the corn-belt route, the way Sonny had it booked, was the Copper Club. We hadn't been back there since the night we planted Spoof—and we didn't feel very good about it.

But a contract isn't anything else.

So we took rooms at the only hotel there ever was in the town. You make a guess which room Sonny took. And we played some cards and bruised our chops and tried to sleep and couldn't. We tossed around in the beds, listening, waiting for the horn to begin. But it didn't. All night long, it didn't.

We found out why, oh yes . . .

Next day we all walked around just about everywhere except in the direction of the cemetery. Why kick up misery? Why make it any harder?

Sonny stayed in his room until ten before opening, and we began to worry. But he got in under the wire.

The Copper Club was packed. Yokels and farmers and high school stuff, a jazz 'connoisseur' here and there—to the beams. Freddie had set up the stands with the music notes all in order, and in a few minutes we had our positions.

Sonny came out wired for sound. He looked—powerful; and that's a hard way for a five-foot four-inch bald-headed white man to look. At any time. Rose-Ann threw me a glance and I threw it back and collected it from the rest. Something bad. Something real bad. Soon.

Sonny didn't look any which way. He waited for the applause to die down, then he did a quick One-Two-Three-Four and we swung into *The Jimjam Man,* our theme.

I mean to say, that crowd was with us all the way—they smelled something.

Sonny did the thumb-and-little-finger signal and we started *Only Us Chickens*. Bud Meunier did the intro on his bass, then Henry took over on the piano. He played one hand racing the other. The front cats hollered "Go! Go!" and Henry went. His left hand crawled on down over the keys and scrambled and didn't fuzz once or slip once and then walked away, cocky and proud, like a mouse full of cheese from an unsprung trap.

"Hooo-boy! Play, Henry, play!"

Sonny watched and smiled. "Bring it on out," he said, gentle, quiet, pleased. "Keep bringin' it out."

Henry did that counterpoint business that you're not supposed to be able to do unless you have two right arms and four extra fingers, and he got that boiler puffing, and he got it shaking, and he screamed his Henry Walker "WoooooOOOOO!" and—he finished. I came in on the tubs and beat them up till I couldn't see for the sweat, hit the cymbal and waited.

Mr. 'T,' Lux and Jimmy fiddlefaddled like a coop of capons talking about their operations for a while. Rose-Ann chanted: "Only us chickens in the hen-house, Daddy, Only us chickens here, Only us chickens in the hen-house, Daddy, Ooo-bab-a-roo. Ooo-bob-a-roo . . ."

Then it was horn time. Time for the big solo.

Sonny lifted the trumpet—One! Two!—He got it into sight—Three!

We all stopped dead. I mean we stopped.

That wasn't Sonny's horn. This one was dented-in and beat-up and the tip-end was nicked. It didn't shine, not a bit.

Lux leaned over—you could have fit a coffee cup into his mouth. "Jesus God," he said. "Am I seeing right?"

I looked close and said: "Man, I hope not."

But why kid? We'd seen that trumpet a million times.

It was Spoof's.

Rose-Ann was trembling. Just like me, she remembered how we'd buried the horn with Spoof. And she remembered how quiet it had been in Sonny's room last night . . .

I started to think real hop-head thoughts, like—where did Sonny get hold of a shovel that late? and how could he expect a horn to play that's been under the ground for two years? and—

That blast got into our ears like long knives.

Spoof's own trademark!

Sonny looked caught, like he didn't know what to do at first, like he was hypnotized, scared, almighty scared. But as the sound came out, rolling out, sharp and clean and clear—new-trumpet sound—his expression changed. His eyes changed: they danced a little and opened wide.

Then he closed them, and blew that horn. Lord God of the Fishes, how he blew it! How he loved it and caressed it and pushed it up, higher and higher and higher. High C? Bottom of the barrel. He took off, and he walked all over the rules and stamped them flat.

The melody got lost, first off. Everything got lost, then, while that horn flew. It wasn't only jazz; it was the heart of jazz, and the insides, pulled out with the roots and held up for everybody to see; it was blues that told the story of all the lonely cats and all the ugly whores who ever lived, blues that spoke up for the loser lamping sunshine out of iron-gray bars and every hop-head hooked and gone, for the bindlestiffs and the city slicers, for the country boys in Georgia shacks and the High Yellow hipsters in Chicago slums and the bootblacks on the corners and the fruits in New Orleans, a blues that spoke for all the lonely, sad and anxious downers who could never speak themselves . . .

And then, when it had said all this, it stopped and there was a quiet so quiet that Sonny could have shouted:

"It's okay, Spoof. It's all right now. You'll get it said, all of it—I'll help you. God, Spoof, you showed me how, you planned it—I'll do my best!"

And he laid back his head and fastened the horn and pulled in air and blew some more. Not sad, now, not blues—but not anything else you could call by name. Except . . . Jazz. It was jazz.

Hate blew out that horn, then. Hate and fury and mad and fight, like screams and snarls, like little razors shooting at you, millions of them cutting, cutting deep . . .

And Sonny only stopping to wipe his lip and whisper in the silent room full of people: "You're saying it, Spoof! You are!"

God Almighty Himself must have heard that trumpet, then; slapping and hitting and hurting with notes that don't exist and never existed. Man! Life took a real beating! Life got groined and sliced and belly-punched and the horn, it didn't stop until everything had all spilled out, every bit of the hate and mad that's built up in a man's heart.

Rose-Ann walked over to me and dug her nails into my hand as she listened to Sonny.

"Come on now, Spoof! Come on! We can do it! Let's play the rest and play it right. You know it's got to be said, you know it does. Come on, you and me together!"

And the horn took off with a big yellow blast and started to laugh. I mean it laughed! Hooted and hollered and jumped around, dancing, singing, strutting through those notes that never were there. Happy music? Joyful music? It was chicken dinner and an empty stomach; it was big-butted women and big white beds; it was country walking and windy days and freshborn crying and—Oh, there just doesn't happen to be any happiness that didn't come out of that horn.

Sonny hit the last high note—the Spoof blast—but so high you could just barely hear it.

Then Sonny dropped the horn. It fell onto the floor and bounced and lay still.

And nobody breathed. For a long long time.

Rose-Ann let go of my hand, at last. She walked across the platform, slowly, and picked up the trumpet and handed it to Sonny.

He knew what she meant.

We all did. It was over now, over and done . . .

Lux plucked out the intro. Jimmy Fritch picked it up and kept the melody.

Then we all joined in, slow and quiet, quiet as we could. With Sonny—I'm talking about *Sonny*—putting out the kind of sound he'd always wanted to.

And Rose-Ann sang it, clear as a mountain wind—not just from her heart, but from her belly and her guts and every living part of her.

For The Ol' Massuh, just for him. Spoof's own song:

Black Country.

Herbert Gold

All Married Women Are Bad, Yes?

November 1955

No fiction writer was so identified with the *Playboy* of the 1950s through the 1970s as the prolific Herb Gold. Here is his very first story for the magazine, which eventually published more than fifty of them, sometimes as many as four or five a year. He had already written three novels by the time he reached *Playboy* and many more followed. Born in Cleveland in 1924, Gold is now a well-known figure on the San Francisco literary scene, as well as a sometime resident of Haiti, the setting for a number of his stories and articles. Some of his best-known novels are *The Man Who Was Not With It* (1954), *Fathers* (1966), *Swifty the Magician* (1974), and *A Girl of Forty* (1986).

Herbert Gold

All Married Women Are Bad, Yes?

"I wouldn't marry you if you were the greatest French violinist in Haiti," Maureen told Patreek. "I'm sick of everything. I'm bored. Life is just one god damn voodoo ceremony after another."

"Poor Maureen," Patreek cooed, "she is so sensitive, so . . . Have you been picking your sunburn again? Whoever said I wanted to marry you? Eric? Give me one of those cigarettes—only American cigarettes can make me forget I am merely the greatest violinist in the Hotel des Arts."

"Sh!" cried Eric, padding up on his huaraches. "That should be enough. It is forbidden to be unhappy. It's not even chic this season."

"I could bawl," said Maureen.

"And a match?" Patreek asked. Maureen lit his cigarette.

Eric went into his little speech for such occasions, scratching the hairs under his pink mesh shirt while he recited. "Haiti is paradise—the Hotel is Haiti—and have I introduced you to the Sturtevant family? They are divine, my friends. He has a regular job and she is well-stacked."

The creative tourists to Port-au-Prince love this gingerbread place, the Hotel des Arts, all crumbling and filigree and termite grandeur. They love the green scum and the split-eyed frogs sunning on its swimming pool. They love the toothless waiters who grin and bow and sing, "Yesss, O yesss!" as if they understand English. They adore the cheap rum, primitive art, and erotic adventure which, more than Pan-American Airways' free meals on board, are the special pomp of a vacation under the glittering royal palms of Haiti.

The manager, Eric von Roitsch ("But please don't call me Baron—I hardly ever use the title anymore"), understands the importance of retaining the Hotel's old-world charm, which is defined by introducing single men to lonely girls and never cleaning the scum off the swimming pool. This job is only a temporary one while Eric awaits his entrance visa to the U. S. of A. His inside dope on the scandals of culture, his talent for tongues, and his special passion for America contribute to making the Hotel des Arts the natural choice of that gifted class of tourists who work in "the arts," that is, television, advertising, airline hostessing, and other fields which require the creative personality. A busy man in a pink sleeveless tail-out shirt, tirelessly smiling, Eric communes devotedly with the clientele. His intuition floods him with exactly the proper bar-talk for a fashion photographer ("The camera is the great Twentieth Century art form, doncha know, but ruined? Prostituted!"), for an author of station-break commercials ("If you want to grasp modern life, it's sad but you have to suffer from it"), or for a sturdy middle-aged widow who had graduated from a creative writing course ("Let me introduce you to a dear friend who knows the *real* Haiti!").

These days, however, Eric is worried that the climate of his mountain slope may have softened that old original cosmopolitan perspicacity. You can buy heavy drapes and smart conversation for a salon in Haiti, but voodoo drums and the hawing of donkeys would embroil the spirit even in the Boubourg St.-Germain. *Embroil* is Eric's word; he felt embroiled by the refusal of Maureen Koot and Patreek St. Coppe, two of his year-round pensionaires, to come to order. Maureen, a girl with blond hair in a pony tail and a married daughter in New Haven, arrived in Haiti almost ten years ago on the income of her third divorce. A painter, she claims to be the first and most authentic of the Haitian primitives. "Why, I invented all that stuff. The Haitian painters were just houseboys until I told them how to be brutal, forceful, voodoo," she says. "*Create,* I told them. Discovered the real thing in a vision one night."

Patreek St. Coppe, a French musician, is hired by the Haitian government to train and direct the Army band. Upon his arrival he gave a violin recital, but since then, discouraged by the ticket sale, he has settled down to a career of teaching sergeant trumpeters to use pipe cleaners on their mouthpieces in order to prevent that sticky buzz. "It is fierce, the military life," he complains, but otherwise seems to have adjusted to modern civilization.

Where Eric's intuition failed was in the assumption that Maureen and Patreek would find themselves made for each other. They dined together. They smoked each other's cigarettes. They even sometimes went out for a rum-soda together. But Patreek is young and finicky, and Maureen is showing her age fast, as too-long-young women sometimes do, so that cigarettes and friendship were all that they exchanged. A great deception for Eric. He was embroiled.

During the sleepy summer months when the tiny lizards called anolis cling to the walls of the Hotel des Art, making their odd shivering spraddle-legged jump at the distant rumble of heat thunder, puffing out their warty craws, digesting with difficulty, Eric is so bored that he has started to write a novel. This indicates how little he had on his mind, apart from the visa, which was slow, slow, slow to come. The few pensionaires besides Maureen and Patreek require little care. Eric retreated into the joys of literature, telling of a White Russian ballet dancer named Serge who collaborated with the Gestapo in France but was really giving messages to the Resistance, brief codes which he communicated by clapping his ankles together in the pas-de-deux of "Swan Lake." Serge made deliberate mistakes in classical form, thus raising the moral issue of the conflict between Art and Freedom, while the crease-necked German officers foolishly called him "decadent" or, in their own barbarous tongue, "dekadent."

"It's not Serge Lifar," Eric confided to Maureen. "I knew him well. It's another Serge."

▪ ▪ ▪

But a surprising event prevented Eric from carrying *Swan Lake* through to its victorious conclusion for the Allies. A group of dancers, led by one of the several million former partners of Katherine Dunham, arrived in Port-au-Prince and descended upon the Hotel des Arts. On the same day, a fine young couple (he a theatrical scene designer, she a painter but pretty enough to need no other recommendation) registered and asked for the best room in the house. As Eric liked fine young American couples, they would have been given it anyway, but asking the question cost them two-fifty more per day. The Hubert Wilkinson dancers, trying to scavenge up enough money to get home to Philadelphia, were soon busy rehearsing, shrieking, and stretching their pectorals on the great vine-entangled gallery of the Hotel. The fine young couple, Sam and Tilly Sturtevant, were celebrating their fifth wedding anniversary by an idea-hunting trip. Cheap sandals, straw bags, and mahogany bowls were all the ideas they had found so far. Someone else had already found Haitian painting.

It was one big happy boardinghouse at mealtimes. Eric's wintertime stories were sprinkled with rum and brought out for the economical delectation of those who took advantage of the summer rates. "And nobody ever explained how the crocodile got up the steps of the National Palace," one concluded. Another favorite was: "And when his wife came back all she would say was she had been initiated into voodoo."

Tilly Sturtevant was a delight. She laughed readily, as pretty women sometimes fear to do, having a mistaken notion that the sight of tonsils is a blemish upon beauty. She had a shock of close-cropped dark hair and did not wear a cap when she went swimming. Her small face quick as a monkey's, a pretty and human monkey, she was confident enough to let her strapless blouses slip halfway down before she gave them the yank required by occidental custom. Everybody liked her.

"A lady," Eric breathed, certain that she could hear him. "A queen of the beautiful American race."

Patreek was thoroughly fetched. He gazed, brooded, and worried. For the first time in weeks he played his violin and brushed his teeth. At last he confided his trouble to Maureen Koot. "Another girl like this may not descend at the Hotel before the season of winter," he pointed out. "I have terribly the *beguin*. I am so neurosthenic over her that my chaconne came out Leibestraum. Jean-Sebastien Bach is turning around in his tomb. Do you find that she notices?"

"Now Patreek, don't be anxious," Maureen said. "Remember how we girls don't care for anxious men. It makes it too anxious all the way around."

"But she is too ravishing!"

"You know how to light her cigarette. Speak French with her. Tell how you were a young genius for violinning."

"But her husband is so close to her—like that close to her—always so close," he mused. "I could put a curse on him, but he's *already* married."

"Well, darling, worried cat never ate tasty rat," Maureen advised.

"Listen me, Maureen. Do not cat me. I am in vacations to the end of this month here, and I no have not cash for Cuba even. Then is it not that I am destined to fall in love? I must! I adore her, darling. I am amorous."

At last Maureen took pity. She would see what she could do.

With the wisdom of a long apprenticeship at the Hotel des Arts, Patreek developed his friendship with Sam, Tilly's husband. This serves the dual purpose of putting the fresh young cuckold at his ease, the better to keep him from rearing and stamping and pawing the ground when one fits on the horns, and at the same time it arouses a worried itch which is the next thing to jealousy on the part of the adored lady. It usually has her staring for minutes at a time into the mirror behind the bar. In order to avoid excessive discouragement, Patreek looked long into her eyes when he whipped out a kitchen match and made fire for her cigarette against his horny and blackened thumbnail. Then he turned hungrily back to Sam for news of the degeneration of the Broadway stage set.

This was one day's work. The next day would bring leanings, bendings, brushings, and shy confidences about the sadness which kept him from composing really great music, his true vocation. "Piquant—one must be spice for a lady, Maureen." By the third or fourth day, it would be only the question of finding an opportunity.

That was the way Patreek had it figured, and Maureen agreed with him. They had observed many American tourists at the Hotel des Arts. After all, a two-week vacation is only ten days long (travelling, adjusting, curing the runs), and then you are back among memories and secret yearnings and the workaday world. Straw placemats and mahogany salad tools will be scant comfort when your spouse is sitting absent in the realms of "Dragnet" or "The Danny Thomas Show." Where else to clean the psyche of its forbidden impulses if not at the Hotel des Arts in the midst of the real Haiti?

"But," as Patreek said, desperate, "she is not marching."

"You're losing the old magic, darling," Maureen teased him. All the same, it was an insult that Patreek showed no interest in being consoled by her, who was so willing to march. She yawned to cover a secret grin of satisfaction.

"No, I think she is willing, but that husband—! So defiant."

"You mean suspicious. He never leaves her alone?"

"Nev-vair! A person atrocious."

They dropped into a brooding silence at their corner of the bar. Alois fortified their glasses. They pursed their lips and gathered strength.

"Say, Maureen, who is this McCarran Act?" Eric asked, coming up with a portfolio full of papers. "The consul tells me I'll have trouble getting admitted to the States because of the McCarran Act."

"Think they're a trapeze team. High divers or something," Maureen murmured, not really listening. She was in that gelatinous mood that caused her to invent Haitian painting. It was nice for ideas.

Patreek inhaled all the way down to low C below middle C and said, "I am truly bewitching of her. I am miserable."

Eric carried his troubles away to his desk. There was no manager to listen to *him*; yet he had to be constantly ready to embroil with sympathy at the merest suggestion of a beetle in a shower. Maureen followed her thoughts, and they led her far. She was worrying over a gesture of generosity which could mark a turning point in her career. It was possible. Even George Arliss went from matinee idoling to taking the part of the house of Rothschild. Yes, it was even probable. Yes, all it needed was a small bit of ingenious maneuvering which would be child's play to the inventress of primitive Haitian painting.

Maureen, whose studio occupied a separate little cottage just next door to the main buildings of the Hotel, had agreed to do the posters for the dance recital of the Hubert Wilkinson troupe. Ordinarily she refused all commissions except for innocent, unspoiled, primitive Haitian paintings, but they had asked her in such a nice way and cash is cash, especially during the slow summer season. However, she considered lettering such captions as, "The Great Interpreters of African Dance, Direct from Philadelphia," in English and French, beneath the dignity of a painter whose first husband had studied privately with Derain in Paris. Besides, she was sure to put too many l's in Philadelphia, and then they would make a fuss about paying her. Why not ask Tilly to help?

Why not indeed?

Why not work alone with Tilly in Maureen's cottage? Why not then be called to town on important business to do with decorating an authentic voodoo temple for some friendly natives? Why then could not Patreek just happen by?

"O darleeng, why not?" Patreek asked.

"Because," Maureen pouted. "Just because."

"Please! For me!" He leaned and touched her sun-roughened cheek. "Please, darleeng, I pray you. I need something to compose again."

Maureen relaxed into tenderness and smiled the toothy, long-nosed, sad-eyed smile of the madam. "Then I'll have to find Sam and get him to take me someplace. If necessary I will have to get him drunk. It's important that you feel secure, Patreek. I hope he has enough money in his pockets."

"She weel march, I know she weel," Patreek ecstatically cried. "Darleeng, you are a pall."

■ ■ ■

Nice Tilly was so glad to help Maureen with the lettering that Eric almost decided that she knew what was planned. Sam was so willing to trot off with his camera for some color photography on the murals of the Episcopal Cathedral that you would have thought him Patreek's dearest collaborator. Sly Patreek remarked casually that he would drive Sam down "on my route someparts"—namely, on his route back to Tilly in Maureen's cottage.

Eric, who now ate lunch with them at a table separate from the long board over which the Hubert Wilkinson dancers frolicked at their food, observed the charming, deep-clefted, monkey-faced Tilly and meditated fluently upon the embroiling fates which had carried a genuine Baron to Haiti and a girlish wife with a waist like a dream into the clutches of Maureen and Patreek. Naturally, Patreek had confided the project to the man at the Hotel who most admired elegant arrangements. Eric hummed the Creole folk song which goes:

Marié bon, marié pas bon
Toute femme marié mauvais, oui?
Marriage is good, is not good
All married women are bad, yes?

"What's that?" Sam asked.

"Oh just a ballet Satie wrote for Lifar," Eric replied. *"Eros and the Mechanical Genius."* Performed it only once. Not even Cocteau liked it."

"Thought so," said Sam. "I can't stand that French impressionism—it gets on the nerves, it'll never sell."

After the melted ice cream and the sharp jolt of Haitian coffee, they all chatted a moment with the dancers who were prancing down to the swimming pool to chip away the algae and cool off. Then Tilly and Maureen headed for Maureen's cottage; Patreek led Sam to his automobile; Eric borrowed a bottle of Rhum Barbancourt to help him fill out still another form for the greedy files of the United States Immigration Service.

Ten minutes later Sam had set up his tripod before a huge Bigaud mural that would have to be taken in sections. Patreek gazed at the tripod from heavy-lidded eyes and took his farewell.

Outside in a bar, Patreek called the Hotel. The gods were generous so far. The telephone worked. Fils-Pierre, who answered, went for Maureen. "For me?" she inquired.

"Yesss, O yesss!" exclaimed Fils-Pierre.

Maureen tightened her bandana and took her time about getting to the desk.

Let Patreek sweat a little, she decided. Good for the appreciation. Really, an attractive girl like Maureen shouldn't have to keep her friends by such tricks. It wasn't as if she really showed all her years. "Hello," she said.

"Hokay," said Patreek, and hung up. He was all atremble.

Maureen scuffed back to the cottage in her espadrilles, mournful but committed, and said to Tilly, "I have to run down to the National Museum. Fellow there wants to buy one of my paintings for the permanent collection. You don't mind doing the lettering yourself?"

"It's perfectly all right, really," Tilly said. "You can help me finish when you get back."

"That's a darling." Maureen then headed toward Sam's tripod while Patreek rushed up to Maureen's cottage. Their paths crossed at the Place des Heros de l'Independance, a former racetrack, and they exchanged waves, Patreek elated in his little buglike Renault, Maureen disconsolate in the afternoon heat.

Patreek pushed the screen door open, saying, "Allo, Teelee." At certain moments his accent came especially strong on him.

Tilly looked up from the easel where she was working and said, "Oh, it's you. Light me a cigarette, will you, Patreek? My hands are all paint."

Patreek lipped the cigarette deliciously and then placed it in her mouth.

Meanwhile, at the Cathedral, Maureen stood behind a pillar and watched Sam move his camera from one panel to the next. It took him almost two hours because he was the cautious type. Not a true artist. No free spirits rampaging in Sam Sturtevant. Maureen, watching, felt more and more bitter about Patreek. She had contracted to give him the entire afternoon. When Sam was just beginning to fold up his tripod, Maureen put all her remaining teeth and as much of her goodwill as she could summon into a smile and came running up to him.

"Oh, dear Sam, what luck. I'm so tired," she said. "I just left Tilly—big New York dealer wants me to have a one-man show. Not unless it's on 57th Street, that's what I told him. Come on, buy me a rum, I'm dying."

"What about Tilly?"

"Fine, just great. I lent her one of my nicest smocks. They want an affiche for every public building in town and what they're paying me hardly even goes for the paint. I'm too generous. Well, everybody has a fault. Please, Sam, do you want me to collapse right here and be charged with heat exhaustion?"

The plan was for Maureen to force enough rum down Sam's gullet, sodaed or sec, to keep him out of pain for the rest of the afternoon. As he was thirsty and hot, Maureen made a good start on him. However, as she was thirsty, hot and discontented, she made an even better start on herself. They were sitting almost alone at the Pigalle Café, next to the outdoor Theatre de Verdure, looking out over the bay of La Gonave with the fat sad afternoon flies buzzing about the sticky spots on the table and an occasional blunt-toed peasant woman wandering past with her basket of mangoes or bananas.

Somehow this time the rum did not calm the Caribbean heat which swept over Maureen. She felt a strange ennui with local color: she almost regretted having invented Haitian painting. Sam's tropical lethargy was the desired quality upon this occasion, a willingness to sit quietly, a philosophic brooding over the meaning of life and the chance of selling his color transparencies; but Maureen felt increasingly sad, hot, and worst of all, unimportant. Pretty soon her life's story began to manifest itself.

"You were in Paris in those days?" Sam inquired politely. "What hotel you stay in?"

Maureen's own brief hour of romance and love and heavy spending came flying back to her. Big dollar dinners in 1932. That was real money, those days. Gifts of perfume enough to paddle in. Her head thrown back on a convertible. Mad, crazy, beautiful life. Red convertible with retractible top. O she was lovely then, Sam, with no more than twenty-four inches round the waist except when she ate fried foods, and that skin you loved to touch. 1928, too, she was but a mere girl, a lissome creature who never went for that flat-chest flapper stuff. Beauty is all that matters, look at me! Those were her very words to the boy who took her to the Army-Navy game. He was nuts for her and they honeymooned in Paris—her first husband he was, and poor? No goddamn money at all. "A fool I was," she said bitterly. "Let's live it up, Sam. A double rum sec for me."

"Go on, it's fascinating," Sam said. "Personally, I was always commercial."

Then came an unpleasant incident about an Al Jolson record and her first divorce. She wasn't used to divorcing yet and it broke up her painting for months. Then Pete, the literary agent, he talked big but that was all there was to it, talk. Said he had Pearl Buck, Vance Bourjaily, James Hilton's "Lost Horizon." Only Jim he had was James T. Farrell. It only lasted two years—she knew Farrell would never sell in hard covers—but Pete gave her the daughter. For the kid's sake she tried psychoanalysis. Nope. Then there was her show in Boston and Frederic, no k, Lowell, in some ways the most unsatisfactory of them all but at least he settled a little something on her—

"Do you think," Sam asked, "maybe Tilly is finished by this time?"

"Why, how fast is she? One more double rum and we'll go. We're up to the war, Sam. I volunteered for psychological and propaganda, but the abstractionists had already taken over the Army—"

Gradually stirring up Beauty and Truth about the world until she found herself in Haiti, Maureen finally brought Sam abreast of contemporary events. She was reminded. Patreek! Straight from the Taboo ad! She wouldn't have let him hold her furs in the old days. Now he could just squeeze her and throw her away like an old tube of Japalac. No, Japalac comes in cans. Sam, it was awful how low an artist can fall. Anything for love, for passion, for creative people. What a filthy business was being honest with yourself!

Maureen sniffed.

Maureen choked up internally, oxidizing the rum at an accelerated rate.

Maureen burst into tears.

"Maureen," Sam said soothingly, "everything's all right, really. Please don't cry, I'm too susceptible. Anyway, I always try to be philosophic about other people's troubles. That's it, stiff lip, girl. No sense trying to mop up spilt milk."

Maureen stopped up her sobs with a curled mouth and an oh-yeah-Sam. Everybody was against her. No one even tried to understand her anymore. They would be sorry. Maureen was a girl you had to reckon with. Therefore, in a few well-chosen words, she informed Sam of Patreek's plan for the afternoon.

▪ ▪ ▪

Sam took the first cab he saw, although on principle he preferred busses and saving his money for other things. This seemed as important as most of the other things. On the trip, a matter of a few minutes, Sam felt like a drowning man with a speech defect: his entire life passed through his head. When he spied the wooden parapets and sagging balconies of the Hotel des Arts, its untended wilderness of palms keeping it damp out of the sun, he leaned forward up the hill. He cracked his knuckles. A queasiness in his belly reminded him that he had forgotten his sulphaguanadine today; it may have been his heart turning over. When the cab arrived, he leapt out without asking for change. He charged up the steps toward Maureen's cabin.

"Hey, buddy," the cab driver called in New York English to the empty air, "you still owe me a dime. Well, what the hell, the man's in a real hurry."

Eric caught sight of Sam and thought he had better come along to protect the furniture.

Back at the Pigalle, Maureen ordered another rum sec and worried about whether things would ever again be the same between Patreek and her.

Sam threw himself against the screen door to Maureen's cottage. As it was not locked, he spilled inside onto the floor, smearing his hair in a wet poster which argued: "HUBERT WILKINSON: DANSEUR UNIQUE!" in great red letters and "HUBERT WILKINSON: UNIQUE DANCER," in smaller, discreet, tourist-colored letters.

"Darling!" cried Tilly. "What on earth happened to you? I told you not to slip and break your neck in those sandals without heels."

He stood up with a piece of DANSEUR UNIQUE sticking to his hair. He stared at Patreek, who gloomily stared back, hot and red-faced, a cigarette in one corner of his mouth. "You," he said, "you lousy fiddler." Patreek acknowledged the salute with a slight bow. Shaking, Sam moved toward him. "What do you think you're doing here?"

"Comb the paint out of your hair, darling. Want some turp?"

Sam ignored his wife and advanced upon Patreek.

"Now remember," Eric warned from the doorway, "we have a complete inventory. The mirror is twenty-three dollars. The table is fifteen. The lamps are all written down."

Patreek retreated by one step. Tilly looked at Eric and shrugged. Sam was gaining on Patreek. Back to the wall, Patreek crunched against Maureen's favorite swatch of driftwood (no stated value).

Tilly clapped her hands. The smile of comprehension on her pretty little face widened until it made noises of joyous flattered laughter, light pitter-pattering sounds showering over a deep note of womanly pleasure. "Oh Sam," she cried, "it's so wonderful of you."

Everywhere Sam stepped he kicked a drying poster, but he still moved toward Patreek, slightly stooped, fists clenched and a vein throbbing in his forehead. Patreek, having already been put through a struggle, raised his hands in a fatigued gesture of assent to manly combat.

Tilly ran to Sam and put her paint-spattered hand on his arm. "Darling Sam, look at me. I'm all covered with Japalac. Come look at the lettering. I've almost finished. Some of it's practically dry, some is damp, some is wet as can be. Look, I've been working steadily."

His eyes widened and he gazed as if he could see at the posters scattered in disarray about the room—propped against the walls, on the tables, over the bed. "It's true," he whispered.

"Patreek tried, but I just laughed at him, darling!"

"It's true," said Sam. "Showcard color can't just be slapped on."

Patreek slipped by him and out the door.

"Yes, darling," said Tilly, "you have to work it and keep it from running."

Sam made a move to try the dampness of one of the posters with his finger, but did not and turned to take his wife in his arms. "I trust you," he announced briefly. Their breathing mingled in a tropical kiss of the sort which Eric did not expect from his married guests.

Eric stood bemused in the doorway, thoroughly embroiled, murmuring to an anolis with its cocked head chomping at termites, "Logic! Understanding! Trust! Then what is there for me in America?"

Richard Matheson

A Flourish of Strumpets

November 1956

Richard Matheson, born in 1926, was already, in the 1950s, a well-known horror and science-fiction writer whose novels—*I Am Legend* (1954) and *The Shrinking Man* (1956)—had been adapted for the movies. Like Charles Beaumont (and sometimes in collaboration with him), Matheson wrote memorable scripts for *The Twilight Zone,* and he also scripted a whole series of movies based on Edgar Allan Poe stories. Two of his stories appeared in *Playboy* in 1956, the year that the magazine stopped reprinting fiction and began to look for original material. Matheson, who lives in California, was never a prolific writer of short stories, but when from time to time one of his innovative, horrific tales would appear ("Distributor," March 1958; "Prey," April 1969, and then two more in 1970), it usually caused something of a stir, bringing in a quantity of mail, mostly positive, from readers.

Richard Matheson

A Flourish of Strumpets

One evening in 1969 the doorbell rang.

Frank and Sylvia Gussett had just settled down to watch television. Frank put his gin-and-tonic on the table and stood. He walked into the hall and opened the door.

It was a woman.

"Good evening," she said. "I represent the Exchange."

"The Exchange?" Frank smiled politely.

"Yes," said the woman. "We're beginning an experimental program in this neighborhood. As to our service—"

Their service was a venerable one. Frank gaped.

"Are you *serious?*" he asked.

"Perfectly," the woman said.

"But . . . good Lord, you can't—come to our very houses and—and—that's against the law! I can have you arrested!"

"Oh, you wouldn't want to do *that*," said the woman. She absorbed blouse-enhancing air.

"Oh, wouldn't I?" said Frank and closed the door in her face.

He stood there breathing hard. Outside, he heard the sound of the woman's spike heels clacking down the porch steps and fading off.

Frank stumbled into the living room.

"It's unbelievable," he said.

Sylvia looked up from the television set. "What is?" she asked.

He told her.

"What!" She rose from her chair, aghast.

They stood looking at each other a moment. Then Sylvia strode to the phone and picked up the receiver. She spun the dial and told the operator, *"I want the police."*

"Strange business," said the policeman who arrived a few minutes later.

"Strange indeed," mused Frank.

"Well, what are you going to *do* about it?" challenged Sylvia.

"Not much we *can* do right off, ma'am," explained the policeman. "Nothing to go on."

"But my description—" said Frank.

"We can't go around arresting every woman we see in spike heels and a white blouse," said the policeman. "If she comes back, you let us know. Probably just a sorority prank, though."

"Perhaps he's right," said Frank when the patrol car had driven off.

Sylvia replied, "He'd better be."

▪ ▪ ▪

"Strangest thing happened last night," said Frank to Maxwell as they drove to work.

Maxwell snickered. "Yeah, she came to our house too," he said.

"She did?" Frank glanced over, startled, at his grinning neighbor.

"Yeah," said Maxwell. "Just my luck the old lady had to answer the door."

Frank stiffened. "*We* called the police," he said.

"What for?" asked Maxwell. "Why fight it?"

Frank's brow furrowed. "You mean you—don't think it was a sorority girl prank?" he asked.

"Hell, no, man," said Maxwell. "It's for real." He began to sing:

I'm just a poor little
door-to-door whore;
A want-to-be-good
But misunderstood . . .

"What on earth?" asked Frank.

"Heard it at a stag party," said Maxwell. "Guess this isn't the first town they've hit."

"Good Lord," muttered Frank, blanching.

"Why not?" asked Maxwell. "It was just a matter of time. Why should they let all that home trade go to waste?"

"That's *execrable,"* declared Frank.

"Hell it is," said Maxwell. "It's progress."

▪ ▪ ▪

The second one came that night; a black-root blonde, slit-skirted and sweatered to within an inch of her breathing life.

"*Hel*-lo, honey," she said when Frank opened the door. "The name's Janie. Interested?"

Frank stood rigid to the heels. "I—" he said.

"Twenty-three and fancy free," said Janie.

Frank shut the door, quivering.

"Again?" asked Sylvia as he tottered back.

"Yes," he mumbled.

"Did you get her address and phone number so we can tell the police?"

"I forgot," he said.

"Oh!" Sylvia stamped her mule. "You said you were going to."

"I know." Frank swallowed. "Her name was—Janie."

"That's a *big* help," Sylvia said. She shivered. "*Now* what are we going to do?"

Frank shook his head.

"Oh, this is *monstrous,*" she said. "That we should be exposed to such . . ." She trembled with fury.

Frank embraced her. "Courage," he whispered.

"I'll get a dog," she said. "A vicious one."

"No, no," he said, "we'll call the police again. They'll simply have to station someone out here."

Sylvia began to cry. "It's monstrous," she sobbed, "that's all."

"Monstrous," he agreed.

▪ ▪ ▪

"What's that you're humming?" she asked at breakfast.

He almost spewed out whole wheat toast.

"Nothing," he said, choking. "Just a song I heard."

She patted him on the back. "Oh."

He left the house, mildly shaken. It *is* monstrous, he thought.

That morning, Sylvia bought a sign at a hardware store and hammered it into the front lawn. It read NO SOLICITING. She underlined the SOLICITING. Later she went out again and underlined the underline.

"Came right to your door you say?" asked the FBI man Frank phoned from the office.

"Right to the door," repeated Frank, "bold as you please."

"My, my," said the FBI man. He clucked.

"Notwithstanding," said Frank sternly, "the police have refused to station a man in our neighborhood."

"I see," said the FBI man.

"Something has got to be done," declared Frank. "This is a gross invasion of privacy."

"It certainly is," said the FBI man, "and we will look into the matter, never fear."

After Frank had hung up, the FBI man returned to his bacon sandwich and thermos of buttermilk.

"I'm just a poor little—" he had sung before catching himself. Shocked, he totted figures the remainder of his lunch hour.

▪ ▪ ▪

The next night it was a perky brunette with a blouse front slashed to forever.

"No!" said Frank in a ringing voice.

She wiggled sumptuously. "Why?" she asked.

"I do not have to explain myself to you!" he said and shut the door, heart pistoning against his chest.

Then he snapped his fingers and opened the door again. The brunette turned, smiling.

"Changed your mind, honey?" she asked.

"No, I mean *yes,*" said Frank, eyes narrowing. "What's your address?"

The brunette looked mildly accusing.

"Now, honey," she said. "You wouldn't be trying to get me in trouble, would you?"

"She wouldn't tell me," he said dismally when he returned to the living room.

Sylvia looked despairing. "I phoned the police again," she said.

"And—?"

"And *nothing*. There's the smell of corruption in this."

Frank nodded gravely. "You'd better get that dog," he said. He thought of the brunette. "A *big* one," he added.

▪ ▪ ▪

"Wowee, that Janie," said Maxwell.

Frank down shifted vigorously and yawed around a corner on squealing tires. His face was adamantine.

Maxwell clapped him on the shoulder.

"Aw, come off it, Frankie-boy," he said, "you're not fooling me any. You're no different from the rest of us."

"I'll have no part in it," declared Frank, "and that's all there is to it."

"So keep telling that to the Mrs.," said Maxwell. "But get in a few kicks on the side like the rest of us. Right?"

"Wrong," said Frank. "*All* wrong. No *wonder* the police can't do anything. I'm probably the only willing witness in town."

Maxwell guffawed.

▪ ▪ ▪

It was a raven-haired, limp-lidded vamp that night. On her outfit spangles moved and glittered at strategic points.

"Hel-*lo*, honey lamb," she said. "My name's—"

"What have you done with our dog?" challenged Frank.

"Why, nothing, honey, nothing," she said. "He's just off getting acquainted with my poodle Winifred. Now about *us* . . ."

Frank shut the door without a word and waited until the twitching had eased before returning to Sylvia and television.

Semper, by God oh God, he thought as he put on his pajamas later, *fidelis*.

▪ ▪ ▪

The next two nights they sat in the darkened living room and, as soon as the women rang the doorbell, Sylvia phoned the police.

"Yes," she whispered, furiously, "they're right out there *now*. Will you please send a patrol car *this instant?"*

Both nights the patrol car arrived after the women had gone.

"Complicity," muttered Sylvia as she daubed on cold cream. "Plain out-and-out complicity."

Frank ran cold water over his wrists.

▪ ▪ ▪

That day Frank phoned city and state officials who promised to look into the matter.

That night it was a redhead sheathed in a green knit dress that hugged all that was voluminous and there was much of that.

"Now see here—" Frank began.

"Girls who were here before me," said the redhead, "tell me you're not interested. Well, I always say, where there's a disinterested husband there's a listening wife."

"Now you see here—" said Frank.

He stopped as the redhead handed him a card. He looked at it automatically.

39-26-36

MARGIE
(specialties)

By appointment only

"If you don't want to set it up here, honey," said Margie, "you just meet me in the Cyprian Room of the Hotel Fillmore."

"I *beg* your pardon," said Frank and flung the card away.

"Any evening between six and seven," Margie chirped.

Frank leaned against the shut door and birds with heated wings buffeted at his face.

"Monstrous," he said with a gulp. "Oh, m-*monstrous*."

"Again?" asked Sylvia.

"But with a difference," he said vengefully. "I have traced them to their lair and tomorrow I shall lead the police there."

"Oh, Frank!" said Sylvia, embracing him. "You're wonderful."

"Th-thank you," said Frank.

▪ ▪ ▪

When he came out of the house the next morning he found the card on one of the porch steps. He picked it up and slid it into his wallet.

Sylvia mustn't see it, he thought.

It would hurt her.

Besides, he had to keep the porch neat.

Besides, it was important evidence.

That evening he sat in a shadowy Cyprian Room booth revolving a glass of sherry between two fingers. Juke box music softly thrummed; there was the mumble of post-work conversation in the air.

Now, thought Frank. *When Margie arrives, I'll duck into the phone booth and call the police, then keep her occupied in conversation until they come. That's what I'll do. When Margie—*

Margie arrived.

Frank sat like a Medusa victim. Only his mouth moved. It opened slowly. His gaze rooted on the jutting opulence of Margie as she waggled along the aisle, then came to gelatinous rest on a leather-topped bar stool.

Five minutes later he cringed out a side door.

"Wasn't *there?"* asked Sylvia for the third time.

"I *told* you," snapped Frank, concentrating on his breaded cutlet.

Sylvia was still a moment. Then her fork clinked down.

"We'll have to move, then," she said. "Obviously, the authorities have no intention of doing *anything."*

"What differences does it make *where* we live?" he mumbled.

She didn't reply.

"I mean," he said, trying to break the painful silence, "well, who knows, maybe it's an inevitable cultural phenomenon. Maybe—"

"Frank Gussett!" she cried. *"Are you defending that awful Exchange?"*

"No, no, of course not," he blurted. "It's execrable. Really! But—well, maybe it's Greece all over again. Maybe it's Rome. Maybe it's—"

"I don't care *what* it is!" she cried. "It's *awful!"*

He put his hand on hers. "There, there," he said.

39-26-36, he thought.

That night, in the frantic dark, there was a desperate reaffirmation of their love.

"It *was* nice, *wasn't* it?" asked Sylvia, plaintively.

"Of course," he said. *39-26-36.*

▪ ▪ ▪

"That's right!" said Maxwell as they drove to work the next morning, "a cultural phenomenon. You hit it on the head, Frankie-boy. An inevitable goddamn cultural phenomenon. First the houses. Then the lady cab drivers, the girls on street corners, the clubs, the teen-age pick-ups roaming the drive-in movies. Sooner or later they had to branch out more; put it on a door-to-door basis. And, naturally, the syndicates are going to run it, pay off complainers. Inevitable. You're so right, Frankie-boy; so right."

Frank drove on, nodding grimly.

Over lunch he found himself humming, *"Mar-gie. I'm always thinkin' of you—"*

He stopped, shaken. He couldn't finish the meal. He prowled the streets until one, marble-eyed. The mass mind, he thought, that evil old mass mind.

Before he went into his office he tore the little card to confetti and snowed it into a disposal can.

In the figures he wrote that afternoon the number *39* cropped up with dismaying regularity.

Once with an exclamation point.

. . .

"I almost think you *are* defending this—this *thing,"* accused Sylvia. "You and your cultural phenomenons!"

Frank sat in the living room listening to her bang dishes in the kitchen sink. Cranky old thing, he thought.

MARGIE

(specialties)

Will you stop! he whispered furiously to his mind. That night while he was brushing his teeth, he started to sing, *"I'm just a poor little—"*

"Damn!" he muttered to his wild-eyed reflection.

That night there were dreams. Unusual ones.

The next day he and Sylvia argued.

The next day Maxwell told him his system.

The next day Frank muttered to himself more than once, "I'm so tired of it all."

. . .

The next night the women stopped coming.

"Is it *possible?"* said Sylvia. "Are they actually going to leave us alone?"

Frank held her close. "Looks like it," he said faintly. *Oh, I'm despicable,* he thought.

A week went by. No women came. Frank woke daily at six A.M. and did a little dusting and vacuuming before he left for work.

"I like to help you," he said when Sylvia asked. She looked at him strangely. When he brought home bouquets three nights in a row she put them in water with a quizzical look on her face.

It was the following Wednesday night.

The doorbell rang. Frank stiffened. They'd *promised* to stop coming!

"I'll get it," he said.

"Do," she said.

He clumped to the door and opened it.

"Evening, sir."

Frank stared at the handsome, mustached young man in the jaunty sports clothes.

"I'm from the Exchange," the man said. "Wife home?"

Ray Bradbury

In a Season of Calm Weather

January 1957

The magazine had its eye on Ray Bradbury right from the beginning; he and Roald Dahl were the only young contemporary authors whose published work was chosen for reprint in the earliest issues. By the time *Playboy* was able to publish an original Bradbury story—the first of many—it was already in a position to illustrate it with several Picasso line drawings. Bradbury, the author of *The Martian Chronicles, Dandelion Wine, Fahrenheit 451,* and *The October Country,* among many other books, is America's most famous fantasist, and no dab hand as a horror writer. He has also written detective novels and movie scripts, notably for John Huston's *Moby Dick.* Born in Illinois in 1920, he has long lived in Los Angeles, where the recent television series, *The Ray Bradbury Theatre,* based on his stories was produced. He continues to be one of *Playboy*'s favorite writers, with new stories appearing nearly every year.

Ray Bradbury

In a Season of Calm Weather

George and Alice Smith detrained at Biarritz one summer noon and in an hour had run through their hotel onto the beach, into the ocean, and back out to bake upon the sand.

To see George Smith sprawled burning there, you'd think him only a tourist flown fresh as iced lettuce to Europe and soon to be trans-shipped home. But here was a man who loved art more than life itself.

"There . . ." George Smith sighed. Another ounce of perspiration trickled down his chest. Boil out the Ohio tapwater, he thought, then drink down the best Bordeaux. Silt your blood with rich French sediment so you'll see with native eyes!

Why? Why eat, breathe, drink everything French? So that, given time, he might really begin to understand the genius of one man.

His mouth moved, forming a name.

"George?" His wife loomed over him. "I know what you've been thinking. I can read your lips."

He lay perfectly still, waiting.

"And?"

"Picasso," she said.

He winced. Someday she would learn to pronounce that name.

"Please," she said. "Relax. I know, you heard the rumor this morning, but you should see your eyes—your tic is back. All right, Picasso's here, down the coast a few miles away, visiting friends in some small fishing town. But you must forget it or our vacation's ruined."

"I wish I'd never heard the rumor," he said honestly.

"If only," she said, "you liked other painters."

Others? Yes, there were others. He could breakfast most congenially on Caravaggio still-lifes of autumn pears and midnight plums. For lunch: those fire-squirting, thick-wormed Van Gogh sunflowers, those blooms a blind man might read with one rush of scorched fingers down fiery canvas. But the great feast? The paintings he saved his palate for? There, filling the horizon, like Neptune risen, crowned with limeweed, alabaster, coral, paintbrushes clenched like tridents in horn-nailed fists, and with fishtail vast enough to fluke summer showers out over all Gibraltar—who else but the creator of *Girl Before a Mirror* and *Guernica?*

"Alice," he said, patiently. "How can I explain? Coming down on the train I thought, Good Lord, it's *all* Picasso country!"

But was it really, he wondered. The sky, the land, the people, the flushed pink bricks here, scrolled electric blue ironwork balconies there, a mandolin ripe as a fruit in some man's thousand-fingerprinting hands, billboard tatters blowing like confetti in night winds—how much was Picasso, how much George Smith staring round the world with wild Picasso eyes? He despaired of answering. That old man had distilled turpentines and linseed oils so thoroughly through George Smith that they shaped his being all Blue Period at twilight, all Rose Period at dawn.

"I keep thinking," he said aloud, "if we saved our money . . ."

"We'll never have five thousand dollars."

"I know," he said quietly. "But it's nice thinking we might bring it off some day. Wouldn't it be great to just step up to him, say 'Pablo, here's five thousand! Give us the sea, the sand, that sky, or any old thing you want, we'll be happy . . .' "

After a moment, his wife touched his arm.

"I think you'd better go in the water now," she said.

"Yes," he said. "I'd better do just that."

White fire showered up where he cut the waves.

During the afternoon George Smith came out and went into the ocean with the vast spilling motions of now warm, now cool people who at last, with the sun's decline, their bodies all lobster colors and colors of broiled squab and guinea hen, trudged for their wedding-cake hotels.

The beach lay deserted for endless mile on mile, save for two people. One was George Smith, towel over shoulder, out for a last devotional.

Far along the shore another, shorter, square-cut man walked alone in the tranquil weather. He was deeply tanned, his close-shaven head dyed almost mahogany by the sun, and his eyes were clear and bright as water in his face.

So the shoreline stage was set, and in a few minutes the two men would meet. And once again Fate fixed the scales for shocks and surprises, arrivals and departures. And all the while these two solitary strollers did not for a moment think on coincidence, that unswum stream which lingers at man's elbow with every crowd in every town. Nor did they ponder the fact that if man dares dip into that stream he grabs a wonder in each hand. Like most they shrugged at such folly, and stayed well up the bank lest Fate should shove them in.

The stranger stood alone. Glancing about, he saw his aloneness, saw the waters of the lovely bay, saw the sun sliding down the late colors of the day, and then half-turning spied a small wooden object on the sand. It was no more than the slender stick from a lime ice-cream delicacy long since melted away. Smiling, he picked the stick up. With another glance around to re-insure his solitude, the man stooped again and holding the stick gently with light sweeps of his hand began to do the one thing in all the world he knew best how to do.

He began to draw incredible figures along the sand.

He sketched one figure and then moved over and still looking down, completely focussed on his work now, drew a second and a third figure and after that a fourth and a fifth and a sixth . . .

George Smith, printing the shoreline with his feet, gazed here, gazed there, and then saw the man ahead. George Smith, drawing nearer, saw that the man, deeply tanned, was bending down. Nearer yet, and it was obvious what the man was up to. George Smith chuckled. Of course, of course . . . alone on the beach this man, how old? Sixty-five? Seventy? was scribbling and doodling away. How the sand flew! How the wild portraits flung themselves out there on the shore! How . . .

George Smith took one more step and stopped, very still.

The stranger was drawing and drawing and did not seem to sense that anyone stood immediately behind him and the world of his drawings in the sand. By now he was so deeply enchanted with his solitudinous creation that depth-bombs, set off in the bay, might not have stopped his flying hand nor turned him round.

George Smith looked down at the sand. And, after a long while, looking, he began to tremble.

For there on the flat shore were pictures of Grecian lions and Mediterranean goats and maidens with flesh of sand like powdered gold and satyrs piping on hand-carved horns and children dancing, strewing flowers along and along the beach with lambs gamboling after and musicians skipping to their harps and lyres, and unicorns racing youths toward distant meadows, woodlands, ruined temples and volcanos. Along the shore in a never-broken line, the hand, the wooden stylus of this man bent down in fever and raining perspiration, scribbled, ribboned, looped around over and up, across, in, out, stitched, whispered, stayed, then hurried on as if this traveling bacchanal must flourish to its end before the sun was put out by the sea. Twenty, thirty yards or more the nymphs and driads and summer founts sprung up in unraveled hieroglyph. And the sand, in the dying light, was the color of molten copper on which was now slashed a message that any man in any time might read and savor down the years. Everything whirled and poised in its own wind and gravity. Now wine was being crushed from under the grape-blooded feet of dancing vintners' daughters, now steaming seas gave birth to coin-sheathed monsters while flowered kites strewed scent on blowing clouds . . . now . . . now . . . now . . .

The artist stopped.

George Smith drew back and stood away.

The artist glanced up, surprised to find someone so near. Then he simply stood there, looking from George Smith to his own creations flung like idle foot-prints down the way. He smiled at last and shrugged as if to say, look what I've done; see what a child? you will forgive me, won't you? one day or another we are all fools . . . you, too, perhaps? so allow an old fool this, eh? Good! Good!

But George Smith could only look at the little man with the sun-dark skin and the clear sharp eyes and say the man's name once, in a whisper, to himself.

They stood thus for perhaps another five seconds, George Smith staring at the sand-frieze, and the artist watching George Smith with amused curiosity. George Smith opened his mouth, closed it, put out his hand, took it back. He stepped toward the pictures, stepped away. Then he moved along the line of fig-ures, like a man viewing a precious series of marbles cast up from some ancient ruin on the shore. His eyes did not blink, his hand wanted to touch but did not dare to touch. He wanted to run but did not run.

He looked suddenly at the hotel. Run, yes! Run! What? Grab a shovel, dig, excavate, save a chunk of this all-too crumbling sand? Find a repairman, race him back here with plaster-of-paris to cast a mould of some small fragile part of these? No, no. Silly, silly. Or . . . ? His eyes flicked to his hotel window. The camera! Run, get it, get back, and hurry along the shore, clicking, changing film, clicking, until . . .

George Smith whirled to face the sun. It burned faintly on his face, his eyes were two small fires from it. The sun was half underwater and as he watched, it sank the rest of the way in a matter of seconds.

The artist had drawn nearer and now was gazing into George Smith's face with great friendliness as if he were guessing every thought. Now he was nodding his head in a little bow. Now the ice-cream stick had fallen casually from his fin-gers. Now he was saying good night, good night. Now he was gone, walking back down the beach toward the south.

George Smith stood looking after him. After a full minute, he did the only thing that he could possibly do. He started at the beginning of the fantastic frieze of satyrs and fauns and wine-dipped maidens and prancing unicorns and piping youths and he walked slowly along the shore. He walked a long way, looking down at the free-running bacchanal. And when he came to the end of the animals and men he turned around and started back in the other direction, just staring down as if he had lost something and did not quite know where to find it. He kept on doing this until there was no more light in the sky, or on the sand, to see by.

He sat down at the supper-table.

"You're late," said his wife. "I just had to come down alone. I'm ravenous."

"That's all right," he said.

"Anything interesting happen on your walk?" she asked.

"No," he said.

"You look funny. George, you didn't swim out too far, did you, and almost drown? I can tell by your face. You *did* swim out too far, didn't you?"

"Yes," he said.

"Well," she said, watching him closely. "Don't ever do that again. Now—what'll you have?"

He picked up the menu and started to read it and stopped suddenly.

"What's wrong?" asked his wife.

He turned his head and shut his eyes for a moment.

"Listen."

She listened.

"I don't hear anything," she said.

"Don't you?"

"No. What is it?"

"Just the tide," he said, after awhile, sitting there, his eyes still shut. "Just the tide, coming in."

James Jones

Just Like the Girl

January 1958

James Jones's first story for *Playboy,* "The King," a gritty, realistic jazz tale, appeared in 1955. His novel of army life, *From Here to Eternity,* published in 1951, had been an enormous popular and critical success, and for the still relatively new magazine to acquire a story by the literary lion of the moment was a coup and a signal to other writers that *Playboy* was a market to take seriously. Jones (1921–1977) was just what *Playboy* was looking for, a certified tough guy who wrote affecting prose. The magazine excerpted his later novels—*Some Came Running* (1957), *The Thin Red Line* (1962)—and even, in 1991, years after his death, some previously unpublished work.

James Jones

Just Like the Girl

"Now listen carefully," John's mother said, and her voice was rushed and breathless.

She took him by his left arm, and her skin-flaky hand—which, as she said, was "rurned" from washing dishes—went clear around the thinness of his arm. She pulled him close to her and talked into his ear as if they were not alone in the house.

"He'll be home in a minute," she said to him, her eyes bright and nervous. "It's after six now and he never stays at the office later than five. He's been somewheres drinking, I could tell by his voice over the phone. He'll come home with that great big ugly nasty belly tight as a drum with beer again."

"Yes, Ma'm," John said. He was scared by the intensity of her voice, and she was gripping his arm so hard he could hardly keep from wincing.

"Here is what I want you to do for me, John. I want you to do this for your mother who loves you. When he brings the groceries in, you run out and get in the car. You understand?"

"Yes, Ma'm," John said. "All right, Mother." He knew this was important, because she was shaking his arm hard. "But what for?"

"Be still. Listen to me. I asked him please not to go back downtown in his condition. I asked him to stay home. I only just hope the operator was listening. Mrs. Haddock says they always do. God knows I've lived with it long enough and tried to hide it and hold our heads up," she said. "And he just laughed at me. Like he always does. But I've always done my duty, in the eyes of God and society. I've done all I could be expected to do."

John was nodding his head. His arm hurt and his mother was still shaking him; he was wondering how, if he was to go in the car, they would be able to go to the Sugar Bowl and the show. This was Saturday and Saturday night his mother always took him and Jeannette to the Sugar Bowl and they ate coney islands or barbecues and they had a malted and then they went to the show. And the malteds at the Sugar Bowl were thick, boy. It was their Saturday treat and he hated to miss it, even if his mother always did make them sit with her at the show instead of down front with the other kids and she stopped outside the show to talk to the other ladies and always made them stand right beside her because, as she told the ladies, John was grown up and taking his father's place like a little man. But then that was what you had to do if you wanted to go.

"Aren't we going to the show tonight, Mother?" he said.

"No we're not going to the show tonight, Mother. Aren't you listening to me? I want you to go in the car with your father. I want you to get in the back seat and keep out of sight. Get down on the floor and stay hid. You watch where he goes and when he comes home you tell me every place he went. I want you to do this for me."

"I don't care about the show, Mother," John said.

"Maybe we'll go tomorrow. If you love your mother like you say, you'll do this for her. You'll hide in the back of the car and find out who it is your father meets, and find out what her name is if you can, and then when I go away I'll take you with me and we'll go away for ever."

"Will Jeannette go too, Mother?" John said.

"Yes. We'll take Jeannette with us too," she said to him and there were tears in her bright eyes. "He isn't fit to have children. Him with those great big arms and strong as a bull. He hurts everything he touches, he'd kill any woman. We'll go far away where he can never find us, with his big talk of education and making fun of my Science and Mrs. Eddy, making everybody think he's so intelligent and saddled with a dumb wife."

"You're not dumb, Mother," John said. "You're smart. You're my mother." He blinked tears from his own eyes, he felt very sorry for his mother. A diworce, he thought, we're going to get a diworce.

"I've given my whole life to you children." His mother let go of his arm and he was glad of that. It was a little numb, but he didn't rub it because his mother put her hands on his shoulders. "You're all I have left now. You and Jeannette. Since your brother Tom grew up and left me. Everybody said I was the most beautiful woman in this county and he was lucky to get me. Now he's cast me aside, for any hot-assed bitch that walks the streets."

John nodded, memorizing the phrase. He learned lots of good swearwords the other kids never heard, listening to his mother and dad when they were mad, although he never said them around her, except when he forgot, because she always washed his mouth out with soap, holding him by the back of the neck, and turning the washrag around wrapped over her fingers and rubbing it hard over his tongue and the roof of his mouth, whenever she heard him swear.

"Someday women will be free," his mother said. She knelt down on the floor beside him and put her arms around him. "Your mother loves you, Johnny, even if she is the ugliest old hag in town."

"You're not ugly, Mother," John said. "You're beautiful and you're my mother." He patted the cook-sweating broadness of his mother's back. It was almost like the game where someone asks the question and you have to give the right answer or pay a forfeit, except he always got so scared it wasn't any fun.

"If you really love your mother, you'll stand by her."

"Sure I will, Mother," John said. "I'll do anything for you. Someday, Mother, I'll make a million dollars and I'll give it all to you."

"No," his mother said. "No, you won't. Someday you'll do just like your brother did. You'll grow up and forget all your mother ever did for you. You'll remember the money your father gives you and I don't have to give you and you'll turn on your ugly mother just like your brother did and go over to your father."

"No I won't either," John protested, feeling guilty. He knew his mother didn't have the money to give him quarters and half dollars like his father did. He knew how hard up they were because his father threw so much money away on beer and whiskey, and then tried to buy his son's affection with quarters and half dollars. Every time he sneaked up in the garage loft to play with his secret collection of extra soldiers and guns, he felt guilty.

"I'll always stand by you, Mother," he said. "I won't be like Tom. Honest I won't. I'm not like Tom."

"Will you prove it to me? Will you find out who your father goes out with tonight?"

"Sure I will, Mother. Didn't I say I would?"

His mother stood up. "All right. You wait out on the front porch where he won't see you. When he brings the groceries in you run out and get in. But be careful: He bought groceries for over Sunday and he'll probably have to make two trips to the car."

"All right, Mother," John said. "You can trust me, Mother."

His mother was on her way back to the kitchen. "Don't let him see you out on the porch."

"OK, Mother," John said.

He went out the front door and sat down in the porch swing to wait for his father to come home. The moon was full, and it reminded him of the quarters and half dollars his father tried to buy his affection with every now and then. It was so bright it made shadows under the trees just like daytime. It made everything hazy like a lace curtain. He sat and swung the swing and listened to the chain creak and rubbed his arm where it still hurt and watched the lace curtain of moonlight.

I'll fool him, he thought. I won't let him buy me away from Mother with quarters and half dollars like he did Tom. I'll take the quarters and half dollars, but I won't let him kid *me*. It made him feel a little better, a little less guilty, but still he knew, guiltily, that he shouldn't take them, any of them.

Once his father had given him a half dollar right in front of his mother. It was the time she hit him with the kitchen fork when she was frying chicken. He was standing by the stove bothering her with questions and making a nuisance of himself, and it was a hot day long, long years ago, and she just got mad and hit him with the fork. The fork cut his forehead and broke his glasses and the blood ran down into his eyes. It did not hurt much but the blood in his eyes scared him because he couldn't see and thought maybe he was going to die. His mother threw the fork down on the floor and started crying and that scared him worse because then he was sure he was going to die and he did not want to die yet, when he was still just such a little boy. She phoned the doctor and his father, and she kept wringing her hands and crying "O what have I done! My poor little boy! My darling son!" and he had felt very sorry for her and put his arms around her and told her it was all right and it didn't hurt much and for her not to worry, he did not really mind dying when he was still such a little boy, but it only made her cry worse. He knew she did not really mean to do it because she cried so much and she sacrificed everything for him and Jeannette and loved them better than anything in the world. So when the doctor and his father came, he and his mother told them he fell down and cut his forehead on the edge of the table. His father gave him a half dollar right in front of his mother and squatted down and put his arm around him. If he had been cut over both eyes he bet his father would have given him a whole dollar.

Other kids' fathers didn't give them whole dollars when they got cut over both eyes, and his father really looked tough when he got mad. He bet there wasn't anybody would tackle his father when he got mad, even if he was a drunkard and ran around with hot-assed bitches and had those great big arms and belly and strong as a bull and would kill any woman. Sitting in the swing he wondered what the hot-assed bitch looked like. He hoped he would get to see them doing it.

Suddenly in his mind he saw his father sitting at the kitchen table, all alone, holding the diworce, drinking a bottle of beer, playing with a pile of quarters and half dollars that he did not have anybody to give them to, that was the way it would be when they were gone. He blinked tears from his eyes, he felt very sorry for his father. A diworce, he thought, we're going to get a diworce.

When his father drove in the driveway he got down on his hands and knees behind the brick railing and watched through the four-cornered hole like a diamond while his father opened the back door of the big square Studebaker and took two huge paper sacks of groceries in his big arms and carried them to the back door. Looking through the trees into the clearing Hawkeye leveled his cap-n-ball-long-rifle and let the big Indian have it, right in the chest, and the two big paper sacks of dynamite tumbled unhurt to the ground; Hawkeye had fired between them carefully because the dynamite was needed to blow the Indian village up the river. He aimed over his finger and fired; and his father walked on to the house.

Then he waited, just as his mother had told him, grinning at how he was outsmarting his father. After the second trip he ran lightly out into the yard, carrying his rifle at trail and loading her as he ran, the Indians called him The Man Whose Gun Was Always Loaded, opened the back door of the car and hit the dirt. It was dusty on the floor and the dust got in his nose and choked him up but he did not mind because he had made it across the clearing unseen and had slipped into the enemy general's limousine.

He heard them talking loud in the kitchen and guessed they were having another big argument. His father came out and slammed the door and got in the car and he lay, laughing to himself, very excited.

His father drove down toward town and every corner John concentrated hard on which way they turned and tried to see the corner in his mind. There was a place on the road through the forest the enemy general's truck was following that it was of the greatest importance he jump out the back of the truck unseen. Some enemy soldiers were holding Priscilla Jenkins captive and going to torture her with red-hot irons. In his mind he saw Priscilla, a great lady now, standing tied to a tree, her clothes torn clear off of her and the enemy soldiers stepping up to put a red-hot iron against her thing—just as he leaped into the circle of firelight wearing his fringed buckskins of a scout and the two enemy soldiers were deaders and Priscilla was very happy to be saved from a fate worse than death and they did it there in the firelight with the two deaders staring open-eyed at the sky.

When his father stopped the car it was the spot, and it was of the greatest importance that he know where it was, and he picked Meeker's Restaurant. He waited till his father got out and was gone and then peeked over the bottom of the window. Instead of Meeker's Restaurant they were in front of the old American Legion. It was very bad, because Priscilla was a deader unless he could figure something out.

He lay there on the floor a long time, wishing his father would hurry up and come back with the hot-assed bitch so he could see them do it, he had never seen anybody do it, but he was tired of laying on the floor and he was getting sleepy. He lay with the sleepiness and the Saturday night noises coming loud suddenly, then going far away, and coming and going and coming and going and he heard his father speak from behind a curtain and far away the car doors opened and his father and someone else got in. Then suddenly he was back inside himself again and listening hard. None of the kids had ever really seen anybody do it. They wouldn't care if he was a drunkard's son or not, if he told how he had seen them do it and just what they did.

"Give me the bottle," he heard his father say. "You mark what I'm saying, Lab. It won't be ten years."

John recognized with disappointment the other voice that answered. It was no hot-assed bitch at all, it was only old Lab Wallers from the American Legion, and he felt he had been cheated of a great adventure.

"I still say she wouldn't want you to go, Doc," it said.

"I don't know," his father said. "Sometimes I think she would. I know she would. She'd be damned glad to get rid of a no-good like me. And I guess I don't blame her any. Anyway," he said, "I'll be too old."

"There won't be another war anyway," Lab Wallers said. "Thas why we won the last one, so there wouldn't be no more. Wilson was a good man, and he knew what he was doin'."

"He couldn't do anything with a Republican congress," his father said.

"Well, he was smarter than this Coolidge, Doc, you don't want your boys to grow up and get drug into something like we did," Lab Wallers said.

"Hell, no," his father said. "But there's no way out. Give your son luck, and throw him into the sea. That's what the Spaniards say. That's all any man can do. I tell you it won't be ten years."

That's me, John thought, they're talking about me. He was a little surprised because everybody knew there wouldn't be any more war. He had always been sorry when he thought how he would never get to be in a war like his father. He lay there, excited, thinking how he would save Priscilla Jenkins from the enemy just as they were about to burn her thing with the red-hot iron. He would come home a great hero and everybody would think he was a fine upstanding man. He wouldn't drink at all, and maybe he would marry Priscilla Jenkins.

Following the pictures in his mind the sleepiness came back and the voice talking began to come and go, loud and faint, like the band concert across town sounded in a shifting summer wind.

"She's a fine woman, Doc," Lab Wallers said. "They don't come any finer. My wife's always talkin' about how fine she is."

"I know she is," his father said. "Everybody knows it. Nobody has to tell me that. I know it's my fault. I know I'm a bum and a drunk."

"We don't deserve the women we got, Doc," Lab Wallers said, his voice thick. "Neither one of us. *None* of us."

"If it wasn't for the kids I'd light out tonight," his father said. "Give her a chance. But it's awful hard to leave your kids, your own kids. What you've done lives on in your kids, if nowhere else."

"She loves you though," Lab Wallers said. "Don't you forget it."

"No she doesn't," his father said, "and I don't blame her. I know what I am," he said. "I know what I've done."

"Give me the bottle," Lab Wallers said. "I don't know where I'd be if it wasn't for my wife. Or you either. Where would the world be, without the wives?

Where would our kids be, if it wasn't for their mothers? Where would this nation be, if it wasn't for the women?"

"She was the most beautiful woman in this part of the country when I married her," his father said. "I was lucky to get her. Everybody says so. If she just wouldn't devil me so. Goddamn it, Lab, someday the men will be free.

"What time is it? I have to be back in town by ten. I have to see somebody. Goddamn it, a man has to live, Lab . . ."

John didn't hear the rest. He was very sleepy and none of it made sense. He just shut his eyes for a minute, only a minute, because he really had to stay awake.

He woke up surprised, because he wasn't in the car anymore. As he came awake he realized he was being carried. His father was carrying him in his arms. John noticed sleepily that his father was wearing some funny new kind of sweet shaving lotion. He did not know where they were at first, but then he saw they were at home at the house. His father carried him inside.

Upstairs, his father laid him down on his bed in his own room and began to undress him, fumbling the buttons. He lay very still, his eyes shut, letting his father undress him and put him to bed. It made him feel good. When he was under the covers, he opened his eyes and smiled at his father. His father smiled back, and John could tell by his eyes that he was pretty drunk.

"Here," his father said, reaching in his pocket. "Put this under your pillow. You earned it. You're a damned good man. You've got a lot of guts and I'm proud you are my son."

John reached out his hand and took it. He rolled over sleepily in the bed. Gee, he thought, a quarter and *two* half dollars *both*. Gee. But he held them in his hand and did not put them under his pillow, because he was suddenly thinking of his mother. I really oughtn't to take them, he thought, thinking guiltily about his brother Tom. I ought to give them back.

"Guts are what a man needs," his father said. "You're going to need a lot of guts, Johnny boy, someday. Someday you'll need guts bad."

His father paused and patted him on the head and then he rubbed his strong stubby-fingered hand over his chin that needed a shave. He got up from the bed slowly. "Always remember: If a man's got guts, he'll come out all right. You got to have the guts to stand up for yourself even when you're bad and wrong," he said, "or you're dead. You'll never be a man again." He stood beside the bed looking down and smiling sadly.

There was Priscilla, the soldiers getting ready to put the iron against her, hard; and there was the general and he was handing him two thousand dollars to go away and forget he had seen it, like every good spy should. And it wasn't even Priscilla. It was just some woman. And a good spy had work to do at the front.

But this time it didn't work, because over the scene in the forest John could see his mother's face with her bright bright eyes looking at him. He wished it *would* work, because he wanted to keep the money. But this time it was not real.

It wasn't a real game at all. It was only playlike. It wasn't two thousand dollars at all, it was only a quarter and two half dollars both.

And there was Mother watching him who didn't think he loved her anymore. He could almost see her. Mother thought he was going to be like Tom. He could almost see her looking at him if he took the money.

"Dad," John said, looking at the silver moons. "Here, Dad," he made himself extend his arm. "I don't want your money."

His father stood looking down at him, his big face and the muscles around his eyes getting a crinkledy look that frightened John, and his eyes seemed to go out of focus and swing around back and forth behind themselves, from one side of John to the other. Then he took the coins and looked at them and put them in his pocket.

"All right, buddyboy," he said in a voice John could hardly hear. "Good night, old man." Carefully with his big hands, gently, he turned off the light and went out of the room and slowly shut the door.

That look on his father's face still scared John a little, but it gave him great pleasure to know he was not like Tom. Mother would be proud of him. He can't buy my affection, John thought proudly, I'm not like Tom.

Roald Dahl

A Fine Son

December 1959

Roald Dahl (1916–1990) is remembered as the author of the children's classics *James and the Giant Peach* and *Charlie and the Chocolate Factory.* But he was also an accomplished short story writer, a master of macabre elegance in the British style. As in Bradbury's case, the *Playboy* editors had thought highly enough of Dahl's work to reprint stories from his first collection, *Someone Like You* (1953), in the early issues. "A Fine Son" was his first original story for the magazine, but most of Dahl's later stories appeared in its pages, as did an excerpt from his only novel, *My Uncle Oswald,* which in turn was based on a *Playboy* story, "The Visitor" (May, 1965).

Roald Dahl

A Fine Son

"Everything is normal," the doctor was saying. "Just lie back and relax." His voice was miles away in the distance and he seemed to be shouting at her. "You have a son."

"What?"

"You have a fine son. You understand that, don't you? A fine son. Did you hear him crying?"

"Is he all right, Doctor?"

"Of course he is all right."

"Please let me see him."

"You'll see him in a moment."

"You are certain he is all right?"

"I am quite certain."

"Is he still crying?"

"Try to rest. There is nothing to worry about."

"Why has he stopped crying, Doctor? What happened?"

"Don't excite yourself, please. Everything is normal."

"I want to see him. Please let me see him."

"Dear lady," the doctor said, patting her hand. "You have a fine strong healthy child. Don't you believe me when I tell you that?"

"What is the woman over there doing to him?"

"Your baby is being made to look pretty for you," the doctor said. "We are giving him a little wash, that is all. You must spare us a moment or two for that."

"You swear he is all right?"

"I swear it. Now lie back and relax. Close your eyes. Go on, close your eyes. That's right. That's better. Good girl . . ."

"I have prayed and prayed that he will live, Doctor."

"Of course he will live. What are you talking about?"

"The others didn't."

"What?"

"None of my other ones lived, Doctor."

The doctor stood beside the bed looking down at the pale exhausted face of the young woman. He had never seen her before today. She and her husband were new people in the town. The innkeeper's wife, who had come up to assist in the delivery, had told him that the husband worked at the local customshouse on the border and that the two of them had arrived quite suddenly at the inn with one trunk and one suitcase about three months ago. The husband was a drunkard, the innkeeper's wife had said, an arrogant, overbearing, bullying little drunkard, but the young woman was gentle and religious. And she was very sad. She never smiled. In the short time she had been here, the innkeeper's wife had never once seen her smile. Also there was a rumor that this was the husband's third marriage, that one wife had died and that the other had divorced him for unsavory reasons. But that was only a rumor.

The doctor bent down and pulled the sheet up a little higher over the patient's chest. "You have nothing to worry about," he said gently. "This is a perfectly normal baby."

"That's exactly what they told me about the others. But I lost them all, Doctor. In the last eighteen months I have lost all three of my children, so you mustn't blame me for being anxious."

"Three?"

"This is my fourth . . . in four years."

The doctor shifted his feet uneasily on the bare floor.

"I don't think you know what it means, Doctor, to lose them all, all three of them, slowly, separately, one by one. I keep seeing them. I can see Gustav's face now as clearly as if he were lying here beside me in the bed. Gustav was a lovely boy, Doctor. But he was always ill. It is terrible when they are always ill and there is nothing you can do to help them."

"I know."

The woman opened her eyes, stared up at the doctor for a few seconds, then closed them again.

"My little girl was called Ida. She died a few days before Christmas. That is only four months ago. I just wish you could have seen Ida, Doctor."

"You have a new one now."

"But Ida was so beautiful."

"Yes," the doctor said. "I know."

"How can you know?" she cried.

"I am sure that she was a lovely child. But this new one is also like that." The doctor turned away from the bed and walked over to the window and stood there looking out. It was a wet gray April afternoon, and across the street he could see the red roofs of the houses and the huge raindrops splashing on the tiles.

"Ida was two years old, Doctor . . . and she was so beautiful I was never able to take my eyes off her from the time I dressed her in the morning until she was safe in bed again at night. I used to live in holy terror of something happening to that child. Gustav had gone and my little Otto had also gone and she was all I had left. Sometimes I used to get up in the night and creep over to the cradle and put my ear close to her mouth just to make sure that she was breathing."

"Try to rest," the doctor said, going back to the bed. "Please try to rest." The woman's face was white and bloodless, but there was a slight bluish-gray tinge around the nostrils and the mouth. A few strands of damp hair hung down over her forehead, sticking to the skin.

"When she died . . . I was already pregnant again when that happened, Doctor. This new one was a good five months on its way when Ida died. 'I don't want it!' I shouted after the funeral. 'I won't have it! I have buried enough children!' And my husband . . . he was strolling among the guests with a big glass of beer in his hand . . . he turned around quickly and said, 'I have news for you, Klara, I have good news.' Can you imagine that, Doctor? We have just buried our third child and he stands there with a glass of beer in his hand and tells me that he has good news. 'Today I have been posted to Braunau,' he says, 'so you can start packing at once. This will be a new start for you, Klara,' he says. 'It will be a new place and you can have a new doctor. . . .' "

"Please don't talk anymore."

"You *are* the new doctor, aren't you, Doctor?"

"That's right."

"And here we are in Braunau."

"Yes."

"I am frightened, Doctor."

"Try not to be frightened."

"What chance can the fourth one have now?"

"You must stop thinking like that."

"I can't help it. I am certain there is something inherited that causes my children to die in this way. There must be."

"That is nonsense."

"Do you know what my husband said to me when Otto was born, Doctor? He came into the room and he looked into the cradle where Otto was lying and he said, 'Why do *all* my children have to be so small and weak?' "

"I am sure he didn't say that."

"He put his head right into Otto's cradle as though he were examining a tiny insect and he said, 'All I am saying is why can't they be better *specimens?* That's all I am saying.' And three days after that, Otto was dead. We baptized him quickly on the third day and he died the same evening. And then Gustav died. And then Ida died. All of them died, Doctor . . . and suddenly the whole house was empty. . . ."

"Don't think about it now."

"Is this one so very small?"

"He is a normal child."

"But small?"

"He is a little small, perhaps. But the small ones are often a lot tougher than the big ones. Just imagine, this time next year he will be almost learning how to walk. Isn't that a lovely thought?"

She didn't answer this.

"And two years from now he will probably be talking his head off and driving you crazy with his chatter. Have you settled on a name for him yet?"

"A name?"

"Yes."

"I don't know. I'm not sure. I think my husband said that if it was a boy we were going to call him Adolfus because it has a certain similarity to Alois. My husband is called Alois."

"Excellent."

"Oh no!" she cried, starting up suddenly from the pillow. "That's the same question they asked me when Otto was born! It means he is going to die! You are going to baptize him at once!"

"Now, now," the doctor said, taking her gently by the shoulders. "You are quite wrong. I promise you you are wrong. I was simply being an inquisitive old man, that is all. And look—here he comes now."

The innkeeper's wife, carrying the baby high up on her enormous bosom, came sailing across the room toward the bed. "Here is the little beauty!" she cried, beaming. "Would you like to hold him, my dear? Shall I put him beside you?"

"Is he well wrapped?" the doctor asked. "It is extremely cold in here."

"Certainly he is well wrapped."

The baby was tightly swaddled in a white woolen shawl, and only the tiny pink head protruded. The innkeeper's wife placed him gently on the bed beside the mother. "There you are," she said. "Now you can lie there and look at him to your heart's content."

"I think you will like him," the doctor said, smiling. "He is a fine little baby."

"He has the most lovely hands!" the innkeeper's wife exclaimed. "Such long delicate fingers!"

The mother didn't move. She didn't even turn her head to look.

"Go on," cried the innkeeper's wife. "He won't bite you."

"I am frightened to look. I don't dare to believe that I have another baby and that he is all right."

"Don't be so stupid."

Slowly, the mother turned her head and looked at the small, incredibly serene face that lay on the pillow beside her.

"Is this my baby?"

"Of course."

"Oh . . . oh . . . but he is beautiful."

The doctor turned away and went over to the table and began putting his things into his bag. The mother lay on the bed gazing at the child and smiling and touching him and making little noises of pleasure. "Hello, my son," she whispered.

"Ssshh!" said the innkeeper's wife. "Listen! I think your husband is coming."

The doctor walked over to the door and opened it and looked out into the corridor. "Come in, please," he said.

A small man in a dark-green uniform stepped softly into the room and looked around him.

"Congratulations," the doctor said. "You have a son."

The man had a pair of enormous whiskers meticulously groomed after the manner of the Emperor Franz Josef, and he smelled strongly of beer. "A son?"

"Yes."

"How is he?"

"He is fine. So is your wife."

"Good." The father turned and walked with a curious little prancing stride over to the bed where his wife was lying. "Well, Klara," he said, smiling through his whiskers. "How did it go?" He bent down to take a look at the baby. Then he bent lower. In a series of quick jerky movements, he bent lower and lower until his face was only about twelve inches from the baby's head. The wife lay sideways on the pillow, staring up at him with a kind of supplicating look.

"He has the most marvelous pair of lungs," the innkeeper's wife announced. "You should have heard him screaming just after he came into this world."

"But my God, Klara . . ."

"What is it, dear?"

"This one is even smaller than Otto was!"

The doctor took a couple of quick paces forward. "There is nothing wrong with that child," he said.

Slowly, the husband straightened up and turned away from the bed and looked at the doctor. He seemed bewildered and stricken. "It's no good lying, Doctor," he said. "I know what it means. It's going to be the same all over again."

"Now you listen to me," the doctor said.

"But do you *know* what happened to the others, Doctor?"

"You must forget about the others. Give this one a chance."

"But so small and weak!"

"My dear sir, he has only just been born."

"Even so . . ."

"What are you trying to do?" cried the innkeeper's wife. "Talk him into his grave?"

"That's enough!" the doctor said sharply.

The mother was weeping now. Great sobs were shaking her body.

The doctor walked over to the husband and put a hand on his shoulder. "Be good to her, Herr Hitler," he whispered. "Please. It is very important." Then he squeezed the husband's shoulder hard and began pushing him forward surreptitiously to the edge of the bed. The husband hesitated. The doctor squeezed harder, signaling to him urgently through fingers and thumb. At last, reluctantly, the husband bent down and kissed his wife lightly on the cheek.

"All right, Klara," he said. "Now stop crying."

"I have prayed so hard that Adolfus will live."

"Yes."

"Every day for months I have gone to the church and begged on my knees that this one will be allowed to live."

"Yes, Klara, I know."

"Three dead children is all that I can stand, don't you realize that?"

"Of course."

"He *must* live, Alois. He *must,* he must . . . Oh God, be merciful unto him now. . . ."

Shirley Jackson

A Great Voice Stilled

March 1960

Nearly everyone knows Shirley Jackson (1919–1965) for her sensational short story of a brutal ritual in small-town America, "The Lottery" (1948), which holds the record for bringing in more outraged mail—and canceled subscriptions—than *The New Yorker* has ever received for any other piece. Apparently many readers thought it was journalism, not fiction at all. Nearly as famous are the great (and frequently imitated, though never so well) haunted-house novel *The Haunting of Hill House* (1959) and *We Have Always Lived in the Castle,* which won the National Book Award in 1962. Born in San Francisco, but a Vermonter in adult life, Jackson was something of an eccentric—she claimed to be a practicing witch. This was her only story to be published in *Playboy,* and it was the first fiction by a woman to appear in the magazine's pages. Hardly more than a sketch, it neatly parodies the pretensions of the intellectual smart set of the 1950s.

Shirley Jackson

A Great Voice Stilled

The hospital waiting room was an island of inefficiency in the long echoing and white-painted and silenced stretches of the hospital. In the waiting room there were ashtrays and crackling wicker furniture and uneven brown wooden benches and clearly unswept corners; the business of the hospital did not go on with the intruders waiting restlessly, and with every bed in every wing of the hospital filled, it was perfectly all right with the hospital administration to see the wicker chairs and wooden benches in the waiting room empty and wasting space. Katherine Ashton, who had not wanted to come anywhere near the hospital, who had wanted to stay at home in the apartment on this dark Sunday afternoon, who had wanted to cry a little in private and then dine later in some small unobtrusive restaurant—perhaps the one where they did sweetbreads so nicely—and linger over a melancholy brandy; Katherine Ashton came into the waiting room behind her husband, saying, "I wish we hadn't come. I tell you I hate hospitals and death scenes and anyway how does anyone know he's going to die today?"

"You'd always be sorry if you hadn't come," Martin said. When he saw that the waiting room was empty, he turned back and looked hopefully up and down the hospital hall. "You think we could go upstairs right now?"

"They won't *possibly* let us upstairs. Not *possibly.*"

"We got here first," Martin said reasonably. "As soon as they let anyone go upstairs, it ought to be us, because we certainly got here ahead of the rest."

"I'm going to feel like a fool," Katherine said. "Suppose he doesn't die? Suppose no one else comes?"

"Look." Martin stopped walking back and forth from the window to the door and came to stand in front of her, as though he were lecturing to one of his classes. "He's *got* to die. Here Angell is flying down from Boston. And practically the whole staff of *Dormant Review* up all night working on obituaries and remembrances and his American publisher already getting together a *Festschrift,* and the wife flying in from Majorca if they weren't able to stop her. And Weasel calling every major literary critic from here to California to get them here in time. You think the man would have the *gall* to live after that?"

"But when I tried to call the doctor—"

"In my business," Martin said, "you've got to be in the right places at the right times. Like a salesman or something. Just by being here I get a chance to meet Angell, for instance—how long could I go, otherwise, trying to get to meet Angell? And if I swing it right *Dormant* could even—"

"Here's Joan," Katherine said. "She's still crying."

Martin moved swiftly to the doorway. "Joan, dear," he said. "How *is* he?"

"Not . . . very well," Joan said. "Hello, Katherine."

"Hello, Joan," Katherine said.

"I finally got hold of the doctor," Joan said. "I called and called and finally *made* him talk to me. It sounds pretty . . . black." She put her hand across her mouth as though she wanted to stop her lips from trembling.

"A matter of hours," she said.

"My God," Martin said.

"How awful," Katherine said.

"Angell's flying down from Boston, did you hear?" Joan sat tentatively on the edge of a bench. "Anybody upstairs with him?"

"They won't let anyone go up," Katherine said.

"Maybe they're giving him a bath, or something. Or do they bother, if it's only a matter of . . ."

"I don't know," Katherine said, and Joan sobbed.

"But it's pretty certain to be today?" Martin asked, with a kind of reluctant delicacy.

"You know how doctors talk." Joan sobbed again. "They had to take me home this morning and give me a sedative, I was crying so. I haven't had any sleep or anything to eat since yesterday. I was right here all the time until they took me home this morning and gave me a sedative."

"Very touching," said Martin. "Katherine and I thought it would look better if there weren't so many people around, so we haven't come until today."

"John Weasel said he'd bring in some sandwiches and stuff later. I plan to stay right here, now, until the end."

"So do we," Martin said firmly.

"The Andersons are coming over, and probably those people he was visiting last weekend, they're probably coming down from Connecticut. And—we all thought it was so sweet—the bar, you know, the one where he had the attack, well, they're sending over flowers. We all thought it was so sweet."

"It was nice of them," Katherine said.

"I only hope Angell gets here in time. Weasel's got the Smiths and their car at the airport and he even called the police station to ask for a police escort, but of course you can't ever make *them* understand. I'm still crying so I can't stop. I haven't stopped since yesterday."

"Someone's coming," Martin said, and Joan sobbed. "Weasel," Martin said. "Weasel, dear old fellow. Any news?"

"I called the doctor. Katherine, hello. Joan, my dear, you shouldn't be here, you really *shouldn't;* you promised me you'd try and get some rest. Now I *am* cross with you."

"I'm sorry." Joan looked up tearfully. "I couldn't bear it, not being near him."

"What a *day* I've had." Weasel sighed and sat down on a bench and let his hands fall wearily. "The *police,* honestly! I told them and *told* them the light of the literary world was going out right here, and so could we *please* just get some kind of an escort to bring the country's foremost literary critic over from the airport to hear his last words and close his eyes and what-not, but I swear, darling, it's exactly like talking to a pack of *prairie* dogs. Calling me 'sir' and asking me who *I* was, and—" he sat up and slapped his forehead violently, "the *wife*, great Bacchus, don't *ask* me about the wife! Cables to Majorca all day yesterday and phone calls to Washington and clearance on the plane and all those cousins of hers pulling strings just simply *every*where and she's arriving with absolutely *no* baggage!"

"You mean his wife *is* coming?" Joan stared open-mouthed.

"Darling, she'll be here practically any *minute;* I kept *pleading* with the woman, I swear I did, positively *entreating* her—no place to put her up, no one free to take care of her, we're *perfectly* capable of making all arrangements this end, and she literally would not listen to a word I said. I swear that that woman would not listen to a blessed word I said. I *knew* you'd be *furious,"* he said to Joan.

Joan wailed. "Naturally we'd send her the *body."*

Martin was pacing back and forth again, from the door to the window. "When will they let us go upstairs?" he demanded irritably.

Joan looked at him, surprised. "You think *you're* going upstairs?"

"We were here first," Martin said.

"But you didn't even *know* him."

"Katherine knew him exactly as well as you did," Martin said flatly. "Besides, he had dinner with us Tuesday night."

"Katherine certainly did *not* know him as well as I did," Joan said.

"He did *not* have dinner with you," Weasel said. "Not *Tuesday.* Tuesday he—"

"I certainly did," Katherine said. "If you care for a public comparison—"

Joan opened her mouth to interrupt, then sobbed and turned as more people came into the waiting room. "That's Philips, from *Dormant,"* Martin said in Katherine's ear. "The woman is Martha something-or-other; she writes those nasty reviews. I don't know the other man." He went forward, so that Weasel would have to introduce him, but more people came in, and he was suddenly involved in a group, talking in lowered voices, asking one another how long it would probably take, telling one another the names of people in the room. Through and around the quiet conversations went the soft half-moan which was Joan's crying.

Katherine, unable to leave the bench where she was sitting because of the crowd around her, turned and said to a strange man sitting next to her, "Someone told me once how you could train yourself to endure physical torture without yielding."

"Could it have been Neilson?" the man asked. "He did a nice piece on torture."

"You pretend it's happening to someone else," Katherine said. "You withdraw your own mind and you just leave your body behind."

"Did you know *him?"* the man asked, gesturing. "Upstairs?"

"Yes," Katherine said. "I knew him very well."

Somebody seemed to have brought a paper milk carton full of vodka, and somebody else went into the hospital hall and came back with a stack of paper cups. Martin pushed through the crowd to bring Katherine a paper cup with vodka in it, and said, "Angell's here. He did make it. No one knows anything about the wife. The man in the blue suit by the door is Arthur B. Arthur, and the dark-haired girl next to him is that little kid he married."

Near Katherine, Weasel was explaining to someone "—stopped off in the chapel to pray. He's thinking of being converted, *anyway,* you know."

The man next to Katherine leaned over and asked her, "Who's doing the Memorial Fund?"

"Weasel, probably," she said.

"Don't *ask* me," Weasel said beside her. "Simply don't ask *me*. Any more dealings with that shrew of a wife, and I will positively be ready to die my*self*. I will simply *have* to get back to Bronxville for a long rest after all this; it's been perfectly *frightful* ever since Friday morning; I haven't been home since he had the attack, I came right down from Bronxville and I've had to stay in the Andersons' place over on the West Side and it's been just *awful."*

From the little group by the door, there was a little rustle of quick, hushed laughter.

"I want Angell to do the Memorial Fund, anyway," Weasel said. "His name always looks so much *better* on a thing like that."

Joan was crying loudly now, struggling in the arms of the tall man in the blue suit. "I want to go to him," she was shouting. Vodka from her paper cup spilled onto the floor of the hospital hall.

"There's a nurse," someone said. "They're not trying to offer her a *drink?"* someone else said. "Be *quiet,* everybody," Weasel said, struggling to get through to the doorway.

"Is he dead?" the man next to Katherine asked her, "did the nurse say he was dead?"

"About three minutes ago," someone else said. "About three minutes ago. He died."

"We missed *every*thing?" Weasel's voice rose despairingly. "Because this just *finishes* it, that's all. They promised to *call* us," he said wildly to the nurse. "That's just about the lowest *I've* ever seen."

"You wouldn't let me go to him," Joan said to the nurse; her voice was heartbroken. "You wouldn't let me go to him."

"We weren't even *there,"* Weasel said. "This poor child . . ." He put an arm tenderly around Joan.

"Mrs. Jones was with him," the nurse said.

"What?" Weasel fell back dramatically. "They sneaked her in? No one let me know? She got here?"

"Can we go up now, anyway?" Martin asked.

"Mrs. Jones is with him," the nurse said. "Mrs. Jones will no doubt want to thank all of you at another time. Now . . ." she gestured, slightly but unmistakably; she was indicating the hall which led to the outside doors of the hospital.

"Well." Weasel tightened his lips. "How about the Service?" he said. "I suppose Mrs. Jones wants to run *that,* too? She's never read a *word* of his work, *naturally.* I was planning to read the passage on death from his *Evil Man,"* he explained to Angell, "you remember: it begins with that marvelous description of the flies? He used to recite it when he was drunk. Mrs. Jones will simply *have* to come down here," he said to the nurse. "How can we make any *arrangements?"*

"Mrs. Jones will no doubt be in touch with you," the nurse said. She stood back a little, and this time her gesture was a shade more emphatic.

There was a minute of silent hesitation, and then Angell said, " 'Within the twilight chamber spreads apace the shadow of white Death, and at the door invisible Corruption waits . . .' "

"A great voice has been stilled," Weasel said reverently.

"My one, truest love," Joan mourned.

"He writes now with a golden pen."

"A great writer is a great man writing."

"It was worth coming down for," Martin said, coming over to take Katherine's arm. "I talked to Angell for a minute, and he said to call him tomorrow." Impatient now, Martin led Katherine through the crowd to the doorway and out into the hall.

"Goodbye," the nurse said.

Slowly, a little ahead of the others, who lingered, laughing a little now, gathering around Joan, listening to Weasel, Katherine and Martin went down the hospital hallway. "He might have a spot for me now in that lecture series," Martin said. He gestured upwards. "Now that *he's* gone, I could do a talk on *his* work. His personal tragedy, maybe."

"It was hot in there," Katherine said.

Weasel caught up with them, and said quickly, "We're all going on to Joan's. I don't think she should be alone right now. You two coming along?"

"Thanks," Martin said, "but Katherine's pretty broken up, too. I'm going to take her directly home."

Weasel glanced quickly at Katherine and said, "Terribly sad, the whole business, wasn't it? I nearly *died* when I heard he was gone, and absolutely *no* one there who cared. I mean really *cared.*"

"We paid him what tribute we could," Martin said.

"The responsibility of the intellectual," Weasel said vaguely. "Come over to Joan's later if you can make it?"

He pattered away, back down the hall to Joan, and Martin and Katherine came down the steps of the hospital into the unexpectedly dark afternoon.

"My only, truest love," Katherine said.

"Hm?" said Martin. "You ask me something?"

"No," said Katherine, and laughed.

"Anyplace special you want to go for dinner?" Martin asked.

"Yes," Katherine said. "That nice little place where they make sweetbreads. I was thinking about it earlier."

Bruce Jay Friedman

The Killer in the TV Set

August 1961

Prominent among the new American writers of the 1960s were the "black humorists," with Bruce Jay Friedman in the front rank. They took the traditional magazine story a contemporary step further, giving it an extra dose of body English and irony. Friedman, a New York writer who also did time in Hollywood, is the author of *A Mother's Kisses* and *Stern*. He continues to contribute both fiction and articles to the magazine. "The Killer in the TV Set" is a good example of early black humor.

Bruce Jay Friedman

The Killer in the TV Set

At first, Mr. Ordz noticed only that the master of ceremonies or star of the television show wore a bad toupee, one that swept up suddenly and pointily like an Elks' convention cap. It seemed to be a late-hour "talk" arrangement, leading off with a singer named Connie who did carefully ticked-off rhythm gestures; one to connote passion, another, unabashed frivolity, and a third naiveté and first love. The show was one Mr. Ordz did not recognize, although this was beside the point since his main concern was to avoid going upstairs to Mrs. Ordz, a plump woman who had discovered sex in her early forties. In curlers, she waited each night for Mr. Ordz to come unravel her mysteries so that she might, in her own words, "fly out of control and yield forth the real me." Mr. Ordz had had several exposures to the real her and now scrupulously ducked opportunities for others.

Four male dancers came out now and surrounded the singer, flicking their fingers out toward her, and keeping up a chant that went "Isn't she a doll?" then hoisting her up on their shoulders for the finale.

"Doesn't she just bash you over the head?" asked the m.c., pulling up a chair. The setting was spare, a simple wall with a chair or two lined up against it, much in the style of the "intellectual" conversation show. "I'd like to bash you over the head, too," said the m.c., "but I can't and I've got to get you some other way." Mr. Ordz snickered, sending the snicker out through his nose. It was a laugh he used both for registering amusement and also slight shock, and it served the side function of clearing his nasal passages. "All right now," the m.c. said, "I used Connie to hook you, although I've no doubt I can keep you once you're watching awhile. Hear me now and hear me good. I've got exactly one week to kill you or I don't get my sponsor. Funny how you fall into these master-of-ceremony jokes just being up here in front of a camera and with all this television paraphernalia. Let me nail down that last remark a little better. I don't mean kill you with laughter or entertainment. I mean really stop your heart, Ordz, for Christ's sake, make you die. I've done work on you and I know I can do it."

Mr. Ordz thought the man had said "hard orbs" but then the m.c. said, "Heart, Ordz, stop your heart, Ordz. All right, then, *Mr.* Ordz. For Christ's sake listen because I just told you I've only got a week."

Mr. Ordz turned the dial and watched test patterns which is all he could get at two in the morning. He looked at a two-week-old *TV Guide* and saw there was no listing for a panel show that hour on Tuesday morning and then he called the police. "I'm getting a crazy channel," he said, "and wonder if you can come over and look at it."

"Wait till tomorrow morning and see if it goes away," said the police officer. "We can't just run out for you people."

"All right," said Mr. Ordz, "but I never call the police and I'm really getting something crazy."

He went to bed then, tapping his wife gently on the shoulder and whispering, "I got something crazy on TV," but when she heaved convulsively Mr. Ordz sneaked into the corner of the bed and pretended he wasn't there.

The following evening Mr. Ordz buried his head in a book on Scottish grottoes and read on late into the night, but when two in the morning came, he put aside the book and flipped on the television set. "It'll be better if you put me on earlier," said the m.c., wearing a loud checkered jacket and smiling without sincerity. "You'll noodle around and put me on anyway, so why don't you just put a man on. All right, here's your production number, Ordz. I don't see any point to doing them. It's sort of like fattening up the calf, but I'm supposed to give you one a night for some damned reason."

The singer of the previous evening came out in a Latin American festival costume, clicking her fingers furiously and doing a rhythm number with lyrics that went "Vadoo, vadoo, vadoo vey. Hey, hey, hey, hey, vadoo vey." She finished up with the word "Yeah" and did a deep, humble bow, and the m.c. said, "It'll go hard if you turn me off. I don't mean I can reach out and strike you down. That's the thing I want to explain. I can't shoot you from in here or give you a swift, punishing rabbit punch. It isn't that kind of arrangement. In ours, I've got six days to kill you, but I'm not actually allowed to do it directly. Now, what I'm going to do is try to shake you up as best I can, Ordz, and get you to, say, go up to your room and have a heart attack. I don't know whether you have heart trouble and another thing is I'm not allowed to ask you questions over this thing. But I *have* researched you, incidentally. It doesn't matter whether I like you or not—the main thing is getting myself a sponsor—but I might as well tell you I don't really care for you at all. You're such a damned small person and your life is such a drag.

Now I'm saying this half because I mean it, and, to be honest, half because I want to shake you up and see if I can bring on that heart attack. And now the news. The arrangement is I'm to bring you only flashes on airplane wrecks and major disasters. It was a compromise and I think I did well. At first I was supposed to give you politics, too."

Mr. Ordz watched the first one, some coverage of a DC-7 explosion in Paraguay and then switched off the show and called the police again. He got a different officer and said, "I called about the crazy television show last night."

"I don't know who you got," said the officer. "We get a lot of calls about television and can't just come out."

"All right," said Mr. Ordz, "but even though I called last night I don't go around calling the police all the time."

The only one Mr. Ordz knew in television was his cousin, Raphael, who was an assistant technical director in video tape. He went to see Raphael during lunch hour the next day. It was a short interview.

"I don't think that's any way to get a man," said Mr. Ordz. "I can see a practical joke but I don't think you should draw them out over a week. What if I *did* get a heart attack?"

"What do you mean?" said Raphael, eating a banana. He was on a banana diet and took several along for his lunch hour.

"The television set," said Mr. Ordz. "What's going on with it is what I mean."

"I'll fix it, I'll fix it," said Raphael. "What are you so ashamed of? If you were a cloak and suiter, as a relative I'd come to you for jackets. I don't see that any shame is involved. The real shame is beating around the bush. If your set is broken, I'll fix it. It doesn't matter that I work on the damned stuff all day long. You won't owe me a thing. Buy me a peck of bananas and we'll call it even. This is a lousy diet if you can't kid yourself a little. And I can kid myself."

"You don't understand what's going on," said Mr. Ordz, helplessly, "and I don't have the energy to tell you."

He went back to his job and late that night, instead of making an effort to stay away, he flicked on the set promptly at two. The m.c. was wearing a Halloween costume. "All right, it's Wednesday," he said, "and the old . . ."

Mr. Ordz cut the m.c. off in mid-sentence by turning the dial to another channel. He waited four or five minutes, feeling his heart beating and then getting nervous about it and squeezing his breast as though to slow it down. He turned back the dial and the m.c. continued the sentence, ". . . heart is still beating, but what you've got to remember is that . . ." Mr. Ordz flipped the dial again and waited roughly ten minutes this time, squeezing down his heart again, then flipped back and picked up the same sentence again: ". . . this thing is cumulative. It looks better for me, it's more realistic, if I bring it off at the tail end of the week. Sort of build tension and then finish up the deal, finish you up that is, right under the wire. What's that?"

The m.c. cupped his hand to his ear and peered off into the wings, then said, "All right, Ordz, they tell me you've been fooling around with the dial and it shocks you that you can't really miss a thing even if you switch off awhile. I don't care if you're shocked or not and the more shocks the better, although I'd rather you didn't go till the end of the week."

Mr. Ordz stood up in front of the television set then and said, "I haven't talked to you yet, but you're getting me mad. It doesn't mean a damned thing when I get mad unless I hit a certain plateau and then I don't feel any pain. I'm not afraid of heart attacks then or doctors or punches in the mouth, and I can spit in death's eye, too. It has no relation to my size or my weak wrists and abdomen. I'm just saying I'm mad now and when I am I'm suddenly articulate, fear no one and can get people. I don't care where you are. You've just come in here and done this to me and I swear I'll get you and I know I can do it because there are no obstacles when I feel this way."

"Calm down," said the m.c., lighting a cigarette. "Just sit down. All right, I admit I'm a little rattled now but it doesn't affect anything, I'm in a studio all right, but it's cleverly disguised and no one in the world would guess where we're set up. So all the anger in the world isn't going to change anything. Just calm down awhile and you'll see what I mean. Sing, Connie."

The hard-faced singer came out as a college coed in sweater and skirt. She pawed naively at the ground, waiting for the lift music and Mr. Ordz shouted, "And I don't want to hear her either."

"Who told you?" said the m.c., rising in a panic. "That's more work for me. You can't keep a damned secret in television. All right, I suppose you know you can have three alternates. The Elbaya flamenco dancers, Orson's Juggling Giants or Alonzo's Acrobatorama."

"I'll take the Acrobatorama," said Mr. Ordz, shaking his fist at the set again. "But it doesn't mean I'm going along with any of this or that I don't want to get you just as bad as ever. I just like acrobats, that's all, and never miss a chance to see them. Then I'm going to watch your damned news and I'm going to bed." Mr. Ordz settled back to watch the acrobats who did several encores.

The m.c. came on again. He had changed his Halloween costume to a dinner jacket and he was puffing away at a cigarette. "All right, I'm going to go right into the news tonight. I *am* a little rattled and there's no point denying it. Do you think that this is what I wanted to be doing this week? I just want to get my damned sponsor and get out of here. That's all for tonight and here is your disaster coverage. I like you more than I thought I would and I got them to allow some sports. It's about a carload of pro football players that overturned in New Mexico, but it's sports in a way."

The following day Mr. Ordz went to see his doctor about a pain in his belly. "It's either real or imagined," he said to the doctor.

"Can you describe it?" asked the doctor.

"It's sort of red with gray edges and is constant."

"It'll probably go away," said the doctor. "If it turns blue let me know and we'll take it from there."

"Are you kidding me?" asked Mr. Ordz.

"I'm a doctor," said the doctor.

Mr. Ordz stayed in town that night to see a foreign film about a tempestuous goat farm. When it was over he went down into the lounge. He was all alone and the TV set was on. His m.c. was dressed like the *La Strada* carnival man.

"I expected this," said the m.c. "The research showed you have to peek under bandages. If a doctor said, 'Your life depends on it,' you'd have to sneak a peek anyway. So I knew you'd stay away from your set tonight, but I also knew you'd have to peek at *some* set. Whoever knocked research is crazy. Now look, forget last night when I said I was rattled. I know one thing. I've got to have a sponsor or I go nowhere. If I could reach out there and personally slit your gizzard I'd do it without batting an eyelash. As it is, I'll just have to torment your tail until you go by yourself. Incidentally, I can tell you the details. Research said you'd be here tonight, so by some finagling around I was able to get on much earlier, almost prime time. You can pick up the disaster flashes when you get home at two. Here's your Acrobatorama and if anyone comes in while we're on, we turn into a trusted, familiar network giveaway show."

When Alonzo's men had taken their third encore, Mr. Ordz took the train home and rode between the cars. At one point, he dipped his foot way down outside the car giddily, but then retrieved it and rode home for the two o'clock disasters.

The following night, Friday, Mrs. Ordz joined Mr. Ordz on the television chaise and showered him with love bites on the nose. "I'll erupt," she said, her matronly bosom heaving with tension. "I warn you I'll erupt right down here and we don't have a door shutter."

"Hold off," said Mr. Ordz. "I don't tell you things, but I've got to tell you this thing." He told her the story of the secret channel and the m.c.'s threats, but her lids were closed and she whispered, "You're speaking words, but I hear only hoarse animal sounds. Tame me, boobsie, tame me, or I'll erupt before the world."

"I can't get through to anyone because I'm too nervous to say what I mean," said Mr. Ordz. "If I get angry enough, if only I can get angry enough, everyone will hear me loud and clear."

"Wild," she said through clenched teeth. "You're wild as the wind."

"I wish you would hold off," said Mr. Ordz, but his wife would not be shunted aside and he finally carried her stocky body upstairs, getting back downstairs at two-thirty A.M. The hard-faced female singer said, "He told me to tell you that he had a cold but that he'd be back tomorrow night if it killed him. I don't know his name either. He said he didn't have time to line up a replacement and that you should just go to bed, unless you want to hear me sing."

"No," said Mr. Ordz. "I don't care what you do. I'm not going along with this. I just want to see how far the whole thing carries."

"Oh, that's right, you're the one who wanted acrobats. Do you think I'd do this crummy show if I had something else? But I figure one exposure is better than none and you might have some connections. I also do figure modeling. We're skipping the news tonight. Since you don't want me to warble a few, I have a modeling date tonight. I only do work for legit photogs."

In the morning, Mr. Ordz called in his secretary and said, "It's in defense bonds, savings stamps and cash, but it works out to six thousand dollars and I want my wife to get it."

"So just give it to her then," said the girl. "I don't know what you mean."

"I want you to know that it's for her if something happens to me."

"Don't you feel well, Mr. Ordz?" asked the girl. "You're supposed to put that in a will and it doesn't mean anything if you just tell it to a person."

"I'm not bothering around with any wills. I told it to you and you know it and that's all."

"But I can't enforce anything," said the girl.

"Don't argue with me. You just know."

The m.c. was wearing an intern's costume when the show came on much later, and was blowing his nose. "It was a pip all right. I used to get one a winter and I guess I still get them. All right then, now that it's come down to the wire I'd be teasing if I didn't admit it has crossed my mind that your heart might *not* stop and here I'd be without a sponsor. Research did tell me about the pain in the belly though, and of course that did relax me. You're on your way. I get your life tonight, Ordz. Now look, this is the equivalent of your smoking a last cigarette. You're sick of me, I'm sick of you. If you go upstairs right this second and drink a bottle of iodine, the deal is you don't have to sit through the whole damned show. Fair enough?"

Mr. Ordz dropped his cheesettes and said, "So help me God I'm getting mad."

"And believe me," said the m.c., "the show stinks tonight. I do a whole series of morbid parodies of songs, real bad ones like *Ghoul That I Am,* and we've got a full hour of on-the-spot coverage of a children's school bus combination fire and explosion. Go upstairs, get yourself a regimental tie or two . . ."

"I'm getting to the crazy point where I can spit in death's eye," said Mr. Ordz, rising from his chaise.

". . . Rig them up noose-style to the shower nozzle, slip your head in there snugly and we'll all go home early."

"I'll get you," shouted Mr. Ordz. And with that he smashed his hand through the television screen, obliterating the picture and opening something stringy in his wrist. Blood spurted out across Mr. Ordz's six volumes of Churchill's war memoirs, sprinkling *The Gathering Storm* and completely drenching *Their Finest Hour.* Mr. Ordz studied his wrist and, until he began to feel faint, poked at it, watching it pour forth with renewed frenzy at each of the pokes. On hands and knees then, he went up to his sleeping wife and clutched at her nightgown. "I erupt, I erupt," she said, in a stupor, and then opened her eyes. "Jeez," she said, "are they open at the hospital?" She got on a robe, and by this time Mr. Ordz had lost consciousness. Blood soaked Mrs. Ordz' nightgown as she gathered her husband up in her stocky arms and said, "God forgive me, but even this is sexy." She got him into the car, relieved to see some twitching going on in his neck, and at the hospital a young doctor said, "Get him right in here. I've treated bee bites before. Oh, isn't he the bee-bite man?"

Mrs. Ordz said, "I could just give interns a good pinch. That's how cute they are to me."

The doctor finally got a tourniquet and bandage on Mr. Ordz, who miraculously regained consciousness for a brief moment and peeked quickly under the bandage. "There are still people I have to get," he said. But then a final jet of blood whooshed forward onto the hospital linoleum and then Mr. Ordz closed his eyes and said no more.

When he began to see again, people were patting lotions on his face. "You're getting me ready for a pine box," he said, but there was no reply. More solutions were patted on his face. He was helped into a tuxedo and then lugged somewhere.

Out of the corner of his eye he saw his m.c. and two distinguished executive-type gentlemen soar out of the top of the building or enclosure he was in. The executives were holding the m.c. by the elbows and all three had sprouted wings. Then Mr. Ordz was shoved forward. Hot lights were brought down close to his face and cameras began to whir. A giant card with large words on it was lowered before his eyes and one of the lotion people said, "Smile at all times. All right, begin reading."

"I don't want to," said Mr. Ordz, "and I'm getting angry enough to spit in all your eyes, even if I *am* dead." But no sound came from his mouth. The lights got hotter. Then he looked at the card, felt his mouth force into an insincere smile and heard himself saying to a strange man who sat opposite him in a kind of living room, munching on some slices of protein bread, "All right now, Simons, I've got exactly one week to kill you. And I'm not using entertainment talk or anything. I really mean take your life, stop you from breathing. There's nothing personal about all this. It's just that I've got to get a sponsor. But before we go any further, for your viewing entertainment, the Tatzo Trapeze Twins."

James Thurber

Brother Endicott

December 1962

James Thurber (1894–1961), one of the best-known American magazine writers and cartoonists of the twentieth century, is so closely associated with *The New Yorker* that it may be a surprise to see him here. According to the "Playbill" introducing the story, " 'Brother Endicott' was still on Thurber's writing table at the time of his death. His widow, aware of our affection for the gentle humorist, made the story available to us for first publication. It will appear in *Credos and Curios,* a new Thurber collection." There had to be more to it than that—and whose idea was it to dub the notoriously cranky Thurber "gentle"? Latent, or not so latent, exasperation was his specialty, as this story about frat men abroad demonstrates. He turned this fizzling annoyance to his advantage even in his classic children's books—*Many Moons* (1945), *The Thirteen Clocks* (1950), *The Wonderful O* (1957)—and it was at full boil in his unique cartoons and many stories and fables for adults. A good selection of these appeared after his death in *A Thurber Carnival* (1962).

James Thurber

Brother Endicott

The man stared at the paper in his typewriter with the bleak look of a rain-soaked spectator at a dull football game, and then ripped it out of the machine. He lit a cigarette, put another sheet of paper in the wringer, and began a letter to his publisher, without salutation: "Why you imbeciles have to have a manuscript three months ahead of publication is, by God—" And out came that sheet. Somewhere a clock began striking three, but it was drowned out by a sudden upsurge of Paris night noises.

The street noises of Paris, staccato, *profundo,* momentary and prolonged, go on all through the summer night, as if hostile hosts were fiercely taking, losing and regaining desperately disputed corners, especially the bloody angle of the Rue de Rivoli and the Rue de Castiglione, just beneath the windows of the writer's hotel room. Presently he heard the jubilant coming of the Americans, late but indomitable, sleepless but ever fresh, moving in, like the taxis of the Marne, from the Right Bank and the Left, shouting, laughing, amiably cursing, as they enveloped and captured the lobby of the hotel. They loudly occupied corridors and rooms, leaving the King's English sprawled and bleeding on the barricades of night. A detachment of foot cavalry trooped past the writer's door, one of the men singing *Louise* in a bad imitation of Chevalier.

American reinforcements kept on arriving at the hotel, and below his window the writer heard a young feminine voice crying, "For God's sake, Mother, why not? S'only three o'clock!" Her mother's voice cried back at her, "Your father's dead and so am I—that's why not." There was no report from the father, and the writer visualized him lying on the sidewalk, his wallet deflated, a spent and valiant victim of the battle of Paris. The writer emptied a clogged ashtray into a metal wastebasket, switched off the lights in the sitting room of his suite and sprawled on one of the twin beds in the other room. "It may be the Fourth of July to everybody else," he said aloud, as if talking to someone he didn't like, "but it's just two weeks past deadline to me." He turned over the phrase, "The fourteenth of Deadline," decided there was nothing in it, and was about to take off his right shoe when he heard a knock at the door. He looked at his wristwatch; it was a few minutes past three o'clock.

The late caller was a young woman he had never seen before. She murmured something that sounded like, "My husband—I thought maybe—" and he stood aside to let her in, apologizing for his shirt-sleeves.

"I was afraid it was the fellas looking for a tenor," he said. "I'm a baritone myself, but out of practice and not in the mood." He put the lights on again in the sitting room, waved casually at a chair and, just as casually, she sat in it. *"Voici le salon,* as they call it," he said. "Makes it sound very proper. What can I do for you? My name's Guy Farland."

"I know," she said. "I've heard you typing at night before. I asked at the desk once, and they said you were here. My name is Marie Endicott."

He reached for his tie and jacket, but she said with a faint smile, *"Ne vous dérangez pas.* It's too warm."

"Before we get around to your problem," he said, "how about a drink?" He moved to a table containing bottles and glasses and an ice bucket. She nodded when he put his hand on the Scotch bottle. "Not too strong, please," she said. "A lot of soda."

"I mix drinks my own way," he told her, "and I'm said to be good at it. Besides, this is my castle." He took her in as he fixed the highball, figured that she was not more than twenty-three and that she had had quite a few drinks already, rather desperate ones, which she hadn't enjoyed much. He set her drink down on a table beside her chair. "If I were a younger writer I would say, 'She looked like a chic Luna moth in her light-green evening gown, as she stood there clutching it, just holding it," he said. "And I'm a middle-aged writer, not a young one," he added.

She picked up her drink but didn't taste it. "I've read your *Lost Corner* four times," she said. He went back to mix himself a drink, saying, "It isn't quite that good. I'm trying to finish another book, but you can't think against this goddamn racket. I had got used to the Paris taxi horns and their silence makes me edgy. They have cut out the best part of the noise and left in the worst."

"The goddamn motorcycles," she said tonelessly. He sat down, and they both listened to the tumult outside the window for a moment.

"The noise has loused me up—I choose the precise word for it," he said. "It would certainly rain in Verlaine's heart if he could hear it." She was looking at him as though he were an actor in a spotlight, and he responded with a performance. "I was thinking how silent Paris must have been the night François Villon vanished into immortality through the snows of yesteryear. If your husband has vanished, maybe I can help you find him. I'm a husband myself, and I know where they go. On the Fourth of July, of course, it's a little harder, especially in a foreign country." He had left the door to the suite ajar, and they could hear the male quartet somewhere down the hall dwelling liquidly on *The Sweetheart of Sigma Chi.*

"Edward isn't lost," she said. "He's the bass. Edward Francis Endicott." She seemed to add a trace of bitters to the name. "Wisconsin Alpha. They're in Rip Morgan's room, with a couple of Americans they picked up at this night club. Edward and Rip insisted on singing *On, Wisconsin*—I don't know why we weren't put out—and these strange men knew the words and joined in, but they are from Illinois, and so then they all sang *Loyal to You, Illinois.* Our honeymoon has been like that ever since Edward ran into Rip Morgan in Rome." She gave the word "honeymoon" a tart inflection.

The quartet down the hall now had *Dear Old Girl* in full swing, and Farland got up and closed the door. "They sound a little older than juniors or seniors," he said, coming back to his chair. She took a long swallow of her drink and set the glass down.

"Edward will be forty-six next week," she said, in the tone of a patient on a psychiatrist's couch, and Farland leaned back for the flow he felt was coming. "He still wears his fraternity pin. He wore it on his pajamas on our wedding night. It's the Nelson Merit Pin. He got it one year for being the biggest Boopa Doopa Chi in the whole damn country. He has a smaller one, too. Fraternity is his life. Maybe you've heard of Endicott Emblems, Incorporated. Well, he's the president. They make fraternity pins, and signet rings, and everything. He goes around all the time, even over here, with his right hand out like this." She separated the thumb and little finger of her right hand from the other fingers. "He gives everybody the grip, in the American Express and at the Embassy, and everywhere he sees an American man. I don't know much about fraternities. I thought it was something men got over, like football practice. I went to Smith." Farland noticed that she kept glancing over her right shoulder at the door.

"Brother Endicott won't break in on us," he said reassuringly. "Quartets never notice that wives are missing. As for my wife, she's in Italy."

"I knew she wasn't here," Marie Endicott said, and Farland followed her gaze about the room, which must have revealed instantly to his visitor the lack of a woman's touch. There were books and papers on the floor, and that unmistakable masculine rearrangement of chairs and lamps which a man finds comfortable and a woman intolerable. "Nancy is going to pick up our daughters in Italy—we have two. They are coming over on one of the Export ships because they wanted to see Gibraltar. I don't work at night when Nancy's here. Wives don't think it's healthy."

"Ellen Morgan went to bed," said the girl, "and Edward thinks I'm in bed, too." She took several long swallows of her drink this time and sat forward in her chair. "The reason I'm here, the thing is," she began, with a flash of firmness, and then leaned back with a helpless flutter of her left hand. Farland gave her a cigarette and held a match for her.

"Don't get a blockage," he said easily. "I'm the one with the blockage, I was thinking of throwing the heroine of my novel out of a window, but you can't do that in novels, only in real life." The girl wasn't listening.

"Edward can't stand any foreign country," she said, "because it isn't God's country, and they don't use God's money, and you can't get God's martinis, or God's anything." Her eyes drifted toward an unopened bottle of bourbon on the table. "Or God's whiskey," she said. "Bourbon is God's whiskey, you know."

"He must have trouble getting God's ice, too," Farland put in, "especially at this hour."

"They don't supply soap at most French hotels," she went on. "In the hotel in Le Havre he called downstairs and said, 'Some of you cave dwellers come up here with some soap and make it snappy. Endicott wants soap.' He speaks of himself in the third person a lot of the time. He doesn't know any French except *combien* and *trop cher* and *encore le méme chose* and *où est le cabinet?* He calls terraces sit-downs, and he's terrible when a dinner check runs into four figures, like 3800 francs. He says, *'Pas si* goddamn *vite'* to taxi drivers. He learned what he calls doughboy French from his brother Harry. Harry is much older. He was in the First World War. You know doughboy French? *'Restez ici* a minute. *Je retourner après cet* guy *partirs.'* " She drank some more and went back to brother Harry. "Harry thinks he's dying," she said. "He thinks he's dying of everything, but there isn't anything the matter with him. He ought to go to a psychiatrist, and he actually did once, but the doctor said something like, 'If you're not sick, and you think you're sick, you're sick.' And Harry slammed out of his office."

"Nice slamming," Farland said. "I think I would have, too."

The girl in the green dress took in a long sad breath and exhaled slowly. "Harry carries a little mirror, like a woman, and keeps looking at his mouth, even in public," she said. "He thinks there's something the matter with his uvula."

"I'm sorry you told me that," Farland said. "It is the only part of my body I have never been conscious of. Can you die of uvulitis or something?"

"Harry and his wife were over here," the girl continued, "but they flew back last week, thank God. He suddenly got the idea in the middle of the night that his doctor had secretly called Irene and told her he was dying—Harry, I mean. 'This is my last vacation,' he screamed, waking Irene up. She thought he had lost his mind in his sleep. 'I'm not going to die in Naples or any other foreign city!' he yelled. 'I'm going to die in Buffalo!' *We* live in Milwaukee. It isn't far enough from Buffalo."

"You were just about to tell me why you came here. I don't mean to Europe, I mean to my chambers, tonight—this morning," Farland said, but she postponed the reason for her call with a wave of her hand. He sat back and let her flow on.

"Edward is a collector," she said. "Big heavy things, like goalposts. He's football-crazy, too. I thought he was really crazy once when we were having a cocktail and he lifted his glass and said, 'Here's to Crazy Legs!' That's Roy Hirsch," she explained. "One of the Wisconsin gridiron immortals. He also drinks to the Horse. That's Ameche. He's immortal, too."

"I'm trying to figure out what you saw in Edward Endicott," Farland said, a flick of impatience in his tone. "It's supposed to be a human mystery, I know, but there's usually a clue of some kind."

She gestured with her hand again and frowned. "He has more drums than anybody else in the world," she went on. "He began collecting them when he was a little boy, and now he has African drums and Maori drums and some from the Civil War and one from the Revolution. He even has a drum that was used in the road company of *The Emperor Jones,* and one of the forty or fifty that were used in *Valencia* during a big production number at the Casino de Paris in 1925, I think it was." She shuddered slightly, as if she heard all the Endicott drums approaching. "Is collecting goalposts Freudian?" she asked.

Farland decided to think that over while he freshened the drinks. "I don't think so," he said. "Goalposts are trophies, a sign your side won. The Indians had it worked out better, of course. Scalping the captain of the losing team would be much simpler. Where does he keep the goalposts?"

"In the attic," she said, "except for the one in the guest room. It belonged to Southern Cal. or SMU, or somebody we didn't expect to beat and did." She managed a small evil inflection on "we."

"All right, let's have it," Farland said. "Why did you come here tonight? All this is overture, I can tell that."

She sat forward suddenly again. "Tom will be here, I mean right here, in your suite, in a few minutes," she said, hurriedly. "He sent me a message by a waiter at the night club, while Edward was trying to get the little French orchestra to play *Back in Your Own Backyard.* Tom must have followed me there. I had to think quick, and all I could think of was your room, because you're always up late."

Farland got up and put on his tie and coat. "I ought to look more *de rigueur* for Tom," he said. "You're not constructing this very well. You don't just hit your readers with a character named Tom. They have a right to know who he is and what he wants."

"I'm sorry," she said. "I mean about asking him to come here. He's awfully difficult, but at least he isn't predictable. He loves to sweep everything off the mantelpiece when he's mad, but he doesn't use a straight razor and strop it all the time, like Edward. Tom and I were engaged for years, but he didn't want to get married until he got through his Army service, so we broke up about that. Everybody else got married and went to camp with their husbands. They had four million babies last year, the American girls."

"American girls often marry someone they can't stand to spite someone they can," he said. "That's a pretty rough generalization, but I haven't got time to polish it up. Is that where Brother Endicott came in?"

"I don't really know what state Tom is in," she said. "He just got out of the service, and I was afraid he would follow me here. It's a long story about how I met Edward. I wanted to come back to Paris. You see, I had spent my junior year here, and I loved Paris. Of course, my mother went completely to pieces. I had a job in New York, but every evening when I got home, Mother was waiting for me. Sometimes crocked. She always wanted to have a little talk. We had more little talks than all the mothers and daughters in the world. I was going crazy, and then I met Edward. He seemed so strong and silent and—" She groped for a word and came up with "attentive." Farland gave her another cigarette. "He wasn't really strong and silent. He was just on the wagon. Tom hadn't written for months, and I thought maybe he had another girl, and Edward promised to bring me to Paris, and so—I don't know."

"Paris seems to be full of American girls who are hiding out from their mothers," he said. This caused a flash of lightning in her eyes.

"Mother belongs to the damn Lost Generation," she said. "The trouble with the Lost Generation is it didn't get lost enough. All the damn lost mothers had only one child," she went on, warming to what was apparently a familiar thesis. "They all think their daughters are weak enough to do the things they thought they were strong enough to do. So we have to pay for what they did. I'm glad I missed the 1920s. God!"

"They've stopped singing," Farland said. "They must be taking a whiskey break. How do I fit into this—for Tom, I mean? I don't want to be knocked cold when he gets here. I seem to be in the middle."

As if it were an entrance cue, there were two sharp raps on the door. Farland hurried out and opened it. A tall young man breezed past him and into the sitting room. "Are you all right?" he demanded of the girl.

"No," Farland said. "Do you want a drink?"

"This is Mr. Farland, Mr. Gregg," said Mrs. Endicott. Mr. Gregg scowled at his host. "I don't get this," he said. "What is that baboon doing now? Could I have a straight Scotch?" Farland put some Scotch and ice in a glass and gave it to him.

"They're probably running out of whiskey," the girl said. "I don't want Edward to find me gone."

"He might as well get used to it," said Tom. He began pacing. "I was hanging around out front when you left the hotel," he said, "and I followed you to that night club. It cost me five bucks for one drink, five bucks and taxi fare to write that note." He suddenly pulled the girl up out of her chair and into his arms.

"This is pretty damned unplanned," Farland said.

"I got to have half an hour with Marie. We've got to settle some things," Tom said peremptorily. "I'm sorry I was so abrupt." He held out the hand that swept things off mantelpieces. He had a quick, firm grip. "I haven't got any plans, except to get her away from that monkey," he said.

"The law is on his side, of course," Farland put in, "and the Church and all that sort of thing." The girl had freed herself and sat down again, and Tom resumed his pacing.

"Do you know the grip?" Farland asked her suddenly. "I think it may be mine. Don't hit me," he said to the young man.

"Tom threw his pledge pin across the room at a chapter meeting, I think they call it," the girl said.

"Somebody said something," Tom snarled. Farland nodded. "People have a way of doing that," he said. "Human failing." He held out his right hand to the girl and she gave him the grip. "Now I do *this,"* he said, pressing her wrist.

"And I do *this,"* she said, returning the pressure. Each then pressed the other's thumb.

"Don't you wiggle your ears, for crissake?" Tom snarled.

"Brother Endicott," Farland sighed, "shake hands with Brother Farland. Pennsylvania Gamma." He picked up the unopened bottle of bourbon and the ice bucket. "I think I can promise you your half hour undisturbed," he said. "God's whiskey and the grip ought to do it, and besides, I know the words of *Back in Your Own Backyard.* I also know the *Darling* song."

"God!" said Marie Endicott.

Tom stopped pacing and looked at Farland. "Damned white of you," he said, "but I don't know why you're doing it."

"Lady in distress," Farland said. "Cry for help in the night. I don't know much about drums, but I can talk about Brother Hunk Elliot."

"Ohio Gamma," said Mrs. Endicott bleakly. "Greatest by God halfback that ever lugged a football, even if he did beat Wisconsin three straight years. Crazy Legs and the Horse don't belong to Boopa Doopa Chi, so they don't rate with Brother Elliot."

"The protocol of fraternity is extremely complicated and uninteresting," Farland said.

"Nuts," snapped Tom, who had begun to crack his knuckles. "Why doesn't that goddamn racket stop?" He suddenly leaped at the open window of the salon and shouted into the night, "Cut down that goddamn noise!"

"Do you want everybody *in* here?" the girl asked nervously.

"I don't see why I shouldn't go down there myself and bust him a couple," he said. "I don't see why you had to marry him anyway. Nobody in her right mind would marry a man old enough to be her father, and live in Milwaukee." He whirled and stared at Farland. "I don't see what you're getting out of this," he said, "acting like her fairy godfather or somebody."

"I—" Farland began, but Mrs. Endicott cut in on him. There was a new storm in her eyes. "He's done more for me in one night than you have in two years!" she said. "You never wrote, and when you did, nobody could read it, the way you write. How do I know who you were running around with in Tacoma? You're not really in love with me, you just want something somebody else has got." Farland tried to get in on it again, but Tom Gregg gave him a little push and turned to the girl again.

"It wasn't Tacoma," he said. "You didn't even bother to find out what camp I was at."

"Seattle, then," she said. "Fort Lawton. And everybody else got married. I know ten girls who went to camp with their husbands and three of them were in Tacoma."

"We couldn't get married on nothing," he said. "I happen to have a job now, a good job."

"Everybody else got married on nothing," she said.

"I'm not everybody else!" he yelled. "I'm not just anybody else, either. 'Miss Withrow, I want you to meet Mr. Endicott.' 'How do you do, Miss Withrow. Will you marry me?' 'Sure, why not? I think I'm engaged to a guy named Tacoma or something, but that's OK.' "

"I'll hit you, I really will!" cried the former Miss Withrow.

Farland hastily put the bottle and the ice bucket on the floor and stepped between them. "I'm not anybody's fairy godfather," he said. "I'm just an innocent bystander. I was about to go to bed when all this hell broke loose, and I'll be goddamned if I'm going down to that room and sing with a lot of big fat emblem-makers if you're going to spend your time fighting." His voice was pitched even louder than theirs. The telephone rang. Farland picked up the receiver and listened for three seconds to a voice on the other end speaking in French. "It's the Fourth of July!" he yelled, and slammed down the receiver.

"I'm sorry about this," Tom said. "I'm willing to talk it over rationally if she is. I got to fly back to work day after tomorrow."

"Oh, sure," said Marie.

"I don't usually lose my temper," Farland apologized, "but I'm stuck in a book I'm writing, and it makes me jumpy." He picked up the bottle and the ice bucket again. "I'll give you until four o'clock," he said. "I'll knock four times, with an interval after the third."

"You probably haven't got your key," Marie said. She spied it, put it in Farland's pocket, and kissed him on the forehead.

"Do you have to keep doing that?" Tom shouted.

"I haven't *been* doing that," Marie said.

"Please!" Farland said. "I'm tossing her aside like a broken doll, anyway." He grinned. "How in hell can I open this door with my arms loaded?" Marie crossed over and opened the door for him. "For God's sake, don't kiss me again," he whispered, "and stop fighting and get something worked out." He raised his voice and spoke to both of them. "Goodnight," he said, "and shut up." He stepped out into the hall and the girl in the green dress quietly closed the door after him . . .

A short, heavy-set man in his middle 40s opened the door, and seemed to block the way aggressively until he caught sight of the American face of the visitor and the things he was carrying. "I heard the Yankee Doodle sounds," Farland told him, and introduced himself. "I thought maybe you needed reinforcements from SOS." The room exploded into American sounds, as if the newcomer had dropped a lighted match in a box of fireworks. Somebody took the bourbon from him and somebody else the ice bucket. "My God, it's real ice!" someone said, and "Brother, you've saved our lives!"

"An American shouldn't spend this night alone," Farland said above the hubbub. The biggest man in the room, who wore no coat or tie, but on whose vest a fraternity pin gleamed, held out his hand in three parts. Farland gave him the full-dress grip. "Ed Endicott, Wisconsin Alpha!" bawled the big man.

"Pennsylvania Gamma," Farland said.

"For crissake, it's a small world!" Endicott said. "Rip, shake hands with Brother Farland, give him the old grip. Brother Morgan and I belong to the same chapter. Wisconsin Alpha has two national presidents to its credit," he told Farland, "and I was one of them, if I do say so myself. These other poor guys took the wrong pins, but they're OK." He managed somehow to get his right arm around the shoulders of both the other men in the room. "This is Sam Winterhorn, Phi Gam from Illinois, and this is Red Perry, also Illini—Red's a Phi Psi. Maybe you heard us doing *Fiji Honeymoon* and *When DKE Has Gone to Hell*. Put 'er there again, fella."

Farland was glad when he was finally given a glass to hold instead of a man's right hand. "Here's to all the brothers, whatever sky's above 'em," Endicott said, clinking his glass against Farland's. He took a great gulp of his drink, and it seemed to Farland that his face brightened like a full moon coming out from behind a cloud. "Endicott is a curly wolf this night, Guy, and you can write that home to your loved ones!" he roared. "Endicott is going to shake hands with the pearly fingered dawn this day. Endicott is going to ring all the bells and blow all the whistles in hell. Any frog that don't like it can bury his head in the Tooleries." Farland managed to get out part of a word, but Brother Endicott trampled on it. "The girls have gone to bed," he said. "Wish you could meet Marie, but we'll be around a couple more days. Marie's Eastern women's college, but Brenda—that's my first wife—was a Kappa. So's Ellen Morgan, Rip's wife. Brenda hated drums. I got the greatest little drum collection in the world, Guy. Once, when a gang of us got up a storm in my house—this was six-seven years ago—damned if Brenda didn't call the cops! One of them turned out to be real mean with the sticks, but the other guy was a surly bastard. I tried to give him the grip, and he got sore as hell. Don't ever try to give a cop the grip, Guy. They think you're queer. Sons of bitches never get through high school."

Farland put on his fixed grin as Endicott rambled on, moving among the disarranged chairs like a truck. He paused in front of one in which Brother Morgan now lay back relaxed, with his eyes closed. "Judas Priest, our tenor's conking out," he said.

" 'Way," mumbled Morgan sleepily.

"Let him sleep," said the man named Perry. "What the hell, we still got a quartet. Anyway, what good's a sleepy tenor unless you're doing *Sleepy Time Gal?"*

"Sleepy Time Gal!" bawled Endicott, and he suddenly started in the middle of the old song, biting a great hunk out of the lyric. The phone rang, and Endicott smote the night with a bathroom word and jerked up the receiver. "Yeah?" he began truculently and, as the voice at the other end began protesting in French, he said to the revelers, "It's one of them *quoi-quois."* He winked heavily at Farland and addressed the transmitter. *"Parlez-vous la langue de Dieu?"* he asked. Farland realized he had been rehearsing the question quite a while. *"Bien,* then," Endicott went on. "You people ought to be celebrating, too. If we hadn't let Lafayette fight on our side, he would have gone to the goddamn guillotine. The way it was, even Napoleon didn't dare lay a hand on him. They cut the heads off Rabelais and Danton, but they couldn't touch Lafayette, and that's on account of the good old thirteen States." The person at the other end had apparently hung up, but Endicott went on with his act. "Get yourselves a bottle of grenadine and a pack of cubebs and raise a little hell for Lafayette," he said, and hung up.

"Not Rabelais," Farland couldn't help saying. "Robespierre."

"Or old Roquefort!" Endicott bawled. "They all sound like cheese to me, rich old *framboise,* and they all look alike. Let's hit the *Darling* song again."

They got through *Three O'Clock in the Morning* and *Linger Awhile* and *Over There* and *Yankee Doodle Dandy* and *You're the B-E-S-T Best* and by that time it was ten minutes after four. "Don't keep looking at your Benrus," Endicott told Farland. "Nobody's going anywhere. What the hell, we've got all day." Rip Morgan's troubled unconscious greeted this with a faint moaning sound. Farland's tone grew firm and terminal, and the Illinois men joined him and began the final round of handshakes. Farland picked up the ice bucket, which had been empty for some time now, and started for the door.

"We'll all meet in the bar downstairs at six," Endicott commanded. *"Be there!"* The three departing Americans said they would be there, but none of them meant it. "I'm going to stay stiff till they pour me on the plane," Endicott went on. Farland's hand felt full of fingers after he had shaken hands again with the Illinois men and they had gone. Brother Endicott, he felt sure, would have his hands full for at least fifteen minutes, putting Brother Morgan to bed . . .

Farland rapped on the door of his suite three times, paused, then rapped again. There was no response, and he unlocked the door and went in. All the lights in the sitting room were out except one, and he turned it off and began undressing before he reached the bedroom. The battle of the Paris night still went on, and it seemed louder than ever. Farland put on the bottom of his pajamas, couldn't find the top, said, "The hell with it," and went into the bathroom and brushed his teeth. "Everything happens to you," he sneered at the man in the mirror. "What's the matter, don't you know how to duck anymore?"

He was about to throw himself on his bed when he noticed the note on his pillow. It read simply "You are the B-E-S-T Best" and it was signed, obviously in Mrs. Endicott's handwriting, "Tom and Marie." In spite of the noise and his still tingling right hand, Farland fell asleep. When he woke up, he picked up the telephone and called the *renseignement* desk. He looked at his watch. It was nine thirty-five. "I want to get a plane out of here for Rome this afternoon," he said when the information desk answered. "One seat. And I don't care what line. There is just one thing. It has *got* to leave before six o'clock."

Bernard Malamud

Naked Nude

August 1963

Bernard Malamud's (1914–1986) first novel, *The Natural* (1952), was the source for the Robert Redford movie. His short-story collection, *The Magic Barrel,* won the National Book Award in 1958. A decade later, in 1967, he won both the National Book Award and the Pulitzer Prize for *The Fixer.* "Naked Nude" stars Arthur Fidelman, a recurring character in Malamud's fiction who, like the author, emerges from the insular Russian Jewish community in Brooklyn to see a great deal of the world. The story was a favorite at *Playboy* and won the annual fiction prize.

Bernard Malamud

Naked Nude

Fidelman listlessly doodled all over a sheet of yellow paper. Odd indecipherable designs, ink-spotted blotched words, esoteric ideographs, tormented figures in a steaming sulphurous lake, including a stylish nude rising newborn from the water. Not bad at all, though more mannequin than Cnidian Aphrodite. Scarpio, sharp-nosed on the former art student's left, looking up from his cards, inspected her with his good eye.

"Not bad, who is she?"

"Nobody I really know."

"You must be hard up."

"It happens in art."

"Quiet," rumbled Angelo, the *padrone,* on Fidelman's right, his two-chinned face molded in lard. He flipped the top card.

Scarpio then turned up a deuce, making eight-and-a-half and out. He cursed his Sainted Mother, Angelo wheezing. Fidelman showed four and his last hundred lire. He picked a cautious ace and sighed. Angelo, with seven showing, chose that passionate moment to get up and relieve himself.

"Wait for me," he ordered. "Watch the money, Scarpio."

"Who's that hanging?" Scarpio pointed to a long-coated figure loosely dangling from a gallows rope amid Fidelman's other drawings.

Who but Susskind, surely, a figure out of the far-off past.

"Just a friend."

"Which one?"

"Nobody you know."

"It better not be."

Scarpio picked up the yellow paper for a closer squint.

"But whose head?" he asked with interest. A long-nosed severed head bounced down the steps of the guillotine platform.

A man's head or his sex? Fidelman wondered. In either case, a terrible wound.

"Looks a little like mine," he confessed. "At least, the long jaw."

Scarpio pointed to a street scene. In front of American Express, here's this starving white Negro pursued by a hooting mob of cowboys on horses. Embarrassed by the recent past, Fidelman blushed.

It was long after midnight. They sat motionless in Angelo's stuffy office, a small lit bulb hanging down over a square wooden table on which lay a pack of puffy cards, Fidelman's naked hundred-lire note, and a green bottle of Munich beer that the *padrone* of the Hotel du Ville, Milano, swilled from, between hands or games. Scarpio, his major-domo and secretary-lover, sipped an espresso, and Fidelman only watched, being without privileges. Each night they played *sette e mezzo,* jeenrummy or baccarat and Fidelman lost the day's earnings, the few meager tips he had garnered from the whores for little services rendered. Angelo said nothing and took all.

Scarpio, snickering, understood the street scene. Fidelman, adrift penniless in the stony gray Milanese streets, had picked his first pocket, of an American tourist staring into a store window. The Texan, feeling the tug, and missing his wallet, had bellowed murder. A *carabiniere* looked wildly at Fidelman, who broke into a run, another well-dressed *carabiniere* on a horse clattering after him down the street, waving his sword. Angelo, cleaning his fingernails with his penknife in front of his hotel, saw Fidelman coming and ducked him around a corner, through a cellar door, into the Hotel du Ville, a joint for prostitutes who split their fees with the *padrone* for the use of a room. Angelo registered the former art student, gave him a tiny dark room and, pointing a gun, relieved him of his passport, recently renewed, and the contents of the Texan's wallet. He warned him that if he so much as peeped to anybody, he would at once report him to the *questura,* where his brother presided, as a dangerous alien thief. The former art student, desperate to escape, needed money to travel, so he sneaked into Angelo's room one morning and from the strapped suitcase under the bed, extracted fistfuls of lire, stuffing all his pockets. Scarpio, happening in, caught him at it and held a pointed dagger to Fidelman's ribs—Fidelman fruitlessly pleaded they could both make a living from the suitcase—until the *padrone* appeared.

"A hunchback is straight only in his grave." Angelo slapped Fidelman's face first with one fat hand, then with the other, till it turned red and the tears freely flowed. He chained him to the bed in his room for a week. When Fidelman promised to behave he was released and appointed *mastro delle latrina,* having to clean thirty toilets every day with a stiff brush, for room and board. He also assisted

Teresa, the asthmatic, hairy-legged chambermaid, and ran errands for the whores. The former art student hoped to escape, but the *portiere* or his assistant was at the door twenty-four hours a day. And thanks to the card games and his impassioned gambling, Fidelman was without sufficient funds to go anywhere, if there was anywhere to go. And without passport, so he stayed put.

Scarpio secretly felt Fidelman's thigh.

"Let go or I'll tell the *padrone*."

Angelo returned and flipped up a card. Queen. Seven-and-a-half on the button. He pocketed Fidelman's last hundred lire.

"Go to bed," Angelo commanded. "It's a long day tomorrow."

Fidelman climbed up to his room on the fifth floor and stared out the window into the dark street to see how far down was death. Too far, so he undressed for bed. He looked every night and sometimes during the day. Teresa, screaming, had once held onto both his legs as Fidelman dangled half out of the window until one of the girls' naked customers, a barrel-chested man, rushed into the room and dragged him back. Sometimes Fidelman wept in his sleep.

. . .

He awoke, cringing. Angelo and Scarpio had entered his room but nobody hit him.

"Search anywhere," he offered, "you won't find anything except maybe half a stale pastry."

"Shut up," said Angelo. "We came to make a proposition."

Fidelman slowly sat up. Scarpio produced the yellow sheet he had doodled on. "We notice you draw." He pointed a dirty fingernail at the nude figure.

"After a fashion," Fidelman said modestly. "I doodle and see what happens."

"Could you copy a painting?"

"What sort of painting?"

"A nude. Tiziano's *Venus of Urbino*. The one after Giorgione."

"That one," said Fidelman. "I doubt that I could."

"Any fool can."

"Shut up, Scarpio," Angelo said. He sat his bulk at the foot of Fidelman's narrow bed. Scarpio, with his good eye, moodily inspected the cheerless view from the window.

"On Isola Bella in Lago Maggiore, about an hour from here," said Angelo, "there's a small *castello* full of lousy paintings, except for one which is a genuine Tiziano, authenticated by three art experts, including a brother-in-law of mine. It's worth half-a-million dollars but the owner is richer than Olivetti and won't sell, though an American museum is breaking its head to get it."

"Very interesting," Fidelman said.

"Exactly," said Angelo. "Anyway, it's insured for at least four hundred thousand dollars. Of course if anyone stole it it would be impossible to sell."

"Then why bother?"

"Bother what?"

"Whatever it is," Fidelman said lamely.

"You'll learn more by listening," Angelo said. "Suppose it was stolen and held for ransom. What do you think of that?"

"Ransom?" said Fidelman.

"Ransom," said Scarpio.

"At least three hundred thousand dollars," said Angelo. "It would be a bargain for the insurance company. They'd save a hundred thousand on the deal."

He outlined a plan. They had photographed the Titian on both sides, from all angles and several distances and had collected from art books the best color plates. They also had the exact measurements of the canvas and every figure on it. If Fidelman could make a decent copy they would duplicate the frame and on a dark night sneak the reproduction into the *castello* gallery and exit with the original. The guards were stupid, and the advantage of the plan—instead of just slitting the canvas out of its frame—was that nobody would recognize the substitution for days, possibly longer. In the meantime they would row the picture across the lake and truck it out of the country down to the French Riviera. The Italian police had fantastic luck in recovering stolen paintings; one had a better chance in France. Once the picture was securely hidden, Angelo back at the hotel, Scarpio would get in touch with the insurance company. Imagine the sensation! Recognizing the brilliance of the execution, the company would have to kick in with the ransom money.

"If you make a good copy, you'll get yours," said Angelo.

"Mine? What would that be?" Fidelman asked.

"Your passport," Angelo said cagily. "Plus two hundred dollars in cash and a quick goodbye."

"Five hundred dollars," said Fidelman.

"Scarpio," said the *padrone* patiently, "show him what you have in your pants."

Scarpio unbuttoned his jacket and drew a long mean-looking dagger from a sheath under his belt. Fidelman, without trying, could feel the cold blade slowly sinking into his ribs.

"Three-fifty," he said. "I'll need plane fare."

"Three-fifty," said Angelo. "Payable when you deliver the finished reproduction."

"And you pay for all supplies?"

"I pay all expenses within reason. But if you try any monkey tricks—snitch or double cross you'll wake up with your head gone, or something worse."

"Tell me," Fidelman asked after a minute of contemplation, "what if I turn down the proposition? I mean in a friendly way?"

Angelo rose sternly from the creaking bed. "Then you'll stay here for the rest of your life. When you leave you leave in a coffin, very cheap wood."

"I see," said Fidelman.

"What do you say?"

"What more can I say?"

"Then it's settled," said Angelo.

"Take the morning off," said Scarpio.

"Thanks," Fidelman said.

Angelo glared. "First finish the toilet bowls."

▪ ▪ ▪

Am I worthy? Fidelman thought. Can I do it? Do I dare? He had these and other doubts, felt melancholy, and wasted time.

Angelo one morning called him into his office. "Have a Munich beer."

"No, thanks."

"Cordial?"

"Nothing now."

"What's the matter with you? You look like you have just buried your mother."

Fidelman set down his mop and pail with a sigh and said nothing.

"Why don't you put those things away and get started?" the *padrone* asked. "I've had the *portiere* move six trunks and some broken furniture out of the storeroom where you have two big windows. Scarpio wheeled in an easel and he's bought you brushes, colors and whatever else you need."

"It's west light, not very even."

Angelo shrugged. "It's the best I can do. This is our season and I can't spare any rooms. If you'd rather work at night we can set up some lamps. It's a waste of electricity, but I'll make that concession to your temperament if you work fast and produce the goods."

"What's more, I don't know the first thing about forging paintings," Fidelman said. "All I might do is just about copy the picture."

"That's all we ask. Leave the technical business to us. First do a decent drawing. When you're ready to paint I'll get you a piece of 16th Century Belgian linen that's been scraped clean of a former picture. You prime it with white lead and when it's dry you sketch. Once you finish the nude, Scarpio and I will bake it, put in the cracks and age them with soot. We'll even stipple in fly spots before we varnish and glue. We'll do what's necessary. There are books on these subjects and Scarpio reads like a demon. It isn't as complicated as you think."

"What about the truth of the colors?"

"I'll mix them for you. I've made a life study of Tiziano's work."

"Really?"

"Of course."

But Fidelman's eyes still looked unhappy.

"What's eating you now?" the *padrone* asked.

"It's stealing another painter's ideas and work."

The *padrone* wheezed. "Tiziano will forgive you. Didn't he steal the figure of the *Urbino* from Giorgione? Didn't Rubens steal the Andrian nude from

Tiziano? Art steals and so does everybody. You stole a wallet and tried to steal my lire. It's the way of the world. We're only human."

"Isn't it sort of a desecration?"

"Everybody desecrates. We live off the dead and they live off us. Take, for instance, religion."

"I don't think I can do it without seeing the original," Fidelman said. "The color plates you gave me aren't true."

"Neither is the original anymore. You don't think Rembrandt painted in those *sfumato* browns, do you? As for painting the *Venus,* you'll have to do the job here. If you copied it in the *castello* gallery, one of those cretin guards might remember your face and the next thing you know you'd have trouble. So would we, probably, and we naturally wouldn't want that."

"I still ought to see it," Fidelman said obstinately.

The *padrone* then, reluctantly, consented to a one-day excursion to Isola Bella, assigning Scarpio to closely accompany the copyist.

▪ ▪ ▪

On the *vaporetto* to the island, Scarpio, wearing dark glasses and a light straw hat, turned to Fidelman.

"In all confidence, what do you think of Angelo?"

"He's all right, I guess."

"Do you think he's handsome?"

"I haven't given it a thought. Possibly he was, once."

"You have many fine insights," said Scarpio. He pointed in the distance where the long blue lake disappeared amid towering Alps. "Locarno, sixty kilometers."

"You don't say." At the thought of Switzerland so close by, freedom swelled in Fidelman's heart but he did nothing about it. Scarpio clung to him like a long-lost brother and sixty kilometers was a long swim with a knife in your back.

"That's the *castello* over there," the major-domo said. "It looks like a joint."

The *castello* was pink on a high terraced hill amid tall trees in formal gardens. It was full of tourists and bad paintings. But in the last gallery, "infinite riches in a little room," hung the *Venus of Urbino* alone.

What a miracle, thought Fidelman.

The golden-brown-haired Venus, a woman of the real world, lay on her couch in serene beauty, her hand lightly touching her intimate mystery, the other holding red flowers, her nude body her truest accomplishment.

"I would have painted somebody in bed with her," Scarpio said.

"Shut up," said Fidelman.

Scarpio, hurt, left the gallery.

Fidelman, alone with Venus, worshiped the painting. What magnificent flesh tones, what extraordinary flesh that can turn the body into spirit.

While Scarpio was out talking to the guard, the copyist hastily sketched the

Venus, and with a Leica Angelo had borrowed from a friend for the purpose, took several new color shots.

Afterward he approached the picture and kissed the lady's hands, thighs and breasts, but as he was murmuring "I love you," a guard struck him hard on the head with both fists.

That night as they returned on the *rapido* to Milano, Scarpio fell asleep, snoring. He awoke in a hurry, tugging at his dagger, but Fidelman hadn't moved.

. . .

The copyist threw himself into his work with passion. He had swallowed lightning and hoped it would strike what he touched. Yet he had nagging doubts he could do the job right and feared he would never escape alive from the Hotel du Ville. He tried at once to paint the Titian directly on canvas, but hurriedly scraped it clean when he saw what a garish mess he had made. The Venus was insanely disproportionate and the maids in the background foreshortened into dwarfs. He then took Angelo's advice and made several drawings on paper to master the composition before committing it again to canvas.

Angelo and Scarpio came up every night and shook their heads over the drawings.

"Not even close," said the *padrone*.

"Far from it," said Scarpio.

"I'm trying," Fidelman said, anguished.

"Try harder," Angelo said grimly.

Fidelman had a sudden insight. "What happened to the last guy who did?"

"He's still floating," Scarpio said.

"I'll need some practice," the copyist coughed. "My vision seems tight and the arm tires easily. I'd better go back to some exercises to loosen up."

"What kind of exercises?" Scarpio inquired.

"Nothing physical, just some warm-up nudes to get me going."

"Don't overdo it," Angelo said. "You've got about a month, not much more. There's a certain advantage in making the exchange of pictures during the tourist season."

"Only a month?"

The *padrone* nodded.

"Maybe you'd better trace it," Scarpio said.

"No."

"I'll tell you what," said Angelo. "I could get you an old reclining nude you could paint over. You might get the form of this one by altering the form of another."

"No."

"Why not?"

"It's not honest. I mean to myself."

Everyone tittered.

"Well, it's your headache," Angelo said.

Fidelman, unwilling to ask what happened if he failed, feverishly drew faster after they had left.

■ ■ ■

Things went badly for the copyist. Working all day and often into the very early morning hours, he tried everything he could think of. Since he always distorted the figure of Venus, though he carried it perfectly in his mind, he went back to a study of Greek statuary with ruler and compasses to compute the mathematical proportions of the ideal nude. Scarpio accompanied him to one or two museums. Fidelman also worked with the Vitruvian square in the circle, experimented with Dürer's intersecting circles and triangles and studied Leonardo's schematic heads and bodies. Nothing doing. He drew paper dolls, not women, certainly not Venus. He drew girls who would not grow up. He then tried sketching every Venus he could lay eyes on in the art books Scarpio brought him from the library, from the Esquiline goddess to *Les Demoiselles d'Avignon.* Fidelman copied, not badly, many figures from classical statuary and modern painting, but when he returned to his Venus, with something of a laugh she eluded him. What am I, bewitched, the copyist asked himself, and if so by what? It's only a copy job, so what's taking so long? He couldn't even guess until he happened to see a naked whore cross the hall and enter a friend's room. Maybe the idea is cold and I like it hot? Nature over art? Inspiration—the live model? Fidelman knocked on the door and tried to persuade the girl to pose for him, but she wouldn't for economic reasons. Neither would any of the others—there were four girls in the room.

A redhead among them called out to Fidelman, "Shame on you, Arturo, are you too good to bring up pizzas and coffee anymore?"

"I'm busy on a job for Angelo."

The girls laughed.

"Painting a picture, that is. A business proposition."

They laughed louder.

Their laughter further depressed his spirits. No inspiration from whores. Maybe too many naked women around made it impossible to draw a nude. Still he'd better try a live model, having tried everything else and failed.

In desperation, practically on the verge of panic because time was going so fast, he thought of Teresa, the chambermaid. She was a poor specimen of feminine beauty, but the imagination could enhance anything. Fidelman asked her to pose for him, and Teresa, after a shy laugh, consented.

"I will if you promise not to tell anybody."

Fidelman promised.

She got undressed, a meager, bony girl, breathing heavily, and he drew her with flat chest, distended belly, thin hips and hairy legs, unable to alter a single detail. Van Eyck would have loved her. When Teresa saw the drawing she wept profusely.

"I thought you would make me beautiful."

"I had that in mind."

"Then why didn't you?"

"It's hard to say," said Fidelman.

"I'm not in the least bit sexy," she wept.

Considering her body with half-open eyes, Fidelman told her to go borrow a long slip.

"Get one from one of the girls and I'll make you sexy."

She returned in a frilly white slip and looked so attractive that instead of painting her, Fidelman, with a lump in his throat, got her to lie down with him on a dusty mattress in the room. Clasping her slip-encased form, the copyist shut both eyes and concentrated on his elusive Venus. He felt about to recapture a rapturous experience and was looking forward to it with pleasure, but at the last minute it turned into a Limerick he didn't know he knew:

Whilst Titian was mixing rose madder,
His model was crouched on a ladder;
Her position to Titian
Suggested coition,
So he stopped mixing madder and had 'er.

Angelo, entering the storeroom just then, let out a furious bellow. He fired Teresa, on her naked knees pleading with him not to, and Fidelman had to go back to latrine duty the rest of the day.

"You might just as well keep me doing this permanently," Fidelman, disheartened, told the *padrone* in his office afterward. "I'll never finish that cursed picture."

"Why not? What's eating you? I've treated you like a son."

"I'm blocked, that's what."

"Get to work, you'll feel better."

"I just can't paint."

"For what reason?"

"I don't know."

"Because you've had it too good here." Angelo angrily struck Fidelman across the face. When the copyist turned and wept, he booted him hard in the rear.

That night Fidelman went on a hunger strike but the *padrone,* hearing of it, threatened force-feeding.

After midnight Fidelman stole some clothes from a sleeping whore, dressed quickly, tied on a kerchief, made up his eyes and lips, and walked out through the door past Scarpio sitting on a bar stool, enjoying the night breeze. Having gone a block, fearing he would be chased, Fidelman broke into a high-heeled run, but it was too late. Scarpio had recognized him in aftermath and called the *portiere.* Fidelman kicked off his slippers and ran furiously, but the skirt impeded him. The major-domo and the *portiere* caught up with him and dragged him, kicking and struggling, back to the hotel. A *carabiniere,* hearing the commotion, appeared on the scene, but seeing how Fidelman was dressed, would do nothing for him. In the cellar, Angelo hit him with a short rubber hose until he collapsed.

▪ ▪ ▪

Fidelman lay in bed three days, refusing to eat or get up.

"What'll we do now?" Angelo, worried, whispered. "What about a fortune-teller? Either that or let's bury him."

"Astrology is better," Scarpio advised. "I'll check his planets. If that doesn't work, we'll try psychology."

"Well, make it fast," said Angelo.

The next morning Scarpio entered Fidelman's room with an American breakfast on a tray and two thick books under his arm. Fidelman was still in bed, smoking a butt. He wouldn't eat.

Scarpio set down his books and took a chair close to the bed.

"What's your birthday, Arturo?" he asked gently, feeling Fidelman's pulse.

Fidelman told him, also the hour of birth and the place: Newark, New Jersey.

Scarpio, consulting the zodiacal tables, drew up Fidelman's horoscope on a sheet of paper and studied it thoroughly with his good eye. After a few minutes he shook his head. "It's no wonder."

"What's wrong?" Fidelman sat up weakly.

"You're a Gemini and your Uranus and Venus are both in bad shape."

"My Venus?"

"She rules your fate." He studied the chart. "Taurus ascending, Venus afflicted. That's why you're blocked."

"Afflicted by what?"

"Uranus, in the twelfth house."

"What's she doing there?"

"Shh," said Scarpio. "I'm checking your Mercury."

"Concentrate on Venus, when will she be better?"

Scarpio consulted the tables, jotted down some numbers and signs and slowly turned pale. He searched through a few more pages of tables, then got up and stared out the dirty window.

"It's hard to tell. Do you believe in psychoanalysis?"

"Sort of."

"Maybe we'd better try that. Don't get up."

Fidelman's head fell back on the pillow.

Scarpio opened a thick book to its first chapter. "The thing to do is associate freely."

"If I don't get out of this whorehouse soon I'll surely die," said Fidelman.

"Do you have any memories of your mother?" Scarpio asked. "For instance, did you ever see her naked?"

"She died at my birth," Fidelman answered, on the verge of tears. "I was raised by my sister Bessie."

"Go on, I'm listening," said Scarpio.

"I can't. My mind goes blank."

Scarpio turned to the next chapter, flipped through several pages, then rose with a sigh.

"It might be a medical matter. Take a physic tonight."

"I already have."

The major-domo shrugged. "Life is complicated. Anyway, keep track of your dreams. Write them down as soon as you have them."

Fidelman puffed his butt.

That night he dreamed of Bessie about to bathe. He was peeking at her through the bathroom keyhole as she was preparing her bath. Openmouthed, he watched her remove her robe and step into the tub. Her hefty well-proportioned body then was young and full in the right places; and in the dream Fidelman, then fourteen, looked at her with longing that amounted to anguish. The older Fidelman, the dreamer, considered doing a *La Baigneuse* right then and there, but when Bessie began to soap herself with Ivory soap, the boy slipped away into her room, opened her poor purse, filched fifty cents for the movies, and went on tiptoe down the stairs.

He was shutting the vestibule door with great relief when Arthur Fidelman awoke with a headache. As he was scribbling down this dream he suddenly remembered what Angelo had said: "Everybody steals. We're all human."

A stupendous thought occurred to him: Suppose he personally were to steal the picture?

A marvelous idea all around. Fidelman heartily ate that morning's breakfast.

▪ ▪ ▪

To steal the picture he had to paint one. Within another day the copyist successfully sketched Titian's painting and then began to work in oils on an old piece of Flemish linen that Angelo had hastily supplied him with after seeing the successful sketch. Fidelman underpainted the canvas and after it was dry began the figure of Venus as the conspirators looked on, sucking their breaths.

"Stay relaxed," begged Angelo, sweating. "Don't spoil it now. Remember you're painting the appearance of a picture. The original has already been painted. Give us a decent copy and we'll do the rest with chemistry."

"I'm worried about the brush strokes."

"Nobody will notice them. Just keep in your mind that Tiziano painted resolutely with few strokes, his brush loaded with color. In the end he would paint with his fingers. Don't worry about that. We don't ask for perfection, just a good copy."

He rubbed his fat hands nervously.

But Fidelman painted as though he were painting the original. He worked alone late at night, when the conspirators were snoring, and he painted with what was left of his heart. He had caught the figure of the *Venus*, but when it came to her flesh, her thighs and breasts, he never thought he would make it. As he painted, he seemed to remember every nude that ever had been done, Fidelman satyr, with Silenus beard and goat legs dancing among them, piping and peeking at backside, frontside, or both, at the *Rokeby Venus, Bathsheba, Suzanna, Venus Anadyomene, Olympia,* at picnickers in dress or undress, bathers ditto, Vanitas or Truth, Niobe or Leda, in chase or embrace, *Hausfrau* or whore, amorous ladies modest or brazen, single or in crowds at the Turkish bath, in every conceivable shape or position, while he sported or disported until a trio of maenads pulled his curly beard and he galloped after them through the dusky woods. He was, at the same time, choked by remembered lust for all the women he had ever desired, from Bessie to Annamaria Oliovino, and for their garters, underpants, slips or half-slips, brassieres and stockings. Although thus tormented, Fidelman felt himself falling in love with the one he painted, every inch of her, including the ring on her pinky, bracelet on arm, the flowers she touched with her fingers, and the bright green earring that dangled from her eatable ear. He would have prayed her alive if he weren't certain she would fall in love, not with her famished creator, but surely with the first *Apollo Belvedere* she laid eyes on. Is there, Fidelman asked himself, a world where love endures and is always satisfying? He answered in the negative. Still, she was his as he painted, so he went on painting, planning never to finish, to be happy as he was in loving her, thus forever happy.

But he finished the picture on Saturday night, Angelo's gun pressed to his head. Then the *Venus* was taken from him and Scarpio and Angelo baked, smoked, stippled, varnished and framed Fidelman's masterwork as the artist lay on his bed in his room in a state of collapse.

"The *Venus of Urbino, c'est à moi.*"

▪ ▪ ▪

"What about my three hundred and fifty?" Fidelman asked Angelo during a card game in the *padrone*'s stuffy office several days later. After completing the painting the copyist was again back on janitorial duty.

"You'll collect when we've got the Tiziano."

"I did my part."

"Don't question decisions."

"What about my passport?"

"Give it to him, Scarpio."

Scarpio handed him the passport. Fidelman flipped through the booklet and saw the pages were intact.

"If you skiddoo now," Angelo warned him, "you'll get spit."

"Who's skiddooing?"

"So the plan is this: You and Scarpio will row out to the *castello* after midnight. The caretaker is an old man and half-deaf. You hang our picture and breeze off with the other."

"If you wish," Fidelman suggested, "I'll gladly do the job myself. Alone, that is."

"Why alone?" said Scarpio suspiciously.

"Don't be foolish," Angelo said. "With the frame it weighs half-a-ton. Now listen to directions and don't try to give any. One reason I detest Americans is that they never know their place."

Fidelman apologized.

"I'll follow in the putt-putt and wait for you halfway between Isola Bella and Stresa in case it should happen we need a little extra speed at the last minute."

"Do you expect trouble?"

"Not a bit. If there's any trouble it'll be your fault. In that case, watch out."

"Off with his head," said Scarpio. He played a deuce and took the pot.

Fidelman laughed politely.

▪ ▪ ▪

The next night, Scarpio rowed a huge weather-beaten rowboat, both oars muffled. It was a moonless night with touches of Alpine lightning in the distant sky. Fidelman sat in the stern, holding with both hands and balancing against his knees the large framed painting, heavily wrapped in monk's cloth and cellophane, and tied around with rope.

At the island, the major-domo docked the boat and securely tied it. Fidelman, peering around in the dark, tried to memorize where they were. They carried the picture up two hundred steps, both puffing when they got to the formal gardens on top.

The *castello* was black except for a square of yellow light from the caretaker's turret window high above. As Scarpio snapped the lock of an embossed heavy wooden door with a strip of Celluloid, the yellow window slowly opened and an old man peered down. They froze against the wall until the window was drawn shut.

"Fast," Scarpio hissed. "If anyone sees us they'll wake the whole island."

Pushing open the creaking door, they quickly carried the painting, growing heavier as they hurried, through an enormous room cluttered with cheap statuary, and by the light of the major-domo's flashlight, ascended a narrow flight of spiral stairs. They hastened in sneakers down a deep-shadowed, tapestried hall into the picture gallery, Fidelman stopping in his tracks when he beheld the *Venus,* the true and magnificent image of his counterfeit creation.

"Let's get to work." Scarpio quickly unknotted the rope and they unwrapped Fidelman's painting and leaned it against the wall. They were taking down the Titian when footsteps sounded unmistakably in the hall. Scarpio's flashlight went out.

"Shh, it's the caretaker. If he comes in, I'll have to conk him."

"That'll destroy Angelo's plan—deceit, not force."

"I'll think of that when we're out of here."

They pressed their backs to the wall, Fidelman's clammy, as the old man's steps drew nearer. The copyist had anguishing visions of losing the picture and made helter-skelter plans somehow to reclaim it. Then the footsteps faltered, came to a stop, and after a moment of intense hesitation, moved in another direction. A door slammed and the sound was gone.

It took Fidelman several seconds to breathe. They waited in the dark without moving until Scarpio shone his light. Both *Venuses* were resting against the same wall. The major-domo closely inspected each canvas with one eye shut, then signaled the painting on the left. "That's the one, let's wrap it up."

Fidelman broke into a profuse sweat.

"Are you crazy? That's mine. Don't you know a work of art when you see it?" He pointed to the other picture.

"Art?" said Scarpio, removing his hat and turning pale. "Are you sure?" He peered at the painting.

"Without a doubt."

"Don't try to confuse me." He tapped the dagger under his coat.

"The lighter one is the Titian," Fidelman said through a dry throat. "You smoked mine a shade darker."

"I could have sworn yours was the lighter."

"No. Titian's. He used light varnishes. It's a historical fact."

"Of course." Scarpio mopped his brow with a soiled handkerchief. "The trouble is with my eyes. One is in bad shape and I overuse the other."

"Tsk-tsk," said Fidelman.

"Anyway, hurry up. Angelo's waiting on the lake. Remember, if there's any mistake he'll cut your throat first."

They hung the darker painting on the wall, quickly wrapped the lighter and hastily carried it through the long hall and down the stairs, Fidelman leading the way with Scarpio's light.

At the dock the major-domo nervously turned to Fidelman. "Are you absolutely sure we have the right one?"

"I give you my word."

"I accept it, but under the circumstances I'd better have another look. Shine the flashlight through your fingers."

Scarpio knelt to undo the wrapping once more, and Fidelman, trembling, brought the flashlight down hard on Scarpio's straw hat, the light shattering in his hand. The major-domo, pulling at his dagger, collapsed.

Fidelman had trouble loading the painting into the rowboat but finally got it in and settled, and quickly took off. In ten minutes he had rowed out of sight of the dark, castled island. Not long afterward he thought he heard Angelo's putt-putt behind him, and his heart beat erratically, but the *padrone* did not appear. He rowed as the waves deepened.

Locarno, sixty kilometers.

A wavering flash of lightning pierced the broken sky, lighting the agitated lake all the way to the Alps, as a dreadful thought assailed Fidelman: Had he the right painting, after all? After a minute he pulled in his oars, listened once more for Angelo, and hearing nothing, stepped to the stern of the rowboat, letting it drift as he frantically unwrapped the *Venus*.

In the pitch black, on the lake's choppy waters, he saw she was indeed his, and by the light of numerous matches adored his handiwork.

Philip Roth

An Actor's Life for Me

January 1964

Philip Roth was only twenty-six when he won the National Book Award in 1959 for a collection of six stories called *Goodbye Columbus,* which introduced America to Brenda Potamkin and Jewish country-club life. The movie came out ten years later, in 1969, the year that *Portnoy's Complaint* shocked and delighted readers on its way up the best-seller list, inspiring countless masturbation jokes. Roth is a prolific writer whose novels since the 1970s have played and replayed with the question of identity, sometimes using his alter ego, the Jewish writer Zuckerman, and sometimes himself as protagonist. The most recent of these are *The Counterlife* (1986), *The Facts* (1988), *Deception* (1990), and *Operation Shylock* (1993). He has written few short stories since the early days, however. It seems a pity, for, as "An Actor's Life for Me" demonstrates, he can pack a world of urban neurosis into a few paragraphs. Roth lives in Connecticut and London with his wife, the actress Claire Bloom.

Philip Roth

An Actor's Life for Me

Instantly, Walter Appel knew what the man across the way was up to. Walter had left his study and come into the living room out of pique with himself, really. He could not keep his mind off Tarsila Brown; he was supposed to be sitting there paying the bills, and all he could think about was whether he would call her. And whether he would did not seem to depend on whether he should. For he knew that he shouldn't. Only a fool had to learn the same lesson twice in six months, a fool or a child, and he made it a point in life to try not to act like either. Tarsila had arrived in New York from London; he had read the news in a gossip column. Would he call her? What good could possibly come of it?

He left his checkbook and came into the living room. Looking for nothing except perhaps release from the unfamiliar discomfort of irresolution, Walter peered between the curtains. In the window facing onto the rear of the Appel apartment, he saw the naked man strolling back and forth.

His first impulse—he had none. He did not throw open his own window and call, "Hey you—will you please pull your shades!" He did not rush to telephone the police, or Bellevue. He did not go immediately around to Juliet's study to see if the curtains were drawn. Walter had no sharp impulse to act. The apartment across the courtyard had been empty for several weeks; the man must have recently moved in—and without a doubt he was trying to expose himself to Juliet. All Walter did, knowing this, was to drop the edge of the curtain and return to his desk where he tried once again to pay the previous month's bills.

Ridiculous! Pushing up from his chair, he raced out of the study, down the hall, and into the living room again. He took three lurching steps to the curtains, pitching forward like some monster—and then got control of himself.

Walter switched on a lamp. He chose a record and placed it on the turntable. All the while he deliberately kept his back to the curtains. If you live in a city like New York, you were bound to catch glimpses through the window . . . But the fellow had been exhibiting himself; his intent was made very clear by the very way in which he moved his limbs, so slowly, so languorously . . .

Walter adjusted the volume of the phonograph; he adjusted the tone. Then he walked around to Juliet's study. And there he had his second intuition. He realized what it was that Juliet was doing behind her door. For a week now she had been going off to her study after dinner to spend an hour or two writing, or so she had said. He had not bothered to question her; she was not very much of a writer, Walter believed, but he allowed her her enthusiasms; he had to. He knew now that she was not writing at all. One and one suddenly made two. He could hardly believe it. He only rapped on the door. "Brandy?"

There was no answer. If he tried the handle he would find it locked—so he believed—so he feared. "Juliet?"

The door swung open. Juliet was fully dressed. He looked immediately past her into the room. The curtains were closed. But just as she snapped out the lights, he saw that the soft folds of blue velvet—the drapes she herself had sewn—were swinging to and fro, as though the wind were blowing them, or as though they had just been pulled shut.

▪ ▪ ▪

Juliet and Walter were not a perfectly happy couple. There had been setbacks and there had been hard times, though discretion being a virtue of both, even when they had chosen for a while to separate, hardly anyone had known of their trouble. For reasons of their own, they had no children. Until only a short time ago, it had been to the expression of their talents that each had devoted himself. At an age when other young men and women were disappearing into small suburban houses, or sailing romantically off to Europe on five dollars a day, Juliet and Walter were living out of choice in one dark room over the truck traffic on Hudson Street. Once, to an impressionable girlfriend down from college, Juliet had offhandedly referred to their place as "a pad in the Village"; when they were alone again, Walter had bawled her out for it. He and Juliet lived where they did, as they did, because they wanted to be themselves—which, at that time, meant that Juliet wanted to be an actress, and Walter a playwright.

But Juliet's career never really got off the ground: She had majored in drama and the dance at a series of permissive girls' schools, she had played most of the leads in college, but in New York the only parts she received were walk-ons in plays put on in vacant churches and downtown lofts, where sometimes to meet the fire regulations was as difficult as finding an audience. The one Broadway role she was ever in the running for—a small one, at that—she did not get because, said the director, she looked too much like Katharine Hepburn: at least that was how Juliet reported his remarks to Walter when she arrived home. Immediately she went out and cut her hair, bought a pair of pendulous copper earrings, and, in the next few days, tried on a crash diet of peanut butter and bananas to change her general appearance. But on the fifth morning, when she mounted the scale, she announced, "I've actually *lost* two pounds," and for a whole day, instead of going back to the director, as she had planned, or to her acting class, or even downstairs to get something for them to eat for dinner, she lay in bed and sobbed. Pathetically she thrashed about on the bed, waiting, Walter knew, for him to do something, or to say something, that would put things right for her. He was her rock. He had a stocky frame, and a strong chin, and in his early twenties his straight black hair had already begun to go gray at the sides. His neck was thick, his body hairy; he had always a tendency to look older and shorter than he was. To a girl like Juliet, so full of airy hopes and dreams, how like granite Walter must have seemed. But now all he could do for her, despite the graying sideburns and the forward thrust of his head, was feel sorry for her, and smooth her hair, and tell her that she ought to be flattered to be told that she looked like Katharine Hepburn, who was a beautiful woman.

The night of Juliet's collapse, Walter read over the five plays he had so industriously written during the three years of their marriage. How much longer could *he* keep it up? He too had been a hot-shot in the theater department, at a liberal-arts college in Pennsylvania, a pretty little place up in the Allegheny Mountains that used the local high-school auditorium in which to put on plays. His drama professor had believed that Walter Appel had written the best one-act play by anyone who had ever attended the school. But Walter was in New York now; though it might be that the producers were commercial, and stupid, and Philistine (as Juliet assured him they were), it might also be that he was not a very gifted man. On the bed in the corner of the room, Juliet whimpered the night through in dreams of loss, while in his writing chair, Walter read his plays and admitted to himself that there was really no more chance of his becoming a playwright than of Juliet's becoming an actress. It was time to stop being an adolescent.

The next morning he put on a tie and jacket, and with the decision firmly made to change his life, he went off to look for work that he could do. Through Harvey Landau, who had met the young couple and taken to them in a fatherly way, Walter found a job in the business end of the theater. Perhaps it was not what he had hoped to do, but it was what he could do. In fact, it was only a short while before he found himself feeling much more like a man, doing a regular day's work, and doing it well.

The Appels were soon able to move from the squalid room on Hudson Street to a good-sized apartment in a brownstone on the Upper West Side. Juliet went around telling people about their high ceilings for a month, in an effort, Walter knew, to forget about her failure as an actress. As the months passed, he was surprised to find her clinging so to her illusions; but then he was surprised that for all his display of seriousness and purpose, he had actually been a victim of illusion himself.

At home Juliet began to practice her French with records. Did she believe they were going to move to France? He did not ask; he let her be. She went for a month to a German woman in the East 80s who taught her how to sew her own clothes. She enrolled in a writing course at the New School, and came home in tears one night, because the instructor had made fun of her story in class. Everything pointed in the same direction: it was time to have a baby. One night Walter had a dream of a little girl whose name was Allison. It was their daughter. But dreams are one thing, Walter well knew, and life another. Unfortunately it was not time to have a baby at all. For, some eight months after discovering their limitations as actress and playwright, the Appels discovered in themselves yet another limitation; it seemed as though they had fallen out of love.

Not that they appeared to care less for each other. What made the predicament so trying was that in all ways but one the marriage seemed to be what it was before: Juliet, between enthusiasms, leaning upon Walter, and Walter there to be leaned upon. During the day there were even moments when Walter thought that perhaps they should have a baby so as to prevent the marriage from falling apart, if that was what was beginning to happen. Yet at night he could not blind himself to the change that had taken place, though it was a change which at first he did not entirely understand. Why should they be indifferent to one another in their bed?

Though they had no baby, their life together went on. At parties Walter would even find himself rubbing his wife's back, as she sat beside him with a drink in her hand. He saw the other men admire her tall, good looks, her vivacity, the way she walked and laughed—he admired these things himself, her spiritedness had always seemed to him the feminine counterpart of his own diligence, but now it pained him to think that when she laughed she was not actually happy. Of course, they did not turn completely from one another; in the middle of the night, they would sometimes reach across the dark bed, and in a dreamy half-sleep, arouse each other's passions. But often it was not until he was on the subway the following morning that Walter remembered that during the previous eight hours he and Juliet had made love, and even then he was not always sure.

One evening at dinner Juliet dropped her fork and stared dully into the candles. "I don't know what the matter is," she said, and put her head in her hands.

Walter thought to move around to her chair and comfort her. But was she any more deprived than he was? "I don't either," he said.

She slammed the table. "What is it! Why do you find me so distasteful!"

"Why do you find me!" he shot back.

She began to cry. "Walter, I didn't mean that. I do know better than that. It's both of us, somehow. Yet we never really fight. You're so thoughtful and solid, you're so good to me—and I'm so dependent on you, whether you know it or not. I think it has to do with our fitting together *too* well."

But that sounded ridiculous to both of them. Juliet blew her nose, Walter helped clear the table, and then each went off as though nothing had happened. At his desk Walter thought to himself, "We should have had a baby a long time ago. The actress business was silly from the start . . ." But then how could he have known that *at* the start?

In five minutes each was back in the living room. "Walter," she said, "do you think we should be divorced?"

"Do *you?"* he demanded.

"Well—*no,"* she said, and hopelessly dropped into a chair.

He dropped into one opposite. "Neither do I," he said.

"Then," asked Juliet, tossing up her arms, "what should we do?"

Walter decided for them: they would separate for a little while. Maybe *that* would do something. Walter telephoned Harvey Landau and asked if he could get away for a few weeks: without even telling Harvey what the trouble was, Walter discovered that Harvey understood. Harvey said, "Do whatever you have to, boy. Just don't run off half-cocked."

"Juliet's going to be alone," said Walter, worried for her.

"We'll have her over for dinner. We'll take care of her." Softly Harvey added, "It happens to everybody."

"Thanks, Harvey." He hung up feeling so relieved that he did not even know why he was going away in the first place.

That night, in bed, his wife said, "Walter?"

"Yes?"

"I don't care who you sleep with. Just don't tell me about it when we meet again."

She was being so brave, so game. How she needed him! Why was he even leaving her? Was he a boy, expecting what a boy expects, or was he a man? Still, he answered with what seemed to him common sense. "The same for you."

There was a pause. "OK," she whispered, and they lay there back to back in an astonished silence.

Where should he go? South? Though it had been a wet and dreary winter, it didn't seem right for him to be lolling on a beach, spending their savings, while Juliet stayed behind in New York. This wasn't supposed to be a pleasure trip, anyway.

He took a train north, and got off in a small town upstate where he rented an inexpensive room; he had the idea that he would read, and walk, and mostly, think things through. But by the end of the first day he found he hadn't made much headway with his thinking. What was he supposed to think about? There was a broken-down ski lodge only a few miles away, and so after dinner, he hiked up the hill and sat at the bar, and watched the few guests sit around trying to think of folk songs to sing. Within the hour he met a young woman who was on vacation from her job as a secretary in Oneonta. They spent some time talking about where Oneonta was and drawing maps on napkins. He knew he could go to her room with her as soon as they began to talk. What he discovered was that he wanted to. His heart began to beat unnaturally. Never before had he committed adultery, yet he went off with the woman without much of an inner struggle. Juliet had said it was OK, and he had something to find out.

She had a room with a fireplace. Before he got into bed, she asked him to build a fire so that they would have it to look into afterward. The draft was bad, and Walter had to get up every few minutes to smash at the logs with the poker, whose handle kept coming off. But the young woman seemed unable to bear the idea of the fire going out, as she was taking half her summer vacation in the winter.

Walter slept in her bed every night for a week. Where Juliet was long in the thigh, the secretary from Oneonta was short; where Juliet was brunette, she was light. Did these few inconsequentialities make the difference? Were they what made him ravenous with her? No, she was just somebody different, a perfect stranger, though he attended to her breasts as though she were a dear friend. And the truth was he couldn't stand her.

On Friday he was ready to take the train down. It was not for this that he had come away. But the separation had been so short; he decided to stay on another night.

He awoke Saturday morning in disgust. After lunch, he went on a long walk with the secretary. The sun was shining on the snow, and they held hands. Absurd. He caught the train to New York just after dinner: he had to rush so to make it that he hadn't time to call the young woman, whose name was Sheila Kay, or Kaye, and tell her that he would not be seeing her that evening, as they had planned.

When he met Juliet at Grand Central, where she was waiting at the information booth, he felt himself go red; fortunately she did not see because she did not look directly at him. They walked across to the Commodore to have a drink, addressing each other like youngsters on a blind date. He handed Juliet a package and waited for her to open it. Inside was a lovely white ski sweater; he had written no note, for he did not know what she would want him to say. He did not know what had happened to her.

"I have a surprise for you, too," she said.

"My God," he thought, "she has found somebody!"

But all Juliet had to tell him was that in his absence she had gone off and gotten a job as Leo Kittering's girl Friday. Kittering was a young man of independent means who was forever trying to start a repertory company in New York; Walter remembered having met him once at a party. For his own reasons, he was so relieved to hear the news that for the first time he took her hands in his. Juliet beamed: she was hardly being paid a fortune, she said, but that wasn't the point. She told Walter she was a new person: she hoped she was through with self-pity.

That night they eventually grew tired of talking and had to go off to bed.

"I'm so tense," whispered Juliet, when he moved in beside her. "It's ridiculous, but I am."

"It's not ridiculous," said Walter.

"Tomorrow . . ." said Juliet.

"OK," he said, for he was not without tension himself, despite his success with the secretary from Oneonta, whom he tried with all his heart not to think of.

When he opened his eyes, it was tomorrow. Walter knew what must be done. They were really as close as people could be—a husband and wife! So, amidst the white sheets, with the yellow curtains blowing in, and a garbage truck roaring away down on the street, Walter looked unflinchingly into Juliet's eyes, and she into his, and they performed the act of love. The noise of the truck grew so loud that at one point Walter wanted to get up and pull down the window. But he stayed where he was and did what had to be done—which turned out to be more than having intercourse once again with his mate. They were telling each other that they wanted each other. When it was over and both lay panting in the strong light, Walter was willing to believe that their crisis was behind them, and that they were about to enter a new stage of marriage.

And so they did. That it could not be forever what it had been four years back on Hudson Street, and in Juliet's room before that, Walter had realized the night before the separation; now he accepted it. Nevertheless, he could not put his finger on why and how it had happened to *them.* Were they resentful of one another? disappointed in one another? too close to one another, whatever that meant? Or was it only time, the diminishing of passion that must one day come to every last husband and every last wife?

Whatever, Walter lowered the expectations of earlier days. He was not seventeen years old, or even twenty-one. He was almost thirty. Not having to be divorced, he came to tell himself, was going to have to cost a little something. He hoped that was as clear to Juliet as it was to him; she too, he hoped, had lowered expectations that were perhaps unreal to begin with. Or were they? There was really no way to tell.

■ ■ ■

In June, Harvey Landau flew to London and took Walter with him. Harvey was going to look over some plays that were opening in the West End. Walter was thrilled—surely he was on the rise—and so too was Juliet thrilled for him; yet when her husband suggested that she come along, at his expense, she had to decline. Kittering had said to her that if she went away just now it would be for him like losing an arm, a statement that Juliet rushed home and repeated to Walter with a charming, open sense of her own importance. Walter understood, agreed, but was not happy. Alone in London it would be business followed by loneliness. But he did not know that he had a right to take her from what she clearly did not want to give up. The pleasures of the new job were filling a gap in her life that he was perhaps not responsible for, but with which he seemed to have something to do. Because, in this vague and ill-defined way, he suspected himself, he had not yet suggested that they fill the gap (if such there really was) with a baby, though of course the idea had occurred to him more than once.

He was on his own, then, when he met Tarsila Brown. She was an actress of Sardinian and American parentage, the wife of the playwright Foxie Brown, one of the noisier of the young Englishmen who had come to be called "angry." Foxie had recently been in two fistfights that had made the papers: the first was with an M.P., who happened to be passing Hyde Park Corner one morning, where Foxie—still in dinner dress from the evening before—had gathered about himself an audience and was imitating the Prime Minister. When the M.P., a man of temper, came charging at Foxie with his umbrella raised, Foxie knocked him cold. The second incident involved Tarsila, also knocked unconscious by Foxie—who had boxed first for his college at Oxford—outside their Hampstead home one afternoon. In the courtroom, Foxie had a gay time of it with the judge, to whom he insisted (or so the papers said) that his dispute with his wife had also been over "political matters"—"whether the woman ought to nationalize herself or be content to stay at home by the fire with me." When Walter met Tarsila, Foxie Brown had just flown off to America.

At a party thrown for Harvey Landau by an English producer, Walter sipped a glass of whiskey and watched Tarsila do the twist. She had been pointed out to him as Foxie's newest estranged wife. When they were introduced she tried to stare him down. When it had obviously for some time been his turn to speak, all he could think to say was, "Your eyes are really black."

She said, "Don't put me on, all right?"

"All right," he said, though actually he admired her eyes, and her dancing had excited him.

But was it her eyes, he wondered, back in his hotel room; was it her dancing; was it that she was so much more voluptuous a woman than Juliet; or was it that she was Foxie Brown's wife?

Late the following afternoon, while deciding what to do with his evening, Walter took a stroll through Soho. Even though he kept his eyes open, and referred from time to time to his guidebook, he knew he was not seeing as much as he would if Juliet were with him. He missed her. He read the little cards posted to the bulletin boards outside the shops. They gave the names and addresses of women advertising themselves as "The Piquant Miss Terry," and "Jessica, a strict disciplinarian," and "Mademoiselle Madeline, authentic French lessons." He passed a simple wooden building with a laundry on the first floor; the Chinaman inside smiled out at him, and pointed upstairs. Walter shook his head, and went to meet Harvey at the hotel.

But after an hour of business, Walter excused himself for a moment. He did not telephone Tarsila because she was married to Foxie Brown; for all of Brown's success as a playwright, Walter would not have traded places with him for the world—the fellow behaved like an ass. Walter was calling Tarsila because he was a man, and she was an exciting-looking woman. But even as he dialed her number, that seemed to him no less shabby a motive than the first.

"Next time," she said, "don't call at the last minute."

He said, "I didn't know I'd be free. Business . . ."

"I just don't want you to think I like men who are offhand. As a matter of fact, I hate them."

Oh yes, thought Walter, and what is Foxie Brown? But he did not see the wisdom in saying anything of a skeptical nature and so, for whatever the reasons, he and Tarsila came together.

He had never before been with anyone like her. Such women he had only fantasized behind locked doors in the delirium of puberty. For the first time in his life, a woman dug her nails into his back. She moaned; she trembled; she cried out, "Oh don't, *don't!*" and this after they were already under way. "Walter," she whispered, "you're like I am. You're crazy for it, too." When he touched her hair, she said, "It's dark, coarse hair. It's Sardinian hair."

Consequently, he saw her the next night, too. And the night after; and the night after. How could he not? Coming out of restaurants they embraced in the street. What was the difference? Who did he know here? It did not seem as though it was he who was here anyway. *He* had a wife in America: *he* was in London on business; *he* knew about kidding yourself . . .

In the taxi rides to her flat she would sometimes jump the gun.

"The driver," moaned Walter, whereupon Tarsila, mysteriously, excitingly, moaned back, "You." And Walter had to admit that it did not make a damn bit of difference about the taxi driver: he was only the back of a head, or eyes in the rearview mirror. It was just that when Walter and Juliet took a taxi, it was to get somewhere; that was what he had grown used to.

Then one night, when she put her arms around him, Walter said, "I'm just beginning to heal."

"Shh."

"No nails, Tarsila—"

She dropped away from him, and rolled onto her side.

"What's the matter?" he asked.

"It's not passion with you," she said. "Your mind's working."

"It's not working."

"It is. You're not thinking about what we're doing. You're thinking about going home to your wife."

"Look," he said, a man laying his cards on the table. "I *am* going back. In two days."

To his surprise—or was it chagrin?—she did not jump up and say, "Then the hell with you!" She didn't dress in a huff and go storming off, leaving him as he had been before they had met. Rather, she pulled his mouth to hers, and said, "You have such sweet breath."

"You heard me?"

"You're so different, Walter. So solid. So steady. Why go home?"

Afterward, Tarsila said, "Do you know my old man?"

"Pardon?"

"Do you know Foxie?"

"Never met him," said Walter, lighting a cigarette.

"You know what he would say after a night like this? That it took the next day's writing out of him. But you—you're so solid-looking, Walter. You're so there."

She said only these words, and in perfect seriousness, but Walter was overcome with humiliation and shame. What was Tarsila's life, or Foxie Brown's for that matter, but so much theatrics? An act. He had really understood what she was the very first night, when he had had a sensation, momentary (but to the point, he now saw), that beneath him Tarsila was floating in an inflated bag, a swollen invisible membrane, inside of which she carried on her contortions all alone. She told him he was so solid, so there, so this, so that, but how innocent of him to believe that it was he who prompted her passion, and not Tarsila, the fantasist, the pretender, the actress, who really prompted her own. "Oh, you are a king, Walter!" she cried, when they came together again that night, but he did not believe that she meant it.

The next night he saw her again. Why not, if he had seen her every night previously? But what of the night after? He would be home.

Even while he walked down Regent Street, shopping for a present for his wife, he asked himself the question Tarsila had asked, and which he believed he had found entirely sufficient reason to dismiss. Why go home?

At four or five the following morning, he was awakened from sleep with a searing pain down his right side. So intense was it that he believed he was having some kind of stroke. At thirty? Oh no! Is everything over? *What has there been!* In the midst of his terror, however, he was thankful that he had returned to his hotel instead of staying until morning at Tarsila's. He was thankful for what Juliet would be spared.

He flailed out for the phone. Within minutes he was in an ambulance bound for the hospital, where his appendix nearly burst in the surgeon's hand. He could not help but believe that the attack had something to do with his activities of the past six days. Otherwise there was no explanation, though of course he did not doubt the physician when he assured him there did not have to be.

Tarsila came to see him only a few minutes after he had spoken long-distance to Juliet. When she slipped off the jacket to her yellow dress, he saw on her arm a mark that he must have made with his mouth.

She put her hand to the top of his hospital pajamas. "Chest hair drives me wild," she said. Did it really? How could it?

As Tarsila went out, Harvey Landau came in. They nodded, natural enemies. Though Harvey had seemingly paid no attention to what Walter did with his free hours, Walter had several times been on the edge of saying to him, "Look, you won't let on to Juliet?" However, he was a grown man and had a right to do what he wanted; consequently, he said nothing in defense of himself. He even began to think of the silent Harvey as Stuffy Harvey and Bourgeois Harvey: secretly Harvey wouldn't mind doing the very same thing—Walter was sure—but the man was twenty years too old and forty pounds too fat and he hadn't the guts . . .

But the older man had only to open his mouth for Walter to see that his boss had nobody's interests at heart but Walter's own. "Do you mind if I give you some advice, big shot?" Harvey said at last.

Walter shook his head. "You don't have to."

"Oh, don't I?"

"No. She's a fake, Harv."

"And you're not a schoolkid," said Harvey, and the next day, with the doctor's permission, Walter left the hospital in a wheelchair and flew home. His wife was at the airport to meet him, and together they resumed their life.

▪ ▪ ▪

Neither the evening that Walter had seen the man across the courtyard, nor the morning after, did he speak of it to Juliet. Nor did she say anything to him. In a way, that was why he said nothing to her . . .

But the question remained: *had* the man revealed himself intentionally? He might only have been walking back and forth before his window . . . But Walter would not talk himself out of what was apparent simply because it was not pleasant. He must only be careful not to assume what was *not* obvious: that Juliet had willingly been a witness. But the curtains had been swaying. And he simply knew it to be so. Of adultery he had never suspected her; yet of this . . .

During the nights that followed, the lights were on across the way and the draperies pulled back, but when Walter stole through his own dark living room and peered between the drawn curtains, he saw nothing of the naked man. Juliet emerged from her study at nine on the second night; on the third, after a nonchalant trip to the kitchen, she returned to spend practically the entire evening behind the closed door. But before she disappeared into the study, she did something unusual: she looked to him as though she were going to explain herself—rather, as though she were going to offer up some lie. And when had he ever demanded an explanation?

"Yes?" he said from the sofa, where he sat pretending to leaf through a magazine.

She shook her head—flushing he saw—and went into the study. For a moment so astonished was he that he tried to tell himself he was only imagining things. He went quickly into the kitchen, from which Juliet had just emerged, and saw no evidence that she had even had a glass of water.

On Saturday evening, they went to a dinner party, and on Sunday out to visit friends in the country. There were two trains back to the city: one would get them in at seven, the other at midnight. It had been a dull day, full of peppy children and loving dogs, but when their hosts asked them to stay on for dinner and take the late train back, Walter immediately said yes. Juliet, however, grasped her forehead and said she wasn't feeling well, and the result was they took the early train.

"Do you really feel ill?" asked Walter, as soon as they boarded.

"Quiet. They're looking through the window. Wave."

The train began to move. "Juliet, do you feel ill or don't you?"

"Walter, I was so bored."

"Well, of all the damn things."

"Weren't you?"

"I said I wanted to stay for dinner. Didn't you hear me?"

"I thought you were being polite. You weren't bored?" she asked. "The big dog kept licking you more than anybody."

"I wasn't bored, Juliet."

"But you were."

"I was not!"

"Well—how am I supposed to know!" she replied, and though to a stranger it might have looked mundane enough, another marital spat, Walter knew, with a sinking of the stomach, that it was not. They did not speak the rest of the way back to the city.

At home, Juliet went into the bathroom, slamming the door behind her, and Walter rushed to the curtains, pushed them back an inch—and across the way, no lights.

When Juliet came out of the bathroom, she said, "If you don't *mind,* I'm going to my study."

Walter was stretched out on the sofa. "Fine."

"I happen to be writing something," said Juliet, belligerently.

"Fine." But his smugness faded the instant she disappeared.

At the close of dinner the following night, Walter actually felt a burning sensation in his chest when he saw his wife take her coffee in two gulps. She mumbled something about what she was writing, and went off to her study. "OK," he said to himself. "So she is writing again." Where he was able to give up on some plan proven impossible with a clean and sharp break, Juliet's unrealistic and unrealizable aspirations had to move through a series of filters, until at last they disappeared. "OK, that is the woman. I should have known that when I married her." It was incredible even to him how strenuously he was trying to believe her.

He sat down at his desk to look through his mail. Then he got up, silently opened his door, and moved back down the hallway. Tonight the lights were back on, but there seemed to be nobody at home. Down below in the courtyard, he saw the reflection from Juliet's study window.

The Wednesday night previously he had not been hallucinating; the man had been there, he was sure. But was he hallucinating the rest? Had all this to do with learning that Tarsila was in town? Since Wednesday he had not thought about her at all. What with his new problem at home, the problem of whether he would call her had disappeared. Or had he invented the one so as to be relieved of the other?

Reason upon reason he continued to offer himself so as not to believe what he had known in an instant on that first night. Tarsila's arrival was nothing more than coincidental; he could not use her to explain away his suspicions of Juliet. In the seven months since his return from London, he had hardly even thought of her; and when he had, it was along with half the other people in New York: the occasion of her divorce from Brown had been treated in the tabloids with gusto. At the very end, there had been a slugfest at a house party in Limehouse, during which someone had pushed Foxie through an open window that let out onto the Thames. Tarsila had lost only a tooth, but the newspaper photograph of the poor woman, her hand over her mouth, had only further convinced Walter of his luck in having been stricken with appendicitis that last night in London. Had he been healthy and able, what foolish, impulsive decision might he have been tempted to make?

He was totally without regret then at having left Tarsila. Yet when the pathetic picture of her had appeared in one of the daily papers, with the caption "Tigress Loses Fang to Britain's Angry Man," Walter's first thought had been: *With that tigress I spent a week.* For about half a block, on the way to lunch, he had had an overpowering urge to mention his exploit to his companion, someone he hardly knew. But at the corner he shot the paper into a wastebasket and, himself again, walked on.

. . . He was standing at the curtains looking for a man who was not there? Why?

But then he saw what he was looking for. Or part of it. He saw an unshod foot. For nights Walter must have looked at the pale spot on the rug without realizing it was human flesh. But he needed only this, the ocular proof, for the last measure of doubt—of hope—to fade away. The man was there, sitting in a chair, in a corner of his living room, out of Walter's range, but directly in Juliet's. That first night he had been pacing up and down so as to get her attention, or recapture it, or God knows what. He sat now exposed to Juliet's eyes.

And in her study, what was Juliet doing? Pretending to write, and catching sidewise glances? Openly staring? Or was she unclothed too? To this had all her dreaming led her! To this! Looking from between the drapes at that bare foot, he cursed all those damn girls' schools his wife had been to, all the impossible aspirations they had spawned in her. But then, as was proper, he blamed himself. He should have forced her to have a child years ago.

▪ ▪ ▪

His decision to call Tarsila he made so simply that he knew it must be connected with what was happening in his home each night. To revenge himself on Juliet? Why revenge, when what he felt for her, as the next night passed, and the next, was not anger or jealousy, but only a terrible pity. He felt pity, he did nothing. He could not at first figure out how to reveal what he knew, without precipitating a full-scale crisis. Might she not, after all, be on the edge of a breakdown? On the other hand, the whole affair might come to an end in another night or two. "Perhaps it is only some passing disturbance, some weird quirk," he told himself. "At any rate, don't lose your head."

But what might that man take it into his head to do next? In the early hours of the morning, fear of the consequences would so shake Walter, that he was ready to awaken Juliet then and there and get the thing out in the open. But when he looked at his sleeping wife, he was not able to disturb her, for he suddenly found himself thinking, "She could be married to anyone, for all that I have made her happy."

As though that were reason to let such insanity continue! As though it were even true! He must *do* something! Yet he did nothing, except to telephone Tarsila.

The instant Tarsila asked "Who is it?" he remembered that first conversation they had ever had, when she had cautioned him not to be offhand. But *she* was the offhand person, the one who did not know about deep attachments, about loyalty and sacrifice and dedication. Foxie was her second husband; he had been, he was sure, her umpteenth lover. He should hang up. She was an inferior person, an unreal person—a fake.

"I want to see you," he said, as calmly as he could.

"Oh?"

"Yes."

"When you left London, you didn't make that too clear."

"No, I suppose I didn't. I would like to see you, however."

"As I remember, you didn't make anything clear. You just left it the way I remember it."

"Well, that's true."

She didn't answer.

"I was in the hospital, Tarsila. Then I was due back in New York."

"Well, I'm glad you arrived safely. Goodbye, squirt."

Walter did not immediately realize that there was no longer anyone at the other end of the line. He hung up and went back to his office.

At 8:30 that evening, Juliet went off to her study. Walter did not know what else to do but go off to his own. But for what? Once again, he came back into the living room, peered momentarily between the curtains, saw the foot, and then sat down in the dark.

Squirt. Or square? He could not remember now which she had said. The two words began to rise and drop inside him, one, then the other, as though they had in fact been addressed to him from one who really mattered.

As though they were *words* that mattered! What was going on? Juliet was his wife—he was her husband! "Enough!" he thought, *"I want Juliet back again,"* following which he thought, "Now there is no chance of having Tarsila on the side," and he was appalled at the kind of people he and his wife seemed to have become, almost overnight. No—only himself overnight. Juliet had really never accepted what she was, what marriage was, what a husband was. At long last he had to admit that his wife was a problem larger than he could handle. It was hard to believe that all this had come to be.

▪ ▪ ▪

The next evening he waited until dinner was over before he told her what, at last, he had decided.

"I want to ask you a question," he said, starting slowly.

"Yes?"

"To say something ..."

"What?"

"This may seem out of the blue to you. However, it's something I've been thinking about for some time."

"Well, what is it?"

"I want us to go to talk to a psychiatrist about some things."

Juliet sat down. "What's the matter?" she asked.

He did not know whether to look directly at her, to catch her betraying herself, or look at the floor, so that she could save face until she was safely inside the doctor's office. "I thought *you* might think there were some things the matter."

"With you?" she asked.

Patience. She is caught, and she knows it. Poor Juliet, you are quite an actress after all. "With our marriage," said Walter kindly.

"—I don't think anything's the matter." But she had hesitated.

"Perhaps if we talked it out," he said.

"What out?"

He gave no answer.

"Well, what out? You always say all those people in analysis are only kidding themselves. That it's a matter of willpower."

"I never said all."

"Well, I don't understand what you're getting at. Well, don't look at me like that. I *don't.*"

"Don't you?"

She threw down her napkin. "No!"

"I don't see why you won't come with me, Juliet."

"Because I don't know what you're getting at! You're trying to say there's something wrong with me."

"I'm not talking about you."

"You're talking about me, Walter, and I know it." There were tears in her eyes. "I know why you think I need a psychiatrist."

He dropped his gaze. "OK, Juliet. Why?"

No answer. When he looked back up, she was glaring at him. "You can't stand that I'm trying to write a play, that's why! You can't stand that I work for Leo—you think that's a waste of time, too!"

"I didn't say anything about either. I thought you were writing a story."

"I *told* you a play."

"You didn't, Juliet."

"I did!"

He shook his head. But had she? A play?

"You can't stand it," she was grumbling. "You want me to see a psychiatrist about it."

He felt for a moment as though he had stepped off into nothing. Why was she writing a play? But she wasn't!

"You've never really had any respect for anything I've tried to do," said Juliet.

"That's not true. And it's not what I'm talking about."

"You always think I'm kidding myself."

Wearily, he shook his head.

"Anybody else would have continued acting, do you know that, Walter? How can you tell anything about yourself at twenty-five, if you don't give yourself a chance? But I only quit—you know why?—because I knew you thought I was making a fool of myself!"

"That's not so. You don't remember what happened."

"I remember what happened to *me!* I remember what *I* thought about. How do *you* know what *I* think!"

"Look"—again, he had to shake off her words—"maybe if you talk to someone about this—"

"Oh damn it! You never let me be what I am! You think I'm silly! You think I waste time!" And then, with a sob, she said, "And what if I do! Suppose I fritter away my whole life! What's the difference anyway? It's *my* life. If I don't do what you think, you think I'm kidding myself. Well, I'm not!" she shouted at him. "Or I am—I don't care!" and she raced from the dining room to the study, where she slammed the door and locked it.

He had accomplished nothing. They were due at the psychiatrist's office the next afternoon; he had not told Juliet that he had already made an appointment for her, or, as he would have put it, for them. Now must he drag her? Was it time to pound on the study door and demand to be let in? Why hadn't he made her confess that very first night? She had been making a fool of herself, humiliating herself—taking into her hands all that was her life!—and he had been letting her.

He had let her! She was right now—in spite, in anger, in bewilderment—taking off her clothes, moving to the window. *And he was letting her.*

He stood up and charged into the darkened living room, toward the study, but wound up at the rear window, peeking between the curtains; and all his fury turned suddenly to suspicion of himself. These past nights, had he not been giving himself some secret pleasure by peeking, imagining . . . ?

Then he saw what had happened across the way. The man had changed his seat. He had moved several feet into the room, in view not only of Juliet's window, but of the living-room window as well. He was settled back in a chair, his legs crossed at the ankles, and his head tipped back, showing the length of his pale throat. He was pretending to be watching TV. In the nude. Very slowly and deliberately, in a way that looked to Walter to be wholly salacious, he was smoking a cigarette.

"Oh God," said Walter, and he found he had tears in his eyes. Was he about to cry for Juliet? For the man across the way? He pulled upon the drawstrings of the curtains and stood in the dark, behind the big window, and looked down upon the strange man. Walter could not turn away from what he saw. "Oh," thought Walter, "I am," and aloud and in exhaustion, like one capitulating, he said, "I am so ordinary."

He pulled off the sweater he was wearing and threw it to the floor. And what did that signify? He began to pull at his clothes. He seemed to himself to be angry. What was he doing? For the moment he did not care to know. His clothing, very shortly, was at his feet. Instantly, he moved back into the room: but once there he only turned on the lamps. Then, drawn by the sight of it, he returned to where the heap of clothing lay and slowly, before the window, he paced off the width of the room, from one side to the other, as though he were awaiting someone's arrival or trying out a pair of shoes. And he said words to himself. *OK—I am naked! In the light! In the window! I am doing this!* In a dizzying moment—as though all the uncertainties of the preceding weeks had come upon him in a single blow—he spun toward the window and, leaning upon the sill, presented himself there, in his socks and his watch. Down in the courtyard below, as evidence that he actually was doing it, he confronted his own elongated shadow. *Yes, I can do anything. Who are you to be so smug? You're not even a person! I am a person! I am at my window—Juliet is at hers—he is at his—*

What am I doing?

He heard a noise, or thought he did. "Yee!" he cried, and in the next instant, pulled at the drawstrings of the curtains. He raced out from the room, yanking at the chains of the lamps as he flew past. In his study, he hurled himself upon the sofa and, trembling in every limb, he whined into his bundle of clothing, "You drove me to it—you were never satisfied," and this time believed he was addressing his wife, as earlier, with his shadow, he must have been addressing Tarsila Brown.

▪ ▪ ▪

Upon awakening the next morning, Walter found that his wife wasn't talking to him. Only silence through breakfast, then coldness on the bus, which they took down to the City Market on First Avenue. On Saturday mornings Juliet liked to shop at the big barn of a market and often Walter accompanied her; it had always been their pleasure to do little domestic things together. Once they had been such an amiable couple—why had she always to dream of the impossible! This was all her fault!

But he tagged along, despite the bad feeling between them, despite the fact that he did not know what to do next with his wife, or for his wife—or himself.

Call the psychiatrist and tell him to forget it—or go alone? And if the phone rang—pick it up? Suppose it was the man across the way! If only he could obliterate last night!

It had taken two-and-a-half barbiturates, the largest potion Walter had ever swallowed, to obliterate enough of it for him even to fall asleep. He had taken the pills and, burrowing beneath the blankets of their bed—to which his wife had not yet come—he had waited for unconsciousness, praying all the while that the telephone would not ring. In the morning, he felt like a man who had been piling bricks all night; in sleep his body had been punished, though he could not remember how.

Marriage is strange. *So* strange, thought Walter, for when he and his wife moved into the crowded market, they took hold of one another's hands. It was what they always did, in order not to lose each other in the crowd. So they did it now. How close we are! Husband and wife—isn't that enough?

"Hey—" said Juliet.

"I'm sorry . . ."

"What's the matter with you?" He had squeezed her hand, but surely not too hard. Nevertheless, she shook loose of him.

"I'm sorry . . ." he said.

They moved through the market now, past bulky bins of vegetables, wheels of cheese, vats of pickles, mounds of fish, past all the hubbub and color that had always appealed to the young couple and made them, usually, so tender with one another, as they shopped. Never had they thought of themselves as people insensitive to what was vivid in life, or to life's pleasures. No, they were not narrow . . .

Oh, what next! Juliet, what is happening?

She turned from the cheese counter. "Walter, look, if you don't want to be with me this morning . . ."

"Let's buy some fennel," he said. He did not know what else to say.

"I bought fennel."

"—Seeded Italian bread," he said.

Petulantly, she started away. She had bought seeded Italian bread, too. So what? So *what!* He saw suddenly how much he hated her. Had there ever been a time in their marriage when she had not been a burden to him? Never! She started down the aisle, and he did not care if he never saw her again. What had she done to make *him* happy?

Then by the fish counter, toward which Juliet was moving, he caught sight of a familiar face. For the moment he was unable to place it. He imagined it might be some actor they had known years ago . . . then he knew. Momentarily he had not recognized him, because, of course, in the market he was dressed. Walter looked back into the crowd—and there he was, wearing a Tyrolean hat, a raincoat . . . Heads moved; he was gone. When he came into view again, Walter turned quickly away, so as not to be seen looking. The fellow did not appear now so languid as he did reclining on a chair in his apartment; nor was his gaze focusless, statuelike, as it was from a distance; nor was his skin like enamel, as it looked in that soft light. His complexion was actually somewhat ruddy. In no obvious way did he appear a person less respectable than Walter himself—but it was the man.

He's followed us!

Immediately, Walter began to push forward, to where he saw his wife moving directly up to the fish counter.

He made a grab for her arm.

"Ex*cuse*—" She turned, pulling herself free. "Walter!"

"Your fault!" he thought with murder in his heart. He caught hold of her a second time, and began to drag her with him to the exit.

"Look, I *bought* bread. Walter, you're pulling, Walter—" And indeed, with all his strength, he did pull her, while with his free hand he pushed to the side elbows, knees, shopping bags . . .

Toward the exit—but toward the man! In the crowd of shoppers Walter had again lost sight of him—but the crowd shifted, surged, and there was the hat, bobbing along, only yards from where they must pass to make it to the street, to home, and then—God, to where? What had they done! Walter fastened his grip on Juliet and prepared for the push to the street.

"Walter!" Juliet demanded, *"what—"* And at the sound of her voice, questioning him, he seemed all at once—on the very edge of escape—to lose his purpose. Or it changed; or it burst forth. The impulse to drag her away with him became its opposite. It lasted but a second, a desire to cry out, "Oh, *take her!"* Then he heard her sobbing his name and, shoving and butting, dragging her with him, he made it through the exit and into the sunlit street.

She fell against him. "Walter—"

He wanted a cab—but even more, he wanted to shake her and shake her, so that every stupid longing might come clattering out of her head.

"Darling Walter—"

He waved at taxis speeding by. "Home," he said. "We're going home! We're getting out of here—"

"Don't be angry with me—"

He turned on her. *"Wait till we're home!"*

She was sobbing. "I'm so sorry. It's you I'm married to. Not that play."

Oh! Enough! He grabbed her by both shoulders. The truth, at last! *"What* play?"

"It stinks, anyhow," she moaned. "Oh, you're hurting me."

The taxi pulled up. He pushed Juliet into the cab, jumped in himself and pulled the door shut behind them. A crowd had gathered on the sidewalk—Walter took a last look, and saw, with relief, no sign of the Tyrolean hat. And Juliet was sobbing, still.

"OK," he demanded. *"What* play?"

"It's only *one* act. I wasn't competing, *really* I wasn't. You think—"

"Damn you, Juliet. *What play!*"

"—Wrong, Walter. I didn't mean to. It doesn't have to do with you, really." But she buried her head in his chest, as though she did not even believe herself. And she could not control the sobbing.

"Listen—" he said, lifting her face, "listen to me! *What play!*" But she only sobbed the same poor answers, over and over. He himself repeated his question two or three more times—and then the truth, like a sharp edge, fell upon him at last. It fell like a guillotine, an unexpected horror of a whack, for all that it had been hanging overhead beforehand, gleaming away. "No!" he cried to himself. "No! It's *her!*" But the truth seemed to be that this time it was only himself.

▪ ▪ ▪

She would never know; no one would.

He called Kittering and told him that Juliet was ill. It gave him pleasure—if such was possible on so awful a day—to say to Kittering, "She'll have to resign." He called Harvey next to say he must have two weeks' vacation: Juliet was not well, and they had to get away. If Harvey said no, then Walter would quit and take the two weeks on his own. He was not going to stop short now of obliterating the night before, and the nights prior to that as well. A moment before dialing, he thought he might be being too extreme—until he reflected upon the extremity of what he had done. So he dialed: Harvey was a friend as well as a boss, and said yes. Then Walter telephoned a travel agency; after that, a real-estate agency uptown. He said he would need an apartment within a few weeks, and described what he was after. In the meantime he saw to it that all the drapes in the apartment were pulled shut; when the phone rang, he did not answer. He hovered over it, to be sure that Juliet did not answer either. But she wanted only to lie on their bed and tearfully confess to him, when he appeared in the doorway, that he had been right and she had been wrong and in her wretchedness, she said she was sorry; he was reminded of the day on Hudson Street, years ago, when she had given up acting . . . and the next evening they were in the Bahamas.

Only when the plane touched down at the airport did Walter at last begin to feel safe. "My God, am I lucky." So he addressed himself as they took a taxi to the hotel; as they had dinner that evening; as they danced later to the music on the terrace; and later still when, at his suggestion, they went like lovers down by the bay, took off their shoes and walked along the water's edge, holding hands. It did not matter that whatever Juliet did she did obligingly; nor did it matter that she was unable to laugh, or even smile, with any conviction: at least it didn't matter to him yet. "I am lucky," he thought, "very lucky."

They walked along the beach. The air was soft and blue. The man across the courtyard was over a thousand miles away. Walter found he could be very clearheaded about him at last. The crisis had passed, and he could think. Who had the man been? What had he been up to? What had he wanted?

Did he just like to sit around naked watching television? Then why didn't he pull the drapes!

Walter managed to do nothing to reveal his astonishment. In fact, he spoke some words to Juliet about the stars overhead. But he began to feel so foolish . . . Had they fled to the Bahamas for no good reason; were they moving for no good reason . . . ?

Not so. He had to flee. He could not have remained in the apartment to be eaten up by worry, to die every time the phone rang or the downstairs buzzer went off. Innocent as the man across the way might actually have been—and what proof was there of that, really?—there was his own performance to keep in mind. He would have to remember it, even while forgetting it.

So then, what he had been chanting all day was true: he was a lucky man. "And I am going to stay lucky," he told himself, and they turned and headed back to their room where, upon the bed, he took what he believed to be the next necessary step in his marriage. To assert once again what he was, what his wife was—at any rate, what they must be—he mounted Juliet, who had appeared all day to be so chastened, and while she held her breath, he proceeded to reproduce himself.

Jack Kerouac

Good Blonde

January 1965

Like the rest of the country, *Playboy* was fascinated by the Beat Generation, and the last issue of the 1950s appropriately featured "Before the Road"—Dean Moriarty as a teenager—by the daddy-o of Beat novelists, Jack Kerouac (1922–1969). *On the Road* had caused a sensation in 1957, and, together with Allen Ginsberg and William Burroughs, Kerouac was hailed as the voice of his generation. His other novels of disaffected wanderers, high on drugs and Eastern religions—*The Dharma Bums, The Subterraneans, Dr. Sax*—seemed like posters pointing the way to the 1960s. The short-story form was not comfortable for the prolix Kerouac, and he wrote few of them. In "Good Blonde," he's on the road again, with a Benzedrine buzz and a gorgeous chick in a bathing suit.

Jack Kerouac

Good Blonde

This old Greek reminded me of my Uncle Nick in Brooklyn who'd spent fifty years of his life there after being born in Crete, and wandered down the gray streets of Wolfe Brooklyn, short, in a gray suit, with a gray hat, gray face, going to his various jobs as elevator operator and apartment janitor summer winter and fall, and was a plain old ordinary man talking about politics but with a Greek accent, and when he died it seemed to me Brooklyn hadn't changed and would never change, there would always be a strange sad Greek going down the gray streets. I could picture this man on the beach wandering around the white streets of San Francisco, looking at girls, "wandering around and looking at things as they are" as the Chinese say, "patting his belly," even, as Chuang-tse says. "I like these shells." He showed me a few shells he'd picked. "Make nice ashtray, I have lots ashtrays in my house."

"What do you think? You think all this is a dream?"

"What?"

"Life."

"Here? Now? What you mean a dream, we're awake, we talk, we see, we got eyes for to see the sea and the sand and the sky, if you dream you no see it."

"How we know we're not dreaming?"

"Look my eyes are open ain't they?" He watched me as I washed my dishes and put things away.

"I'm going to try to hitchhike to San Francisco or catch a freight, I don't wanta wait till tonight."

"You mens always in hurry, hey, he he he he" and he laughed just like Old Uncle Nick, hands clasped behind his back, stooped slightly, standing over sand caves his feet had made, kicking little tufts of sand grass. In his green gray eyes which were just like the green gray sea I saw the yawning eternity not only of Greece but of America and myself.

"Well, I go now," says I hoisting my pack to my shoulder.

"I walk you to the beach." Long before we'd stopped talking I'd seen the girl come out of the bushes, shameful and slow, and stroll on back to the bathhouse, then the boy came out, five minutes later. It made me sad I didn't have a girl to meet me in the bushes, in the exciting sand among leaves, to lie there swapping breathless kisses, groping at clothes, squeezing shoulders. Me and the old Greek sighed to see them sneak off. "I was a young man once," he said. At the bathhouse we shook hands and I went off across the mainline track to the little store on the corner where I'd bought the wine and where now they were playing a football game from Michigan loud on the radio and just then the sun came out anyway and I saw all the golden wheatfields of America Football Time stretching out clear back to the East Coast.

"Damn," said I, "I'll just hitchhike on that highway" (101) seeing the fast flash of many new cars. The old Greek was still wandering on the mystical margin mentioned by Whitman where sea kisses sand in the endless sigh kiss of time. Like the three bos in Lordsburg New Mexico his direction in the void seemed so much sadder than my own, they were going east to hopeless sleeps in burlap in Alabama fields and the eventual Texas chaingang, he was going up and down the beach alone kicking sand . . . but I knew that in reality my own direction, going up to San Francisco to see the gang and whatever awaited me there, was no higher and no lower than his own humble and unsayable state. The little store had a tree in front, shade, I laid my pack down and went in and came out with a ten-cent ice cream on a stick and sat awhile eating, resting, then combed my hair with water out of an outside faucet and went to the highway all ready to thumb. I walked a few blocks up to the light and got on the far side and stood there, pack at my feet, for a good half hour during which time I got madder and madder and finally I was swearing to myself "I will never hitchhike again, it's getting worse and worse every goddamn year." Meanwhile I kept a sharp eye on the rails a block toward the sea watching for convenient freight trains. At the moment when I was the maddest, and was standing there, thumb out, completely infuriated and so much so that (I remember) my eyes were slitted, my teeth clenched, a brand new cinnamon colored Lincoln driven by a beautiful young blonde in a bathingsuit flashed by and suddenly swerved to the right and put to a stop in the side of the road for me. I couldn't believe it. I figured she wanted road information. I picked up my pack and ran. I opened the door and looked in to smile and thank her.

She said "Get in. Can you drive?" She was a gorgeous young blonde girl of about twenty-two in a pure white bathingsuit, barefooted with a little ankle bracelet around her right ankle. Her bathingsuit was shoulderless and low cut. She sat there in the luxurious cinnamon sea in that white suit like a model. In fact she was a model. Green eyes, from Texas, on her way back to the City.

"Sure I can drive but I don't have a license."

"You drive all right?"

"I drive as good as anybody."

"Well I'm dog tired, I've been driving all the way from Texas without sleep, I went to see my family there" (by now she had the heap jet gone up the road and went up to sixty and kept it there hard and clean on the line, driving like a good man driver). "Boy," she said, "I sure wish I had some Benzedrine or sumptin to keep me awake. I'll have to give you the wheel pretty soon."

"Well how far you going?"

"Far as you are I think . . . San Francisco."

"Wow, great." (To myself: who will ever believe I got a ride like this from a beautiful chick like that practically naked in a bathingsuit, wow, what does she expect me to do next?) "And Benzedrine you say?" I said. "I've got some here in my bag, I just got back from Mexico, I got plenty."

"Crazy!" she yelled. "Pull it out. I want some."

"Baby you'll drive all the way when you get high on that stuff, Mexican you know."

"Mexican Shmexican just give it to me."

"OK." Grinning I began dumping all my dirty old unwashed rags and gear and claptraps of cookpot junk and pieces of food in wrapper on the floor of her car searching feverishly for the little tubes of Benny suddenly I couldn't find anymore. I began to panic. I looked in all the flaps and sidepockets. "Goddamnit where is it!" I kept worrying the smell of my old unwashed clothes would be repugnant to her, I wanted to find the stuff as soon as possible and repack everything away.

"Never mind man, take your time," she said looking straight ahead at the road, and in a pause in my search I let my eye wander to her ankle bracelet, as damaging a sight as Cleopatra on her poop of beaten gold, and the sweet little snowy bare foot on the gas pedal, enough to drive a man mad. I kept wondering why she'd really picked me up.

I asked her. "How come you picked up a guy like me? I never seen a girl alone pick up a guy."

"Well I tell you I need someone to help me drive to the City and I figured you could drive, you looked like it anyway . . ."

"O where are those Bennies!"

"Take your time."

"Here they are!"

"Crazy! I'll pull into that station up ahead and we'll go in and have a Coke and swallow them down." She pulled into the station which also had an inside luncheonette. She jumped out of the car barefooted in her low-cut bathingsuit as the attendant stared and ordered a full tank as I went in and bought two bottles of Coke to go out, cold. When I came back she was in the car with her change, ready to go. What a wild chick. I looked at the attendant to see what he was thinking. He was looking at me enviously. I kept having the urge to tell him the true story.

"Here," and I handed her the tubes, and she took out two. "Hey, that's too many, your top'll fly out . . . better take one and a half, or one. I take one myself."

"I don't want no one and a half, I want two."

"You've had it before?"

"Of course man and everything else."

"Pot too?"

"Sure pot . . . I know all the musicians in L.A. and the City, when I come into the Ramador Shelly Manne sees me coming and stops whatever they're playing and they play my theme song which is a little bop arrangement."

"How does it go?"

"Ha! and it goes: boop boop be doodleya dap."

"Wow, you can sing."

"I walk in, man, and they play that, and everybody knows I'm back." She took her two Bennies and swigged down, and buzzed the car up to a steady seventy as we hit the country north of Santa Barbara, the traffic thinning and the road getting longer and straighter. "Long drive to San Francisco, four hundred miles just about. I hope these Bennies are good, I'd like to go all the way."

"Well if you're tired I can drive," I said but hoped I wouldn't have to drive, the car was so brand new and beautiful. It was a '55 Lincoln and here it was October 1955. Beautiful, lowslung, sleek. Zip, rich. I leaned back with my Benny in my palm and threw it down with the Coke and felt good. Up ahead suddenly I realized the whole city of San Francisco would be all bright lights and glittering wide open waiting for me this very night, and no strain, no hurt, no pain, no freight train, no sweating on the hitchhike road but up there zip zoom inside about eight hours. She passed cars smoothly and went on. She turned on the radio and began looking for jazz, found rock 'n' roll and left that on, loud. The way she looked straight ahead and drove with no expression and sending no mincing gestures my way or even telepathies of mincingness, you'd never believe she was a lovely little chick in a bathingsuit. I was amazed. And in the bottom of that scheming mind I kept wondering and wondering (dirtily) if she hadn't picked me up because she was secretly a sexfiend and was waiting for me to say "Let's park the car somewhere and make it" but something so inviolately grave about her prevented me from saying this, more than that my own sudden bashfulness (as the holy Benny began taking effect) prevented me from making such an importunate and really insulting proposition seeing I'd just met the young lady. But the thought stuck and stuck with me. I was afraid to turn and look at her and only occasionally dropped my eyes to that ankle bracelet and the little white lily foot on the gas pedal. And we talked and talked. Finally the Benny began hitting us strong after Los Alamos and we were talking a blue streak, she did most of the talking. She'd been a model, she wanted to be an actress, so forth, the usual beautiful-California-blonde designs but finally I said "As for me I don't want anything . . . I think life is suffering, a suffering dream, and all I wanta do is rest and be kind somewhere, preferably in the woods, under a tree, live in a shack."

"Ain't you ever gonna get married?"

"Been married twice and I've had it."

"Well you oughta take a third crack at it, maybe this time you'd hit a homerun."

"That ain't the point, in the first place I wouldn't wanta have children, they only born to die."

"You better not tell that to my mom and dad, they had eight kids in Texas, I was the second, they've had a damn good long life and the kids are great, you know what my youngest brother did when I walked in the house last week and hadn't seen him for a year: he was all grown up tall and put on a rock-'n'-roll record for me and wanted me to do the lindy with him. O what laughs we had in the old homestead last week. I'm glad I went."

"I'll bet when you were a little girl you had a ball there in Texas huh hunting, wandering around."

"Everything man, sometimes I think my new life now modeling and acting in cities ain't half as good as that was."

"And there you were on long Texas nights Grandma readin the Bible right?"

"Yeah and all the good food we made nowadays I have dates in good restaurants and man—"

"Dates . . . you ain't married hey?"

"Not yet, pretty soon."

"Well what does a beautiful girl like you think about?" This made her turn and look at me with bland frank green eyes.

"What do you mean?"

"I don't know . . . I'd say, for a man like me, what I say is best for him . . . but for a beautiful girl like you I guess what you're doing is best." I wasn't going to say get thee to a nunnery, she was too gone, too pretty too, besides she wouldn't have done it by a long shot, she just didn't care. In no time at all we were way up north of Los Alamos and coming into a little bumper to bumper traffic outside Santa Maria where she pulled up at a gas station and said:

"Say do you happen to have a little change?"

"About a dollar and a half."

"Hmmmm . . . I want to call longdistance to South City and tell my man I'll be in at eight or so."

"Call him collect if he's your man."

"Now you're talkin like a man" she said and went trottin barefoot to the phone booth in the driveway and got in and made a call with a dime. I got out of the car to stretch out, high and dizzy and pale and sweating and excited from the Benzedrine, I could see she was the same way in the phone booth, chewing vigorously on a wad of gum. She got her call and talked while I picked up an orange from the ground and wound up and did the pitcher-on-the-mound bit to stretch my muscles. I felt good. A cool wind was blowing across Santa Maria, with a smell of the sea in it somehow. The palm trees waved in a cooler wind than the one in Barbara and L.A. Tonight it would be the cool fogs of Frisco again! After all these years! She came out and we got in.

"Who's the guy."

"He's my man, Joey King, he runs a bar in South City . . . on Main Street."

"Say I used to be a yardclerk in the yards there and I'd go to some of those bars on Main Street for a beer . . . with a little cocktail glass neon in front, with a stick in it?"

"All the bars have that around here" she laughed and gunned on up the road fast. Pretty soon, yakking happily about jazz and even singing a lot of jazz, we got to San Luis Obispo, went through town, and started up the pass to Santa Margarita.

"There you see it," I said, "see where the railroad track winds around to go up the pass, I was a brakeman on that for years, on drizzly nights I'd be squattin under lumber boards riding up that pass and when I'd go through the tunnels I'd hold my bandanna over my nose not to suffocate."

"Why were you riding on the outside of the engine."

"Because I was the guy assigned to puttin pops up and down, air valves, for mountain brakes, all that crap . . . I don't think it would interest you."

"Sure, my brother's a brakeman in Texas. He's about your age."

"I'm thirty-three."

"Well he's a little younger but his eyes are greener than yours, yours are blue."

"Yours are green."

"No, mine are hazel."

"Well that's what green-eyed girls always say."

"What do hazel-eyed girls always say?"

"They say, hey now." We were (as you see) talking like two kids and completely unself-conscious and by this time I'd quite forgotten the lurking thought of us sexing together in some bushes by the side of the road, though I kept smelling her, the Benny sweat, which is abundant, and perfumy in the way it works, it filled the car with a sweet perfume, mingled with my own sweat, in our noses if not in our minds there was a thought of sweating love . . . at least in my mind. Sometimes I felt the urge to just lay my head in her lap as she drove but then I got mad and thought "Ah hell it's all a dream including beauty, leave the Angel Alone you dirty old foney Duluoz" which I did. To this day I never know what she wanted, I mean, what she really secretly thought of me, of picking me up, and she got so high on the Benny she drove all the way anyway, or perhaps she woulda drove all the way anyway, I don't know. She balled up over the pass in the gathering late afternoon golden shadows of California and came out on the flats of the Margarita plateau, where we stopped for gas, where in the rather cool mountain wind she got out and ran to the ladies room and the gas attendant said to me:

"Where'd you pick her up?" thinking the car was mine.

"She picked *me* up, pops."

"Well I oughta be glad if I was you."

"I ain't unglad."

"Sure is a nice little bundle."

"She's been wearing that bathingsuit clear from Texas."

"Geez." She came out and we went up the Salinas valley as it got dark slowly with old orange sunsets behind the rim where I'd seen bears as a brakeman, at night, standing by the track as we'd in the Diesel ball by with a hundred-car freight behind us, and one time a cougar. Wild country. And the floor of the dry Salinas riverbottom is all clean white sand and bushes, ideal for bhikkuing (outdoor camping where nobody bothers you) because you can hide good and hide your campfire and the only people to bother you are cattle, and snakes I guess, and beautiful dry climate with stars, even now at dusk, I could see flashing in the pale plank of heaven, like bhaghavat nails. I told Pretty about it:

"Someday I'm gonna bring my pack and a month's essential groceries right down to that riverbottom and build a little shelter with twigs and stuff and a tarpaulin or a poncho and lay up and do nothing for a month."

"What you wanta do that for? There's no fun in that."

"Sure there is."

"Well I can't figure all this out but . . . it's all right I guess." At times I didn't like her, at one point I definitely didn't like her because there was something so cold and yawny distant about her, I felt that in her secret bedroom she probably yawned a lot and didn't know what to do with herself and to compensate for that had a lot of boyfriends who bought her expensive presents (just because she was beautiful, which compensated not for her inside unbeautiful feeling), and going to restaurants and bars and jazz clubs and yooking it up because there was nothing else inside. And I thought: "Truly, I'm better off *without* a doll like this . . . out there in that riverbottom, pure and free, what immensities I'd have, in real riches . . . alone, in old clothes, cooking my own food, finding my own peace . . . instead of sniffin around her ankles day in day out wonderin whether in some mean mood she's going to throw me out anyway and then I would have to clap her one or something and all of it a crock for sure—" I didn't dare tell her all this, besides the point being she wouldn't have been interested in the least. It got dark, we flew on, soon we saw the sealike flats of Salinas valley stretching on both sides of us, with occasional brown farmlamps, the stars overhead, a vast storm cloud gathering in the night sky in the east and the radio announcer predicting rain for the night, then finally far up ahead the jeweled cluster of Salinas the city and airport lights. Outside Salinas on the four lane, about five miles, suddenly she said "The car's run out of gas, Oho" and she began wobbling the car from side to side in a graceful dance.

"What you doin that for?"

"That's to splash what's left of the gas into the carburetor . . . I can do this for a few miles, let's pray we see a station or we don't get to South City by eight." She swayed and wobbled along, grinning faintly over her wheel, and in the cuddly dark and little emergency of the night, I began to love her again and thought "Ah well and what a strong sweet angel to spend the rest of your life with, though, damn." Pretty soon the wobbles were wider and the speed slower and she finally pulled over by the side of the road and parked and said "That's that, we're out of gas."

"I'll go out and hail a car."

"While you're doing that I'll go in the backseat and put something over my bathingsuit, it's getting cold," which it was. I unsuccessfully tried to hail down cars for five minutes or so, they were all zipping at a steady seventy, and I said:

"Say when you're ready to come on out, when they see *you* they'll stop." She came out and we joked a bit in the dark dancing and showing our legs at the cars and finally a big truck stopped and I ran after it to talk to him. It was a big burly guy eager to help, he'd seen the blonde. He got out a chain and tied her car on and off we went at about fifteen miles per hour to the gas station three miles down. He had airbrakes and she was worried about ramming him and hoped he wouldn't go too fast. He went perfect. In the gas station driveway he got out to admire her some more.

"Boy, that's a little bit of sumptin" he said to me as she went to the toilet.

"She picked me up in Santa Barbara, she's been driving all the way from Texas alone."

"Well, well, you're a luck hitchhiker." He undid the chain. She came out and stood around chatting with the big truckdriver and the attendant. Now she was clad in tightfitting black slacks and a neat keen throwover of some kind, and sandals, in which she padded like a little tightfit Indian. I felt humble and foolish with the two men staring at her and me waiting by the car for my poor world ride. She came back and off we went, getting through Salinas and out on the dark road and now finally we found some real fine jazz from San Francisco, the Pat Henry show or some other show, and we didn't speak much anymore but just sang with the music and kept our eyes glued on the headlamp swatch and the inwinding kiss-in of the white line in the road where it again became a two-laner. Soon we were going through Watsonville, a little behind schedule.

"Here's where I did most of my work as a brakeman . . . insteada sleeping in the railroad dormitory I'd go out to the sandbottom of that river, the Pajaro, and cook woodfires and eat hotdogs like last night and sleep in the sand . . ."

"You're always in some riverbottom or other." The music on the radio got louder and louder as we began to approach San Jose and the City. The storm to the east hadn't formed yet. It was exciting to be coming into the City now. On Bayshore we really felt it, all the cars flashing by both ways in the lanes, the lights, the roadside restaurants, the antennas, nothing had looked like that all day, the big city, "The Apple," I said, "the Apple of California but have you ever been to *the* Apple, New York!" to which she replied: "Yeah man."

"But nothing wrong with this little old town, it's got everything . . . isn't it . . . don't you feel a funny feeling in your belly coming into the City."

"Yeah man I always do." We agreed on that and talked about it, and soon we were coming into South San Francisco where I suddenly realized she was going to let me out in only a few minutes and I hadn't anticipated parting from her ever, somehow. She pulled up right smack in front of the little station where I'd worked as a yardclerk and there were the same old tracks, I knew every number and name of them, and the same old overpass, and the spurs leading off to the slaughterhouses Armour and Swift east, the same sad lamps and sad dim red switchlights in the darkness. The car stopped, our bodies were still vibrating as we sat in the stillness, the radio booming.

"Well I'll get out and let you get home," I said, "and I needn't tell you how great it was and how glad I am you gave me this great ride."

"Oh man, nothing, it was fun."

"Why don't you give me your phone, I'll call you and we'll go down and hear Brue Moore, I hear he's in town."

"Oh he's my favorite tenor, I've seen him . . . OK, I'll give you my address, I haven't got a phone in yet."

"OK." She wrote out the address in my little breastpocket notebook and I could see she was anxious to get on home to her man so I said "OK, here I go," and got my bag and went out and stuck my hand in to shake and off she went, up Main Street, probably to her pad to take a shower and dress up and go down to her man's bar. And I put my bag on my back and walked down the same old homey familiar rail and felt glad . . . probably gladder than she did, but who knows? It almost brought tears to my eyes to see my old railyards again, as though I'd been brought up to them on a magic carpet just to see them and remember, the whole trip had been so ephemeral and easy and fast, in fact the whole trip from Mexico City four thousand gory miles away . . . as though some ruling God in the sky had said "Jack I want you to cry when you remember your past life, and to accomplish this, I'm going to shoot you to that spot" and there I was, walking numbly on the same old railside cinders and there across the way the long sorrowful pink neon saying BETHLEHEM WEST COAST STEEL about five long blocks of it and I used to take down the numbers of boxcars and gons in drags that were even longer than that and measure their length by the length of the huge neon: beyond which you could hear frogs croaking in the airport marsh, where mountains of tin scrap soaked in scum water, and rats scurried, and occasional pure Chinese birds sailed around (at night, bats). I went into the old station (actually a brand new little station still fresh with new bricks) and consulted the timetable and saw that I had a train to the City in five minutes, everything perfect. As of yore, to celebrate, I stuck a nickel in my old candy machine and got out a Pay Day and munched on that on the platform, stole a newspaper from the rack, and it was just like old times, eleven-fifteen going home with work done. But the train had changed, it came being pulled by a new type of small engine I'd never seen (electric) and the cars were doubledeckers with commuters sitting up and below like dolls in the bright lights of the new ceilings. "Too new, too fancy" I thought, regretting it, and got on and got my ticket punched by a conductor whose face I vaguely remembered from the trainmen's lockers at Third and Townsend. On we went to the City. Bayshore Yards appeared after a while, with the old redbrick 1890 roundhouse gloomy like *Out Our Way* cartoons of 1930 factories in the night, smoke of steam-pots beyond, the distant marvel and visible miracle of Oakland suddenly seen casting its infinitesimal and as-if-innumerable lights on the far bay waters, and then swosh into the tunnel, coming out right smack in the City with white tenements and houses on grassy cliffs by the side of the dug-in rail canyon, and then the long slow curve, the long slow appearance of the skyscrapers of downtown San Francisco, so sad, so reddish, so mysterious and Chinese, and the general purple brownness of the yards, red and green switchlights, funny switchmen at the crossings and the train slowing down as it comes into the station to the dead-end blocks to stop.

Everybody got up and got out. I went slowly to savor everything. The smell of San Francisco was great, it is always the same, at night, a compoundment of sea, fog, cinders, coalsmoke, taffy and dust. And somehow the smell of wine, maybe from all the broken bottles on Third Street. Now I was really exhausted and headed up Third Street, after a slow nostalgic survey of the Third and Townsend station, looking desultorily if there was anybody I knew, like maybe Cody, or Mal. I went straight to the little old Cameo Hotel on the corner of Harrison and Third, where for seventy-five cents a night you could always get a clean room with no bedbugs and nice soft mattresses with soft old clean sheets, clean enough, not snow-white Fab by any means but better, and nice quilts, and old frayed carpets and quiet sleep: that's the main thing. The clerk in the cage was the same Hindu I'd known there in 1954, he didn't remember me or the night he'd told me the long story of his boyhood in India and his father who owned seven hundred camels and the time he'd peeked at a woman's religious ritual where he claimed there were some virgins and barren women walking around a stone phallus and sitting on it. I didn't bring it up but followed him up the stairs and down the sad old hall to my door, and the room. I took all my clothes off and got in the cool smooth sheets and said "Now I'll just lay like this for fifteen minutes in the dark and rest and then I'll get up, dress and go down to Chinatown and have a nice feed: I'll have sweet and sour prawn and cold broiled duck, yessir, I'll splurge a dollar and a half on that" and I uncapped my little poorboy of tokay wine I'd bought in the store downstairs and took a swig and in fifteen minutes, after three swigs and dreamy thoughts with a serene smile realizing I was at last back in my beloved San Francisco and surely must have a lot of crazy adventures ahead of me, I was asleep. And slept the sleep of the justified.

James Baldwin

The Manchild

January 1966

Born in Harlem, James Baldwin (1924–1987) emigrated to Paris in 1948 and spent most of his life abroad; he was living in Istanbul when this story was published. Nevertheless, because so much of his writing concerned race, and because he never forgot his roots, he is strongly associated with the American civil rights movement. Baldwin began as a novelist *(Go Tell It on the Mountain,* 1953), but became perhaps more famous for his eloquent essays, collected in *Notes of a Native Son* (1955), *Nobody Knows My Name* (1961), and *The Fire Next Time* (1963). He wrote for *Playboy* fairly often, with his last essay appearing shortly before his death. His short stories were few, however, and this dark but memorable tale was something of a change of pace for him.

James Baldwin

The Manchild

The city is like an experienced whore, night comes and goes in her, she is indifferent to his approach and is left unchanged at his departure—but for the countryside, it is a different matter. There night watches his opportunity, bides his time, is patient with the silly, upbraiding sun. He knows that she must go, even though her farewells at the western threshold are interminable. The countryside seems to shudder as the door at last closes behind the sun, leaving her alone with that lover who will never be denied. At this moment the countryside seems like a girl who cannot bear the idea of possession, who cannot live without being possessed. Night has been visiting the countryside these many ages, but she has never ceased to thrill to his approach. Only the city has found a way of dealing with the night, and this way is indifference; which is, perhaps, why night is so cruel in the city and so voluptuous in the fields. Yes, the sun goes down. One watches her, slow-moving, changing, superbly preparing for her mighty exit, at the very edge of the world. Having scolded, tortured and nourished the fields all day, she now gives her parting warning—which the fields, already anticipating night's long touch, seem not to heed. Then, abruptly, in the middle, as it were, of a sentence, the sun is gone. Gone—dropped in an instant below the farthest hill, the last field, the most distant tree. Gone; and where she was is a long, long silence. Then, night, coming on, lets fall his warrior's mantle, gray and blue and black, and hangs up on the walls of the world his overwhelming trophies; and falls on the countryside, his lover forever, in love and lust and endless whispering.

Night is like that in the country and in the small villages set here and there like hives, where lights go out in his honor, where windows are barred and all but the most mysteriously driven footfall stilled. Night is like that for the people who live there, who drive their cows home, put their children to bed, for *the sandman is coming!* and turn, turn, turn, together or alone throughout the tumultuous darkness, whose power it has not occurred to them to challenge.

All children feel this power, and are frightened by it; they have, but only yesterday, come shrieking out of darkness. Old men feel this power and, with what rage or terror or gladness no one knows, prepare themselves to keep the appointment made so long ago by the absolutely faithful true lover of all the world. For children, who, alone among the living, do not know that the night has made an appointment with them, too, the night is simply the kingdom of evil, of crimes unnamed, unnamable, of spirits roaming the earth for vengeance, taking the shapes of trees, of rocks, taking the sounds of birds, of crickets, sometimes taking the shapes and sounds of men.

As the sun began preparing for her exit, and he sensed the waiting night, Eric, blond and eight years old and dirty and tired, started homeward across the fields. Eric lived with his father, who was a farmer and the son of a farmer, and his mother, who had been captured by his father on some far-off, unblessed, unbelievable night, who had never since burst her chains. She did not know that she was chained any more than she knew that she lived in terror of the night. One child was in the churchyard, it would have been Eric's little sister and her name would have been Sophie; for a long time, then, his mother had been very sick and pale. It was said that she would never, really, be better, that she would never again be as she had been. Then, not long ago, there had begun to be a pounding in his mother's belly, Eric had sometimes been able to hear it when he lay against her breast. His father had been pleased. *I did that,* said his father, big, laughing, dreadful and red, and Eric knew how it was done, he had seen the horses and the blind and dreadful bulls. But then, again, his mother had been sick, she had had to be sent away, and when she came back the pounding was not there anymore, nothing was there anymore. His father laughed less, something in his mother's face seemed to have gone to sleep forever.

. . .

Eric hurried, for the sun was almost gone and he was afraid the night would catch him in the fields. And his mother would be angry. She did not really like him to go wandering off by himself. She would have forbidden it completely and kept Eric under her eye all day, but in this she was overruled: Eric's father liked to think of Eric as being curious about the world and as being daring enough to explore it, with his own eyes, by himself.

His father would not be at home. He would be gone with his friend, Jamie, who was also a farmer and the son of a farmer, down to the tavern. This tavern was called The Rafters. They went each night, as his father said, imitating an Englishman he had known during a war, *to destruct The Rafters, sir.* They had been destructing The Rafters long before Eric had kicked in his mother's belly, for

Eric's father and Jamie had grown up together, gone to war together, and survived together—never, apparently, while life ran, were they to be divided. They worked in the fields all day together, the fields which belonged to Eric's father. Jamie had been forced to sell his farm, and it was Eric's father who had bought it.

Jamie had a brown-and-yellow dog. This dog was almost always with him; whenever Eric thought of Jamie, he thought also of the dog. They had always been there, they had always been together: in exactly the same way, for Eric, that his mother and father had always been together, in exactly the same way that the earth and the trees and the sky were together. Jamie and his dog walked the country roads together, Jamie walking slowly in the way of country people, seeming to see nothing, head slightly bent, feet striking surely and heavily the earth, never stumbling. He walked as though he were going to walk to the other end of the world and knew it was a long way but knew that he would be there by the morning. Sometimes he talked to his dog, head bent a little more than usual and turned to one side, a slight smile playing about the edges of his granite lips; and the dog's head snapped up, perhaps he leaped upon his master, who cuffed him down lightly, with one hand. More often he was silent. His head was carried in a cloud of blue smoke from his pipe. Through this cloud, like a ship on a foggy day, loomed his dry and steady face. Set far back, at an unapproachable angle, were those eyes of his, smoky and thoughtful, eyes which seemed always to be considering the horizon. He had the kind of eyes which no one had ever looked into—except Eric, only once. Jamie had been walking these roads and across these fields, whistling for his dog in the evenings as he turned away from Eric's house, for years, in silence. He had been married once, but his wife had run away. Now he lived alone in a wooden house and Eric's mother kept his clothes clean, and Jamie always ate at Eric's house.

Eric had looked into Jamie's eyes on Jamie's birthday. They had had a party for him. Eric's mother had baked a cake and filled the house with flowers. The doors and windows of the great kitchen all stood open on the yard and the kitchen table was placed outside. The ground was not muddy as it was in winter, but hard, dry and light brown. The flowers his mother so loved and so labored for flamed in their narrow borders against the stone wall of the farmhouse; and green vines covered the gray stone wall at the far end of the yard. Beyond the wall were the fields and barns and Eric could see, quite far away, the cows nearly motionless in the bright-green pasture. It was a bright, hot, silent day, the sun did not seem to be moving at all.

This was before his mother had had to be sent away. Her belly had been beginning to grow big, she had been dressed in blue and had seemed—that day, to Eric—younger than she was ever to seem again.

Though it was still early when they were called to table, Eric's father and Jamie were already tipsy and came across the fields, shoulders touching, laughing and telling each other stories. To express disapproval and also, perhaps, because she had heard their stories before and was bored, Eric's mother was quite abrupt with them, barely saying, "Happy birthday, Jamie'" before she made them sit down. In the nearby village, church bells rang as they began to eat.

It was perhaps because it was Jamie's birthday that Eric was held by something in Jamie's face. Jamie, of course, was very old. He was thirty-four today, even older than Eric's father, who was only thirty-two. Eric wondered how it felt to have so many years and was suddenly, secretly glad that he was only eight. For today, Jamie *looked* old. It was perhaps the one additional year that had done it, this day, before their very eyes—a metamorphosis that made Eric rather shrink at the prospect of becoming nine. The skin of Jamie's face, which had never before seemed so, seemed wet today, and that rocky mouth of his was loose: loose was the word for everything about him, the way his arms and shoulders hung, the way he sprawled at the table, rocking slightly back and forth. It was not that he was drunk. Eric had seen him much drunker. Drunk, he became rigid, as though he imagined himself in the Army again. No. He was old. It had come upon him all at once, today, on his birthday. He sat there, his hair in his eyes, eating, drinking, laughing now and again, and in a very strange way, and teasing the dog at his feet so that it sleepily growled and snapped all through the birthday dinner.

"Stop that," said Eric's father.

"Stop what?" asked Jamie.

"Let that stinking, useless dog alone. Let him be quiet."

"Leave the beast alone," said Eric's mother—very wearily, sounding as she often sounded when talking to Eric.

"Well, now," said Jamie, grinning, and looking first at Eric's father and then at Eric's mother, "it *is* my beast. And a man's got a right to do as he likes with whatever's his."

"That dog's got a right to bite you, too," said Eric's mother, shortly.

"This dog's not going to bite me," said Jamie, "he knows I'll shoot him if he does."

"That dog knows you're not going to shoot him," said Eric's father. "Then you *would* be all alone."

"All alone," said Jamie, and looked around the table. "All alone." He lowered his eyes to his plate.

Eric's father watched him. He said, "It's pretty serious to be all alone at *your* age." He smiled. "If I was you, I'd start thinking about it."

"I'm thinking about it," said Jamie. He began to grow red.

"No, you're not," said Eric's father, "you're dreaming about it."

"Well, goddamnit," said Jamie, even redder now, "it isn't as though I haven't tried!"

"Ah," said Eric's father, "that was a *real* dream, that was. I used to pick *that* up on the streets of town every Saturday night."

"Yes," said Jamie, "I bet you did."

"I didn't think she was as bad as all that," said Eric's mother, quietly. "*I* liked her. I was surprised when—she ran away."

"Jamie didn't know how to keep her," said Eric's father. He looked at Eric and chanted: *"Jamie, Jamie, pumpkin-eater, had a wife and couldn't keep her!"* At this, Jamie at last looked up, into the eyes of Eric's father. Eric laughed out of fear. Jamie said:

"Ah, yes, you can talk, you can."

"It's not my fault," said Eric's father, "if you're getting old—and haven't got anybody to bring you your slippers when night comes—and no pitter-patter of little feet—"

"Oh, leave Jamie alone," said Eric's mother, "he's *not* old, leave him alone."

Jamie laughed a peculiar, high, clicking laugh which Eric had never heard before, which he did not like, which made him want to look away and, at the same time, want to stare. "Hell, no," said Jamie, "I'm not old. I can still do all the things we used to do." He put his elbows on the table, grinning. "I haven't ever told you, have I, about the things we used to do?"

"No, you haven't," said Eric's mother, "and I certainly don't want to hear about them now."

"He wouldn't tell you anyway," said Eric's father, "he knows what I'd do to him if he did."

"Oh, sure," said Jamie, and laughed again. He picked up a bone from his plate. "Here," he said to Eric, "why don't you feed my poor mistreated dog?"

Eric took the bone and stood up, whistling for the dog, who moved away from his master and took the bone between his teeth. Jamie watched with a smile and opened the bottle of whiskey and poured himself a drink. Eric sat on the ground beside the dog, beginning to be sleepy in the bright, bright sun.

"Little Eric's getting big," he heard his father say.

"Yes," said Jamie, "they grow up fast. It won't be long now."

"Won't be long *what?"* he heard his father ask.

"Why, before he starts skirt-chasing like his daddy used to do," said Jamie. There was mild laughter at the table in which his mother did not join; he heard, instead, or thought he heard, the familiar, slight, exasperated intakes of her breath. No one seemed to care whether he came back to the table or not. He lay on his back, staring up at the sky, wondering—wondering what he would feel like when he was old—and fell asleep.

When he awoke, his head was in his mother's lap, for she was sitting on the ground. Jamie and his father were still sitting at the table; he knew this from their voices, for he did not open his eyes. He did not want to move or speak. He wanted to remain where he was, protected by his mother, while the bright day rolled on. Then he wondered about the uncut birthday cake. But he was sure, from the sound of Jamie's voice, which was thicker now, that they had not cut it yet; or if they had, they had certainly saved a piece for him.

"—ate himself just as full as he could and then fell asleep in the sun like a little animal," Jamie was saying, and the two men laughed. His father—though he scarcely ever got as drunk as Jamie did, and had often carried Jamie home from The Rafters—was a little drunk, too.

Eric felt his mother's hand on his hair. By opening his eyes very slightly, he could see, over the curve of his mother's thigh, as through a veil, a green slope far away, and beyond it the everlasting, motionless sky.

"—she was a no-good *bitch,*" said Jamie.

"She was beautiful," said his mother, just above him.

Again, they were talking about Jamie's wife.

"Beauty!" said Jamie, furious. "Beauty doesn't keep a house clean. Beauty doesn't keep a bed warm, either."

Eric's father laughed. "You were so—poetical—in those days, Jamie," he said. "Nobody thought you cared much about things like that. I guess she thought you didn't care, either."

"I cared," said Jamie, briefly.

"In fact," Eric's father continued, "I *know* she thought you didn't care."

"How do you know?" asked Jamie.

"She told me," Eric's father said.

"What do you mean," asked Jamie, "what do you mean she told you?"

"I mean just that. She told me."

Jamie was silent.

"In those days," Eric's father continued after a moment, "all you did was walk around the woods by yourself in the daytime and sit around The Rafters in the evenings with me."

"You two were always together then," said Eric's mother.

"Well," said Jamie, harshly, "at least that hasn't changed."

"Now, you know," said Eric's father, gently, "it's not the same. Now I got a wife and kid—and another one coming."

Eric's mother stroked his hair more gently, yet with something in her touch more urgent, too, and he knew she was thinking of the child who lay in the churchyard, who would have been his sister.

"Yes," said Jamie, "you really got it all fixed up, you did. You got it all—the wife, the kid, the house, and all the land."

"I didn't steal your farm from you. It wasn't my fault you lost it. I gave you a better price for it than anybody else would have done."

"I'm not blaming you. I know all the things I have to thank you for."

There was a short pause, broken, hesitantly, by Eric's mother. "What I don't understand," she said, "is why, when you went away to the city, you didn't *stay* away. You didn't really have anything to keep you here."

There was the sound of a drink being poured. Then, "No. I didn't have nothing—*really*—to keep me here. Just all the things I ever knew—all the things—*all* the things—I *ever* cared about."

"A man's not supposed to sit around and mope," said Eric's father, wrathfully, "for things that are over and dead and finished, things that can't *ever* begin again, that can't ever be the same again. That's what I mean when I say you're a dreamer—and if you hadn't kept on dreaming so long, you might not be alone now."

"Ah, well," said Jamie, mildly, and with a curious rush of affection in his voice, "I know you're the giant killer, the hunter, the lover—the real old Adam, that's you. I know you're going to cover the earth. I know the world depends on men like you."

"And you're damn right," said Eric's father, after an uneasy moment.

Around Eric's head there was a buzzing, a bee, perhaps, a bluefly, or a wasp. He hoped that his mother would see it and brush it away, but she did not move her hand. And he looked out again, through the veil of his eyelashes, at the slope and the sky, and then he saw that the sun had moved and that it would not be long now before it would be going.

"—just like you already," Jamie said.

"You think my little one's like me?" Eric knew that his father was smiling—he could almost feel his father's hands.

"Looks like you, walks like you, talks like you," said Jamie.

"*And* stubborn like you," said Eric's mother.

"Ah, yes," said Jamie, and sighed. "You married the stubbornest, most determined—most selfish—man I know."

"I didn't know you felt that way," said Eric's father. He was still smiling.

"I'd have warned you about him," Jamie added, laughing, "if there'd been time."

"Everyone who knows you feels that way," said Eric's mother, and Eric felt a sudden brief tightening of the muscle in her thigh.

"Oh, *you,*" said Eric's father, "I know *you* feel that way, women like to feel that way, it makes them feel important. But," and he changed to the teasing tone he took so persistently with Jamie today, "I didn't know my fine friend, Jamie, here—"

It was odd how unwilling he was to open his eyes. Yet he felt the sun on him and knew that he wanted to rise from where he was before the sun went down. He did not understand what they were talking about this afternoon, these grownups he had known all his life; by keeping his eyes closed he kept their conversation far from him. And his mother's hand lay on his head like a blessing, like protection. And the buzzing had ceased, the bee, the bluefly or the wasp seemed to have flown away.

"—if it's a boy this time," his father said, "we'll name it after you."

"That's touching," said Jamie, "but that really won't do me—or the kid—a hell of a lot of good."

"Jamie can get married and have kids of his own any time he decides to," said Eric's mother.

"No," said his father, after a long pause, "Jamie's thought about it too long."

And, suddenly, he laughed and Eric sat up as his father slapped Jamie on the knee. At the touch, Jamie leaped up, shouting, spilling his drink and overturning his chair, and the dog beside Eric awoke and began to bark. For a moment, before Eric's unbelieving eyes, there was nothing in the yard but noise and flame.

His father rose slowly and stared at Jamie. "What's the matter with you?"

"What's the matter with me!" mimicked Jamie, "what's the matter with me? What the hell do you care what's the matter with me! What the hell have you been riding me for all day like this? What do you want? What do you *want?"*

"I want you to learn to hold your liquor, for one thing," said his father, coldly. The two men stared at each other. Jamie's face was red and ugly and tears stood in his eyes. The dog, at his legs, kept up a furious prancing and barking. Jamie bent down and, with one hand, with all his might, slapped his dog, which rolled over, howling, and ran away to hide itself under the shadows of the far gray wall.

Then Jamie stared again at Eric's father, trembling, and pushed his hair back from his eyes.

"You better pull yourself together," Eric's father said. And, to Eric's mother: "Get him some coffee. He'll be all right."

Jamie set his glass on the table and picked up the overturned chair. Eric's mother rose and went into the kitchen. Eric remained sitting on the ground, staring at the two men, his father and his father's best friend, who had become so unfamiliar. His father, with something in his face that Eric had never before seen there, a tenderness, a sorrow—or perhaps it was, after all, the look he sometimes wore when approaching a calf he was about to slaughter—looked down at Jamie where he sat, head bent, at the table. "You take things too hard," he said. "You always have. I was only teasing you for your own good."

Jamie did not answer. His father looked over to Eric, and smiled.

"Come on," he said. "You and me are going for a walk."

Eric, passing on the side of the table farthest from Jamie, went to his father and took his hand.

"Pull yourself together," his father said to Jamie. "We're going to cut your birthday cake as soon as me and the little one come back."

Eric and his father passed beyond the gray wall where the dog still whimpered, out into the fields. Eric's father was walking too fast and Eric stumbled on the uneven ground. When they had gone a little distance his father abruptly checked his pace and looked down at Eric, grinning.

"I'm sorry," he said. "I guess I said we were going for a walk, not running to put out a fire."

"What's the matter with Jamie?" Eric asked.

"Oh," said his father, looking westward where the sun was moving, pale orange now, making the sky ring with brass and copper and gold—which, like a magician, she was presenting only to demonstrate how variously they could be transformed—"Oh," he repeated, "there's nothing wrong with Jamie. He's been drinking a lot," and he grinned down at Eric, "and he's been sitting in the sun—

you know, his hair's not as thick as yours," and he ruffled Eric's hair, "and I guess birthdays make him nervous. Hell," he said, "they make me nervous, too."

"Jamie's *very* old," said Eric, "isn't he?"

His father laughed. "Well, Butch, he's not exactly ready to fall into the grave yet—he's going to be around awhile, is Jamie. Hey," he said, and looked down at Eric again, "you must think I'm an old man, too."

"Oh," said Eric, quickly, "I know you're not as old as Jamie."

His father laughed again. "Well, thank you, son. That shows real confidence. I'll try to live up to it."

They walked in silence for a while and then his father said, not looking at Eric, speaking to himself, it seemed, or to the air: "No, Jamie's not so old. He's not as old as he should be."

"How old *should* he be?" asked Eric.

"Why," said his father, "he ought to be his age," and, looking down at Eric's face, he burst into laughter again.

"Ah," he said, finally, and put his hand on Eric's head again, very gently, very sadly, "don't you worry now about what you don't understand. The time is coming when you'll have to worry—but that time hasn't come yet."

Then they walked till they came to the steep slope that led to the railroad tracks, down, down, far below them, where a small train seemed to be passing forever through the countryside, smoke, like the very definition of idleness, blowing out of the chimney stack of the toy locomotive. Eric thought, resentfully, that he scarcely ever saw a train pass when he came here alone. Beyond the railroad tracks was the river where they sometimes went swimming in the summer. The river was hidden from them now by the high bank where there were houses and where tall trees grew.

"And this," said his father, "is where your land ends."

"What?" said Eric.

His father squatted on the ground and put one hand on Eric's shoulder. "You know all the way we walked, from the house?" Eric nodded. "Well," said his father, "that's your land."

Eric looked back at the long way they had come, feeling his father watching him.

His father, with a pressure on his shoulder, made him turn; he pointed: "And over there. It belongs to you." He turned to him again. "And that," he said, "that's yours, too."

Eric stared at his father. "Where does it end?" he asked.

His father rose. "I'll show you that another day," he said. "But it's farther than you can walk."

They started walking slowly, in the direction of the sun.

"When did it get to be mine?" asked Eric.

"The day you were born," his father said, and looked down at him and smiled.

"My father," he said, after a moment, "had some of this land—and when he died, it was mine. He held onto it for me. And I did my best with the land I had, and I got some more. I'm holding onto it for you."

He looked down to see if Eric was listening. Eric was listening, staring at his father and looking around him at the great countryside.

"When I get to be a real old man," said his father, "even older than old Jamie there—you're going to have to take care of all this. When I die it's going to be yours." He paused and stopped; Eric looked up at him. "When you get to be a big man, like your poppa, you're going to get married and have children. And all this is going to be theirs."

"And when *they* get married?" Eric prompted.

"All this will belong to *their* children," his father said.

"Forever?" cried Eric.

"Forever," said his father.

They turned and started walking toward the house.

"Jamie," Eric asked at last, "how much land has *he* got?"

"Jamie doesn't have any land," his father said.

"Why not?" asked Eric.

"He didn't take care of it," his father said, "and he lost it."

"Jamie doesn't have a wife anymore, either, does he?" Eric asked.

"No," said his father. "He didn't take care of her, either."

"And he doesn't have any little boy," said Eric—very sadly.

"No," said his father. Then he grinned. "But *I* have."

"*Why* doesn't Jamie have a little boy?" asked Eric.

His father shrugged. "Some people do, Eric, some people don't."

"Will I?" asked Eric.

"Will you what?" asked his father.

"Will *I* get married and have a little boy?"

His father seemed for a moment both amused and checked. He looked down at Eric with a strange, slow smile. "Of course you will," he said at last. "Of course you will." And he held out his arms. "Come," he said, "climb up. I'll ride you on my shoulders home."

So Eric rode on his father's shoulders through the wide green fields that belonged to him, into the yard which held the house that would hear the first cries of his children. His mother and Jamie sat at the table talking quietly in the silver sun. Jamie had washed his face and combed his hair, he seemed calmer, he was smiling.

"Ah," cried Jamie, "the lord, the master of this house arrives! And bears on his shoulders the prince, the son and heir!" He described a flourish, bowing low in the yard. "My lords! Behold your humble, most properly chastised servant, desirous of your—compassion, your love and your forgiveness!"

"Frankly," said Eric's father, putting Eric on the ground, "I'm not sure that this is an improvement." He looked at Jamie and frowned and grinned. "Let's cut the cake."

Eric stood with his mother in the kitchen while she lit the candles—thirty-five, one, as they said, to grow on, though Jamie, surely, was far past the growing age—and followed her as she took the cake outside. Jamie took the great, gleaming knife and held it with a smile.

"Happy birthday!" they cried—only Eric said nothing—and then Eric's mother said, "You have to blow out the candles, Jamie, before you cut the cake."

"It looks so pretty the way it is," Jamie said.

"Go ahead," said Eric's father, and clapped him on the back, "be a man."

Then the dog, once more beside his master, awoke, growling, and this made everybody laugh. Jamie laughed loudest. Then he blew out the candles, all of them at once, and Eric watched him as he cut the cake. Jamie raised his eyes and looked at Eric and it was at this moment, as the suddenly blood-red sun was striking the topmost tips of trees, that Eric had looked into Jamie's eyes. Jamie smiled that strange smile of an old man and Eric moved closer to his mother.

"The first piece for Eric," said Jamie then, and extended it to him on the silver blade.

▪ ▪ ▪

That had been near the end of summer, nearly two months ago. Very shortly after the birthday party, his mother had fallen ill and had had to be taken away. Then his father spent more time than ever at The Rafters; he and Jamie came home in the evenings stumbling drunk. Sometimes, during the time that Eric's mother was away, Jamie did not go home at all, but spent the night at the farmhouse; and once or twice Eric had awakened in the middle of the night, or near dawn, and heard Jamie's footsteps walking up and down, walking up and down, in the big room downstairs. It had been a strange and dreadful time, a time of waiting, stillness and silence. His father rarely went into the fields, scarcely raised himself to give orders to his farm hands—it was unnatural, it was frightening, to find him around the house all day, and Jamie was there always, Jamie and his dog. Then one day Eric's father told him that his mother was coming home but that she would not be bringing him a baby brother or sister, not this time, nor in any time to come. He started to say something more, then looked at Jamie, who was standing by, and walked out of the house. Jamie followed him slowly, his hands in his pockets and his head bent. From the time of the birthday party, as though he were repenting of that outburst, or as though it had frightened him, Jamie had become more silent than ever.

When his mother came back she seemed to have grown older-old; she seemed to have shrunk within herself, away from them all, even, in a kind of storm of love and helplessness, away from Eric; but, oddly, and most particularly, away from Jamie. It was in nothing she said, nothing she did—or perhaps it was in everything she said and did. She washed and cooked for Jamie as before, took him into account as much as before as a part of the family, made him take second helpings at the table, smiled good night to him as he left the house—it was only that something had gone out of her familiarity. She seemed to do all that she did out of memory and from a great distance. And if something had gone out of her ease, something had come into it, too, a curiously still attention, as though she had been startled by some new aspect of something she had always known. Once or twice at the supper table, Eric caught her regard bent on Jamie, who, obliviously, ate. He could not read her look, but it reminded him of that moment at the birthday party when he had looked into Jamie's eyes. She seemed to be looking at Jamie as though she were wondering why she had not looked at him before; or as though she were discovering, with some surprise, that she had never really liked him but also felt, in her weariness and weakness, that it did not really matter now.

Now, as Eric entered the yard, he saw her standing in the kitchen doorway, looking out, shielding her eyes against the brilliant setting sun.

"Eric!" she cried, wrathfully, as soon as she saw him, "I've been looking high and low for you for the last hour. You're getting old enough to have some sense of responsibility and I wish you wouldn't worry me so when you know I've not been well."

She made him feel guilty at the same time that he dimly and resentfully felt that justice was not all on her side. She pulled him to her, turning his face up toward hers, roughly, with one hand.

"You're filthy," she said, then, "Go around to the pump and wash your face. And hurry, so I can give you your supper and put you to bed."

And she turned and went into the kitchen, closing the door lightly behind her. He walked around to the other side of the house, to the pump.

On a wooden box next to the pump was a piece of soap and a damp rag. Eric picked up the soap, not thinking of his mother, but thinking of the day gone by, already half asleep; and thought of where he would go tomorrow. He moved the pump handle up and down and the water rushed out and wet his socks and shoes—this would make his mother angry, but he was too tired to care. Nevertheless, automatically, he moved back a little. He held the soap between his hands, his hands beneath the water.

He had been many places, he had walked a long way and seen many things that day. He had gone down to the railroad tracks and walked beside the tracks for a while, hoping that a train would pass. He kept telling himself that he would give the train one more last chance to pass; and when he had given it a considerable number of last chances, he left the railroad bed and climbed a little and walked through the high, sweet meadows. He walked through a meadow where there were cows and they looked at him dully with their great dull eyes and mooed among each other about him. A man from the far end of the field saw him and shouted, but Eric could not tell whether it was someone who worked for his father or not and so he turned and ran away, ducking through the wire fence. He passed an apple tree, with apples lying all over the ground—he wondered if the apples belonged to him, if he were still walking on his own land or had gone past it—but he ate an apple anyway and put some in his pockets, watching a lone brown horse in a meadow far below him nibbling at the grass and flicking his tail. Eric pretended that he was his father and was walking through the fields as he had seen his father walk, looking it all over calmly, pleased, knowing that everything he saw belonged to him. And he stopped and peered as he had seen his father do, standing wide-legged and heavy in the middle of the fields; he pretended at the same time to be smoking and talking, as he had seen his father do. Then, having watered the ground, he walked on, and all the earth, for that moment, in Eric's eyes, seemed to be celebrating Eric.

Tomorrow he would go away again, somewhere. For soon it would be winter, snow would cover the ground, he would not be able to wander off alone.

He held the soap between his hands, his hands beneath the water; then he heard a low whistle behind him and felt a rough hand on his head and the soap fell from his hands and slithered between his legs onto the ground.

He turned and faced Jamie, Jamie without his dog.

"Come on, little fellow," Jamie whispered. "We got something in the barn to show you."

"Oh, did the calf come yet?" asked Eric—and was too pleased to wonder why Jamie whispered.

"Your poppa's there," said Jamie. And then: "Yes. Yes, the calf is coming now."

And he took Eric's hand and they crossed the yard, past the closed kitchen door, past the stone wall and across the field, into the barn.

"But *this* isn't where the cows are!" Eric cried. He suddenly looked up at Jamie, who closed the barn door behind them and looked down at Eric with a smile.

"No," said Jamie, "that's right. No cows here." And he leaned against the door as though his strength had left him. Eric saw that his face was wet, he breathed as though he had been running.

"Let's go see the cows," Eric whispered. Then he wondered why he was whispering and was terribly afraid. He stared at Jamie, who stared at him.

"In a minute," Jamie said, and stood up. He had put his hands in his pockets and now he brought them out and Eric stared at his hands and began to move away. He asked, "Where's my poppa?"

"Why," said Jamie, "he's down at The Rafters, I guess. I have to meet him there soon."

"I have to go," said Eric. "I have to eat my supper." He tried to move to the door, but Jamie did not move. "I have to go," he repeated, and, as Jamie moved toward him, the tight ball of terror in his bowels, in his throat, swelled and rose, exploded: he opened his mouth to scream, but Jamie's fingers closed around his throat. He stared, stared into Jamie's eyes.

"That won't do you any good," said Jamie. And he smiled. Eric struggled with pain and fright. Jamie relaxed his grip a little and moved one hand and stroked Eric's tangled hair. Slowly, wondrously, his face changed, tears came into his eyes and rolled down his face.

Eric groaned—perhaps because he saw Jamie's tears or because his throat was so swollen and burning, because he could not catch his breath, because he was so frightened—he began to sob in great, unchildish gasps. "Why do you hate my father?"

"I love your father," Jamie said. But he was not listening to Eric. He was far away—as though he were struggling, toiling inwardly up a tall, tall mountain. And Eric struggled blindly, with all the force of his desire to live, to reach him, to stop him before he reached the summit.

"Jamie," Eric whispered, "you can have the land. You can have all the land."

Jamie spoke but not to Eric: "I don't want the land."

"I'll be your little boy," said Eric. "I'll be your little boy forever and forever and forever—and you can have the land and you can live forever! Jamie!"

Jamie had stopped weeping. He was watching Eric.

"We'll go for a walk tomorrow," Eric said, "and I'll show it to you, all of it—really and truly—if you kill my father I can be your little boy and we can have it all!"

"This land," said Jamie, "will belong to no one."

"Please!" cried Eric. "Oh, please! Please!"

He heard his mother singing in the kitchen. Soon she would come out to look for him. The hands left him for a moment. Eric opened his mouth to scream, but the hands then closed around his throat.

Momma. Momma.

The singing was farther and farther away. The eyes looked into his, there was a question in the eyes, the hands tightened. Then the mouth began to smile. He had never seen such a smile before. He kicked and kicked.

Momma. Momma. Momma. Momma.

Far away, he heard his mother call him.

Momma.

He saw nothing, he knew that he was in the barn, he heard a terrible breathing near him, he thought he heard the sniffing of beasts, he remembered the sun, the railroad tracks, the cows, the apples and the ground. He thought of tomorrow—he wanted to go away again somewhere tomorrow. *I'll take you with me,* he wanted to say. He wanted to argue the question, the question he remembered in the eyes—wanted to say, *I'll tell my poppa you're hurting me*. Then terror and agony and darkness overtook him, and his breath went violently out of him. He dropped on his face in the straw in the barn, his yellow head useless on his broken neck.

Night covered the countryside and here and there, like emblems, the lights of houses glowed. A woman's voice called, "Eric! Eric!"

▪ ▪ ▪

Jamie reached his wooden house and opened his door; whistled, and his dog came bounding out of darkness, leaping up on him; and he cuffed it down lightly, with one hand. Then he closed his door and started down the road, his dog beside him, his hands in his pockets. He stopped to light his pipe. He heard singing from The Rafters, then he saw the lights; soon, the lights and the sound of singing diminished behind him. When Jamie no longer heard the singing, he began to whistle the song he had heard.

Irwin Shaw

Where All Things Wise and Fair Descend

February 1967

Irwin Shaw (1913–1984) was another *Playboy* favorite, sending in stories from his home in Klosters, Switzerland, and occasionally descending on New York for a prolonged party. Shaw was famous for his appreciation of the good life, and other writers—and *Playboy* editors—loved to join him for memorable meals and nights on the town, in both Europe and the United States. Shaw's long World War II novel, *The Young Lions* (1948), put him on the literary map and was made into a movie with Marlon Brando. Many hefty best-sellers followed, but, unlike many novelists, especially commercial novelists (and he turned out to be more commercial than literary in the long run), Shaw retained a deft hand with a short story. *Playboy* was the beneficiary, publishing most of Shaw's later stories as well as a number of essays. He was versatile: some stories were satiric, some, like this one about youthful grief, entirely serious.

Irwin Shaw

Where All Things Wise and Fair Descend

He woke up feeling good. There was no reason for him to wake up feeling anything else.

He was an only child. He was twenty years old. He was over six feet tall and weighed one hundred eighty pounds and had never been sick in his whole life. He was number two on the tennis team and back home in his father's study there was a whole shelf of cups he had won in tournaments since he was eleven years old. He had a lean, sharply cut face, topped by straight black hair that he wore just a little long, which prevented him from looking merely like an athlete. A girl had once said he looked like Shelley. Another, like Laurence Olivier. He had smiled noncommittally at both girls.

He had a retentive memory and classes were easy for him. He had just been put on the dean's list. His father, who was doing well up North in an electronics business, had sent him a check for one hundred dollars as a reward. The check had been in his box the night before.

He had a gift for mathematics and probably could get a job teaching in the department if he wanted it upon graduation, but he planned to go into his father's business. He would then be exempt from the draft and Vietnam.

He was not one of the single-minded equational wizards who roamed the science departments. He got A's in English and history and had memorized most of Shakespeare's sonnets and read Roethke and Eliot and Ginsberg. He had tried marijuana. He was invited to all the parties. When he went home, mothers made obvious efforts to throw their daughters at him.

His own mother was beautiful and young and funny. There were no unbroken silver cords in the family. He was having an affair with one of the prettiest girls on the campus and she said she loved him. From time to time he said he loved her. When he said it he meant it. At that moment, anyway.

Nobody he had ever cared for had as yet died and everybody in his family had come home safe from all the wars.

The world saluted him.

He maintained his cool.

No wonder he woke up feeling good.

■ ■ ■

It was nearly December, but the California sun made a summer morning of the season and the girls and boys in corduroys and T-shirts and bright-colored sweaters on their way to their ten-o'clock classes walked over green lawns and in and out of the shadows of trees that had not yet lost their leaves.

He passed the sorority house where Adele lived and waved as she came out. His first class every Tuesday was at ten o'clock and the sorority house was on his route to the arts building in which the classroom was situated.

Adele was a tall girl, her dark, combed head coming well above his shoulder. She had a triangular, blooming, still-childish face. Her walk, even with the books she was carrying in her arms, wasn't childish, though, and he was amused at the envious looks directed at him by some of the other students as Adele paced at his side down the graveled path.

" 'She walks in beauty,' " Steve said, " 'like the night/Of cloudless climes and starry skies;/And all that's best of dark and bright/Meet in her aspect and her eyes.' "

"What a nice thing to hear at ten o'clock in the morning," Adele said. "Did you bone up on that for me?"

"No," he said. "We're having a test on Byron today."

"Animal," she said.

He laughed.

"Are you taking me to the dance Saturday night?" she asked.

He grimaced. He didn't like to dance. He didn't like the kind of music that was played and he thought the way people danced these days was devoid of grace. "I'll tell you later," he said.

"I have to know today," Adele said. "Two other boys've asked me."

"I'll tell you at lunch," he said.

"What time?"

"One. Can the other aspirants hold back their frenzy to dance until then?"

"Barely," she said. He knew that with or without him, Adele would be at the dance on Saturday night. She loved to dance and he had to admit that a girl had every right to expect the boy she was seeing almost every night in the week to take her dancing at least once on the weekend. He felt very mature, almost fatherly, as he resigned himself to four hours of heat and noise on Saturday night.

But he didn't tell Adele that he'd take her. It wouldn't do her any harm to wait until lunch.

He squeezed her hand as they parted and watched for a moment as she swung down the path, conscious of the provocative way she was walking, conscious of the eyes on her. He smiled and continued on his way, waving at people who greeted him.

It was early and Mollison, the English professor, had not yet put in an appearance. The room was only half full as Steve entered it, but there wasn't the usual soprano-tenor tuning-up sound of conversation from the students who were already there. They sat in their chairs quietly, not talking, most of them ostentatiously arranging their books or going through their notes. Occasionally, almost furtively, one or another of them would look up toward the front of the room and the blackboard, where a thin boy with wispy reddish hair was writing swiftly and neatly behind the teacher's desk.

"Oh, weep for Adonais—he is dead!" the red-haired boy had written. "Wake, melancholy Mother, wake and weep!"

Yet wherefore? Quench within their burning bed
Thy fiery tears, and let thy loud heart keep
Like his a mute and uncomplaining sleep;
For he is gone where all things wise and fair
Descend. Oh, dream not that the amorous Deep
Will yet restore him to the vital air;
Death feeds on his mute voice, and laughs at our despair.

Then, on a second blackboard, where the boy was finishing the last lines of another stanza, was written:

He has outsoared the shadow of our night;
Envy and calumny and hate and pain,
And that unrest which men miscall delight,
Can touch him not and torture not again;
From the contagion of the world's slow stain
He is secure, and now can never mourn
A heart grown cold, a head grown gray in vain;

Professor Mollison came bustling in with the half-apologetic smile of an absent-minded man who is afraid he is always late. He stopped at the door, sensing by the quiet that this was no ordinary Tuesday morning in his classroom. He peered nearsightedly at Crane writing swiftly in rounded chalk letters on the blackboard.

Mollison took out his glasses and read for a moment, then went over to the window without a word and stood there looking out, a graying, soft-faced rosy-cheeked old man, the soberness of his expression intensified by the bright sunlight at the window.

"Nor," Crane was writing, the chalk making a dry sound in the silence,

when the spirit's self has ceased to burn,
With sparkless ashes load an unlamented urn.

When Crane had finished, he put the chalk down neatly and stepped back to look at what he had written. A girl's laugh came in on the fragrance of cut grass through the open window and there was a curious hushing little intake of breath all through the room.

The bell rang, abrasively, for the beginning of classes. When the bell stopped, Crane turned around and faced the students seated in rows before him. He was a lanky, skinny boy, only nineteen, and he was already going bald. He hardly ever spoke in class and when he spoke, it was in a low, harsh whisper.

He didn't seem to have any friends and he never was seen with girls and the time he didn't spend in class he seemed to spend in the library. Crane's brother had played fullback on the football team, but the brothers had rarely been seen together, and the fact that the huge, graceful athlete and the scarecrow bookworm were members of the same family seemed like a freak of eugenics to the students who knew them both.

Steve knew why Crane had come early to write the two verses of Shelley's lament on the clean morning blackboard. The Saturday night before, Crane's brother had been killed in an automobile accident on the way back from the game, which had been played in San Francisco. The funeral had taken place yesterday, Monday. Now it was Tuesday morning and Crane's first class since the death of his brother.

Crane stood there, narrow shoulders hunched in a bright tweed jacket that was too large for him, surveying the class without emotion. He glanced once more at what he had written, as though to make sure the problem he had placed on the board had been correctly solved, then turned again to the group of gigantic, blossoming, rosy California boys and girls, unnaturally serious and a little embarrassed by this unexpected prolog to their class, and began to recite.

He recited flatly, without any emotion in his voice, moving casually back and forth in front of the blackboards, occasionally turning to the text to flick off a little chalk dust, to touch the end of a word with his thumb, to hesitate at a line, as though he had suddenly perceived a new meaning in it.

Mollison, who had long ago given up any hope of making any impression on the sun-washed young California brain with the fragile hammer of Nineteenth Century romantic poetry, stood at the window, looking out over the campus, nodding in rhythm from time to time and occasionally whispering a line, almost silently, in unison with Crane.

" '. . . an unlamented urn,' " Crane said, still as flat and unemphatic as ever, as though he had merely gone through the two verses as a feat of memory. The last echo of his voice quiet now in the still room, he looked out at the class through his thick glasses, demanding nothing. Then he went to the back of the room and sat down in his chair and began putting his books together.

Mollison, finally awakened from his absorption with the sunny lawn, the whirling sprinklers, the shadows of the trees speckling in the heat and the wind, turned away from the window and walked slowly to his desk. He peered nearsightedly for a moment at the script crammed on the blackboards, then said, absently, "On the death of Keats. The class is excused."

For once, the students filed out silently, making a point, with youthful good manners, of not looking at Crane, bent over at his chair, pulling books together.

Steve was nearly the last one to leave the room and he waited outside the door for Crane. *Somebody* had to say something, do something, whisper "I'm sorry," shake the boy's hand. Steve didn't want to be the one, but there was nobody else left. When Crane came out, Steve fell into place beside him and they went out of the building together.

"My name is Dennicott," Steve said.

"I know," said Crane.

"Sure." There was no trace of grief in Crane's voice or manner. He blinked through his glasses at the sunshine, but that was all.

"Why did you do that?"

"Did you object?" The question was sharp but the tone was mild, offhand, careless.

"Hell, no," Steve said. "I just want to know why you did it."

"My brother was killed Saturday night," Crane said.

"I know."

" 'The death of Keats. The class is excused.' " Crane chuckled softly but without malice. "He's a nice old man, Mollison. Did you ever read the book he wrote about Marvell?"

"No," Steve said.

"Terrible book," Crane said. "You really want to know?" He peered with sudden sharpness at Steve.

"Yes," Steve said.

"Yes," Crane said absently, brushing at his forehead. "You would be the one who would ask. Out of the whole class. Did you know my brother?"

"Just barely," Steve said. He thought about Crane's brother, the fullback. A gold helmet far below on a green field, a number (what number?), a doll brought out every Saturday to do skillful and violent maneuvers in a great wash of sound, a photograph in a program, a young, brutal face looking out a little scornfully from the page. Scornful of what? Of whom? The inept photographer? The idea that anyone would really be interested in knowing what face was on that numbered doll? The notion that what he was doing was important enough to warrant this attempt to memorialize him, so that somewhere, in somebody's attic fifty years from now, that young face would still be there, in the debris, part of some old man's false memory of his youth?

"He didn't seem much like John Keats to you, did he?" Crane stopped under a tree, in the shade, to rearrange the books under his arm. He seemed oppressed by sunshine and he held his books clumsily and they were always on the verge of falling to the ground.

"To be honest," Steve said, "no, he didn't seem much like John Keats to me."

Crane nodded gently. "But I knew him," he said. "I knew him. And nobody who made those goddamned speeches at the funeral yesterday knew him. And he didn't believe in God or in funerals or those goddamned speeches. He needed a proper ceremony of farewell," Crane said, "and I tried to give it to him. All it took was a little chalk, and a poet, and none of those liars in black suits. Do you want to take a ride today?"

"Yes," Steve said without hesitation.

"I'll meet you at the library at eleven," Crane said. He waved stiffly and hunched off, gangling, awkward, ill-nourished, thin-haired, laden with books, a discredit to the golden Coastal legend.

▪ ▪ ▪

They drove north in silence. Crane had an old Ford without a top and it rattled so much and the wind made so much noise as they bumped along that conversation would have been almost impossible, even if they had wished to talk. Crane bent over the wheel, driving nervously, with an excess of care, his long pale hands gripping the wheel tightly. Steve hadn't asked where they were going and Crane hadn't told him. Steve hadn't been able to get hold of Adele to tell her he probably wouldn't be back in time to have lunch with her, but there was nothing to be done about that now. He sat back, enjoying the sun and the yellow, burnt-out hills and the long, grayish-blue swells of the Pacific beating lazily into the beaches and against the cliffs of the coast. Without being told, he knew that this ride somehow was a continuation of the ceremony in honor of Crane's brother.

They passed several restaurants alongside the road. Steve was hungry, but he didn't suggest stopping. This was Crane's expedition and Steve had no intention of interfering with whatever ritual Crane was following.

They rocked along between groves of lemon and orange and the air was heavy with the perfume of the fruit, mingled with the smell of salt from the sea.

They went through the flecked shade of avenues of eucalyptus that the Spanish monks had planted in another century to make their journeys from mission to mission bearable in the California summers. Rattling along in the noisy car, squinting a little when the car spurted out into bare sunlight, Steve thought of what the road must have looked like with an old man in a cassock nodding along it on a sleepy mule, to the sound of distant Spanish bells, welcoming travelers. There were no bells ringing today. California, Steve thought, sniffing the diesel oil of a truck in front of them, has not improved.

The car swerved around a turn, Crane put on the brakes and they stopped. Then Steve saw what they had stopped for.

There was a huge tree leaning over a bend of the highway and all the bark at road level on one side of the tree had been ripped off. The wood beneath, whitish, splintered, showed in a raw wound.

"This is the place," Crane said, in his harsh whisper. He stopped the engine and got out of the car. Steve followed him and stood to one side as Crane peered nearsightedly through his glasses at the tree. Crane touched the tree, just at the edge of the wound.

"Eucalyptus," he said. "From the Greek, meaning well covered; the flower, genus of plants of the N.O. Myrtaceae. If I had been a true brother," he said, "I would have come here Saturday morning and cut this tree down. My brother would be alive today." He ran his hand casually over the torn and splintered wood, and Steve remembered how he had touched the blackboard and flicked chalk dust off the ends of words that morning, unemphatically, in contact with the feel of things, the slate, the chalk mark at the end of the last "s" in Adonais, the gummy, drying wood. "You'd think," Crane said, "that if you loved a brother enough you'd have sense enough to come and cut a tree down, wouldn't you? The Egyptians, I read somewhere," he said, "were believed to have used the oil of the eucalyptus leaf in the embalming process." His long hand flicked once more at the torn bark. "Well, I didn't cut the tree down. Let's go."

He strode back to the car, without looking back at the tree. He got into the car behind the wheel and sat slumped there, squinting through his glasses at the road ahead of him, waiting for Steve to settle himself beside him. "It's terrible for my mother and father," Crane said, after Steve had closed the door behind him. A truck filled with oranges passed them in a thunderous whoosh and a swirl of dust, leaving a fragrance of a hundred weddings on the air. "We live at home, you know. My brother and I were the only children they had, and they look at me and they can't help feeling, If it had to be one of them, why couldn't it have been *him?* And it shows in their eyes and they know it shows in their eyes and they know I agree with them and they feel guilty and I can't help them." He started the engine with a succession of nervous, uncertain gestures, like a man who was just learning how to drive. He turned the car around in the direction of Los Angeles and they started south. Steve looked once more at the tree, but Crane kept his eyes on the road ahead of him.

"I'm hungry," he said. "I know a place where we can get abalone about ten miles from here."

▪ ▪ ▪

They were sitting in the weather-beaten shack with the windows open on the ocean, eating their abalone and drinking beer. The jukebox was playing *Downtown.* It was the third time they were listening to *Downtown.* Crane kept putting dimes into the machine and choosing the same song over and over again.

"I'm crazy about that song," he said. "Saturday night in America. Budweiser Bacchanalia."

"Everything all right, boys?" The waitress, a fat little dyed blonde of about thirty, smiled down at them from the end of the table.

"Everything is perfectly splendid," Crane said in a clear, ringing voice.

The waitress giggled. "Why, that sure is nice to hear," she said.

Crane examined her closely. "What do you do when it storms?" he asked.

"What's that?" She frowned uncertainly at him.

"When it storms," Crane said. "When the winds blow. When the sea heaves. When the young sailors drown in the bottomless deeps."

"My," the waitress said, "and I thought you boys only had one beer."

"I advise anchors," Crane said. "You are badly placed. A turn of the wind, a twist of the tide, and you will be afloat, past the reef, on the way to Japan."

"I'll tell the boss," the waitress said, grinning. "You advise anchors."

"You are in peril, lady," Crane said seriously. "Don't think you're not. Nobody speaks candidly. Nobody tells you the one-hundred-percent honest-to-God truth." He pushed a dime from a pile at his elbow, across the table to the waitress. "Would you be good enough to put this in the box, my dear?" he said formally.

"What do you want to hear?" the waitress asked.

"Downtown," Crane said.

"Again?" The waitress grimaced. "It's coming out of my ears."

"I understand it's all the rage," Crane said.

The waitress took the dime and put it in the box and *Downtown* started over again.

"She'll remember me," Crane said, eating fried potatoes covered with ketchup. "Every time it blows and the sea comes up. You must not go through life unremembered."

"You're a queer duck, all right," Steve said, smiling a little, to take the sting out of it, but surprised into saying it.

"Ah, I'm not so queer," Crane said, wiping ketchup off his chin. "I don't behave like this ordinarily. This is the first time I ever flirted with a waitress in my life."

Steve laughed. "Do you call that flirting?"

"Isn't it?" Crane looked annoyed. "What the hell is it if it isn't flirting?" He surveyed Steve appraisingly. "Let me ask you a question," he said. "Do you screw that girl I always see you with around the campus?"

Steve put down his fork. "Now, wait a minute," he said.

"I don't like the way she walks," Crane said. "She walks like a coquette. I prefer whores."

"Let's leave it at that," Steve said.

"Ah, Christ," Crane said, "I thought you wanted to be my friend. You did a friendly, sensitive thing this morning. In the California desert, in the Los Angeles Gobi, in the Camargue of Culture. You put out a hand. You offered the cup."

"I want to be your friend, all right," Steve said, "but there're limits . . ."

"The word friend has no limits," Crane said harshly. He poured some of his beer over the fried potatoes, already covered with ketchup. He forked a potato, put it in his mouth, chewed judiciously. "I've invented a taste thrill," he said. "Let me tell you something, Dennicott, friendship is limitless communication. Ask me anything and I'll answer. The more fundamental the matter, the fuller the answer. What's your idea of friendship? The truth about trivia—and silence and hypocrisy about everything else? God, you could have used a dose of my brother." He poured some more beer over the gobs of ketchup on the fried potatoes. "You want to know why I can say Keats and name my brother in the same breath?" he asked challengingly, hunched over the table. "I'll tell you why. Because he had a sense of elation and a sense of purity." Crane squinted thoughtfully at Steve. "You, too," he said, "that's why I said you would be the one to ask, out of the whole class. You have it, too—the sense of elation. I could tell—listening to you laugh, watching you walk down the library steps holding your girl's elbow. I, too," he said gravely, "am capable of elation. But I reserve it for other things." He made a mysterious inward grimace. "But the purity—" he said. "I don't know. Maybe you don't know yourself. The jury is still out on you. But I knew about my brother. You want to know what I mean by purity?" He was talking compulsively. Silence would have made memory unbearable. "It's having a private set of standards and never compromising them," he said. "Even when it hurts, even when nobody else knows, even when it's just a tiny, formal gesture, that ninety-nine out of a hundred people would make without thinking about it."

Crane cocked his head and listened with pleasure to the chorus of *Downtown,* and he had to speak loudly to be heard over the jukebox. "You know why my brother wasn't elected captain of the football team? He was all set for it, he was the logical choice, everybody expected it. I'll tell you why he wasn't, though. He wouldn't shake the hand of last year's captain, at the end of the season, and last year's captain had a lot of votes he could influence any way he wanted. And do you know why my brother wouldn't shake his hand? Because he thought the man was a coward. He saw him tackle high when a low tackle would've been punishing, and he saw him not go all the way on blocks when they looked too rough. Maybe nobody else saw what my brother saw or maybe they gave the man the benefit of the doubt. Not my brother. So he didn't shake his hand, because he didn't shake cowards' hands, see, and somebody else was elected captain. That's what I mean by purity," Crane said, sipping at his beer and looking out at the deserted beach and the ocean. For the first time, it occurred to Steve that it was perhaps just as well that he had never known Crane's brother, never been measured against that Cromwellian certitude of conduct.

"As for girls," Crane said. "The homeland of compromise, the womb of the second best—" Crane shook his head emphatically. "Not for my brother. Do you know what he did with his first girl? And he thought he was in love with her, too, at the time, but it still didn't make any difference. They only made love in the dark. The girl insisted. That's the way some girls are, you know, darkness excuses all. Well, my brother was crazy about her, and he didn't mind the darkness if it pleased her. But one night he saw her sitting up in bed and the curtains on the window moved in the wind and her silhouette was outlined against the moonlight, and he saw that when she sat like that she had a fat, loose belly. The silhouette, my brother said, was slack and self-indulgent. Of course, when she was lying down it sank in, and when she was dressed she wore a girdle that would've tucked in a beer barrel. And when he saw her silhouette against the curtain, he said to himself, This is the last time, this is not for me. Because it wasn't perfect, and he wouldn't settle for less. Love or no love, desire or not. He, himself, had a body like Michelangelo's *David* and he knew it and he was proud of it and he kept it that way, why should he settle for imperfection? Are you laughing, Dennicott?"

"Well," Steve said, trying to control his mouth, "the truth is, I'm smiling a little." He was amused, but he couldn't help thinking that it was possible that Crane had loved his brother for all the wrong reasons. And he couldn't help feeling sorry for the unknown girl, deserted, without knowing it, in the dark room, by the implacable athlete who had just made love to her.

"Don't you think I ought to talk about my brother this way?" Crane said.

"Of course," Steve said. "If I were dead, I hope my brother could talk like this about me the day after the funeral."

"It's just those goddamned speeches everybody makes," Crane whispered. "If you're not careful, they can take the whole idea of your brother away from you."

He wiped his glasses. His hands were shaking. "My goddamned hands," he said. He put his glasses back on the table, so they wouldn't shake.

"How about you, Dennicott?" Crane said. "Have you ever done anything in your whole life that was unprofitable, damaging, maybe even ruinous, because it was the pure thing to do, the uncompromising thing, because if you acted otherwise, for the rest of your life you would remember it and feel shame?"

Steve hesitated. He did not have the habit of self-examination and had the feeling that it was vanity that made people speak about their virtues. And their faults. But there was Crane, waiting, himself open, naked. "Well, yes . . ." Steve said.

"What?"

"Well, it was never anything very grandiose . . ." Steve said, embarrassed, but feeling that Crane needed it, that in some way this exchange of intimacies helped relieve the boy's burden of sorrow. And he was intrigued by Crane, by the violence of his views, by the almost comic flood of his reminiscence about his brother, by the importance that Crane assigned to the slightest gesture, by his searching for meaning in trivialities, which gave the dignity of examination to every breath of life. "There was the time on the beach at Santa Monica," Steve said. "I got myself beaten up and I knew I was going to be beaten up . . ."

"That's good," Crane nodded approvingly. "That's always a good beginning."

"Oh, hell," Steve said, "it's too picayune."

"Nothing is picayune," said Crane. "Come on."

"Well, there was a huge guy there who always hung around and made a pest of himself," Steve said. "A physical-culture idiot, with muscles like basketballs. I made fun of him in front of some girls and he said I'd insulted him, and I had, and he said if I didn't apologize, I would have to fight him. And I was wrong, I'd been snotty and superior, and I realized it, and I knew that if I apologized, he'd be disappointed and the girls'd still be laughing at him—so I said I wouldn't apologize and I fought him there on the beach and he must have knocked me down a dozen times and he nearly killed me."

"Right." Crane nodded again, delivering a favorable judgment. "Excellent."

"Then there was this girl I wanted . . ." Steve stopped.

"Well?" Crane said.

"Nothing," Steve said. "I haven't figured it out yet." Until now he had thought that the episode with the girl reflected honorably on him. He had behaved, as his mother would have put it, in a gentlemanly manner. He wasn't sure now that Crane and his mother would see eye to eye. Crane confused him. "Some other time," he said.

"You promise?" Crane said.

"I promise."

"You won't disappoint me, now?"

"No."

"OK," Crane said. "Let's get out of here."

They split the check.

"Come back again sometime, boys," the blonde waitress said. "I'll play that record for you." She laughed, her breasts shaking. She had liked having them there. One of them was very good-looking, and the other one, the queer one with the glasses, she had decided, after thinking about it, was a great joker. It helped pass the long afternoon.

▪ ▪ ▪

On the way home, Crane no longer drove like a nervous old maid on her third driving lesson. He drove very fast, with one hand, humming *Downtown,* as though he didn't care whether he lived or died.

Then, abruptly, Crane stopped humming and began to drive carefully, timidly, again. "Dennicott," he said, "what are you going to do with your life?"

"Who knows?" Steve said, taken aback by the way Crane's conversation jumped from one enormous question to another. "Go to sea, maybe, build electronic equipment, teach, marry a rich wife . . ."

"What's that about electronics?" Crane asked.

"My father's factory," Steve said. "The ancestral business. No sophisticated missile is complete without a Dennicott supersecret what-do-you-call-it."

"Nah," Crane said, shaking his head, "you won't do that. And you won't teach school, either. You don't have the soul of a didact. I have the feeling something adventurous is going to happen to you."

"Do you?" Steve said. "Thanks. What're you going to do with *your* life?"

"I have it all planned out," Crane said. "I'm going to join the forestry service. I'm going to live in a hut on the top of a mountain and watch out for fires and fight to preserve the wilderness of America."

That's a hell of an ambition, Steve thought, but he didn't say it. "You're going to be awfully lonesome," he said.

"Good," Crane said. "I expect to get a lot of reading done. I'm not so enthusiastic about my fellow man, anyway. I prefer trees."

"What about women?" Steve asked. "A wife?"

"What sort of woman would choose me?" Crane said harshly. "I look like something left over after a New Year's party on skid row. And I would only take the best, the most beautiful, the most intelligent, the most loving. I'm not going to settle for some poor, drab Saturday-night castaway."

"Well, now," Steve said, "you're not so awful." Although, it was true, you'd be shocked if you saw Crane out with a pretty girl.

"Don't lie to your friends," Crane said. He began to drive recklessly again, as some new wave of feeling, some new conception of himself, took hold of him. Steve sat tight on his side of the car, holding onto the door, wondering if a whole generation of Cranes was going to meet death on the roads of California within a week.

They drove in silence until they reached the university library. Crane stopped the car and slouched back from the wheel as Steve got out. Steve saw Adele on the library steps, surrounded by three young men, none of whom he knew. Adele saw him as he got out of the car and started coming over to him. Even at that distance, Steve could tell she was angry. He wanted to get rid of Crane before Adele reached him. "Well, so long," Steve said, watching Adele approach. Her walk *was* distasteful, self-conscious, teasing.

Crane sat there, playing with the keys to the ignition, like a man who is always uncertain that the last important word has been said when the time has come to make an exit.

"Dennicott," he began, then stopped, because Adele was standing there, confronting Steve, her face set. She didn't look at Crane.

"Thanks," she said to Steve. "Thanks for the lunch."

"I couldn't help it," Steve said. "I had to go someplace."

"I'm not in the habit of being stood up," Adele said.

"I'll explain later," Steve said, wanting her to get out of there, away from him, away from Crane, watching soberly from behind the wheel.

"You don't have to explain anything," Adele said. She walked away. Steve gave her the benefit of the doubt. Probably she didn't know who Crane was and that it was Crane's brother who had been killed Saturday night. Still . . .

"I'm sorry I made you miss your date," Crane said.

"Forget it," Steve said. "She'll get over it."

For a moment he saw Crane looking after Adele, his face cold, severe, judging. Then Crane shrugged, dismissed the girl.

"Thanks, Dennicott," Crane said. "Thanks for coming to the tree. You did a good thing this afternoon. You did a friendly thing. You don't know how much you helped me. I have no friends. My brother was the only friend. If you hadn't come with me and let me talk, I don't know how I could've lived through today. Forgive me if I talked too much."

"You didn't talk too much," Steve said.

"Will I see you again?" Crane asked.

"Sure," said Steve. "We have to go back to that restaurant to listen to *Downtown* real soon."

Crane sat up straight, suddenly, smiling shyly, looking pleased, like a child who has just been given a present. If it had been possible, Steve would have put his arms around Crane and embraced him. And with all Crane's anguish and all the loneliness that he knew so clearly was waiting for him, Steve envied him. Crane had the capacity for sorrow and now, after the day Steve had spent with the bereaved boy, he understood that the capacity for sorrow was also the capacity for living.

"Downtown," Crane said. He started the motor and drove off, waving gaily, to go toward his parents' house, where his mother and father were waiting, with the guilty look in their eyes, because they felt that if one of their sons had to die, they would have preferred it to be him.

Steve saw Adele coming back toward him from the library steps. He could see that her anger had cooled and that she probably would apologize for her outburst. Seeing Adele suddenly with Crane's eyes, he made a move to turn away. He didn't want to talk to her. He had to think about her. He had to think about everything. Then he remembered the twinge of pity he had felt when he had heard about the fat girl erased from her lover's life by the movement of a curtain on a moonlit night. He turned back and smiled in greeting as Adele came up to him. Crane had taught him a good deal that afternoon, but perhaps not the things Crane had thought he was teaching.

"Hello," Steve said, looking not quite candidly into the young blue eyes on a level with his own. "I was hoping you'd come back."

But he wasn't going to wake up, automatically feeling good, ever again.

John Cheever

The Yellow Room

January 1968

Like Thurber, John Cheever (1912–1982) was a writer mainly associated with *The New Yorker.* A few stories made their way to *Playboy,* perhaps because the other magazine, more straitlaced then than now, found them a little risqué. Illegitimacy is a theme of "The Yellow Room," while homosexuality, prostitution, masturbation, and premarital sex—"carnal roughhouse"—turn up casually, but it might have been the heavy drinking (Cheever was himself a heavy drinker) that *The New Yorker* shied away from. At any rate, "The Yellow Room" remains a splendid calling-card from one of the finest short-story writers in America's literary history.

John Cheever

The Yellow Room

I was born out of wedlock—the son of Franklin Faxon Taylor and Gretchen Shurz Oxencroft, his onetime secretary. I have not met my mother for several years, but I can see her now—her gray hair flying and her fierce blue eyes set plainly in her face like the water holes in a prairie. She was born in an Indiana quarry town, the fourth and by far the plainest of four daughters. Neither of her parents had more than a high school education. The hardships and boredom of the provincial Middle West forced them into an uncompromising and nearly liturgical regard for the escape routes of learning. They kept a volume of the complete works of Shakespeare on their parlor table like a sort of mace. Her father was a Yorkshireman with thick light-brown hair and large features. He was slender and wiry and was discovered, in his forties, to have tuberculosis. He began as a quarry worker, was promoted to quarry foreman and then, during a drop in the limestone market, was unemployed. In the house where she was raised there was a gilt mirror, a horsehair sofa and some china and silver that her mother had brought from Philadelphia. None of this was claimed to prove lost grandeur or even lost comfort, but Philadelphia! Philadelphia!—how like a city of light it must have seemed in the limestone flats. Gretchen detested her name and claimed at one time or another to be named Grace, Gladys, Gwendolyn, Gertrude, Gabriella, Giselle and Gloria. In her adolescence, a public library was opened in the village where she lived and through some accident or misdirection, she absorbed the complete works of John Galsworthy. This left her with a slight English accent and an immutable clash between the world of her reveries and the limestone country. Going home from the library one winter afternoon on a trolley car, she saw her father standing under a street lamp with his lunch pail. The driver did not stop for him and Gretchen turned to a woman beside her and exclaimed: "Did you *see* that poor creature! He signaled for the tram to stop, but the driver *quite* overlooked him." These were the accents of Galsworthy in which she had been immersed all afternoon, and how could she fit her father into this landscape? He would have failed as a servant or gardener. He might have passed as a groom, although the only horses he knew were the wheel horses at the quarry. She knew what a decent, courageous and cleanly man he was and it was the intolerable sense of his aloneness that had forced her, in a contemptible way, to disclaim him. Gretchen—or Gwendolyn, as she then called herself—graduated from high school with honors and was given a scholarship at the university in Bloomington. A week or so after her graduation from the university, she left the limestone country to make her fortune in New York. Her parents came down to the station to see her off. Her father was wasted. Her mother's coat was threadbare. As they waved goodbye, another traveler asked if they were her parents. It was still in her to explain in the accents of Galsworthy that they were merely some poor people she had visited, but instead she exclaimed: "Oh, yes, yes, they are my mother and father."

There is some mysterious, genetic principality where the children of anarchy are raised, and Gretchen (now Gloria) carried this passport. She had become a socialist in her last year at the university and the ills, injustices, imperfections, inequities and indecencies of the world made her smart. She more or less hurled herself at the city of New York and was hired shortly as a secretary for Franklin Faxon Taylor. He was a wealthy and visionary young man and a member of the Socialist Party. Gretchen became his secretary and presently his lover. They were by all accounts very happy together. What came between them—or so my father claimed—was that at this point her revolutionary ardor took the form of theft or kleptomania. They traveled a great deal and whenever they checked out of a hotel, she always packed the towels, the table silver, the dish covers and the pillowcases. The idea was that she would distribute them among the poor, although he never saw this happen. "Someone *needs* these things," she would exclaim, stuffing their suitcases with what did not belong to her. Coming into her Hay-Adams room in Washington once, he found her standing on a chair, removing the crystals from the chandelier. "Someone can *use* these," she said. At the Commodore Perry in Toledo, she packed the bathroom scale, but he refused to close the suitcase until she returned it. She stole a radio in Cleveland and a painting from the Palace Hotel in San Francisco. This incurable habit of thieving—or so he claimed—led them to bitter quarrels and they parted in New York. In the use of any utensils—toasters, irons and automobiles—Gretchen had been dogged by bad luck and, while he had been well equipped with birth-control material, her bad luck overtook her again. She discovered soon after the separation that she was pregnant.

Taylor did not mean to marry her. He paid the costs of her accouchement and gave her an income and she took a small apartment on the West Side. She always introduced herself as Miss Oxencroft. She meant to be disconcerting. I suppose she saw some originality in our mutual illegitimacy. When I was three years old, I was visited by my father's mother. She was delighted by the fact that I had a head of yellow curls. She offered to adopt me. After a month's deliberation, my mother—who was never very consistent—agreed to this. She felt that it was her privilege, practically her vocation, to travel around the world and improve her mind. A nursemaid was gotten for me and I went to live in the country with Grandmother. My hair began to turn brown. By the time I was eight, my hair was quite dark. My grandmother was neither bitter nor eccentric and she never actually reproached me for this, but she often said that it had come to her as a surprise. I was called Paul Oxencroft on my birth certificate, but this was thought unsatisfactory and a lawyer came to the house one afternoon to settle this. While they were discussing what to call me, a gardener passed the window, carrying a hammer, and so I was named. A trust had been established to provide Gretchen with a decent income and she took off for Europe. This ended her imposture as Gloria. Her checks, endorsements and travel papers insisted that she be Gretchen and so she was.

When my father was a young man, he summered in Munich. He had worked out all his life with bar bells, dumbbells, etc., and had a peculiar physique that is developed by no other form of exercise. In Munich he posed, out of vanity or pleasure, for the architectural sculptor Feldspar, who ornamented the façade of the Prinz-Regenten Hotel. He posed as one of those male caryatids who hold on their shoulders the lintels of so many opera houses, railroad stations, apartment buildings and palaces of justice. The Prinz-Regenten was bombed in the forties, but long before this, I saw my father's recognizable features and overdeveloped arms and shoulders supporting the façade of what was then one of the most elegant hotels in Europe. Feldspar was popular at the turn of the century and I saw my father again, this time in full figure, holding up the three top floors of the Hotel Mercedes in Frankfurt am Main. I saw him in Yalta, Berlin and upper Broadway and I saw him lose caste, face and position as this sort of monumental façade went out of vogue. I saw him lying in a field of weeds in West Berlin. But all of this came much later, and any ill feeling about my illegitimacy and the fact that he was always known as my uncle was overcome by my feeling that he held on his shoulders the Prinz-Regenten, the better suites of the Mercedes and the Opera House in Malsberg that was also bombed. He seemed very responsible and I loved him.

I once had a girl who kept saying that she knew what my mother must be like. I don't know why an affair that centered on carnal roughhouse should have summoned memories of my old mother, but it did. The girl had it all wrong, although I never bothered to correct her. "Oh, I can imagine your mother," the girl would sigh. "I can see her in her garden, cutting roses. I know she wears chiffon and big hats." If my mother was in the garden at all, she was very likely on her hands and knees, flinging up weeds as a dog flings up dirt. She was not the frail and graceful creature that my friend imagined. Since I have no legitimate father,

I may have expected more from her than she could give me, but I always found her disappointing and sometimes disconcerting. She now lives in Kitzbühel until the middle of December—whenever the snow begins to fall—and then moves to a pension in Estoril. She returns to Kitzbühel when the snow melts. These moves are determined more by economic reasons than by any fondness she has for the sun.

I graduated from Choate and Yale. In my sophomore year, Grandmother died and left me some money. After my graduation, I moved to Cleveland and invested fifty thousand dollars in a textbook firm. I lost this investment in less than a year. I don't think there was any connection, because I still had plenty of money, but about this time I found my appetite for men, women, children, athletics—everything—mysteriously curtailed and I had begun to suffer, for no apparent reason, from melancholy, a *cafard* or form of despair that sometimes seemed to have a tangible approach. Once or twice I seemed to glimpse some of its physical attributes. It was covered with hair—it was the classical bête noire—but it was as a rule no more visible than a column of thin air. I decided then to move to New York. I had majored in Italian literature and my plan was to translate the poetry of Eugenio Montale, but my *cafard* made this impossible. I took a furnished apartment in the East 50s. I seemed to know almost no one in the city and this left me alone much of the time and much of the time with my *cafard*.

It overtook me on trains and planes. I would wake feeling healthy and full of plans to be crushed by the *cafard* while I shaved or drank my first cup of coffee. It was most powerful and I was most vulnerable when the noise of traffic woke me at dawn. My best defense, my only defense, was to cover my head with a pillow and summon up those images that represented for me the excellence and beauty I had lost. The first of these was a mountain—it was obviously Kilimanjaro. The summit was a perfect, snow-covered cone, lighted by a passing glow. I saw the mountain a thousand times—I begged to see it—and as I grew more familiar with it, I saw the fire of a primitive village at its base. The vision dated, I guess, from the Bronze or the Iron Age. Next in frequency I saw a fortified medieval town. It could have been Mont-Saint-Michel or Orvieto or the grand lamasery in Tibet, but the image of the walled town, like the snow-covered mountain, seemed to represent beauty, enthusiasm and love. I also saw less frequently and less successfully a river with grassy banks. I guessed these were the Elysian fields, although I found them difficult to arrive at and at one point it seemed to me that a railroad track or a throughway had destroyed the beauty of the place. As often as I saw these places I would, to fend off the *cafard,* recite a sort of incantation or primitive prayer. I would pick the name of some virtue I had lost—love, valor, compassion or excellence—and repeat the word a hundred times. As in Zen, I would exhale and inhale; for example: "Compassion" (exhale), "Compassion" (inhale), etc. However, this was not like Zen counting; that is to say, there was nothing contemplative in my incantation. It was wrung from me in despair. I suppose I could have organized a church in which the congregation got to their knees and shouted "Valor, Valor" (exhale, inhale) a thousand times. One could do worse.

I had begun to drink heavily to lick the *cafard* and one morning—I had been in New York for about a month—I took a hooker of gin while I shaved. I then went back to bed again, covered my head with a pillow and tried to evoke the mountain, the fortified town or the green field.

I stayed in bed that day until 11 or later. What I wanted then was a long, long, long sleep and I had enough pills to accomplish this. I flushed the pills down the toilet and called one of my few friends and asked for the name of his doctor. I then called the doctor and asked him for the name of a psychiatrist. He recommended a man named Doheny.

Doheny saw me that afternoon. His waiting room had a large collection of magazines, but the ashtrays were clean, the cushions were unrumpled and I had the feeling that perhaps I was his first customer in a long time. Was he, I wondered, an unemployed psychiatrist, an unsuccessful psychiatrist, an unpopular psychiatrist, did he while away the time in an empty office like an idle lawyer, barber or antique dealer? He presently appeared and led me into a consultation room that was furnished with antiques. There were no diplomas on the wall. I wondered then if some part of a psychiatrist's education was the furnishing of his consultation room. Did they do it themselves? Did their wives do it? Was it done by a professional? Doheny had large brown eyes in a long face. When I sat in the patient's chair, he turned the beam of his brown eyes onto me exactly as a dentist turns on the light above his drills, and for the next fifty minutes I basked in his gaze and returned his looks earnestly to prove that I was truthful and manly. He seemed, like some illusion of drunkenness, to have two faces and I found it fascinating to watch one swallow up the other. He charged a dollar a minute.

Doheny was intensely interested in my parents—he seemed to find them entertaining. My mother writes to me from Kitzbühel once or twice a month, and I gave Doheny her most recent letter. "I dreamed an entire movie last night," she wrote, "not a scenario but a movie in full color about a Japanese printer named Chardin. And then I dreamed I went back to the garden of the old house in Indiana and found everything the way I had left it. Even the flowers I'd cut so many years ago were on the back porch, quite fresh. There it all was, not as I might remember it, for my memory is failing these days and I couldn't recall anything in such detail, but as a gift to me from some part of my spirit more profound than memory. After that, I dreamed that I took a train. Out of the window I could see blue water and blue sky. I wasn't quite sure where I was going, but looking through my handbag, I found an invitation to spend a weekend with Robert Frost. Of course, he's dead and buried and I don't suppose we would have gotten along for more than five minutes, but it seemed like some dispensation or bounty of my imagination to have invented such a visit.

"My memory is failing in some quarters, but in others it seems quite tenacious and even tiresome. It seems to perform music continuously. I seem to hear music all the time. There is music running through my mind when I wake and it plays all day long. What mystifies me is the variety in quality. Sometimes I wake to the slow movement of the finest Rasoumovsky. You know how I love that. I may have a Vivaldi concerto for breakfast and some Mozart a little later. But sometimes I wake to a frightful Sousa march followed by a chewing-gum commercial and a theme from Chopin. I loathe Chopin. Why should my memory torment me by playing music that I loathe?

"I suppose you think all of this foolish but at least I don't go in for tarot cards or astrology and I do not, as my friend Elizabeth Howland does, feel that my windshield wiper gives me sage and coherent advice on my stock-market investments. She claimed only last month that her windshield wiper urged her to invest in Merck chemicals, which she did, making a profit of several thousand. I suppose she lies about her losses as gamblers always do. As I say, windshield wipers don't speak to me, but I do hear music in the most unlikely places—especially in the motors of airplanes. Accustomed as I am to the faint drone of transoceanic jets, it has made me keenly aware of the complicated music played by the old DC-7s and Constellations that I take to Portugal and Geneva. Once these planes are airborne, their engines sound to my ears like some universal music as random and free of reference and time as the makings of a dream. It is far from jubilant music, but one would be making a mistake to call it sad. The sounds of a Constellation seem to me more contrapuntal—and in a way less universal than a DC-7's. I can trace, as clearly as anything I ever heard in a concert hall, the shift from a major chord to a diminished seventh, the ascent to an eighth, the reduction to a minor and the resolution of the chord. The sounds have the driving and processional sense of Baroque music, but they will never, I know from experience, reach a climax and a resolution. The church I attended as a girl in Indiana employed an organist who had never completed his musical education, because of financial difficulties or a wayward inability to persevere. He played the organ with some natural brilliance and dexterity, but since his musical education had never reached the end of things, what had started out as a forthright and vigorous fugue would collapse into formlessness and vulgarity. The Constellations seem to suffer from the same musical irresolution, the same wayward inability to persevere. The first, second and third voices of the fugue are sounded clearly, but then, as with the organist, the force of invention collapses into a series of harmonic meanderings. The engines of a DC-7 seem both more comprehensive and more limited. One night on a flight to Frankfurt, I distinctly heard the props get halfway through Gounod's vulgar variations on Bach. I have also heard Handel's *Water Music,* the death theme from *Tosca,* the opening of the *Messiah,* etc. But boarding a DC-7 one night in Innsbruck—the intense cold may have made the difference—I distinctly heard the engines produce some exalting synthesis of all life's sounds. Boats and train whistles and the creaking of iron gates and bedsprings and drums and rain winds and thunder and footsteps and the sounds of singing all seemed woven into a rope or cord of air that ended when the stewardess asked us to observe the NO SMOKING sign (RAUCHEN VERBOTEN), an announcement that has come to mean to me that if I am not at home, I am at least at my destination.

"Of course, I know that you think all of this unimportant. It is no secret to me that you would have preferred a more conventional mother—someone who sent you baked goods and remembered your birthday—but it seems to me that in our knowledge and study of one another, we are circumspect and timid to an impractical degree. In our struggle to glimpse the soul of a man—and have we ever desired anything less?—we claim to have the honesty of desperation, whereas, in fact, we set up whole artificial structures of acceptable reality and stubbornly refuse to admit the terms by which we live. I will, before I end my letter, bore you with one more observation of fact. What I have to say must be well known to most travelers, and yet I would not dare confide my knowledge to an intimate friend, lest I be thought mad. Since you already think me mad, I suppose no harm can be done.

"I have noticed, in my travels, that the strange beds I occupy in hotels and pensions have a considerable variance in atmosphere and a profound influence on my dreams. It is a simple fact that we impress something of ourselves—our spirits and our desires—on the mattresses where we lie, and I have more than ample evidence to prove my point. One night in Naples last winter, I dreamed of washing a drip-dry wardrobe, which is, as you well know, something I would never do. The dream was quite explicit—I could see the articles of clothing hanging in the shower and smell the wet cloth, although this is no part of my memories. When I woke, I seemed surrounded by an atmosphere unlike my own—shy, earnest and chaste. There was definitely some presence in the room. In the morning, I asked the desk clerk who had last occupied my bed. He checked his records and said that it had last been occupied by an American tourist—a Miss Harriet Lowell—who had moved to a smaller room but who could then be seen coming out of the dining room. I then turned to see Miss Lowell, whose white, drip-dry dress I had already seen in my dreams and whose shy, chaste and earnest spirit still lingered in the room she had left. You will put this down to coincidence, I know, but let me go on. Sometime later, in Geneva, I found myself in a bed that seemed to exhale so unsavory and venereal an atmosphere that my dreams were quite disgusting. In them I saw two naked men, mounted like a horse and rider. In the morning, I asked the desk clerk who the earlier tenants had been and he said: *'Oui, oui, deux tapettes.'* They had made so much noise they had been asked to leave. After this, I made a practice of deciding who the previous occupant of my bed had been and then checking with the clerk in the morning. In every case I was correct—in every case, that is, where the clerk was willing to cooperate. In cases involving prostitutes, they were sometimes unwilling to help. If I found no presence in my bed, I would judge that the bed had been vacant for a week or ten days. I was always correct. Traveling that year, I shared the dreams of businessmen, tourists, married couples, chaste and orderly people, as well as whores. My most remarkable experience came in Munich in the spring.

"I stayed, as I always do, at the Bristol and I dreamed about a sable coat. As you know, I detest furs, but I saw this coat in great detail—the cut of the collar, the honey-colored skins, the yellow silk with which it was lined and, in one of the silk pockets, a pair of ticket stubs for the opera. In the morning, I asked the maid who brought me coffee if the previous occupant of the room had owned a fur coat. The maid clasped her hands together, rolled her eyes and said yes, yes, it was a Russian sable coat and the most beautiful coat that she, the maid, had ever seen. The woman had loved her coat. It was like a lover to her. And did the woman who owned the coat, I asked, stirring my coffee and trying to seem unexceptional, ever go to the opera? Oh, yes, yes, said the maid, she came for the Mozart festival and went to the opera every night for two weeks, wearing her sable coat.

"I was not deeply perplexed—I have always known life to be overwhelmingly mysterious—but wouldn't you say that I possess indisputable proof of the fact that we leave fragments of ourselves, our dreams and our spirits in the rooms where we sleep? But what could I do with this information? If I confided my discovery to a friend, I would likely be thought mad; and was there, after all, any usefulness in my ability to divine that my bed had been occupied by a spinster or a prostitute or by no one at all? Was I gifted or were these facts known to all travelers and wouldn't giftedness be a misnomer for a faculty that could not be exploited? I have finally concluded that the universality of our dreams includes everything—articles of clothing and theater ticket stubs—and we truly know one another so intimately mightn't we be closer than we imagine to a peaceable world?"

After I had been going to Doheny for a month or longer, he asked me to masturbate when I got home and report my reactions to him. I did as he asked and reported that I felt ashamed of myself. He was delighted with this news and said that sexual guilt was the source of my *cafard*. I was a repressed, transvestite homosexual. The fact that the image of my father supported hotels, palaces of justice and opera houses had intimidated me and forced me into an unnatural way of life. I told him to go to hell and that I was through. I said that he was a charlatan and that I was going to report him to the American Psychiatric Association. If he wasn't a charlatan, I asked, why didn't he have diplomas hung on his wall like other doctors? He got very angry at this, threw open his desk drawer and pulled out a pile of diplomas. He had diplomas from Yale, Columbia and the Neurological Institute. Then I noticed that all these documents were made out to a man named Howard Shitz and I asked if he hadn't picked them up in a secondhand bookstore. He said he had changed his name when he went into practice, for reasons that any dunce would understand. I left.

I was no better after Doheny—I was worse—and I began to wonder seriously if the ubiquitousness of my father's head and shoulders, carved in limestone, had not been crippling; but if it had been, what could I do? The opera house in Malsberg and the Prinz-Regenten had been demolished, but I couldn't remove him from his position on upper Broadway and he was still holding up the Mercedes in Frankfurt. I went on drinking—almost a quart a day—and my hands had begun to shake terribly. When I went into a bar, I would wait until the bartender turned his back before I tried to get the glass up to my mouth. I sometimes spilled gin all over the bar. This amused the other customers. I went out to Pennsylvania one weekend with some heavy-drinking friends and came back on a local train that got me into Penn Station about eleven Sunday night. The station was then being razed and reconstructed and it was such a complex of ruins that it seemed like a frightening projection of my own confusions and I stepped out into the street, looking for a bar. The bars around the station were too brightly lighted for a man whose hands were shaking and I started walking east, looking for some dark saloon where my infirmity would not be so noticeable. Walking down a side street, I saw two lighted windows and a room with yellow walls. The windows were uncurtained. All I could see were the yellow walls. I put down my suitcase to stare at the windows. I was convinced that whoever lived there lived a useful and illustrious life. It would be a single man like myself, but a man with a continent nature, a ruling intelligence, an efficient disposition. The pair of windows filled me with shame. I wanted my life to be not merely decent but exemplary. I wanted to be useful, continent and at peace. If I could not change my habits, I could at least change my environment, and I thought that if I found such a room with yellow walls, I would cure my *cafard* and my drunkenness.

The next afternoon, I packed a bag and took a cab across town to the Hotel Dorset, looking for that room where I could begin my illustrious life. They gave me a room on the second floor, looking out onto an air shaft. The room had not been made up. There was an empty whiskey bottle and two glasses on the bureau and only one of the two beds had been used. I called the desk to complain and they said the only other vacancy they had was a suite on the tenth floor. I then moved to this. I found a parlor, a double bedroom and a large collection of flower pictures. I ordered some gin, vermouth and a bucket of ice and got stoned. This was not what I intended and in the morning I moved to the Madison Hotel.

My room at the Madison was furnished with the kind of antiques Doheny had had in his consultation room. The desk, or some part of it, had once been a spinet. The coffee table was covered with leather that had been tooled, gilded and burned by many cigarettes. There were mirrors on all the walls, so that I could not escape my own image. I saw myself smoking, drinking, dressing and undressing and when I woke in the morning, the first thing I saw was myself. I left the next day for the Waldorf, where I was given a pleasant, high-ceilinged room. There was a broad view. I could see the dome of St. Bartholomew's, the Seagram building and one of those yellow bifurcated buildings that has a terraced and a windowed front and a flat, yellow-brick backside with no sign of life but a rain gutter. It seemed to have been sliced with a knife. Almost anywhere in New York above the fifteenth floor, your view includes a few caryatids, naiads, homely water tanks and Florentine arches, and I was admiring these when it occurred to me how easy it would be to escape the *cafard* by jumping into the street, and I checked out of the Waldorf and took a plane to Chicago.

In Chicago I took a room at the Palmer House. This was on the sixteenth floor. The furniture seemed to be of some discernible period, but the more I examined it, the more it seemed to be an inoffensive improvisation, and then I realized that it was the same furniture I had seen in my room at the Waldorf. I flipped open the Venetian blinds. My window looked out into an enclosure where I could see, upward, downward and sidewise, a hundred hundred windows exactly like mine. The fact that my room had no uniqueness seemed seriously to threaten my own uniqueness: I suffered an intense emotional vertigo. The fear was not of falling but of vanishing. If there was nothing in my room to distinguish it from a hundred hundred others, there might be nothing about me to set me apart from other men, and I snapped the Venetian blinds shut and went out of the room. Waiting for the elevator, a man gave me that bland, hopeful gaze of a faggot on the make and I thought that he might have been driven by the sameness of the hotel windows to authenticate his identity by unnatural sexual practices. I lowered my eyes chastely to the floor. Downstairs I drank three martinis and went to a movie. I stayed in Chicago two days and took the Zephyr to San Francisco. I thought a train compartment might be the environment where I could begin my new life, but it was not. In San Francisco I stayed two nights at the Palace and two nights at the St. Francis and then flew down the coast and checked in at the Los Angeles Biltmore. This was the furthest from what I wanted and I moved from there to the Chateau Marmont. I moved from there to the Beverly Hills and a day later took a plane to London on the northerly route. I tried to get a room at the Connaught, but they were full and so I went instead to the Dorchester, where I lasted two days. I then flew to Rome and checked in at the Eden. My *cafard* had followed me around the world and I was still drinking heavily. Lying in bed in the Eden one morning with a pillow over my face, I summoned up Kilimanjaro and its ancient village, the Elysian fields and the fortified town. It occurred to me then that I had thought the town might be Orvieto. I rented a Fiat from the concierge and started north.

It was after lunch when I got into Umbria and I stopped in a walled town and had some pasta and wine. The country was wheat country, more heavily forested than most of Italy and very green. Like most travelers, I kept stupidly observing the sameness of things, kept telling myself that on the evidence of what I saw, I might be in New Hampshire or the outskirts of Heidelberg. What for? It was nearly seven o'clock when I came down the winding road into the broad valley that surrounds Orvieto.

I had been wrong about the towers, but everything else seemed right. The city was high, its buildings seemed to be a variation of the stone butte and it looked like the place I had seen in fending off the *cafard*. It seemed to correspond to my vision. I was excited. My life, my sanity were involved. The papal cathedral, in its commanding position, excited, as it was meant to do, awe, admiration and something like dread, as if some part of my memory was that of a heretic on my way to be questioned by the bishops. I drove through the lower town up to the city on the butte and checked in at the Hotel Nazionali, where I was given a large, deluxe European room with a massive armoire and a glass chandelier. It was not the room I was looking for. I wandered around the streets and just before dark, in a building not far from the cathedral, I saw the lighted windows and the yellow walls.

I seemed, looking up at them from the sidewalk, to be standing at the threshold of a new life. This was not a sanctuary, this was the vortex of things, but this was a place where the *cafard* could not enter. The door of the building was open and I climbed some stairs. The pair of yellow rooms was on the second floor. They were unfurnished, as I knew they would be, and freshly painted. Everything was ready for my occupancy. There was a man putting up shelves for my books. I spoke to the man and asked him whom the rooms belonged to. He said they were his. I asked if they were for sale or for rent and he smiled and said no. Then I said I wanted them and would pay whatever he asked for them, but he went on smiling and saying no. Then I heard some men in the hallway, carrying something heavy. I could hear their strained voices, their breathing and the object, whatever it was, bumping against the wall. It was a large bed, which they carried into the second of the yellow rooms. The owner explained to me then that this was his marriage bed. He was going to be married next day in the chapel of the cathedral and begin his married life here. I was still so convinced that the rooms were, spiritually at least, my property that I asked him if he wouldn't prefer to live in one of the new apartments in the lower town. I would pay the difference in the rent and was prepared to give him a large present for his wedding. He was impervious, of course. Like any groom, he had imagined so many hundreds of times the hour when he would bring his bride back to the yellow rooms that no amount of money would dislodge the memory from its place in his mind. I wished him well anyhow and went down the stairs. I had found my yellow rooms and I had lost them. I left Orvieto in the morning for Rome and left Rome the next day for New York.

I spent one night in my apartment, during which I drank almost a quart of whiskey. The next afternoon I drove out to Pennsylvania to visit a classmate of mine—Charlie Masterson—and his wife. They were heavy drinkers and we ran out of gin before dinner. I drove into the little village of Blenville and bought a fresh supply at the liquor store and started back. I made a wrong turn and found myself on a narrow red dirt lane that seemed to lead nowhere. Then on my left, set back from the road and a little above it, I saw the yellow walls for the third time.

I turned off the motor and the lights and got out of the car. There was a brook between the road and the house and I crossed this on a wooden bridge. A lawn or a field—the grass needed cutting—sloped up to a terrace. The house was stone—rectangular—an old Pennsylvania farmhouse, and the yellow room was the only room lighted. The walls were the same color I had seen in Orvieto. I went up onto the terrace, as absorbed as any thief. A woman sat in the yellow room, reading a book. She wore a black dress and high-heeled shoes and had a glass of whiskey on a table at her side. Her face was pale and handsome. I guessed she was in her twenties. The black dress and the high-heeled shoes seemed out of place in the country and I wondered if she had just arrived from town or were just about to leave, although the size of the whiskey glass made this seem unlikely. But it was not the woman but the room I wanted—square, its lemon-yellow walls simply lighted, and I felt that if I could only possess this, I would be myself again, industrious and decent. She looked up suddenly, as if she sensed my presence, and I stepped away from the window. I was very happy. Walking back to the car, I saw the name Emmison painted on a mailbox at the end of the driveway. I found my way back to the Mastersons and asked Mrs. Masterson if she knew anyone named Emmison. "Sure," she said. "Dora Emmison. I think she's in Reno."

"Her house was lighted," I said.

"'What in the world were you doing at her house?"

"I got lost."

"Well, she was in Reno. I suppose she's just come back. Do you know her?" she asked.

"No," I said, "but I'd like to."

"Well, if she's back, I'll ask her for a drink tomorrow."

She came the next afternoon, wearing the black dress and the same high heels. She was a little reserved, but I found her fascinating, not because of her physical and intellectual charms but because she owned the yellow room. She stayed for supper and I asked about her house. I presently asked if she wouldn't like to sell it. She was not at all interested. Then I asked if I could see the house and she agreed indifferently. She was leaving early and if I wanted to see the place, I could come back with her, and so I did.

As soon as I stepped into the yellow room, I felt that peace of mind I had coveted when I first saw the walls in a walk-up near Pennsylvania Station. Sometimes you step into a tack room, a carpenter's shop or a country post office and find yourself unexpectedly at peace with the world. It is usually late in the day. The place has a fine smell (I must include bakeries). The groom, carpenter, postmaster or baker has a face so clear, so free of trouble that you feel that nothing bad has ever or will ever happen here, a sense of fitness and sanctity never achieved, in my experience, by any church.

She gave me a drink and I asked again if she would sell the place. "Why should I sell my house?" she asked. "I like my house. It's the only house I have. If you want a place in the neighborhood, the Barkham place is on the market and it's much more attractive than this."

"This is the house I want."

"I don't see why you're so crazy about this place. If I had a choice, I'd rather have the Barkham place."

"Well, I'll buy the Barkham place and exchange it for this."

"I simply don't want to move," she said. She looked at her watch.

"Could I sleep here?" I asked.

"Where?"

"Here, here in this room."

"But what do you want to sleep here for? The sofa's hard as a rock."

"I'd just like to."

"Well, I guess you can if you want to. No monkey business."

"No monkey business."

"I'll get some bedding."

She went upstairs and came down with some sheets and a blanket and made my bed. "I think I'll turn in myself," she said, going toward the stairs. "I guess you know where everything is. If you want another drink, there's some ice in the bucket. I think my husband left a razor in the medicine cabinet. Good night." Her smile was courteous and no more. She climbed the stairs.

I didn't make a drink. I didn't, as they say, need one. I sat in a chair by the window feeling the calm of the yellow walls restore me. Outside I could hear the brook, some night bird, moving leaves and all the sounds of the night world seemed endearing, as if I quite literally loved the night as one loves a woman, loved the stars, the trees, the weeds in the grass as one can love with the same ardor a woman's breasts and the apple core she has left in an ashtray. I loved it all and everyone who lived. My life had begun again and I could see, from this beginning, how far I had gone from any natural course. Here was the sense of reality—a congenial, blessed and useful construction to which I belonged. I stepped out onto the terrace. It was cloudy, but some stars could still be seen. The wind was shifting and smelled of rain. I walked down to the bridge, undressed and dove into a pool there. The water was buoyant and a little brackish from the bogs in which it rose, but it had, so unlike the disinfected sapphire of a pool, a strong and unmistakably erotic emphasis. I dried myself on my shirttails and walked naked back to the house, feeling as if the earth were paved for my contentment. I brushed my teeth, turned out the light and, as I got into my bed, it began to rain.

For a year or more, the sound of the rain had meant merely umbrellas, raincoats, rubbers, the wet seats of convertibles; but now it seemed like some enlargement of my happiness, some additional bounty. It seemed to increase my feeling of limberness and innocence and I fended off sleep to listen to it with the attention of curiosity with which we follow music. When I did sleep, I dreamed in this order of the mountain, the walled town and the banks of the river, and when I woke at dawn, there was no trace of the *cafard*. I dove into the pool again and dressed. In the kitchen I found a melon, made some coffee and fried some bacon. The smell of coffee and bacon seemed like a smell of newness and I ate with a good appetite. She came down later in a bathrobe and thanked me for having made the coffee. When she raised the cup to her lips, her hands shook so that the coffee spilled. She went into the pantry, returned with a bottle of whiskey and spiked her coffee. She neither apologized nor explained this, but the spike steadied her hand.

I asked her if she wouldn't like me to cut the grass. "Well, I would, frankly," she said, "if you don't have anything better to do. It's terribly hard to find anyone around here to do anything. All the young men leave home and all the old ones die. The mower's in the tool shed and I think there's some gasoline."

I found the mower and gasoline and cut the grass. It was a big lawn and this took me until noon or later. She was sitting on the terrace reading and drinking something—ice water or gin. I joined her, wondering how I could build my usefulness into indispensability. I could have made a pass at her, but if we became lovers, this would have meant sharing the yellow room and that was not what I wanted. "If you want a sandwich before you go, there's some ham and cheese in the refrigerator," she said. "A friend of mine is coming out on the four o'clock, but I suppose you'll want to go back before then."

I was frightened. Go back, go back, go back to the greasy green waters of the Lethe, back to my contemptible cowardice, back to the sanctuary of my bed, where I cowered before thin air, back to anesthetizing myself with gin in order to eat a plate of scrambled eggs. I wondered about the sex of her visitor. If it was a woman, mightn't I stay on as a sort of handy man, eating my supper in the kitchen and sleeping in the yellow room? "If there's anything else you'd like me to do," I said. "Firewood?"

"I buy my firewood in Blenville."

"Would you like me to split some kindling?"

"Not really," she said.

"The screen door in the kitchen is loose," I said. "I could repair that."

She didn't seem to hear me. She went into the house and returned a little later with two sandwiches. "Would you like mustard?" she asked.

"No, thank you," I said.

I took the sandwich as a kind of sacrament, since it would be the last thing I could approach with any appetite until I returned to the yellow room, and when would that be? I was desperate. "Is your visitor a man or a woman?" I asked.

"I really don't think that concerns you," she said.

"I'm sorry."

"Thank you for cutting the grass," she said. "That needed to be done, but you must understand that I can't have a strange man sleeping on my sofa without a certain amount of damage to my reputation, and my reputation isn't absolutely invincible."

"I'll go," I said.

I drove back to New York then, condemned to exile and genuinely afraid of my inclination to self-destruction. As soon as I closed the door of my apartment, I fell into the old routine of gin, Kilimanjaro, scrambled eggs, Orvieto and the Elysian fields. I stayed in bed until late the next morning, performing my incantation. Courage. Inhale. Courage. Exhale. I drank some gin while I shaved and went out onto the street to get some coffee. In front of my apartment house I ran into Dora Emmison. She wore black—I never saw her in anything else—and said that she had come into town for a few days to do some shopping and go to the theater. I asked if she'd have lunch with me, but she said she was busy. As soon as we parted, I got my car and drove back to Blenville.

The house was locked, but I broke a pane of glass in the kitchen window and let myself in. To be alone in the yellow room was everything I had expected. I felt happy, peaceful and strong. I had brought the Montale with me and I spent the afternoon reading and making notes. The time passed lightly and the sense that the hands of my watch were Procrustean had vanished. At six o'clock I went for a swim, had a drink and made some supper. She had a large store of provisions and I made a note of what I was stealing so that I could replace it before I left. After dinner I went on reading, taking a chance that the lighted windows would not arouse anyone's curiosity. At nine o'clock I undressed, wrapped myself in a blanket and lay down on the sofa to sleep. A few minutes later I saw the lights of a car come up the drive.

I got up and went into the kitchen and shut the door. I was, of course, undressed. If it were she, I supposed I could escape out the back door. If it were not she, if it were some friend or neighbor, they would likely go away. Whoever it was began to knock on the door, which I had left unlocked. Then a man opened the door and asked softly, "Doree, Doree, you sleeping? Wake up, baby, wake up, it's Tony, the old loverboy." Climbing the stairs, he kept asking: "Doree, Doree, Doree," and when he went into her bedroom and found the bed empty, he said, "Aw, shit." He then came down the stairs and left the house and I stayed, shivering in the kitchen until I heard his car go down the road.

I got back onto the sofa and had been there for perhaps a half hour when another car came up the drive. I retired again to the kitchen and a man named Mitch went through more or less the same performance. He climbed the stairs, calling her name, made some exclamation of disappointment and went away. All of this left me uneasy and in the morning I cleaned up the place, emptied the ashtrays and drove back to New York.

Dora had said that she would be in the city for a few days. Four is what is usually meant by a few and two of these had already passed. On the day that I thought she would return to the country, I bought a case of the most expensive bourbon and started back to Blenville, late in the afternoon. It was after dark when I turned up the red-dirt road. Her lights were on. I looked in at the window and saw that she was alone and reading, as she had been when I first found the place. I knocked on the door and when she opened it and saw me, she seemed puzzled and irritated. "Yes?" she asked. "Yes? What in the world do you want now?"

"I have a present for you," I said. "I wanted to give you a present to thank you for your kindness in letting me spend the night in your house."

"That hardly calls for a present," she said, "but I do happen to have a weakness for good bourbon. Won't you come in?"

I brought the case into the hall, tore it open and took out a bottle. "Shouldn't we taste it?" I asked.

"Well, I'm going out," she said, "but I guess there's time for a drink. You're very generous. Come in, come in and I'll get some ice."

She was, I saw, one of those serious drinkers who prepare their utensils as a dentist prepares his utensils for an extraction. She arranged neatly on a table near her chair the glasses, ice bucket and water pitcher, as well as a box of cigarettes, an ashtray and a lighter. With all of this within her reach, she settled down and I poured the drinks.

"Chin, chin," she said.

"Cheers," I said.

"Did you just drive out from New York?" she asked.

"Yes," I said.

"How is the driving?" she asked.

"It's foggy on the Turnpike," I said. "It's quite foggy."

"Damn," she said. "I have to drive up to a party in Havenswood and I hate the Turnpike when it's foggy. I do wish I didn't have to go out, but the Helmsleys are giving a party for a girl I knew in school and I've promised to show up."

"Where did you go to school?"

"Do you really want to know?"

"Yes."

"Well, I went to Brearley for two years. Then I went to Finch for a year. Then I went to a country day school called Fountain View for two years. Then I went to a public school in Cleveland for a year. Then I went to the International School in Geneva for two years, the Parioli School in Rome for a year and when we came back to the United States, I went to Putney for a year and then to Masters for three years. I graduated from Masters."

"Your parents traveled a lot?"

"Yes. Dad was in the State Department. What do you do?"

"I'm translating Montale."

"Are you a professional translator?"

"No."

"You just do it to amuse yourself."

"To occupy myself."

"You must have some money," she said.

"I do."

"So do I, thank God," she said. "I'd hate to be without it."

"Tell me about your marriage," I said. This might have seemed importunate, but I have never known a divorced man or woman unwilling to discuss his marriage.

"Well, it was a mess," she said, "an eight-year mess. He drank and accused me of having affairs with other men and wrote anonymous letters to most of my friends, claiming that I had the principles of a whore. I bought him off, I had to, I paid him a shirtful and went out to Reno. I came back last month. I think I'll have another little drink," she said, "but first I'm going to the john."

I filled her glass again. We were nearly through the first bottle. When she returned from the toilet, she was not staggering, not at all, but she was walking much more lithely, with a much more self-confident grace. I got up and took her in my arms, but she pushed me away—not angrily—and said: "Please don't, please don't. I don't feel like that tonight. I've been feeling terrible all day and the bourbon has picked me up, but I still don't feel like that. Tell me all about yourself."

"I'm a bastard," I said.

"Oh, really? I've never known any bastards. What does it feel like?"

"Mostly lousy, I guess. I mean, I would have enjoyed a set of parents."

"Well, parents can be dreadful, of course, but I suppose dreadful parents are better than none at all. Mine were dreadful." She dropped a lighted cigarette into her lap, but retrieved it before it burned the cloth of her skirt.

"Are your parents still living?"

"Yes, they're in Washington, they're very old." She sighed and stood. "Well, if I'm going to Havenswood," she said, "I guess I'd better go." Now she was unsteady. She splashed a little whiskey into her glass and drank it without ice or water.

"Why do you have to go to Havenswood?" I asked. "Why don't you telephone and say there's a fog on the Turnpike or that you've got a cold or something?"

"You don't understand," she said hoarsely. "It's one of those parties you have to go to like birthdays and weddings."

"I think it would be better if you didn't go."

"Why?" Now she was bellicose.

"I just think it would be, that's all."

"You think I'm drunk?" she asked.

"No."

"You do, don't you? You think I'm drunk, you nosy son of a bitch. What are you doing here, anyhow? I don't know you. I never asked you to come here and you don't know me. You don't know anything about me excepting where I went to school. You don't even know my maiden name, do you?"

"No."

"You don't know anything about me, you don't even know my maiden name, and yet you have the cheek to sit there and tell me I'm drunk. I've been drinking, that's true, and I'll tell you why. I can't drive safely on the goddamned Jersey Turnpike sober. That road and all the rest of the freeways and throughways were engineered for clowns and drunks. If you're not a nerveless clown, then you have to get drunk. No sensitive or intelligent man or woman can drive on those roads. Why, I have a friend in California who smokes pot before he goes onto the freeway. He's a great driver, a marvelous driver, and if the traffic's bad, he uses heroin. They ought to sell pot and bourbon at the gas stations. Then there wouldn't be so many accidents."

"Well, let's have another drink, then," I said.

"Get out," she said.

"All right."

I went out of the yellow room onto the terrace. I watched her from the window. She was reeling. She stuffed some things into a bag, tied a scarf around her hair, turned out the lights and locked the door. I followed her at a safe distance. When she got to her car, she dropped the keys in the grass. She turned on the lights and I watched her grope in the grass until she recovered the keys. Then she slammed the car down the driveway and clipped the mailbox post with her right headlight. I heard her swear and a moment later I heard the noise of falling glass, and why is this sound so portentous, so like a doomcrack bell? I was happy to think that she would not continue up to Havenswood, but I was mistaken. She backed the car away from the mailbox post and off she went. I spent the night in a motel in Blenville and telephoned the Turnpike police in the morning. She had lasted about fifteen minutes.

My lawyer arranged for the purchase of the house. I was able to get the place and eight acres of land for $35,000. Her mother came up from Washington and removed her personal effects and I moved into the house three weeks later, but during the time the house had been empty, it had filled up with mice. Mice ran across the floor while I tried to work, kept me awake at night and ate my provisions. I asked about getting a cat in the village and the druggist said that he had a mouser I could have. He produced a black cat named Schwartz and I took Schwartz home with me.

I never found out much about Schwartz' past. I guess he was a middle-aged cat and he seemed to have a cranky disposition, if such a thing is possible in an animal, but he was an excellent mouser. I fed him canned cat food twice a day. There was a brand of cat food he disliked and if I forgot and gave him this, he would go into the yellow room and shit in the middle of the floor. He made his point and so long as I fed him what he liked, he behaved himself. We worked out a practical and unaffectionate relationship. I don't like having cats in my lap, but now and then I would dutifully pick him up and pat him to prove that I was a good scout. He rid the house of mice in a week or so and I was proud of Schwartz, but at the height of his efficiency as a mouser, Schwartz vanished. I let him out one night and in the morning he failed to return. I don't know much about cats, but I guessed they were loyal to their homes and I supposed that a dog or a fox had killed my friend. One morning, a week later (a light snow had fallen), Schwartz returned. I fed him a can of his favorite brand and gave him a few dutiful caresses. He smelled powerfully of French perfume. He had either been sitting in the lap of someone who used perfume or had been sprayed with it. It was an astringent and musky scent. The nearest house to mine was owned by some Polish farmers and the woman, I happened to know, smelled powerfully of the barnyard and nothing else. The next nearest house was shut for the winter and I couldn't think of anyone in Blenville who would use French perfume. Schwartz stayed with me that time for a week or ten days and then vanished again for a week. When he returned, he smelled like the street floor of Bergdorf Goodman's during the Christmas rush. I buried my nose in his coat and felt a moment's nostalgia for the city and its women. That afternoon I got into my car and drove over the back roads between my place and Blenville, looking for some place that might house a bewitching woman. I felt that she must be bewitching and that she was deliberately tempting me by dousing my cat with perfume. All the houses I saw were either farms or places owned by acquaintances and I stopped at the drugstore and told my story. "Schwartz," I said, "that cat, that mouser you gave me, he goes off every other week and comes home smelling like a whorehouse on Sunday morning."

"No whorehouses around here," said the druggist.

"I know," I said, "but where do you suppose he gets the perfume?"

"Cats roam," said the druggist.

"I suppose so," I said, "but do you sell French perfume? I mean, if I can find who buys the stuff. . . ."

"I don't remember selling a bottle since last Christmas," the druggist said. "The Avery boy bought a bottle for his girlfriend."

"Thank you," I said.

That night after dinner, Schwartz went to the door and signaled to be let out. I put on a coat and went out with him. He went directly through the garden and into the woods at the right of the house, with me following. I was as excited as any lover on his way. The smell of the woods, heightened by the dampness of the brook, the stars overhead, especially Venus, seemed to be extensions of my love affair. I thought she would be raven-haired with a marbly pallor and a single blue vein at the side of her brow. I thought she would be about thirty. Now and then Schwartz let out a meow, so that it wasn't too difficult to follow him. I went happily through the woods, across Marshman's pasture and into Marshman's woods. These had not been cleared for some years and the saplings lashed at my trousers and my face. Then I lost Schwartz. I called and called. Schwartz, Schwartz, here, Schwartz. Would anyone, hearing my voice in the dark woods, recognize it as the voice of a lover? I wandered through the woods calling my cat, until a tall sapling dealt me a blinding blow across the eyes and I gave up. I made my way home feeling frustrated and lonely.

Schwartz returned at the end of the week and I seized him and smelled his coat to make sure that she was still setting out her lures. She was. He stayed with me that time ten days. A snow had fallen on the night he vanished and in the morning I saw that his tracks were clear enough to follow. I got through Marshman's woods and came, at the edge of them, upon a small frame house, painted gray. It was utilitarian and graceless and might have been built by some hardworking amateur carpenter on Saturdays and Sundays and those summer nights when the dark comes late. I had seriously begun to doubt that it was the lair of a raven-haired beauty. The cat's tracks went around the house to a back door. When I knocked, an old man opened the door.

He was small, smaller than I, anyhow, with thin gray hair, pomaded and combed. There was a white button in his right ear, connected to a cord. From the lines and the colorlessness of his face, I would guess that he was close to seventy. Some clash between the immutable facts of vanity and time seemed to animate him. He was old, but he wore a flashy diamond ring, his shoes were polished and there was all that pomade. He looked a little like one of those dapper men who manage movie theaters in the badlands.

"Good morning," I said. "I'm looking for my cat."

"Ah," he said. "Then you must be the master of dear Henry. I've often wondered where Henry was domiciled when he was not with me. Henry, Henry, your second master has come to pay us a call." Schwartz was asleep on a chair. He did not stir. The room was a combination kitchen and chemistry laboratory. There was the usual kitchen furniture and, on a long bench, an assortment of test tubes and reports. The air was heavy with scent. "I don't know anything about the olfactory capacities of cats, but Henry does seem to enjoy perfumes, don't you, Henry? May I introduce myself. I'm Gilbert Hansen, formerly head chemist for Beauregarde et Cie."

"Hammer," I said. "Paul Hammer."

"How do you do. Won't you sit down?"

"Thank you!" I said. "You manufacture perfume here?"

"I experiment with scents," he said. "I'm no longer in the manufacturing end of things, but if I hit on something I like, I'll sell the patent, of course. Not to Beauregarde et Cie, however. After forty-two years with them, I was dismissed without cause or warning. However, this seems to be a common practice in industry these days. I do have an income from my patents. I am the inventor of Etoile de Neige, Chou-Chou, Miguet de Nuit and Naissance de Jour."

"Really," I said. "How did you happen to pick a place like this—way off in the woods—for your experiments?"

"Well, it isn't as out of the way as it seems. I have a garden and I grow my own thyme, lavender, iris, roses, mint, wintergreen, celery and parsley. I buy my lemons and oranges in Blenville and Charlie Hubber, who lives at the four corners, traps beaver and muskrat for me. I find their castors as lasting as civet and I get them for a fraction of the market price. I buy gum resin, methyl salicylate and benzaldehyde. Flower perfumes are not my forte, since they have very limited aphrodisiac powers. The principal ingredient of Chou-Chou is cedar bark and parsley and celery go into Naissance de Jour."

"Did you study chemistry?"

"No. I learned my profession as an apprentice. I think of it more as alchemy than as chemistry. Alchemy is, of course, the transmutation of base metals into noble ones and when an extract of beaver musk, cedar bark, heliotrope, celery and gum resin can arouse immortal longings in a male, we are close to alchemy, wouldn't you say?"

"I know what you mean," I said.

"The concept of man as a microcosm, containing within himself all the parts of the universe, is Pythagorean. The elements are constant. The distillations and transmutations release their innate power. This not only works in the manufacture of perfume; I think these transmutations can work in the development of character."

A young woman then came into the room. "This is my granddaughter Gloria," he said. "Gloria takes care of me. Gloria, this is Mr.—"

"Hammer," I said. "Paul Hammer."

"How do you do," she said. She lighted a cigarette and said: "Nineteen."

"How many yesterday?" the old man asked.

"Twenty-two." She frowned, then brightened. "It was only fifteen the day before. What do you want for supper?"

"Oh, some sort of meat," he said. "A chop."

The grace with which she moved seemed so accomplished that I wondered if she hadn't had some theatrical training or some theatrical ambitions. I don't mean that she moved like a dancer. I don't like the way serious dancers move. They have a toe-heel, toe-heel way of progressing that gives me the creeps. I mean she moved with the grace of an actress—nothing spectacular—an ingénue in the national company of Figs & Thistles. Six weeks in Chicago. Her hair was yellow and naturally so, I guess, although it's hard to tell, now that they've got the bugs out of hair dye. Her hair was short and straight, with two modest pieces of hardware on either side, which were meant, I suppose, to produce spit curls for the evening. Teeth have never played any discernible part in my romantic or erotic life, and yet her teeth filled me with tenderness. They were very small and set apart. I don't mean there were gaps, but you could see where they were divided. They stirred me like music. Her mouth was small and very pretty, but what I remember most about her then was her brightness, her fairness; she seemed as she moved her arms and legs to generate luminousness, although when I got to know her better, I discovered that she was not especially fair-skinned and that her face, when she was disturbed, provoked or amorous, could seem quite dark and opaque. Her eyes were blue and very bright. The effect of beautiful women on me is first to make my knees weak and then to give me the feeling that their coloring and features—all their charms—form a kind of liquid in which I swim like a goldfish in a bowl. I seemed to lose my head while she talked with the old man about the groceries. I was really swimming. This sensation, powerful in any case, was heightened by the heavy air of the kitchen.

"Well, I'll get some chops, then," she said. "I'll get some lamb chops and something for a salad."

"Where do you do your shopping?" I asked.

"I go to the UP Supermarket in Readwell," she said. "It was nice to have met you." She took the hardware out of her hair, gave her hair a shake and went out the door.

"Well, I'll leave Schwartz with you," I said to the old man. "Goodbye, Schwartz," I said to the cat. "Come home whenever you feel like it."

I walked and ran and walked through the snowy woods to my house, got my car, drove to Readwell and parked at the supermarket. I found her picking over salad greens. "Gloria," I said, and I held out my arms. She stepped, one, two, three, into my embrace. Her kiss was light and dry and she pressed lightly against me those parts of her that meant she was serious. I took her hand and led her toward the door. "But I have to get the chops for Grandpa," she said insincerely.

She came along with me to my car, where I kissed her several times, but people going to and from the market could see us there. Readwell is a small town and you might think it easy to find some privacy there, but it wasn't easy. First I drove over the hill by the wireworks, but there was lots of traffic there. Then I went up Chilton Avenue past Main Street, heading for the Roman Catholic cemetery, and got stuck in the middle of a funeral procession. The road was narrow and I had to stay in line until we got past the cemetery gates. From there I went down Chilton Lane, where the houses are set far apart but not far enough apart to afford any privacy. I stopped the car, anyhow, and gathered her up in my arms. "We can't do it here," she said. "Everybody can see us. We'll get arrested." I started the car again, turned right on Townsend Road and left on Shinglehouse Lane, but there was a development there. Then I turned onto 114, took the Eastlake exit and parked in the driveway of what seemed to be an empty house. I won't go into the anatomical details, which were complicated by the fact that my car is a two-seater Jaguar with a stick shift. I then drove her back to the supermarket to get Grandfather's chops and she promised to come to my house at five.

So that's the way it is. Beginning with a *cafard,* I ended up with a girl, a part-time mouser and my yellow walls. It's spring now and I wake early, swim in the pool, eat a large breakfast and settle down to my translation at a table in the yellow room. I work happily until one or sometimes later, when I eat a bowl of soup. I've bought some tools—an ax, chain saw, and so forth, and spend the afternoons clearing the woods around the house. She comes every day at five to make the rain fall, scatter the ghosts and mend the wreath of hair. What a kingdom it is! After supper I study German until half-past ten, when I go to bed, feeling limber, clean and weary. I no longer have any need for the mountain, the valley and the fortified city, and if I dream at all, my dreams are of an exceptional innocence and purity.

John Updike

I Am Dying, Egypt, Dying

September 1969

There is no question that John Updike, the fourth *New Yorker* writer presented here (Shirley Jackson, like Thurber and Cheever, wrote mainly for that magazine), occasionally preferred a more relaxed sexual atmosphere for his stories than the magazine would tolerate in the 1960s and 1970s. Thus Updike's stylish stories and excerpts from some of his major novels—*The Witches of Eastwick, Rabbit Is Rich*—have been appearing in *Playboy* for nearly a quarter-century. Updike, together with Joyce Carol Oates, is the most prolific literary figure in America today—a critic, essayist, poet, playwright, and children's book author as well as a novelist; it may come as a surprise to know that he originally aspired to be a cartoonist. Updike was born in Pennsylvania in 1932 and set the four Rabbit novels in that state, but he has long lived in New England and, like Cheever, is associated with the region. Many of his *Playboy* stories, from this first one to the most recent, are set abroad, though this seems to be no more than coincidence. Updike won the National Book Award in 1963 for *The Centaur,* pulled off publishing's triple crown in 1981 with *Rabbit Is Rich,* which won the National Book Critics Circle award, the American Book Award, and the Pulitzer, then was awarded a second Pulitzer in 1990 with *Rabbit at Rest.*

John Updike

I Am Dying, Egypt, Dying

Clem came from Buffalo and spoke in the neutral American accent that sends dictionary makers there. His pronunciation was clear and colorless, his manners impeccable, his clothes freshly laundered and appropriate no matter where he was, however far from home. Rich and unmarried, he traveled a lot; he had been to Athens and Rio, Las Vegas and Hong Kong, Leningrad and Sydney and now Cairo. His posture was perfect, but he walked without swing; people at first liked him, because his apparent perfection reflected flatteringly upon them, and then distrusted him, because his perfection revealed no flaw. As he traveled, he studied the guidebooks conscientiously, picked up phrases of the local language, collected prints and artifacts. He was serious but not humorless; indeed, his smile, a creeping but finally complete revelation of utterly even and white front teeth, with a bit of tongue flirtatiously pinched between them, was one of the things that led people on, that led them to hope for the flaw, the entering crack. There were hopeful signs. At the bar he took one drink too many, the hurried last drink that robs the dinner wine of taste. Though he enjoyed human society, he couldn't dance. He had a fine fair square-shouldered body, surely masculine and yet somehow neutral, which he solicitously covered with oil against the sun that, as they moved up the Nile, grew sharper and more tropical. He fell asleep in deck chairs, beautifully immobile, glistening, as the two riverbanks at their safe distance glided by—date palms, taut green fields irrigated by rotating donkeys, pyramids of white round pots, trapezoidal houses of elephant-colored mud, mud-colored children silently waving, and the roseate desert cliffs beyond, massive parentheses. Glistening like a mirror, he slept in this gliding parenthesis with a godlike calm that possessed the landscape, transformed it into a steady dreaming. Clem said of himself, awaking, apologizing, smiling with that bit of pinched tongue, that he slept badly at night, suffered from insomnia. This also was a hopeful sign. People wanted to love him.

There were not many on the boat. The war discouraged tourists. Indeed, at Nag Hammadi they did pass under a bridge in which Israeli commandos had blasted three neat but not very conclusive holes; a wooden ramp had been laid on top and the traffic of carts and rickety lorries continued. And at Aswan they saw antiaircraft batteries defending the High Dam. But for the cruise between, the war figured only as a luxurious amount of space on deck and a pleasant disproportion between the seventy crewmen and the twenty paying passengers. These twenty were:

Three English couples, middle-aged but for one miniskirted wife, who was thought for days to be a daughter.

Two German boys; they wore bathing trunks to all the temples, yet seemed to know the gods by name and perhaps were future archaeologists.

A French couple, in their sixties. The man had been tortured in World War Two; his spine had fused in a curve as he moved over the desert rubble and uneven stairways with tiny shuffling steps and studied the murals by means of a mirror hung around his neck. Yet he, too, knew the gods and would murmur worshipfully.

Three Egyptians, a man and two women, in their thirties, of a professional class, teachers or museum curators, cosmopolitan and handsome, given to laughter among themselves, even while the guide, a cherubic old Bedouin called Poppa Omar, was lecturing.

A fluffy and sweet, ample and perfumed American widow and her escort, a short bald native of New Jersey who for twenty years had run tours in Africa, armed with a fancy fly whisk and an impenetrable rudeness toward natives of Africa.

An amateur travelogist from Green Bay working his way south to Cape Town with two hundred pounds of photographic equipment.

A stocky blond couple, fortyish, who kept to themselves, hired their own guides and were presumed to be Russian.

A young Scandinavian woman, beautiful, alone.

Clem.

Clem had joined the cruise at the last minute; he had been in Amsterdam and become oppressed by the low sky and tight-packed houses, the cold canal touring boats and the bad Indonesian food and the prostitutes illuminated in their windows like garish great candy. He had flown to Cairo and not liked it better. A cheeseburger in the Hilton offended him by being gamy. In the plaza outside, a man rustled up to him and asked if he had had any love last night. The city, with its incessant twinkle of car horns and furtive-eyed men in pajamas, seemed unusable, remote. The museum was full of sandbags. The heart of King Tut's treasure had been hidden in case of invasion; but his gold sarcophagus, feathered in lapis lazuli and carnelian, did touch Clem, with a whisper of death, of flight, of floating. A pamphlet in the Hilton advertised a six-day trip up the Nile, Luxor to Aswan, in a luxurious boat. It sounded passive and educational, which appealed to Clem; he had gone to college at the University of Rochester and felt a need to keep rounding off his education, to bring it up to Ivy League standards. Also, the tan would look great back in Buffalo.

Stepping from the plane at the Luxor airport, he was smitten by the beauty of the desert roseate and motionless around him. His element, perhaps. What was his traveling, his bachelorhood, but a search for his element? He was thirty-four and still seemed to be merely visiting the world. Even in Buffalo, walking the straight shaded streets where he had played as a small boy, entering the homes and restaurants where he was greeted by name, sitting in the two-room office where he put in a few hours of telephoning that managed the parcel of securities and property fallen to him from his father's death, he felt somehow light, limited to forty-four pounds of luggage, dressed with the unnatural correctitude people assume at the outset of a trip. A puff of air off Lake Erie and he would be gone, and the city, with its savage blustery winters, its deepset granite mansions, its factories, its iron bison in the railroad terminal, would not have noticed. He would leave only his name in gilt paint on a list of singles tennis champions above the bar of his country club. But he knew he had been a methodical joyless player to watch, too full of lessons to lose.

He knew a lot about himself: He knew that this lightness, the brittle unmarred something he carried, was his treasure, which his demon willed him to preserve. Stepping from the airplane at Luxor, he had greeted his demon in the air—air ideally clean, with the poise of a mirror. From the window of his cabin he sensed again, in the glittering width of the Nile, bluer than he had expected, and in the unflecked alkaline sky, and in the tapestry strip of labored green between them, that he would be happy for this trip. He liked sunning on the deck that first afternoon. Only the Scandinavian girl, in an orange bikini, kept him company. Both were silent. The boat was still tied up at the Luxor dock, a flight of stone steps; a few yards away, across a gulf of water and paved banking, a traffic of peddlers and cart drivers stared across. Clem liked that gulf and liked it when the boat cast loose and began gliding between the fields, the villages, the desert. He liked the first temples: gargantuan Karnak, its pillars upholding the bright blank sky; gentler Luxor, with its built-in mosque and its little naked queen touching her king's giant calf; Hollywoodish Dendera—its restored roofs had brought in darkness and dampness and bats that moved on the walls like intelligent black gloves.

Clem even, at first, liked the peddlers. Tourist-starved, they touched him in their hunger, thrusting scarabs and old coins and clay mummy dolls at him, moaning and grunting English: "How much? How much you give me? Very fine. Fifty. Both. Take both. Both for thirty-five." Clem peeked down, caught his eye on a turquoise glint and wavered; his mother liked keepsakes and he had friends in Buffalo who would be amused. Into this flaw, this tentative crack of interest, they stuffed more things, strange sullied objects salvaged from the desert, alabastar vases, necklaces of mummy heads. Their brown hands probed and rubbed; their faces looked stunned, unblinking, as if, under the glaring sun, they were conducting business in the dark. Indeed, some did have eyes whitened by trachoma. Hoping to placate them with a purchase, Clem bargained for the smallest thing he could see, a lapis-lazuli bug the size of a fingernail. "Ten, ten," the old peddler said, irritably making the "give me" gesture with his palm. Holding his wallet high, away from their hands, Clem leafed through the big notes for the absurdly small five-piaster bills, tattered and silky with use. The purchase, amounting to little more than a dime, excited the peddlers: ignoring the other tourists, they multiplied and crowded against him. Something warm and hard was inserted into his hand, his other sleeve was plucked, his pockets were patted and he wheeled, his tongue pinched between his teeth flirtatiously, trapped. It was a nightmare; the dream thought crossed his mind that he might be scratched.

He broke away and rejoined the other tourists in the sanctum of a temple courtyard. One of the Egyptian women came up to him and said, "I do not mean to remonstrate, but you are torturing them by letting them see all those fifties and hundreds in your wallet."

"I'm sorry." He blushed like a scolded schoolboy. "I just didn't want to be rude."

"You must be. There is no question of hurt feelings. You are the man in the moon to them. They have no comprehension of your charm."

The strange phrasing of her last sentence, expressing not quite what she meant, restored his edge and dulled her rebuke. She was the shorter and the older of the two Egyptian women; her eyes were green and there was an earnest mischief, a slight pressure, in her upward glance. Clem relaxed, almost slouching. "The sad part is, some of their things, I'd rather like to buy."

"Then do," she said, and walked away, her hips swinging. So a move had been made. He had expected it to come from the Scandinavian girl.

▪ ▪ ▪

That evening the Egyptian trio invited him to their table in the bar. The green-eyed woman said, "I hope I was not scolding. I did not mean to remonstrate, merely to tell."

"Of course," Clem said. "Listen. I was being plucked to death. I needed rescuing."

"Those men," the Egyptian man said, "are in a bad way. They say that around the hotels the shoeshine boys are starving." His face was triangular, pockmarked, saturnine. A heavy weary courtesy slowed his speech.

"What did you buy?" the other woman asked. She was sallower than the other, and softer. Her English was the most British-accented.

Clem showed them. "Ah," the man said, "a scarab."

"The incarnation of Khepri," the green-eyed woman said. "The symbol of immortality. You will live forever." She smiled at everything she said; he remembered her smiling with the word "remonstrate."

"They're jolly things," the other woman pronounced, in her stately way. "Dung beetles. They roll a ball of dung along ahead of them, which appealed to the ancient Egyptians. Reminded them of themselves, I suppose."

"Life is that," the man said. "A ball of dung we push along."

The waiter came and Clem said, "Another whiskey sour. And another round of whatever they're having." Beer for the man, Scotch for the taller lady, lemonade for his first friend.

Having bought, he felt, the right to some education, Clem asked, "Seriously. Has the"—he couldn't bring himself to call it a war, and he had noticed that in Egypt the word Israeli was never pronounced—"trouble cut down on tourism?"

"Oh, immensely," the taller lady said. "Before the war, one had to book for this boat months ahead. Now, my husband was granted two weeks and we were able to come at the last moment. It is pathetic."

"What do you do?" Clem asked.

The man made a self-deprecatory and evasive gesture, as a deity might have, asked for employment papers.

"My brother," the green-eyed woman stated, smiling, "works for the government. In, what do you call it, planning?"

As if in apology for having been reticent, her brother abruptly said, "The shoeshine boys and the dragomen suffer for us all. In everyone in my country, you have now a deep distress."

"I noticed," Clem said, very carefully, "those holes in the bridge we passed under."

"They brought *jeeps* in, jeeps. By helicopter. The papers said bombs from a plane, but it was jeeps by helicopters from the Red Sea. They drove onto the bridge, set the charges and drove away. We are not warriors. We are farmers. For thousands of years now, we have had others do our fighting for us—Sudanese, Libyans, Arabs. We are not Arabs. We are Egyptians. The Syrians and Jordanians, they are Arabs. But we, we don't know who we are, except we are very old. The man who seeks to make warriors of us creates distress."

His wife put her hand on his to silence him while the waiter brought the drinks. His sister said to Clem, "Are you enjoying our temples?"

"Quite." But the temples within him, giant slices of limestone and sun, lay mute. "I also quite like," he went on, "our guide. I admire the way he says everything in English to some of us and then in French to the rest."

"Most Egyptians are trilingual," the wife stated. "Arabic, English, French."

"Which do you think in?" Clem was concerned, for he was conscious in himself of an absence of verbal thoughts; instead, there were merely glints and reflections.

The sister smiled. "In English, the thoughts are clearest. French is better for passion."

"And Arabic?"

"Also for passion. Is it not so, Amina?"

"What so, Leila?" She had been murmuring with her husband.

The question was restated in French.

"Oh, *c'est vrai, vrai.*"

"How strange," Clem said. "English doesn't seem precise to me; quite the contrary. It's a mess of synonyms and lazy grammar."

"No," the wife said firmly—she never, he suddenly noticed, smiled—"English is clear and cold, but not *nuancé* in the emotions, as is French."

"And is Arabic *nuancé* in the same way?"

The green-eyed sister considered. "More *angoisse.*"

Her brother said, "We have ninety-nine words for camel dung. All different states of camel dung. Camel dung, we understand."

"Of course," Leila said to Clem, "Arabic here is nothing compared with the pure Arabic you would hear among the Saudis. The language of the Koran is so much more—can I say it?—gutsy. So guttural, nasal; strange, wonderful sounds. Amina, does it still affect you inwardly, to hear it chanted? The Koran."

Amina solemnly agreed, "It is terrible. It tears me all apart. It is too much passion."

Italian rock music had entered the bar via an unseen radio and one of the middle-aged English couples was trying to waltz to it. Noticing how intently Clem watched, the sister asked him, "Do you like to dance?"

He took it as an invitation: he blushed. "No, thanks, the fact is I can't."

"Can't dance? Not at all?"

"I've never been able to learn. My mother says I have Methodist feet."

"Your mother says that?" She laughed: a short shocking noise, the bark of a fox. She called to Amina, *"Sa mère dit que l'Américain a les pieds méthodistes!"*

"Les pieds méthodiques?"

"Non, non, aucune méthode, la secte chrétienne—méthodisme!"

Both barked, and the man grunted. Clem sat there rigidly, immaculate in his embarrassment. The girl's green eyes, curious, pressed on him like gems scratching glass. The three Egyptians became overanimated, beginning sentences in one language and ending in another, and Clem understood that he was being laughed at. Yet the sensation, like the blurred plucking of the scarab salesmen, was better than untouched emptiness. He had another drink before dinner, the drink that was one too many, and when he went in to his single table, everything—the tablecloths, the little red lamps, the waiting droves of waiters in blue, the black windows beyond which the Nile glided—looked triumphant and glazed.

▪ ▪ ▪

He slept badly. There were bumps and scraping above him, footsteps in the hall, the rumble of the motors and, at four o'clock, the sounds of docking at another temple site. Once, he had found peace in hotel rooms, strange virgin corners where his mind could curl into itself, cut off from all nagging familiarities, and painlessly wink out. But he had known too many hotel rooms, so they had become themselves familiar, with their excessively crisp sheets and boastful plumbing and easy chairs one never sat in but used as clothes racks. Only the pillows varied—neck-cracking fat bolsters in Leningrad, in Amsterdam hard little wads the size of a lady's purse, and as lumpy. Here on the floating hotel Osiris, two bulky pillows were provided and, toward morning, Clem discovered it relaxed him to put his head on one and his arms around the other. Some other weight in the bed seemed to be the balance his agitated body, oscillating with hieroglyphs and sharp remonstrative glances, was craving. In his dream, the Egyptian woman promised him something marvelous and showed him two tall limestone columns with blue sky between them. He awoke unrefreshed but conscious of having dreamed. On his ceiling there was a dance of light, puzzling in its telegraphic rapidity, more like electronic art than anything natural. He analyzed it as sunlight bouncing off the tremulous Nile through the slats of his Venetian blinds. He pulled the blinds and there it was again, stunning in its clarity: the blue river, the green strip, the pink cliffs, the unflecked sky. Only the village had changed. The other tourists—the Frenchman being slowly steered, like a fragile cart, by an Arab boy—were already heading up a flight of wooden stairs toward a bus. Clem ran after them, into the broad day, without shaving.

Their guide, Poppa Omar, sat them down in the sun in a temple courtyard and told them the story of Queen Hatshepsut. "Remember it like this," he said, touching his head and rubbing his chest. "Hat—cheap—suit. She was wonderful woman here. Always building the temples, always winning the war and getting the nigger to be slaves. She marry her brother Tuthmosis and he grow tired here of jealous and insultation. He say to her, 'OK, you done a lot for Egypt, take it more easy now.' She say to him, 'No, I think I just keep rolling along.' What happen? Tuthmosis die. The new king also Tuthmosis, her niece. He is a little boy. Hatshepsut show herself in all big statues wearing false beard and all flatness here." He rubbed his chest. "Tuthmosis get bigger and go say to her now, 'Too much jealous and insultation. Take it easy for Egypt now.' She say, 'No.' Then she die, and all over Egypt here, he take all her statue and smash, hit, hit, so not one face of Hatshepsut left and everywhere her name in all the walls here, become Tuthmosis!" Clem looked around, and the statues had, indeed, been mutilated, thousands of years ago. He touched his own face and the whiskers scratched.

On the way back in the bus, the Green Bay travelogist asked them to the top so he could photograph a water wheel. A tiny child met them, weeping, on the path, holding one arm as if crippled. "Baksheesh, baksheesh," he said. "Musha, musha." One of the British men flicked at him with a whisk. The bald American announced aloud that the child was faking. Clem reached into his pocket for a piaster coin, but then remembered himself as a torturer. Seeing his gesture, the child, and six others, chased after him. First they shouted, then they tossed pebbles at his heels. From within the haven of the bus, the tourists could all see the child's arm unbend. But the weeping continued and was evidently real. The travelogist was still doing the water wheel and the peddlers began to pry open the window and thrust in scarabs, dolls, alabaster vases not without beauty. The window beside Clem's face slid back and a brown hand insinuated an irregular parcel about six inches long, wrapped in brown cloth. "Feesh mummy," a disembodied voice said, and to Clem it seemed hysterically funny. He couldn't stop laughing; the tip of his tongue began to hurt from being bitten. The Scandinavian girl, across the aisle, glanced at him hopefully. Perhaps the crack in his glaze was appearing.

Back on the Osiris, they basked in deck chairs. The white boat had detached itself from the brown land and men in blue brought them lemonade, daiquiris, salty peanuts called *soudani*. Though Clem, luminous with suntan oil, appeared to be asleep, his lips moved in answer to Ingrid beside him. Her bikini was chartreuse today. "In my country," she said, "the summers are so short, naturally we take off our clothes. But it is absurd, this myth other countries have of our paganism, our happy sex. We are a harsh people. My father, he was like a man in the Bergman films. I was forbidden everything growing up—to play cards, lipstick, to dance."

"I never did learn to dance," Clem said, slightly shifting.

"Yes," she said, "I saw in you, too, a stern childhood. In a place of harsh winters."

"We had two yards of snow the other year," Clem told her. "In one storm. Two *yards.*"

"And yet," Ingrid said, "I think the thaw, when at last it comes in such places, is so dramatic, so intense." She glanced toward him hopefully.

Clem appeared oblivious within his gleaming placenta of suntan oil.

The German boy who spoke a little English was on the other side of him. By now, the third day, the sun bathers had declared themselves: Clem, Ingrid, the two young Germans, the bald-headed American, the young English wife, whose skirted bathing suits were more demure than her ordinary dresses. The rest of the British sat on the deck in the shade of the canopy and drank; the three Egyptians sat in the lounge and talked: the supposed Russians kept out of sight altogether. The travelogist was talking to the purser about the immense chain of tickets and reservations that would get him to Cape Town; the widow was in her cabin with Egyptian stomach and a burning passion to play bridge; the French couple sat by the rail, in the sun but fully dressed, reading guidebooks, his chair tipped back precariously, so he could see the gliding landscape.

The German boy asked Clem, "Haff you bot a caftan?"

He had been nearly asleep, beneath a light, transparent headache. He said, *"Bitte?"*

"*Ein* caftan. You shoot. In Luxor: go back tonight. He will measure you and haff it by morning ven ve go. Sey are good—wery cheap."

Hatcheapsuit, Clem thought, but granted that he might do it. His frozen poise contended within him with something promiscuous and American, that must go forth and test, and purchase. He felt, having spurned so many scarabs and alabaster vases, he owed Egypt some of the large-leafed money that fattened his wallet uncomfortably.

"It vood be wery handsome on you."

"Ravishing," the young English wife said behind them. She had been listening. Clem sometimes felt like a mirror that everyone glanced into before moving on.

"You're all kidding me," he announced. "But I confess, I'm a sucker for costumes."

"Again," Ingrid said, "like a Bergman film." And languorously she shifted her long arms and legs; the impression of flesh in the side of his vision disturbingly merged, in his sleepless state, with a floating sensation of hollowness, of being in parentheses.

That afternoon they toured the necropolis in the Valley of the Kings. King Tut's small two-chambered tomb; how had they crammed so much treasure in? The immense tunnels of Ramses III; or was it Ramses IV? Passageways hollowed from the limestone chip by chip, lit by systems of tilted mirrors, painted with festive stiff figures banqueting, fishing, carrying offerings of fruit forward, which was always slightly down, down past pits dug to entrap grave robbers, past vast false chambers, toward the real and final one, a square room that would have made a nice night club. Its murals had been left unfinished, sketched in gray ink but uncolored. The tremors of the artist's hand, his nervous strokes, were still there. Abdul, the Egyptian planner, murmured to him, "Always they left something unfinished; it is a part of their religion no one understands. It is thought perhaps they dreaded finishing, as closing in the dead, limiting the life beyond." They climbed up the long slanting passageway, threaded with electric lights, past hundreds of immaculate bodies carried without swing. "The dead, you see, are not dead. In their language, the word for death and the word for life are the same. The death they feared was the second one, the one that would come if the tomb lacked provisions for life. In the tombs of the nobles, more than here, the scenes of life are all about, like a musical—you say score?—that only the dead have the instrument to play. These hieroglyphs are all instructions to the dead man, how to behave, how to make the safe journey."

"Good planning," Clem said, short of breath.

Abdul was slow to see the joke, since it was on himself.

"I mean the dead are much better planned for than the living."

"No," Abdul said flatly, perhaps misunderstanding. "It is the same."

Back in Luxor, Clem left the safe boat and walked toward the clothing shop, following the German boy's directions. He seemed to walk a long way. The narrowing streets grew shadowy. Pedestrians drifted by him in a steady procession, carrying offerings forward. No peddlers approached him; perhaps they kept businessmen's hours, went home and totaled up the sold scarabs and fish mummies in impeccable lined ledgers. Radio Cairo blared and twanged from wooden balconies. Dusty intersections flooded with propaganda (or was it prayer?) and faded behind him. The air was dark by the time he reached the shop. Within its little cavern of brightness, a young woman was helping a small child with homework, and a young man, the husband and father, lounged against some stacked bolts of cloth. All three persons were petite; Egyptian children, Clem had noticed before, are proportioned like miniature adults, with somber staring dolls' heads. He felt oversize in this shop, whose reduced scale was here and there betrayed by a coarse object from the real world—a steam press, the inflated pastel of Nasser on the wall. Clem's voice, asking if they could make a caftan for him by morning, seemed to boom; as he tuned it down, it cracked and trembled. Measuring him, the small man touched him all over; and touches that at first had been excused as accidental declared themselves as purposeful, determined.

"Hey," Clem said, blushing.

Shielded from his wife by the rectangular bulk of Clem's body, the young man, undoing his own fly with a swift light tailor's gesture, exhibited himself. "I can make you very happy," he muttered.

"I'm leaving," Clem said.

He was at the doorway instantly, but the tailor had time to call, "Sir, when will you come back tomorrow?" Clem turned; the little man was zipped, the woman and child had their heads bent together over the homework. Nasser, a lurid ocher, scowled toward the future. Clem had intended to abandon the caftan but pictured himself back in Buffalo, wearing it to New Year's Eve at the club, with sunglasses and sandals. The tailor looked frightened. His little mustache twitched uncertainly and his brown eyes had been worn soft by worry and needlework.

Clem said he would be back no later than nine. The boat sailed south after breakfast. Outside, the dry air had chilled. From the tingling at the tip of his tongue, he realized he had been smiling hard.

▪ ▪ ▪

Ingrid was sitting at the bar in a backwards silver dress, high in the front and buckled at the back. She invited herself to sit at his table during dinner; her white arms, pinched pink by the sun, shared in the triumphant glaze of the tablecloth, the glowing red lamp. They discussed religion. Clem had been raised as a Presbyterian, she as a Lutheran. In her father's house, north of Stockholm, there had been a guest room held ready against the arrival of Jesus Christ. Not quite seriously, it had been a custom, and yet . . . she supposed religion had bred into her a certain *expectancy.* Into him, he thought, groping, peering with difficulty into that glittering blank area, which in other people, he imagined, was the cave of life, religion had bred a *dislike of litter*. It was a disappointing answer, even after he had explained the word litter. He advanced in its place the theory that he was a royal tomb, once crammed with treasure, that had been robbed. Her white hand moved an inch toward him on the tablecloth, intelligent as a bat, and he began to cry. The tears felt genuine to him, but she said, "Stop acting."

He told her that a distressing thing had just happened to him.

She said, "That is your flaw; you are too self-conscious. You are always in costume, acting. You must always be beautiful." She was so intent on delivering this sermon that only as an afterthought did she ask him what had been the distressing thing.

He found he couldn't tell her; it was too intimate, and his own part in provoking it had been, he felt, unspeakably shameful. The tailor's homosexual advance had been, like the child's feigning a crippled arm, evoked by his money, his torturing innocence. He said, "Nothing. I've been sleeping badly and don't make sense. Ingrid: Have some more wine." His palms were sweating from the effort of pronouncing her name.

After dinner, though fatigue was making his entire body shudder and itch, she asked him to take her into the lounge, where a three-piece band from Alexandria was playing dance music. The English couples waltzed and Gwenn, the young wife, frugged with one of the German boys. The green-eyed Egyptian woman danced with the purser. Egon, the German boy who knew some English, came and, with a curt bow and a curious hard stare at Clem, invited Ingrid. She danced, Clem observed, very close, in the manner of one who, puritanically raised, thinks of it only as a substitute for intercourse. After many numbers, she was returned to him unmarred, still silver, cool and faintly admonitory. Downstairs, in the corridor where their cabin doors were a few steps apart, she asked him, her expression watchful and stern, if he would sleep better tonight. Compared with her large eyes and long nose, her mouth was small; she pursed her lips in a thoughtful pout, holding as if in readiness a small slot of dark space between them.

He realized that her face was stern because he was a mirror in which she was gauging her beauty, her power. His smile sought to reassure her. "Yes," he said, "I'm sure I will, I'm dead."

And he did fall asleep quickly, but woke in the dark, to escape a dream in which the hieroglyphs and Pharaonic cartouches had left the incised walls and inverted and become stamps, sharp-edged stamps trying to indent themselves upon him. Awake, he identified the dream blows with the thumping of feet and furniture overhead. But he could not sink back into sleep; there was a scuttling, an occasional whispering in the corridor that he felt was coming toward him, toward his door. But once, when he opened his door, there was nothing in the corridor but bright light and several pairs of shoes. The problem of the morning prevented him from sinking back. If he went to pick up his caftan, it would seem to the tailor a submission. He would be misunderstood and vulnerable. Also, there was the danger of missing the boat. Yet the caftan would be lovely to have, a shimmering striped polished cotton, with a cartouche containing Clem's monogram in silver thread. In his agitation, his desire not to make a mistake, he could not achieve peace with his pillows; and then the telegraphic staccato of sunlight appeared on his ceiling and Egypt, that green thread through the desert, was taut and bright beyond his blinds. Leaving breakfast, lightheaded, he impulsively approached the bald American on the stairs. "I beg your pardon; this is rather silly, but could you do me an immense favor?"

"Like what?"

"Just walk with me up to this shop where something I ordered should be waiting. Uh . . . it's embarrassing to explain."

'The boat's pulling out in half an hour."

"I know. It wouldn't leave if two of us were missing."

The man sized Clem up—his clean shirt, his square shoulders, his open hopeful face—and grunted. "OK. I left my whisk in the cabin, I'll see you outside."

"Gee, I'm very grateful, uh—"

"Walt's the name."

Ingrid, coming up the stairs late to breakfast, had overheard. "May I come, too, on this expedition that is so dangerous?"

"No, it's stupid," Clem told her. "Please eat your breakfast. I'll see you on the deck afterward."

Her face attempted last night's sternness, but she was puffy beneath her eyes from sleep, and he revised upward his estimate of her age. Like him, she was over thirty. How many men had she passed through to get here, alone; how many self-forgetful nights, traumatic mornings of separation, hung-over heartbroken afternoons? It was epic to imagine, her history of love: she loomed immense in his mind, a monumental statue, forbidding and foreign, even while under his nose she blinked, puckered her lips and went into breakfast, rejected.

On the walk to the shop, Clem tried to explain what had happened the evening before. Walt impatiently interrupted. "They're scum," he said. "They'll sell their mother for twenty piasters." His accent still had nasal Newark in it. A boy ran shyly beside them, offering them *soudani* from a bowl. "Amscray," Walt said, brandishing his whisk.

"Is very good," the boy said.

"You make me puke," Walt told him.

The woman and the boy doing homework were gone from the shop. Unlit, it looked dingy; Nasser's glass was cracked. The tailor sprang up when they entered, pleased and relieved. "I work all night," he said.

"Like hell you did," Walt said.

"Try on?" the tailor asked Clem.

In the flecked dim mirror, Clem saw himself gowned; a shock, because the effect was not incongruous. He looked like a husky woman, a big-boned square-faced woman, quick to blush and giggle, the kind of naïve healthy woman, with money and without many secrets, that he tended to be attracted to. He had once loved such a girl, and she had snubbed him to marry a Harvard man. "It feels tight under the armpits," he said.

The tailor rapidly caressed and patted his sides. "That is its cut," he said.

"And the cartouche was supposed to be in silver thread."

"You said gold."

"I said silver."

"Don't take it," Walt advised.

"I work all night," the tailor said.

"And here," Clem said. "This isn't a pocket, it's just a slit."

"No, no, no pocket. Supposed to let the hand through. Here, I show." He put his hand in the slit and touched Clem until Clem protested, "Hey."

"I can make you very happy," the tailor murmured.

"Throw it back in his face," Walt said. "Tell him it's a god-awful mess."

"No," Clem said. "I'll take it. The fabric is lovely. If it turns out to be too tight, I can give it to my mother." He was sweating so hard that the garment became stuck as he tried to pull it over his head, and the tailor, assisting him, was an enveloping blur of caresses.

From within the darkness of cloth, Clem heard a slap and Walt's voice snarl, "Hands off, sonny." The subdued tailor swiftly wrapped the caftan in brown paper. As Clem paid, Walt said, "I wouldn't buy that rag. Throw it back in his face." Outside, as they hurried back toward the boat, through crowded streets where women clad in black mantles stepped aside, guarding their faces as if from evil eyes—a cloud of faces in which one or two hung with a startled, unpainted beauty—Walt said, "The little queer."

"I don't think it meant anything, it was just a nervous habit. But it scared me. Thanks a lot for coming along."

Walt asked him, "Ever try it with a man?"

"No. Good heavens."

Walt said, "It's not bad." He nudged Clem in walking and Clem shifted his parcel to that side, as a shield. All the way to the boat, Walt's conversation was anecdotal and obscene, describing a night he had had in Alexandria and another in Khartoum. Twice Clem had to halt and shift to Walt's other side, to keep from being nudged off the sidewalk. "It's not bad," Walt insisted. "It'd pleasantly surprise you." Back on the Osiris, Clem locked the cabin door while changing into his bathing suit. The engines shivered: the boat glided away from the Luxor quay. On deck, Ingrid asked him if his dangerous expedition had been successful. She had reverted to the orange bikini.

"I got the silly thing, yes. I don't know if I'll ever wear it."

"You must model it tonight; we are having Egyptian Night."

Her intonation saying this was firm with reserve. Her air of pique cruelly pressed upon him in his sleepless, sensitive, brittle state. Ingrid's lower lip jutted in profile; her pale eyes bulged beneath the spears of her lashes. He tried to placate her by describing the tailor shop—its enchanted smallness, the woman and child bent over schoolwork.

"It is a farce," Ingrid said, with a bruising positiveness, "their schooling. They teach the poor children the language of the Koran, which is difficult and useless. The literacy statistics are nonsense."

Swirls of Arabic, dipping like bird flight from knot to knot, wound through Clem's brain and gently tugged him downward into a softness where Ingrid's tan body stretching beside him merged with the tawny strip of desert gliding beyond the ship's railing. Lemonade was being served to kings around him. On the ceiling of one temple chamber that he had seen, the goddess Nut was swallowing the sun in one corner and giving birth to it in another, all out of the same body. A body was above him and words were crashing into him like stones. He opened his eyes; it was the American widow, a broad cloud of cloth eclipsing the sun, a perfumed mass of sweet-voiced anxiety resurrected from her cabin, crying out to him, "Young man, you *look* like a bridge player. We're *des*perate for a fourth!"

▪ ▪ ▪

The caftan pinched him under the arms; and then, later in Egyptian Night, after the meal, Ingrid danced with Egon and disappeared. To these discomforts the American widow and Walt added that of their company. Though Clem had declined her bridge invitation, his protective film had been broken and they had plunked themselves down around the little table where Clem and Ingrid were eating the buffet of *foule* and pilaf and *qualeema* and filafil and maamoule. To Clem's surprise, the food was to his taste—nutty, bland, dry. Then Ingrid was invited to dance and failed to return to the table, and the English couples, who had befriended the widow, descended in a cloud of conversation.

"This place was a hell of a lot more fun under Farouk," said one old man with a scoured red face.

"At least the poor *fellah,*" a woman perhaps his wife agreed, "had a little glamor and excitement to look up to."

"Now what does the poor devil have? A war he can't fight and Soviet slogans."

"They *hate* the Russians, of course. The average Egyptian, he loves a show of style, and the Russians don't have any. Not a crumb."

"The poor dears."

And they passed on to ponder the inability, mysterious but a thousand times proven, of Asiatics and Africans—excepting, of course, the Israelis and the Japanese—to govern themselves or, for that matter, to conduct the simplest business operation efficiently. Clem was too tired to talk and too preoccupied with the pressure chafing his armpits, but they all glanced to his face and found their opinions reflected there. In a sense, they deferred to him, for he was prosperous and young and as an American the inheritor of their colonial wisdom.

All had made attempts at native costume. Walt wore his pajamas, and the widow, in bed sheet and sunglasses and *kúfíyah,* did suggest a fat sheik, and Gwenn's husband had blacked his face with an ingenious paste of Bain de Soleil and instant coffee. Gwenn asked Clem to dance. Blushing, he declined, but she insisted. "There's nothing to it—you simply bash yourself about a bit," she said, and demonstrated.

She was dressed as a harem girl. For her top, she had torn the sleeves off one of her husband's shirts and left it unbuttoned, so that a strip of skin from the base of her throat to her navel was bare; she was not wearing a bra. Her pantaloons were less successful: yellow St. Tropez slacks pinned in loosely below the knees. A blue-gauze scarf across her nose—setting her hectic English cheeks and Twiggy eyes oddly afloat—and gold chains around her ankles completed the costume. The band played *Delilah.* As Clem watched Gwenn's feet, their shuffle, and the glitter of gold circlets, and the ten silver toenails, seemed to be rapidly writing something indecipherable. There was a quick half step she seemed unaware of, in counterpoint with her swaying head and snaking arms. "Why—oh—whyyy, De-liii-lah," the young Egyptian sang in a Liverpool whine. Clem braced his body, hoping the pumping music would take it. His feet felt sculpturally one with the floor; it was like what stuttering must be for the tongue. The sweat of incapacity fanned outward from the pain under his arms, but Gwenn obliviously rolled on, her pantaloons coming unpinned, her shirt loosening so that as she swung from side to side, one shadowy breast, and now the other, was exposed. She had shut her eyes, and in the haven of her blindness Clem did manage to dance a little, to shift his weight and jerk his arms, though he was able to do it only by forgetting the music. The band changed songs and rhythms without his noticing; he was conscious mostly of the skirt of his caftan swinging around him, of Gwenn's red cheeks turning and turning below sealed slashes of mascara, and of her husband's face. He had come onto the dance floor with the American widow; as the Bain de Soleil had sunk into his skin, the instant coffee had powdered his *gallabíyah.* At last the band took a break. Gwenn's husband claimed her, and the green-eyed Egyptian woman, as Clem passed her table, said remonstratingly, "You can dance."

"He is a dervish," Amina stated.

"All Americans are dervishes," Abdul sighed. "Their energy menaces the world."

"I am the world's worst dancer; I'm hopeless," Clem said.

"Then you should sit," Leila said. All three Egyptians were dressed, with disdainful chic, in Western dress. Clem ordered a renewal of their drinks and a brandy for himself.

"Tell me," he begged Abdul. "Do you think the Russians have no style?"

"It is true," Abdul said. "They are a very ugly people. Their clothes are very baggy. They are like us, Asiatic. They are not yet convinced that this world absolutely matters."

"Mon mari veut ètre un mystique," Amina said to Clem.

Clem persisted. Fatigue made him desperate and dogged. "But," he said, "I was surprised, in Cairo, even now, with our ambassador kicked out, how many Americans were standing around the lobby of the Hilton. And all the American movies."

"For a time," Amina said, "they tried films only from the Soviet Union and China, about farming progressively. The theater managers handed their keys in to the government and said, 'Here, you run them.' No one would come. So the Westerns came back."

"And this music," Clem said, "and your clothes."

"Oh, we love you," Abdul said, "but with our brains. You are like the stars, like the language of the Koran. We know we cannot be like that. There is a sullen place"—he moved his hand from his head to his stomach—"where the Russians make themselves at home. I speak in hope. There must be some compensation."

The waiter brought the drinks and Amina said "Shh" to her husband.

Leila said to Clem, "You have changed girlfriends tonight. You have many girlfriends."

He blushed. "None."

Leila said, "The big Swede, she danced very close with the German boy. Now they have both gone off."

"Into the Nile?" Amina asked. "Into the desert? How jolly romantic."

Abdul said slowly, as if bestowing comfort, "They are both Nordic. They are at home within each other. Like us and the Russians."

Leila seemed angry. Her green eyes burned and Clem feared they would seek to scratch his face. Instead, her ankle touched his beneath the table; he flinched. "They are both," she said, "ice—ize—? They hang down in winter."

"Icicles?" Clem offered.

She curtly nodded, annoyed at needing rescue. "I have never seen one," she said in self-defense.

"Your friends the British," Abdul said, indicating the noisy table where they were finger-painting on Gwenn's husband's face, "understood us in their fashion. They had read Shakespeare. It is very good, that play. How we turned our sails and ran. Our cleverness and courage are all female."

"I'm sure that's not so," Clem said, to rescue him.

Leila snapped, "Why should it not be so? All countries are women, except horrid Uncle Sam." And though he sat at their table another hour, her ankle did not touch his again.

Floating on three brandies, Clem at last left the lounge, his robe of polished cotton swinging around him. The Frenchman was tipped back precariously in a corner, watching the dancers. He lifted his mirror in salute as Clem passed. Though even the Frenchman's wife was dancing, Ingrid had not returned, and this added to Clem's lightness, his freedom from litter. Surely he would sleep. But when he lay down on his bed, it was trembling and jerking. His cabin adjoined that of the unsociable plump couple thought to be Russian. Clem's bed and one of theirs were separated by a thin partition. His shuddered as theirs heaved with a playful, erratic violence; there was a bump, a giggle, a hoarse male sibilance. Then the agitation settled toward silence and a distinct rhythm, a steady, mounting beat that put a pulsing into the bed taut under Clem. Two or three minutes of this. "Oh": the woman's exclamation was middle-pitched, totally curved, languageless; a man's guttural grunt came right on top of it. Clem's bed, in its abrupt stillness, seemed to float and spin under him. Then from beyond the partition some murmurs, a sprinkling of laughter and a resonant heave as one body left the bed. Soon, faint snoring. Clem had been robbed of the gift of sleep.

After shapeless hours of pillow wrestling, he went to the window and viewed the Nile gliding by, the constellations of village lights, the desert stars, smaller than he had expected. He wanted to open the window to smell the river and the desert, but it was sealed shut, in deference to the air conditioning. Clem remembered Ingrid and a cold silver rage, dense as an ingot, upright as an obelisk, filled his body. "You bitch," he said aloud and, by repeating those two words, over and over, leaving his mind no space to entertain any other images, he managed to wedge himself into a few hours' sleep, despite the tempting, problematical scuttle of presences in the hall, who now and then brushed his door with their fingernails. *You bitch, you bitch, you. . . .* He remembered nothing about his dreams, except that they all took place back in Buffalo, amid people he had thought he had forgotten.

▪ ▪ ▪

Temples. Dour dirty heavy Isna sunk in its great pit beside a city market where Clem, pestered by flies and peddlers, nearly vomited at the sight of ox palates, complete with arcs of teeth, hung up for sale. Vast sun-struck Idfu, an endless square spiral climb up steps worn into troughs toward a dizzying view, the amateur travelogist calmly grinding away on the unparapeted edge. Cheery little Kom Ombo, right by the Nile, whiter and later than the others. In one of them, dead Osiris was resurrected by a hawk alighting on his phallus: in another, Nut the sky god flowed above them nude, swimming amid gilt stars. A god was having a baby, baby Horus. Poppa Omar bent over and tenderly patted the limestone relief pitted and defaced by Coptic Christians. "See now here," he said, "the lady squat, and the other ladies hold her by the arms so, here, and the baby Horus, out he comes here. In villages all over Egypt now, the ladies there still have the babies in this manner, so we have too many the babies here." He looked up at them and smiled with ancient benevolence. His eyes, surprisingly, were pale blue.

The man from Wisconsin was grinding away, the man from New Jersey was switching his whisk, the widow was fainting in the shade, beside a sphinx. Clem helped the Frenchman inch his feet across some age-worn steps; he was like one of those toys that walks down an inclined ramp but easily topples. The English and Egyptians were bored; too many temples, too much Ramses. Ingrid detached herself from the German boys and came to Clem. "How did you sleep?"

"Horribly. And you?"

"Well. I thought," she added, "you would be soothed by my no longer trying to rape you."

At noon, in the sun, as the Osiris glided toward Aswan, she took her accustomed chair beside Clem. When Egon left the chair on the other side of him and clamorously swam in the pool, Clem asked her, "How is he?"

"He is very nice," she said, holding her bronze face immobile in the sun. "Very earnest, very naïve. He is a revolutionary."

"I'm glad," he said, "you've found someone congenial."

"Have I? He is very young. Perhaps I went with him to make another jealous." She added, expressionless, "Did it?"

"Yes."

"I am pleased to hear it."

In the evening, she was at the bar when he went up from an unsuccessful attempt at a nap. They had docked for the last time; the boat had ceased trembling. She had reverted to the silver dress that looked put on backward. He asked, "Where are the Germans?"

"They are with the Egyptians in the lounge. Shall we join them?"

"No," Clem said. Instead, they talked with the lanky man from Green Bay, who had ten months of advance tickets and reservations to Cape Town and back, including a homeward cabin on the Queen Elizabeth II. He spoke mostly to women's groups and high schools, and he detested the Packers. He said to Clem, "I take pride in being an eccentric, don't you?" and Clem was frightened to think that he appeared eccentric, he who had always been praised, even tested, by his mother as typically American, as even *too* normal and dependable. She sometimes implied that he had disappointed her by not defying her, by always returning from his trips.

After dinner, he and Ingrid walked in Aswan: a receding quay of benches, open shops burning a single light bulb, a swish of vehicles, mostly military. A true city, where the appetites did not beg. He had bought some postcards and let a boy shine his shoes. He paid the boy ten piasters, shielding his potent wallet with his body, like a grenade that might explode. They returned to the Osiris and sat in the lounge watching the others dance. A chaste circle around them forbade intrusion; or perhaps the others, having tried to enter Clem and failed, had turned away. Clem imagined them in the eyes of the others, both so composed and now so tan, two stately cool children of harsh winters. Apologizing, smiling, after three iced arracks, he bit his tongue and rose. "Forgive me, I'm dead. I must hit the hay. You stay and dance."

She shook her head, with a preoccupied stern gesture, gathered her dress tight about her hips and went with him. In the hall before his door, she stood and asked, "Don't you want me?"

A sudden numbness lifted from his stomach and made him feel unreally tall. "Yes," he said.

"Then why not take me?"

Clem looked within himself for the answer, saw only glints refracted and distorted by a deep fatigue. "I'm frightened to," he told her. "I have no faith in my right to take things."

Ingrid listened intently, as if his words were continuing, clarifying themselves; she looked at his face and nodded. Now that they had come so far together and were here, her gaze seemed soft, as soft and weary as the tailor's. "Go to your room," she said. "If you like, then, I will come to you."

"Please do." It was as simple as dancing—you simply bash yourself about a bit.

"Would you like me to?" She was stern now, could afford to be guarded.

"Yes. *Please* do."

He left the latch off, undressed, washed, brushed his teeth, shaved the second time that day, left the bathroom light on. The bed seemed immensely clean and taut, like a sail. Strange stripes, nonsense patterns, crossed his mind. The sail held taut, permitting a gliding, but with a tipping. The light in the cabin changed. The door had been opened and shut. She was still wearing the silver dress; he had imagined she would change. She sat on his bed; her weight was the counterweight he had been missing. He curled tighter, as if around a pillow, and an irresistible peace descended, distinctly, from the four corners of space, along forty-five-degree angles marked in charcoal. He opened his eyes, discovering thereby that they had been shut, and the sight of her back—the belling solidity of her bottom, the buckle of the backward belt, the scoop of cloth exposing the nape of blonde neck and the strong crescent of shoulder waiting to be touched—covered his eyes with silver scales. On one of the temple walls, one of the earlier ones, Poppa Omar had read off the hieroglyphs that spelled WOMAN IS PARADISE. The ship and its fittings were still and, confident she would not move, he postponed the beginning for one more second.

He awoke feeling rich, full of sleep. At breakfast, he met Ingrid by the glass dining-room doors and apologetically smiled, blushing and biting his tongue. "God, I'm sorry," he said. He added in self-defense, "I told you I was dead."

"It was charming," she said. "You gave yourself to me that way."

"How long did you sit there?"

"Perhaps an hour. I tried to insert myself into your dreams. Did you dream of me?" She was a shade shy, asking.

He remembered no dreams but did not say so. Her eyes were permanently soft now toward him; they had become windows through which he could admire himself. It did not occur to him that he might admire her in the same fashion; in the morning light, he saw clearly the traces of age on her face and throat, the little scars left by time and a presumed promiscuity, for which he, though not heavily, did blame her. His defect was that, though accustomed to reflect love, he could not originate light within himself; he was as blind as the silvered side of a mirror to the possibility that he, too, might impose a disproportionate glory upon the form of another. The world was his but slid through him.

In the morning, they went by felucca to Lord Kitchener's gardens, and the Aga Khan's tomb, where a single rose was fresh in a vase. The afternoon expedition, and their last, was to the Aswan High Dam. Cameras were forbidden. They saw the anti-aircraft batteries and the worried brown soldiers in their little wooden cartoon guardhouses. The desert became very ugly: no longer the rose shimmer that had surrounded him at the airport in Luxor, it was a merciless gray that had never entertained a hope of life, not even fine in texture but littered to the horizon with black flint. And the makeshift pitted roads were ugly, and the graceless Russian machinery clanking and sitting stalled, and the styleless, already squalid propaganda pavilion containing a model of the dam. The dam itself, after the straight, elegantly arched dam the British had built upriver, seemed a mere mountain of heaped rubble, hardly distinguishable from the inchoate desert itself. Yet at its heart, where the turbines had been set, a plume like a cloud of horses leaped upward in an inverted Niagara that dissolved, horse after horse, into mist before becoming the Nile again and flowing on. Startled greenery flourished on the gray cliffs that contained the giant plume. The stocky couple who had been impassive and furtive for six days now beamed and crowed aloud; the man roughly nudged Clem to wake him to the wonder of what they were seeing. Clem agreed: "*Khorosho*." He waited but was not nudged again. Gazing into the abyss of the trip that was over, he saw that—sparks struck and lost within a waterfall—he had been happy.

Joyce Carol Oates

Saul Bird Says: Relate! Communicate! Liberate!

October 1970

Sometimes it seems that one can hardly open a magazine, large or tiny, without finding a piece of writing—a story, poem, review, or essay, always worth reading—by Joyce Carol Oates. *Playboy* has published many stories, of which this was the first. Written at a time when universities, even in Canada (Oates was teaching there at the time), were adjusting to the turmoil of the 1960s, it focuses a wry mirror on the period. Oates has won most of the important American literary honors, including the National Book Award for *Them* (1969) and *Playboy*'s fiction award for this story. Born in 1938 in a small town near Buffalo in upstate New York, Oates frequently uses that landscape to create her own form of Hudson River Gothic; critics of her work sometimes shy at the violence and fear that often characterize it. She now lives in Princeton, where, in addition to her prolific literary output, she continues to teach. Among her most recent novels were *Because It Is Bitter, And Because It Is My Heart,* a finalist for the National Book Award in 1990, and *Black Water* in 1992.

Joyce Carol Oates

Saul Bird Says: Relate! Communicate! Liberate!

Wanda Barnett, born in 1945, received her bachelor's degree at Manhattanville College of the Sacred Heart in 1965, as class valedictorian, received a fellowship from the University of Michigan for graduate studies in English in the fall of that year and, in the spring of 1969, accepted a temporary lectureship at Hilberry University, a school in southern Ontario with an enrollment of about five thousand students. On September 9, 1969, she met Saul Bird; someone appeared in the doorway of her office at the university, rapping his knuckles loudly against the door. Wanda had been carrying a heavy box of books, which she set down at once.

"How do you do, my name is Saul Bird," he said. He shook hands briskly with her. His voice was wonderfully energetic; it filled the narrow room and bounced off the empty walls, surrounding her. Wanda introduced herself, still out of breath from carrying the books; she smiled shyly. She leaned forward attentively, listening to Saul Bird, trying to understand what he was saying. He talked theatrically, elegantly. His voice wound about her like fine ribbon. She found herself stooping slightly so that she might seem less obviously taller than he.

"What are your values? Your standards? Everything in you will be questioned, eroded here, every gesture of spontaneity—if you love teaching, if you love working with young people, you've certainly come to the wrong university. Are you a Canadian? Where are you from? Have you found an apartment? I can help you find one if you haven't."

"I have to look for an apartment today—"

"The economy is maniacal here. Are you a Canadian?"

"No, I'm from New York."

"Oh. New York." His voice went flat. He took time to light a cigarette and Wanda stared at him, bewildered. He had blond hair that was bunched and kinky about his face, like a cap; his face had looked young at first—the eyebrows that rose and fell dramatically, the expressive little mouth, the nose that twitched slightly with enthusiasm—but, really, it was the face of a forty-year-old, with fine, straight lines on the forehead and around the mouth. His complexion was both dark and pale—darkish pale, an olive hue, difficult to describe. He had a hot, busy, charming face. "I'm from New York, too. I don't actually approve—I want to state this clearly—of this university's persistent policy of hiring Americans to fill positions that could be filled by Canadians, though I myself am an American, but I hope not contaminated by that country's madness. I am going to form a committee, incidentally, to investigate the depth of the Americanization of this university. Do you have a Ph.D.?"

"I'm writing my dissertation now," Wanda said quickly.

"On what?"

"Landor."

"Landor," he said flatly. The set of his face was now negative. He did not approve. Wanda nervously wiped her hands on her skirt. With one foot, Saul Bird turned a box of books around to read their titles. "All this is dead. Dried crap."

She stared at him in dismay.

His eyes darted quickly about her office. His profile was stern, prompt, oddly morose; the lines deepened about the small mouth. "These books. This office. The desk you've innocently inherited—from Jerry Renling, whom you will never meet, since they fired him last spring for taking too much interest in his students. All this is dead, finished. Where is your telephone?"

He turned back abruptly to her, as if impatient with her slowness. She came awake and said, "Here, it's here, let me move all this. . . ." She tried to pick up another box of books, but the box gave way and some books fell onto the floor. She was very embarrassed. She cleared a space for him. He sat on the edge of her desk and dialed a number.

Wanda waited awkwardly. Should she leave her office while he telephoned? But he seemed to take no notice of her. His blond hair appeared to vibrate with electricity. On the bony ridge of his nose, his black-rimmed glasses were balanced as if by an act of fierce will. . . . Why was her heart pounding so absurdly? It was the abrasive charge of his voice—that demanding, investigative air—it put her in mind of men she had admired, public men she had known only from a distance, a meek participant in a crowd. Saul Bird had a delicate frame, but there was something powerful in the set of his shoulders and the precise, impatient way he dialed the telephone.

"Any messages there?" he said, without introducing himself. "What? Who? When will he call back?" He paused for a moment. Wanda brushed her short hair back nervously from her face. Was he talking to his wife? "We have four more signatures on the petition. Yes. I *told* you to forget about that. It's twelve-ten now; can you get down here at one and pick me up? Why not? There's someone here looking for an apartment—"

Wanda stared at him. At that moment, Saul Bird turned and smiled—fond, friendly, an intimate smile—or was she imagining it? He looked like a child in his dark turtleneck sweater and brown trousers. He wore sandals; the grimy straps looked gnawed. Wanda, in her stockings and new shoes, in her shapeless dress of dark cotton, felt foolishly tall in his sight: *Why* had she grown so tall?

When he hung up, he said, "My wife's coming. We'll find you an apartment."

"But I really don't—"

Someone appeared in the doorway, leaning in. "Saul?" He was a young man in a soiled trench coat.

"Come in, I've been waiting for you," Saul Bird said. He introduced Wanda to the young man. "Wanda, this is Morris Kaye in psychology, my friend 'K.' This is Wanda Barnett. Susannah and I are going to find her an apartment this afternoon."

"Something has come up. Can I talk to you?"

"Talk."

"But it's about—I mean—" The young man glanced nervously at Wanda. He was about twenty-three, very tall, wearing a white T-shirt and shorts under his trench coat. His knees were pale beneath tufts of black hair. His face, dotted with small blemishes that were like cracked veins, had a strange glow, an almost luminous pallor. Wanda could feel his nervousness and shied away from meeting his eyes.

"We may as well introduce Wanda to the high style of this place," Saul Bird said. "I was given notice of nonrenewal for next year. Which is to say, I've been fired. Why do you look so surprised?"

Wanda had not known she looked surprised—but now her face twitched as if eager to show these men that she was surprised, yes. "But what? Why?"

"Because they're terrified of me," Saul Bird said with a cold smile.

▪ ▪ ▪

Susannah Aptheker Bird, born in 1929, earned doctoral degrees in both history and French from Columbia University. In the fall of 1958, she met and married Saul Bird. Their child, Philip, and Susannah's formidable book on Proust both appeared in 1959. The next year, Susannah taught at Brandeis, while Saul Bird taught at a small experimental college in California; the following year, they moved to Baton Rouge, where Susannah worked on her second book. When Saul Bird was dismissed from Louisiana State University, Susannah accepted an appointment at Smith College. The following year, however, she received a Frazer Foundation grant to complete her second book—*The Radical Politics of Absurd Theater*—and decided to take a year's leave from teaching. Saul Bird had been offered a last-minute appointment from a small Canadian university on the American border. The two of them flew up to Hilberry University to look it over: They noted the ordinary, soot-specked buildings, the torn-up campus, the two or three "modern" buildings under construction, the amiable, innocuous student faces. They noted the grayness of the sky, which was the same sky that arched over Buffalo, New York, and which was fragrant with gaseous odors and ominous, as if the particles of soot were somehow charged with energy, with electricity; not speaking, not needing to speak, the Birds felt a certain promise in the very dismalness of the setting, as if it were not yet in existence, hardly yet imagined.

They could bring it into existence.

On September ninth, after Saul Bird called, Susannah changed her clothes, taking off her pajama bottoms and putting on a pair of blue jeans. The pajama top looked like a shirt—it was striped green and white—so she did not bother to change it. "Get dressed, your father wants us to pick him up at the university," she said to the boy, Philip. "I'm not leaving you here alone."

"Why not?" the boy said cheerfully. "Think I'd kill myself or something?"

"To spite your father and me."

The boy snickered.

She drove to the university. Saul was standing with a small group—K and a few students, Doris and David and Homer, and a young woman whom Susannah did not recognize. Saul introduced them: "This is Wanda Barnett, who is anxious to get an apartment." Everyone piled into the car. Wanda, demure and homely, seemed not to know what to do with her hands. She squeezed in next to Susannah. She smiled shyly; Susannah did not smile at all.

That was at one o'clock. By five that afternoon, they had located an apartment—not exactly within walking distance of the university—but a fairly good apartment, just the same, though quite expensive. "Someone will have to wash these walls," Saul Bird declared to the manager. "You don't expect this young woman to sign a lease for such filth, do you? This city is still in the Nineteenth Century! Well, Wanda, are you pleased with this?"

He turned to face her. She was exhausted, her stomach upset from the day's activity. Anxious not to disappoint Saul Bird, she could only nod mutely. She felt how the others in the room—everyone except the child had come up—were waiting for her reaction, watching her keenly.

"Yes," she said shakily, "yes, it's perfect."

Saul Bird smiled. "I'm on my way to a private conference with Hubben. I must leave, but we want you to have dinner with us tonight. I might be stopping at T. W.'s apartment to see what they've heard. Wanda, you're not busy tonight?"

"I really can't—"

"Why not?" Saul Bird frowned. He put out his arms and a cigarette burned eloquently in his fingers. Wanda felt the others watching her, waiting. Susannah Bird stood with her arms folded over the striped, sporty shirt she wore.

"I have work to do of my own, and I can't intrude upon you," Wanda said miserably.

"Relax. You take yourself too seriously," Saul Bird said. "You must reassess yourself. You may be on the verge of a new life. You are in Canada, a country not free of bourgeois prostitution but relatively innocent, free, at any rate, of a foreign policy, a country that is a *possibility.* You grant me Canada's a possibility?"

Wanda glanced at the others. Saul Bird's wife had a thin, ravaged, shrewd face; it was set like stone, with patches of black hair like moss about it. A blank. K was staring at Wanda's shoes, as if waiting painfully for her response. The students—Homer McCrea and David Rose—eyed her suspiciously. Their young nostrils widened with the rapidity of their breathing. Clearly, they did not trust her. Both were very thin. Their faces were eaglelike and intense; in imitation of Saul Bird, perhaps, they wore turtleneck sweaters that emphasized their thinness, and blue jeans and sandals. Their feet were grimy. Their toes were in perpetual movement, wiggling, appearing to signal the unbearable tension of the moment. David Rose wore a floppy orange-felt hat that was pulled down upon his head; his untidy hair stuck out around it. Homer McCrea, hatless, had a head of black curly hair and wore several rings on his fingers.

Wanda thought: *I must get away from these people.*

But Saul Bird said swiftly, as if he had heard her thoughts, "Why are you so nervous, Wanda? You look very tired. You look a little sick. Your problem is obvious to me—you do not relax. Always your mind is working and always you're thinking, planning, you're on guard, you're about to put up your hands to shield your private parts from us—why must you be so private? Why are you so terrified?"

"I—I don't know what you—"

"Come, we must leave. Susannah will make us all stuffed breast of veal."

A wave of nausea rose in Wanda.

▪ ▪ ▪

Erasmus Hubben, born in Toronto in 1930, completed his doctoral work in 1955 with an 800-page study called "The Classical Epistemological Relativism of Ernst Cassirer." Every summer, Hubben traveled in Europe and northern Africa; friends back in Canada received postcards scribbled over with his fine, enigmatic prose—sprinkled with exclamation points and generally self-critical, as if Hubben were embarrassed for himself. He was conscious of himself, always: Students could not quite understand his nervous jokes, the facial tics and twitches that were meant to undercut the gravity of his pronouncements, the kind of baggy shuffling dance he did when lecturing. His face, seen in repose, was rather sorrowful, the eyebrows scanty, accenting the hard bone of his brow, the nose long and pale as wax, the lips thin and colorless; in company, his face seemed to flesh out, to become muscular with the drama of conversation, the pupils of the eyes blackening, the lips moving rapidly, so that tiny flecks of saliva gathered in the corners of his mouth. He was a good, generous man, and the somewhat clownish look of his clothes (seedy, baggy trousers with fallen seats; coats with elbows worn thin; shoes splotched with old mud) was half deliberate, perhaps—while Hubben suggested to his colleagues, evasively and shyly, that they must play Monopoly with him sometime (he had invented a more complicated game of Monopoly), at the same time he waved away their pity for his loneliness by the jokes, the puns, the difficult allusions, the jolly cast of his face and dress alike . . . and he carried in his wallet the snapshot of a smiling, beefy young woman, which he took out often to show people as if to assure them that he had someone, yes, there was someone back in Toronto, someone existed somewhere who cared for Erasmus Hubben.

He came to Hilberry University in 1967, having resigned from another university for reasons of health. He taught logic, but his real love was poetry, and he had arranged for a private printing of a book of his poems. They were always short, often ending with queries.

Actual adversaries
are not as prominent as quivering
speculations

When you think of me, my dear,
do you think of
anything?

He took teaching very seriously. He liked students, though he did not understand them; he liked their energy, their youth, their *foreignness*. During his first year at Hilberry, he prepared for as many as twenty hours for a single lecture. But his teaching was not successful. He could not understand why. So he worked harder on his lectures, taking notes by hand so as not to disturb the family he lived with. (He boarded with a colleague and his family.) Late in the winter of 1968, a student named David Rose came to see him. This student did not attend class very often and he was receiving a failing grade, but when he sat in class with his arms folded, his face taut and contemptuous beneath a floppy orange-felt hat, he impressed Hubben as a superior young man. Wasn't that probably a sign of superiority, his contempt? Erasmus Hubben shook hands with him, delighted that a student should seek him out, and made a joke about not seeing him very often. David Rose smiled slowly, as if not getting the joke. He was very thin and intense. "Dr. Hubben," he said, "I have been designated to approach you with this question—would you like your class liberated?" Hubben was leaning forward with an attentive smile—*liberated?* "Yes. Your course is obviously a failure. Your subject is not entirely hopeless, but you are unable to make it relevant. Your teaching methods are dead, dried up, finished. Of course, as a human being, you have potential," the boy said. Hubben blinked. He could not believe what he was hearing. The boy went on to explain that a certain professor in English, Saul Bird, was conducting experimental classes and that the other Hilberry professors would do well to learn from him before it was too late. Saul—everyone called him Saul—

did not teach classes formally at all; he had "liberated" his students; he met with them at his apartment or in the coffee shop or elsewhere, usually at night; his students read and did anything they wanted, and some skipped all sessions, since in any case, they were going to be allowed to grade themselves at the end of the year. "The old-fashioned grading system," David Rose said angrily, "is only imperialistic sadism!"

Hubben stared at the boy. He had been hearing about Saul Bird for a long time, and he had seen the man at a distance—hurrying across campus, usually dressed badly, with a few students running along with him—but he had never spoken to him. Something about Saul Bird's intense, urbane, theatrical manner had frightened Hubben off. And then there was the matter of his being a Jew, his being from New York. . . . Hubben's family was a little prejudiced, and though Hubben himself was free of such nonsense, he did not exactly seek out people like Saul Bird. So he told David Rose, with a gracious smile, that he would be delighted to talk with "Saul" sometime. He hoped he wasn't too old to learn how to teach! David Rose did not catch this joke but gravely and politely nodded. "Yes, the whole university better learn. It better learn from Saul or go under," he said.

Soon, Hubben began to hear of little else except Saul Bird. Bird had been fired and would fulfill only the next year's contract. His department—English—and the dean of arts and sciences had voted to dismiss him. Now, it seemed that many of Hubben's students were also "Saul's" students. They sat together in the classroom, when they came to class, their arms folded, their eyes beady and undefeated, though Hubben's finely wrought lectures obviously bored them. David Rose had enrolled for another course, still wearing his orange hat; a girl named Doris had joined him, perhaps his girlfriend—Doris, all angles and jutting lines, very thin, with stringy blonde hair and sweaters pulled down to her bony hips as if they were men's sweaters, her voice sometimes rising in a sarcastic whine that startled the other students, "Professor Hubben, doesn't this entirely contra*dict* what you said the other day?" Another boy, Homer McCrea, had black curly hair and a dramatic manner that put Hubben in mind of Saul Bird. Sometimes he took notes all period long (were these lecture notes going to be used against him?—Hubben wondered), sometimes he sat with his arms folded, his expression distant and critical. Hubben began to talk faster and faster, he spiced up his lectures with ironic little jokes of the sort that superior students would appreciate, but nothing worked—nothing worked.

Saul Bird came to see him the first week in September, striding into his office. "I'm Saul Bird. I would like your signature on a petition," he said. Hubben spent many minutes reading the petition, examining its syntax, to give himself time to think. Saul Bird's presence in this small room upset him. The man was very close, physically close to Hubben—and Hubben could not stand to be touched—and he was very *real*. He kept leaning over Hubben's shoulder to point out things in the petition. "*That* is the central issue. *That* will break someone's back," Saul Bird said.

Hubben, rattled, could not make much sense of the petition except that it seemed to support excellence in teaching and the need for dedication to students and for experimentation to prevent "the death of the humanities." Hubben could not see that it had much to do with the case of Saul Bird at all. But he said, not meeting Saul Bird's stare, "I really must decline. I'm afraid I don't sign things."

"You what?"

"I'm afraid I don't—"

"You refuse to involve yourself?" Saul Bird said sharply.

Hubben sat staring at the petition. He read it over again. Would this awful man not go away?

"I think you'll reconsider if you study my case," Saul Bird said. "Most of the faculty is going to support me, once the injustice of the case is aired. Here is my own file—read it tonight and tell me what your response is." And he gave Hubben a manila folder of Xeroxed memos, outlines, programs, personal letters from students in praise of Saul Bird, dating back to March of the year that Saul Bird had signed a contract with Hilberry. Hubben sat dizzily looking through these things. He had his own work to do. . . . What sense could he make of all this?

On September ninth, he was to meet with Saul Bird at four in the afternoon, but the hour came and went. He was immensely relieved. He prepared to go home, thinking of how much better it was to stay away from people, really. No close relationships. No intimate ties. Of course, he liked to "chat" with people—particularly about intellectual subjects—and he enjoyed the simple-minded family dinners in the Kramer household, where he boarded. He liked students at a distance. Women made him extremely nervous. His female students were as colorful as partridges and as unpredictable—so many sudden flutterings, the darting of eyes and hands! The young men in his classes were fine human beings, but, up close, the heat of their breath was disturbing. Better to keep people at a distance. . . . And as Hubben thought this clearly to himself the telephone rang and Doris Marsdell announced that Saul Bird was on his way. "But he's an hour late and I'm going home," Hubben protested.

"You hadn't better go home," the girl said.

"What?" said Hubben. "What did you say, Miss Marsdell?"

"This is a matter of extreme importance, more to you than to Saul. You *hadn't better go home*." Shaken, Hubben looked around his dingy, cluttered office as if seeking help—but he was alone. The girl went on quickly, "Saul is a genius, a saint. You people all know that! You're jealous of him! You want to destroy him, because you're jealous, you're terrified of a real genius in your midst!"

"Miss Marsdell," Hubben said, "are you joking? You must be joking."

"I don't joke," the girl said and hung up.

When Saul Bird arrived fifteen minutes later, he was in an excellent mood. He shook hands briskly, lit a cigarette and sat on the edge of Hubben's desk. "Did you read my file? Are you convinced of the injustice of this university?"

Hubben was extremely warm. "I'm not sure—"

"Most of your colleagues in philosophy are going to sign in my behalf," Saul Bird said. "What is your decision?"

"I wasn't aware that most of them were—"

"Of course not. People are afraid to talk openly of these matters."

"I still don't think—"

"My wife wants you to have dinner with us tonight. We'll talk about this quietly, sanely. Intelligent discourse between humanists is the only means of bringing about a revolution—until the need for violence is more obvious, I mean," Saul Bird said with a smile.

"Violence?" Hubben stared. He felt something in his blood warming, opening, coming to life in arrogant protestation against himself, his own demands. He was very warm. Saul Bird, perched on the edge of his desk, eyed him through glasses that looked as if they might slightly magnify the images that came through them.

"People like you," Saul Bird said softly, "have been allowed to live through books for too long. That's been your salvation—dust and the droppings of tradition—but all that is ending, as you know. You'll change. You'll be changed. My wife would like you to come to dinner. You're rooming with the Kramers, aren't you? Old Harold Kramer and his 'ethics of Christianity' seminar?"

Hubben wanted to protest that Kramer was only forty-six.

"People like Kramer, according to the students, are hopeless. They must go under. People like *you*—and a very few others—are possibilities. The students do admit certain possibilities. They are very wise, these twenty-year-olds, extraordinarily wise. The future belongs to them, of course. You are not anti-student, are you?"

"Of course not, but—"

"Telephone Kramer's wife and tell her you're eating out tonight," Saul Bird said.

Hubben hesitated. Then something in him surrendered: Really, it would not harm him to have dinner with the Birds. He was curious about them, after all. And then, it could not be denied that Saul Bird was a fascinating man. His face was shrewd, peaked, oddly appealing. He was obviously very intelligent—his students had not exaggerated. Hubben had heard, of course, that Saul Bird had been fired for incompetence and "gross misconduct." He did not teach his classes, evidently. He did not assign any examinations or papers and his students were allowed to grade themselves. But in the man's presence, these charges faded, they did not seem quite *relevant*. . . . Hubben made up his mind. He would spend the evening with the Birds. Wasn't it a part of the rich recklessness of life, to explore all possibilities?

And so it all began.

▪ ▪ ▪

The group met informally at Saul Bird's apartment, at first two or three times a week, then every evening. Wanda went as often as she could—she had to work hard on her class preparations and on her dissertation, she was often exhausted, a little sick to her stomach and doubtful of her subject (*Landor,* Saul Bird had said flatly)—but still she showed up, shy and clumsy about this new part of her life. Saul Bird and his group were so passionate! They were so wise! They asked her bluntly how she could devote her intelligence to the analysis of a *medieval* writer when the world about her was so rotten. It was based on hypocrisy and exploitation, couldn't she see? The world was a nightmarish joke, unfunny. Nothing was funny. It was a fact of this life, Saul Bird lectured to his circle, that *nothing was funny.*

And he would stare openly at Erasmus Hubben, whose nervous jokes had annoyed the circle at first.

Hubben was transformed gradually. How had he been blind for so long? His students told him that half the faculty was going to be fired, hounded out, shamed out of existence, if Saul Bird was not rehired. When Saul Bird was rehired, however, he would not be gratefully silent but would head a committee of activist faculty and students to expose the hypocrisy of the rest of the faculty. Their findings would be published. Would he, Erasmus, like to contribute anything to help with printing costs? As the fall semester went on, Hubben turned up at Saul Bird's more and more often, he stayed later, he became quite dependent upon these nightly meetings. How was it possible that he had known so little about himself? about his own stultifying life? He began to speak wildly, parodying his own professorial manner, and the saliva flew from his lips. He believed that Saul Bird listened closely to him. The very air of Saul Bird's crowded little apartment was exhilarating to Hubben; he and the two other faculty members who showed up regularly began to feel younger, to dress in an untidy, zestful, youthful manner. Hubben gained a new respect for Morris Kaye, whom he had never taken seriously. And a new lecturer, a young woman named Wanda, attracted Hubben's eye: Vague in her speech, flat-chested, her eyes watery with emotion or shyness, she did not upset Hubben at all and she seemed to admire his speeches.

On the walls of the apartment there were many posters and photographs, and those that caught Hubben's eye most often were of blazing human beings—Buddhist monks and nuns, and a Czechoslovakian university student. A human being in flames! Maniacal flames leaping up from an oddly rigid, erect human being, sitting cross-legged in a street! It was unimaginable. But it had happened, it had been photographed. Hubben had the idea as the weeks passed that only so dramatic an act, so irreparable an act, would impress Saul Bird.

When Wanda could not go to the apartment, she thought about the group and could not concentrate on her work. What were they talking about? They usually talked for hours—sometimes quietly, sometimes noisily. The air would be heavy with smoke. Everyone except Wanda smoked; even Saul Bird's little boy showed up, smoking. (The Birds did not exactly live together. Susannah had an apartment on the top floor of a building and Saul had a smaller apartment on the second floor, in the rear.) The little boy, Philip, would come down to visit and stand behind his father's chair, watching everyone. He was a fascinating child, Wanda thought. She feared children, usually, but Philip did not seem to be a child; he was dwarfish rather than small, wise and almost wooden, with thick kinky hair a little darker than his father's and his father's cool, intelligent face. He would not attend public schools and the Birds supported him. (Some kind of legal case was going on over this.) He said little, unlike other children Wanda had known, and she was very pleased one day when the Birds asked her to take Philip out to get a pair of shoes. She took him on the bus. He was silent except for one remark: "Don't fall in love with my father, please."

Wanda laughed hysterically.

She began to lie awake at night, thinking about Saul Bird. He often looked directly at her, pointedly at her. He often nodded in support of her remarks. If only they could talk alone!—but the apartment was always crowded with students who were staying overnight, some of them even bringing their sleeping bags along. The young man with the orange hat, David Rose, had moved out of his parents' house and Saul Bird had gladly agreed to house him, for nothing. The telephone was always ringing. Susannah sometimes showed up around midnight, silent and dark. She reminded Wanda of a crow. But the woman was brilliant, her book on Proust was brilliant. Wanda despaired of such brilliance herself. Susannah had a deft, witchlike, whimsical style, her small face sometimes breaking into a darting, razorish smile that was really charming. And her wit frightened everyone—"If my husband could function normally, he would function normally," she said once, winking. And Hubben was always there. He sent out for pizzas and chop suey and hamburgers. K—"I am a character out of Kafka, pure essence," he declared—was always there. And the students, always the students. They seemed to live on air, disdaining Hubben's offers of food. They did not need food. They lived on the hours of intense, intoxicating dialog:

SAUL BIRD: What conclusions have you come to?
DORIS: That I was an infant. I was enslaved.
SAUL BIRD: And what now?
DORIS: Now I am totally free.
SAUL BIRD: You're exaggerating to gain our respect.
DORIS: No, I'm free. I'm free. I detest my parents and everything they stand for—I'm free of them—I am my own woman, entirely!

During the day, Hubben began to notice that his colleagues at the university were jealous of him. They were probably curious about the renewed interest in his notoriously difficult subject, logic. How strange that young people should begin to hang around Erasmus Hubben's office! Hubben spent hours "chatting" with them. *I must get closer. I must wake up to reality,* he thought. His colleagues were not only jealous of his popularity but fearful of it. He began closing his office door and opening it only to Saul Bird's circle. He took around Saul Bird's petition and tried to argue people into signing it. When Kramer would not sign it, Hubben became extremely angry and moved out of the Kramer home and into a cheap river-front hotel. He told the Kramers that their attitude toward Saul Bird was disgusting. They were sick people, he could not live under the same roof with such sick, selfish people! Kramer, a professor of ethics, an old-fashioned Catholic layman, was brought to tears by Hubben's accusations. But Hubben would not move back. He would not compromise with his new ideals.

I have friends now. I have real friends, he thought fifty times a day, in amazement. He doodled little poems, smiling at their cryptic ingenuity—

One savage kiss is worth
a thousand savage syllogisms—

and showed them to Saul Bird, who shrugged his shoulders. Though he was a professor of English, Saul had not much interest in poetry. He argued that the meaning of life was *action,* involvement with other *human beings;* the trappings of the past were finished—books, lectures, classrooms, buildings, academic status! He, Saul Bird, was being fired only because he represented the future. The establishment feared the future. In a proclamation sent to the local newspaper, calling for an investigation of the financial holdings of the university's board of governors, he stated: "Because it is my duty to liberate the students of this university, I am being fired. Because people like myself—and we are numerous in Canada and the United States—are loyal to our students and not to the establishment, we are being persecuted. But we are going to fight back."

"We certainly are going to fight back!" Hubben cried.

He hurried about the university with a wild, happy look. He felt so much younger! Though living in the White Hawk Hotel did not agree with him, he felt much younger these days; it was mysterious. He and the young lecturer Wanda Barnett often sought each other out at the university to discuss the change in their lives. At first, they were shy; then, guessing at their common experiences, they began to talk quite openly. "I was always lonely. I was always left out. I was always the tallest girl in my class," Wanda said, gulping for breath.

Hubben, feeling a kind of confused, sparkling gratitude for this woman's honesty, admitted that he, too, had been lonely, isolated, overly intelligent, a kind of freak. "And I was selfish, so selfish! I inherited from my father—a pious old fraud!—an absolute indifference to moral and political commitment. I skipped a stage in the natural evolution of mankind! But thanks to Saul—"

"Yes, thanks to Saul—" Wanda said at once.

Just before the break at Christmas, the university's Appeals Committee turned down the Saul Bird case.

"And now we must get serious," Saul Bird said to the circle.

They began to talk of tactics. They talked of faculty resignations, of the denunciation of the university by its student population; guardedly, at first, they talked of demonstrations and breakage and bombings. They would certainly occupy the humanities building and only violent police action could get them out—maybe not even that, if they were armed. They could stay in the building for weeks and force the university's administration to rehire Saul Bird. As they spoke, they became more excited, more certain of themselves. The blazing suicides on Saul Bird's walls were luminous, as if in sympathy with their cause.

How could one live in such a rotten society? Why not destroy it with violence?

The telephone was always ringing. Sometimes Wanda answered, sometimes one of the girl students; if Saul Bird nodded, they handed the receiver to him; if he shook his head, they made excuses for him. He was not always available to everyone. This pleased them immensely, his belonging to *them*. When they did not talk directly of forcing the administration to rehire him, they talked about him, about his effect on their lives. They were frank and solemn. A first-year arts student, a girl, clasped her hands before her and said breathlessly, "Saul has changed me. No cell in me is the same."

K, enormously moved, sat on the floor and confessed, "He revolutionized my concept of reality. It's like that corny *Gestalt* of George Washington's face—once it's pointed out to you, you can't see anything else. Not lines and squiggles but only Washington's face. That is fate."

But sometimes, very late at night, the discussions became more intimate. It was in January that Saul Bird turned to Hubben, who had been unusually noisy that evening, and said, "You assure us you've been transformed. But I doubt it. I doubt that you are ready yet to face the truth about yourself."

"The truth?"

"The truth. Will you tell us?"

It was so late—around four in the morning—that only about twelve students remained, as well as Wanda, K and a recent convert, a peppy, bearded sociology lecturer. The air was suddenly quite tense. Everyone looked at Hubben, who tugged at the collar of his rumpled shirt.

"I don't know what you mean, Saul," he said.

"Of course you know what I mean."

"That I'm prejudiced? Against certain races . . . or creeds . . . ?"

Saul Bird was silent.

"I admit to a slight primitive fear . . . an entirely irrational fear of people different from myself. It's Toronto instinct! Good old Anglo-Saxon stock!" Hubben laughed.

"We know all that," David Rose said coldly.

"How do you know that? Did you—did you know that?" Hubben said. He looked around the room. Wanda Barnett was watching him, her face drawn with the late hour. K's look was slightly glazed. "But I like all human beings personally, as—as human beings. Today I was chatting in the lounge with Franklin Ambrose, and it never occurred to me, not once, that he was a—that he was a Negro—"

Hubben looked miserably at Saul Bird.

"Franklin Ambrose is not a Negro," said Saul Bird shrewdly.

Everyone barked with laughter. It was true: Frank Ambrose, a black man of thirty, whose Ph.D. was from Harvard, who dressed expensively and whose clipped high style was much appreciated by his female students, was not really a "Negro" at all.

"What about Jews, Erasmus?" Doris Marsdell said suddenly.

"Jews? I don't think about Jews. I have no feelings one way or another. I do not think about people as Jews—or non-Jews—"

"Tell us more," another student said with a snicker.

"Yes, tell us."

"Tell us about your most intimate instinct," Saul Bird said. He leaned forward to stare down at Hubben, who was sitting on the floor. "What is the truth about your feeling for me?"

"Extreme admiration—"

"Come, come. I think we all know. You might as well admit it."

"Admit what?"

"Your inclinations."

"But what—what are my inclinations?"

"Your obsession."

Hubben stared. "What do you mean?"

"Tell us."

"But what—what do you mean?"

"Your desire for me," Saul Bird said.

"I don't—"

"Your homosexual desire for me," Saul Bird said flatly.

Hubben sat without moving.

"Well?" said Saul Bird. "Why are you so silent?"

"I don't—I don't—" Hubben wiped his forehead with both hands. He could not bear the gaze of Saul Bird, but there was nowhere else to look. And then, suddenly, he heard his own voice saying, "Yes, I admit it. It's true."

Saul Bird lifted his hands in a gesture that matched the lifting of his eyebrows. "Of course it's true," he said.

The discussion leaped at once to another topic: tactics for the occupation of the humanities building. Hubben took part vociferously in this discussion. He stayed very late, until only he and a few students remained, and Saul Bird said curtly, "I forgot to tell you that Susannah and I are flying to New York this morning. Will you all go home, so that I can get some sleep?"

"You're going away?" everyone said.

A weekend without Saul Bird was a lonely weekend. Hubben did not leave the White Hawk Hotel: Wanda, staying up in Susannah's apartment in order to take care of Philip, hoped for a telephone call. While the child read books on mathematical puzzles, or stared for long periods of time out the window, Wanda tried to prepare her Chaucer lectures. But she could not concentrate: She kept thinking of Saul Bird.

Who could resist Saul Bird?

The White Hawk Hotel was very noisy and its odors were of festivity and rot. Hubben, unable to sleep, telephoned members of the Saul Bird circle during the night, chatting and joking with them, his words tumbling out, saliva forming in the corners of his mouth. Sometimes he himself did not know what he was saying. After talking an hour and a half with K about the proper wording of their letters of resignation, he caught himself up short and asked, startled, "Why did you call me? Has anything happened?"

The next Monday, on his way to class, he overheard two students laughing behind him. He whirled around; the boys stared at him, their faces hardening. No students of his. He did not know them.

But perhaps they knew him?

Getting his mail in the departmental office, he noticed that the secretary—a young woman with stacked blonde hair—was eying him strangely. He glanced down at himself—frayed trouser cuffs, unbuckled overshoes. She was so absurdly overdressed that she must sneer at an intellectual like him, in self-defense. She must.

And yet, perhaps she had heard . . . ?

He went over to the English department to see Wanda, but she stammered an apology: "A student is coming to see me right now. About the special edition of the paper."

"The special edition? Can't I stay and listen?"

"Not right now," Wanda said, confused.

Hubben had donated five hundred dollars for a special edition of the student newspaper, which was going to feature an interview with "Saul Bird: Teacher Extraordinary."

He walked quickly back to his office and closed the door. His head pounded. He covered his face with his hands and wept.

Saul Bird. . . .

Saul Bird returned in three days and the activities of the circle were resumed. It was necessary to begin plans for the occupation of the humanities building in earnest. They must be prepared for violence. Now the telephone was ringing more than ever: The local newspaper wanted an interview to run alongside an interview with the president of the university; a professor in civil engineering, of all fields, wanted Saul Bird to come to dinner, because it was "time we all communicated"; the head of Saul's department wanted an explanation of all this intrigue; David Rose's father called to demand angrily what was happening to his son; long-distance calls came in from Toronto, in response to a full-page advertisement

Hubben had paid for in the Toronto *Globe and Mail,* headlined "WHY IS HILBERRY UNIVERSITY PERSECUTING A MAN NAMED SAUL BIRD?"

Wanda walked through a cold sleeting rain to watch a television interview show at the home of the Episcopal chaplain, Father Mott, a young, balding man who was Saul Bird's newest disciple. The show was a local production, rather amateurish, but Saul Bird spoke clearly and strongly and made an excellent impression. Wanda stared, transfixed, at his image on the screen. It was impossible to tell how short he was! He talked for fifteen minutes in his urbane, imploring voice: "It must be smashed so that it can live! Those of us who are prepared to smash it are feared, especially by our own generation; but this fear is hopeless, it will stop nothing—the future will come, it will be heard! We may have to destroy higher education in both Canada and the United States in order to save our young people!"

"Dr. Bird," said the interviewer, "may I ask a more personal question? We've been hearing about a possible occupation of one of the university's buildings. Is there any basis to this threat?"

"Absolutely not," said Saul Bird.

The occupation had been planned for the following Tuesday, the second week in February. Wanda, who had been staying up almost every night, got so nervous that she could not sit still. She could not even stay in her office for long. She imagined that people were staring at her. The older faculty members, unsympathetic to Saul Bird, in some cases hating Saul Bird, began to look at her in a most unpleasant way. In the faculty lounge, Wanda believed that they laughed at her because she came in so rushed, her short hair untidy about her face, her books clumsily cradled in her arms. She blushed miserably.

February was dim and cold and few students showed up at her morning classes. Inspired by Saul Bird, she had announced that all students enrolled in her sections would be allowed to grade themselves at the end of the year. Saul Bird had predicted a renewed enthusiasm on the students' part, but in fact, the students were disappearing; what had gone wrong? Didn't they understand her devotion to them? She was so nervous that she had to hurry to the women's rest room before classes, fearing nausea. Sometimes she did throw up. And then, shaken, pale, distraught, she hurried across the windy quadrangle to her classroom, arriving five minutes late, her glasses steamed over.

As the date of the occupation approached, she became even more nervous. She could not sleep. If she telephoned Saul Bird, it often happened that someone else answered—it sounded like Doris Marsdell—and said loftily, "Saul is not available at the moment!" If she telephoned Susannah, the phone went unanswered. Erasmus Hubben, at his hotel, would snatch up his telephone receiver and say hello in so panicked a voice that Wanda could not identify herself. So the two of them would sit, listening to each other's frightened breathing, until they both hung up.

She kept thinking and rethinking about the past several months. Her mind raced and would not let her sleep. For some reason, she kept glancing at her wrist watch. What was wrong? What was happening? She caught a bad cold waiting for a bus to take her to Saul Bird's apartment and could not get rid of it. When she met other faculty members in the halls, she stammered and looked away. She could not concentrate on her dissertation. That could wait; it had nothing to do with real life. But people were looking at her oddly. When she hurried into the coffee shop to sit with K and a few students, it seemed that even these people glanced oddly at her. But it was Erasmus Hubben they were analyzing. "People just want to discredit his ad in the Toronto *Globe and Mail!*" Doris Marsdell said sourly. She had a very thin, grainy face, rubbed too raw and drawn with exhaustion; her blonde hair hung in strands. When she waved her arms excitedly, she did not smell good. "Sanity and insanity, Saul says, are bourgeois distinctions we don't need to observe. It's all crap! If society tries to say that Erasmus is unbalanced, that is *their* distinction and not ours. Society wants to categorize us in order to get power over us! Sheer primitive imperialist power!"

▪ ▪ ▪

The occupation began on February tenth, at ten-thirty p.m. Saul Bird's supporters—about forty students and eight faculty members and the wiry little Episcopal chaplain—approached the humanities building with their sleeping bags, helmets, goggles and food, but the campus police must have been tipped off, because they were waiting. These police—about five of them—blocked the entrance to the building and asked for identification cards.

Erasmus Hubben pushed his way through the shivering little group. "Are you the Gestapo?" he cried. "The thought police? What is *your* identification?" A few of the students began shoving forward. They broke past the campus police—who were middle-aged, portly men in uniforms that looked like costumes—and ran into the building. "Fascists! Gestapo!" Hubben cried. His long dark overcoat was unbuttoned and swung open. Wanda, whose throat was very sore, wondered if she should not try to calm Erasmus. But something about the rigidity of his neck and head frightened her. "I dare you to arrest me! I dare you to use your guns on me! I am an associate professor employed by this university, I am a Canadian citizen, I will use all the powers of my station and my intellect to expose you!" he cried. The students inside the building were now holding the doors shut against the police, but this prevented the other students from getting in. The policemen moved slowly, like men in a dream. Erasmus was pulling at one of them, a plump, catfaced, frightened man in his mid-fifties, and was shouting, "Are we threatened with being fired, indeed? Are these loyal students threatened with expulsion? Indeed, indeed? And who will fire us and who will expel us when this university is burned to the ground and its corrupt administration put to public shame?"

"Somebody put a gag on him!" one of the students muttered.

Then something happened that Wanda did not see. Did Erasmus shove the policeman or did the policeman shove Erasmus? Did Erasmus truly spit in the man's face, as some claimed gleefully, or did the policeman just slip accidentally on the steps? People began to shout. The policeman had fallen and Erasmus was trying to kick him. Someone pulled at his arm. Hubben screamed, "Let me at him! They are trying to castrate us! All my life, they have tried to castrate me!" He took off his overcoat and threw it behind him and it caught poor Father Mott in the face. Before anyone could stop him, Erasmus tore off his shirt and began undoing his trousers. Wanda could not believe her eyes—she saw Erasmus Hubben pull down his trousers and step out of them! And then, eluding everyone, he ran along the side of the building, through the bushes, in his underclothes.

"Get him, get him!" people cried. A few students tried to head him off, but he turned suddenly and charged right into them. He was screaming. Wanda, confused, stood on the steps and could not think what to do—then two young girls ran right into her, uttering high, shrill, giggling little screams. They were from her Chaucer class. They ran right into her and she slipped on the icy steps and fell. She could not get up. Someone's foot crashed onto her hand. About her head were feet and knees; everyone was shouting. Someone stumbled backward and fell onto Wanda, knocking her face down against the step, and she felt a violent pain in her mouth.

She began to weep helplessly.

▪ ▪ ▪

Saul Bird, who had thought it best to stay away from the occupation, telephoned Wanda at three o'clock in the morning. He spoke rapidly and angrily. "Come over here at once, please. Susannah and I are driving to Chicago in an hour and we need you to sit with Philip. I know all about what happened—spare me the details, please."

"But poor Erasmus—"

"How soon can you get here?"

"Right away," Wanda said. Her mouth was swollen—one of her teeth was loose and would probably have to be pulled. But she got dressed and called a taxi and ran up the steps into Saul Bird's apartment building. In the foyer, a few students were waiting. Doris Marsdell cried, "What are you doing? Is he letting you come up to see him?" Her eyes were pink and her voice hysterical. "Did anything happen? Is he still alive? He didn't attempt suicide, did he?"

"He asked me to take care of Philip for a few days," Wanda said.

"*You?* He asked *you?*" Doris cried in dismay.

Susannah answered the door. She was wearing a yellow-tweed pants suit and hoop earrings; her mouth was a dark, heavy pink. "Come in, come in!" she said cheerfully. The telephone was ringing. Saul Bird, knotting a necktie, appeared on the run. "Don't answer that telephone!" he said to Susannah. The boy, Philip, stood in his pajamas at a window, his back to the room. Everywhere there were suitcases and clothes. Wanda tried to cover her swollen mouth with her hand, ashamed of looking so ugly. But Saul Bird did not seem to look at her. He was rummaging through some clothes. "Wanda, we'll contact you in a few days. We're on our way out of this hellhole," he said curtly.

She helped them carry their suitcases down to the car.

Then, for three days, she stayed in the apartment and "watched" Philip. She fingered her loose tooth, which was very painful; she wept, knotting a handkerchief in her fingers. She could not shake loose her cold. "Do you think—do you think your father will ever recover from this?" she asked, staring at the little boy.

He spent most of his time reading and doodling mathematical puzzles. When he laughed, it was without humor, a short, breathy bark.

Saul Bird did not telephone until the following Saturday, and then he had little to say. "Put Philip on the Chicago flight at noon. Give him the keys to both apartments."

"But aren't you coming back?"

"Never," said Saul Bird.

"But what about your teaching? Your students?" Wanda cried.

"I've had it at Hilberry University," Saul Bird said.

She was paralyzed.

Preparing Philip for the trip, she walked about in a kind of daze. She kept saying, "But your father must return. He must fight them. He must insist upon justice." Philip did not pay much attention to her. A cigarette in the center of his pursed lips, he combed his thick hair carefully, preening in the mirror. He was a squat, stocky and yet attractive child—like his father, his face wooden and theatrical at once, a sickly olive hue. Wanda stared at him. He was all she had now, her last link with Saul Bird. "Do you think he's desperate? Will he be hospitalized like poor Erasmus Hubben? What will happen?"

"Nothing," said Philip.

"What do you mean?"

"He has found another job, probably."

"What? How do you know?" Wanda cried.

"This has happened before," said Philip.

In the taxi to the airport, she began to weep desperately. She kept touching the child's hands, his arms. "But what will happen to us . . . to me . . . ? The year is almost gone. I have nothing to show for it. I resigned from the university and I cannot, I absolutely cannot ask to be rehired like the others. . . . I cannot degrade myself! And my dissertation, all that is dead, dried up, all that belongs to the past! What will happen to me? Will your father never come back, will I never see him again?"

"My father," said Philip coldly, "has no particular interest in women."

Wanda hiccuped with laughter. "I didn't mean—"

"He makes no secret of it. I've heard him talk about it dozens of times," Philip said. "He was present at my birth. Both he and my mother wanted this. He watched me born . . . me being born . . . he watched all that blood, my mother's insides coming out . . . all that blood. . . ." The child was dreamy now, no longer abrasive and haughty; he stared past Wanda's face as if he were staring into a mystery. His voice took on a softened, almost bell-like tone. "Oh, my father is very articulate about that experience. . . . Seeing that mess, he said, made him impotent forever. Ask him. He'd love to tell you about it."

"I don't believe it," Wanda whispered.

"Then don't believe it."

She waited until his flight was called and walked with him to the gate. She kept touching his hands, his arms, even his bushy dark-blond hair. He pulled away from her, scowling; then, taking pity on her, staring with sudden interest at her bluish, swollen lip, he reached out to shake hands. It was a formal handshake, a farewell.

"But what will I do with the rest of my life?" Wanda cried.

The child shook his head. "You are such an obvious woman," he said flatly.

Gabriel García Marquez

The Handsomest Drowned Man in the World

November 1971

The celebrated Colombian novelist, born in Bogota in 1928, became a bestselling author in America with *One Hundred Years of Solitude* in 1970, a book that was embraced as an instant classic and focused the attention of the literary world on Latin America. García Marquez had been a journalist and columnist, mainly in Mexico, before turning to fiction. He won the Nobel Prize for Literature in 1982. Later novels were *Chronicle of a Death Foretold* (1983) and the bestselling *Love in the Time of Cholera* (1988). This fine short piece appeared in the 1993 collection, *Strange Pilgrims,* together with two other stories that first appeared in English in *Playboy,* "Miss Forbes' Summer of Happiness" (January 1986) and "The Trail of Your Blood on the Snow" (January 1984). The latter helped the magazine to win a National Magazine Award for Fiction in 1985.

Gabriel García Marquez

The Handsomest Drowned Man in the World

The first children who saw the dark and slinky bulge approaching through the sea let themselves think it was an enemy ship. Then they saw it had no flags nor masts and they thought it was a whale. But when it washed up on the beach, they removed the clumps of seaweed, the jellyfish tentacles and the remains of fish and flotsam and only then did they see that it was a drowned man. And so they made a toy of him.

They had been playing with him all afternoon, burying him in the sand and digging him up again, when someone chanced to see them and spread the alarm in the village. The men who carried him to the nearest house noticed that he weighed more than any dead man they had ever known, almost as much as a horse, and they said to each other that maybe he'd been floating too long and the water had got into his bones. When they laid him on the floor, they said he'd been taller than all other men, because there was barely enough room for him in the house, but they thought that maybe the ability to keep on growing after death was part of the nature of certain drowned men. He had the smell of the sea about him and only his shape gave one to suppose that it was the corpse of a human being, because the skin was covered with a crust of mud and scales.

They did not have to clean off his face to know that the dead man was a stranger. The village was made up of only twenty-odd wooden houses that had stone courtyards with no flowers and that were spread about on the end of a desertlike cape. There was so little land that mothers always went about with the fear that the wind would carry off their children and the few dead that the years had caused among them had to be thrown off the cliffs. But the sea was calm and bountiful and all the men fit into seven boats. So when they found the drowned man, they simply had to look at one another to see that they were all there.

That night they did not go out to work at sea. While the men went to find out if anyone was missing in neighboring villages, the women stayed behind to care for the drowned man. They took the mud off with grass swabs, they removed the underwater stones entangled in his hair and they scraped the crust off with tools used for scaling fish. As they were doing that, they noticed that the vegetation on him came from faraway oceans and deep water and that his clothes were in tatters, as if he had sailed through labyrinths of coral. They noticed, too, that he bore his death with pride, for he did not have the lonely look of other drowned men who came out of the sea nor that haggard, needy look of men who drowned in rivers. But only when they finished cleaning him off did they become aware of the kind of man he was and it left them breathless. Not only was he the tallest, strongest, most virile and best-built man they had ever seen but, even though they were looking at him, there was no room for him in their imagination.

They could not find a bed in the village large enough to lay him on nor was there a table solid enough to use for his wake. The tallest men's holiday pants would not fit him nor the fattest ones' Sunday shirts nor the shoes of the one with the biggest feet. Fascinated by his huge size and his beauty, the women then decided to make him some pants from a large piece of sail and a shirt from some bridal brabant linen, so that he could continue through his death with dignity. As they sewed, sitting in a circle and gazing at the corpse between stitches, it seemed to them that the wind had never been so steady nor the sea so restless as on that night and they supposed that the change had something to do with the dead man. They thought that if that magnificent man had lived in the village, his house would have had the widest doors, the highest ceiling and the strongest floor, his bedstead would have been made from a midship frame held together by iron bolts and his wife would have been the happiest woman. They thought that he would have had so much authority that he could have drawn fish out of the sea simply by calling their names and that he would have put so much work into his land that springs would have burst forth from among the rocks, so that he would have been able to plant flowers on the cliffs. They secretly compared him with their own men, thinking that for all their lives, theirs were incapable of doing what he could do in one night, and they ended up dismissing them deep in their hearts as the weakest, meanest and most useless creatures on earth. They were wandering through that maze of fantasy when the oldest woman, who as the oldest had looked upon the drowned man with more compassion than passion, sighed:

"He has the face of someone called Esteban."

It was true. Most of them had only to take another look at him to see that he could not have any other name. The more stubborn among them, who were the youngest, still lived for a few hours with the illusion that when they put his clothes on and he lay among the flowers, his name might be Lautaro. But it was a vain illusion. There had not been enough canvas, the poorly cut and worse-sewn pants were too tight and the hidden strength of his heart popped the buttons on his shirt. After midnight, the whistling of the wind died down and the sea fell into its Wednesday drowsiness. The silence put an end to any last doubts: He was Esteban. The women who had dressed him, who had combed his hair, had cut his nails and shaved him were unable to hold back a shudder of pity when they had to resign themselves to his being dragged along the ground. It was then that they understood how unhappy he must have been with that huge body, since it bothered him even after death. They could see him in life, condemned to going through doors sideways, cracking his head on crossbeams, remaining on his feet during visits, not knowing what to do with his soft, pink, sea-lion hands while the lady of the house looked for her most resistant chair and begged him, frightened to death, sit here, Esteban, please, and he, leaning against the wall, smiling, don't bother, ma'am, I'm fine where I am, his heels raw and his back roasted from having done the same thing so many times whenever he paid a visit, don't bother, ma'am, I'm fine where I am, just to avoid the embarrassment of breaking up the chair and never knowing, perhaps, that the ones who said don't go, Esteban, at least wait till the coffee's ready, were the ones who later on would whisper the big boob finally left, how nice, the handsome fool has gone. That was what the women were thinking beside the body a little before dawn. Later, when they covered his face with a handkerchief so that the light would not bother him, he looked so forever dead, so defenseless, so much like their men that the first furrows of tears opened in their hearts. It was one of the younger ones who began the weeping. The others, coming to, went from sighs to wails, and the more they sobbed, the more they felt like weeping, because the drowned man was becoming all the more Esteban for them, and so they wept so much, for he was the most destitute, most peaceful and most obliging man on earth, poor Esteban. So when the men returned with the news that the drowned man was not from the neighboring villages either, the women felt an emptiness of jubilation in the midst of their tears.

"Praise the Lord," they sighed, "he's ours!"

The men thought the fuss was only womanish frivolity. Fatigued because of the difficult nighttime inquiries, all they wanted was to get rid of the bother of the newcomer once and for all, before the sun grew strong on that arid, windless day. They improvised a litter with the remains of foremasts and gaffs, tying it together with rigging, so that it would bear the weight of the body until they reached the cliffs. They wanted to tie the anchor from a cargo ship to him, so that he would sink easily into the deepest waves, where fish are blind and divers die of nostalgia, and bad currents would not bring him back to shore, as had happened with other bodies. But the more they hurried, the more the women thought of ways to waste time. They walked about like startled hens, pecking with the sea charms on their breasts, some interfering on one side to put a scapular of the good wind on the drowned man, some on the other side to put a wrist compass on him, and after a great deal of get away from there, woman, stay out of the way, look, you almost made me fall on top of the dead man, the men began to feel mistrust in their livers and started grumbling about why so many main-altar decorations for a stranger, because no matter how many nails and holy-water jars he had on him, the sharks would chew him all the same, but the women kept piling on their junk relics, running back and forth, stumbling, while they released in sighs what they did not in tears, so that the men finally exploded with since when has there ever been such a fuss over a drifting corpse, a drowned nobody, a piece of cold meat. One of the women, mortified by so much lack of care, then removed the handkerchief from the dead man's face and the men were left breathless, too.

He was Esteban. It was not necessary to repeat it for them to recognize him. If they had been told Sir Walter Raleigh, even they might have been impressed with his gringo accent, the macaw on his shoulder, his cannibal-killing blunderbuss, but there could be only one Esteban in the world and there he was, stretched out like a sperm whale, shoeless, wearing the pants of an undersized child and with those stony nails that had to be cut with a knife. They had only to take the handkerchief off his face to see that he was ashamed, that it was not his fault that he was so big or so heavy or so handsome, and if he had known that this was going to happen, he would have looked for a more discreet place to drown in, seriously, I even would have tied the anchor from a galleon around my neck and staggered off a cliff like someone who doesn't like things, in order not to be upsetting people now with this Wednesday dead body, as you people say, in order not to be bothering anyone with this filthy piece of cold meat that doesn't have anything to do with me. There was so much truth in his manner that even the most mistrustful men, the ones who felt the bitterness of endless nights at sea fearing that their women would tire of dreaming about them and begin to dream of drowned men, even they and others who were harder still shuddered in the marrow of their bones at Esteban's sincerity.

That was how they came to hold the most splendid funeral they could conceive of for an abandoned drowned man. Some women who had gone to get flowers in the neighboring villages returned with other women, who could not believe what they had been told, and those women went back for more flowers when they saw the dead man, and they brought more and more, until there were so many flowers and so many people that it was hard to walk about. At the final moment, it pained them to return him to the waters as an orphan and they chose a father and mother from among the best people, and aunts and uncles and cousins, so that through him all the inhabitants of the village became kinsmen. Some sailors who heard the weeping from a distance went off course and people heard of one who had himself tied to the mainmast, remembering ancient fables about sirens. While they fought for the privilege of carrying him on their shoulders along the steep escarpment by the cliffs, men and women became aware for the first time of the desolation of their streets, the dryness of their courtyards, the narrowness of their dreams as they faced the splendor and the beauty of their drowned man. They let him go without an anchor, in order that he might come back if he wished and whenever he wished, and they all held their breath for the fraction of centuries the body took to fall into the abyss. They did not need to look at one another to realize that they were no longer all present, that they would never be. But they also knew that everything would be different from then on, that their houses would have wider doors, higher ceilings and stronger floors, so that Esteban's memory could go everywhere without bumping into the beams and so that no one in the future would dare whisper the big boob finally died, too bad, the handsome fool has finally died, because they were going to paint their house fronts gay colors to make Esteban's memory eternal and they were going to break their backs digging for springs among the stones and planting flowers on the cliffs. In future years, at dawn the passengers on great liners would awaken, suffocated by the smell of gardens on the high seas, and the captain would have to come down from the bridge in his dress uniform, with his astrolabe, his polestar and his row of war medals and, pointing to the promontory of roses on the horizon, he would say in fourteen languages, look there, where the wind is so peaceful now that it's gone to sleep beneath the beds, over there, where the sun's so bright that the sunflowers don't know which way to turn, yes, over there, that's Esteban's village.

—Translated from the Spanish by Gregory Rabassa

Vladimir Nabokov

The Dashing Fellow

December 1971

Some critics consider the Russian-born American writer Vladimir Nabokov (1899–1977) to be the greatest writer of the twentieth century. He became world-famous for the controversial *Lolita* (1955), which was written in English, as were *Pnin* (1957), *Pale Fire* (1962), and *Ada* (1969 and excerpted in *Playboy*). Nabokov's verbal dexterity and vivid narrative, his eccentricities and fondness for both puns and butterflies were well known. He was trilingual, with French as his third language, but even after he left the United States to live in Switzerland, he continued to write in English. His highly praised early short stories had been in Russian, and *Playboy* was fortunate enough to publish most of the few he wrote in English. This is not one of them. A tale of seduction, Russian-style, it dates back to his younger days and was translated for the magazine by Nabokov himself, working with his son, Dmitri.

Vladimir Nabokov

The Dashing Fellow

Our suitcase is carefully embellished with bright-colored stickers: Nürnberg, Stuttgart, Köln—and even Lido (but that one is fraudulent). We have a swarthy complexion, a network of purple-red veins, a black mustache, trimly clipped, and hairy nostrils. We breathe hard through our nose as we try to solve a crossword puzzle in an *émigré* paper. We are alone in a third-class compartment—alone and, therefore, bored.

Tonight we arrive in a voluptuous little town. Freedom of action! Fragrance of commercial travels! A golden hair on the sleeve of one's coat! Oh, woman, thy name is Goldie! That's how we called Momma and, later, our wife, Katya. Psychoanalytic fact: Every man is Oedipus. During the last trip, we were unfaithful to Katya three times, and that cost us thirty reichsmarks. Funny—they all look a fright in the place one lives in, but in a strange town they are as lovely as antique hetaerae. Even more delicious, however, might be the elegancies of a chance encounter: Your profile reminds me of the girl for whose sake years ago. . . . After one single night we shall part like ships. . . . Another possibility: She might turn out to be Russian. Allow me to introduce myself: Konstantin. . . . Better omit the family name—or maybe invent one? Obolenski. Yes, relatives.

We do not know any famous Turkish general and can guess neither the father of aviation nor an American rodent. It is also not very amusing to look at the view. Fields. A road. Birches-smirches. Cottage and cabbage patch. Country lass, not bad, young.

Katya is the very type of a good wife. Lacks any sort of passion, cooks beautifully, washes her arms as far as the shoulders every morning and is not overbright; therefore, not jealous. Given the sterling breadth of her pelvis, one is surprised that for the second time now, she has produced a stillborn babikins. Laborious years. Uphill all the way. *Absolut marasmus* in business. Sweating twenty times before persuading one customer. Then squeezing out the commission drop by drop. God, how one longs to tangle with a graceful gold-bright little devil in a fantastically lit hotel room! Mirrors, orgies, a couple of drinks. Another five hours of travel. Railroad riding, it is proclaimed, disposes one to this kind of thing. Am extremely disposed. After all, say what you will, but the mainspring of life is robust romance. Can't concentrate on business unless I take care first of my romantic interests. So here is the plan: starting point, the café that Lange told me about. Now, if I don't find anything there—

Crossing gate, warehouse, big station. Our traveler let down the window and leaned upon it, elbows wide apart. Beyond a platform, steam was issuing from under some sleeping cars. One could vaguely make out the pigeons changing perches under the lofty glass dome. Hot dogs cried out in treble, beer in baritone. A girl, her bust enclosed in white wool, stood talking to a man, now joining her bare arms behind her back, swaying slightly and beating her buttocks with her handbag, now folding her arms on her chest and stepping with one foot upon the other, or else, holding her handbag under her arm and with a small snapping sound thrusting nimble fingers under her glossy black belt; thus she stood, and laughed, and sometimes touched her companion in a valedictory gesture, only to resume at once her twisting and turning: a sun-tanned girl with a heaped-up hairdo that left her ears bare, and a quite ravishing scratch on her honey-hued upper arm. She does not look at us, but never mind, let us ogle her fixedly. In the beam of the gloating tense glance, she starts to shimmer and seems about to dissolve. In a moment, the background will show through her—a refuse bin, a poster, a bench; but here, unfortunately, our crystalline lens had to return to normality, for everything shifted; the man jumped into the next carriage, the train jerked into motion and the girl took a handkerchief out of her handbag. When, in the course of her receding glide, she came exactly in front of his window, Konstantin, Kostya, Kostenka thrice kissed with gusto the palm of his hand, but his salute passed unnoticed: With rhythmical waves of her handkerchief, she floated away.

He shut the window and, on turning around, saw with pleased surprise that during his mesmeric activities the compartment had managed to fill up: three men with their newspapers and, in the far corner, a brunette with a powdered face. Her shiny coat was of gelatin-like translucency—resisting rain, maybe, but not a man's gaze. Decorous humor and correct eye reach—that's our motto.

Ten minutes later, he was deep in conversation with the passenger in the opposite window seat, a neatly dressed old gentleman; the prefatory theme had sailed by in the guise of a factory chimney; certain statistics came to be mentioned and both men expressed themselves with melancholic irony regarding industrial trends; meanwhile, the white-faced woman dismissed a sickly bouquet of forget-me-nots to the baggage rack and, having produced a magazine from her traveling bag, became engrossed in the transparent process of reading: Through it comes our caressive voice, our commonsensical speech. The second male passenger joined in: He was engagingly fat, wore checked knickerbockers stuck into green stockings and talked about pig breeding. What a good sign—she adjusts every part you look at. The third man, an arrogant recluse, hid behind his paper. At the next stop, the industrialist and the expert on hogs got out, the recluse retired to the dining car and the lady moved to the window seat.

Let us appraise her point by point. Funereal expression of eyes, lascivious lips. First-rate legs, artificial silk. What is better—the experience of a sexy thirty-year-old brunette or the silly young bloom of a bright-curled romp? Today the former is better, and tomorrow we shall see. Next point: Through the gelatin of her raincoat glimmers a beautiful nude, like a mermaid seen through the yellow waves of the Rhine. Spasmodically rising, she shed her coat but revealed only a beige dress with a piqué collaret. Arrange it. That's right.

"May weather," affably said Konstantin, "and yet the trains are still heated."

Her left eyebrow went up and she answered: "Yes, it *is* warm here and I'm mortally tired. My contract is finished, I'm going home now. They all toasted me, the station buffet there is tops, I drank too much, but I never get tipsy, just a heaviness in my stomach. Life has grown hard, I receive more flowers than money and a month's rest will be most welcome; after that I have a new contract, but of course, it's impossible to lay anything by. The potbellied chap, who just left, behaved obscenely. How he stared at me! I feel as if I had been on this train for a long, long time, and I am so very anxious to return to my cozy little apartment far from all that flurry and claptrap and rot."

"Allow me to offer you," said Kostya, "something to palliate the offense."

He pulled from under his backside a square pneumatic cushion, its rubber covered in speckled satin: He always had it under him during his flat, hard, hemorrhoidal trips.

"And what about yourself?" she inquired.

"We'll manage, we'll manage. I must ask you to rise a little. Excuse me. Now sit down. Soft, isn't it? That part is especially sensitive on the road."

"Thank you," she said. "Not all men are so considerate. I've lost quite a bit of flesh lately. Oh, how nice! Just like traveling second-class."

"Galanterie, Gnädigste," said Kostenka, "is an innate property with us. Yes, I'm a foreigner. Russian. Here's an example: One day my father had gone for a walk on the grounds of his manor with an old pal, a well-known general. They happened to meet a peasant woman—a little old hag, you know, with a bundle of firewood on her back—and my father took off his hat. This surprised the general, and then my father said: 'Would your Excellency really want a simple peasant to be more courteous than a member of the gentry?' "

"I know a Russian—I'm sure you've heard his name, too—let me see, what was it? Baretski . . . Baratski. . . . From Warsaw. He now owns a drugstore in Chemnitz. Baratski . . . Baritski. I'm sure you know him?"

"I do not. Russia is a big country. Our family estate was about as large as your Saxony. And all has been lost, all has been burned down. The glow of the fire could be seen at a distance of seventy kilometers. My parents were butchered in my presence. I owe my life to a faithful retainer, a veteran of the Turkish campaign."

"How terrible," she said, "how very terrible!"

"Yes, but it inures one. I escaped, disguised as a country girl. In those days, I made a very cute little maiden. Soldiers pestered me. Especially one beastly fellow. . . . And thereby hangs a most comic tale."

He told his tale. *"Pfui!"* she uttered, smiling.

"Well, after that came the era of wanderings and a multitude of trades. At one time I even used to shine shoes—and would see in my dreams the precise spot in the garden where the old butler, by torchlight, had buried our ancestral jewels. There was, I remember, a sword, studded with diamonds—"

"I'll be back in a minute," said the lady.

The resilient cushion had not yet had time to cool when she again sat down upon it and with mellow grace recrossed her legs.

"And, moreover, two rubies, that big, then stocks in a golden casket, my father's epaulets, a string of black pearls—"

"Yes, many people are ruined at present," she remarked with a sigh, and continued, again raising that left eyebrow: "I, too, have experienced all sorts of hardships. I had a husband, it was a dreadful marriage, and I said to myself: Enough! I'm going to live my own way. For almost a year now, I'm not on speaking terms with my parents—old people, you know, don't understand the young—and it affects me deeply—sometimes I pass by their house and sort of dream of dropping in—and my second husband is now, thank goodness, in Argentina; he writes me absolutely marvelous letters, but I will never return to him. There was another man, the director of a factory, a very sedate gentleman; he adored me, wanted me to bear him a child, and his wife was also such a dear, so warmhearted—much older than he—oh, we three were such friends, went boating on the lake in summer, but then they moved to Frankfurt. Or take actors—such good, gay people—and affairs with them are so *kameradschaftlich,* there's no pouncing upon you, at once, at once, at once. . . ."

In the meantime Kostya reflected: We know all those parents and directors. She's making up everything. Very attractive, though. Breasts like a pair of piggies, slim hips. Likes to tipple, apparently. Let's order some beer from the diner.

"Well, some time later, there was a lucky break, brought me heaps of money. I had four apartment houses in Berlin. But the man whom I trusted, my friend, my partner, deceived me. . . . Painful recollections. I lost a fortune but not my optimism; and now, again, thank God, despite the Depression. . . . Apropos, let me show you something, madam."

The suitcase with the swanky stickers contained (among other meretricious articles) samples of a highly fashionable kind of vanity-bag looking glass: little things neither round nor square, but *Phantasie*—shaped, say, like a daisy or a butterfly or a heart. Meanwhile came the beer. She examined the little mirrors and looked in them at herself; blinks of light shot across the compartment. She downed the beer like a trooper and with the back of her hand removed the foam from her orange-red lips. Kostenka fondly replaced the samples in the valise and put it back on the shelf. All right, let's begin.

"Do you know—I keep looking at you and imagining that we met once years ago. You resemble to an absurd degree a girl—she died of consumption—whom I loved so much that I almost shot myself. Yes, we Russians are sentimental eccentrics, but believe me, we can love with the passion of a Rasputin and the naïveté of a child. You are lonely and I am lonely. You are free and I am free. Who, then, can forbid us to spend several pleasant hours in a sheltered love nest?"

Her silence was enticing. He left his seat and sat next to her. He leered, and rolled his eyes, and knocked his knees together, and rubbed his hands, as he gaped at her profile.

"What is your destination?" she asked.

Kostenka told her.

"And I am returning to—"

She named a city famous for its cheese production.

"All right, I'll accompany you and tomorrow continue my journey. Though I dare not predict anything, madam, I have all grounds to believe that neither you nor I will regret it."

The smile, the eyebrow.

"You don't even know my name yet."

"Oh, who cares, who cares? Why should one have a name?"

"Here's mine," she said and produced a visiting card: Sonja Bergmann.

"And I'm just Kostya. Kostya and no nonsense. Call me Kosta, right?"

An enchanting woman! A nervous, supple, interesting woman! We'll be there in half an hour. Long live life, happiness, ruddy health! A long night of double-edged pleasures. See our complete collection of caresses! Amorous Hercules!

The person we nicknamed the recluse returned from the diner and flirtation had to be suspended. She took several snapshots out of her handbag and proceeded to show them: "This girl's just a friend. Here's a very sweet boy, his brother works for the radio station. In this one I came out appallingly. That's my leg. And here—do you recognize this person? I've put spectacles on and a bowler—cute, isn't it?"

We are on the point of arriving. The little cushion has been returned with many thanks. Kostya deflated it and slipped it into his valise. The train began braking.

"Well, so long," said the lady.

Energetically and gaily he carried out both suitcases—hers, a small fiber one, and his, of a nobler make. The glass-topped station was shot through by three beams of dusty sunlight. The sleepy recluse and the forgotten forget-me-nots rode away.

"You're completely mad," she said with a laugh.

Before checking his bag, he extracted from it a pair of flat folding slippers. At the taxi stand there remained one cab.

"Where are we going?" she asked. "To a restaurant?"

"We'll fix something to eat at your place," said terribly impatient Kostya. "That will be much cozier. Get in. It's a better idea. I suppose he'll be able to change fifty marks? I've got only big bills. No, wait a sec, here's some small cash. Come on, come on, tell him where to go."

The inside of the cab smelled of kerosene. We must not spoil our fun with the small fry of osculatory contacts. Shall we get there soon? What a dreary town. Soon? Urge becoming intolerable. That firm I know. Ah, we've arrived.

The taxi pulled up in front of an old, coal-black house with green shutters. They climbed to the fourth landing and there she stopped and said: "And what if there's somebody else there? How do you know that I'll let you in? What's that on your lip?"

"A cold sore," said Kostya, "just a cold sore. Hurry up. Open. Let's dismiss the whole world and its troubles. Quick. Open."

They entered. A hallway with a large wardrobe, a kitchen and a small bedroom.

"No, please wait. I'm hungry. We shall first have supper. Give me that fifty-mark note, I'll take the occasion to change it for you."

"All right, but for God's sake, hurry," said Kostya, rummaging in his wallet. "There's no need to change anything, here's a nicer tenner."

"What would you like me to buy?"

"Oh, anything you want. I only beseech you to make haste."

She left. She locked him in, using both keys. Taking no chances. But what loot could one have found here? None. In the middle of the kitchen floor, a dead cockroach lay on its back, brown legs stretched out. The bedroom contained one chair and a lace-covered wooden bed. Above it, the photograph of a man with fat cheeks and waved hair was nailed to the spotty wall. Kostya sat down on the chair and in a twinkle substituted the morocco slippers for his mahogany-red street shoes. Then he shed his Norfolk jacket, unbuttoned his lilac braces and took off his starched collar. There was no toilet, so he quickly used the kitchen sink, then washed his hands and examined his lip. The doorbell rang.

He tiptoed fast to the door, placed his eye to the peephole but could see nothing. The person behind the door rang again and the copper ring was heard to knock. No matter—we can't let him in even if we wish to.

"Who's that?" asked Kostya insinuatingly through the door.

A cracked voice inquired: "Please, is *Frau* Bergmann back?"

"Not yet," replied Kostya, "why?"

"Misfortune," the voice said and paused. Kostya waited.

The voice continued: "You don't know when she will be back in town? I was told she was expected to return today. You are *Herr* Seidler, I believe?"

"What's happened? I'll pass her the message."

A throat was cleared and the voice said, as if over the telephone:

"Franz Loschmidt speaking. She does not know me, but tell her, please. . . ."

Another pause and an uncertain query: "Perhaps you can let me come in?"

"Never mind, never mind," said Kostya impatiently. "I'll tell her everything."

"Her father is dying, he won't live through the night: He has had a stroke in the shop. Tell her to come over at once. When do you think she'll be back?"

"Soon," answered Kostya, "soon. I'll tell her. Goodbye."

After a series of receding creaks, the stairs became silent. Kostya made for the window. A gangling youth, death's apprentice, rain-cloaked, hatless, with a small close-cropped smoke-blue head, crossed the street and vanished around the corner. A few moments later from another direction appeared the lady with a well-fitted net bag.

The door's upper lock clicked, then its lower one.

"Phew!" she said, entering. "What a load of things I bought!"

"Later, later," cried Kostya, "we'll sup later. Quick to the bedroom. Forget those parcels. I beseech you."

"I want to eat," she replied in a long-drawn voice.

She smacked his hand away and went into the kitchen. Kostya followed her.

"Roast beef," she said. "White bread. Butter. Our celebrated cheese. Coffee. A pint of cognac. Goodness me, can't you wait a little? Let me go, it's indecent."

Kostya, however, pressed her against the table, she started to giggle helplessly, his fingernails kept catching in the knit silk of her green undies and everything happened very ineffectually, uncomfortably and prematurely.

"Pfui!" she uttered, smiling.

No, it was not worth the trouble. Thank you kindly for the treat. Wasting my strength. I'm no longer in the bloom of youth. Rather disgusting. Her perspiring nose, her faded mug. Might have washed her hands before fingering eatables. "What's that on your lip?" Impudence! Still to be seen, you know, who catches what from whom. Well, nothing to be done.

"Bought that cigar for me?" he inquired.

She was busy taking knives and forks out of the cupboard and did not hear.

"What about that cigar?" he repeated.

"Oh, sorry, I didn't know you smoked. Shall I run down to get one?"

"Never mind, I'll go myself," he replied gruffly and passed into the bedroom, where he put on his shoes and coat. Through the open door he could see her moving gracelessly as she laid the table.

"The tobacconist's right on the corner," she sang out and, choosing a plate, arranged upon it with loving care the cool, rosy slices of roast beef, which she had not been able to afford for quite a time.

"Moreover, I'll get some pastry," Konstantin said and went out. Pastry, and whipped cream, and a chunk of pineapple, and chocolates with brandy filling, he added mentally.

Once in the street, he looked up, seeking out her window (the one with the cacti or the next?), then turned right, walked around the back of a furniture van, nearly got struck by the front wheel of a cyclist and showed him his fist. Farther on there was a small public garden and some kind of stone *Herzog*. He made another turn and saw at the very end of the street, outlined against a thundercloud and lit up by a gaudy sunset, the brick tower of the church, past which, he recalled, they had driven. From there it was but a step to the station. A convenient train could be had in a quarter of an hour: In this respect, at least, luck was on his side. Expenses: bag check, 30 pfennigs; taxi, 1.40; she, ten marks (five would have been enough). What else? Yes, the beer, 55 pfennigs, with tip. In all: 12 marks and 25 pfennigs. Idiotic. As to the bad news, she was sure to get it sooner or later. I spared her several sad minutes by a deathbed. Still, maybe I should send her a message from here? But I've forgotten the house number. No, I remember: 27. Anyway, one may assume I forgot it—nobody is obliged to have such a good memory. I can imagine what a rumpus there would have been if I had told her at once! The old bitch. No, we like only small blondes—remember that once and for all.

The train was crammed, the heat stifling. We feel out of sorts but do not quite know if we are hungry or drowsy. But when we have fed and slept, life will regain its looks and the American instruments will make music in the merry café described by our friend Lange. And then, sometime later, we die.

—Translated from the Russian by Dmitri Nabokov in collaboration with his father.

Nelson Algren

The Last Carrousel

February 1972

Chicago's own Nelson Algren (1909–1981), best remembered for *The Man with the Golden Arm* (1949) and *A Walk on the Wild Side* (1956), was one of the tough guys of letters, taking his material from the slums where he grew up and turning them into raw, realistic portraits of the mean streets and their inhabitants. He achieved another kind of fame as Simone de Beauvoir's American lover; she wrote about him both in her autobiography and in a novel. He would seem to have been a natural for *Playboy,* but in fact he contributed only a couple of stories. During the Depression, Algren worked for a while as a carnival shill down in Bonnie and Clyde country, where this story is set. He claimed that it cured him of the urge ever to work again—saying that writing was a way of avoiding the need to do so.

Nelson Algren

The Last Carrousel

I wonder whether there stands yet, on a lonesome stretch of the Mexican border, a green legend welcoming Spanish-speaking motorists to an abandoned gas station:

SINCLAIR *se habla español* SINCLAIR

A sign I once sat beneath, between a chaparral jungle and a state highway, shelling black-eyed peas. With a burlap sack, a pan and a pocket-size English-Spanish dictionary beside me, I shelled through the searing summer of 1932.

I'd painted that green welcome myself. Above a station that was home, storehouse and operational base for me and a long, lopsided cracker named Luther. I was proud to be his partner and proud that the station was in my name. I'd signed the papers.

We were occupying it, ostensibly, to sell Sinclair gas. What we were actually up to was storing local produce, bought or begged, for resale in the border towns. We had sacks, buckets, pails, pans, Mason jars and crates filled to overflowing with black-eyed peas. When word got around to valley wives that they could now buy black-eyed peas already shelled, they'd be driving up from all over southeast Texas. The Sinclair agent would think we weren't selling them anything but gas. By the time he caught on, we'd be rich.

Sitting bolt upright at the wheel of a 1919 Studebaker, under a straw kelly the hue of an old hound's tooth, Luther turned my memory back to the caption on the frontispiece of *The Motor Boys in Mexico:* "We were bowling along at fifteen miles per hour." He lacked only duster and goggles. I feared for the Mexican farmers.

"Protect yourself at all times, son," was Luther's greeting every single morning. "Keep things going *up.*"

I hadn't seen a newspaper for weeks. For news of the world beyond the chaparral, I awaited Luther's evening return. I did the shelling and he did the selling.

There were deer in the chaparral, buzzards in the blue and frogs in the ditch. Once a host of butterflies, all white, came out of the sun and settled about me as though they'd been sent. Then they rose and fled as if they'd been commanded to leave. In the big Rio heat, I shelled on.

Luther was the man who'd discovered the unexploited shelled-pea market. I'd make him foreman of my ranch in return. The Mexican help would love me, too. "Got the whole plumb load for only two dolla'," Luther announced smugly over his latest outwitting of a Mexican farmer: He'd returned with another carload. We sat down to a supper of cold mush and black-eyed peas, in the kerosene lamp's faltering glow. Our kerosene was running low. We were short of everything but peas.

"Collards 'n' black-eyed peas on New Year's Day means silver 'n' gold the whole plumb year," Luther assured me. He was full of great information like that.

"They thought they had Clyde, but they didn't." He gave me the big news once the meal had been eaten.

A sheriff had nearly trapped Clyde Barrow and Ray Hamilton in a farmhouse outside Carlsbad, New Mexico. But Bonnie had held the sheriff off long enough for Clyde to come around the side of the house and get the drop on him with a shotgun. New Mexico police had subsequently brought in a body, found in a ditch beside a highway.

No body was ever Clyde Barrow's.

"They'll never take Clyde alive," I prophesied.

The Sinclair agent had let us have a hundred gallons of gas on credit. As well as a high-posted brass bed whose springs bore rust from damp nights at the Alamo. Our chairs were orange crates. I lugged a five-gallon jug of water, pumped from a Mexican farmer's well, two miles down the highway every morning.

When the Sinclair agent had driven up with papers assigning responsibility for payment for the hundred gallons, Luther had claimed illiteracy. "Mister, Ah cain't but barely handwrite mah own name, far less to read what someone else has print-wrote. But this boy has been to college. He's *right* bright. Got a sight more knowance than Ah'll *evah* git."

The right-bright boy with all that knowance had felt right proud to sign the papers.

"When we git enough ahead to open a packin' shed," Luther assured me after the agent had left, "Ah'm gonna need your services to meet our buyers—Ah'll just see that the fruit gits packed in the back 'n' you set at the desk up front. How do *that* suit you, son?" That suited Son just fine. And if Luther averted his eyes, I realized it was only to conceal gratitude.

Once, at midday, the agent caught me in the middle of my bushels, jars and sacks. "We plan to can them for the winter," was my explanation.

"Well, you'll never get to be a millionaire by askin' for raises," he counseled me.

I already knew that you had to work for nothing or you'd never get rich. Grit counted more than money. All a poor boy had to do to get a foothold on the ladder of success was to climb one rung whenever anyone above him fell off. This made the rise from a filling-station partnership to owning a cattle ranch merely a matter of time and patience. And when the day came that I'd made the top rung, the first thing I'd buy would be a pair of Spanish boots and a John Batterson Stetson hat.

The reason we'd sold only one gallon of gas in that whole autumn season, it looked to me, was that Mexican farmers preferred to buy from Spanish-speaking merchants. *"¿Quiere usted un poco de este asado?"* I would invite myself aloud to dinner while shelling. And, finding the roast beef tasty, would ask for more: *"Dame usted un magro, yo le gusta."* That made a pleasing change from what actually went on in our mush-encrusted pan.

So I'd painted the sign that invited the Spanish-speaking world to our two pumps: with fifty gallons of gas beneath each pump. I'd gotten as far as *"Acérquese usted tengo que decirle una cosa"* when a Mexican drove up, hauling a trailer. I raced to give the crank forty-five or fifty spins. But the bum didn't want gas. He wanted tequila. What were we doing out here in the brush if we weren't selling whiskey? He turned his coat inside out to prove he wasn't a revenue agent. He couldn't believe that we were actually trying to *sell* black-eyed peas. Laughing, he swept his hand toward the chaparral: Black-eyed peas were as common as cactus. We *must* be kidding him.

Still convinced that we had tequila cached somewhere, he showed me a coin, representing itself as an American quarter, to prove he could pay. It was smaller than any quarter I'd ever seen. I wouldn't have taken it even if I'd had whiskey to sell. He wheeled away.

One night I woke up because someone kept snoring. "Is that you, Luther?" I asked.

"No," he grunted, "I thought that was you."

The snoring came again. From under the bed. "Who's under there?" Luther asked, leaning far over. For an answer he got another snort.

He got up, dressed in a union suit, though the night was steaming. He probed under the bed and looked in all the corners with the help of our kerosene lamp. Finally, we both got up and played the lamp under the station's floor: A wild pig was rooting under our heads.

"SOOOO-*eeeee,* soooo-*eeeee!* Git out of there, you dern ole hawg!" Luther challenged it. But no amount of soooo*eeeee*ing could get the brute out. Or stop its snorting.

The next morning, I piled into the front seat of the Studebaker beside Luther. I wanted to go to Harlingen, too. "Now, if we had an accident on the way," Luther pointed out, "with both of us settin' up front, both of us'd be kilt. But if one of us was in the back, he'd likely git off just bein' crippled but still able to carry on our work."

I climbed into the back seat. Luther smiled, smugly yet approvingly, into the rearview mirror. "Done forgot what I told you about protectin' yourself at all times, didn't you, son?"

I picked up a week-old San Antonio paper in town. Four youths had driven up to a dance hall in Atoka, Oklahoma, arguing among themselves. Two officers had come up to pacify them and both had been shot down. Other youths had grabbed the officers' guns and given chase. The outlaws had abandoned their car when it had lost a wheel, had kidnapped a farmer in his car, had set him free at Clayton, had stolen another car at Seminole and then had disappeared themselves. One of the officers survived.

"That *got* to be Ray Hamilton and Clyde Barrow," I decided.

"*And* Bonnie Parker," Luther was just as certain.

In the window of the jitney jungle in Harlingen, Luther pointed out a Mason jar of black-eyed peas I'd packed for the industry myself. I could hardly have been more proud. "You're practically the black-eyed pea king of the whole dern Rio Grande Valley awready," Luther congratulated me. I felt the responsibility.

Sheltered from the sun in the station's shadow, my fingers forgot their cunning in a dream of a Hoover-colored future, wherein I supervised a super Sinclair Station wearing a J. B. Stetson hat. Never a yellow kelly.

"I never been North"—Luther came up with curious news—"but my family been struck by the Lincoln disease all the same."

"What disease is that, Luther?"

"The one that stretches your bones. My Auntie Laverne growed to over six feet before she was fifteen, same as Abe Lincoln. Her shoe was fifteen and five eighths inches, it were that long. Same as Lincoln's. It caused her nipples to grow inward. Which made her ashamed. Later she went blind but recovered her sight 'n' spent the rest of her days blessing the light God had sent her personally."

The next night I wakened to hear a motor running that wasn't Luther's Studebaker. Yet I could make out his long lank figure in the dark, bent above the gas tank. I thought he was drunk and trying to vomit, because he had both hands to his mouth. There was someone at the roadster's wheel whose face I couldn't make out. "*Llévame a casa*" had been chalked on one side of its windshield and "Take me home" on the other.

"Feeling badly, Luther?" I called. He made a long, sucking sound for reply. Then he climbed into the roadster and off he wheeled with the mysterious stranger.

He'd siphoned the last drop of gas out of tank number one. I wasn't going to be the black-eyed-pea king of the Rio Grande Valley after all.

So I filled the Studebaker from the other tank. Then I dumped a bushel of peas into that tank, added five cans of Carnation milk, two plates of dried mush and a can of bacon grease. Then went back to bed content. Toward morning I heard the roadster return. I hoped I hadn't flavored the tank too richly. I didn't want Luther to choke on anything. After he'd emptied it, he wheeled away once more.

In the forenoon I went bowling along in the Studebaker at fifteen miles per hour. On a day so blue, so clear, it took my breath away to breathe it.

The *Llévame a casa*—Take me home roadster was parked out on a shoulder of the road on the last curve into Harlingen. Luther came out of it wigwagging. I pushed my speed to eighteen miles per hour and he had to jump for it. In the rearview mirror I saw him standing with his hands hanging at his sides like a disappointed undertaker's.

Now he'd walk into town to save a nickel phone call. And report to the agent that I'd absconded with a hundred gallons of Sinclair gas in a stolen Studebaker. Would the agent telephone Dallas to alert the Rangers? Would I have to run a roadblock at Texarkana? Would my picture be posted in every P.O. in Texas: WANTED DEAD OR ALIVE?

Clyde, Bonnie, Ray Hamilton and I were at large. I'd never felt so elated in my life.

I sold the heap to a garage in McAllen for eleven dollars without being recognized. I treated myself to *tortillas* and chili in a Mexican woman's lunch counter that leaned toward the Southern Pacific tracks. She didn't recognize me either.

I took cover behind a water tower until a northbound freight came clanking. I climbed into a boxcar, slid the big door shut and fell asleep in a corner. I slept for a long time, waking only to hum contentedly:

Dead or alive, boys, dead or alive
How do I look, boys, dead or alive?

Until in sleep I heard music, like children calling, between the beating of the wheels. Little lights were pursuing one another under the boxcar door. A calliope's high cry came clearly. I slid the big door open just an inch. Great silver-circling lights were mounting like steps into a Ferris-wheeling sky. A city of pennoned tents was stretching under those mounting lights. Then a tumult of merry-go-rounding children came on a wind that blew the pennons all one way.

I hit the dirt on a run, leaped a ditch, jumped a fence, fell into a bush, crept under a billboard, straddled a low brick wall and followed a throng of Mexicans under a papier-mâché arch into the Jim Hogg County Fair. And the name of that carnival town was Hebbronville.

A banner, strung between two poles in front of a tent and lit by carbon lights, showed two boxers squaring off. Someone began banging on an iron ring. A big woman, tawny as a gypsy, with a yellow bandanna binding her hair, mounted a bally and began barking: "*¡Avanza! ¡Avanza! ¡Avanza!* Hurry! Hurry! Hurry! See the two strongest men on earth battle to the death! See Hannah the Half-Girl Mystery! See the Human Pincushion!"

A dozen rubes were already gaping. A skinny boy, wearing white boxing trunks and muddy tennis shoes, climbed up the bally beside her. "Say hello to the folks, Melvin," the gypsy instructed the boy. The boy grinned stupidly.

"I never saw anything like it!" a roughneck in farmer's jeans exclaimed beside me.

I didn't see anything that remarkable. The boy looked to be about fifteen, thin as a long-starved hound, with legs that had little more than knobs for knees. His shoulders were so narrow there was just room for his goiterish neck between them. His chin receded so far an ice-cream cone would have had to be inserted beneath his upper lip before he'd be able to lick it. The Human Pincushion looked as if a pin stuck into his egg-shaped skull could cause him no pain, while his hair had the look of bitten-off pink threads.

Two young huskies, one in a tattered red bathrobe and the other in a faded blue one, trotted from opposite sides of the tent and climbed onto the bally, one beside the boy and the other beside the woman. "The Birmingham Strong Boy!" the woman held up the hand of the red-robed terror, who merely looked sullenly out toward the midway. "The Okefenokee Grizzly!" she held up blue-robe's arm. Grizzly merely frowned. Both men were high-cheekboned blonds, unshaven and looking enough alike to be brothers.

The Mexican sheriff came down the midway, checking the joints.

"Keep movin', tin-can cop," Strong Boy challenged him. "Keep movin' or I'll come down there 'n' whup you!" Grizzly, the woman and the Pincushion grappled with him to keep him from assaulting the officer. The sheriff kept on walking, smiling faintly. The rubes grinned knowingly.

"The man is an *animal,*" the roughie whispered to me confidentially.

"You must have seen the show before," I took a guess.

Grizzly threw off his robe, began pounding his chest with his fists and roaring. Strong Boy immediately threw off *his* robe, pounded his chest and roared back. They created such an uproar that one Mexican came on the run, leaving his wife and two children standing on the midway. Melvin and the woman got between the two monsters and the roughie jumped up onto the bally to keep them from tearing each other to bloody shreds publicly.

"The boys are going to settle their differences inside!" the woman announced after the two had been cooled momentarily. "Mountain style! No holds barred!"

"I don't want to miss *this!*" Roughie chortled at the crowd and headed for the tent, with the rubes following him like sheep following a bell ram. Melvin jumped down and began taking dimes. His chest, I noticed as I paid him mine, appeared to be mosquito bitten.

Someone had painted both sides of the tent with figures intended to be those of seductive women, but had succeeded only in creating two lines of whorish dwarfs. The angle at which the tent was pitched amplified the breasts and foreshortened the legs, so that each grotesque leaned forward as if she'd been impaled at her ankles. The artist had used too much red. Some whores.

Roughie, standing in front of a curtained closet no higher than himself, announced, "Hannah the Half-Girl Mystery!"—and opened the curtain. Swinging gently there on a child's swing, against a background of velvety black, a girl in a purple-and-cream-colored sweater looked down upon us with long, dark, indolent Indian eyes. Her body apparently ended at her waist.

"As you see," she explained in a voice as low and husky as a child's, "I have no visible means of support and still I don't run around nights. Thank you thank you thank you, ladies and gentlemen. Thank you one all. *Señoras y señores, gracias.*" The crowd sighed, as one man, with pity and love.

"She tires easily," Roughie explained and drew the curtain.

"You *believe* that?" a simple-looking fellow, in need of confirming his own doubt, asked me.

"Might be she got run over by a train," I took another guess.

He looked at me with the indignation a simple mind feels when confronted with a mind even simpler. "You dern *fool,*" he accused me. "Couldn't you even tell that girl was a-layin' on her belly?"

"Step this way, gentlemen," Roughie commanded us and nodded to the mosquito-bitten boy. *"Melvin the Human Pincushion!"*

Melvin shuffled onto the bally with a sheepish look and began pinning red-white-and-blue campaign buttons into his skin. Some were for William Gibbs McAdoo. When he used a Hoover button, I thought he'd surely bleed. He didn't bleed for either McAdoo or Hoover. He was a bipartisan pincushion.

Then he jabbed a huge horse-blanket pin into his shoulder and Roughie went face forward in a dead faint. Strong Boy and Grizzly, both in their fighting robes, carried him off. I was glad to see they'd made up their differences in this emergency.

The dark woman handed Melvin a small blackboard and a piece of chalk. He drew a line beside three lines already drawn and held the board up for us all to see. " 'N' that's the number of people has fainted during my performance just today!" he announced triumphantly and jumped off the bally without waiting for applause. That was a good idea, because there wasn't any applause.

"In this cawneh!"—and here came Roughie again, now in white referee's trousers, into the center of the makeshift ring—"in this cawneh, at two hundred and fifty-two pounds, the champion of the Florida Coast Guard—*the Okefenokee Grizzly!"* Pause for scattered applause. " 'N' in this cawneh, the champion of the Panama Canal Zone—*the Birmin'ham Strong Boy!"* Scattered applause by the same hands. "These boys are about to settle a long-standin' grudge, so any of you men who faint easy, kindly leave now. No money refunded once the battle has begun!"

"How about yerself?" Someone had to remind Roughie; but he paid no heed. "Now, this event is presented at no extra cost and no hat passing, because you men are all lovers of good clean sport, auspices of the Rio Grande Valley Wrestlin' Association." He turned to the wrestlers. "Boys, remember you're professional athletes at the top of your class, representin' the honor of the Florida Coast Guard and the American fleet in Panama, respectively, and I'm here to enforce the rules. Now, shake hands, return to your corners, come out fighting and may the best man win!"

Grizzly put out his paw, but Strong Boy, hateful fellow, struck it down. Then he turned on his heel back to his corner, handed his robe to the dark woman and flexed his limbs while holding the ropes.

"You'll pay dearly for *that,* Strong Boy!" The Human Pincushion threatened him from Grizzly's corner.

"Watch your mouth or I'll whup *both* of you!" the dark woman answered. Strong Boy, still grasping the ropes, spat across the ring directly at the opposing corner. The yokels loved it.

Strong Boy and Grizzly began circling each other, both frowning, yet not closing. Somebody booed. Grizzly went to the ropes, scanned the faces looking up through a haze made of tobacco and heat.

"What do you want for a dime?" he challenged the whole tent. "Blood?"

"Look out!" Pincushion warned him too late.

Strong Boy leaped on Grizzly from behind and they went to the canvas, rolling over and under from rope to rope in a roaring fury. The canvas shook, the tent poles trembled and the carbon lamps swung. Strong Boy clamped a headlock on Grizzly that nothing human could break. But Grizzly—being subhuman—broke it, sending Strong Boy staggering, his hands waving before his eyes in the throes of blinding shock. Grizzly backed against the ropes to gain leverage, then propelled himself half across the ring. Strong Boy stepped lightly aside, grabbed Grizzly's ankles as he flew past and brought him crashing down on his face. Strong Boy had only been *pretending* to be hurt! Swiftly applying a double scissors, a toe hold, a half nelson and a Gilligan guzzler with one hand, he began poking his opponent's eyes out with the other.

"*Give* it to him, Strong Boy!" the crowd came on in full cry, uncaring which of the two brutes got it, as long as one of them was punished murderously. "*Wreck* him, Birmingham!"

The blood lusters hadn't reckoned on the Human Pincushion. Melvin slipped through the ropes carrying a length of hose and now it was the dark woman who cried warning—*"Watch out, Strong Boy!"*—just as Melvin conked him behind the ear and knocked him flat on his face.

The referee snatched the hose length from the boy's hand and began loping about the ring, holding it aloft and crying, *"I'm here to enforce the rules! Here to enforce the rules!,"* as if waving a hose length proved that that was what he was doing; while Strong Boy still lay stretched defenselessly with Melvin kneeling in the small of his back. Grizzly, instead of helping Melvin, merely loped after the referee with his fists clasped in the victory sign. A bear's head was tattooed on his right biceps: a grizzly with small red eyes.

Then Strong Boy lurched to his knees, sending Melvin spinning, got to his feet and went loping counterclockwise to Grizzly, holding *his* fists aloft in victory. They passed each other twice making the same claim. Then both climbed out of the ring, followed by Melvin. Roughie paused to announce the results, *"Draw! Draw! Two falls out of three for the world's free-style championship! Final fall in one hour!"* Then he climbed out, too.

"*That* were the worst fake fight I ever seen my whole born days." A voice behind me drawled its disappointment.

"The holler 'n' uproar was pretty fair," a woman observed. Fake fight or real, the holler 'n' uproar had been fair enough to fill the tent with marks, some of whom had now brought women.

"And now, if the ladies will allow, I'll talk to the gentlemen *privately,"* the dark woman said, then waited. The half-dozen women in the crowd retreated, huddled and sheepish, as their fine bold fellows inched forward. "And I know you *are* gentlemen," she resumed, using a more intimate tone. "Do you see this little bell I hold in my hand?" raising a small tin bell and holding it high until every gentleman had seen it. "Now, I know what you men are here to see. I was young once myself—ha-ha-ha—and although you're gentlemen, you're still hot-blooded Americans." Her eyes scanned their ashen and chinless faces in which most of the teeth were missing. "But there's a city ord'nance against presenting young women in the *ex-treem nood* within forty feet of the midway—but back *there,* gentlemen, back *there* our young women are only waitin' for me to tinkle this bell so's they can start *goin' the whole hawg!"*

One tinkle and we'd be off! The men craned their necks like trackmen, but she lowered the bell, as if having second thoughts. Then suddenly threw up her hands, as if pleading. "For God's sake, men, don't go tellin' total strangers what you're about to see! You'll spoil it for your friends!" She waited to assure herself nobody was going to tell. Several more marks joined us from the midway while she still held the bell aloft.

"Gentlemen! If there's anyone here who can't control his passions when we get back there, I'll have to ask him to step forward and have his money refunded at the box office! No money refunded once the performance has begun!" Nobody stepped forward. She tinkled the bell at last.

"Awful sex acts goin' on right this way, gentlemen," the Roughie-referee directed us. "Step this way, gentlemen, for *awful* sex acts!" He was holding a sombrero into which we each dropped a dime as we passed into the partitioned rear of the tent.

"You handle quite a few jobs around here," I observed as I paid him.

"Why not?" he remarked cheerfully. "It's my tent."

A crude wooden cubicle, octagonal, with shutters at the height of a man's eyes, waited in the flickering gloom. We stood around it while crickets began choiring to a generator's beat. The Roughie came in, wearing a coin bag around his neck. "Get your nickels here, boys," he advised us, "two for a dime and five for a quarter, see the little ladies shiver and shake. You pay for the ridin', but the rockin' is free!" I had to wait in line to get change for a dime. A gramophone began playing inside the cubicle:

Ain't she sweet?
See her coming down the street!

I put in a nickel, the shutter lifted and Hannah the Half-Girl Mystery's long, indolent eyes looked straight into mine. She was wearing a red veil tied in a great bow about her hips and a green veil about her breasts. She moved her hips and breasts gently as the gramophone droned on:

Now I ask you very confidentially
Ain't she sweet?

The shutter closed. I put in my other nickel hurriedly. This time she had closed her eyes and was smiling faintly. The gramophone began another inquiry:

How come you do me like you do?. . .
I ain't done nuth-in' to you.

And *click*. Another nickel shot.

"Mighty short nickel's worth," I complained to the ex-referee.

"Ain't *nothin'* to what's comin' next, son," he assured me, "and no charge *whatsoever* for this next show—just keep your voice and your head down, right this way." I stooped to keep from bumping my head as he raised the next flap and then stepped into the ultimate mystery of a wide and stilly night. A full moon was just starting to rise. I stumbled across tent stakes until I'd regained the midway.

Under the new moon's coppery light, the fair seemed strangely changed. The dust that rose down its long midway, catching that light, looked like metallic flecks restlessly drifting. A glow, like beaten bronze, burnished the sides of tents that by day had been mottled gray. And the faces of the men and women behind the wheels and the stands and the galleries looked out more ominously than before.

The dark woman's plea of "*¡Avanza!*" sounded more pleading and the calliope cried *La Paloma* more urgently now. An air of haste stirred the dark pennons, as if to hurry the tempo of pleasure along. Everyone began moving a little faster, as though time were running out: All lights might darken at the same moment and never come on again.

"Spin 'er, mister!" Someone was challenging the wheel in a wheel-of-fortune tent. "Doublin' up! Let 'er spin! This is *my* night! Cash on the barrel!" A clinking of silver dollars followed and I hurried over to watch.

If the aging man in the paint-stained cap was having a winning night, he looked to me it must be the first winning night of his life. "Takin' the six!" he announced like an auctioneer. "*And* the nine!"

"Only one number to a player," said the wheelman, refusing the Cap's double bet. He looked worried.

"Afeerd I'll beat you *both* numbers, mister?" the Cap taunted the wheelman, yet the wheelman still refused him. I felt the Cap slipping a silver dollar into my hand as he whispered, *"Put this on the nine for me, son."* I immediately liked his plan of putting something over on the wheelman.

The wheel clicked fast, slowed at 5-6-7-8, then nudged onto 9 and stopped. All the poor wheelman could do was shake his head ruefully and complain, "This is the worst streak of bad luck I've *ever* run into," while he paid me twelve silver dollars. When I slipped them to my backer, he returned one as a token of his appreciation, whispering, "Play this for yourself, son." I was careful to wait until the wheelman stepped back from the wheel before I put it down. Nobody was working monkey business on *me*.

I put the dollar on 7. The wheel almost stopped on 6, then nudged over onto 7!

"We're killing him!" the Cap cried joyously.

The wheelman stacked the twelve dollars I'd won just out of my reach. Then stacked twenty of his own beside them and asked me casually, "Try for the jackpot, son?"

"Take him up," the Cap urged me in the same hoarse whisper.

"I don't know how it works," I confessed in a whisper almost as hoarse.

"You get the chance at the twenty-dollar jackpot because you won twice in a row, son. You don't have to bet on a number, you can bet on color 'n' that gives you a fifty-fifty instead of just a thirteen–one chance, 'n' if you bet on both color and number and you hit both, you get paid double on top of thirteen–one, making twenty-six–one 'n' a chance at the twenty-dollar gold piece—"

"Red!" I shouted. But the wheelman just stood waiting.

"It costs a dollar to bet on the color, because the fifty-fifty pay-off gives you too big an edge over the house—that's the rules of the game, son." I put a dollar of my own down and the wheel, sure enough, stopped on the red 5.

"Hit *again!* I never seen anything like it!" the Cap exulted and I wished he weren't so loud about it. He was attracting the attention of people on the midway. "Whoo-*eee!* This kid is a *gambler! Pay the kid off, mister!*" he threatened the wheelman loudly enough for the whole fair to hear. I didn't see any need for threats, because the man was already stacking my winnings in three neat piles.

I decided not to press my luck. "I'll just take my thirty-two," I told him.

"Play," the Cap hissed in my ear. *"You can't quit now."* Only this time, he wasn't advising. Now he was *telling*. I felt someone standing right behind me, but I didn't turn to see if it was anyone I knew. I just gave the Cap a fixed smile and then turned it on the wheelman so he wouldn't think I liked the Cap more than I liked him.

"Try for sixty, sport?" he asked.

"Sure thing," Sport agreed. "Make it or break it on the black."

"It costs five dollars to try for sixty," the Cap informed me. "Rules of the game." Could he be making those rules up as he went along?

"I don't have five, I have only two," I lied, because I didn't want to go into my right shoe.

"Let him try for two," a voice behind me commanded. The wheelman spun for two. If I won again, I'd have to make a run for it—but it stopped on red 0. The house had recovered its losses, plus three dollars of my own. I turned to go. Nobody was standing behind me.

"Sport!" the wheelman called me back and handed me two quarters. "Get yourself something to eat at a grabstand and come back. If you want to go to work."

I went wandering down the thronging midway, clicking my two consolation coins. One was smaller than the other. Why was it somebody was always trying to slip me phony money? I turned it over and saw it had Washington's head engraved upon it. I gave it to a woman selling *tacos* just to try it out. She gave me fifteen cents change. Well, I be dawg. That Mexican had been on the up-and-up, after all. With the ten-dollar bill in my shoe and forty cents in my hand, I had enough to go courting! I worked my way through the throng toward Hannah the Half-Girl's tent.

The ex-referee was sitting on the bally stand chewing a blade of grass, looking as if he'd been put together with wire, then sprayed with sand. A sinewy, freckled, sandy-haired, pointy-nosed little terrier of a fellow of any age between thirty and fifty.

"Stick around for the girlie show, son," he hustled me the moment he saw me. "You never seen anything like it."

"I've already seen the show, sir," I let him know. "May I ask you something?"

"Ask away."

"Is that wheel down the midway on the up-and-up?"

"Every show on the grounds is honest, son," he assured me, looking me straight in the eye.

"Reason I ask is that I lost three dollars playing it and that gave rise to some doubt," I explained. "I feel better now."

"Nobody wins *all* the time, son."

The dark woman came up, walking as though she were wearied out. Behind her the Half-Girl put her head and torso out of the tent. I hoped that that *really* wasn't *all* there was to her. Then the rest of her emerged on two sturdy legs and began moving toward us. I kept my eyes on the man and the woman. When she came up, I caught a faint scent of clove and lavender.

"Oh, they're nice enough," I hastened to assure the tent people. "One of them loaned me half a dollar and told me to come back if I wanted to go to work. It's the wheel with the Navaho blanket nailed up in back."

"That's Denver Dixon's," the man informed me. "You're in good hands, son." He added, to the girl, "Dixon has offered this young man a position." All three then looked me up and down, as though one thought were in all their minds.

"I can see how he'd prove useful," the woman decided for them all.

"We take care of Dixon's boardinghouse," the girl put in. "It's where you'll stay if you work for him. If you come back here at closing, we'll drive you out."

"I appreciate your hospitality, miss," I assured her.

The man put out his hand. "Name of Bryan Tolliver," he told me. "My wife Jessie. My daughter Hannah."

"That's spelled T-a-l-i-a-f-e-r-r-o," the girl explained. Now, how had a sandy little man held together by wire and a woman as weary and heavy as that gotten themselves a girl so lovely?

WELCOME TO
DIXON'S SHOWFOLKS BOARDING HOME
SPANISH COUSINE A SPECIALTY

Everything was settled, yet nothing was settled. Hard times had taken the people apart and hard times had put them back together: some with parts missing, some with parts belonging to others, some with parts askew, yet others with extra parts they hadn't learned how to handle. The times themselves had come apart and been put together askew.

Doggy Hooper, the shill in the paint-stained cap, had been a railroad clerk on the Atchison, Topeka & Santa Fe for twenty years. Now he showed me how he'd made Denver Dixon's wheel stop at 9 by a wire attached to his shoe, how he'd stopped it at 7, and then how he'd stopped it on red 0 when I'd bet on the black 11. Doggy replayed such small triumphs with the air of a man who'd made a killing on Wall Street.

" 'N' that's the way we flap the jays!" he grinned up at me, but a bit to the side, because his right eye was slightly turned out. "It's how we move the minches 'n' give the rubes dry shaves"—and he did a bit of a jig.

"Son," he suddenly said seriously, "do you have so much as a flash notion of how much people will pay for the chance of losing their shirts?"

I didn't have a flash notion. He showed me a pair of dice, which I had only to weigh in my palm to tell were loaded.

"I wouldn't play against you with these," I told him.

"Even if I told you *beforehand* they were loaded, that what I had in mind was to cheat you?"

"Surely not."

He stuck a finger at my chest. "You wouldn't *now*. But you will, son. You will." And he walked away.

The Atchison, Topeka & Santa Fe had made a good move in getting this old man away from their rolling stock, I concluded. He'd sprung a coupling and been left on a spur.

Doggy Hooper's parts didn't match. But then, nothing else around that old strange house matched. Upstairs or down. There were hens in the yard, but when you looked for a rooster, here came a capon.

Denver Dixon himself belonged somewhere else. Six feet one and slim in the hips, wearing a dark suit sharply pressed, walking so lightly in his Spanish boots with the yellow string of his Bull Durham pouch dangling from his lapel pocket, keeping his face half-shadowed by his Stetson and his drawl pitched to the Pecos, nothing he wore or said would indicate that he'd been born and brought up in Port Halibut, Massachusetts.

Had his big red-white-and-blue boardinghouse sign stood near the state highway, instead of being smeared across the side of a dilapidated stable, that would have seemed less fanciful. Chicken wire, nailed across the stable to prevent horses from leaping its half door, would have made sense had there been a horse inside. But all the stable held was a domino table teetering on a scatter of straw. Where harness and saddles should have been, fishing tackle hung. Kewpies of another day that once had smiled on crowds tossing colored confetti smiled on, though their smiles were now cracked and all the confetti had long been thrown. Along shelves were ducks of wood and cats of tin remembering, among paint cans in which the paint had dried, their shooting-gallery days. An umbrella hung above the Kewpies—what was *that* doing here? A burlap sack marked FEED held nothing but dusty joint togs discarded by belly dancers whose bellies by now had turned to dust.

The deep-sea tackle belonged to Doggy, who'd never come closer to a creature of the deep than to a crawfish in a backwater creek. Yet nobody considered the man strange because he practiced casting, with rod and reel, in ranching country. Once, showing me how to reel in bass, he hooked his line into a bristlecone pine. Then stood purely dumbfounded that anything like that could happen to a man in a country of cactus and bristlecone pine. If a blue whale could have been hooked in alfalfa, Doggy Hooper was the man with the bait, sinker and line to haul the awful brute in.

Doggy *liked* beating marks. He liked beating *me*. He beat me at dominoes and he beat me pitching horseshoes—and every time he beat me, he called me sport. But he never beat me for money again.

One forenoon I found him crouching before an orange crate half-covered with tar paper. Chicken bones, recently gnawed, littered the crate's uncovered side. A hole, sufficiently large for a small animal to enter, had been cut into the top of the covered section. I thought I heard a faint scurrying in there.

"What is it, Doggy?" I asked. He was too preoccupied with what was going on inside that crate to reply. He drew back without taking his eyes off that hole.

"Did you catch something, Doggy?" I asked. Doggy nodded as much as to say he'd caught something but wasn't pleased about it.

"What did you catch, Doggy?" I asked after another minute. "What's in there?"

"What's in there? What's in there?" he mocked me. "The Thing That Fights Snakes, fool! Now, stand back while I rile it up a little." I backed off.

He drew on a pair of canvas gloves, lowered his cap to protect his eyes and bent to the box once more. He appeared puzzled about something. "Damned little bugger just et 'n' now he's hongry again," he reported, shaking his head reflectively.

"It *is* a pure wonder to me, though," he reflected, turning back to his captive, "that it'd want *another* rattler so *soon*. Barely had time to digest *that* one. Where *am* I to find *another'n?"* he asked himself, then answered, "I just plain don't *know."* He stood up, appearing relieved. "Sleeping," he confided to me in a whisper. I bent down over the crate with utmost caution.

The top sprang open and a silver-streaking fury, all fur and fangs, flew at my face. I stumbled backward, wigwagging frantically to protect my eyes, then recovered myself and peered down through my fingers. An eviscerated squirrel, its fur painted silver, lay coiled at my feet. A spring had been wired to its tail and a set of old dentures joined to its jaws.

Doggy began leaping about the yard, his laughter breaking like crockery cracking on stone, holding his stomach for sheer joy of his prank. One can't expect too much of a semiliterate booze fighter, I thought, walking to the house and registering contempt with every step.

Jessie was in her rocker on the porch with a copy of the *Valley Morning Star* on her lap. I took the rocker beside her. A column of coal smoke kept rising from a Southern Pacific switch engine directly across the rutted road into a cloudless and windless sky. Voices, from the *iglesia metodista* just down the road, rose in praise of that same sky.

"En la cruz, en la cruz
Yo primera vi la luz
Y las manchas de mi alma yo lavé
Fue alli por fe yo vi a Jesús
Y siempre feliz con él seré."

"The papers keep puttin' every killing in Texas on Clyde and Bonnie," Jessie complained. "I know for a fact that Bonnie was in jail at Kaufman when them gas stations at Lufkin was robbed. 'N' it wasn't them that shot down the grocerman at Sherman. That was Hollis Hale 'n' Frank Hardy. Clyde 'n' Bonnie was up in Kansas gettin' married by razzle-dazzle."

"By what?" I asked politely.

"By razzle-dazzle. Flat-ride. Carrousel."

"Merry-go-round?"

"No. A merry-go-round is the gambling wheel you're working with Doggy. Could a couple fixing to get married ride *that?"* As a victim of one practical joke that day, and the day still short of noon, I thought it best not to pursue the matter.

"Just one of Mother's pipe dreams," Hannah advised me from the door. She was wearing some kind of hand-me-down burlesque gown, ripped under one arm, to which a few silver sequins still clung. The sun glinted on them so sharply that she canted one arm to shield her eyes, exposing a dark tangle of hair in the pit of the arm. Again I caught that faint scent of lavender or clove, touched now by perspiration.

"If you think me and your pa got married in church," Jessie reminded her sharply, "you'd do well to check with Bill Venable's steam razzle-dazzle in Joplin—'cause it was on that your pa and me got bound in wedlock, holy or not, 'n' don't you go forgettin' it."

And here came Doggy shuffling along with his cap pulled too low over his eyes. Well, let the poor geek tell his sorry joke, I thought, I'll go along with the laugh.

Yet the old man spoke not a word. Simply braced his back against the sun-striped wall with his cap low over his eyes. But when he glanced up, blinking toward the light, I saw his eyes looking inward and his cheeks pale as ash. Jessie gave me a flicker, as if to say she understood something I did not.

"I wasn't *disputing* you, Mother," the girl explained, "I just purely doubt that Bonnie Parker and Clyde Barrow married that way. After all, they're *not* carnies."

"They wouldn't be the first outlaws rode the flat-ride because they couldn't risk walkin' through a J.P.'s door," Jessie suspected.

"*I'm* not an outlaw, Mother," the girl caught Jessie up.

"And not much of a carny, neither," Jessie put her down quite as fast.

"All the more reason for me to be married in church instead of on a merry-go-round."

"We don't call it a merry-go-round," I put in authoritatively, "we call it a flat-ride or razzle-dazzle. Merry-go-round is a gambling wheel. Or a lay-down."

"Now," Jessie exulted at Hannah's expense, "you hear *that?* Here's an eye tinerant college boy turned carny bare a week 'n' he talks better carny than you who was born 'n' bred to tent life."

"*I* didn't attend college," Hannah explained, taking the rocker beside her mother's. "I want a *church* marriage. By a *preacher*. I'm just not goin' to set on top of some dumb wood brewery horse with a calliope blowing 'n' call *that* marriage."

"Your pa and me rode wood horses driven by steam 'n' *we* called it marriage," Jessie said reproachfully, " 'n' the flat-ride *we* rode we could have set atop a zebra or a lion if we'd wanted—*that* razzle-dazzle had a whole *jungle* on it. If we find you a steam-driven ride with a zebra, will you like that better, honey?"

"Mother, *try* to be serious."

I had the impression that this fanciful debate had been fought, uphill and down, numerous times before. Always about whether it would be a carny or a church wedding; and never a reference to a groom.

It had, of course, to be one of the half brothers who alternated nightly in the roles of the Strong Boy and the Grizzly. Lon Bethea, at 233 pounds, outweighed Vinnie by less than four pounds. Yet their combined 462 pounds of sinew, with the sheen of youth and the shine of health and the poise of power upon it, could hardly have left Hannah Taliaferro less impressed.

When they took her into their Model A in a kind of protective custody each evening, she sat in the back seat flipping the pages of a magazine, while they sat up front matching her indifference with their own.

"It's up to Vinnie and Hannah," Lon would say, resigning himself too easily to losing Hannah.

"If Hannah 'n' Lon make the ride, I'll be their best man." Vinnie was equally gallant. "I'm not agoing to stand in my own brother's way."

"It's awright with me if you marry 'em *both,* sis," Melvin came to his own decision—for which he caught a fast clap on his ear from her.

The Bethea boys hurled themselves into battle night after night, applying airplane spins and turnover scissors, hammer-locking each other, then butting like bulls: stomping each other's feet, barking each other's shins, then choking each other purple with Gilligan guzzlers; yet they breathed nothing but good will toward men by day.

The S. P. engine shunted a boxcar onto a siding, then raced backward, tootling all the way. "What's *that* fool got to toot about?" Jessie feigned indignation at the engineer. "Because he's driving a yard pig?"

"Goin' backwards is when folks blows their whistles loudest," Doggy decided, "or when they got no mail whatsoever to pick up. Don't I do a lot of tootlin' myself?" he asked. "And what have *I* got to tootle about? Ain't I been goin' backwards ever since I was born?" he asked in a voice prepared to grieve the whole bright day away.

"I cheated on my folks by playin' hooky," Doggy mourned on, unheeding. "I cheated on my wife with other women. I cheated on my kids by hittin' the bottle. I even cheated countin' boxcar numbers for the Atchison, Topeka 'n' Santa Fe." He paused for dramatic effect. "What else *could* I do? I were only a child.

"Giving the Atchison, Topeka 'n' Santa Fe a wrong count on boxcar numbers wasn't cheating," he explained to clear that point up, "it was a subconscious matter I haven't to this day been able to understand myself." He waited to see if we were interested in this mystery. Nobody was.

"I couldn't report a three if I was counting *inside,*" he recalled. "I had to go outside to do it. I could *not* form that number within walls. Inside, my fingers simply would not *do* it. Had to write another number or go out in the rain."

The little engine raced all the way back toward us, as if the engineer had been listening to our conversation and wanted to put in a word himself. Surely our voices, in that clear bright air, carried far down the tracks. Then he raced back down to the roundhouse and out of sight. Jessie turned toward Hannah.

"And if you're making plans to sew that seam under your arm before it's ripped to your belly button, young woman, I'll loan *you* a proper needle."

Doggy poked his ferrety face out from under his cap. "Aren't no proper thread." Then he pulled his head back under his cap and began singing challengingly:

> *"If he's good enough for Lindy*
> *He's good enough for me*
> *Herbert Hoover is the only man*
> *To be our nation's chief."*

"Good enough for Lindbergh ain't good enough for me," Jessie derided the President, the pilot, Doggy and the song. "Franklin D. Roosevelt is the man to set *this* country free."

"I'll tell you about Roosevelt," Doggy offered: "He's like the bottom part of a double boiler—gets all worked up but don't know what's cookin'. 'N' I'll tell *you* something, sport." He turned to me. "Any time you get into a town where the cops don't have uniforms, you can be sure the chow is going to be lousy." Doggy seemed to be coming out of his mood nicely.

"Is Mr. Dixon up yet, Mother?" Hannah asked.

"Gone to town bright 'n' early to pick up the Jew fella," Jessie reported. "Took them two fool wrasslers along." The "Jew fella" was Dixon's wheelman, Little British.

Although Hannah Taliaferro was a sturdy girl, she gave an impression of fragility. She was quick in mind and movement, but, even more, the impression came from that strange personal scent that seemed to mingle clove and lavender with perspiration. Men who fixed their eyes on a distant point when she stood directly before them looked perfect fools to me. I avoided looking the fool simply by shutting my eyes until her mother called her away.

The true mystery about Hannah the Half-Girl Mystery was not how her lower body disappeared at tent time, then reappeared as she swept floors, made beds and turned hot cakes the next morning. It was how, whether bending, walking, turning, resting, stretching itself or just standing still, it became more voluptuous at every reincarnation.

Her carelessness toward her own charms was not the least of her charm. She went about barefoot, wearing nothing but a hand-me-down burlesque gown, once red, now faded to brown. Her nipples, always pointing, as if forever taut, stretched the dress's thin fabric. When she bent down over the table to serve a dish, I saw a skin so tawny that the circles about the nipples were only a hue darker than the breasts themselves.

After that, I'd go upstairs to rest.

Doggy got so drunk, between the stable and the town, that he lay all day Sunday, on his garret cot, paralyzed by exhaustion. By Monday noon, however, he'd recuperated sufficiently to go about consumed with remorse: "No, you don't get a cigarette," I heard him pronouncing various penances upon himself—"*you* had *yours* Saturday. No, you don't get any lunch today. *You* had *yours* Saturday." All day Monday he denied himself, and part of Tuesday, too. Thursday evening he began letting up a bit on himself. By Saturday, we all knew, he'd be ready for an all-night bender once again.

▪ ▪ ▪

On September 1, 1932, the moon moved across the face of the sun and I heard an owl hoot in Dixon's stable just before noon. It was lighter than night, yet darker than day. I'd never seen an owl.

So I went searching the stable's shadows, with a flashlight, in hope of seeing that curious bird. All I saw was Doggy Hooper huddled in a corner, his eyes staring at me so fixedly I wondered whether it might have been himself who'd hooted. "You playing owl on us, Doggy?" I asked, playing the flashlight on his face.

"Gonna be a shakedown an' a shake*up!*" he cried without blinking right into the flashlight's beam. "Union's gonna throw old Doggy out! Roman black snakes after old Doggy!"

An uncorked pint lay on its side, seeping darkly onto the straw. "You're losing good whiskey, Doggy," I told him. His head wobbled, trying to focus on the figure behind the flashlight.

"Awright, Dixon," he muttered, "you come to collect"—he struggled to his feet, holding the wall of the stall for support—"this is the showdown! Show*down*. Show*up*. *Shakedown!* Shake*up!* I'll never borrow another nickel off you the rest of my life! I'll be your swore enemy!" I had to catch my swore enemy to keep him from falling and support him into the yard. Hannah came out to help. Between us, we got him up the narrow stairs to the room above the stable.

A Navaho blanket, torn and stained by tobacco juice and whiskey, covered Doggy's cot. A cheap alarm clock ticked on the floor. But Doggy wouldn't lie down. He sat stubbornly on the cot's edge and began croaking lonesomely:

"Mother's voice is gone from the kitchen.
She's teaching the angels to sing—"

"Try to sleep it off, Doggy, dear," Hannah pleaded with him, spoon-feeding hot black coffee into him.

"I'll do anything you fellows can force me to do," he finally conceded. "I'll take anything you can give me so long as I don't have to like it." He took a few spoonfuls of coffee from the girl, then looked at her drowsily. "If you don't behave yourself," he warned her, "I'll stop taking your money." And with that threat he fell back, rolled onto his face and sank into a snoring sleep.

Later I wandered down the road paralleling the S. P. tracks, up to the *iglesia metodista*. The doors were open, though no service was being held. Candles burned in the church's dusty gloom. I sat on the steps and waited for a train to pass in either direction. There was no train nor a rumor of one down the bright rails.

I wandered back to the house and around to the stable, wondering vaguely whether there might be anything left in the bottle Doggy had abandoned. There were half a dozen drops, no more. I drank them and pitched the bottle into a corner. Then saw, in the shadow, the crate that held the Thing That Fights Snakes. The Thing still lay coiled inside. I fooled around with its spring until I got it to leap. Then I put the cage in full view of the kitchen window.

"How was the tip Saturday night, sport?" Hannah put her head out the window to ask.

My back toward her, I contemplated the cage and made no reply.

"Did you have a good tip Saturday night, sport?" she repeated a bit louder. I held my silence and my pose. Her bare feet came padding up behind me. "Something happening?" I heard her ask softly.

"Shhh," I shushed her, "it's not finished eating."

"What's eating *what?"* She came up right beside the box. Apparently, Doggy's contraption was new to her. "What's not finished eating what?"

"Shhh, I might have to rile it up a bit."

"Rile *what* up, for God's sake? What *have* you got in there?"

She reached for the box, but I held her back with my hand and shouted, "The Thing That Fights Snakes, fool! *Back!* Stand *back!"*

That girl wouldn't back for tigers. Hannah put her eye to the opening. I sprang the catch. The Thing flew, claws, fur and silvered teeth, into her face. She fell back, waving her hands before her eyes, yet made no outcry. For a moment, she stood looking down, until the crazed look in her eyes subsided.

She turned the Thing over with her bare foot. As she turned it onto its back once more, a smile too sly formed on her lips.

Then she came right at me.

Around and around the stable I fled her rage. I had to keep running until she ran out of rage or breath, or stepped on a nail, or all three. Her fingers closed on my shirt, but I ripped away, feinted as if to double back and leaped ahead, gaining enough yardage to take me halfway around the stable once more. Then I stopped short and wheeled about. She barreled head down right into me, spinning me backward into the stable, crashing me against the domino table as she bore her whole weight down on me. The table collapsed above us in a cascade of dominoes. I clapped my hands about her buttocks, arching myself against her. She broke my hold by straddling me and we both lay a long minute then, struggling for breath. She recovered hers first, because I had her weight on my chest. I tried to push her off with my hands against her shoulders, but she pinned both my arms and slipped her tongue deep into my mouth. That kiss drained my remaining strength.

"Your buckle is hurting me," she complained, and released my arms to unbuckle it. Instead, I got my hands around her buttocks again. They were round and firm as new melons. I hauled her panties down nearly to her knees. She slipped half on her side to kick them off; when they caught on her ankles, she gave a wild kick and sent them flying toward the stable wall. That gave me my chance to roll out from under. I got halfway out and pressed her back with all the strength I had.

She was nearly pinned before she gathered her own strength and I felt myself being forced back inch by inch. In a flash it came to me why she was evading those heavy brothers. This girl wasn't going to be pinned under *anybody:* She could not bear it. Either *she* did the pinning or nothing was going to happen. She entwined her thighs about mine. I thrust upward at the same moment that she thrust down. She gasped with the pain that turns so quickly to pleasure. There was a fast flash of light behind her shoulder and I knew the stable door was standing wide. Then I heard a hoarse cry from far away. I blacked out.

I came to hearing my own cry dying hoarsely in my throat. A moment later, utterly spent, eyes closed, I felt her weight leaving me at last. When I opened my eyes I saw Hannah, silhouetted against the light, scuffling through the straw of the stable floor.

"Lose something?" I asked her.

"My underpants."

"What color were they?"

She glanced over at me. "What kind of question is *that?"*

"Because if they were pink, it must be somebody else's white pair hangin' over that paint can over your head."

I'd caught the sun's glint on the panties' white fringe, draped across the can out of which a brush was still sticking. It stood on a shelf behind and above her head. She snatched the panties down. Then, half rueful and half laughing, she held them up for me to see.

"Now, look what that Doggy Hooper done!"

The panties were dripping with silver hoof paint. It seemed that Doggy had half roused himself from sleep and had come down to do some redecorating. He was gone now, but he had daubed everything within reach. This brought heavy worry to my mind.

"Give me a couple minutes to get to the house," I asked her. "I don't want to spoil your marriage plans."

"Those boys wouldn't hurt you even if they did find out," she assured me. I wasn't that sure. I took a long swing around the house, so that I could approach from the front.

Jessie and Lon were taking their ease in the front-porch rockers. The rocker holding Lon looked ready to crumble beneath all that brawn. He was shirtless. That bear's head, tattooed on his right biceps, began studying me with its two small red eyes.

"I suppose Doggy went and told you of the practical joke he pulled on me," I asked as soon as I reached the step, my plan being to start asking questions before anyone started asking me anything.

"He jumped a dead squirrel out of a box on me once," Lon recalled. "I hit him with the box. He ain't tried it again."

But where was Vinnie? Had he been watching the athletics in the stable from his upstairs room? Had he come down the back stairs softly to see what was going on? Had he then conferred with Lon? Had they already set up a plan to catch me that night on the carny grounds? Had they taken Jessie and Bryan in on it? If they consulted Denver Dixon, would *he* speak a word in my defense?

"Clyde Barrow 'n' Bonnie Parker kidnapped an officer of the law," Jessie said. "Drove him around New Mexico all day before letting him go."

I couldn't have cared less that the law had been outwitted again. "I reckon I'll ride out tonight with Mr. Dixon," I said, forestalling Lon's usual offer.

"Suit yourself, sport," he said cheerfully.

"There won't be much of a tip tonight," Jessie guessed. "The sand is starting to blow."

I went up the footworn stairs to the little room beneath the eaves. Heat was piling up between the walls. A small clock was making a muted ticking, like news of some lost time too dear for losing.

Fifty-odd years from the bourn of his mother, twenty-two dollars in debt to Dixon, face down on the cot where he always fell, one palm outflung as if to say *"Spent it all!,"* Doggy Hooper was sleeping it off, fully clothed.

I stretched out on my cot, hearing voices mingling on the porch below. I fell asleep thinking I'd heard Lon speaking my name to Vinnie. Or was it Vinnie to Lon?

In sleep I felt something near and endangering. I struggled to waken. And quite clearly, though framed by a bluish mist, two massive dogs, sitting their haunches, waited for me to waken.

When I woke at last, Doggy was gone. Sand was tapping the eaves. I listened for something else but heard nothing. The small clock had stopped ticking and the wind was blowing up.

The carny folks were gathered about Dixon's board; but I passed the door as if I had somewhere else to go. I went out onto the porch and watched the wind swirling sand between the S. P. ties.

Dixon and Little British drove up, British at the wheel. I climbed into the rear seat.

"Doggy's off on a bender," I told Dixon. British made a U turn. As he straightened the car out toward the state highway, I glanced back and saw, briefly yet clearly, a pair of silver-colored panties hanging above the stable door like a challenge.

Like a challenge? It *was* a challenge. A challenge to Jessie and Bryan, as well as to the Betheas. That girl was going to bring on a family row *deliberately.*

To get out of marrying either of the brothers? Or to get out of her role as the Half-Girl? It had to be one or both. Because Hannah wasn't so thoughtless as to hang her silver-colored panties up to dry on a chicken wire in full view of the kitchen. There simply was no way of explaining away that garment, shining with silver hoof paint. She was going to blow up the family circle. And whether I got my neck broken in the ensuing row was, it was plain enough, a matter of no concern at all to Hannah.

My heart didn't spin with the wheel that night. Everything, it seemed, had stopped with Doggy Hooper's clock. Something had ended; yet nothing new had begun. And in that interval, I had to be more alert than usual, because I was working with Dixon instead of Doggy. In Doggy's absence, Dixon had wired the gaff to his own shoe, while I fronted the marks for him, one by one.

"Don't let your luck get away, mister," I encouraged a Mexican old enough to know better. "All you have to do is hit the red to get the thirty-dollar jackpot!"

It cost that one two dollars to try for the thirty-dollar jackpot, while signals went flying between Dixon and British. When they had eight dollars of the man's money, British wanted to get rid of him, but Dixon felt he'd stand more gaffing. They built the fool up to a one-hundred-dollar jackpot, and I helped by confusing and encouraging him at the same time, until the man had gone for thirty dollars out of his own pocket. Then he turned back to the midway with his collar awry, sweat on his forehead and a dazed look in his eye.

As Jessie had foreseen, the tip was thin that evening. Some of the tent flaps were already down, though it was still two hours until closing. Only the flat-ride seemed to be doing normal business, I judged, by its calliope crying *La Paloma* without ceasing. When I told Dixon I wanted to walk down to a grabstand because I'd missed supper, he gave me the nod to leave.

As I made the rounds of the joints, chewing a *taco*, sand was blowing so high that the lights of the Ferris wheel's lower half looked like lights seen under shifting waters.

I'd known, as soon as I'd seen that girl's panties above the stable door, that this was my last night at the Jim Hogg County Fair. But my mind was so dull from the heat and the heavy day, I couldn't think clearly about a means of getting away.

When I went back to Dixon's wheel, there was an old woman in a black-lace mantilla waving her arms at Dixon and British. That is, her tears and Spanish cries made her seem old, but when I went up, I saw she was hardly thirty. I hung back, trying to understand a few words of her Spanish rage.

All I caught was "thieves" and "husband." That cleared matters up. She was, most likely, the wife of the Mexican we'd just sheared.

By rights, as one of the hands in the shearing, I ought to be right up there taking some of the fire. On the other hand, what was *I* doing flapping the jays, anyhow? I didn't belong on any midway.

She was pointing a finger directly at Little British, feeling that *he* was the villain of the plot. Then Dixon put one hand on her shoulder and I saw him reaching for his wallet with the other. He wasn't going to risk having the sheriff shut his wheel down. And possibly the whole fair.

I took two steps backward, turned slowly away and began walking through the dust storm like a man walking through rising waters. I put a bandanna to my mouth and nose, as if to keep out sand. But it was also, I felt, a disguise. I held it there while moving against the crowd of marks coming in, despite the dust, under the papier-mâché arch with its legend: JIM HOGG COUNTY FAIR.

Then I ran for it.

I got over the same fence I'd scaled a week before and mounted the embankment before I looked back. In those few moments of flight, the whole sky had darkened. A swirling darkness was enwrapping the tents. Yet the calliope went on crying.

And the merry-go-round kept circling, circling, though its red, yellow, blue and green lights were blind with dust. Finally, the calliope began to subside. The merry-go-round was going around for the last time.

Then the music stopped and pennons and tents, grabstands and galleries, Kewpies and carnies and gaff wheels and all, were lost in a rising dust wind.

Blowing forever away from home.

Nadine Gordimer

The Conservationist

March 1973

Beginning with Shirley Jackson in 1960, women have published fiction in *Playboy,* though they are in the minority. Some women's fiction simply doesn't suit the male audience for which the magazine is edited, and some women writers don't want to appear in it. Nadine Gordimer, one of the world's most acclaimed authors, has been both willing and able for many years. Born in Johannesburg in 1923, she still lives in South Africa, where she is known as a passionate and eloquent foe of racial apartheid. Indeed, it might fairly be said that the international attention following her Nobel Prize for Literature in 1991 had a distinct effect on South Africa's political future. Her most recent book is *Why Haven't You Written?* (1992) and her best-known might be *Burger's Daughter* (1979). "The Conservationist" was her first story for *Playboy,* and a fine example of her observant, unsentimental writing.

Nadine Gordimer

The Conservationist

Pale, freckled eggs. Swaying over the ruts to the gate of the third pasture, Sunday morning, the owner of the farm suddenly sees: a clutch of pale, freckled eggs set out before a half circle of children. Some are squatting; the one directly behind the eggs is cross-legged, like a vendor in a market. There is pride of ownership in that grin lifted shyly to the farmer's gaze. The eggs are arranged like marbles, the other children crowd round, but you can tell they are not allowed to touch unless the cross-legged one gives permission. The bare soles, the backsides of the children have flattened a nest in the long dead grass for both eggs and children. The emblem on the car's bonnet, itself made in the shape of a prismatic flash, scores his vision with a vertical-horizontal sword of dazzle. This is the place at which a child always appears, even if none has been in sight, racing across the field to open the gate for the car. But today the farmer puts on the brake, leaves the engine running and gets out. One very young boy, wearing a jersey made long ago for much longer arms but too short to cover a naked belly, runs to the gate and stands there. The others all smile proudly round the eggs. The cross-legged one (wearing a woman's dress, but it may be a boy) puts out his hands over the eggs and gently shuffles them a little closer together, letting a couple of the outer ones roll back into his palms. The eggs are a creamy buff, their glaze pored and lightly spotted, their shape more pointed than a hen's, and the palms of the small black hands are translucent-looking apricot pink. There is no sound but awed, snuffling breathing through snotty noses.

The farmer asks a question of the cross-legged one and there are giggles. He points down at the eggs but does not touch them, and asks again. The children don't understand the language. He goes on talking, with many gestures. The cross-legged child puts his head on one side, draws in his lower lip, smiling as if under the weight of praise, and cups one of the eggs from one hand to the other.

Eleven pale, freckled eggs. A whole clutch of guinea-fowl eggs.

The baby at the gate is still waiting. The farmer goes back to the car, switches off the ignition and walks in the direction from which he has driven. He has left the road and struck out across the veld, leaping the dry donga to land with a springy crackle on dead cosmos and khaki weed that bordered it last summer. Over the hard ground his thick rubber soles scuff worn scrubbing brushes of closely grazed dead grass. He is making for the kraal; it is up beside the special paddock where the calves are kept at night. But the neat enclosure with oil drums cut in two to make feed troughs is empty; no one is about. From a line of rooms built of gray breeze blocks the sound of radio music winds like audible smoke in the clean fine morning: It's Sunday. A woman appears from behind the lean-tos of wire and tin that obscure or are part of the habitations. When she sees him approach, she stands quite still, one of those figures with the sun in its eyes caught in a photograph. He asks where the chief herdsman is. Without moving, but grimacing as if she strains to understand, she makes an assenting noise and then answers. He repeats what she has said, to be sure, and she repeats the assenting noise, long and reassuring, like the grunting sigh of a satisfied sleeper. Her gaze steers his back in the direction she has indicated.

He is crossing a lucerne field. The last late cutting of autumn must have been made sometime that week; although the shriveled scraps (like bits of busted balloon) that remain have lost their clover shapes and faded to gray-green, underfoot they give out now and then a sweet sickish whiff of summer—breath from the mouth of a cow or the mouth of a warm sleepy woman turned to in the morning. Involuntarily he draws it deep into his lungs and it disappears into a keener pleasure, the dry, cool and perfect air of a high-veld autumn, which, shut up in the car that carried with it the shallow breath of the city, he has not yet taken. Not this morning, not for a week. As the air plunges in him, his gaze widens and sweeps: Down along the river the willows have gone blond, not yet at their palest, combed out into bare strands but still lightly spattered and delicately streaked with yellowed leaves. Around them is a slight smudgy *ambiance,* a mauvish-smoky blend between their outline and the bright air . . . extraordinary.

Eleven. A whole clutch of guinea-fowl eggs. Eleven. Soon there'll be nothing left. In the country. The continent. The oceans, the sky.

Suddenly he sees the figure of the black man, Jacobus, making for *him.* He must have come out of the mealies on the other side of the road beyond the lucerne and is lunging across the field with the particular stiff-hipped hobble of a man who would be running if he were younger. But it's *he* who's looking for Jacobus; there's a mistake somewhere—how could the man already know that he is wanted? Some semaphore from the kraal? The farmer gives himself a little impatient, almost embarrassed snigger—and continues his own progress, measuredly, resisting the impulse to flag the man down with a wave of the hand, preparing in his mind what to say about the guinea fowl.

Although it is Sunday, Jacobus is wearing the blue overalls supplied him, and although there has been no rain and none can be expected for four months, he has on the rubber boots meant for wet weather. He's panting, naturally, but stops, as if there were a line drawn there, ten feet away from the farmer, and goes through the formalities of greeting, which include a hand movement as if he had a hat to remove. The farmer approaches unhurriedly. "Jacobus, I was coming to find you. How's everything?"

"No—everything it's all right. One calf he's borned Friday. But I try to phone you, yesterday night—"

"Good, that's from the red cow, eh?"

"No, the red cow she's not ready. This from that young one, that ones you buy last year from Pietersburg—"

Each is talking fast, in the manner of a man who has something he wants to get on to say. There is a moment's pause to avoid collision; but, of course, the right of way is the farmer's. "Look, Jacobus, I've just been down at the third pasture there—"

"I'm try, try to phone last night, master—"

But he has in his mind just exactly how to put it: "The children are taking guinea-fowl eggs to play with. They must've found a nest somewhere in the grass or the reeds and they've taken the eggs."

"There by the river . . . you were there?" The herdsman's lips are drawn back from his decayed horse teeth. He looks distressed, reluctant: Yes, he is responsible for the children, some of them are probably his, and anyway, he is responsible for good order among the dependents of the farm workers and already the farmer has had occasion to complain about the number of dogs they are harboring—a danger to the game birds.

"It's not as if they needed them for food. To eat, no, eh? You've got plenty of fowls. They're just pickanins and they don't know, but you must tell them, those eggs are not to play games with. If they find the eggs in the veld, they are not to touch them, you understand? Mustn't touch or move them, ever." Of course, he understands perfectly well but wears that uncomprehending and pained look to establish he's not to blame, he's burdened by the behavior of all those other people down at the kraal. Jacobus is not without sycophancy. "Master," he pleads. "Master, it's very bad down there by the river. I'm try, try phone you yesterday night. What is happen there. The man is dead there. You see him." And his hand, with an imperious forefinger shaking it, stabs the air, through chest level of the farmer's body, to the line of willows away down behind him.

"A man?"

"There—there"—the herdsman draws back from his own hand as if to hold something at bay. His forehead is raised in three deep wrinkles.

"Somebody's died?"

The herdsman has the authority of dreadful knowledge. "Dead man. Solomon find it yesterday five o'clock."

"Has something happened to one of the boys? What man?"

"No. Yes, we don't know who is it. Or what. Where he come to be dead here on this farm."

"A strange man. *Not* one of our people?"

The herdsman's hands go out wide in exasperation. "Nobody can say who is that man." And he begins to tell the story again: Solomon ran, it was five o'clock, he was bringing the cows back. "Yesterday night, myself, I'm try sometime five time"—he holds up his spread fingers and thumb—"to phone you in town."

"So what have you done?"

"Now when I'm see the car come just now, I run from that side where the mealies are—"

"But with the body?"

This time the jutting chin as well as the forefinger indicate: "The man is *there*. You can see, still there, master, come I show you where is it."

The herdsman stumps past. There is nothing for the farmer to do but follow. Why should he go to look at a dead man near the river? He could just as well telephone the police at once and leave it to the proper channels that exist to deal with such matters. It is not one of the farm workers. It is not anyone one knows. It is a sight that has no claim on him.

But the dead man is on his property. Now that the farmer has arrived, the herdsman Jacobus has found the firmness and support of an interpretation of the event: His determined back in the blue overalls, collar standing away from slightly bent neck, is leading to the intruder. He is doing his duty and his employer has a duty to follow him.

They go back over the lucerne field and down the road. A beautiful morning, already coming into that calm fullness of peace and warmth that will last until the sun goes, without the summer's climax of rising heat. Ten o'clock as warm as midday will be, and midday will be no hotter than three in the afternoon. The pause between two seasons; days as complete and perfectly contained as an egg.

The children are gone; the place where they were might just as well have been made by a cow lying down in the grass.

The two men have passed the stationary car and almost reached the gate. A coyly persuasive voice blaring a commercial jingle comes out of the sky from the direction of the kraal. . . . YOUR GIANT FREE . . . SEND YOUR NAME AND ADDRESS TODAY TO. . . . The baby in the jersey bursts from nowhere but is disconcerted at the sight of the herdsman. Hanging from his plump pubis, his little dusty penis is the trunk of a toy elephant. He stands watching while Jacobus unwinds the loop of rusty wire that encloses the pole of the barbed fence and the pole of the gate, and the gate, which is just a freed section of the fence, falls flat.

The road has ruts and incised patterns from the rains of the season before last, petrified, more like striations made over millennia in rock than marks of wheels, boots and hooves in the live earth. There was no rain this summer, but even in a drought year, the vlei provides some moisture on this farm and the third pasture has patches where a skin of greenish wet has glazed, dried, lifted, cracked, each irregular segment curling at the edges. The farmer's steps bite down on them with the crispness of biscuits between teeth. The river's too low to be seen or heard; as the slope quickens his pace through momentum, there is a whiff held in the dry air as the breath of clover was. A whiff—the laundry smell of soap scum. So the river's there, somewhere, all right.

And the dead man. They are jogging down to the willows and the stretch of reeds, broken, crisscrossed, tangled, collapsed against themselves, stockaded all the way to the other side—which is the rise of the ground again and someone else's land. Nobody goes there. When it is not a drought year, it is impossible to get across and the cows stand in midstream and gaze stupidly toward islands of hidden grass in there that they scent but cannot reach. The half-naked willows trail the tips of whips an inch or two above the threadbare picnic spot, faintly green, with its shallow cairn of stone filled with ashes among which the lettering on a fragment of beer carton may still be read by the eye that supplies the familiar missing letters. With the toe of his rubber sole, the farmer turns, as he goes, a glint where the bed of the river has dropped back; someone lost a ring here last summer. The blue overalls are leading through dead thistle, past occasional swirls of those swamp lilies with long ragged leaves arranged in a mandala, through a patch of tough reeds like the tails of some amphibians that keep their black-green flexibility all through winter. The two men plunge clumsy as cattle into the dry reeds, exploding a little swarm of minute birds, taking against their faces the spider-web sensation of floss broken loose by their passage, from seeding bulrush heads. There lying on his face is the man.

The farmer almost ran onto him without seeing: He was close behind his herdsman and weltering along doggedly. The dead man.

Jacobus is walking around the sight. There is a well-trampled clearing about it—the whole kraal must have been down to have a look. "How is happen? What is happen here? Why he come down here on this farm? What is happen?" He talks on, making a kind of lament of indignation. The farmer is circling the sight, too, with his eyes.

The face is in the tacky mud; the tiny brown ears, the fine, felted hair, a fold or roll where it meets the back of the neck, because whoever he was, he wasn't thin. A brown pin-stripe jacket, only the stubs of button shanks left on the sleeves, that must once have been part of some white man's business suit. Smart tight pants and a wide belt of fake snakeskin with fancy stitching. He might be a drunk, lying there, this city slicker. But his outdated "stylish" shoes are on dead, twisted feet, turned in stiff and brokenly as he was flung down into the reeds. Except for the face, which struck a small break or pocket between clumps, his body isn't actually on the earth at all but held slightly above it on an uneven nest of the reeds it has flattened, made for itself. From here, the only injury he shows is a long red scratch obviously made by a sharp broken reed catching his neck.

The farmer bats at something clinging at his face. No mosquitoes now; bulrush gossamer. "He was dead when Solomon found him?"

"Dead, dead, finish." The herdsman walks over delicately toward the object and, bending toward it a little, turns his face back at his employer and says confidentially, rather as if he had been listening—"And now already is beginning to be little bit. . . ." He wrinkles his nose, exposing the dirty horse teeth.

The farmer breathes quite normally, he does not take in the deep breaths of dry clear air that he did up on the lucerne field, but he does not reduce his intake, either. There is nothing, really nothing; whereas, up there, that sweetish whiff.

"You'd better not touch him. You're sure nobody here knows him? It's got nothing to do with any of you here?" He looks very deeply at his herdsman, lowering his head and hooding his eyebrows over his eyes.

Jacobus puts a hand dramatically on his own breast, where a stained vest shows through the unbuttoned overalls. He swings his head slowly from side to side: "Nobody can know this man. Nothing for this man. This is people from there—there"—he points that same accusing finger away in the direction of the farm's northern boundary.

The skin of the palm of a hand is too insensitive to detect the gossamer, but still it clings. The farmer projects his lower lip and blows sharply, upward over his face. And now he notices a single fly, one of the lingering, persistent kind, hovering just above the neat brown ear down there. The fly is on the side to which the head is fractionally turned, although it is fullface in the mud, the side on which the mouth must be close to being exposed. The fly hovers and lands, hovers and lands, unmolested.

"Just leave it as it is. The police must come."

"Ye-e-es, master," the herdsman says, long drawn out in sympathy for the responsibility that is no longer his. "Ye-e-es . . . is much better."

There is a moment's pause. The fly looks as if it ought to be buzzing but cannot be heard. There is the customary silence down here among the reeds, broken by the rifle crack (so it sounds, in contrast) of a dry stalk snapped by the movement of some unseen bird. The seething of the wind through the green reeds in late summer is seasonal.

They turn and thrash back the way they had come, leaving the man. Behind them, he is lying alone on his face.

The farmer takes the car to get up to the house and Jacobus comes with him, sitting carefully with feet planked flat on the carpeted floor and curled hands together on neat knees—he has the keys, so that he can always get into the house to telephone to town during the week, when the farmer is not a farmer but an industrialist, in pig iron. The house is closed up, because no one lives there all week. They enter through the kitchen door and the farmer goes straight to the telephone in the living room and turns the little crank on the box. The party line is busy and while he waits, he frees from the thin tacky mud on his soles the slivers of dry reed that are stuck in it. He prizes one sole against the other and the mud wrinkles and blobs, like droppings, to the shiny linoleum patterned with orange-and-brown roses. The table is laid ready with hardware for a meal, under a net weighted at the hem with colored beads; an authoritative refrigerator, placed across the angle of a corner, hums to itself. The ring that he is waiting for makes him start. The line is free now and the exchange puts him through to the police station.

He always talks the white man's other language to officials and he is speaking in Afrikaans. "Look—Mehring here, from Vleibos, the Groendal Road. You must send someone. There's a dead man been found on my farm. Down in the vlei. Looks as if he'd been dumped there."

There is a blowing noise, abrupt, at the other end, air is expelled in good-natured exasperation. The voice addresses him as if he were an old friend: "Man . . . on Sunday . . . where'm I going to get someone? The van's out on patrol at the location. I'm alone here, myself. It's a Bantu, ay?"

"Yes. The body's lying in the reeds."

"Your boys have a fight or what?"

"It's a stranger. None of my boys knows who it is."

The voice laughs. "Yes, they're scared, they'll say they don't know. Was it a knife fight, I suppose?"

"I tell you, I've no idea. I don't want to mess about with the body and confuse your investigation. You must send someone."

"Hell, I don't know what I'm going to do about that. I'm only myself, here. The van's at the location. . . . I'll send tomorrow morning."

"But this body was found yesterday, it's been lying there twenty-four hours already."

"What can I do, sir? Man, I'm alone here!"

"Why can't you get hold of some other police station? Let them send someone."

"Can't do that. This's my district."

"Well, what am I to do about a dead body on my property? The man may have been murdered. It's obvious he's been knocked on the head or something and dumped. You can see from his shoes he didn't walk a step in that vlei."

"There's injuries on the head or where?"

"I've told you, that's your affair. I don't want my boys handling someone who's been murdered. I don't want any trouble afterward about this business. You must get a man out here today, Sergeant."

"First thing in the morning. There won't be any trouble for you, don't worry. You're there by the vlei, just near the location, ay? It comes from there, all right, they're a terrible lot of Kaffirs there, we're used to that lot. . . ."

The farmer replaces the receiver and says in English, "Christ Almighty"; and snorts a laugh, softly, so that Jacobus shall not hear.

The herdsman is waiting in the kitchen. "They'll come early tomorrow. I've told them everything. Just keep people away. And dogs. See that no dogs go down there." The herdsman doesn't react at all, although he has no doubt that the farmer didn't know that the dogs that were supposed to be banished from the kraal have quietly reappeared again, not the same individual animals, perhaps, but as a genus.

"Excuse, my master"—he indicates that he wants to pass before him into the living room and tramps, tiptoeing almost, across to a piece of furniture that must once have featured as the pride of a dining-room "suite" for the previous owner of the farm but is now used as a bar (a locked cupboard to which Jacobus has not got a key) and also repository (unlocked drawers) for farm documents, and pulling out one of the stiff drawers by its fancy gilt handle, feels surely under the feed bills tossed there. He has found what he apparently had hidden for safekeeping: He brings in the bowl of his palms a huge, black-dialed watch with broad metal strap and a pair of sunglasses with a cracked right lens. He waits, indicating by the pause that his employer must put out his hand to receive, and formally gives over the property. "From him?" And the herdsman nods heavily.

"All right, Jacobus."

"All right, master."

"Send Alina up about one to make me some lunch, eh?" he calls after him.

So they have touched the thing, lifted the face. Of course, the dark glasses might have been in a pocket. No money. Not surprising; these Friday, payday, murderers are for money, what else? Jacobus took the objects (the Japanese-made steel watch is the kind black men offer surreptitiously for sale on street corners) into safekeeping to show that the people here've got nothing to do with the whole business.

Going to the drawer Jacobus has just shut, he finds a window envelope, already franked, that had carried some circular. The watch, with its flexible steel-mesh strap wrapped close, fits in easily, but the glasses prevent the flap from closing. He doubles a rubber band over his fingers and stretches it to secure envelope and contents. He writes on it, "Watch and Glasses, property of dead man." He adds, "For the Police," and places the envelope prominently on the table, on top of the net, then moves it to the kitchen, putting it on the draining board of the sink, where it cannot fail to be in the line of vision as one walks into the house.

Outside the kitchen door, he distends his nostrils distastefully at the smell of duck shit and three or four pallid kittens whose fur is thin as the bits of duck down that roll softly about in invisible currents of air run from the threatening column of his body. "Psspsspss," he calls, but they cower and one even hisses. He strides away, past the barn, the paddock where the cows about to calve stand hugely in company and the tiny paddock where the bull, used less and less now, with the convenience of artificial insemination available, is always alone, and he continues by way of the mealie fields the long walk around the farm, on a perfect

Sunday morning, he was about to begin when he stopped the car at the third pasture.

The matter of the guinea-fowl eggs has not been settled. He's conscious of this as he walks, because he knows it's no good allowing such things to pass. They must be dealt with. Eleven freckled eggs. It would have been useless to put them under the black Orpingtons; they must have been cold already. A red-legged partridge is taking a dust bath where it thinks it won't be spied, at the end of a row of mealies reaped and ready to be uprooted. But there are no guinea fowl feeding down in the far field where they usually come. Those bloody dogs; their dogs have probably been killing them off all summer. Eleven eggs, pointed, so different from hens' eggs made to lie in the standard depressions of plastic trays, in dozens, subject to seasonal price fluctuation. Soon there will be nothing left. (No good thinking about it: put a stop to it.) The hands of the child round the pale eggs were the color of the underside of an empty tortoise shell held up to the light. The mealies are nearly all reaped, the stalks stacked in pyramids with dry plumy apexes, the leaves peeling tattered. Distance comes back with these reaped fields, the plowed earth stretching away in fan-shaped ridges to its own horizon; the farm extends in size in winter, just as in summer as the mealies grow taller and thicker the horizon closes in, diminishes the farm until it is a series of corridors between walls of stiff green higher than his head. In a good year. If there is going to be a good year again. A cultivator has been left to rust on its side (no rain to rust it, but still, standing out here won't do it any good). Now is the time to clear the cankerweed that plagues this part of the field, near the eucalyptus trees, which have made a remarkable recovery—he can scarcely notice, for new branches, the stumps where they (up at the kraal) had chopped at them for firewood before he bought the place.

Although he had no sign of it when he set out this morning, a Saturday-night headache is now causing pressure on the bridge of his nose; closing his eyes against the light, he pinches the bone there between thumb and finger. He feels pleasantly, specifically thirsty for water. He makes for the windmill near an old stone outbuilding. The cement round the borehole installation is new and the blades of the windmill are still shiny. He puts his head sideways to the stiff tap and the water sizzles, neither warm nor cold, into his mouth. The windmill is not turning and he releases the chain and arm that brake it in order to set it going, but although it noses creakily, it does not begin to turn, because there is no wind today, the air is still, it is a perfect autumn day. He sets the brake again carefully.

A little after one, passing the room of the servant, Alina, beside the fowl run, on his way up to the house, he sees Jacobus talking there to her. He and the herdsman do not acknowledge each other, because they have seen each other before and no greeting is exchanged. He calls out, "You'd better take something—to put over"—his head jerks toward the river—"down there. An old tarpaulin. Or sacks."

John Irving

Brennbar's Rant

December 1974

Several chapters of John Irving's famous novel *The World According to Garp* (1978) appeared in earlier incarnations as short stories in *Playboy.* "Brennbar's Rant," which explores the anguish of zitism, is not one of them. It shows the author in his most antic mood, which, for Irving, is positively zany. Born in New Hampshire in 1942, and strongly associated with New England, Irving worked on and off as a wrestling coach at various preparatory schools even after the breakout success of *Garp,* which rivaled García Marquez's *One Hundred Years of Solitude* as the most successful literary novel to be published in the 1970s. It was, of course, later adapted as a film, as was *The Hotel New Hampshire* (1981). *Garp* was his fourth book—*Setting Free the Bears* in 1969 was the first—and it has been followed by three more, all of them considerable best-sellers, the last being *A Prayer for Owen Meany* in 1989. Irving's work is both spirited and attentive to detail, even in a story as unbuttoned as this one.

John Irving

Brennbar's Rant

My husband, Ernst Brennbar, worked steadily on his second cigar and his third cognac. A slow, rising heat flushed his cheeks. His tongue felt lazy and overweight. He knew that if he didn't try to speak soon, his mouth would loll open and he'd belch—or worse. A bear of guilt shifted in his stomach and he remembered the bottle of '64 Brauneberger Juffer Spatlese that had accompanied his ample portion of *truite Metternich.* His red ears throbbed a total recall of the '61 Pommard Rugiens that had drowned his *boeuf Crespi.*

Brennbar looked across the wasted dinner table at me, but I was lost in a conversation about minority groups. The man speaking to me appeared to be a member of one. For some reason, the waiter was included—perhaps as a gesture meant to absolve class distinctions. Perhaps because the man who spoke with me and the waiter were from the same minority group.

"You wouldn't know anything about it," the man told me, but I'd been watching my blotching husband; I hadn't been paying attention.

"Well," I said defensively. "I can certainly imagine what it must have been like."

"Imagine!" the man shouted. He tugged the waiter's sleeve for support. "This was the real thing. No amount of *imagining* could ever make you feel it like we did. We had to live with it every day!" The waiter guessed he should agree.

Another woman, sitting next to Brennbar, suddenly said, "That's no different from what women have always had to face—what we still have to face today."

"Yes," I said quickly, turning on the man. "For example, you're bullying me right now."

"Look, there's no persecution like religious persecution," the man said, yanking the waiter's arm for accent.

"You might ask a black," I said.

"Or any woman," said the woman next to Brennbar. "You talk as if you had a monopoly on discrimination."

"You're all full of shit," said Brennbar, slowly uncoiling his lounging tongue. The others stopped talking and looked at my husband as if he were a burn hole developing in a costly rug.

"Darling," I said, "we're talking about minority groups."

"As if that counts me out?" Brennbar asked. He made me disappear in a roil of cigar smoke. But the woman next to him seemed to feel provoked by this; she responded recklessly.

"I don't see that you're black," she said, "or a woman or a Jew. You're not even Irish or Italian or something like that, are you? I mean—*Brennbar*—what's that? German?"

"Oui," said the waiter. "That's German, I know it."

And the man whose pleasure had been to abuse me said, "Oh, that's a fine minority group." The others—but not I—laughed. I was familiar with my husband's signals for the control he gradually lost on polite conversation; blowing cigar smoke in my face was a fairly advanced phase.

"My husband is from the Midwest," I said cautiously.

"Oh, you poor man," said the woman next to Brennbar. Her hand lay with facetious sympathy on Brennbar's shoulder.

"How appalling: the Midwest," someone far down the table muttered.

And the man who held the waiter's sleeve with the importance he might lavish on a mine detector said, "Now, there's a minority group!" Laughter embraced the table while I observed my husband's journey through one more lost control he held on polite conversation: the stiff smile accompanied by the studied tossing off of his third cognac and the oversteady pouring of his fourth.

I was so full I felt I'd temporarily lost my cleavage, but I said, "I'd like dessert. Would anyone else have anything else?" I asked, watching the studied tossing off of my husband's fourth cognac and the fantastically deliberate pouring of his fifth.

The waiter remembered his job; he fled to fetch the menu. And the man who had sought in the waiter an ethnic kinship boldly faced Brennbar and said with unctuous condescension, "I was merely trying to establish that religious discrimination—at least historically—is of a more subtle and pervasive kind than those forms of discrimination we have all jumped on the band wagon about lately, with our cries of racist, sexist——"

Brennbar belched: a sharp shot like a brass bedpost ball flung at random into the kitchenware. I was familiar with this phase, too; I knew now that the dessert would come too late and that my husband scarcely needed to pause before he would launch forth.

Brennbar began: "The first form of discrimination I encountered while growing up is so subtle and pervasive that even to this day no group has been able to organize to protest it, no politician has dared mention it, no civil-liberty case has been taken to the courts. In no major, nor in any minor, city is there even a suitable ghetto where these sufferers can support one another. Discrimination against them is so total that they even discriminate against one another; they are ashamed to be what they are, they are ashamed of it when they're alone—and all the more ashamed to be seen together."

"Listen," said the woman next to Brennbar, "if you're talking about homosexuality, what you're saying is no longer the case——"

"I'm talking about pimples," Brennbar said. "Acne," he added, with a meaningful and hurting glance about the table. "Zits," Brennbar said. The others, those who dared, stared into my husband's deeply cratered face as if they were peeking into a disaster ward in a foreign hospital. Alongside that terrible evidence, the fact that we were ordering dessert *after* brandy and cigars was of little consequence. "You all knew people with pimples," Brennbar accused them. "And pimples disgusted you, didn't they?" The diners all looked away from him, but their memory of his pockmarks must have been severe. Those indentations, those pits, appeared to have been made by stones. My God, he was lovely.

Nearby, but coming no nearer, the waiter hovered and held back the dessert menus from this queer party as if he feared the menus could be consumed by our silence.

"Do you think it was easy to go into a drugstore?" Brennbar asked. "A whole cosmetic counter devoted to reminding you, the saleslady grinning at your zits and saying loudly, 'What can I do for you?' As if she didn't know. Even your own parents were ashamed of you! Subtle indications that your pillowcase was not washed with the rest of the laundry and at breakfast your mother would say to you, 'Dear, you know, don't you, that the *blue* washcloth is yours?' Then watch your sister's face pale; she excuses herself from the table and rushes to rewash. Talk about myths involved with discrimination! God, you'd think pimples were more communicative than clap! Some kid after gym class asks if someone has a comb; you offer him yours, you see his mind melt—praying for an alternative, imagining his precious scalp alive with your zits. It was a common fable: If you saw a pimple, you assumed dirt. People who produce pus never washed.

"I swear on my sister's sweet ass," Brennbar said (he has no sister), "I washed my entire body three times a day. One day I washed my face eleven times. Every morning I went to the mirror to read the news. Like a body count in a war. Maybe the acne plaster killed two overnight, but four more have arrived. You learn to expect the greatest humiliation at the worst time: The morning of the night you achieved that blind date, there's a new one pulling your lip askew. Then one day, out of misguided pity or a vast and unfathomable cruelty, those few people who pass for your friends secure you a date with *another* pimple freak! Mortified, you both wait for it to end. Did they expect we would exchange remedies or count our permanent scars?

"Zitism!" Brennbar yelled. "That's what it is, zitism! And you're *zitists,* all of you, I'm sure of it," he muttered. "You couldn't begin to understand how awful. . . ." His cigar was out; apparently shaken, he fumbled to relight it.

"No," said the man next to me. "I mean, yes . . . I can understand how terrible that must have been for you, really."

"It's nothing like your problem," Brennbar said morosely.

"No, well, yes—I mean, really, it *is* sort of what I mean," the man groped. "I can truly imagine how awful——"

"Imagine?" I said, my face alert, my mouth turning toward my best smile. "But what about what you said to me? You can't possibly *feel* it like he did. He had to *live* with it every day." I smiled at my husband. "Those were real pimples," I told my former attacker. "They're not to be imagined." Then I leaned across the table and touched Brennbar's hand affectionately. "Nice work, darling," I said. "You got him."

"Thanks," said Brennbar, totally relaxed. His cigar was relit; he passed the rim of his brandy snifter under his nose like a flower.

The woman next to Brennbar was unsure. She touched him gently, but urgently, and said to him, "Oh, I see, you were kidding—sort of. Weren't you?" Brennbar consumed her in cigar smoke before she could read his eyes; I can always read his eyes.

"Well, not kidding, exactly—were you, darling?" I said. "I think it was a metaphor," I told the others, and they looked at Brennbar with all the more suspicion. "It was a metaphor for growing up with intelligence in a stupid world. It meant that intelligence is so peculiar—so rare—that those of us with any real brains are constantly being discriminated against by the masses of stupidity around us." The entire table looked more pleased. Brennbar smoked; he could be an infuriating man.

"Of course," I went on, "people with intelligence really constitute one of the smallest minority groups. They have to endure the wallowing sheep-mindedness and flagrant idiocy of what's forever being *popular.* Popularity is probably the greatest insult to an intelligent person. Hence," I said, with a gesture to Brennbar, who was resembling a still life, "acne is a perfect metaphor for the feeling of being unpopular, which every intelligent person must suffer. Intelligence is unpopular, of course. Nobody likes an intelligent person. Intelligent people are not to be trusted. We suspect that their intelligence hides a kind of perversity. It's a little like thinking that people with pimples are unclean."

"Well," began the man next to me—he was warming up to the conversation, which he must have felt was returning to more comfortable ground. "Of course, the notion of the intellectual constituting a kind of ethnic group—this is hardly new. America is predominantly anti-intellectual. Look at television. Professor types are all batty eccentrics with the sort of temperaments of grandmothers. All idealists are fanatics or saints, young Hitlers or young Christs. Children who read books wear glasses and secretly wish they could play baseball as well as the other kids. We prefer an armpit evaluation of a man. And we like his mind to be possessed by the kind of stubborn loyalty we admire in dogs. But I must say, Brennbar, to suggest that pimples are analogous to intellect—"

"Not intellect," I said. "Intelligence. There are as many stupid intellectuals as there are stupid baseball players. Intelligence simply means the perception of what is going on." But Brennbar was cloaked in an enigma of cigar smoke and even the woman next to him could not see through to his point of view.

The man who had momentarily experienced the illusion of returning to more comfortable ground said, "I would dispute with you, Mrs. Brennbar, that there are as many stupid intellectuals as there are stupid baseball players."

Brennbar released a warning belch: a long, tunneling and muffled signal like a trash can thrown down an elevator shaft while you were far away, in a shower on the 31st floor ("Who's there?" you'd call out to your empty apartment).

"Dessert?" said the waiter, distributing menus. He must have thought Brennbar had asked for one.

"I'll have the *pommes Normande en belle vue,*" said the faraway man who had found the Midwest appalling. His wife wanted the *pouding alsacien,* a cold dessert.

"I'd like the *charlotte Malakoff aux fraises,*" said the woman next to Brennbar.

I said I'd have the *mousseline au chocolat.*

"Shit," said Brennbar. Whatever he'd meant as a metaphor, his ravaged face was no invention; we could all see that.

"I was just trying to help you, darling," I said, in a shocking new tone.

"Smart bitch," Brennbar said.

The man for whom comfortable ground was now a hazardous free fall away sat in this uneasy atmosphere of warring minority feelings and wished for more intelligence than he had. "I'll have the *clafouti aux pruneaux,*" he said sheepishly.

"You would," said Brennbar. "That's just what I figured you for."

"I got him right, too, darling," I said.

"Did you guess *her?*" Brennbar asked me, indicating the woman next to him.

"Oh, she was easy," I said. "I got everyone."

"I was wrong on yours," Brennbar told me. He seemed troubled. "I was sure you'd try to split the savarin with someone."

"Brennbar doesn't eat dessert," I explained to the others. "It's bad for his complexion."

Brennbar sat more or less still, like a contained lava flow. I knew that in a very short time we would go home. I wanted, terribly, to be alone with him.

John Collier

Asking for It

January 1975

John Collier (1901–1980) was another of the writers *Playboy* published in reprint before beginning to solicit original material. His first original story appeared in 1957 and many followed; this was his last in the magazine. He could be said to be the middle figure between Saki and Roald Dahl in the British version of the wittily well-written, economical, and ironic tale of the macabre. Like many other *Playboy* writers of the 1950s and 1960s (Richard Matheson, Ray Bradbury, Charles Beaumont, Jerome Weidman, Budd Schulberg), Collier spent years as a screenwriter in Hollywood; *The African Queen* is his best-known script. He wrote a novel, *His Monkey Wife, or Married to a Chimp* (1930), and many of his short stories, always in demand by magazines, were collected in *Fancies and Goodnights* (1951) and *The John Collier Reader* (1972).

John Collier

Asking for It

Two young men with junior-executive haircuts were taking a drink together after a long hot day at the office. They worked in the Marseilles branch of the E.T. & Orient Line and it was in Alec Weaver's apartment where they now had their drinks.

Alec's features were not unpleasing and his smile was that of one who is anxious to please. The combination can suggest a certain vulnerability. "I should like," said Alec, "to write a story about a murderee."

His friend was Jay Wisden, who had a face like his name, a face with a pipe in it. He now removed this accessory. At once he looked as naked and surprised as the shortsighted do when they strip off their glasses. "Since when have you had the notion of becoming a writer?"

"Only of this one thing. It might solve a problem that sort of has me hooked. Why should anyone want to get himself bumped off? It's been stuck in my mind for ages. I can almost see the guy. And yet . . . no, I can't see him."

"He probably looks like any other nut."

"What makes him tick? And how does he bring it off?"

"No good asking me, brother. After all, you know the experts."

"At the Striptease, you mean. I wish I'd never taken you there. To me, Louis Camatte is just another businessman."

"Not to me, he's not."

"He lives for his kids. Good schools, nice friends; that's what he wants for them. He's proud of that horrible wedding cake of a villa. He wants to cover Marie with fur coats and diamonds and things."

"They say she needed a bit of covering in the old days."

These words hung in the air as if they had no place to go. Unwilling to take them in, Alec stared out of the window. Far down the street, between high buildings, the water of the port showed as blue as a flag.

Jay wondered if he had said the wrong thing. He reinstated his pipe and, with it, his look of sagacity. "Didn't you tell me one time there was a girl you dreamed up and couldn't stop thinking of? Did you have to write a story about her?"

"No. But, by God, I made one up, though! Under the influence of that shrink I went to in New York. Mimi. A slave."

"Black?"

"No. Just a type. A physical type. Psychological, too. Certainly a sexual type. The slave. Masochistic. Made to be kept down. Crushed flat. Brutalized. And yet—look out! A woman like a snake."

"Treacherous?"

"Asking to be trodden on. But tread on her—and you're done for. Do I make myself clear?"

"Clear enough," said Jay, lighting up. Anything is clear enough to a man who is lighting up.

"It was the summer before I transferred here. I couldn't stop thinking about her. She became so real I thought I might be going round the bend. It was mostly because of her I wasted my money on that shrink. Fifteen hundred bucks! And stuck in the city the whole summer!"

"But he got rid of her?"

"He did, more or less, I suppose. But see what a con the whole thing amounts to. He hooked her up with certain dreams I had and things I remembered from when I was a kid; and he got me believing that this was a nursemaid I had when I was about four. Mamie, her name was. Which seemed to make it plausible."

"Seems to me, I must say." And Jay emitted a judicious smoke ring, which, however, was already disintegrating.

"Wait till you hear what this bird cooked up. When I was five, we spent a couple of weeks in Atlantic City."

"A traumatic experience in itself, I imagine."

"This girl was supposed to take me to the beach in the afternoons. Instead, on certain days, she took me to a cheap lodginghouse. To a back room, up three flights of stairs—dirty stairs. And there she left me hanging about on the landing, while she was in there with a man—a Marine."

"Audibly?"

"Very much so. Until one day I thought she was shouting for me."

"So you opened the door?"

"And there she was! Under him. A hideous, sweating, gobbling brute! Mamie! Crushed down! Brutalized! And, blast her, enjoying it!"

"Classical situation. And I notice the effect lingers."

"Yes. I can see it now. Smell it, too. That shabby landing. The sun coming through a dirty window onto a wall the color of puke. And the waiting. And the wondering. And opening the door. It seems I opened it slowly, because the first thing I saw was the belt and the Marine's cap. On a chair. And then—the bed."

"Well, I can understand your being a bit obsessed with your Mimi or Mamie or whatever you call her. But what's all this got to do with the other character—the murderee?"

"Oh, nothing at all. Absolutely nothing. Nothing to do with him. I was just giving you another example of the way I can get hooked on a person. But wait till you hear the payoff."

Emitting smoke, Jay waited.

Alec, after one of those pauses that seemed to allow for a change of gear, resumed in a steady, precise and reasonable tone. "Nothing could be clearer. Nothing could be more real than that memory. All the same, Jay, it was all a lot of crap. When I got my transfer, I came over here by boat. I think I told you that. Very well, on that boat, out from under the influence of that so-called analyst, walking my ten times around the deck one morning, I suddenly realized that that particular episode could never have happened. Listen to this: My father went broke and had his breakdown when I was four. After that, there wasn't any money for any nursemaid—Mamie or Mimi or anything you like—to take me around. The year after, when I was five, like I said, it's true we did go to Atlantic City. For a cheap couple of weeks. My mother and me, and nobody else at all. No lodging house, no stairs, no back room, no door to open; absolutely nothing at all."

"Might have been something you've seen and forgotten," said Jay. "Something you'd seen in the park."

"In my opinion, it was nothing at all," insisted Alec. "Nothing but a bloody egg laid in my head by that shrink. Hatched out under his expectant silence. You feel you have to say something."

"And you certainly did. But isn't there always some little germ of reality in these things?" asked Jay. "Maybe something you don't even recognize at the time. As, for example, with this murderee who's got stuck in your mind. Somebody's triggered the thought."

"I know nobody like that," said Alec.

"You know one fellow who's certainly asking for it." And Jay lifted up the stem of his pipe and he pointed it at the ceiling of Alec's living room. A little smoke oozed out, as from the barrel of a pistol that has just been fired. The pipe pointed, at an angle slanting up through several floors, to a row of flimsy structures on the roof of this bad modern building; structures such as are called ateliers by the agents and, by the occupants, hutches.

"You can't possibly mean André," said Alec.

"That young man," said Jay, "is my choice as most likely to succeed in ending up at the bottom of one of the *calanques,* with a hole in his head and a couple of yards of heavy chain wrapped around him. Like those two they fished up at Easter."

"You're out of your bloody mind," cried Alec. "You're talking about a guy who loves his life, loves his work——"

"You call it work? Picking out a few bars on the piano and making with the offcolor monolog in between?" Jay blew out long clouds of contempt for this ignoble occupation.

"That's not fair, Jay. That's what he does at the Striptease. Everyone's got to eat. It's what he does in the daytime that matters."

"Exactly," said Jay.

"He composes. People say he's got talent. Certainly he lives for his music, and he—"

But Jay was enveloping himself in a smoke cloud so dense that Alec was forced to stop and look and, hence, to listen. One should beware of voices speaking out of clouds. "It's the music he makes with Marie Camatte I'm thinking of," said Jay.

"How do you know?" cried Alec in almost childish distress. "What have you ever seen to make you say a thing like that? It's not true, and I don't think you should go around saying such things."

Jay was not the man to press a point where he saw it was causing pain. "Well," said he, "the Camattes are your friends, not mine. I've only seen them when you've dragged me to that lousy night club. And all I ever saw, with my own eyes, was the glazed sort of look people wear when they're playing footsie under the table. And maybe what you'd call a smoldering glance or two."

"On the strength of which you take the typical small-town view of the French! No wonder there's all this anti-U.S. feeling over here!"

Magnanimity, even in a pipe smoker, has its limits. Like all limits, they are reached sooner than one expects. "Alec," said Jay, "you're the world's all-time champ at seeing a thing, or saying a thing, and then forgetting it. You told me yourself you'd caught sight of Marie, more than once, on her way out of this building, evidently from André's."

"Only twice," said Alec. "And I thought nothing of it. He's young and he's hard up and talented." This small, weak thought was uttered in a small, weak voice. It seemed anxious to slip away unnoticed.

Jay threw only the smallest of jokes after it; to do less would have been more conspicuous. "You must let me bring a bottle next time," said he, rising. "Now I've got to get home or the kid won't go to sleep."

Alec walked this upright family man to the stair well. Pressing the button, he evoked only the considerable silence of a dead elevator. "These functional dumps are fine," said Jay, "only nothing ever functions." With that, he set off down the stairs and soon the sound of his footfalls died away.

Alec stood for quite a long time, feeling completely empty, unable to think of anything at all. Any period is long if spent doing nothing on an empty landing. Indeed, in the silence, it seemed as if time had come to a stop. It was set going again by the tick, tick, tock not of a stately clock but of a pair of high heels coming down from the upper floors.

In this building, made all of concrete, the elevator was often out of order, and many pairs of high heels descended that naked, echoing, rather grimy staircase. Nevertheless, Alec *knew,* as they say, that this was Marie Camatte who was coming down. He therefore felt a paralyzing sense of the inevitable, like a giant hand on the back of his neck, as she turned on the last landing and came into view.

Marie came from one of those ancient pockets of Marseilles where the houses are eight floors high and the streets scarcely eight feet wide. Those tall houses are linked by rooms erupting from their upper stories, bridging the narrow alleys and running like lava over the roofs of lesser buildings. In each room, a family or a whore. Not infrequently, both.

In the doorways, and in the shadows of shops, you sometimes see the most extraordinary faces: Roman faces, Greek faces, Phoenician faces; faces with the profiles of vipers and the whiteness of those night-blooming flowers that smell sweetly of flesh. They are the faces of the slaves of Tyre and Sidon—and of certain of the queens of silent movies.

Marie had such a face and it seemed at all times ready to tilt unbearably far back under the insolent devouring kiss of its natural mate, the Sheik of Araby, or the mate of the last coaster to dock.

"That face is my fate." Someone else had already said it, but Alec felt it. He felt it every time he saw Marie, and the feeling was accompanied by a heart-laboring, bowel-twisting sensation that tried to pass itself off as passionate love. Actually, it was the ugly sister of the love family—that quite hideous sister, the dull, persistent ache of an unhealable wound.

Those suffering from unhealable wounds readily assume a reproachful expression. This causes people to feel they have been found out, a feeling that can arouse guilt, fear and rage in the best of us. These things showed on Marie's face for a moment. They were quickly covered by the sweetest of smiles, but Alec had seen them. It is not pleasant to be greeted by a look of that sort when one has been waiting on a dirty landing for several minutes, or possibly for 20 years.

Alec stepped in front of Marie without either a smile or an extended hand. "Come into my place," he said. "I've something to say to you."

Marie put on the appropriate look of wonder, but she had observed that Alec spoke as if he had no breath in his lungs. She had learned quite early in life that when a man speaks in that way, he means business. She therefore allowed him to march her through the open door of his apartment, and she was suitably impressed by the backward kick with which he slammed the door shut behind them. "I'm late already," she said. "Louis will wonder what has happened to me."

"No doubt André could tell him."

"André? What has André to do with it?" Marie tried the effect of a look of lofty offense, a period piece as absurd and pathetic as a moth-eaten old fox fur would be, with a bunch of limp and faded artificial violets pinned on it, dragged out of some trunk in the attic. "Is it possible you suggest I was visiting André? Perhaps I have other friends in this building."

Alec permitted himself a look of contempt for this pitiful alibi, so easy to check up on.

Marie, a creature of the alleys, knew a blind one as soon as she set foot in it. "But why should I not tell you the truth?" said she. "It is a little secret, but not from you. Louis has some business friends who are coming from Nice to meet him at the club this evening. So I thought I would tell André one or two funny little things about each of them, for him to work into his act."

"No doubt he had other friends last Thursday. Were they also from Nice?"

"Last Thursday? I fail to see—"

"You failed to see me, but I saw you. And I saw you on Monday, too, you dirty little whore!"

"You're jealous!"

What a relief it is, after a lot of fencing, to get down to brass tacks! The next moment, Marie was plastering herself upon Alec, flickering her fingers like snake's tongues up his arms, along his jaw, around his neck: engulfing the stiff, resentful fool in kisses as red and sticky and sweet as stolen jam, pouring a froth of confessions and reproaches and endearments all over him, telling him that André was a boy, a toy, a mistake, a nothing. "A nothing! A nothing! A nothing! It was all because of you. I love you. You close your eyes. You turn away. You ignore me. You look at me as if I were dirt." All this sounds much better in French, especially if one's French is not of the best.

To Alec it had the magic of that double talk that is uttered by our most discreditable desires, through the mouths of creatures of our own creation, in our dreams. It offered him his love and his slave, an abject repentance and a rival belittled to nothing at all. Nothing was lacking to complete his pleasure, except perhaps pleasure itself.

The fact is, the realization of a fantasy, like the foot of the rainbow on the site of the mirage, inevitably turns out to be just another bit of the same old desert. Alec, seeking it under Marie's skirt, had for a delightful moment the excusable illusion of having found it.

Unfortunately, he could not refrain from just one more question. "But if he was such a mistake, why didn't you drop him right away?"

"Because he is so weak, so stupid. In his despair he'd have done something foolish. Right there in the club, perhaps; right under Louis' eyes. And then . . . you know what Louis is!"

Alec realized that he knew perfectly well what Louis was. Louis was the owner. It is the owner who makes the slave, crushing her down, brutalizing her, devouring her all to himself, keeping other people out on the landing.

"Louis is dangerous," said Marie. "That one"—pointing above—"is nothing but a child. But Louis terrifies me. I am afraid to let myself hate him as much as I want to hate him. I have to pretend always. That is my life. Yours, too, now. He must never, never suspect."

"Oh, I don't know about that," said Alec with one of those smiles one should never indulge in. It might have been a smile on the lips of an unhealable wound. "Perhaps we will let him suspect André."

"Oh, no, no, no!" cried Marie sharply. She had no wish to annoy Alec by a contradiction; the words just slipped out. "He'd kill him."

"You said he was a mistake. You said you couldn't get rid of him. Don't you *want* to get rid of him?"

"But he'd kill me, too."

"Oh, no, my dear. Quite the opposite." Alec was enjoying the intoxicating but rather dangerous sensation of great cleverness. He had seen the whole scene in one of those flashes that, like lightning flashes, are rightly called blinding, because they make us automatically close our eyes, or because after them the darkness is darker than before. "You shall be away somewhere quite safe. Louis will wipe André out. We shall know that he has done it. A word dropped into the right ear—and Louis will be wiped out, too. And you, my love, will be wiped clean." The word wipe passed back and forth over everything he said, as over a dirty windscreen, but with no great gain in visibility.

"You're mad!" said Marie.

"Free of Louis and free of André!" continued Alec in a positive orgasm of fancy. "Clean and free and happy!" He almost added the words "And with the man you love," but considerations of taste restrained him. Instead, he started warbling a solo about transferring to the Colombo office, or Alexandria, or even Osaka.

Completely mad! thought Marie. And, as if prompted by Alec's unuttered phrase, she raised her momentarily tender eyes to heaven, always assuming heaven to be situated just where Jay had pointed with his pipe. Then, narrowing those same eyes a little, she seemed to be gazing with concentration through Alec's nonexistent dirty windscreen, along a dimly seen road that, with all the wiping he had indulged in, was gradually becoming clearer. "It is necessary to be practical," said she.

"You speak of dropping a word into the right ear," she continued. "Whose ear is that? Have you any particular person in mind?"

"Anyone at the commissariat," said Alec. "One policeman is as good as another, I suppose, in a matter of this sort."

"You are very clever," said Marie. "It is because you are so clever that I adore you. But sometimes the little goose knows something that the clever fox doesn't know. One policeman is *not* as good as another. Say your word to the wrong man at the commissariat—and you might be saying it into Louis' own ear.

That is how they are with him, most of them: close—like that! Then you and I, my friend, we would both be wiped out, as you call it."

"Let me think a moment," said Alec.

"No. But listen a moment. There is one of them who is not Louis' friend. Far from it. Out to get him. But he has never been able to make anything stick. Now, forget André. Why should you wish to hurt André, a boy, a mere child: two, three years younger than you are? The police are not going to be interested in what happens to a little nobody like that. But there were two men, men of importance, who had business dealings with Louis. And a little disagreement. And a fishing boat, dragging its anchor—you read about it—caught the chain that was wrapped around one of them and fished him up. And then they found the other.

"They know who did it. This man I spoke of, Inspector Grimeaux—remember that name—knows damn well that Louis did it. But he lacks one thing to make it stick.

"I have it. It is nothing but a scrap of paper, but I found it in my hand and I kept it. For insurance. I will seal it up in an envelope and bring it back to you within the half hour. Meanwhile, call the commissariat and insist on speaking to Inspector Grimeaux. Don't say a word to anyone else. You will get yourself murdered, Alec, if you talk to anyone but Inspector Grimeaux. When he is on the phone, tell him, not talking loudly, that you have just what he needs—a certain letter—in the affair of Louis Camatte and the Calvi brothers. Tell him you will hand it to him in person, at a private rendezvous, somewhere outside the town. He'll tell you a place and an hour when he'll pass by in his car and pick you up. If he has a friend with him, that will be quite all right. Go with them. Give them what I am going to bring you. And everything will go just as you want it to. And I shall have helped you!

"And then, my love," said she, raising her eyes heavenward again, "we shall be free, and happy, and rich—for I know where the money is—and we can go far, far away, and live in Monte Carlo."

Norman Mailer

Trial of the Warlock

December 1976

Norman Mailer's career has been full of controversy and surprises. Born in Brooklyn in 1923—he still lives there—Mailer roared into the literary scene in 1948 with his World War II novel *The Naked and the Dead.* His books have taken us to Hollywood *(The Deer Park),* to outer space *(Of a Fire on the Moon,* 1970), behind bars *(The Executioner's Song,* 1980), to ancient Egypt *(Ancient Evenings,* 1983), and to political events made more significant by his presence *(The Armies of the Night,* which won the Pulitzer prize, as did *The Executioner's Song,* and *Miami and the Siege of Chicago,* both in 1968). Thus to find him in *fin-de-siècle* Paris on intimate terms with "demonologists, alchemists and cabalists"—as well as with Joan of Arc and Gilles de Rais from an earlier century—should come as no real surprise. This story is almost a screen treatment, but much more readable.

Norman Mailer

Trial of the Warlock

We see Paris on an autumn evening. We sense the period: It must be about 1890. Pavements are wet with mist. Carriages go by. We follow Durtal, a writer in his early forties. He has dark hair and a pale complexion, mustache and goatee. He enters a house, rings at a first-floor apartment, is received by a servant, offers up hat and cape, is led into a vast, high-ceilinged drawing room where a party is going on.

On the walls are religious pictures, plus a portrait of the host, Chantelouve, three quarter length, his hand resting on a pile of his works. Chantelouve is small, rotund, with a well-fed stomach, red cheeks, long hair drawn up in crescents along his temples, smooth shaven. His wife, standing for a moment next to him, is considerably younger than himself, a blonde with marvelous eyes, alternately cold and gleaming with sparks, thin sensuous lips. She is voluptuous for a slim woman and remote from the company, as if bored with her duties as a hostess.

Chantelouve: "What an honor! You are becoming the most famous recluse in Paris."

Durtal: "On the contrary. Nobody invites me out. Fame has a way of walking around my books."

Chantelouve: "Everybody assures me you are a marvelous writer."

Durtal, looking around the room, takes in the throng now packed into Chantelouve's library and drawing room and sees a friend. "There's Des Hermies," he says to Chantelouve and moves along. Across the room we see a man who looks out of place. Tall, slender, somewhat pale, his eyes have a cold blue gleam. With his flaxen hair and Vandyke, he might be a Norwegian or an Englishman. His garments are of London make and the long, tight, wasp-waisted coat, buttoned clear up to the neck, encloses him like a box. He is very cold in the presence of strangers.

Durtal makes his way toward Des Hermies. We see faces that might belong to *fin-de-siècle* priests, poets, journalists, actresses, dabblers, occultists, a few scholars.

As Durtal and Des Hermies shake hands formally to greet each other, Des Hermies for the first time shows a friendly expression. "Never go to a party given by a Catholic historian."

"I don't know," Durtal replies. "I would think a priest comes here at the risk of his reputation."

Madame Chantelouve joins them. "What is the value of a reputation," she asks, "if it takes no risks?" She smiles at Durtal. "Tell me, if you will, the book you are working on now."

Durtal: "I confess I have in mind something on Monsieur Gilles de Rais."

Madame Chantelouve: "He was a soldier who fought by the side of Joan of Arc through all the campaigns. He was with her when she was wounded and adored her."

Durtal: "Yes."

Madame Chantelouve: "And with her again at Reims during the coronation of the dauphin. Of course, I remember. But then, there is something else about him that I forget. Something not so nice."

Durtal: "Oh, there's a great deal to him."

Des Hermies: "Wasn't he put on trial for something obscene and immense?"

Durtal: "All of that."

Madame Chantelouve: "I can hardly wait."

She moves on.

Des Hermies: "Let's go. I've seen nothing but patients all day and feel as if I still haven't left the hospital."

As they leave, we hear Madame Chantelouve say in annoyance at Durtal's departure, "The level at which Durtal flirts with the Church reminds me of the way a prostitute works up to entering a brothel. Ah, to be free of the chase and come in from the rain."

▪ ▪ ▪

Durtal's apartment. A small sitting room and smaller bedroom. A fire on the hearth in the sitting room.

The place is furnished without luxury. The sitting room has been converted into a study. Black bookcases crammed with volumes hide the walls. In front of the window is a large table, a leather armchair and a few straight chairs.

In the study, there is a large print of a Crucifixion by Matthias Grünewald. As we hear the conversation of Durtal and Des Hermies, the titles begin and the camera offers us the print to examine.

Christ rises before us nailed to a cross of rough wood. His arms bend under the weight of his body and an enormous spike pierces his feet. Almost ripped out of their sockets, the tendons of his armpits seem ready to snap. His fingers are contorted. His thighs are greasy with sweat. His ribs are like staves. The flesh is swollen, blue, mottled with fleabites, specked with thorns broken off from the lashes of his scourging. These thorns are festering now beneath his skin.

The wound in his side drips thickly, his thigh shows blood congealing. A discharge oozes from his chest and drips to his abdomen and loincloth. His knees are forced together, but his lower legs are held apart. His feet, however, have been crisscrossed one on top of the other. They are turning green where the flesh has swollen over the head of the spike. His toes show horny blue nails.

Christ's head, encircled by a broken, disarrayed crown of thorns, hangs lifeless. One eye half opens with a shudder. All the drooping features weep, while the mouth is unnerved. Its underjaw laughs atrociously.

While we look, Durtal is saying, "As you see, this is not the Christ of the rich, no, not that well-groomed boy with his curly brown hair, elegant beard and those doll-like features. No, this is the man who was abandoned by his Father to die like a thief in his own putrefaction. Yet, for me, this Christ *is* the Son of God."

Des Hermies replies, "Did you know that after we are dead our corpses are devoured by different kinds of worms? It depends on whether you're fat or thin. In fat corpses, the rhizophagous maggot is found. In thin corpses, the phora, an aristocrat, a fastidious maggot that sneers at copious breasts and juicy fat bellies. It looks for a corpse that is chic. Just think, no equality, not even in the way we feed the worms."

Durtal: "Isn't it enough that you are famous for being on intimate terms with demonologists, alchemists and cabalists, without adding maggots to your list?"

Des Hermies: "Dear friend, I respect the innocence of your heart, for it can look on this painting every morning and then eat breakfast. I go back to the worms. There has to be a higher intelligence that designs different worms for the well bred and the obese. Don't look for compassion in that."

"It's not for God to prove the existence of compassion," Durtal answers. "It is for people."

"I agree with you," says Des Hermies.

"You amaze me."

"No, you think I'm interested only in twisted natures. I know a few who are not. Durtal, the time has come to introduce you to the one marvelous man I know, Louis Carhaix. He's an intelligent Catholic who, save us, is not sanctimonious. In fact, he is the one human I know who is without hatred or envy for anyone."

Last of the titles.

▪ ▪ ▪

The Place St.-Sulpice: The square is almost deserted. A few women are going up the church steps, met by beggars who murmur prayers as they rattle their tin cups. An ecclesiastic, carrying a book bound in black cloth, salutes the women. A few dogs are running about. Children are jumping rope.

We see Durtal and Des Hermies. On a stone porch in the flank of the church of St.-Sulpice, they read the placard, TOWER OPEN TO VISITORS.

At the back, a little kerosene lamp, hanging from a nail, lights a door to the tower entrance.

In close to utter darkness, they climb. Turning a corner, Durtal sees a shaft of light, then a door. Des Hermies pulls a bell cord and the door swings back. Above them on a landing they can see feet, whether of a man or of a woman, they cannot tell.

"Ah! It's you, Monsieur Des Hermies." A woman bends over, so that her head is in a stream of light. "Louis is in the tower."

"Permit me to introduce my friend Durtal."

Durtal makes a bow in the darkness.

"Ah, monsieur, how fortunate. Louis is anxious to meet you."

Durtal gropes along behind his friend. Finally, they come to a barred door, open it and find themselves on a balcony.

Beneath them, they can see a formidable array of bells hanging from oak supports lined with iron straps. The dark bell metal looks oiled. Above, in the upper abyss, are more bells. There is a place inside each, worn by the striking of the clapper, that shines golden.

The bells are quiet, but the wind rattles against the shutters, howls along the spiral stair and whines in the bell vases. Suddenly, a light breeze fans Durtal's cheek. He looks up. The current has been set in motion by a great bell beginning to get under way. There is a crash of sound, the bell gathers momentum, and now the gigantic clapper opens a deafening clamor. The tower trembles and the balcony on which Durtal is standing shakes like the floor of a railway coach.

Durtal manages to catch sight of a leg swinging out into space and back again in one of those wooden stirrups, two of which, he notices, are fastened to the bottom of every bell. Leaning out so that he is almost prone on one of the timbers, he finally perceives the bell ringer, clinging with his hands to two iron handles and balancing over the gulf.

Durtal is shocked by the face. Never has he seen such pallor. The man's eyes are blue and bulging, but their expression is contradicted by a truculent Kaiser Wilhelm mustache. The man seems at once a dreamer and a fighter.

He gives the bell stirrup a last yank with his foot and with a heave back to the platform regains his equilibrium. He mops his brow and descends, smiles at Des Hermies.

When he learns Durtal's name, he shakes hands cordially.

"I have read your books, monsieur. I know a man like you can't help falling in love with my bells."

Once more, they grope up the winding stairs in the near dark. Having reached the door to the room beneath the tower roof, Carhaix stands aside to let them pass.

They are in a rotunda that is pierced in the center by a great circular hole that has around it a corroded iron railing orange with rust.

"Don't be afraid to lean over," says Carhaix.

But Durtal feels uneasy. As if drawn toward the chasm, the camera gives a vertiginous view of the fall.

They descend and Carhaix, in silence, opens a door to a large storeroom, containing colossal broken statues of saints, scaly and dilapidated apostles, Saint Matthew legless and armless, Saint Luke accompanied by a fragmentary stone ox, Saint Mark lacking a shoulder and part of his beard, Saint Peter holding up an arm from which the hand holding the keys is broken off.

"What is that over there?" inquires Durtal, perceiving, in a corner, an enormous fragment of rounded metal, like half a gigantic skullcap. On it, dust lies thick, and in the hollow are meshes on meshes of fine web, dotted with the bodies of lurking spiders.

"That? Ah, monsieur!"—there is fire in Carhaix's mild eyes—"That is the skull of an old, old bell whose like is not cast these days. The ring of that bell, monsieur, was like a voice from heaven." Suddenly, he explodes, "Bell ringing is a lost art. People will spend thirty thousand francs on an altar, but mention bells and they shrug their shoulders. Do you know, Monsieur Durtal, there is only one man in Paris besides myself who can still ring chords? Yet there's your real sacred music."

They descend to Carhaix's apartment. It is a vast room, vaulted, with walls of rough stone and lighted by a semicircular window just under the ceiling. The tiled floor is barely covered by a worn carpet and the furniture, very simple, consists of a round dining-room table, some old armchairs covered with slate-blue velvet, a little walnut sideboard on which are a few plates and pitchers of Breton faïence, and opposite the sideboard a little black bookcase, which might contain fifty books.

"If I had a place like this," Durtal says, "I would fix it up and work on my book and take my time about it." He smiles. "I certainly do like your place."

"Oh," says the wife, "it's so cold! And no kitchen—"

"You can't even drive a nail into the wall to hang things on," says Carhaix. "But I like this place too."

Des Hermies rises. All shake hands and Monsieur and Madame Carhaix ask Durtal to come again.

▪ ▪ ▪

"What refreshing people!" exclaims Durtal as he and Des Hermies cross the square. "But why is an educated man like that working as a day laborer?"

"If Carhaix could hear you!" says Des Hermies. "You'd be in trouble. He lives for the bells. They're human to him. A bell, he told me, is baptized like a Christian. Then it's anointed with seven unctions of the oil of the infirm, in order to send a message to the dying. According to Carhaix, bells, like fine wines, mellow with age and lose their raw flavor."

▪ ▪ ▪

The conversation is still with Durtal as he goes to bed. He hears Carhaix saying, "The ring of the bells is your real sacred music." As he lies in bed in his small bedroom, the moonlight of Paris is coming through his window. The sound of the bells starts up in his mind. He drifts on their sounds into a dream of a slow procession of monks kneeling to the call of the Angelus. Chimes sound over narrow medieval streets, over cornet towers and dentilated walls. The chimes shout Prime and Tierce, call out Sext and None, Vespers and Complin.

It is here in Durtal's dream that we receive our first view of Joan of Arc, and she is astride the stirrups that rock the bell in the tower of a church. Her feet are in the ropes like those of Carhaix, the bell ringer, so that she is alternately suspended over space and virtually embracing the bell. The sound of the bell becomes, ideally, married to our first sight of her face. She is lovely, but in no delicate fashion, handsome and strong as a rich peasant, not male nor female so much as quintessentially athletic, with a bright and smiling face, and perhaps by such measure five centuries ahead of her time. Her sexuality has become as simple and as separate from herself as the force of her vigor, and her vigor is a natural force apparent to us in the powerful reverberations of the bell—part of its resonance seems to come out of the gusto of her body.

As the bells stop, she calls down merrily to the market place below. "I told you I could ring them," she cries out. "Once our bell ringer at Domremy slipped and the bell sliced off his leg—what a sound it made when the leg hit the ground"—she makes a thwooping sound with her tongue, not crude but all too comfortable, a soldier's sound—"I was the only one the curé could get to climb up into the tower. The boys were afraid." She gives a great laugh, large as her sense of competition, but surprisingly attractive.

At the foot of the tower is Gilles de Rais. He is twenty-five, also vigorous, a robust, active man immaculately dressed in light armor. His face is angelic in expression. His body is carnal in power. He is unbelievably handsome, a man—as described by contemporaries—"of striking beauty and rare elegance." If he is delighted with the sight of Joan swinging on the bell, she is also, by his measure, taunting him. He quits the soldiers grinning beside him and starts to climb.

In his reverie, Durtal is looking down the fall again from Carhaix's tower at St.-Sulpice and again feels the abysmal vertigo he had known that afternoon. He shudders in his bed. The image of his fall coalesces into the fall below Gilles and Joan, and we see them on opposite sides of the bell, ringing it back and forth. Since the bell is massive enough to provide stirrups on either side, they offer it a powerful momentum, sufficiently intense to suggest that union acrobats can know.

Gilles takes it further. He leaps out of the stirrups, races around the circular catwalk and jumps to grasp the bell rope above her hands. She immediately frees one of her feet to allow him a stirrup, and in this position, facing each other, each with a leg in a stirrup and the other over the abyss, each holding with one arm to the rope, they toll the bell, faces three inches apart.

"I've come to claim a kiss," says Gilles.

"Never."

"Not even for the bravest man in France?"

"I'll give you a kiss after we take Paris—if I give any man a kiss."

She is looking into the face of a diabolical angel.

"Joan, dear Joan," says Gilles. "Think of me as a girl. Leave a kiss on this brave girl's lips."

"You're mad. I wouldn't kiss a girl. I'd sooner eat garlic."

"You do," he says.

She jumps to the catwalk and tries to kick him. He jumps as well and they wrestle on near to equal terms, their armor thumping comically against each other. As they come to a stop, he is in the midst of a speech he has not expected to make and can no longer control. Half muttered, half growled, the words and sounds of a lover near to burned out of his senses come forth in a riprace of confession. "I could eat you. I could drive my hands through your body. I could drink your blood. Drink your blood and be blessed."

She shivers. She sees before her Grünewald's Christ freed of its frame. It is now a man rather than a portrait. As in the picture, however, we see the Virgin keeping watch. Her face is pale and swollen with weeping. The vision fades. Joan says to Gilles in a hoarse voice, "I do not live in my body, Gilles de Rais, as you live in yours."

He kneels on the narrow catwalk and touches his hand to her boot in apology.

"You light up a court of ruffians and bandits, arouse a cowardly king, purify a castle and wash the orgies off black old goats. You rouse everybody out of bed long enough to fight and even induce me to take Communion the morning of a battle. Maid of Orleans, fantastic Maid of Orleans, I confess I love you."

She looks more troubled. "Once," Joan says, "my Lady told me that I must protect the tears of her son from the evil of men. 'Beware of the French,' she said, 'for they are full of greed, and abhor the English, since they are next to Satan.' "

"I live just across the sea from England," he replies.

She looks at the Christ she perceives in the air, that quivering presence of the Grünewald head.

▪ ▪ ▪

We see the same Christ again, back in its picture, back in its frame, there on the mantelpiece of Durtal's apartment. The author is talking to Des Hermies while he pets his cat. "Joan had her visions, and I must say, I am certainly beginning to have mine. I cannot get Gilles de Rais out of my mind. Yet, for all my research, I don't begin to comprehend him. A man of such contrasts is beyond all measure. There's no question he had to experience some mystical emotion when with Joan. Yet not ten years after her death, he is on trial for butchering children. Why? To enrich his Black Masses, he confesses. To bring him nearer to the powers of Satan. How do you comprehend a total paradox? He spoils my sleep. I don't know if I can manage this book."

Des Hermies: "Why don't we visit what's left of his château? Let's take a trip to Tiffauges."

Durtal: "One hundred and forty children, tortured and murdered. What frightful nights there must have been."

▪ ▪ ▪

Durtal and Des Hermies are walking along a country road toward the château. The castle towers over the valleys of the Crûme and the Sèvre, facing hills of granite overgrown with formidable oaks and the roots, protruding out of the ground, resemble nests of snakes.

One could believe oneself in medieval Brittany. The same melancholy heavy sky, the same sun, which seems older than in other parts of France, the gloomy age-old forest.

One feels this iron-gray sky, this starving soil, these roads, bordered with stone walls. One still sees the inhospitable fields and crippled beggars on the road, medieval in their sores and filth. Even the black sheep have blue eyes with a cold, pale gleam. The landscape appears unchanged through the centuries but for a factory chimney in the distance. Within the castle walls, traced by the ruins of the towers, is a miserable produce garden.

A thatched hut has been built in a corner. The peasant inhabitants move only when a silver coin is held up. Seizing it, they hand over some keys.

Durtal points to the cabbages and the carrots. "It may interest you," Durtal says, irritated by their apathy, "that where these vegetables now grow, knights once fought in tournaments."

Peasant (shakes his head): "It came to a bad end."

His wife crosses herself.

Durtal and Des Hermies enter the castle. We see them wandering around the ruins, climbing the towers. There is a great moat at the bottom of which huge trees are growing. The wall of the dungeon is broken and they can see into it near the foot of the moat.

Within, one vaulted room succeeds another, as close together as cabins in the hold of a ship. By spiral stairways they descend into cellar passageways.

In these corridors, so narrow two persons cannot walk along them abreast, they pass cells on whose walls mineral salts sparkle in the light of the lantern like grains of sugar. There are dungeons still beneath. Voices echo here.

As Durtal and Des Hermies make this trip, we begin to see the soldiers of Gilles de Rais, somewhat transparent, not wholly corporeal, standing in the corridors and up on the summits of the towers, as if the past has attempted to materialize for a moment.

The ruins seem to restore themselves. Transparencies of people in costume become manifest in the bare rooms.

The walls reclothe themselves with wainscots of Irish wood and tapestries of gold and thread of Arras. The hard black soil of the courtyard is repaved with green and yellow bricks and black and white flagstones. The roof vaults are starred with gold and crossbows on a field azure. The marshal's cross, sable on shield or, is set shining there.

The furnishings return, each to its own place. Here are high-backed signorial chairs, sideboards with carved bas-reliefs, painted and gilded statues of saints. Great beds are reached by carpeted steps.

Durtal, excited, is speaking all the while: "Why, Gilles was dabbling in alchemy long before he even met Joan. He knew more about perfumes and wines at the age of twenty than anyone alive. He was brilliant. Wrote a play at the age of sixteen to celebrate his own wedding to the local heiress. Nine years later: He's with Joan. But there is so little known about them. It maddens me. He was supposed to be lurking in Rouen for days before she was burned at the stake. Was he plotting her rescue? How could he survive her death? And then to come back here, to these feasts and these debauches."

We see a banquet in a great room. The guests eat and disport. All men. No women. Gilles and his friends are not in their damaskeened field harness but in glittering pleated jackets that belly out in a small flounced skirt at the waist. The legs are shown in dark skintight hose. As they eat, call out, jostle one another, stand up and bow, Durtal's voice gives us a clue to what the camera sees of the bill of fare.

Durtal: "Beef pies, salmon pies, squab tarts, roast heron, stork, crane, peacock, bustard and swan; venison in verjuice: Nantes lampreys; salads of bryony, hops, beard of Judas; vehement dishes seasoned with marjoram and mace, coriander and sage, peony and rosemary, basil and hyssop—-dishes to give one a violent thirst and drinks to spur the guests in this womenless castle to scandalous frenzies of lechery."

Durtal has a passing vision of men embracing men.

"Of course, there's also his wife, Catherine of Thouars," says Durtal.

"I have some recollection," says Des Hermies, "that she was an absolute bitch."

"There's a letter from her to the Duke of Brittany written just a few years after Joan perished at the stake. In the letter, she complains bitterly of Gilles's extravagance."

We see an attractive woman (who looks somehow familiar to us). Dressed with consummate disregard for cost, she is speaking to a scribe who takes down her words. "My husband possesses a grand library with a painter to illuminate his books. He revels in rich materials and dreams of unknown gems, weird stones and uncanny metals. All this is very expensive."

As she speaks, we see the panoply she describes, and again, this evocation of the past sits like an overlay or transparency on the ruins of the château through which Durtal and Des Hermies are exploring.

The wife: "He has a guard of two hundred men and all these people have personal attendants magnificently equipped. The luxury of his chapel is extravagant. He insists on clothing his vicars, treasurers, canons, deacons, scholastics and especially his choirboys. There are vermilion altar cloths, curtains of emerald silk and crimson and violet orphreys of cloth of gold.

"His funds are giving way. He borrows from unscrupulous people. An immense fortune is being squandered.

"Frightened by his mad course, the family of the marshal supplicates the king to intervene." So saying, her image fades.

▪ ▪ ▪

A scene between Gilles de Rais and Jean V, the Duke of Brittany.

Jean V: "Spend less! Abjure alchemy. It is too expensive."

Gilles: "The star under which I was born is so potent that I must discover what no one in the world has found."

He has tried to say this mockingly, but the force of his absolute conviction leaves a vibration in the air.

Jean V: "You have too much lust for the extreme."

Gilles: "I fear neither angels nor demons. In the beyond, all things touch."

Durtal and Des Hermies are following the cracked walls of the ruins. The night is bright. One part of the castle is thrown back into shadow and the other stands forth, washed in silver and blue. Below is the Sèvre, along whose surface streaks of moonlight dart like the backs of fishes. The silence is overpowering. After nine o'clock, not a dog, not a soul.

Durtal (out of the silence): "Satan had to be a vivid figure in the Middle Ages——"

Des Hermies: "He's still about."

Durtal: "What do you mean?"

Des Hermies: "I expect Satanism has come down in an unbroken line from that age to this."

They return to their chamber at the inn, where an old woman, in black, wearing the cornet headdress her ancestors wore in the sixteenth century, waits with a candle to bar the door as soon as they return.

Once in the room, Durtal bursts out, "You believe right now as we talk that the Devil is being evoked and the Black Mass celebrated?"

Des Hermies: "Yes."

Durtal (sardonically): "You have proofs, of course."

Des Hermies (shrugs): "Tomorrow evening, let's dine with Carhaix."

▪ ▪ ▪

At Carhaix's, the table is set country style. Polished glasses, a covered dish of sweet butter, a cider pitcher, a somewhat battered lamp.

The diners are silent, their noses in their plates, their faces brightened by steam from the savory soup.

"I'm inclined toward Manichaeism," Des Hermies is saying. "An old and simple religion that helps explain our abominable mess. There they rule us: the

God of Light and the Power of Darkness, two powers of omnipotence, two equals fighting for our souls. Carhaix, you look distressed by these theories."

"Manichaeism is impossible!" cries the bell ringer. "Two infinities cannot exist together."

"Is it more difficult to comprehend two infinities than one?" Des Hermies asks. But he is waiting till Madame Carhaix, who has got up to remove the plates, will go out of the room to fetch the beef. As soon as she is gone, he whispers, "I can tell you that the worst Manichaeans are no advertisement for their religion. They like to taste excrement."

"Horrible!" exclaims Carhaix.

"I am sure Monsieur Des Hermies has been saying something awful," murmurs Madame Carhaix as she comes back, bearing a platter on which is a piece of beef smothered in vegetables.

They burst out laughing. Carhaix cuts up the meat, while his wife pours the cider and Durtal uncorks a bottle of anchovies.

Carhaix's pale face is lighted up, his great canine eyes are becoming suspiciously moist. Visibly, he is jubilant. He is at table with friends, in his tower. "Empty your glasses. You are not drinking," he says, holding up the cider pot.

"Des Hermies, admit you said yesterday that Satanism has pursued an uninterrupted course since the Middle Ages," says Durtal.

"My thesis embarrasses me not at all. In the fifteenth century, your own Gilles de Rais. By the sixteenth, Catherine de Médicis. In the seventeenth, the 'possessed' of Loudun. In the eighteenth, to give just one example, a certain *Abbé* Guibourg made a spectacle of his abominations. On a table serving as altar, the woman lies down, with her skirts lifted up over her head, arms outstretched. She holds the altar lights during the whole office.

"In this fashion, Guibourg celebrated Masses on the abdomen of Madame de Montespan, Madame d'Argenson and Madame de Saint-Point."

"My heavenly Savior!" sighs the bell ringer's wife. "What a lot of filth."

"That's a change," says Durtal. "In the Middle Ages, the Mass was celebrated on the naked buttocks of a woman."

"These frightful stories seem to have taken away your appetite," says Madame Carhaix. "Come, Monsieur Durtal, a little more salad?"

"No, thanks."

"My friends," says Carhaix, looking troubled, "I must sound the Angelus. Don't wait for me. Have your coffee."

He puts on a heavy coat, lights a lantern and opens the door. A stream of glacial air pours in. White flakes whirl in the blackness.

Once he is gone, his wife says, "Monsieur Des Hermies, here is the coffee. I appoint you to the task of serving it. At this hour of day, I must lie down."

"You were saying," says Durtal, when they have wished her good night, "that the most important element in Satanism is the Black Mass."

"No, I wouldn't ignore witchcraft, incubacy, succubacy."

At this moment, the bell, set in motion in the tower, booms out. The chamber in which they are sitting trembles and waves of sound come out of the walls. Heard in the rooms of the tower, the reverberation is oppressive.

Now the booming of the bell comes more slowly. The humming departs from the air. The tumblers on the table cease to rattle and give off only a tenuous tinkling.

A step is heard on the stairs. Carhaix enters covered with snow.

"Christi, boys, it blows!" He shakes himself, throws his heavy outer garments onto a chair and extinguishes his lantern.

Carhaix goes up to the stove and pokes the fire, then dries his eyes, which the bitter cold has filled with tears, and drinks a great draught of coffee.

"How far did you get with your lecture, Des Hermies?"

"I'd like Durtal to see your friend Gévingey."

"Well, then I will arrange it."

"We'll give you a chance to get to bed."

Carhaix lights his lantern and in single file, shivering, they descend the glacial, pitch-dark, winding stairs.

▪ ▪ ▪

Durtal is in his apartment, studying an alchemistic document, *The Chemical Coitus*. The camera sees mysterious bottles and flasks. Each contains a liquid with a small creature in it. A green lion the size of a frog hangs head downward. Doves no larger than beetles are trying to fly up to the neck of another bottle. The liquid in one jar is black and undulates with waves of carmine and gold. Another is white and granulated with dots of ink. Sometimes these dots take the shape of a bat or a star. Sometimes flames rise from a liquid. As we look, we hear Durtal's voice musing over his documents and his fantasies.

Durtal: "With the aid of the philosopher's stone, provided one could find it, mercury would be transmuted to silver and lead to gold. Where did they not look? In arsenic, saltpeter and niter; in the juices of spurge, poppy and purslane: in the bellies of starved mice and in human urine; in the menstrual fluid of women and in their milk. How Gilles de Rais must have been baffled!"

The second and more oppressive sound of the bells is heard again.

▪ ▪ ▪

We see a small medieval procession, perhaps eight or ten priests, soldiers and servants, approaching the castle of Tiffauges. We see Gilles de Rais crossing a drawbridge over the moat to greet them.

A young priest, exceptionally polished in appearance, approaches. He has features that speak of a formidable intelligence. The two men embrace.

"I salute Marshal Gilles de Rais, the most splendid mind of France," says the young priest.

"Francesco Prelati is the master of Florentine magic. There is no one I have dreamed of meeting more."

They smile. They walk off together. Their bodies move in immediate sympathy to each other.

. . .

We see Gilles de Rais and Francesco Prelati in the great laboratory that occupies one wing of the castle. It is filled with an alchemist's furnace and crucibles and retorts.

Gilles: "I conducted experiments for a year. Nothing but failure. My frustrations were considerable." We have a glimpse, as he is speaking, of flames in many colors and burning powders; we hear the cries of animals being slaughtered sacrificially. "Nothing came near to finding the philosophers' stone."

Prelati: "The secret of alchemy is that no secret can be uncovered without the intervention of Satan."

Gilles does not look happy. "I have come to the same conclusion," he says, "but the thought is not happy. To combine my force with such a force. That is too powerful. Terrible things have happened already."

. . .

We see a sorcerer trace a great circle on the floor of a large empty room. Now he asks De Rais and another nobleman to step inside the circle. The nobleman begins to tremble. Gilles, bolder, stands in the middle of the circle. At the first conjurations, however, he begins to pray to Our Lady. The sorcerer, furious, orders both men out of the room. Gilles and his friend rush through the door and wait below in the courtyard. Howls are suddenly heard from the chamber where the magician is operating alone. There is the sound of blows.

When the groans cease, they open the door and find the sorcerer lying in blood, his body mangled.

Prelati: "Did he live?"

Gilles: "Just about." (With a wry smile) "He doesn't practice sorcery anymore."

Prelati: "Your motive was improper. From the Devil's point of view, you asked for the use of his power yet gave back nothing in return."

Gilles: "What could I offer?"

Prelati: "A crime."

Gilles: "I am ready for any crime."

(We have a glimpse of Gilles and Joan swinging in the tower. The sound of bells is intense.)

Gilles expels his breath. "No," he says, "not yet. Let us, for now, relight the furnaces."

. . .

We are treated to a montage of flames and invocations. Lead is being poured and we see a cross being waved upside down.

Prelati and Gilles are making adjurations. There is no result.

Prelati: "I must try it alone."

Gilles: "No, it is better if we fail together."

Prelati: "We have failed already. Nothing is worse than to stop at this place. That molten lead is now ready to become a pestilence in our organs. We will die of bloated bellies."

Gilles nods and steps back. At a sign from Prelati, he leaves the room.

Now he waits. Suddenly, he hears Prelati screaming. The priest emerges bleeding, staggers into his arms. We see the marshal take Prelati to his room and hold his hand by the side of his bed. The bells sound in the tower. The oppressive second sound of the bells.

"Yes," says Gilles de Rais, "the time has come to open my mind to the horrors of my imagination."

▪ ▪ ▪

The concierge is dusting Durtal's living room. "This came for you," he says, handing over a letter.

"I am a woman of lassitude"—we are treated to a woman's voice as Durtal reads the letter—"who has just finished reading your last book. Though it is always folly to try to capture a desire, will you permit me to meet you some evening in a place which you shall designate? Afterward, we shall return, each of us, into our own lives. Understand, monsieur, I address you only because I consider you a marvelous writer in an era of scribblers. Therefore, this evening, a maid will call on your concierge and ask him if there is a letter for Madame Maubel."

"Hmmm!" says Durtal, folding up the letter. "She must be forty-five years old at least."

In spite of himself, he reopens the letter.

"Still, I commit myself to nothing by going to meet her."

He dashes off a note, looks up. "I better add that I'm in poor health. It'll be an excuse if she seems too energetic." He writes. "Dear Madame Maubel, a serious liaison is impossible."

To the room, he says: "Who knows? Maybe she is good-looking."

▪ ▪ ▪

Durtal is before his desk. Now a number of letters are on it. He shakes his head as he passes through them. " 'Never accuse yourself,' " he reads aloud, " 'of being unable to give me consolation. Let us rather permit our souls to speak to each other—low, very low—as I have spoken to you this night.' "

"Four pages of the same sad tune," Durtal says to his cat.

"There is no misspelling," he says, studying her script, "and the handwriting is nice." He sniffs the envelope. "Discreet scent of heliotrope, pale-green ink. She must be a blonde. Yet I keep seeing her as a brunette." We are offered a flash of his sexual inventories. A blonde and a brunette in Parisian costumes, half undressed, no, three quarters undressed—breasts visible and thighs, corsets, garters, stockings—cavort on either side of him. They are attractive but not wholly materialized. Now they give way to two ugly women, one small and thin, the other huge and fat, both in similar undress. They are hardly in costume to write a letter, but they are all writing letters.

"Last night," says a woman's voice, "your name was burning me. Unbearable shivers came to my flesh as I spoke of you to a common friend of yours and mine. But then, why should I not now tell you that you know me?"

Durtal is seeing women in partial states of nudity. "I wrote," he declares to the empty room, as if the sound of his voice will fortify his sense of irony, "I wrote a burning reply. I, who gave up all carnal relations years ago. I, tranquil little man, dried up, safe from adventures, forgetful of sex for months at a time—why do I find myself aroused by the mystery of these letters?"

Another unseen woman's voice:

"Now you speak of your desire with a crudity of phrase which makes my body tingle. This morning, my husband wished to make love. I began to laugh crazily. 'What would you think,' I asked him, 'of my dream? A woman without a head came to me and said, "I am your chamber succubus." ' 'My dear, you are ill,' he said. 'Worse than you think,' said I. Yes, your letter has unbalanced me." She laughs wildly.

Durtal: "No laughing matter. This woman is married to a man who knows me. But whom? Des Hermies is the only man I would call a friend." Durtal puts down her letter. Now he is seeing more blondes than brunettes, and they are reduced to their stockings. "It is too bad," says Durtal, "that we have both become inflamed at the same time. It's these ecclesiastical and demonic studies." He sighs. "I must see her. If she's good-looking, I'll sleep with her. That will bring peace." The pen shakes in his fingers as he tries to write. "Think of the harm we do ourselves teasing at a distance. Think of the remedy, my poor darling, that we have at hand."

▪ ▪ ▪

Durtal is trying to sleep. It is impossible. His head is ringing with angelic and demonic bells. He hears the cries of Francesco Prelati and in the dark, Durtal's cat metamorphoses into a devil and makes low, spitting, urgent sounds. He sees a blonde removing the costume of Paris in the Nineties and putting on the dress of the early fifteenth century. He can almost see her face, but the image withdraws and he sits up. By the clock, it is not yet midnight.

"Des Hermies must still be awake. He is always complaining of insomnia."

▪ ▪ ▪

Des Hermies: "It's certainly the week for friends and acquaintances to be ill. I've been attending to Chantelouve, who has had an attack of gout. His wife, by the way, whom I would not have taken for an admirer of your books, speaks increasingly of you. For a reserved woman she certainly can't hold back on this enthusiasm."

"I think I'd better be going."

"You just got here. Are you certain you're feeling well?"

"Perfect."

▪ ▪ ▪

We see Durtal walking along the streets of Paris at night. He is accompanied on either side by Madame Chantelouve fully dressed. To his right, she is society woman, reserved and adept, hostess smiling without animation.

On his other arm, he has Madame Chantelouve as a creature. Her eyes are wild, romantic and, by his lights, nymphomaniacal.

"It can't be Madame Chantelouve," he says aloud to the empty streets. "Her husband has written a history of Pope Boniface VIII, a life of the blessed founder of the Annunciate, Jeanne de Valois, and a biography of Venerable Mother Anne de Xaintonge."

Church bells ring out suddenly, discordantly, and he comes close to racing down the dark, cold Paris street.

▪ ▪ ▪

Next afternoon, Durtal is trying to write but puts down his pen. He again has the fantasy of the blonde woman who is changing her costume from Paris in the 1890s to the Brittany of the 1430s. We see Madame Chantelouve in tentered stuffs with tight sleeves, a great collar thrown back over the shoulders, a long train lined with fur. She thrusts her head under a two-horned steeple headdress. From behind the lace, she smiles. We realize that the face of Madame Chantelouve is equal to the face of Catherine of Thouars, the wife of Gilles de Rais.

Once again, Durtal picks up his pen but the doorbell rings. He gets up, opens the door and falls a step backward.

Madame Chantelouve is before him.

Stupefied, he bows. Madame Chantelouve, without a word, goes straight into the study. Durtal follows.

"Won't you please sit down?" He advances an armchair. She makes a vague gesture and remains standing. She is wearing a tight black dress, long fawn-colored suede gloves, a fur cloak and no jewelry except sparkling blue-sapphire eardrops.

In a calm but low voice she says, "It is I who wrote you those mad letters. Since I have come to agree that nothing is possible between us, let us also agree to forget what has happened."

"I love you," he blurts out to his astonishment.

"Love me! You didn't even know who the letters were from."

"I knew very well it was Madame Chantelouve hiding behind the pseudonym of Madame Maubel."

She sits down and bursts out laughing.

Furious at seeing this woman behave differently from her letters, he asks irritably, "Am I to know why you laugh?"

"It's a trick my nerves play. Never mind. Let us talk things over. Chantelouve is a very nice man who loves me. His only crime is that he offers a somewhat insipid happiness. So I started this correspondence with you. But you have beautiful books to write. You don't need a crazy woman. I came to tell you we must remain friends and go no further."

"You wrote those letters. Now you speak of reason."

He takes her hands. She makes no resistance.

He presses her hands more tightly. She regards him with her smoky eyes, her subtly voluptuous face. With a firm gesture, she frees her hands.

"Which saint is that?" she asks, getting up to examine a picture on the wall of a monk on his knees.

"I do not know."

"I will find out for you. I have the lives of all the saints at home."

"I don't care who he is!"

She comes closer.

"Are you angry at me?"

"I've been dreaming about this meeting. Now you tell me it is all over."

She is demure. "If I did not care about you, would I come to explain? No! Let me go." Her voice becomes a hint harder. "Do not squeeze me like that! I swear I will go away and you will never see me again if you do not let me loose." He lets go. "Sit there behind the table," she says. "Do that for me." She adds, in a tone of melancholy, "It is impossible to be friends with a man. It would be nice to come and see you without evil thoughts to fear." She is silent. "Yes, just to see each other."

Then she says, "I must go home."

"You leave me with no hope," he exclaims, kissing her gloved hands.

She does not answer. As he looks pleadingly at her, she says, "Listen. If you will promise to make no demands on me and be good, I will come here night after next at nine o'clock."

He promises. As he raises his head from her hands, she offers her neck to his lips. Then she is gone.

▪ ▪ ▪

The Carhaix apartment:

We see Gévingey climbing the stairs. He is a little man. Has a head like an egg. The skull seems to have grown up out of the hair. His nose is bony and his nostrils open over a toothless mouth hidden by a mustache and goatee. Solemn voice and obsequious manners. Looks like he belongs in a sacristy.

Gévingey, as soon as he has seated himself, puts his hands on his knees. Enormous, freckled with blotches of orange, the fingers are covered with huge rings.

Seeing Durtal's gaze on his fingers, he smiles. "My valuables, monsieur, are of three metals, gold, platinum and silver. This ring bears a scorpion; that with its two triangles reproduces the image of the macrocosm. A story for each of my rings."

"Ah!" says Durtal, somewhat surprised at the man's self-satisfaction.

"Dinner is ready," says the bell ringer's wife.

Gévingey (at table): "Mysticism, astrology and alchemy were the great sciences of the Middle Ages."

Des Hermies: "It is too bad that the astrologers, occultists and cabalists of the present day know absolutely nothing."

Gévingey (nodding wisely): "Ignorant imbeciles. Nonetheless, the old theories can be upheld. Space is peopled by microbes. Why can't it also be crammed with spirits?" He puts his hands on his plump stomach.

Madame Carhaix: "Maybe that is why cats suddenly look at something we can't see."

Carhaix: "I'll be back." Gets up to ring the bells.

The bell ringer's wife bids them good night. Des Hermies gets the kettle and the coffeepot.

"Any help?" Durtal proposes.

"Get the little glasses and uncork the liqueur bottles, if you will."

As he opens the cupboard, Durtal sways from the strokes of the bells that shake the walls.

Carhaix returns, blowing out his lantern.

"I hear, monsieur, that you are occupied with a history of Gilles de Rais," says Gévingey to Durtal.

"Up to my eyes in Satanism with that man."

Des Hermies: "We are going to appeal to your knowledge. You can enlighten my friend on one of the obscure questions."

"Which?"

"Incubacy and succubacy."

Gévingey replies. "The Church, you know, does not like this subject."

"I beg your pardon," says Carhaix. "The Church has never hesitated to declare itself on this detestable matter. The existence of succubi and incubi is certified by Saint Augustine, Saint Thomas, Saint Bonaventure, and many others! The question is settled for every Catholic."

"Yes," says Gévingey, "the Church recognizes succubacy. But let me speak."

"I want to ask you," says Des Hermies, "does a woman receive the visit of the incubus while she is asleep or while she is awake?"

"A distinction has to be made. If the woman consorts willingly with the impure spirit, then she is certainly awake when the carnal act takes place. Of course, here the details are a little dirty." says Gévingey. He blushes. "The organ of the incubus, you see, has two branches." He extends his pinkie and forefinger like horns. "So the incubus is able to penetrate both *vasa* of the lady."

"Whereas, the succubus is a woman," says Des Hermies, "and so has no branches. But does she have four *vasa?"*

Gévingey says in rebuke, "The subject is grave. Messieurs, I slept once in the room of the only modern master Satanism can claim."

"Canon Docre," says Des Hermies.

"Yes. And I can tell you—my sleep was fitful. It was broad daylight. Yet I swear to you the succubus came to me."

"What was she like?" Durtal asks.

"Why, like any naked woman," the astrologer says hesitantly.

"I hear Canon Docre celebrates a Black Mass," Des Hermies remarks.

"With abominable men and women. Some people cross themselves when Docre's name is said in their presence."

"But how did a priest fall so low?" asks Durtal.

"I can't say. If you wish more information about him," says Gévingey, "you might question your friend Chantelouve."

"Chantelouve!" cries Durtal.

"Yes, he and his wife used to be friendly with Canon Docre. I hope for their sakes they have no further dealings with that monster."

▪ ▪ ▪

Durtal's apartment. He is cleaning in preparation for Madame Chantelouve's second visit.

He consults his watch. "I am waiting for a woman," he says aloud. "I, who for years scorned the doings of lovers. Now I look at my watch every five minutes."

There is a gentle ring. "Not nine o'clock yet. It isn't she," he murmurs, opening the door.

He squeezes her hands and thanks her for being so punctual.

She says she is not feeling well. "I came only because I didn't want to keep you waiting in vain."

His heart sinks.

"I have a fearful headache," she says, passing her gloved hands over her forehead.

He takes her furs and motions her to the armchair. He sits down on the stool, but she refuses the armchair and takes a seat beside the table. Rising, he bends over her and catches hold of her fingers.

"Your hand is burning," she says.

"Yes, because I get so little sleep. If you know how much I have thought about you!"

He sits down in front of her. His knee touches hers.

"Listen!" Her voice becomes grave and firm. "I do not wish to spoil the happiness our relation gives me. I do not know if I can explain, but try to comprehend: I am able to possess you in my mind when and how I please"—she snaps her fingers—"just as, for a long time, I have possessed Lord Byron, Baudelaire, Gérard de Nerval, all those writers I love—"

"You mean . . .?"

"I have only to desire them, or desire you, before I go to sleep. . . ."

"And?"

"Dear man, you in your own flesh would have to be inferior to the fabulous writer Durtal who comes to me in my bed. That imaginary man offers caresses that make my night delirious!"

He looks at her and pictures Gévingey lying nude on a bed and Madame

Chantelouve approaching Gévingey as a succubus. "We shall untangle all this later," Durtal says. "Meanwhile—" He takes her gently by the arms, draws her to him and abruptly kisses her mouth.

She rebounds as if she has had an electric shock. With a strange cry, she throws back her head.

He pushes her away. She stands there, pale, her eyes closed. Durtal comes up to her and catches her again, but she cries out, "No! I beseech you, let me go."

He holds her.

"I implore you, let me go."

Her accent is so despairing that he obeys.

She is breathing heavily. She leans, very pale, against the bookcase.

"Good God," he says, marching up and down, knocking into the furniture, "what are you made of?"

"Monsieur, I, too, suffer. Spare me. I have to think of my husband and my confessor." She is silent long enough to regain composure. Then, in a changed voice, she says, "Tell me, will you come to my house tomorrow night? Tell me you will come."

"Yes," he says at last. "I don't know why, but yes."

She readjusts herself and, without saying a word, quits the room.

▪ ▪ ▪

During a storm, we see Gilles de Rais on one of the battlements of Tiffauges. The parapet is narrow, not six inches in width. A fall would be fatal. Gilles is forcing himself to advance. As he does, he calls to a voice he hears on the wind. "I will walk around the walls of Tiffauges," he cries out. "If I fall, I am yours." Then he turns to Prelati, who is standing below in the courtyard. "There is no answer," says Gilles de Rais. He moves and almost slips. The rain is icy. The parapet is slippery.

"Come down."

"He says . . . I hear him."

"Come down."

"He says he has no interest in my fall." Gilles de Rais comes off the parapet. In the rain, he says to Prelati, "The Demon does not want my death. He wishes me to perform the deed."

"Do what he wants."

They have descended to the stone chamber where the marshal sleeps.

Gilles de Rais: "Prelati, I do not fear this Demon, because hell is where I live now. My blood is oppressed. I could meet a wild boar in a forest and it would flee my teeth. Wolves draw back when I go by. I cannot speak of the thoughts I have when young boys pass before my eyes."

"We have had our pleasure with young boys," says Prelati.

"The Demon tells me not to stop at their skins." He lifts his head. "Smell the wind. It stinks worse than any battlefield." He makes a violent move. "Tomorrow, I will disembowel a small boy."

"Who?"

"I have not seen him yet. You, Prelati, will find him for me. I am going to separate his hands from his arms and his eyes from his head."

Prelati crosses himself. Gilles de Rais picks up Prelati's cross and makes the same sign upside down.

"We will use the blood of this child," says Gilles de Rais, "to compose the ink of our formulas. Spirits will flower in that blood."

▪ ▪ ▪

A scene in the same room where Prelati was attacked by the Devil. We see him enter with a few small objects on a tray. They are wrapped in bloody linen. he and Gilles de Rais kneel. With passion, they offer these sacrifices to the Demon. Their words are so thick we can hardly hear them. The both speak at once.

"To Asmodeus and Sammael. . . ."

"By the law of pointed stakes. . . ."

"By fire and grease. . . ."

"In the way of the great work. . . ."

"Through salts and retort. . . .

"In the grand magisterium of the ferment."

"By Xoxe, Xocheon and Xolostosos."

"In blood, in gold."

"Faeces urinam nascimur."

"By the snake of your intestine."

When they are done, we see Prelati gather up the bloodstained objects.

"Recognize," Prelati says to Gilles de Rais, "that the Devil did not attack me."

▪ ▪ ▪

Chantelouve's apartment. Durtal is waiting in the same room where we first saw him at the party.

Monsieur and Madame Chantelouve enter. The lines of her figure are advantageously displayed by a wrapper of white swanskin. She sits down facing Durtal, and he perceives under the wrap her indigo silk stockings in little patent-leather boots with straps across the insteps. They are like the picture he has had of her in fantasy.

Chantelouve is in a dressing gown. "You catch me in the middle of my literary drudgeries," he tells Durtal. "I've taken on the worst kind of job. A quick series of unsigned volumes—unsigned, thank God!—on the lives of the saints."

"Yes," says his wife, laughing; "sadly *neglected* saints."

Chantelouve, also laughing, says, "My publisher has a nose for the unkempt martyrs: Saint Opportuna who never used water because she washed her bed with her tears; Saint Radegunde who never changed her hair shirt. I am asked to draw a golden halo around their heads."

Madame Chantelouve laughs gaily. "This disregard of cleanliness makes me suspicious of your beloved Middle Ages."

"Pardon me, my dear," says her husband, "it is not until the Renaissance that uncleanliness becomes common in France, and our good Henri Quatre will boast of his 'reeking feet and a fine armpit.' "

"For heaven's sake," says madame, "spare us one or two details. My dear," she says, addressing her husband, "you have forgotten to turn up your lampwick. I can smell it smoking from here."

Chantelouve rises, gathers up the skirts of his dressing gown and, with a vaguely malicious smile, excuses himself.

She assures herself the door is closed, then returns to Durtal, who is leaning against the mantel. Without a word, she takes his head between her hands, presses her lips to his mouth and opens it with her tongue.

He grunts with sudden appetite and agitation.

She passes her hands over her forehead. "You won't believe it, but I have to suffer when I think how hard he is working. If he had a few women, it would not be so bad."

Durtal rises to take leave.

"When shall I see you?" she murmurs.

"My apartment tomorrow night?"

She responds by a long kiss.

▪ ▪ ▪

Durtal's apartment.

Madame Chantelouve is buried under the thick coverlet, her lips parted and her eyes closed, but she is studying Durtal through the fringe of her blonde eyelashes. He sits down on the edge of the bed. She draws the cover over her chin.

"Cold, dear?"

"No." She opens wide her eyes. They flash sparks.

He undresses. Her face is hidden in the darkness but is sometimes revealed by a flare of the fire, as a smoldering log suddenly bursts into flame. Swiftly, he slips between the covers. Silently, she kisses his features. They thrash about. He cannot speak for the shower of kisses traveling over his face. It is too much. He pulls away.

"I detest you!" she exclaims.

"Why?"

"I detest you!"

"I can't stand *you.*"

The fire is burning low. He sits up and looks into the darkness. His nightshirt is torn.

Once more, he is enlaced; the woman grips him again. This time, he responds. He tries to crush her with caresses. In a guttural voice, she cries out, "I love it, I love it, oh, piss, shit, I want to eat you." The bodies writhe under the covers, the bed creaks and he finally jumps over her, out of bed, and lights the candles. On the dresser, the cat sits motionless. He chases the animal away.

He puts some more wood on the fire and dresses. She calls him gently. He approaches the bed. She throws her arms around his neck and kisses him hungrily. Then she says, "The deed is done. Will you love me any better?"

He does not have the heart to answer.

▪ ▪ ▪

"A woman of my age doing a mad thing like that!" she says as she emerges from the bedroom fully dressed. "You will sleep tonight," she adds sadly.

He begs her to sit down and warm herself, but she says she is not cold.

"Why," he says, "your body was cold as ice!"

"I am always that way. Winter and summer, my flesh is chilly. Even in August."

▪ ▪ ▪

Durtal and Des Hermies are strolling by the Seine. Notre-Dame is in the background.

"Tell me," Durtal asks Des Hermies, "do you know whether a woman can get a cold body as a result of making love to an incubus?"

"Gévingey told me that women who were attached to an incubus had icy flesh even in the month of August. All the books of the specialists bear witness to that. But now, such ladies show the opposite: a skin that is burning and dry to the touch."

"Odd," says Durtal.

▪ ▪ ▪

Durtal and Madame Chantelouve are in bed. He is looking somewhat relieved the act is done. She puts her arm around his neck and kisses him forcibly—her tongue is not inactive. He remains apathetic. She slips under the sheets, works around, reaches him and he groans.

"Ah," she exclaims, coming up from the covers, "at last I have heard you make a sound."

A little later. They are getting dressed.

"Does your husband suspect us?" he asks.

"He may, but I do not accept his right of control over me. He is free, and I am free, to go where we please. I keep the house for him and watch out for his interests. I love him like a devoted companion. My acts, however, are none of his business."

She has spoken in a crisp, incisive tone.

"You certainly reduce the importance of the role of husband."

"My ideas do not belong to this period we live in. In my first marriage, they created a disaster. You see, I despise deceit. After I was married a few years, I fell in love with a most unusual man. And I proceeded to tell my first husband about that lover."

"How did he take such information?"

"He could not bear it. He called it treason. In one night, his hair turned white. A week later, he killed himself." She has spoken with a nondramatic and resolute air.

"Ah!" says Durtal. "Suppose he had strangled you first?"

She shrugs and picks a cat hair off her skirt.

"The result," he resumes after a silence, "being that you then looked for a new husband who would tolerate—"

"Let us not discuss my second husband. I receive enough trouble on this subject from my confessor."

"Is your confessor hard on you?"

"He is of the old school. Incorruptible. I chose him for that."

"If I were like you, I think I would look for a confessor who was indulgent." Something in her expression excites his intuition. "Of course, there's always the danger of seducing a priest who likes you too much."

"That would be sacrilege," she says quickly. But it is obvious he has guessed something of her past. "Oh," she says, half-pleased with the confession, "I was mad, mad—"

He observes her; sparks glint again in her eyes.

"When you are at home in bed, do you still summon me to make love to you?"

"I do not understand," she says.

"Didn't you used to have a visit from an incubus who resembled me?"

"No need now!"

"But you still receive Canon Docre? As an incubus?" His voice is not without anger. He is jealous at the thought.

"What are you saying?"

"You know him."

"Yes, I do."

"How much truth is there to stories about him?"

"I don't know. Docre was once a confessor to royalty. He would certainly have become a bishop if he had not quit the priesthood."

"You knew him personally?"

"I had him for a confessor."

"Is he young or old, handsome or ugly? Tell me."

"He is forty years old. He is very fastidious of his person."

"Do you believe he celebrates the Black Mass?"

"Possibly."

"Suppose I were to ask if your knowledge of incubacy . . . ?"

"I received it from him. Now I hope you are satisfied."

"I don't know. I think I'm in pain. But I must say I'm curious. Do you know how I can see Canon Docre in person?"

"He's not in Paris."

"Pardon me. He *is* in Paris."

"It would not be good for you to see him."

"You admit he is dangerous?"

"I admit nothing. I deny nothing. I tell you simply: Have nothing to do with him."

"I need new material to stimulate my book."

"Get it from somebody else." Shaking her finger at him, she leaves with the remark, "Don't think too much about Canon Docre."

"Devil take you," he says after he closes the door.

▪ ▪ ▪

Durtal is writing at his desk.

"From 1432 to 1440, the children of Brittany begin to disappear. Shepherds are abducted from the fields. Little boys who go to play in the woods fail to return. Whenever the marshal quits one castle for another, he leaves behind a devastation of tears. From Tiffauges to the château de Champtoce, and from La Suze to Nantes, children are missing. Entire regions are devastated. The hamlet of Tiffauges has no more young men. La Suze is without male posterity. At Champtoce, the whole foundation room of a tower is filled with corpses."

Durtal throws down his pen. "I write, but I do not know of what I am writing."

▪ ▪ ▪

We see Gilles speaking. Just his head.

"I took pleasure in butchery. Once I slashed a boy's chest and drank the breath from his lungs. I would open another's stomach and smell it. I took carnal knowledge of the open guts of a third. I knew odors and felt sensations no other man has come near. I was rich in vitality. I lived in a country of my own habitation."

As he speaks, the camera passes over a great fire on a hearth where indistinct objects, the size of their bodies, are burning. Scraps of charred clothing are visible.

We have a clear view of one of Gilles's henchmen scattering ashes to the wind from the top of a tower at Tiffauges on a dark dawn.

We see Gilles snoring in coma. Then we hear his voice, as if out of his sleep, "There is no man on earth who dare do as I have done."

The bell sounds in the tower.

"Who is ringing at this hour?" Gilles cries out.

No answer.

We see him rushing along the solitary corridors of the château. He is in the tower, looking at the bell. The last echoes of its reverberation sound in his ear. He has a partial image of Joan and himself swinging on the bell and howls like a wounded beast. "I swear to do penance," he cries out.

We see his face again, only his face.

"I had hoped to do penance," he declares. "Yet, on the next night, I gouged out the eyes of a child. I crushed its skull with a club."

He grinds his teeth. He laughs.

He is running through the woods.

His henchmen are cleaning stains on the floor of the castle and burying the garments.

More ashes are scattered from the tower.

We see Gilles wandering in the forest surrounding Tiffauges. He sees obscenity in the shape of the trees. Between two limbs, a branch is jammed in a stationary fornication. He sees the act repeated all the way up to the top of the tree. He sees the trunk as a phallus that disappears into a skirt of leaves.

More frightful images rise. The puckered orifice in the bark of an old oak simulates the protruding anus of a beast. In the trunks are incisions that spread out into great lips of vulvas beneath tufts of brown, velvety moss.

The clouds overhead swell into breasts, divided into buttocks, bulge with fecundity. Now they mingle with the somber foliage. Gilles sees images of giant hips, mouths of Sodom, glowing scars, humid wounds. He sees frightful cancers on the trunks and horrible wens. He observes ulcers, sores, chancres.

There, at a detour of the forest aisle, stands a mottled red beech. Tensely, Gilles listens to the wind. Under the falling leaves, he feels spattered by a shower of blood. He runs until he reaches the château. He returns to his room exhausted and crawls to the crucifix like a wolf on all fours. He strains his lips to the feet of the Christ. It is the Grünewald Christ.

He adjures him to have pity, supplicates him to spare a sinner. Then he whimpers. In his own voice, he is hearing the lamentations of children.

▪ ▪ ▪

A bell is ringing. We hear the voice of the bell at last. It says, "I call to the living. I mourn the dead. I break the thunder."

▪ ▪ ▪

Durtal and Madame Chantelouve are walking on a Paris street.

"You're wrong," she says. "I am being consistent. I really don't want you to become acquainted with Canon Docre. But I understand your desire for new material. So I have arranged to let you see a ceremony."

"A Black Mass?"

"Yes. I'm disobeying my confessor in order to take you." She shivers visibly. "You will have no complaint if the spectacle terrifies you."

"Tell me," he asks, "are you still in love with Canon Docre?" A pause. "Admit you are in love with him."

"Not now. But once we were mad about each other. It was because of him that my first husband committed suicide."

"It is really over?"

"I swear it."

▪ ▪ ▪

Durtal's apartment. Madame Chantelouve enters.

Madame Chantelouve: "It's on for tonight. I'll be back at nine. First you must sign this letter." She reads it aloud:

▪ ▪ ▪

"I certify that all I write about the Black Mass is pure invention. I have imagined these incidents."

■ ■ ■

"Your canon distrusts me."

"Of course. You write books."

"What if I refuse to sign?"

"Then you will not go to the Black Mass."

He scratches his signature on the letter.

■ ■ ■

In a fiacre, they go up the Rue de Vaugirard.

The carriage turns up a dark street, swings around and stops.

Durtal and Madame Chantelouve find themselves confronted by a little door cut into a thick unlighted wall.

She rings. A grating opens. She raises her veil. A shaft of lantern light strikes her full in the face, the door opens and they penetrate into a garden.

A woman with a lantern scrutinizes Durtal. He sees, beneath a hood, wisps of gray hair over a wrinkled face, but she does not give him time to examine her.

He follows Madame Chantelouve down a dark lane between rows of palms to the entrance of a building.

"Be careful," she says, going through a vestibule. "There are three steps."

They come out into a court and stop before an old house. She rings. A man greets her in an affected voice. Durtal has a glimpse of cheeks plastered with cosmetics.

"You didn't tell me I was going to be in such company," he whispers to Madame Chantelouve.

"Did you expect to meet saints here?"

They go into a chapel with a low ceiling. The windows are hidden by large drapes. The walls are cracked and dingy. Gusts of moldy air pour out of the heat registers to mingle with an irritating odor of alkali, burnt herbs and the acridity of a new stove. Durtal is choking.

He attempts to accustom his eyes to the half-darkness. The chapel is vaguely lighted by sanctuary lamps suspended from chandeliers of gilded bronze with pink glass pendants. Madame Chantelouve makes a sign to sit down. Durtal notices there are many women and few men present, but his efforts to see anyone's features are somewhat frustrated by the dim light. Not a laugh, not a raised voice is heard, only an irresolute, furtive whispering, unaccompanied by gesture.

A choirboy, dressed in red, advances to the end of the chapel and lights a stand of candles. Then the altar becomes visible. It is an ordinary church altar on a tabernacle. Above it stands a statue in parody of Christ. The head has been raised and the neck lengthened. Wrinkles, painted in the cheeks, transform the grieving face to a comic and bestial one twisted into a mean laugh. The figure is naked. Where the loincloth should have been, a virile phallus projects from a bush of horsehair. In front of the tabernacle, the chalice is covered with a pall. The choirboy, reaching up to light the black tapers, wiggles his hips, stands tiptoe on one foot and flips his arms, as if to fly away like a cherub.

Durtal recognizes him as the man in rouge and lipstick who guarded the chapel entrance.

Another choirboy now exhibits himself. Hollow-chested, racked by coughs, made up with white grease paint and vivid carmine, he approaches the tripods flanking the altar, stirs the smoldering incense pots and throws in leaves and chunks of resin.

Now Madame Chantelouve conducts Durtal to a seat far in the rear, behind all the rows of chairs.

"What's the matter with you?" she asks, looking at him closely.

"The odor from the incense burners is unbearable. What are they burning?"

"Asphalt and henbane; nightshade and myrrh. Perfumes delightful to Satan." She is speaking in the same guttural voice she uses in bed. "Here he comes!" she murmurs suddenly. The women in front of them kneel.

Preceded by the two choirboys, the canon enters wearing a scarlet bonnet with two horns of red cloth. Durtal examines him as he marches toward the altar. Canon Docre is tall but not well built. His large chest is out of proportion to the rest of his body. His forehead makes one line with his straight nose. His lips and cheeks bristle with beard. The eyes are close together and phosphorescent. An evil face, and energetic.

The canon kneels before the altar. Then he mounts the steps and begins to say Mass. Durtal now sees that he has nothing on beneath his sacrificial habit. One can see his black socks and the flesh of his thighs bulging over his garters, which have been attached high on his legs. His chasuble has the shape of an ordinary chasuble but is the dark-red color of dried blood. In the middle is a triangle surrounding the figure of a black billy goat showing its horns.

Docre makes the genuflections specified by ritual. The kneeling choirboys sing the Latin responses; their voices trill on the final syllables of the words.

"It's a simple Low Mass," says Durtal to Madame Chantelouve.

She shakes her head. At that moment, the choirboys pass behind the altar and bring back copper chafing dishes and censers, which they distribute to the congregation. The women envelop themselves in smoke. Some hold their heads right over the chafing dishes and then, close to fainting, they unlace their bodices and make raucous sighs. As Canon Docre proceeds through the following invocation, so do they open their clothing and expose themselves.

"Master of Slanders," says Docre, descending the steps backward and kneeling on the last one, "Dispenser of the benefits of crime, Administrator of sumptuous sins and great vices, we bow to thee, Satan, thee we adore, for you are our reasonable God, our just God!

"You save the honor of families by aborting wombs impregnated in the forgetfulness of illicit fornication; you are the mainstay of the Poor and the Vanquished, for you endow them with hypocrisy, that they may defend themselves against the Rich, who are the only children to whom God speaks.

"Treasurer of old Humiliations, you alone fertilize the mind of a man whom injustice has crushed; you breathe the idea of vengeance, incite him to murder; you furnish the abundant joy of reprisal."

As he speaks, the choirboys tinkle prayer bells. The women fall to the carpet and writhe.

One of them seems to be worked by a spring. She throws herself prone and waves her legs in the air. Another stands with her mouth open, the tongue turned back, the tip cleaving to the palate. Another, pupils dilated, lolls her head back over her shoulders, then tears her breast with her nails. Another undoes her skirts and draws forth a rag. Her tongue, which she cannot control, sticks out, bitten at the edges, harrowed by red teeth, from a bloody mouth. As these acts continue, so does Docre's voice. Standing erect, with arms outstretched, he speaks in a ringing voice of hate:

"Jesus, Chief of Hoaxes, Thief of Homage, Counterfeit of Affection, hear! Since the day when thou did issue from the bowels of a Virgin, thou hast broken all thy promises. Centuries have wept, awaiting thee, mute God! Thou were to redeem man and thou hast not, thou were to appear in thy glory but slept. Thou dost say to the wretch who appeals to thee. 'Be patient and hope; the angels will assist thee.' Impostor! The angels abandon thee!

"Thou hast forgotten the poverty thou didst preach. Thou hast seen the weak crushed beneath the press of profit; thou hast heard the death whine of the weak paralyzed by famine and thou hast caused thy commercial agents, thy Popes, to answer by excuses and promises.

"We wish to violate the quiet of thy body, cursed Nazarene, do-nothing King, coward God!"

"Amen!" trill the soprano voices of the choirboys.

A silence succeeds the litany. The chapel is foggy with smoke.

Contemplating the Christ surmounting the tabernacle, Canon Docre says loudly. "Piss, Shit, Fuck and Blood. *Hoc est enim corpus meum.*" He faces the congregation, haggard, dripping with sweat. The two choirboys raise the chasuble to display his naked belly. Docre passes the host around his groin and then sails it, tainted and soiled, into the congregation.

Hysteria shakes the room. While the choirboys sprinkle holy water on the naked pontiff, women rush upon the Eucharist. They crawl in front of the altar, clawing the bread.

A crone tears her hair, whirls around and around, and falls beside a young girl who is writhing in convulsions. Durtal sees the red horns of Docre. The canon is seated now. He is in a spasm of activity as he chews up sacramental wafers, takes them out of his mouth, wipes himself and distributes them to the women. They struggle over each other to get hold of the bread.

The place is a pandemonium. One could be looking at a congress of prostitutes and maniacs. Now the choirboys offer their buttocks to two of the men present. A woman climbs up onto the altar to take hold of the phallus of Christ. A young girl bends over and barks like a dog. Durtal looks for Madame Chantelouve. She is no longer at his side. He catches sight of her close to the canon and, stepping over writhing bodies, reaches her. She is in a trance. She is breathing the effluvia of the incense, the couples and the acts.

"Let's get out of this!"

She hesitates a moment, then follows him. He elbows his way through the crowd, jostling women whose teeth look as ready to bite as any snarling animal's. He pushes Madame Chantelouve to the entrance, crosses the court, traverses the vestibule, opens the door in the wall and finds himself in the street.

There he stops and looks at her. "Confess you would like to go back."

"No, these scenes shatter me," she says with an effort. "I need a glass of water."

She leans on him as they walk up the street to a nearby wineshop. Two day laborers are playing cards. They turn around and laugh at the sight of Durtal in his frock coat. The proprietor takes an excessively short-stemmed pipe from his mouth and spits into the sawdust. He seems not at all surprised to see this fashionably gowned woman in his dive. Durtal, who is watching him, surprises a look of complicity between the proprietor and Madame Chantelouve.

The proprietor lights a candle and mumbles into Durtal's ear, "Monsieur, you can't drink here with these people watching. I'll take you to a room where you can be alone."

"This," says Durtal to Madame Chantelouve as they climb an old wooden staircase, "is a lot of fuss for a glass of water!"

But she has already entered a room with paper peeling from walls, and a dirty bed. Her eyes are wild. She embraces Durtal.

"No!" he shouts, furious at having fallen into this trap. "I've had enough."

She does not even hear him.

"I want you," she says, and throws her skirts onto the floor. Lying on the bed, she rubs her spine over the coarse grain of the sheets. A look of ecstasy he has not seen before is in her eyes.

Durtal is shuddering in a bed strewn with fragments of dirty hosts. The bells are sounding in his brain. "I call to the living. I mourn the dead. I break the thunder."

. . .

An ecclesiastical courtroom. Massive and dark, it is upheld by heavy Roman pillars. An array of bishops presides over a troop of deans, jurists, advocates, curates and chancellors. Row on row of clerics form the juridical ranks of the court.

Gilles de Rais is speaking in a loud voice. "I do not recognize the competence of this tribunal," we hear him say. "I protest the nature of my arrest and the evidence collected against me."

"May the court rule," says the prosecutor, "that the objection of the accused is null in law and frivolous."

"So does the court rule. Proceed to inform the accused of those counts on which he will be tried."

Now the prosecutor begins to invoke the separate crimes of heresy, blasphemy, sacrilege and magic. "He has polluted and slain little children. He has violated the immunities of the Holy Church at St. Etienne de Mer Morte."

Gilles cries out, "The prosecutor is a liar and a traitor."

The prosecutor extends his hand toward the crucifix. "I swear," he declares, "that my list is a true list. Will the marshal take an oath that he tells the truth?"

Gilles shouts. "I make no vows before God, you filthy liar!"

After a silence, the prosecutor demands that Gilles be struck with double excommunication, first as an evoker of demons, a heretic, apostate and renegade; second as a sodomist and perpetrator of sacrilege.

Gilles loses control of himself. He is in a greater rage than any we have witnessed until now. "You call yourselves judges and me a sodomist. On your knees, clergy. Let my pollutions drip from your mouth. Recognize yourselves as clowns, you buggered asses." He bellows like an animal in pain.

"Do you answer the questions?" asks the court.

"I answer no questions. I declare my presence to be equal in magnitude to this court."

"You are prepared to refute nothing?" asks the court.

"My refutation is my silence."

"You are in contempt. This court pronounces upon you the sentence of excommunication. The hearing will be continued tomorrow before a civil court that will decide the penalties."

"I am innocent in the eyes of Satan and God. Through me, they find peace with each other."

■ ■ ■

Gilles is in his cell. He is trying to evoke the image of Joan of Arc but cannot succeed in making her wholly visible. Glimpses of her, elusive as wings, glide by. The bells are muffled. Now his attempt betrays him and the sound of the bells becomes the sound of his bellow in court. Gilles is swinging on the bell, but a wild boar swings on the other side.

He hears a woman's voice. "When do you return to the Church?"

"I am excommunicated," he shouts. "The Church must return to me."

"But I am burning."

We see Gilles's face; but it is Joan's voice that issues from his face. "Why did you not rescue me at Rouen when I began to burn?" she asks out of his mouth.

He stares into the walls of his cell. We see Joan on the stake. We see the pain on her face. Now we see Gilles standing in the crowd that watches. He is a hundred feet away, staring at the burning stake.

Gilles (his own voice): "I could not rescue you. If you lived, I would have had to follow you for the rest of my life." He cries out, "Better to love a dead woman than obey a live one. I was born to follow no one."

Joan: "You did not follow me. You followed my voices."

Gilles: "I wanted to hear my own voices. They told me that I was born to be the master of discovery. The planets were holding their secrets for me. And the minerals and the beasts. You were as blind as the muscle of my arm. Do you comprehend? I needed a greater courage than yours."

"Why?"

"Because I had to violate every holy covenant that resisted the advance of my knowledge."

Joan: "I am still burning."

Several times he is about to speak; several times he clamps shut his jaws. Finally, the words come out:

"Why, Joan, why do you continue to burn?"

"I do not know."

"Perhaps," he says, "you continue to burn because you are not a saint but a demon."

"I do not know what I am."

"Maybe the Devil is stronger than God," he says.

She shrieks through his lips.

He shrieks back in his own voice.

"I pray for you," Joan says. "In the flames of my fire, I pray for you. Yet the more I pray, the more you torture others."

"My desire to become evil," he says with pride, "is larger than your power to remain good."

Now she appears before him. Suddenly, he sees her speaking to him out of her own face. "My strength was my faith in My Lady, but I continued to think of you. That diminished my strength. I could not bear it when you did not save me from the flames. The odor of my flesh was ugly as I burned."

He moans.

She disappears.

He is left alone in his cell. As light changes through the day and into the night, he meditates.

In the dawn, he stands. "I will speak," he says aloud, "out of all the arrogance of the Devil and in all the compassion of the Lord. Those priests will hear a truth like none heard before."

The trial recommences. Peasants in every variety of good and poor dress are sitting on the stairs, standing in the corridors, filling the neighboring courts, blocking the streets and lanes. From twenty miles around, they have come.

Suddenly, the trumpets blare, the room is lighted up. The bishops enter the civil court. Their golden miters flame like lightning. About their necks are brilliant collars with orphreys crusted. In silent processional, they advance and seat themselves in the front row. Their jewels animate the pale sun of a rainy day. They make the black vestments of the civil judges look wholly somber in contrast.

Under the escort of men-at-arms, Gilles enters. He has aged twenty years in one night. He declares that he is ready to begin a full recital of his crimes.

In a slow, hoarse voice, he states, "I have committed countless abductions of children. I murdered hundreds. Before I killed them, I violated them. I have heard every sound of pain. I am able to reproduce in my ear the hoarse sound that is made by the rattle of a dying throat." He looks about him. "Does the court shudder? Hear that I confess to having wallowed in the warmth of open intestines. I have also held in my hands the sweet-smelling hearts I had just ripped out from wounds that opened before my fingers like ripe fruit." He holds up his hands.

Gasps rise from the audience. With the eyes of a somnambulist, he looks at his fingers. We see only a shaking hand. He sees blood still dripping. "Once, I had congress in the belly of a wound," he says. "That provided me with more pleasure than nature ever offered through *her* orifice. I found no pain in such an act. Previously, taking the way of nature, between the thighs of a woman, it hurt like a knife in my loins." Now the camera is once again close to his face and unlocated to anything else—"I even opened the incision in one stomach so wide that I could seat myself in it. As I squatted there, I had a vision of how in years to come there will be doctors who look like nuns in white. They will make just such cuts and slashes. They will transport organs from one body to another." (A quick view of an operating room where open-heart surgery takes place. It is, even by his scale, a bloody sight.) "But," says Gilles de Rais, "such doctors would never dare to defecate in the wound they created. Gentlemen, I was happier in the enjoyment of tortures, tears, fright and blood than in any other pleasure. There was nothing I did not do—I had only to think of it! I was looking, you see, for the philosophers' stone."

The audience is as silent as a forest after an animal has just been killed.

Tempered in extremes of medieval confession, familiar with demonomania and torture, the bishops, nonetheless have never heard anything like this. As Gilles de Rais speaks, each is constantly making the sign of the cross. Now the presiding bishop rises and veils the face of Christ.

"Some nights," Gilles goes on, "I would sit in reverie over which of the three young heads arrayed before me might be most beautiful to kiss. No one knows so well as I the peace that resides in the chill of dead lips." The marshal is bathed in sweat. He looks at the crucifix whose head is now covered. Only the crown of thorns thrusts up a shape beneath the veil. "I knew the loneliness of such a man," he says, pointing to Christ.

Gilles de Rais finishes his narrative with a look of surprise. "My God," he cries aloud, "I have boasted too much."

He falls over abruptly like a tree, true in its fall. On the floor, he begins to beat the flagstones with his forehead. "O my God, I smell the odor of her burning flesh."

The bishop Jean de Malestroit leaves his seat and raises the accused, raises him to his knees. "He laments his fault," says the bishop to the court.

Gilles de Rais is weeping. With his head down and his arms extended, he looks to the audience at the rear of the court. "Will the parents who have lost their children be able to pray for me?" he asks.

A sound of anguish comes up from the men and women in the court. Woe, rage, pity and outrage are heard, and terrible cries of pain. In the convulsions of these sounds can also be heard the murmur of prayer.

In the babble, the judge of the civil hearings, Pierre de l'Hôpital, intones, "Dispose yourself to die in good state with a great repentance for having committed such crimes."

▪ ▪ ▪

Gilles de Rais is alone again in his cell. He is staring at the moon. "I now know," he says aloud, "a peace I have not known since I was born. Maybe I was born to commit a thousand murders and find peace.

"Maybe I have accomplished something I cannot quite name.

"Certainly, I have no fear. That is curious."

▪ ▪ ▪

We are back on the cheap bed with the crumbs and fragments of soiled bread on the floor, on the bed linen and on Madame Chantelouve's face. "Dress," says Durtal. "Let's get out of here."

He picks up a piece of the host. "I am a rational man and do not think the Savior ever resided in this"—suddenly aware of where *this* has been, he flips it away, as if holding a cockroach—"still . . ." He does not finish.

They go out. Below, in the cheap bar, they face the smiles of the laborers. He pays and leaves without waiting for change.

▪ ▪ ▪

They are traveling in a cab. It comes to her door.

"Soon?" she asks.

"No."

"You are not a big man."

"By your measure, I am now a determined little man."

She leaves.

He gives the cabman his address.

▪ ▪ ▪

Des Hermies and Durtal, at a café.

Durtal: "Carhaix has been ill?"

Des Hermies: "He almost died two nights ago."

Durtal: "I was at a Black Mass two nights ago."

Des Hermies (a pause): "The older I get, the more I conclude that medieval reason is not utterly without logic."

Durtal: "I would like to see Carhaix. But I don't know if I have the right."

Des Hermies: "See him. Your Black Mass has probably had more power at a distance than it will in the same room."

Durtal: "Maybe I'll tell him about my researches on Gilles de Rais's trial. The end is surprising, you see."

▪ ▪ ▪

At Carhaix's: Durtal is talking. Carhaix is in bed and the others sit around him. Durtal speaks animatedly, trying to interest the invalid.

"From his dungeon, Gilles de Rais appeals to the bishop to intercede with the fathers and mothers of the children Gilles has killed. Will they consent to be present at his execution?

"On the day, by nine in the morning, people are marching through the city in processional.

"Many of the parents are actually weeping in pity. Contemporary documents describe their sentiments as follows: They see a demonic nobleman who now knows the emotions of a poor man. He is about to confront divine wrath. What a fearsome journey must await him! So they take vows to fast three days for the repose of the marshal's soul. Isn't that incredible? I know no story that so captures the spirit of the Middle Ages," says Durtal. "Is it not touching?"

Unwilling to be overcome by such sentiment, Des Hermies remarks, "It's a long way from the lynch law of those crazy Americans."

"At eleven that morning," Durtal goes on, "they wait at the prison for Gilles de Rais. There, at the prison gate, he prays to the Virgin. One document describes his conversation with Prelati. ' "Farewell, Francesco, my friend," ' he is reputed to say, ' "we shall never see each other again in this world. But I pray God we meet again in great joy in paradise." ' In *paradise,* mind you," Durtal says.

"He goes to the stake. The clergy, the peasants and the people join in the strophes of the chant for the departed."

At last, we see the scene. The camera passes over the market place, the great square, the fiery stake and the thousands assembled on their knees in prayer. Hundreds are weeping. We hear the chant. We have a last look at the face of Gilles de Rais in the flames.

"Nos timemus diem judicii
Quia mali et nobis conscii
Sed tu, Mater summi concilii,
Para nobis locum refugii
O Maria"

The chant fades. The flames fade. We hear Durtal's voice again. "As he burns, we are without a clue to his last thoughts."

Des Hermies: "Whatever they were, those peasants know enough to weep for him. They may have been naïve then, but they were not as stupid as people today."

"That," cries Carhaix, "is because the great majority no longer believe Satan exists. That is what is frightening."

"Do you know," says Durtal, "when I think of the decades to come, I feel terror."

"No," says Carhaix, "don't say that. In the future, there will be light." With bowed head, he prays.

. . .

Durtal walks up into the tower by himself. He has a note from Madame Chantelouve and hears her voice in his ear as he reads.

> *"You might at least have permitted a comradeship that would have allowed me to leave my sex at home so I could spend an evening with you now and then."*

He gives a low laugh and descends the tower.

. . .

Walking along the street, he thinks aloud, "I wonder if I will ever comprehend Gilles de Rais. That man has such conviction. Even in his doom, he can think only of paradise. He must be the very monster who brought science to the modern world."

As Durtal continues to walk, the streets of Paris go through a metamorphosis. The hacks become taxicabs. The horse-buses turn into autobuses. High-rise apartments go up in the *banlieues*. Traffic increases until we are witnessing scenes from Godard's *Weekend*. The sound of the bells becomes an electronic shriek and the low animal roar of the Demon turns into the shriek of jet planes at Orly. Durtal in his costume of 1890 is not at all out of date as he walks among all the recapitulations of the costumes of the past hundred years that tourists and hippies are wearing in line at the ticket counters and in the plastic seats of the arcades and concourses.

"Dig those threads," says an adolescent to his sister as Durtal goes by. "Is *it* a boy or a girl?" And we see that Durtal has long hair, something like make-up and his stern nineteenth-century expression has moved into the clown's look of modern androgyny. Yes, we are suddenly aware that the nearest waiting room at Orly is filled with androgynous couples. But Durtal is seeing Gilles de Rais in his mind and the fires of the great crucible in the castle of Tiffauges at night. As he pictures those flames, a rocket lifts slowly out of the same great fires and the moon gives a cry like a wounded child.

Jorge Luis Borges

The Other

May 1977

The first language of the famous Argentine novelist, poet, and critic was English, which he learned from his English mother, although he always wrote in Spanish. Jorge Luis Borges (1899–1986) was one of the first of the Latin American "magic realists," using fantastic themes and inversions in his stories, often parodically, as here. *Fictions,* which appeared in English in 1962, was a collection of short pieces closely studied by other writers and probably the most widely read of his books. He also wrote takeoffs on hard-boiled American detective stories, with Don Isidro Parodi as his Buenos Aires–based private eye. "The Other" was his first publication in *Playboy.*

Jorge Luis Borges

The Other

It was in Cambridge, back in February 1969, that the event took place. I made no attempt to record it at the time, because, fearing for my mind, my initial aim was to forget it. Now, some years later, I feel that if I commit it to paper others will read it as a story and, I hope, one day it will become a story for me as well. I know it was horrifying while it lasted—and even more so during the sleepless nights that followed—but this does not mean that an account of it will necessarily move anyone else.

It was about ten o'clock in the morning. I sat on a bench facing the Charles River. Some five hundred yards distant, on my right, rose a tall building whose name I never knew. Ice floes were borne along on the gray water. Inevitably, the river made me think about time—Heraclitus' millennial image. I had slept well; my class on the previous afternoon had, I thought, managed to hold the interest of my students. Not a soul was in sight.

All at once, I had the impression (according to psychologists, it corresponds to a state of fatigue) of having lived that moment once before. Someone had sat down at the other end of the bench. I would have preferred to be alone, but not wishing to appear unsociable, I avoided getting up abruptly. The other man had begun to whistle. It was then that the first of the many disquieting things of that morning occurred. What he whistled, what he tried to whistle (I have no ear for music), was the tune of *La Tapéra,* an old *milonga* by Elias Regules. The melody took me back to a certain Buenos Aires patio, which has long since disappeared, and to the memory of my cousin Alvaro Melían Lafinur, who has been dead for so many years. Then came the words. They were those of the opening line. It was not Alvaro's voice but an imitation of it. Recognizing this, I was taken aback.

"Sir," I said, turning to the other man, "are you a Uruguayan or an Argentine?"

"Argentine, but I've lived in Geneva since 1914," he replied.

There was a long silence. "At number seventeen Malagnou—across from the Orthodox church?" I asked.

He answered in the affirmative.

"In that case," I said straight out, "your name is Jorge Luis Borges. I, too, am Jorge Luis Borges. This is 1969 and we're in the city of Cambridge."

"No," he said in a voice that was mine but a bit removed. He paused, then became insistent. "I'm here in Geneva, on a bench, a few steps from the Rhone. The strange thing is that we resemble each other, but you're much older and your hair is gray."

"I can prove I'm not lying," I said. "I'm going to tell you things a stranger couldn't possibly know. At home we have a silver maté cup with a base in the form of entwined serpents. Our great-grandfather brought it from Peru. There's also a silver washbasin that hung from his saddle. In the wardrobe of your room are two rows of books: the three volumes of Lane's *Arabian Nights,* with wood engravings and with notes in small type at the end of each chapter; Quicherat's Latin dictionary; Tacitus' *Germania* in Latin and also in Gordon's English translation; a *Don Quixote* published by Garnier; Rivera Indarte's *Tablas de Sangre,* inscribed by the author; Carlyle's *Sartor Resartus;* a biography of Amiel; and, hidden behind the other volumes, a book in paper covers about sexual customs in the Balkans. Nor have I forgotten one evening on a certain second floor of the Place Dubourg."

"Dufour," he corrected.

"Very well—Dufour. Is this enough, now?"

"No," he said. "These proofs prove nothing. If I am dreaming you, it's natural that you know what I know. Your catalog, for all its length, is completely worthless."

His objection was to the point. I said, "If this morning and this meeting are dreams, each of us has to believe that he is the dreamer. Perhaps we have stopped dreaming, perhaps not. Our obvious duty, meanwhile, is to accept the dream just as we accept the world and being born and seeing and breathing."

"And if the dream should go on?" he said anxiously.

To calm him and to calm myself, I feigned an air of assurance that I certainly did not feel. "My dream has lasted seventy years now," I said. "After all, there isn't a person alive who, on waking, does not find himself with himself. It's what is happening to us now—except that we are two. Don't you want to know something of my past, which is the future awaiting you?"

He assented without a word. I went on, a bit lost. "Mother is healthy and well in her house on Charcas and Maipú, in Buenos Aires, but Father died some thirty years ago. He died of heart trouble. Hemiplegia finished him; his left hand, placed on his right, was like the hand of a child on a giant's. He died impatient for death but without complaint. Our grandmother had died in the same house. A few days before the end, she called us all together and said, 'I'm an old woman who is dying very, very slowly. Don't anyone become upset about such a common, everyday thing.' Your sister Norah married and has two sons. By the way, how is everyone at home?"

"Quite well. Father makes his same antireligious jokes. Last night he said that Jesus was like the Gauchos, who don't like to commit themselves, and that's why he preached in parables." He hesitated and then said, "And you?"

"I don't know the number of books you'll write, but I know they'll be too many. You'll write poems that will give you a pleasure that others won't share and stories of a somewhat fantastic nature. Like your father and so many others of our family, you will teach."

It pleased me that he did not ask about the success or failure of his books. I changed my tone and went on. "As for history, there was another war, almost among the same antagonists. France was not long in caving in; England and America fought against a German dictator named Hitler—the cyclical battle of Waterloo. Around 1946, Buenos Aires gave birth to another Rosas, who bore a fair resemblance to our kinsman. In 1955, the province of Córdoba came to our rescue, as Entre Ríos had in the last century. Now things are going badly. Russia is taking over the world; America, hampered by the superstition of democracy, can't make up its mind to become an empire. With every day that passes, our country becomes more provincial. More provincial and more pretentious—as if its eyes were closed. It wouldn't surprise me if the teaching of Latin in our schools were replaced by Guarani."

I could tell that he was barely paying attention. The elemental fear of what is impossible and yet what is so dismayed him. I, who have never been a father, felt for that poor boy—more intimate to me even than a son of my flesh—a surge of love. Seeing that he clutched a book in his hands, I asked what it was.

"*The Possessed,* or, as I believe, *The Devils,* by Fyodor Dostoievsky," he answered, not without vanity.

"It has faded in my memory. What's it like?" As soon as I said this, I felt that the question was a blasphemy.

"The Russian master," he pronounced, "has seen better than anyone else into the labyrinth of the Slavic soul."

This attempt at rhetoric seemed to me proof that he had regained his composure. I asked what other volumes of the master he had read. He mentioned two or three, among them *The Double*. I then asked him if on reading them he could clearly distinguish the characters, as you could in Joseph Conrad, and if he thought of going on in his study of Dostoievsky's work.

"Not really," he said with a certain surprise.

I asked what he was writing and he told me he was putting together a book of poems that would be called *Red Hymns.* He said he had also considered calling it *Red Rhythms.*

"And why not?" I said. "You can cite good antecedents. Rubén Dario's blue verse and Verlaine's gray song."

Ignoring this, he explained that his book would celebrate the brotherhood of man. The poet of our time could not turn his back on his own age, he went on to say. I thought for a while and asked if he truly felt himself a brother to everyone—to all funeral directors, for example, to all postmen, to all deep-sea divers, to all those who lived on the even-numbered side of the street, to all those who were aphonic, etc. He answered that his book referred to the great mass of the oppressed and alienated.

"Your mass of oppressed and alienated is no more than an abstraction," I said. "Only individuals exist—if it can be said that anyone exists. 'The man of yesterday is not the man of today,' some Greek remarked. We two, seated on this bench in Geneva or Cambridge, are perhaps proof of this."

Except in the strict pages of history, memorable events stand in no need of memorable phrases. At the point of death, a man tries to recall an engraving glimpsed in childhood; about to enter battle, soldiers speak of the mud or of their sergeant. Our situation was unique and, frankly, we were unprepared for it. As fate would have it, we talked about literature; I fear I said no more than the things I usually say to journalists. My alter ego believed in the invention or discovery of new metaphors; I, in those metaphors that correspond to intimate and obvious affinities and that our imagination has already accepted. Old age and sunset, dreams and life, the flow of time and water. I put forward this opinion, which years later he would put forward in a book. He barely listened to me. Suddenly, he said, "If you have been me, how do you explain the fact that you have forgotten your meeting with an elderly gentleman who in 1918 told you that he, too, was Borges?"

I had not considered this difficulty. "Maybe the event was so strange I chose to forget it," I answered without much conviction.

Venturing a question, he said shyly, "What's your memory like?"

I realized that to a boy not yet twenty, a man of over seventy was almost in the grave. "It often approaches forgetfulness," I said, "but it still finds what it's asked to find. I study Old English, and I am not at the bottom of the class."

Our conversation had already lasted too long to be that of a dream. A sudden idea came to me. "I can prove at once that you are not dreaming me," I said. "Listen carefully to this line, which, as far as I know, you've never read."

Slowly I entoned the famous verse, *"L'hydre-univers tordant son corps écaillé d'astres."* I felt his almost fearful awe. He repeated the line, low-voiced, savoring each resplendent word.

"It's true," he faltered. "I'll never be able to write a line like that."

Victor Hugo had brought us together.

Before this, I now recall, he had fervently recited that short piece of

Whitman's in which the poet remembers a night shared beside the sea when he was really happy.

"If Whitman celebrated that night," I remarked, "it's because he desired it and it did not happen. The poem gains if we look on it as the expression of a longing, not the account of an actual happening."

He stared at me openmouthed. "You don't know him!" he exclaimed. "Whitman is incapable of telling a lie."

Half a century does not pass in vain. Beneath our conversation about people and random reading and our different tastes, I realized that we were unable to understand each other. We were too similar and too unalike. We were unable to take each other in, which makes conversation difficult. Each of us was a caricature copy of the other. The situation was too abnormal to last much longer. Either to offer advice or to argue was pointless, since, unavoidably, it was his fate to become the person I am.

All at once, I remembered one of Coleridge's fantasies. Somebody dreams that on a journey through paradise, he is given a flower. On waking, he finds the flower. A similar trick occurred to me. "Listen," I said. "Have you any money?"

"Yes," he replied. "I have about twenty francs. I've invited Simon Jichlinski to dinner at the Crocodile tonight."

"Tell Simon that he will practice medicine in Carouge and that he will do much good. Now, give me one of your coins."

He drew out three large silver pieces and some small change. Without understanding, he offered me a five-franc coin. I handed him one of those not very sensible American bills that, regardless of their value, are all the same size. He examined it avidly.

"It can't be," he said, his voice raised. "It bears the date 1964. All this is a miracle," he managed to say, "and the miraculous is terrifying. Witnesses to the resurrection of Lazarus must have been horrified."

We have not changed in the least, I thought to myself. Ever the bookish reference. He tore up the bill and put his coins away. I decided to throw mine into the river. The arc of the big silver disk losing itself in the silver river would have conferred on my story a vivid image, but luck would not have it so. I told him that the supernatural, if it occurs twice, ceases to be terrifying. I suggested that we plan to see each other the next day, on that same bench, which existed in two times and in two places. He agreed at once and, without looking at his watch, said that he was late. Both of us were lying and we each knew it of the other. I told him that someone was coming for me.

"Coming for you?" he said.

"Yes. When you get to my age, you will have lost your eyesight almost completely. You'll still make out the color yellow and lights and shadows. Don't worry. Gradual blindness is not a tragedy. It's like a slow summer dusk."

We said goodbye without having once touched each other. The next day, I did not show up. Neither would he.

I have brooded a great deal over that meeting, which until now I have related to no one. I believe I have discovered the key. The meeting was real, but the other man was dreaming when he conversed with me, and this explains how he was able to forget me: I conversed with him while awake, and the memory of it still disturbs me.

The other man dreamed me, but he did not dream me exactly. He dreamed, I now realize, the date on the dollar bill.

—Translated from the Spanish by Norman Thomas di Giovanni

Isaac Bashevis Singer

A Party in Miami Beach

June 1978

Isaac Bashevis Singer (1904–1991) began publishing stories in *Playboy* in 1967 and continued to do so for the rest of his life. Singer was born in Poland, came to the United States in 1935, and worked for the *Yiddish Daily Forward,* which serialized most of his novels before they were translated into English. The fact that he wrote in Yiddish and often set his stories in Poland or Russia did not seem to stand in the way of his English-language popularity. His best-known novel may be *The Magician of Lublin* (1960), but Singer was even more celebrated for his short stories, collected in *Gimpel the Fool* (1957), *The Spinoza of Market Street* (1961), *Short Friday* (1964), and other volumes. He won National Book Awards in 1970 and 1974; and the Nobel Prize for Literature in 1978. Unlike many of his stories, this one is set in America, but Singer's America has many old-country Polish parallels.

Isaac Bashevis Singer

A Party in Miami Beach

My friend the humorist Reuben Kazarsky called me on the telephone in my apartment in Miami Beach and asked, "Menashe, for the first time in your life, do you want to perform a *mitzvah?"*

"Me a *mitzvah?"* I countered. "What kind of word is that—Hebrew? Aramaic? Chinese? You know I don't do *mitzvahs,* particularly here in Florida."

"Menashe, it's not a plain *mitzvah*. The man is a multimillionaire. A few months ago, he lost his whole family in a car accident—a wife, a daughter, a son-in-law and a baby grandchild of two. He is completely broken. He has built here in Miami Beach, in Hollywood and in Fort Lauderdale maybe a dozen condominiums and rental houses. He is a devoted reader of yours. He wants to make a party for you, and if you don't want a party, he simply wants to meet you. He comes from somewhere around your area—Lublin or how do you call it? To this day, he speaks a broken English. He came here from the camps without a stitch to his back, but within fifteen years, he became a millionaire. How they manage this I'll never know. It's an instinct like for a hen to lay eggs or for you to scribble novels."

"Thanks a lot for the compliment. What can come out from this *mitzvah?"*

"In the other world, a huge portion of the leviathan and a Platonic affair with Sarah, daughter of Tovim. On this lousy planet, he's liable to sell you a condominium at half price. He is loaded and he's been left without heirs. He wants to write his memoirs and for you to edit them. He has a bad heart; they've implanted a pacemaker. He goes to mediums or they come to him."

"When does he want to meet me?"

"It could even be tomorrow. He'll pick you up in his Cadillac."

At five the next afternoon, my house phone began to buzz and the Irish doorman announced that a gentleman was waiting downstairs. I rode down in the elevator and saw a tiny man in a yellow shirt, green trousers and violet shoes with gilt buckles. The sparse hair remaining around his bald pate was the color of silver, but the round face reminded me of a red apple. A long cigar thrust out of the tiny mouth. He held out a small, damp palm, pressed my hand once, twice, three times, then said, in a piping voice:

"This is a pleasure and an honor! My name is Max Flederbush."

At the same time, he studied me with smiling brown eyes that were too big for his size—womanly eyes. The chauffeur opened the door to a huge Cadillac and we got in. The seat was upholstered in red plush and was as soft as a down pillow. As I sank down into it, Max Flederbush pressed a button and the window rolled down. He spat out his cigar, pressed the button again and the window closed.

He said, "I'm allowed to smoke about as much as I'm allowed to eat pork on Yom Kippur, but habit is a powerful force. It says somewhere that a habit is second nature. Does this come from the Gemara? The Midrash? Or is it simply a proverb?"

"I really don't know."

"How can that be? You're supposed to know everything. I have a Talmudic concordance, but it's in New York, not here. I'll phone my friend Rabbi Stempel and ask him to look it up. I have three apartments—one here in Miami, one in New York and one in Tel Aviv—and my library is scattered all over. I look for a volume here and it turns out to be in Israel. Luckily, there is such a thing as a telephone, so one can call. I have a friend in Tel Aviv, a professor at Bar-Ilan University, who stays at my place—for free, naturally—and it's easier to call Tel Aviv than New York or even someone right here in Miami. It goes through a little moon, a Sputnik or whatever. Yes, a satellite. I forget words. I put things down and I don't remember where. Our mutual friend, Reuben Kazarsky, no doubt told you what happened to me. One minute I had a family, the next—I was left as bereft as Job. Job was apparently still young and God rewarded him with new daughters, new camels and new asses, but I'm too old for such blessings. I'm sick, too. Each day that I live is a miracle from heaven. I have to guard myself with every bite. The doctor does allow me a nip of whiskey, but only a drop. My wife and daughter wanted to take me along on that ride, but I wasn't in the mood. It actually happened right here in Miami. They were going to Disney World. Suddenly, a truck came up driven by some drunk and it shattered my world. The drunk lost both of his legs. Do you believe in Special Providence?"

"I don't know how to answer you."

"According to your writings, it seems you do believe."

"Somewhere deep inside, I do."

"Had you lived through what I have, you'd grow firm in your beliefs. Well, but that's how man is—he believes and he doubts."

The Cadillac had pulled up and a parking attendant had taken it over. We walked inside a lobby that reminded me of a Hollywood supercolossal production—rugs, mirrors, lamps, paintings. The apartment was in the same vein. The rugs felt as soft as the upholstery in the car. The paintings were all abstract. I stopped before one that reminded me of a Warsaw rubbish bin on the eve of a holiday when the garbage lay heaped in huge piles. I asked Mr. Flederbush what and by whom this was, and he replied:

"Trash like the other trash. Pissako or some other bluffer."

"Who is this Pissako?"

Out of somewhere materialized Reuben Kazarsky, who said, "That's what he calls Picasso."

"What's the difference? They're all fakers," Max Flederbush said. "My wife, may she rest in peace, was the expert, not me."

Kazarsky winked at me and smiled. He had been my friend even back in Poland. He had written a half-dozen Yiddish comedies, but they had all failed. He had published a collection of vignettes, but the critics had torn it to shreds and he had stopped writing. He had come to America in 1939 and later had married a widow twenty years older than he. The widow died and Kazarsky inherited her money. He hung around rich people. He dyed his hair and dressed in corduroy jackets and hand-painted ties. He declared his love to every woman from fifteen to seventy-five. Kazarsky was in his sixties, but he looked no more than fifty. He let his hair grow long and wore side whiskers. His black eyes reflected the mockery and abnegation of one who has broken with everything and everybody. In the cafeteria on the Lower East Side, he excelled at mimicking writers, rabbis and party leaders. He boasted of his talents as a sponger. Reuben Kazarsky suffered from hypochondria and because he was by nature a sexual philanthropist, he had convinced himself that he was impotent. We were friends, but he had never introduced me to his benefactors. It seemed that Max Flederbush had insisted that Reuben bring us together. He now complained to me:

"Where do you hide yourself? I've asked Reuben again and again to get us together, but according to him, you were always in Europe, in Israel or who knows where. All of a sudden, it comes out that you're in Miami Beach. I'm in such a state that I can't be alone for a minute. The moment I'm alone, I'm overcome by a gloom that's worse than madness. This fine apartment you see here turns suddenly into a funeral parlor. Sometimes I think that the real heroes aren't those who get medals in wartime but the bachelors who live out their years alone."

"Do you have a bathroom in this palace?" I asked.

"More than one, more than two, more than three," Max answered. He took my arm and led me to a bathroom that bedazzled me by its size and elegance. The lid of the toilet seat was transparent, set with semiprecious stones and a two-dollar bill implanted within it. Facing the mirror hung a picture of a little boy urinating in an arc while a little girl looked on admiringly. When I lifted the toilet-seat lid, music began to play. After a while, I stepped out onto the balcony that looked directly out to sea. The rays of the setting sun scampered over the waves. Gulls still hunted for fish. Far off in the distance, on the edge of the horizon, a ship swayed. On the beach, I spotted some animal that from my vantage point, 16 floors high, appeared like a calf or a huge dog. But it couldn't be a dog and what would a calf be doing in Miami Beach? Suddenly, the shape straightened up and turned out to be a woman in a long bathrobe digging for clams in the sand.

After a while, Kazarsky joined me on the balcony. He said, "That's Miami. It wasn't he but his wife who chased after all these trinkets. She was the businesslady and the boss at home. On the other hand, he isn't quite the idle dreamer he pretends to be. He has an uncanny knack for making money. They dealt in everything—buildings, lots, stocks, diamonds, and eventually she got involved in art, too. When he said buy, she bought; and when he said sell, she sold. When she showed him a painting, he'd glance at it, spit and say, 'It's junk, they'll snatch it out of your hands. Buy!' Whatever they touched turned to money. They flew to Israel, established Yeshivas and donated prizes toward all kinds of endeavors—cultural, religious. Naturally, they wrote it all off in taxes. Their daughter, that pampered brat, was half-crazy. Any complex you can find in Freud, Jung and Adler, she had it. She was born in a DP camp in Germany. Her parents wanted her to marry a chief rabbi or an Israeli prime minister. But she fell in love with a gentile, an archaeology professor with a wife and five children. His wife wouldn't divorce him and she had to be bought off with a quarter-million-dollar settlement and a fantastic alimony besides. Four weeks after the wedding, the professor left to dig for a new Peking man. He drank like a fish. It was he who was drunk, not the truck driver. Come, you'll soon see something!"

Kazarsky opened the door to the living room and it was filled with people. In one day, Max Flederbush had managed to arrange a party. Not all the guests could fit into the large living room. Kazarsky and Max Flederbush led me from room to room and the party was going on all over. Within minutes, maybe two hundred people had gathered, mostly women. It was a fashion show of jewelry, dresses, pants, caftans, hairdos, shoes, bags, make-up, as well as men's jackets, shirts and ties. Spotlights illuminated every painting. Waiters served drinks. Black and white maids offered trays of hors d'oeuvres.

In all this commotion, I could scarcely hear what was being said to me. The compliments started, the handshakes and the kisses. A stout lady seized me around and pressed me to her enormous bosom. She shouted into my ear, "I read you! I come from the towns you describe. My grandfather came here from Ishishok. He was a wagon driver there and here in America, he went into the freight business. If my parents wanted to say something I wouldn't understand, they spoke Yiddish, and that's how I learned a little of the language."

I caught a glimpse of myself in the mirror. My face was smeared with lipstick. Even as I stood there, trying to wipe it off, I received all kinds of proposals. A cantor offered to set one of my stories to music. A musician demanded I adapt an opera libretto from one of my novels. A president of an adult-education program invited me to speak a year hence at his synagogue. I would be given a plaque. A young man with hair down to his shoulders asked that I recommend a publisher, or at least an agent, to him. He declared, "I *must* create. This is a physical need with me."

One minute all the rooms were full, the next—all the guests were gone, leaving only Reuben Kazarsky and myself. Just as quickly and efficiently, the help cleaned up the leftover food and half-drunk cocktails, dumped all the ashtrays and replaced all the chairs in their rightful places. I had never before witnessed such perfection. Out of somewhere, Max Flederbush dug out a white tie with gold polka dots and put it on.

He said, "Time for dinner."

"I ate so much I haven't the least appetite," I said.

"You must have dinner with us. I reserved a table at the best restaurant in Miami."

After a while, the three of us, Max Flederbush, Reuben Kazarsky and I, got into the Cadillac and the same chauffeur drove us. Night had fallen and I no longer saw nor tried to determine where I was being taken. We drove for only a few minutes and pulled up in front of a hotel resplendent with lights and uniformed attendants. One opened the car door ceremoniously, a second fawningly opened the glass front door. The lobby of this hotel wasn't merely supercolossal but supersupercolossal—complete to light effects, tropical plants in huge planters, vases, sculptures, a parrot in a cage. We were escorted into a nearly dark hall and greeted by a headwaiter who was expecting us and led us to our reserved table. He bowed and scraped, seemingly overcome with joy that we had arrived safely. Soon, another individual came up. Both men wore tuxedos, patent-leather shoes, bow ties and ruffled shirts. They looked to me like twins. They spoke with foreign accents that I suspected weren't genuine. A lengthy discussion evolved concerning our choice of foods and drinks. When the two heard I was a vegetarian, they looked at each other in chagrin, but only for a second. Soon they assured me they would serve me the best dish a vegetarian had ever tasted. One took our orders and the other wrote them down. Max Flederbush announced in his broken English that he really wasn't hungry, but if something tempting could be dredged up for him, he was prepared to give it a try. He interjected Yiddish expressions, but the two waiters apparently understood him. He gave precise instructions on how to roast his fish and prepare his vegetables. He specified spices and seasonings. Reuben Kazarsky ordered a steak and what I was to get, which in plain English was a fruit salad with cottage cheese.

When the two men finally left, Max Flederbush said, "There were times if you would have told me I'd be sitting in such a place eating such food, I would have considered it a joke. I had one fantasy—one time before I died to get enough dry bread to fill me. Suddenly, I'm a rich man, alas, and people dance attendance on me. Well, but flesh and blood isn't fated to enjoy any rest. The angels in heaven are jealous. Satan is the accuser and the Almighty is easily convinced. He nurses a longtime resentment against us Jews. He still can't forgive the fact that our great-great-grandfathers worshiped the golden calf. Let's have our picture taken."

A man with a camera materialized. "Smile!" he ordered us.

Max Flederbush tried to smile. One eye laughed, the other cried. Reuben Kazarsky began to twinkle. I didn't even make the effort. The photographer said he was going to develop the film and that he'd be back in three quarters of an hour.

Max Flederbush asked, "What was I talking about, eh? Yes, I live in apparent luxury, but a woe upon this luxury. As rich and as elegant the house is, it's also a Gehenna. I'll tell you something: in a certain sense, it's worse here than in the camps. There, at least, we all hoped. A hundred times a day we comforted ourselves with the fact that the Hitler madness couldn't go on for long. When we heard the sound of an airplane, we thought the invasion had started. We were all young then and our whole lives were before us. Rarely did anyone commit suicide. Here, hundreds of people sit, waiting for death. A week doesn't go by that someone doesn't give up the ghost. They're all rich. The men have accumulated fortunes, turned worlds upside down, maybe swindled to get there. Now they don't know what to do with their money. They're all on diets. There is no one to dress for. Outside of the financial page in the newspaper, they read nothing. As soon as they finish their breakfasts, they start playing cards. Can you play cards forever? They have to, or die from boredom. When they get tired of playing, they start slandering one another. Bitter feuds are waged. Today they elect a president, the next day they try to impeach him. If he decides to move a chair in the lobby, a revolution breaks out. There is one touch of consolation for them—the mail. An hour before the postman is due, the lobby is crowded. They stand with their keys in hand, waiting like for the Messiah. If the postman is late, a hubbub erupts. If one opens his mailbox and it's empty, he starts to grope and burrow inside, trying to create something out of thin air. They are all past seventy-two and they receive checks from Social Security. If the check doesn't come on time, they worry about it more than those who need it for bread. They're always suspicious of the mailman. Before they mail a letter, they shake the cover three times. The women mumble incantations.

"It says somewhere in the Book of Morals that if man will remember his dying day, he won't sin. Here you can as much forget about death as you can forget to breathe. Today I meet someone by the swimming pool and we chat. Tomorrow I hear he's in the other world. The moment a man or a woman dies, the widow or widower starts right in looking for a new mate. They can barely sit out the shivah. Often, they marry from the same building. Yesterday they maligned the other with every curse in the book, today they're husband and wife. They make a party and try to dance on their shaky legs. The wills and insurance policies are speedily rewritten and the game begins anew. A month or two don't go by and the bridegroom is in the hospital. The heart, the kidneys, the prostate.

"I'm not ashamed before you—I'm every bit as silly as they are, but I'm not such a fool as to look for another wife. I neither can nor do I want to. I have a doctor here. He's a firm believer in the benefits of walking and I take a walk each day after breakfast. On the way back, I stop at the Bache brokerage house. I open the door and there they sit, the oldsters, staring at the ticker, watching their stocks jump around like imps. They know full well that they won't make use of these stocks. It's all to leave in the inheritance, and their children and grandchildren are often as rich as they are. But if a stock goes up, they grow optimistic and buy more of it.

"Our friend Reuben wants me to write my memoirs. I have a story to tell, yes I do. I went through not only one Gehenna but ten. This very person who sits here beside you sipping champagne spent three quarters of a year behind a cellar wall, waiting for death. I wasn't the only one—there were six of us men there and one woman. I know what you're going to ask. A man is only a man, even on the brink of the grave. She couldn't live with all six of us, but she did live with two—her husband and her lover—and she satisfied the others as best as she could. If there had been a machine to record what went on there, the things that were said and the dreams that were played out, your greatest writers would be made to look like dunces by comparison. In such circumstances, the souls strip themselves bare and no one has yet adequately described a naked soul. The *szmalcowniks,* the informers, knew about us and they had to be constantly bribed. We each had a little money or some valuable objects and as long as they lasted, we kept buying pieces of life. It came to it that these informers brought us bread, cheese, whatever was available—everything for ten times the actual price.

"Yes, I could describe all this in pure facts, but to give it flavor requires the pen of a genius. Besides, one forgets. If you would ask me now what these men were called, I'll be damned if I could tell you. But the woman's name was Hilda. One of the men was called Edek, Edek Saperstein, and the other—Sigmunt, but Sigmunt what? When I lie in bed and can't sleep, it all comes back as vivid as if it would have happened yesterday. Not everything, mind you.

"Yes, memoirs. But who needs them? There are hundreds of such books written by simple people, not writers. They send them to me and I send them a check. But I can't read them. Each one of these books is poison, and how much poison can a person swallow? Why is it taking so long for my fish? It's probably still swimming in the ocean. And your fruit salad first has to be planted. I'll give you a rule to follow—when you go into a restaurant and it's dark, know that this is only to deceive. The headwaiter is one of the Polish children of Israel, but he poses as a native Frenchman. He might even be a refugee himself. When you come here, you have to sit and wait for your meal, so that later on the bill won't seem too excessive. I'm neither a writer nor a philosopher, but I lie awake half the nights and when you can't sleep, the brain churns like a mill. The wildest notions come to me. Ah, here is the photographer! A fast worker. Well, let's have a look!"

The photographer handed each of us two photos in color and we sat there quietly studying them.

Max Flederbush asked me, "Why did you come out looking so frightened? That you write about ghosts, this I know. But you look here as if you'd seen a real ghost. If you did, I want to know about it."

"I hear you go to séances," I said.

"Eh? I go. Or, to put it more accurately—they come to me. This is all bluff, too; but I *want* to be fooled. The woman turns off the lights and starts talking, allegedly in my wife's voice. I'm not such a dummy, but I listen. Here they come with our food, the Miami *szmalcowniks*."

The door opened and the headwaiter came in leading three men. All I could see in the darkness was that one was short and fat, with a square head of white hair that sat directly on his broad shoulders, and with an enormous belly. He wore a pink shirt and red trousers. The two others were taller and slimmer. When the headwaiter pointed to our table, the heavy-set man broke away from the others, came toward us and shouted in a deep voice:

"Mr. Flederbush!"

Max Flederbush jumped up from his seat.

"Mr. Albeginni!"

They began to heap praises upon each other. Albeginni spoke in broken English with an Italian accent.

Max Flederbush said, "Mr. Albeginni, you know my good friend, Kazarsky, here. And this man is a writer, a Yiddish writer. He writes everything in Yiddish. I was told that you understand Yiddish!"

Albeginni interrupted him. "*A gezunt oyf dein kepele . . . Hock nisht kein tcheinik . . . A gut boychik. . . .* My parents lived on Rivington Street and all my friends spoke Yiddish. On Sabbath, they invited me for gefilte fish, *cholent,* kugel. Who do you write for—the papers?"

"He writes books."

"Books, eh? Good! We need books, too. My son-in-law has three rooms full of books. He knows French, German. He's a foot doctor, but he first had to study math, philosophy and all the rest. Welcome! Welcome! I've got to get back to my friends, but later on we'll—"

He held out a heavy, sweaty hand to me. He breathed asthmatically and smelled of alcohol and hair tonic. The words rumbled out deep and grating from his throat. After he left, Max said:

"You know who he is? One of the Family."

"Family?"

"You don't know who the Family is? Oh! You've remained a greenhorn! The Mafia. Half Miami Beach belongs to them. Don't laugh, but they keep order here.

Uncle Sam has saddled himself with a million laws that, instead of protecting the people, protect the criminal. When I was a boy studying about Sodom in heder, I couldn't understand how a whole city or a whole country could become corrupt. Lately, I've begun to understand. Sodom had a constitution and our nephew, Lot, and the other lawyers reworked it so that right became wrong and wrong—right. Mr. Albeginni actually lives in my building. When the tragedy struck me, he sent me a bouquet of flowers so big it couldn't fit through the door."

"Tell me about the cellar where you sat with the other men and the only woman," I said.

"Eh? I thought that this would intrigue you. I talked to one of the writers about my memoirs and when I told him about this, he said, 'God forbid! You must leave this part out. Martyrdom and sex don't mix. You must write only good things about them.' That's the reason I lost the urge for the memoirs. The Jews in Poland were people, not angels. They were flesh and blood just like you and me. We suffered, but we were men with manly desires. One of the five was her husband. Sigmunt. This Sigmunt was in contact with the *szmalcowniks*. He had all kinds of dealings with them. He had two revolvers and we resolved that if it looked like we were about to fall into murderers' hands, we would kill as many of them as possible, then put an end to our own lives. It was one of our illusions. When it comes down to it, you can't manage things so exactly. Sigmunt had been a sergeant in the Polish army in 1920. He had volunteered for Pilsudski's legion. He got a medal for marksmanship. Later on, he owned a garage and imported automobile parts. A giant, six foot tall or more. One of the *szmalcowniks* had once worked for him. If I was to tell you how it came about that we all ended up together in that cellar, we'd have to sit here till morning. His wife, Hilda, was a decent woman. She swore that she had been faithful to him throughout their marriage. Now, I will tell you who her lover was. No one but yours truly. She was seventeen years older than me and could have been my mother. She treated me like a mother, too. 'The child,' that's what she called me. The child this and the child that. Her husband was insanely jealous. He warned us he'd kill us both if we started anything. He threatened to castrate me. He could have easily done it, too. But gradually, she wore him down. How this came about you could neither describe nor write, even if you possessed the talent of a Tolstoy or a Zeromski. She persuaded him, hypnotized him like Deliah did Samson. I didn't want any part of it. The other four men were furious with me. I wasn't up to it, either. I had become impotent. What it means to spend twenty-four hours out of the day locked in a cold, damp cellar in the company of five men and one woman, words cannot describe. We had to cast off all shame. At night we barely had enough room to stretch our legs. From sitting in one place, we developed constipation. We had to do everything in front of witnesses and this is an anguish Satan himself couldn't endure. We had to become cynical. We had to speak in coarse terms to conceal our shame. It was then I discovered that profanity has its purpose. I have to take a little drink. So . . . *L'chayim!*

"Yes, it didn't come easy. First she had to break down his resistance, then she had to revive my lust. We did it when he was asleep, or he only pretended. Two of the group had turned to homosexuality. The whole shame of being human emerged there. If man is formed in God's image, I don't envy God. . . .

"We endured all the degradation one can only imagine, but we never lost hope. Later, we left the cellar and went off, each his own way. The murderers captured Sigmunt and tortured him to death. His wife—my mistress, so to say—made her way to Russia, married some refugee there, then died of cancer in Israel. One of the other four is now a rich man in Brooklyn. He became a penitent, of all things, and he gives money to the Bobow rabbi or to some other rabbi. What happened to the other three, I don't know. If they lived, I would have heard from them. That writer I mentioned—he's a kind of critic—claims that our literature has to concentrate only on holiness and martyrdom. What nonsense! Foolish lies!"

"Write the whole truth," I said.

"First of all, I don't know how. Secondly, I would be stoned. I generally am unable to write. As soon as I pick up a pen, I get a pain in the wrist. I become drowsy, too. I'd rather read what you write. At times, it seems to me you're stealing my thoughts.

"I shouldn't say this, but I'll say it anyway. Miami Beach is full of widows and when they heard that I'm alone, the phone calls and the visits started. They haven't stopped yet. A man alone and something of a millionaire, besides! I've become such a success I'm literally ashamed before myself. I'd like to cling to another person. Between another's funeral and your own, you still want to snatch a bit of that swinish material called pleasure. But the women are not for me. Some *yenta* came to me and complained, 'I don't want to go around like my mother with a guilt complex. I want to take everything from life I can, even more than I can.' I said to her, 'The trouble is, one cannot. . . .' With men and women, it's like with Jacob and Esau: When one rises, the other falls. When the females turn so wanton, the men become like frightened virgins. It's just like the prophet said, 'Seven women shall take hold of one man.' What will come of all this, eh? What, for instance, will the writers write about in five hundred years?"

"Essentially, about the same things as today," I replied.

"Well, and what about in a thousand years? In ten thousand years? It's scary to think the human species will last so long. How will Miami Beach look then? How much will a condominium cost?"

"Miami Beach will be under water," Reuben Kazarsky said, "and a condominium with one bedroom for the fish will cost five trillion dollars."

"And what will be in New York? In Paris? In Moscow? Will there still be Jews?"

"There'll be only Jews," Kazarsky said.

"What kind of Jews?"

"Crazy Jews, just like you."

—Translated from the Yiddish by Joseph Singer

Paul Theroux

White Lies

May 1979

The most reliably prolific and entertaining new short-story writer *Playboy* acquired in the 1970s was undoubtedly Paul Theroux, whose first work appeared in 1970. Theroux, a Foreign Service officer turned novelist, journalist, and travel writer, has the knack of making the old-fashioned form of the "exotic" adventure tale seem solidly contemporary. "White Lies" is a perfect example, and one of the best. Theroux, born in 1941, is based on Cape Cod near several other members of his large and bookish family. He lives also in London and travels the world by train (*The Great Railway Bazaar,* 1975; *The Old Patagonian Express,* 1979; *Riding the Iron Rooster,* 1988), by boat (*Sailing Through China,* 1983), by foot (*The Kingdom by the Sea,* 1983), and even by kayak (*The Happy Isles of Oceania,* 1992). Perhaps his best-known novel is *The Mosquito Coast* (1981), later made into a movie.

Paul Theroux

White Lies

Normally, in describing the life cycle of ectoparasites for my notebook, I went into great detail, since I hoped to publish an article about the strangest ones when I returned home from Africa. The one exception was *Dermatobia bendiense*. I could not give it my name; I was not its victim. And the description? One word: *Jerry*. I needed nothing more to remind me of the discovery, and though I fully intend to test my findings in the pages of an entomological journal, the memory is still too horrifying for me to reduce it to science.

Jerry Benda and I shared a house on the compound of a bush school. Every Friday and Saturday night, he met an African girl named Ameena at the Rainbow Bar and took her home in a taxi. There was no scandal: No one knew. In the morning, after breakfast, Ameena did Jerry's ironing (I did my own) and the black cook carried her back to town on the crossbar of his old bike. That was a hilarious sight. Returning from my own particular passion, which was collecting insects in the fields near our house, I often met them on the road: Jika in his cook's khakis and skullcap pedaling the long-legged Ameena—I must say, she reminded me of a highly desirable insect. They yelped as they clattered down the road, the deep ruts making the bicycle bell hiccup like an alarm clock. A stranger would have assumed these Africans were man and wife, making an early-morning foray to the market. The local people paid no attention.

Only I knew that this was the cook and mistress of a young American who was regarded at the school as very charming in his manner and serious in his work. The cook's laughter was a nervous giggle—he was afraid of Ameena. But he was devoted to Jerry and far too loyal to refuse to do what Jerry asked of him.

Jerry was deceitful, but at the time I did not think he was imaginative enough to do any damage. And yet his was not the conventional double life that most white people led in Africa. Jerry had certain ambitions: Ambition makes more liars than egotism does. But Jerry was so careful, his lies such modest calculations, he was always believed. He said he was from Boston. "Belmont, actually," he told me, when I said I was from Medford. His passport—*Bearer's address*—said Watertown. He felt he had to conceal it. That explained a lot: the insecurity of living on the lower slopes of the long hill, between the smoldering steeples of Boston and the clean, high-priced air of Belmont. We are probably no more class-conscious than the British, but when we make class an issue, it seems more than snobbery. It becomes a bizarre spectacle, a kind of attention-seeking, and I cannot hear an American speak of his social position without thinking of a human fly, one of those tiny men in grubby capes whom one sometimes sees clinging to the brickwork of a tall building.

What had begun as fantasy had, after six months of his repeating it in our insignificant place, been made to seem like fact. Jerry didn't know Africa: His one girlfriend stood for the whole continent. And of course he lied to her. I had the impression that it was one of the reasons Jerry wanted to stay in Africa. If you tell enough lies about yourself, they take hold. It becomes impossible ever to go back, since that means facing the truth. In Africa, no one could dispute what Jerry said he was: a wealthy Bostonian. From a family of some distinction, adventuring in Third World philanthropy before inheriting his father's business.

Rereading the above, I think I may be misrepresenting him. Although he was undeniably a fraud in some ways, his fraudulence was the last thing you noticed about him. What you saw first was a tall good-natured person in his early twenties, confidently casual, with easy charm and a gift for ingenious flattery. When I told him I had majored in entomology, he called me Doctor. This later became Doc. He showed exaggerated respect to the gardeners and washerwomen at the school, using the politest phrases when he spoke to them. He always said "sir" to the students ("You, sir, are a lazy little creep"), which baffled them and won them over. The cook adored him, and even the cook's cook—who was lame and fourteen and ragged—liked Jerry to the point where the poor boy would go through the compound stealing flowers from the Inkpens' garden to decorate our table. While I was merely tolerated as an unattractive and nearsighted bug collector, Jerry was courted by the British wives in the compound. The wife of the new headmaster, Lady Sarah (Sir Godfrey Inkpen had been knighted for his work in the civil service), usually stopped in to see him when her husband was away. Jerry was gracious with her and anxious to make a good impression. Privately, he said, "She's all tits and teeth."

"Why is it," he said to me one day, "that the white women have all the money and the black ones have all the looks?"

"I didn't realize you were interested in money."

"Not for itself, Doc," he said. "I'm interested in what it can buy."

▪ ▪ ▪

No matter how hard I tried, I could not get used to hearing Ameena's squawks of pleasure from the next room, or Jerry's elbows banging against the wall. At any moment, I expected their humpings and slappings to bring down the boxes of mounted butterflies I had hung there. At breakfast, Jerry was his urbane self, sitting at the head of the table while Ameena cackled.

He held a teapot in each hand. "What will it be, my dear? Chinese or Indian tea? Marmalade or jam? Poached or scrambled? And may I suggest a kipper?"

"Wopusa!" Ameena would say, "Idiot!"

She was lean, angular and wore a scarf in a handsome turban on her head. "I'd marry that girl tomorrow," Jerry said, "if she had fifty grand." Her breasts were full and her skin was like velvet; she looked majestic, even doing the ironing. And when I saw her ironing, it struck me how Jerry inspired devotion in people.

But not any from me. I think I resented him most because he was new. I had been in Africa for two years and had replaced any ideas of sexual conquest with the possibility of a great entomological discovery. But he was not interested in my experience. There was a great deal I could have told him. In the meantime, I watched Jika taking Ameena into town on his bicycle and I added specimens to my collection.

▪ ▪ ▪

Then, one day, the Inkpens' daughter arrived from Rhodesia to spend her school holidays with her parents.

We had seen her the day after she arrived, admiring the roses in her mother's garden, which adjoined ours. She was seventeen, and breathless and damp; and so small I at once imagined this pink butterfly struggling in my net. Her name was Petra (her parents called her Pet) and her pretty bloom was reckless and innocent. Jerry said, "I'm going to marry her."

"I've been thinking about it," he said the next day. "If I just invite her, I'll look like a wolf. If I invite the three of them, it'll seem as if I'm stage-managing it. So I'll invite the parents—for some inconvenient time—and they'll have no choice but to ask me if they can bring the daughter along, too. *They'll* ask *me* if they can bring her. Good thinking? It'll have to be after dark—they'll be afraid of someone raping her. Sunday's always family day, so how about Sunday at eight? High tea. They will deliver her into my hands."

The invitation was accepted. And Sir Godfrey said, "I hope you don't mind if we bring our daughter—"

More than anything, I wished to see whether or not Jerry would take Ameena home that Saturday night. He did—I suppose he did not want to arouse Ameena's suspicions—and on Sunday morning, it was breakfast as usual and "What will it be, my dear?"

But everything was not as usual. In the kitchen, Jika was making a cake and scones. The powerful fragrance of baking, so early on a Sunday morning, made Ameena curious. She sniffed and smiled and picked up her cup. Then she asked: What was the cook making?

"Cakes," said Jerry. He smiled back at her.

Jika entered timidly with some toast.

"You're a better cook than I am," Ameena said in Chinyanja. "I don't know how to make cakes."

Jika looked terribly worried. He glanced at Jerry.

"Have a cake," said Jerry to Ameena.

Ameena tipped the cup to her lips and said slyly, "Africans don't eat cakes for breakfast."

"*We* do," said Jerry, with guilty rapidity. "It's an old American custom."

Ameena was staring at Jika. When she stood up, he winced. Ameena said, "I have to make water." It was one of the few English sentences she knew.

Jerry said, "I think she suspects something."

As I started to leave with my net and my chloroform bottle, I heard a great fuss in the kitchen, Jerry telling Ameena not to do the ironing. Ameena protesting. Jika groaning. But Jerry was angry, and soon the bicycle was bumping away from the house: Jika pedaling, Ameena on the crossbar.

"She just wanted to hang around," said Jerry. "Guess what the bitch was doing? She was ironing a drip-dry shirt!"

▪ ▪ ▪

It was early evening when the Inkpens arrived, but night fell before tea was poured. Petra sat between her proud parents, saying what a super house we had, what a super school it was, how super it was to have a holiday here. Her monotonous ignorance made her even more desirable.

Perhaps for our benefit—to show her off—Sir Godfrey asked her leading questions. "Mother tells me you've taken up knitting" and "Mother says you've become quite a whiz at math." Now he said, "I hear you've been doing some riding."

"Ever so much," said Petra. Her face was shining. "There are some stables near the school."

Dances, exams, picnics, house parties: Petra gushed about her Rhodesian school. And in doing so, she made it seem a distant place—not an African country at all but a special preserve of superior English recreations.

"That's funny," I said. "Aren't there Africans there?"

Jerry looked sharply at me.

"Not at the school," said Petra. "There are some in town. The girls call them nig-nogs." She smiled. "But they're quite sweet, actually."

"The Africans, dear?" asked Lady Sarah.

"The girls," said Petra.

Her father frowned.

Jerry said, "What do you think of this place?"

"Honestly, I think it's super."

"Too bad it's so dark at the moment," said Jerry. "I'd like to show you my frangipani."

"Jerry's famous for that frangipani," said Lady Sarah.

Jerry had gone to the French windows to indicate the general direction of the bush. He gestured toward the darkness and said, "It's somewhere over there."

"I see it," said Petra.

The white flowers and the twisted limbs of the frangipani were clearly visible in the headlights of an approaching car.

Sir Godfrey said, "I think you have a visitor."

The Inkpens were staring at the taxi. I watched Jerry. He had turned pale but kept his composure. "Ah, yes," he said, "it's the sister of one of our pupils." He stepped outside to interrupt her, but Ameena was too quick for him. She hurried past him, into the parlor, where the Inkpens sat dumfounded. Then Sir Godfrey, who had been surprised into silence, stood up and offered Ameena his chair.

Ameena gave a nervous grunt and faced Jerry. She wore the black-satin cloak and sandals of a village Moslem. I had never seen her in anything but a tight dress and high heels; in that long cloak, she looked like a very dangerous fly that had buzzed into the room on stiff wings.

"How nice to see you," said Jerry. Every word was right, but his voice had become shrill. "I'd like you to meet—"

Ameena flapped the wings of her cloak in embarrassment and said, "I cannot stay. And I am sorry for this visit." She spoke in her own language. Her voice was calm and even apologetic.

"Perhaps she'd like to sit down," said Sir Godfrey, who was still standing.

"I think she's fine," said Jerry, backing away slightly.

Now I saw the look of horror on Petra's face. She glanced up and down, from the dark shawled head to the cracked feet, then gaped in bewilderment and fear.

At the kitchen door, Jika stood with his hands over his ears.

"Let's go outside," said Jerry in Chinyanja.

"It is not necessary," said Ameena. "I have something for you. I can give it to you here."

Jika ducked into the kitchen and shut the door.

"Here," said Ameena. She fumbled with her cloak.

Jerry said quickly, "No," and turned as if to avert the thrust of a dagger.

But Ameena had taken a soft gift-wrapped parcel from the folds of her cloak. She handed it to Jerry and without turning to us, flapped out of the room. She became invisible as soon as she stepped into the darkness. Before anyone could speak, the taxi was speeding away from the house.

Lady Sarah said, "How very odd."

"Just a courtesy call," said Jerry, and amazed me with a succession of plausible lies. "Her brother's in form four—a very bright boy, as a matter of fact. She was rather pleased by how well he'd done in his exams. She stopped in to say thanks."

"That's *very* African," said Sir Godfrey.

"It's lovely when people drop in," said Petra. "It's really quite a compliment."

Jerry was smiling weakly and eyeing the window, as if he expected Ameena to thunder in once again and split his head open. Or perhaps not. Perhaps he was congratulating himself that it had all gone so smoothly.

Lady Sarah said, "Well, aren't you going to open it?"

"Open what?" said Jerry, and then he realized that he was holding the parcel. "You mean this?"

"I wonder what it could be," said Petra.

I prayed that it was nothing frightening. I had heard stories of jilted lovers sending aborted fetuses to the men who had wronged them.

"I adore opening parcels," said Petra.

Jerry tore off the wrapping paper but satisfied himself that it was nothing incriminating before he showed it to the Inkpens.

"Is it a shirt?" said Lady Sarah.

"It's a beauty," said Sir Godfrey.

It was red and yellow and green, with embroidery at the collar and cuffs; an African design. Jerry said, "I should give it back. It's a sort of bribe, isn't it?"

"Absolutely not," said Sir Godfrey. "I insist you keep it."

"Put it on!" said Petra.

Jerry shook his head. Lady Sarah said, "Oh, do!"

"Some other time," said Jerry. He tossed the shirt aside and told a long humorous story of his sister's wedding reception on the family yacht. And before the Inkpens left, he asked Sir Godfrey with old-fashioned formality if he might be allowed to take Petra on a day trip to the local tea estate.

"You're welcome to use my car if you like," said Sir Godfrey.

▪ ▪ ▪

It was only after the Inkpens had gone that Jerry began to tremble. He tottered to a chair, lit a cigarette and said, "That was the worst hour of my life. Did you see her? Jesus! I thought that was the end. But what did I tell you? She suspected something!"

"Not necessarily," I said.

He kicked the shirt—I noticed he was hesitant to touch it—and said, "What's this all about, then?"

"As you told Inky—it's a present."

"She's a witch," said Jerry. "She's up to something."

"You're crazy," I said. "What's more, you're unfair. You kicked her out of the house. She came back to ingratiate herself by giving you a present—a new shirt for all the ones she didn't have a chance to iron. But she saw our neighbors. I don't think she'll be back."

"What amazes me," said Jerry, "is your presumption. I've been sleeping with Ameena for six months, while you've been playing with yourself. And here you are, trying to tell me about her! You're incredible."

Jerry had the worst weakness of the liar: He never believed anything you told him.

I said, "What are you going to do with the shirt?"

Clearly, this had been worrying him. But he said nothing.

Late that night, working with my specimens, I smelled acrid smoke. I went to the window. The incinerator was alight: Jika was coughing and stirring the flames with a stick.

▪ ▪ ▪

The next Saturday, Jerry took Petra to the tea estate in Sir Godfrey's gray Humber. I spent the day with my net, rather resenting the thought that Jerry had all the luck. First Ameena, now Petra. And he had ditched Ameena. There seemed no end to his arrogance or—what was more annoying—his luck. He came back to the house alone. I vowed that I would not give him a chance to do any sexual boasting. I stayed in my room, but less than ten minutes after he arrived, he was knocking on my door.

"I'm busy!" I yelled.

"Doc, this is serious."

He entered rather breathless, fever-white and apologetic. This was not someone who had just made a sexual conquest—I knew as soon as I saw him that it had all gone wrong. So I said, "How does she bump?"

He shook his head. He looked very pale. He said, "I couldn't."

"So she turned you down." I could not hide my satisfaction.

"She was screaming for it," he said, rather primly. "She's seventeen, Doc. She's locked in a girls' school half the year. She even found a convenient haystack. But I had to say no. In fact, I couldn't get away from her fast enough."

"Something *is* wrong," I said. "Do you feel all right?"

He ignored the question. "Doc," he said, "remember when Ameena barged in. Just think hard. Did she touch me? Listen, this is important."

I told him I could not honestly remember whether or not she had touched him. The incident was so pathetic and embarrassing I had tried to blot it out.

"I knew something like this would happen. But I don't understand it." He was talking quickly and unbuttoning his shirt. Then he took it off. "Look at this. Have you ever seen anything like it?"

At first, I thought his body was covered by welts. But what I had taken to be welts were a mass of tiny reddened patches, like fly bites, some already swollen into bumps. Most of them were on his back and shoulders. They were as ugly as acne and had given his skin that same shine of infection.

"It's interesting," I said.

"Interesting!" he screamed. "It looks like syphilis and all you can say is it's interesting. Thanks a lot."

"Does it hurt?"

"Not too much," he said. "I noticed it this morning before I went out. But I think they've gotten worse. That's why nothing happened with Petra. I was too scared to take my shirt off."

"I'm sure she wouldn't have minded if you'd kept it on."

"I couldn't risk it," he said. "What if it's contagious?"

He put calamine lotion on it and covered it carefully with gauze, and the next day it was worse. Each small bite had swelled to a pimple, and some of them seemed on the point of erupting: a mass of small warty boils. That was on Sunday. On Monday, I told Sir Godfrey that Jerry had a bad cold and could not teach. When I got back to the house that afternoon, Jerry said that it was so painful he couldn't lie down. He had spent the afternoon sitting upright in a chair.

"It was that shirt," he said. "Ameena's shirt. She did something to it."

I said, "You're lying. Jika burned that shirt—remember?"

"She touched me," he said. "Doc, maybe it's not a curse—I'm not superstitious, anyway. Maybe she gave me syph."

"Let's hope so."

"What do you mean by that?"

"I mean, there's a cure for syphilis."

"Suppose it's not that?"

"We're in Africa," I said.

This terrified him, as I knew it would.

He said, "Look at my back and tell me if it looks as bad as it feels."

He crouched under the lamp. His back was grotesquely inflamed. The eruptions had become like nipples, much bigger and with a bruised discoloration. I pressed one. He cried out. Watery liquid leaked from a pustule.

"That hurt!" he said.

"Wait." I saw more infection inside the burst boil—a white clotted mass. I told him to grit his teeth. "I'm going to squeeze this one."

I pressed it between my thumbs and as I did, a small white knob protruded. It was not pus—not liquid. I kept on pressing and Jerry yelled with shrill ferocity until I was done. Then I showed him what I had squeezed from his back; it was on the tip of my tweezers—a live maggot.

"It's a worm!"

"A larva."

"You know about these things. You've seen this before, haven't you?"

I told him the truth. I had never seen one like it before in my life. It was not in any textbook I had ever seen. And I told him more: There were, I said, perhaps two hundred of them, just like the one wriggling on my tweezers, in those boils on his body.

Jerry began to cry.

. . .

That night, I heard him writhing in his bed, and groaning, and if I had not known better, I would have thought Ameena was with him. He turned and jerked and thumped like a lover maddened by desire; and he whimpered, too, seeming to savor the kind of pain that is indistinguishable from sexual pleasure. But it was no more passion than the movement of those maggots in his flesh. In the morning, gray with sleeplessness, he said he felt like a corpse. Truly, he looked as if he were being eaten alive.

An illness you read about is never as bad as the real thing. Boy scouts are told to suck the poison out of snake bites. But a snake bite—swollen and black and running like a leper's sore—is so horrible I can't imagine anyone capable of staring at it, much less putting his mouth on it. It was that way with Jerry's boils. All the textbooks on earth could not have prepared me for their ugliness, and what made them even more repellent was the fact that his face and hands were free of them. He was infected from his neck to his waist and down his arms; his face was haggard and in marked contrast.

I said, "We'll have to get you to a doctor."

"A witch doctor."

"You're serious!"

He gasped and said, "I'm dying, Doc. You have to help me."

"We can borrow Sir Godfrey's car. We could be in Blantrye by midnight."

Jerry said, "I can't last until then."

"Take it easy," I said. "I have to go over to the school. I'll say you're still sick. I don't have any classes this afternoon, so when I get back, I'll see if I can do anything for you."

"There are witch doctors around here," he said. "You can find one—they know what to do. It's a curse."

I watched his expression change as I said, "Maybe it's the curse of the white worm." He deserved to suffer, after what he had done, but his face was so twisted in fear, I added, "There's only one thing to do. Get those maggots out. It might work."

"Why did I come to this fucking place?"

But he shut his eyes and was silent: He knew why he had left home.

When I returned from the school ("And how is our ailing friend?" Sir Godfrey had asked at morning assembly), the house seemed empty. I had a moment of panic, thinking that Jerry—unable to stand the pain—had taken an overdose. I ran into the bedroom. He lay asleep on his side but woke when I shook him.

"Where's Jika?" I said.

"I gave him the week off," said Jerry. "I didn't want him to see me. What are you doing?"

I had set out a spirit lamp and my tools: tweezers, a scalpel, cotton, alcohol, bandages. He grew afraid when I shut the door and shone the lamp on him.

"I don't want you to do it," he said. "You don't know anything about this. You said you'd never seen this before."

I said, "Do you want to die?"

He sobbed and lay flat on the bed. I bent over him to begin. The maggots had grown larger, some had broken the skin and their ugly heads stuck out like beads. I lanced the worst boil, between his shoulder blades. Jerry cried out and arched his back, but I kept digging and prodding, and I found that heat made it simpler. If I held my cigarette lighter near the wound, the maggot wriggled, and by degrees, I eased it out. The danger lay in their breaking: If I pulled too hard, some would be left in the boil to decay, and that, I knew would kill him.

By the end of the afternoon, I had removed only twenty or so and Jerry had fainted from the pain. He awoke at nightfall. He looked at the saucer beside the bed and saw the maggots jerking in it—they had worked themselves into a white knot—and he screamed. I had to hold him until he calmed down. And then I continued.

I kept at it until very late. And I must admit that it gave me a certain pleasure. It was not only that Jerry deserved to suffer for his deceit—and his suffering was that of a condemned man—but also what I told him had been true: This was a startling discovery for me, as an entomologist. I had never seen such creatures.

It was after midnight when I stopped. My hand ached, my eyes hurt from the glare and I was sick to my stomach. Jerry had gone to sleep. I switched off the light and left him to his nightmares.

▪ ▪ ▪

He was slightly better by morning. He was still pale, and the opened boils were crusted with blood, but he had more life in him than I had seen for days. And yet he was brutally scarred. I think he knew this: He looked as if he had been whipped.

"You saved my life," he said.

"Give it a few days," I said.

He smiled. I knew what he was thinking. Like all liars—those people who behave like human flies on our towering credulity—he was preparing his explanation. But this would be a final reply: He was preparing his escape.

"I'm leaving," he said. "I've got some money—and there's a night bus—" He stopped speaking and looked at my desk. "What's that?"

It was the dish of maggots, now as plump as a rice pudding.

"Get rid of them!"

"I want to study them," I said. "I think I've earned the right to do that. But I'm off to morning assembly—what shall I tell Inky?"

"Tell him I might have this cold for a long time."

He was gone when I got back to the house; his room had been emptied and he'd left me his books and his tennis racket with a note. I made what explanations I could. I told the truth: I had no idea where he had gone. A week later, Petra went back to Rhodesia, but she told me she would be back. As we chatted over the fence, I heard Jerry's voice: *She's screaming for it.* I said, "We'll go horseback riding."

"Super!"

The curse of the white worm: Jerry had believed me. But it was the curse of impatience—he had been impatient to get rid of Ameena, impatient for Petra, impatient to put on a shirt that had not been ironed. What a pity it was that he was not around when the maggots hatched and saw them become flies I had never seen. He might have admired the way I picked some and sealed others in plastic and mounted twenty of them on a tray.

And what flies they were! It was a species that was not in any book, and yet the surprising thing was that in spite of their differently shaped wings (like a Moslem woman's cloak) and the shape of their bodies (a slight pinch above the thorax, giving them rather attractive waists), their life cycle was the same as many others of their kind: They laid their eggs on laundry and these larvae hatched at body heat and burrowed into the skin to mature. Of course, laundry was always ironed—even drip-dry shirts—to kill them. Everyone who knew Africa knew that.

Sean O'Faolain

May I Have Some Marmalade, Please?

December 1980

The novelist, biographer, and short-story writer Sean O'Faolain (1900–1991), a controversial Irish nationalist in his youth, began to publish in *Playboy* in 1971. He and his wife lived in Killiney, a suburb of Dublin, and took frequent trips to Italy and the United States. Ireland, he once said, "drives one, howling with boredom, out of it from time to time, only to lure one back, gently, insistently, until it drives one mad again." O'Faolain, working slowly but steadily on an old Royal portable, became a frequent contributor during the 1970s, turning out story after story with great charm and insight. This was the last one to appear. It illustrates perfectly the complex, passionate, yet ironic view of relationships that O'Faolain found in modern Ireland.

Sean O'Faolain

May I Have Some Marmalade, Please?

When Ellie slammed the front door, he slowed his cup's approach to the coffee table to glance across his shoulder at the clock on the mantelpiece. Six forty-five? Of course. Monday. Her night for bridge, his for the art class. His coffee made a smooth landing. He sank into his armchair, carefully unfolded his evening paper, looked blindly at its headlines for a while, let it fall into his lap. If only! If only! If only they had had a child! All day she had not spoken one word to him since she said at breakfast, "May I have some marmalade, please?" And now she was gone for the night.

Which of them first mooted this crazy idea of one night a week apart? She had been sarcastic about it. "Divorced weekly? A comedy in fifty-two acts."

He had been sour. "The road back to celibacy? Act five."

Probably neither of us began it. Just another knight's move, another oblique assertion of another imaginary speck of precious bloody personality threatened by some other imaginary attack by one on t'other. *Quid pro quo*. My turn now. Tit for tat. Even Stephen. Omens common to every failing marriage? Like her insistence on rising early every Sunday morning for first Mass and his on staying in bed late. His demanding roast leg of lamb on Fridays against her preference for black sole—not that he did not always let her have her way; he liked black sole—or her wanting flowers before her Madonna's statue all through May. It was not the flowers he minded; it was the silent betrayal of her man who had given up "all that" for . . . for what? At which, as if an earth tremor made the ornaments on the mantelpiece tremble, he heard all around him for miles and miles the tide of Dublin's suburban silence. Out there, how many mugs like himself were enjoying the priceless company of their own personalities?

He flung the newspaper onto the carpet, tore off his gray tie and pink shirt, went into his bedroom, dragged on his old black roll-neck Pringle pullover, groped for his old black homburg hat and began to brush it briskly. As good today as the day I brought it in Morgan's in Westmoreland Street for the mother's funeral. He curled a black scarf around his neck, felt for his car keys, switched off the Flo-Glo fire and the electric candles on the walls, checked the bathroom taps and the taps of the electric cooker, put out the hall light and slowly drew the front door behind him until he heard the lock's final click.

Fog. A drear-nighted February. Every road lamp on the estate had its own halo. He drove with care. Bungalow, bungalow, bungalow. Some lighted, most caverns of television's blue flicker. Exactly the kind of night he had first persuaded Father Billy Casey to doff their Roman collars, black jackets, black overcoats, black hats, put on sports jackets, checkered caps, jazzy ties and set off for some, any lounge bar in the city, in search, Father Billy had hooted, rocking with amusement, of what laymen call Life.

He was able to accelerate a bit on the yellow-lighted bus route. After 15 minutes or so, he felt space and damp on his right. The sea. The new hospital. Lights in a church for benediction. Inner suburbia's exclusive gateways. The U.S. embassy. He crossed the canal. The city's moat.

"Whither tonight?" Casey had always said at this point, rubbing his palms. Anywhere west of O'Connell Bridge used to be safe from episcopal spies; the east was less safe, too many people coming and going between the big cinemas, the bars of hotels. The Abbey Theater, the Peacock, the Busáras Theater. There was the same contrast on the other side of the bridge between Dublin's only pricey hub, the cube of Grafton Street, Nassau, Dawson and Saint Stephen's Green on to the east and the old folksy Liberties off to the west. Once you got that bit of geography clear in your head, you knew the only danger left was the moment of exit from the presbytery and your return to it. Holy smoke! Supposing the parish priest caught you dressed in civvies! As Father Billy once put it, a priest in a checkered cap is as inconceivable as a Pope in a bowler hat or, suddenly remembering some scrap of his seminarian's philosophy, if not inconceivable, at least unimaginable. He had enjoyed and hated these small risks, so much so that he could still groan and laugh at the thought of their hairbreadth escape the night they were nearly spotted by the P.P.'s housekeeper coming home late from what she always spoke of as her Fwhishte Diriuve. That was the night Father Billy had in his Edenish innocence pushed him out of the Church.

"Here's to us!" Billy had cheered from where he lay strewn like a podgy Pompeian on the triclinium of his secondhand sofa, his nightcap of malt aloft. "Who have at this triumphant moment once more unarguably demonstrated the undeniable truth that privacy is the last and loveliest of all class luxuries. Look at us! Boozing to our hearts' content in peace and privacy and nobody one penny the wiser. Whereas all the most overpaid, socialist, lefty poor working-man can do when he is thrown out of his pub at closing time is to take home half a dozen bottles of beer in a pack. In a pub, Foley! That's the key word. In a pub! A public house. Subject to public inspection, permission to drink only in public, get drunk in public, puke in public, under the public eye, to public knowledge. But you and I, Foley, privileged nobs by virtue of our exclusive, elitist rank as officers of the Pope's *Grande Armée,* can sit here at our ease, luxuriating in the lordly privacy of Father William Casey's personal sitting room in Saint Conleth's Roman presbytery, and not another soul one penny the wiser."

He had replied coldly:

"You've got it all wrong, Father Billy. We do not drink in lordly privacy. We drink in abject secrecy."

One word and he became aware of the duplicity of all institutions, the Law, the Army, Medicine, the Universities, Parliament, the Press, the Church dominated by the one iron rule, Never let down the side. There was only one kind of people from whom you might get a bit of the truth, not because they are more moral but because they have no side to let down. Outlaws. Join any organization and truth at once takes second place. They went on arguing it down to the bottom of the half bottle of Irish. "Sleep on it, Billy," he had said. "In whishky weritas."

▪ ▪ ▪

A kindled traffic light halted him as he approached O'Connell Bridge. He peered up at the Ballast Office clock, 7:32, and remembered the night—*The* Night—when he had answered Father Billy's ritual "Whither tonight?" with the daredevil cry of "Why don't we try the Long Bar in the basement of the old Met?" which—bang in the middle of O'Connell Street—spelled maximum danger. He was still chuckling at Casey's reply when the green let him through.

"The Long Bar? The short life! Onward to booze, death and glory." Poor Billy! Poor in every sense. All a booze meant to him was a large whisky, or two glasses of ale. He remembered how the two of them had cheered like kids that night when they found a parking spot directly opposite the Long Bar of the Met.

And, behold! Here it was, waiting for him again. He slid smoothly into its arms, sighing, "This is what I should be doing every night, instead of staring into bloody TV or an electric fire!"

He halted at the foot of the stairs, pushed open the glass door, three semicircular steps above the floor of the saloon, and surveyed the babble. He saw one vacant table and his mistake. A mob of youngsters. Mere boys and girls. Pint drinkers. Years of tobacco smoke. Life? Gaiety? Unconventional? Bohemian? It was just any ordinary bar. Or had it changed? Or had he? Or was it she who had transformed it that night? He edged down to the vacant table and gave his order to the bar curate. After two slow dry martinis, he surrendered. He took up his homburg—no other man or woman in the rooms wore a hat—felt for his car keys, foresaw fog, the drive, the empty bungalow. How Father Billy had stared around that night at all the pairs and quartets!

"Well, here it is, Foley! Life! And I can't tell you how glad I am to see it, because only last night I found myself going through the dictionary to find out what the devil the word means. I was as nearly off my rocker as that! I can now reveal to you, Father Foley, that Life is, quote, unquote, that condition which distinguishes animals and plants from inorganic objects and dead organisms by growth through A, metabolism, B, adaptability and C, reproduction. Look around you. Look at us. They are growing up. I put on seven pounds since Easter. Look at their fancy dress. Look at our fancy caps and jackets. We all adapt. Reproduction? Look at 'em, every single one of 'em with a one-way first-class ticket for the double bed. All booked!"

"Not all! Or don't I see over there in the corner two unaccompanied young women? The dark one isn't at all bad-looking. Four people spoiling two tables who could be improving one? Maybe those two young ladies are in search of Life? Come on, Billy Casey! Let's ask them over for a drink."

He had not meant one word of it. What they had already done on half a dozen nights was, every time, an act of the gravest indiscipline. Two soldiers of a victorious empire frolicking in taverns with conquered barbarians? At the sight of Casey's terrified eyes, he had leaned back and laughed so heartily that the dark young woman had looked across and smiled indulgently at their happiness. One second's thought and he would have merely smiled back and resumed his chatter with Casey. He spontaneously lifted his glass to her. Her smile widened whitely. His questioning eyebrows rose, his eye and thumb indicated his table invitingly, hers did the same to hers, he said, "Come on, Billy, in for a penny, in for a pound!" and the unimaginable of five minutes before became reality.

"Ellie," her companion apologized admiringly for her friend, "is very saucy." She was herself a striking redhead, but he thought the dark one much more handsome and she had by her laugh and gesture across the bar suggested a touch of dash and character. As for her looks, she had only one slight flaw; her mouth was by the faintest touch awry, and even this was in itself an attraction, that delicate, that charming fleck of imperfection that never fails to impress a woman's looks unforgettably. Her black hair, divided down the center of her skull, was drawn back boldly like two curtains. Her eyes were as clear as her clarid speech. Their large brown irises, shining like burred chestnuts, harmonized with her willow-colored skin. She was dressed entirely in black, apart from the little white ruff on her high neck that somehow made her look like a nun. He confided to himself the next day that her smiles came and went like the sly sunshine of April.

He introduced himself as Frederick Cecil Swinburne and his companion, to Casey's grinning delight, as Arthur Gordon Woodruffe, both of them final medicals at Trinity College. She said, "I am Ellie Wheeler Wilcox and my friend is Molly Malone," both of them private secretaries to directors of the Irish Sweep. They passed what any casual observer would have seen as a merry hour, as light, bright and gay as a joking and laughing scene in an operetta.

On parting, they all four said they might meet again the next Monday night.

He said a couple of hours later in Father Billy's rooms in the presbytery that the only thing missing was that those two young women should have been nuns in disguise and they should all have burst out into an Offenbach quartet. Casey's solemn reply had infuriated him:

"I am afraid, Father Foley, we went a bit too far tonight. We deceived those two young ladies. We pretended. We were guilty of bad faith."

He responded in exasperation with a whisper of "Well, I'll be damned!"

This restored Father Billy's sense of humor far enough to let him disagree about the damnation bit, though, possibly, there might be an extra couple of thousand years of purgatory in store for them both. All the same, he kept coughing dramatically the following Monday morning to indicate the onset of a bad cold.

The corner table was empty. No Miss Wilcox. No Miss Malone. He sat at the table that he had shared the week before with Father Casey, prolonging three tasteless martinis for an hour. Thereupon, cursing his silliness, he had clapped on his checkered cap and risen to his feet, and there she was on the platform of the three semicircular steps of the entrance door, tall and slim, dressed in black, her eyelashes overflowing her cheeks, her hair as close-fitting as a cap, her high neck extended to assist her searching gaze. He flung up his hand. Smiling back at him, she slowly edged her way between the tables. She sat opposite him though still looking about her, explaining that she had expected to meet her friend Molly Malone, though Molly did mention something today about feeling a cold coming on; but he felt so happy in her presence that he heeded little she said until he got her to talking about herself, her girlhood in the country, in County Offaly, where her father was a national teacher, her two younger sisters, her brother Fonsy, short for Alphonsus, who had emigrated to England and was now married in Birmingham; not that he attended to her chat half so much as he did to the fleeting mobility of her features, her contralto laughter, her vivacious gestures, though he did heed her carefully when she described her Auntie Nan with whom she was lodging in a little house in Ranelagh, and her friends, working mostly in the Irish Sweep, which led her in turn to ask him about what it is like to be a final medical in Trinity College and about his plans when he became a doctor, a question that instantaneously reminded him of Father Billy's words about bad faith. She listened to his lies with such a transparent expression of belief that he felt thrown down beneath her feet by a whirlwind of shame that kept gnawing at him for the rest of the night, until the moment came when he had halted outside her aunt's little red-brick home in that terraced cul-de-sac at Ranelagh. There, drawn up beside the curb, he gripped her hand, not, as she obviously thought and by her warm smile showed, to say a grateful good night but to plead for her trust. He must confess the truth about himself.

"Miss Wilcox, I have been deceiving you."

"The truth? Deceiving me?" Staring, frightened by his intensity and tone.

"I am not a medical student. I made all that up."

If only he could have stopped there. Neither, she could laugh, was she Ella

Wheeler Wilcox. He had to tell her the essence of him. He kept pressing her hand tighter and tighter.

"I am a clerical student. Trying to become a priest. You have been a revelation from heaven to me. I can't go on with it. I no longer want to be a priest."

Her eyelids shot open at that last word. While he went on to half explain, they opened wider and wider, as if she were opening the doors of her soul to him. In the silence that followed, she kept staring at him and he at her. In his celibate ignorance, he was feeling for the first time the full blast of power that Woman when reduced to one special woman possesses by the mere fact of being female. She in her virginal ignorance was transfixed by the power that Man in the person of this one man held over her by the mere fact of being male. Each was at that moment so evenly conqueror and conquered that if the essential god of all lovers had in that blind alley breathed over them so delicately as would not have shaken the filaments of a dandelion in full cloud of seed, they would have sunk into each other's arms.

That they did not, he often thought later, was due less to the gods than to her aunt, or to whatever other hand had suddenly lit the fanlight. What she may have said before she jumped from the car and ran up the brief concrete path to the door beneath the light he was never after to remember verbatim except for the petals of her voice declaring with unarguable clarity that they must never meet again, and her "Very well!" to his wild pleading that they must meet just once more so that neither of them should remember the other ungratefully.

They did meet just once again, and went on meeting just once again for the whole of the next year, propelled as gently and as irresistibly as a yacht before a summer breeze by sympathy, chivalry and self-immolation, until, to his astonishment, one gentle May evening in the stodgy bedroom of her Auntie Nan's dim house in Ranelagh while the old lady was away on holiday in County Cork, a typhoon of passion swallowed them both. After another year, marked by more agonizing and less passion, he extricated himself from his priestly vows. They married.

All that was five years ago, and he had long since accepted that he was never to understand what estranged them, he who had so often in his presbytery given counsel and comfort to young marrieds lost in the same fogged wood. All he knew for certain was that that year of waiting of tenderly comforting each other, or trying to decide what he should do, had been the happiest year of his life, conjoined then by the misery of separation divided now by the disaster of domesticity.

They had never really quarreled, never violently confronted each other, though of course they now and again "had words," the worst being the night he had evaded her clamant desire on the eve of Good Friday, the anniversary of the execution of a great man in whose alleged godliness he no longer believed. She had spat at him, "Your very skin is dyed black! You will never wash yourself of your precious stigmata!" To which he had retorted, "You? you, of all people dare say that to a man who has cast out every last trace of what you call black.

You with your getting up at dawn, your statues and your flowers and your evening benedictions and all the rest of your pietistic falderals and fandago you say that to me?" All of which she dismissed haughtily with the passionate observation that God's world is one—joy and pain, crocuses and the Crucifixion, love and lust, desire and denial, human passion and prayer.

"Dare you deny it?"

Weaponless, he did not.

The only clear hint he ever got anywhere about how marriages break had been vouchsafed to him one morning a bare month ago in the little shop of convenience near their bungalow, managed by an aging man and wife. He had always found each of them normally friendly and loquacious. That day the two were in the shop together. The old man, before attending to him, quietly asked his wife some trivial question concerning their stock. Was it about fire lighters, or washing soda? She answered him in the voice of *ancien régime* courtesy, in the softest voice, with all the formality of a duchess from the good old days before the revolution. She said between politeness and hauteur, "I beg your pawrdon?" He had fled from the shop, horrified by the revelation that this old pair were living out their last days in a state of savage war. Passion ends in politeness. After that, he added to his "If only we could have had a child" the wish that they could have one blazing, battering, bloody row.

▪ ▪ ▪

He jingled his car keys, rose to face the fog, the bungalow, the evening paper already out of date, clapped on his black hat, and saw a vision. His wife was standing on the platform at the end of the stairs, dressed in blacks, her hair as black as thunder, her midnight lashes enlarging her eyes that roved the rooms in search of . . . in search of whom? He flung up the arm of a drowning man. For a moment, she looked across the rooms at him, then her eyelids sank, her eyebrows shot upward; she looked at him again, decided, smiled her small crooked smile at him and edged forward between the tables. She held out her hand with, "Well, after all these years, if it isn't Mr. Swinburne! And what have you been doing with yourself all this time? Medicine?"

"Miss Wilcox!" he said and shook her hand. "You will join me in a drink?"

She gave him her sly smile, took the proffered chair and let silence fall between them as she slowly removed her gloves finger tip by finger tip. He as slowly extracted a cigarette and lit it. At their first far-off meeting, when he had taken her to be an ingenuous miss of about twenty, he had been struck by this same air of assurance. They both asked simultaneously, "Do you often come here?" and chuckled into a fresh silence which she quickly took hold of with "I have been told that some gentlemen have their pet pubs. Is this one of yours, Mr. Swinburne?"

Two seconds' silence during which he wondered if it were one of hers.

"I have no pet pub. I used to come here years ago to meet a girl I used to know."

"What happened to her?"

"She just disappeared." The bar curate stood silently beside them. "Your usual, Miss Wilcox? A dry martini? Make it two. On the rocks."

"Nice of you to remember my favorite drink, Mr. Swinburne."

"I have a good memory. When you stood in that doorway just now, you reminded me very much of my friend. Oddly enough, she also liked a dry martini. Like you, she was tall, dark and queenly."

She lowered her head sideways to deprecate the compliment, smiled to accept it.

"This is odd. When I saw you just now, you reminded me of a man I first met in this bar several years ago. I have not seen him for a long time. He, as you say, disappeared."

"What happened to him?"

Three seconds' pause.

"I have wondered. My friends and I have never been able to agree about what happens to make people disappear."

"Your friends?"

Four seconds' pause, during which she slowly turned her head to look toward a large round table, in an alcove that he had not previously noted, occupied by five or six women of varying ages. They were all looking her way. Her left wrist lifted her palm an inch to greet them. Her chin nodded an unspoken agreement. She turned back to him.

"My friends."

"Your bridge club?"

Five seconds' pause.

"I never play bridge. But we are a club. All married, all botched, all of us working now in the Irish Sweep. We came together by chance. Last summer, I got chatting with Mrs. Aitch, that is the jolly fat woman in the orange head scarf with her back to us. Angela Hanafey. She is about forty-six. Her husband was, is, always will be an AA case. She has four sons, all but one grown up. She just happened to be walking beside me one evening when we were pouring in our hundreds out of the Sweepstakes offices at five o'clock. We had never laid eyes on each other before. 'God!' she said to me. 'I'm starved for a drink. Come and have a quick one on me at the Horseshoe.' We met Mrs. King there. She's the slim, handsome blonde; don't let her see you looking. She is still bitter of her ex. He left her holding three children and slid off to get lost somewhere in England with a slut of seventeen. It was she brought along Kit Ferriter, the baby of the bunch, six months married and glad to be living alone again in her virginal bed-sit. Kit studied sociology for three years at Trinity. She says she learned far more about it in six months of marriage. Three or four others drop in and out. All sorts. One is married to an army captain who batters her. Another to a briefless barrister. Mrs. Aitch calls us the Missusmatched. Monday is club night. No other rules. No premises."

"And you talk about men and sex and marriage."

"Sex? Never. Men? No. Marriage? Occasionally. Not as an important subject. We mostly talk about woman things. Food, cooking, dress, make-up, kids, the cost of living, our jobs, nothing in particular."

"And in your club's view, why do those marrieds have this odd way of disappearing?"

"Why?"

Her eyebrows threw a shrug over her left shoulder. Her eyelids lowered a curtain on the shrug. The corners of her mouth buttoned it down. She leaned back to consider either the question or him. When she tinkled the ice in her glass, it sounded like his idea of Swiss cowbells in far-off valleys. When she laughed her contralto laugh, it hurt him that he had not heard it for a long, long time.

"Yes, why?"

"Why? We solved that months ago, when we invented the Seven Cs. Every marriage, we decided, sinks or swims on any three of"—right finger on left thumb checked them off—"Concupiscence, Comradeship, Contact, Kids, Cash, high or low Cunning and not to give a tinker's Curse about everything in general and anything in particular."

"Ye have left out Love!"

"Mrs. Aitch, our mother hen, dealt ably with that. 'I made a fatal mistake,' says she, 'with my fellow. I led him to think I was the reincarnation of the Blessed Virgin. On our honeymoon, I got a sudden, terrible thirst for tangerines. Afterward, we both found out, too late, that pregnant women get these odd hungers. He would have done anything for me, of course, on our honeymoon. He went to a power of trouble to get me the tangerines, but get them he did! When we were back home, I got a sudden wish for apricots. He rumbled and bumbled about it, but still and all, the poor devil did get me the apricots. A month later, I got an unquenchable longing for nothing less than wild strawberries. Well, by that time, I had a belly on me like a major. He told me to go to hell and find out for myself where anyone could find wild strawberries in the month of November and I knew at once that my dear love had vanished from the earth as if the fairies had got him.' Kit Ferriter, our expert on sociology, told her she was lucky that he didn't batter the other fellow's baby out of her. The dear child insists that Love, which you say we have omitted form our Seven Cs, is a mass-invented delusion with a life expectancy of three weeks."

She rose, holding out her hand. "Nice meeting you again, Mr. Swinburne. It was very pleasant. Now I must join my friends."

He held her hand pleadingly. "Can't we meet again? Say next Monday night. Just for a quick drink?"

She looked around the rooms, said, indifferently, "All right," and joined her welcoming group. As he walked out, he heard behind him again her miraculous laughter.

Back home, he kicked aside the evening paper, switched on his fire, sank into his armchair and fell into a stunned sleep. In the morning, the only time either of them spoke over their breakfastette in their kitchenette across their hinged tablette was when she said, "May I have some marmalade, please? . . . Thank you." On their way into town to work, he as always driving, he did say that next Monday night he would be, as usual, at his art class and she with an air of slight surprise replied that she would, of course, as usual be playing bridge with her friends.

Accordingly, on the following Monday night, she again left home before him to walk to the bus, and he, after taut calculations, followed her in time to be in the Long Bar before her arrival, seated facing the glass doors. Now and again, he glanced furtively toward the women's table in the alcove to his far left. His jury? His judges? His amused witnesses? Again, after two slowly sipped drinks, he jumped to his feet between rage and regret just as she appeared in the doorway. For a moment, she stood there motionless, then slowly descended to the level of the bar, edging between the tables toward him with "So we meet again, Mr. Swinburne," sat, began calmly to deglove. Of the precious ten minutes she allowed him that night, he could afterward recall clearly only one sequence, which he initiated:

"Did they ask if we were related?"

"No. And I did not vouchsafe. You could be only one of two things."

He worked it out.

"Or I could be a new friend?"

"Here? So briefly?"

"Did they say nothing at all about me?"

"Mrs. King said, 'He looks like a priest, all in black, even to the hat.' I said that the first time I met you seven years ago, here, you were dressed in the colors of the rainbow. I left them guessing. I said, 'Maybe he has become a priest since then.' " Ten seconds' silence, looking at each other. She swallowed her last piece of ice, put down her glass smartly, picked up her gloves and handbag, rose, said, "Have you?" and turned to go.

He winced but held her hand to beg for next Monday. He pleaded for it. They had talked so very little. "And I have nowhere else to go."

"Except," she said sympathetically, "back? All right. Then they *will* know!" and left him for her beaming friends.

In this fashion, he continued to meet her every week into the first green promises of spring, until by early May these extemporaneous meetings took on the character of regular assignations and, since they were never mentioned at home, the clandestine air of a double life. He looked forward to these encounters more and more eagerly. As we say, he lived for them, suspected that she enjoyed them equally, noted with excitement that they extended themselves on occasion to fifteen minutes, even to nearly twenty minutes and on one memorable night to fully twenty-five minutes, this being the night when he asked for her opinion as to which of her club's Seven Cs of marriage was the most important of all. She answered promptly.

"The first three, of course, Concupiscence, Comradeship and Contact. Some people think Comradeship comes first, but that is just Con disguising itself as Com. Kids inevitably follow. Then Cash edges forward. Then more and more need arises for high Cunning. But on all occasions thereafter, there is the need for not caring a damn, for the indifference of a divorce-court judge."

Naturally, they started to argue, and they might have gone on arguing if she had not suddenly become aware of radiations of impatience from across the room.

The next morning, she said, "May I have the marmalade, please? Thank you." But then, as lightly as she pasted the preserve on her toast, she added, "By the way, I understood you to say some time ago that your art class meets twice a week. My bridge club is proposing to meet on Mondays and Fridays." He at once decided that their relations had completely changed.

On that following Friday, the women's alcove contained only two elderly men drinking stout. His chest swelled with triumph. She arrived on time. Unasked, he clicked his fingers for the bar attendant and ordered their drinks. Presently, he observed with a tolerant amusement at the transparency of the feminine mind that the conversation had returned to last Monday's question about the primacy in marriage of feelings of fellowship or of desire, to which she referred as "passion" and rather brazenly (he thought) as "lust." In the course of their conversation, she said:

"Of course, in all this, one should first agree about the general principle of the thing. I mean, is it not all largely a question of what in life one most believes in? In poetry or in prose? I happen to see the world as a complex of things beyond all understanding, far too bewildering to be confined or defined by human laws or rules, shalls and shalt nots. I look at it all as a miracle and a mystery, a place of beauty and horror, a spring flower, a tree in bud, a dead child, a husband dying of cancer—Mrs. Aitch's boozy husband is dying that way, and she has fallen in love with him again—a lottery like the Irish Sweep chance, fate, the gods, God, the Madonna, love, lust, passion, a baby at the breast. Everything is one thing. That is why I love to have flowers for the Madonna who had a baby, miraculously according to you, not that it matters how she had it, why I rise in the morning for the first dark Mass, where they celebrate again the execution of a god, or of God, not that that matters either, why I like to go in the evening for the last benediction before the dark night, why I let that friend of mine whom I loved years ago go to bed with me because I thought he saw life the way I do, a poem that anybody can read and that nobody can understand."

Staring at her, taken again by her passion, yes, he could remember those wild talks during that year of blissful agony before. . . .

"Alas!" she smiled her hurt smile. "When we got married, he changed. Looking at him then, I was often reminded of the marvelous thing Keats once said about the greatest quality any human being can possess—the power to live in wonder and uncertainty, mystery and doubt, without ever reaching out after fact and reason. My friend turned out to be a man always looking for fact and reason, a lawmaker, a lawgiver, a law explainer, a policeman, a judge, a proseman, a prosy priest longing for his pulpit."

The bar's chatter, rumble, clinking talk, laughing stopped dead. Silence. Then:

"Did you never consider, Miss Wilcox, that this friend of yours may nevertheless have once dearly loved you?"

She pounced.

"Once? Yes. Once! One night in my aunt's house in Ranelagh while she was on holidays in County Cork with her sister. For a whole year after that night my wild lover wandered around and around in his head in search of fact and reason. I," she smiled crookedly, "was left waiting for more of the poetry."

Unguardedly, he laid a hand on her hand, said, "Ellie!" saw that he had blundered, withdrew. There was a staring silence. Then she looked at the ceiling as if she were listening to a plane passing over Dublin, looked at him once again, pushed back her cuff from her wristlet watch with her index finger, seized her bag and rose.

"You have reminded me, Mr. Swinburne. I promised my Auntie Nan to keep an eye on her little house in Ranelagh while she is gone to Derbyshire to stay with a niece. Would you mind leaving me there on your way home?"

He threw up his palms. Outside, it was raining. They did not speak in their car. She became proprietress of his homburg hat, nursing it on her lap. When they arrived outside the tiny red-brick house, he offered Miss Wilcox to wait and drive her to wherever she lived, it was no night for busing, she had no hope of getting a taxi. She said that that would be most kind of him, "But do come in! This is real rain," and clapped his black hat comically on her head and ran through the rain beside the new-mown patch of grass. He was relieved to see her laughing gaily at him as he also ran, hatless and stooped, through the rain. She left him in the parlor while she went off to do her checking, room by room. He could recognize only two items in the parlor: the aquatint of Christ with the Samaritan woman at the well, its frame painted in ugly commercial gilt (his mind clicked, "They shall not thirst anymore"), and the corded old sofa where he had put his arms around her for the first time. He heard her steps on the linoleum overhead. The photograph of a bearded man on the mantelpiece. What relative? He went into the kitchen. Her aunt's kingdom. An antique iron range. A stoneware sink. A crucifix. Tidy. Cold. He wandered to the stairs. On its side walls, lithographs of castles. He identified Ross Castle in Killarney. Then Blarney Castle in Cork. He paused longest at Reginald's Tower in Waterford, still seeing that corded sofa in the parlor. It had been raining that night, too. That, too, had been May. Through a little shower they had raced for the door.

From the front bedroom, she called him. "Mr. Ess?" When he reached the half-open door, he saw through the vertical aperture between the paneled door and its jamb an object that he recalled clearly, and with emotion, a tall mirror so mounted on its mahogany frame as to be able to tilt forward or backward. In this *cheval* mirror he had, that first night, first seen her completely undressed. Now, modestly undressed, in black bikini and black brassiere, she was smiling into the mirror in the direction of the slowly opening door. He entered, became aware that she was deliberately modeling female allurement, his hat tilted on her head, one wrist back-twisted on her left hip, right knee forward, the other hand airily held aloft.

"Well?" she invited him in the mirror with her minx's smile. "Do you really still love me?"

Between incomprehension and revelation, desire and revulsion, passion and despair, he gestured wildly around the room. Over the bed head in black and white, Pope Pius X in black and white stared like an intolerant boy from under black eyebrows. His mind clicked: Giuseppe Sarto, that bitter antimodernist. By the bed on the wall, a holy-water font. Last thing before sleep. His mind clicked: daring seminarian joke—*Here I lay me down to sleep, upon my little bed; but if I die before I wake, how will I know that I am dead?* On the dressing table, a tiny Infant of Prague, gaudy, pyramidical, pagan.

"Yes!" he said defiantly. "I do still love you. But not this way! Not here! Where everything smells of spinsters and sanctity!"

She turned to him. She handed him back his black hat. He was prepared for her to spit that there is no other way; or that "This room was once heaven to you." If she had said that, he would have said, "Yes! But then I was defying it, now I would be accepting it." Or she might in a sad memory of lost hope say nothing. She said nothing. She looked from his eyes to his feet, and from his feet up to his eyes, and with one fast swing of her fist, she crashed him across the face. Her engagement ring drew a red line in blood across his jaw. He returned the blow, they grappled, swaying and stumbling, screaming bitch and bastard, fell across the bed, where her nails tore at his face until he found himself mastering her on her back and suddenly she was kissing his slavering mouth and groaning over and over, "Give it to me."

▪ ▪ ▪

Whether it was the morning sun milliarding through the window into his face or the boom of a plane just taken off from Dublin, or the sound of a neighboring church bell that woke him, he found himself sitting up in bed startled, bewildered until he was calmed and fully informed by a hand stroking his bare back and her voice soothing him with "It is all right, Swinny! This is Saturday. Neither of us has to work." He sank back on the pillow, closed his eyes, remembered, turned his head toward her face on her palm on her pillow watching him quizzically. Beyond her on the floor, he saw his homburg hat battered flat.

"I'm starving," he announced querulously.

"Love always does that."

Always?

"Can we have breakfast?"

"Here? There's nothing in this house. No bread, no milk, butter. Nothing.

Water and power turned off. No shave, no shower. Where do you live, Swinny? Let's have brekker in your place."

At this inane question, his eyes widened. His lips tightened. He could say, "What the hell is this game you are playing?" or, "I am sick and tired of this fal-lal," or, "How long more are we going to act the parts of cat and mouse?" He said sourly, "I live near Ballybrack. Half an hour away."

While they were hurrying into their clothes, she rudely toed his black hat with, "You might as well throw that out."

He lifted it, dusted it affectionately, punched it, said, "One never knows," and put it on. "Hadn't we better make the bed?" he asked in his disciplined way.

She waved a paw. "She won't be back for a week; I'll drop in someday."

He held her wrist when she was unlocking the street door. "The neighbors?"

She ushered him out. "You are the gas man come to measure the meter."

He took the six-lane Bray Road. She murmured, "I am still sleepy," and leaned back her head and closed her eyes. The morning traffic was floating inward on his right. His outward lane was empty. He would be home in 20 minutes. He pondered the coming confrontation.

Home, she silently prepared breakfast while he showered and shaved, phrasing his ultimatum to his mirror. His cheek received a slim strip of plaster. Back in the kitchen, he found a changeling who spoke silently, as all long-marrieds can, ignoring words, hearing thoughts, interpreting silence, speaking runes. He sat to table and waited for it. Her open palm politely indicated his dish of marmalade. His belly went red with rage. He accepted the challenge. He withheld his marmalade. She looked at him mildly. He yielded the dish and waited. Slowly and seductively, she stroked his marmalade to and fro. Do come a little early. Before the others. My aunt will not be home until Saturday. He was almost certain that the extreme corner of her upper lip stirred. A speck of marmalade clung to her cheek. It made her look agreeably silly. He rubbed brisk palms, grabbed three slices of toast, surveyed his favorite dish of bacon and tomatoes, poured himself coffee, faced a hearty breakfast. But wait! Hold it! Half a sec! This woman? His fists closed like castles on either side of his breakfast. Who is she? My wife? Somebody else's? Nobody's? Is she a bit crazy? Does she mean all this? His memory clicked. Who said "Love is a mood to a man, to a woman life or death"? It was Ella Wheeler Wilcox! Without raising her eyes or ceasing to munch her toast, she slowly pushed the marmalade back to him. He considered the move, and her. The snippet of marmalade kept seductively moving up and down. Pensively he plastered his toast, began to eat and eat his fill. She watched him impassively.

Andre Dubus

Anna

January 1981

The short stories of New Englander Andre Dubus began to make a stir in the literary magazines of the 1970s. Uncompromisingly realistic, many are set in small towns that have seen better days, and the same might be said of his characters. The titles of Dubus's collections give a good idea of his tone: *Adultery and Other Choices* (1977), *We Don't Live Here Anymore* (1984), *The Last Worthless Evening* (1986), *Broken Vessels* (1991). This was his first story to be published in *Playboy*.

Andre Dubus

Anna

Her name was Anna Griffin. She was twenty. Her blonde hair had been turning darker over the past few years, and she believed it would be brown when she was twenty-five. Sometimes she thought of dyeing it blonde, but living with Wayne was still new enough to her so that she was hesitant about spending money on anything that could not be shared. She also wanted to see what her hair would finally look like. She was pretty, though parts of her face seemed not to know it: The light of her eyes, the lines of her lips seemed bent on denial, so that even the rise of her high cheekbones seemed ungraceful, simply covered bone. Her two front teeth had a gap between them and they protruded, the right more than the left.

She worked at the cash register of a Sunnycorner store, located in what people called a square: two blocks of small stores, with a Chevrolet dealer and two branch banks, one of them next to the Sunnycorner. The tellers from that one—women not much older than Anna—came in for take-out coffees, cigarettes and diet drinks. She liked watching them come in: soft sweaters, wool dresses, polyester blouses that in stores she liked rubbing between thumb and forefinger. She liked looking at their hair, too: beauty-parlor hair that seemed groomed to match the colors and cut and texture of their clothing, so it was more like hair on a model or a movie actress, no longer an independent growth to be washed and brushed and combed and cut, but part of the ensemble, as the boots were. They all wore pretty watches, and bracelets and necklaces, and more than one ring. She liked the way the girls moved: They looked purposeful but not harried. One enters the store and stops at the magazine rack against the wall opposite Anna and the counter, and picks up a magazine and thumbs the pages, appearing even then to be in motion still, a woman leaving the job for a few minutes, but not in a hurry; then she replaces the magazine and crosses the floor and waits in line while Anna rings up and bags the cans and bottles and boxes cradled in arms, dangling from hands. They talk to each other, Anna and the teller she knows only by face, as she fills and caps Styrofoam cups of coffee. The weather. Hi. How are you? Bye, now. The teller leaves. Often, behind the counter, with other customers, Anna liked what she was doing; liked knowing where the pimientos were; liked her deftness with the register and bagging; was proud of her cheerfulness; felt in charge of customers and what they bought. But when the tellers were at the counter, she was shy; and if one of them made her laugh, she covered her mouth.

She took new magazines from the rack, one at a time, keeping it under the counter near her tall three-legged stool, until she finished it; then she put it back and took another. So by the time the girls from the bank glanced through the magazine, she knew what they were seeing. For they always chose the ones she did: *People, Vogue, Glamour*. She looked at *Playgirl,* and in *Oui* she looked at the women and read the letters, this when she worked at night, not because there were fewer customers then but because it was night, not day. At first she had looked at them during the day, and felt strange raising her eyes from the pictures to blink at the parking lot, whose presence of cars and people and space she always felt because the storefront was glass, her counter stopping just short of it. The tellers never picked up those magazines, but Anna was certain they had them at home. She imagined that, too: where they lived after work, before work. She gave them large pretty apartments with thick walls so they heard only themselves; stereos and color television, and soft carpets and soft furniture and large brass beds; sometimes she imagined them living with men who made a lot of money, and she saw a swimming pool, a Jacuzzi.

Near the end of her workday, in its seventh and eighth hours, her fatigue was the sort that comes from confining the body while giving neither it nor the mind anything to do. She was restless, impatient and distracted, and while talking politely to customers and warmly to the regular ones, she wanted to be home. The apartment was in an old building she could nearly see from behind the counter; she could see the gray house with red shutters next to it. As soon as she left the store, she felt as if she had not been tired at all; only her feet still were. Sometimes she felt something else, too, as she stepped outside and crossed that line between fatigue and energy: a touch of dread and defeat. She walked past the bank, the last place in the long building of bank, Sunnycorner, drugstore, department store and pizza house, cleared the corner of the building, passed the dumpster on whose lee side teenagers on summer nights smoked dope and drank beer, down the sloping parking lot and across the street to the old near-yardless green wooden apartment house; up three flights of voices and television voices and the smell that reminded her of the weariness she had just left. It was not a bad smell. It bothered her because it was a daily smell, even when old Mrs. Battistini on the first floor cooked with garlic; a smell of all the days of this wood. Up to the third floor, the top of the building, and into the apartment whose smells she noticed only because they were not the scent of contained age she had breathed as she climbed. Then she went to the kitchen table or the bed or shower or couch, either talking to Wayne or waiting for him to come home from Wendy's, where he cooked hamburgers.

At those times, she liked her home. She rarely liked it when she woke in it: a northwest apartment, so she opened her eyes to a twilit room and, as she moved about, she saw the place clearly, with its few pieces of furniture, cluttered only with leavings—tossed clothes, beer bottles, potato-chip bags—as if her night's sleep had tricked her so she would see only what last night she had not. And sometimes, later, during the day or night, while she was simply crossing a room, she would suddenly see herself juxtaposed with the old maroon couch that had been left, along with everything else, by whoever lived there before her and Wayne: the yellow wooden table and two chairs in the kitchen, the blue easy chair in the living room and, in the bedroom, the chest of drawers, the straight wooden chair and the mattress on the floor, and she felt older than she knew she ought to.

▪ ▪ ▪

The wrong car: a 1964 Mercury Comet that Wayne had bought for one hundred sixty dollars two years ago, before she knew him, when the car was already eleven years old, and now it vibrated at sixty miles an hour, and had holes in the floor board; and the wrong weapon: a Buck hunting knife under Wayne's leather jacket, unsheathed and held against his body by his left arm. She had not thought of the car and knife until he put the knife under his jacket and left her in the car, smoking so fast that between drags she kept the cigarette near her face and chewed the thumb of the hand holding it; looking through the wiper-swept windshield and the snow blowing between her and the closed bakery next to the lighted drugstore, at tall Wayne walking slowly with his face turned and lowered away from the snow. She softly kept her foot on the accelerator so the engine would not stall. The headlights were off. She could not see into the drugstore. When she drove slowly past it, there were two customers, one at the cash register and counter at the rear, one looking at display shelves at a side wall. She had parked and turned off the lights. One customer left, a man bareheaded in the snow. He did not look at their car. Then the other one left, a man in a watch cap. He did not look, either, and when he had driven out of the parking lot to the highway it joined, Wayne said OK and went in.

She looked in the rearview mirror, but snow had covered the window; she looked to both sides. To her right, at the far end of the shopping center, the doughnut shop was open; and in front of it, three cars were topped with snow. All the other stores were closed. She would be able to see headlights through the snow on the rear window, and if a cruiser came, she was to go into the store, and if Wayne had not already started, she would buy cigarettes, then go out again, and if the cruiser was gone, she would wait in the car; if the cruiser had stopped, she would go back into the store for matches and they would both leave. Now, in the dark and heater warmth, she believed all of their plan was no longer risky, but doomed, as if by leaving the car and walking across the short space through soft angling snow, Wayne had become puny, his knife a toy. So it was the wrong girl, too, and the wrong man. She could not imagine him coming out with money, and she could not imagine tomorrow or later tonight or even the next minute. Stripped of history and dreams, she knew only her breathing and smoking and heartbeat and the falling snow. She stared at the long window of the drugstore, and she was startled when he came out: He was running, he was alone, he was inside, closing the door. He said Jesus Christ three times as she crossed the parking lot. She turned on the headlights and slowed as she neared the highway. She did not have to stop. She moved into the right lane, and cars in the middle and left passed her.

"A *lot,*" he said.

She reached to him and he pressed bills against her palm, folded her fingers around them.

"Can you see out back?" she said.

"No. Nobody's coming. Just go slow; no skidding, no wrecks. Jesus."

She heard the knife blade slide into the sheath, watched yellowed snow in the headlights and glanced at passing cars on her left; she held the wheel with two hands. He said when he went in he was about to walk around like he was looking for something, because he was so scared, but then he decided to do it right away or else he might have just walked around the store till the druggist asked what he wanted and he'd end up buying tooth paste or something, so he went down along the side wall to the back of the store—he lit a cigarette and she said, "Me, too"; she watched the road and taillights of a distant car in her lane as he placed it between her fingers—and he went around the counter and took out the knife and held it at the druggist's stomach: a little man with gray hair watching the knife and punching open the register.

She left the highway and drove on a two-lane road through woods and small towns.

"Tequila," he said.

In their town, all but one package store closed at ten-thirty; she drove to the one that stayed open until eleven, a corner store on a street of tenement houses where Puerto Ricans lived; on warm nights, they were on the stoops and sidewalks and corners. She did not like going there, even on winter nights when no one was out. She stopped in front of it, looked at the windows and said, "I think it's closed."

"It's quarter to."

He went out and tried the door, then peered in, then knocked and called and tried the door again. He came back and struck the dashboard.

"I can't fucking be*lieve* it. I got so much money in my pockets I got no room for my hands, and we got one *beer* at home. Can you believe it?"

"He must've closed early——"

"No shit."

"Because of the *snow.*"

She turned a corner around a used-car lot and got onto the main street going downhill through town to the river.

"I could use some tequila," she said.

"Stop at Timmy's."

The traffic lights were blinking yellow so people would not have to stop on the hill in the snow; she shifted down and coasted with her foot touching the brake pedal, drove over the bridge and parked two blocks from it at Timmy's. When she got out of the car, her legs were weak and eager for motion and she realized they had been taut all the way home; and, standing at the corner of the bar, watching Johnny McCarthy pour two shots beside the drafts, she knew she was going to get drunk. She licked salt from her hand and drank the shot, then a long swallow of beer that met the tequila's burn as it rose, and held the shot glass toward grinning McCarthy and asked how law school was going: he poured tequila and said, "Long but good," and she drank that and finished her beer and he poured two more shots and brought them drafts. She looped her arm around Wayne's and nuzzled the soft leather and hard biceps, then tongue-kissed him and looked down the bar at the regulars, most of them men talking in pairs, standing at the bar that had no stools; two girls stood shoulder to shoulder and talked to men on their flanks. The room was long and narrow, separated from the dining room by a wall with a half door behind the bar. Anna waved at people who looked at her, and they raised a glass or waved and some called her name and old Lou, who was drinking beer alone at the other end of the bar, motioned to McCarthy and sent her and Wayne a round. Wayne's hand came out of his jacket and she looked at the bill in it: a twenty.

"Set up Lou," he said to McCarthy. *"Lou.* Can I buy you a shot?"

Lou nodded and smiled, and she watched McCarthy pour the whiskey and take it and a draft to Lou, and she wondered if she could tend bar, could remember all the drinks. It was a wonderful place to be, this bar, with her back to the door so she got some of the chill, not all stuffy air and smoke, and able to look down the length of the bar and at the young men crowded into four tables at the end of the room, watching a television set on a shelf on the wall: a hockey game. It was the only place outside of her home where she always felt the comfort of affection. Shivering with a gulp of tequila, she watched Wayne arm-wrestle with Curt: knuckles white and hand and face red, veins showing at his temples and throat. She had never seen either win, but Wayne had told her that till a year ago, he had always won.

"Pull," she said.

His strength and effort seemed to move into the air around her, making her restless; she slapped his back, lit a cigarette, wanted to dance. She called McCarthy and pointed to the draft glasses, then to Curt's highball glass and, when he came with the drinks, told him Wayne would pay after he beat Curt. She was humming to herself, and she liked the sound of her voice. She wondered if she could tend bar. People didn't fight here. People were good to her. They wouldn't— A color television. They shouldn't buy it too soon: but when? Who would care? Nobody watched what they bought. She wanted to count the money but did not want to leave until closing. Wayne and Curt were panting and grunting; their arms were nearly straight up again; they had been going slowly back and forth. She slipped a hand into Wayne's pocket, squeezed the folded wad. She had just finished a cigarette, but now she was holding another and wondering if she wanted it, then she lit it and did. There was only a men's room in the bar. "Draw?" Curt said.

"Draw," Wayne said, and she hugged his waist and rubbed his right biceps and said: "I ordered us and Curt a round. I didn't pay. I'm going piss."

He smiled down at her. The light in his eyes made her want to stay holding him. She walked toward the end of the bar, past the backs of leaning drinkers; some noticed her and spoke; she patted backs, said. "Hi, How you doing? Hey, what's happening?"; big curly-haired Mitch stopped her: Yes, she was still at Sunnycorner; where had he been? Working in New Hampshire. He told her what he did, and she heard, but seconds later she could not remember; she was smiling at him. He called to Wayne and waved. She said, "I'll see you in a minute," and moved on. At the bar's end was Lou. He reached for her, raised the other arm at McCarthy. He held her shoulder and pulled her to him.

"Let me buy you a drink."

"I have to go to the ladies'."

"Well, go to the ladies' and come back."

"OK."

She did not go. Her shot and their drafts were there and she was talking to Lou. She did not know what he did, either. She used to know. He looked sixty. He came every night. His gray hair was short and he laughed often and she liked his wrinkles.

"I wish I could tend bar here."

"You'd be good at it."

"I don't think I could remember all the drinks."

"It's a shot-and-beer place."

His arm was around her, her fingers pressing his ribs. She drank. The tequila was smooth now. She finished the beer, said she'd be back, next round was hers; she kissed his cheek: His skin was cool and tough and his whiskers scraped her chin. She moved past the tables crowded with the hockey watchers: Henry coming out of the men's room moved around her, walking carefully. She went through the door under the television set, into a short hall, glanced down it into the doorless silent kitchen and stepped left into the rear of the dining room: empty and darkened. Some nights she and Wayne brought their drinks in here after the kitchen closed and sat in a booth in the dark. The ladies' room was empty. "Ah." Wayne was right: When you really had to piss, it was better than sex. She listened to the voices from the bar, wanted to hurry back to them. She jerked the paper, tore it.

Lou was gone. She stood where he had been, but his beer glass was gone, the ashtray emptied. He was like that. He came and went quietly. You'd look around and see him for the first time and he already had a beer; some time later, you'd look around and he was gone. Behind Wayne, the front door opened and a blue cap and jacket and badge came in: It was Ryan from the beat. She made herself think in sentences and tried to focus on them, as if she were reading: He's coming in to get warm. He's just cold. She waved at him. He did not see her. She could not remember the sentences. She could not be afraid, either. She knew that she ought to be afraid so she would not make any mistakes, but she was not, and when she tried to feel afraid or even serious, she felt drunker. Ryan was standing next to Curt, one down from Wayne, and had his gloves off and was blowing on his hands. He and McCarthy talked, then he left: at the door, he waved at the bar, and Anna waved. She went toward Wayne, then stopped at the two girls: One was Laurie or Linda, she couldn't remember which: one was Jessie. They were still flanked by Bobby and Mark. They all turned their backs to the bar, pressed her hands, touched her shoulders, bought her a drink. She said tequila and drank it and talked about Sunnycorner. She went to Wayne, told McCarthy to set up Bobby and Mark and Jessie—leaning forward: "Johnny, what is it? Laurie or Linda?"

"Laurie."

She slipped a hand into Wayne's pocket. Then her hand was captive there, fingers on money, his forearm pressing hers against his side.

"I'll get it. Did you see Ryan?"

"Yes."

She tried to think in sentences again. She looked up at Wayne; he was grinning down at her. She could see the grin, or his eyes, but not both at once. She gazed at his lips.

"You're cocked," he said. He was not angry. He said it softly and took her wrist and withdrew it from his pocket.

"I'll do it in the john."

She wanted to be as serious and careful as he was, but looking at him and trying to see all of his face at once weakened her legs; she tried again to think in sentences, but they jumped away from her like a cat her mind chased; when she turned away from him, looked at faces farther away and held the bar, her mind stopped struggling and she smiled and put her hand in his back pocket and said, "OK."

He started to walk to the men's room, stopping to talk to someone, being stopped by another; watching him, she was smiling. When she became aware of it, she kept the smile; she liked standing at the corner of the bar smiling with love at her man's back and profile as he gestured and talked, then he was in the men's room. Midway down the bar, McCarthy finished washing glasses and dried his hands, stepped back and folded his arms and looked up and down the bar; and when he saw nothing in front of her, he said, "Anna? Another round?"

"Just a draft, OK?"

She looked in her wallet; she knew it was empty, but she looked to be sure it was still empty; she opened the coin pouch and looked at lint and three pennies. She counted the pennies. Johnny put the beer in front of her.

"Wayne's got—"

"On me," he said. "Want a shot, too?"

"Why not?"

She decided to sip this one or at least drink it slowly, but, while she was thinking, the glass was at her lips and her head tilted back and she swallowed it all and licked her lips, then turned to the door behind her and, without coat, stepped outside. The sudden cold emptied her lungs, then she deeply drew in the air tasting of night and snow. "Wow." She lifted her face to the light snow and breathed again. Had she smoked a cigarette? Yes. From Lou. Jesus. Snow melted on her cheeks. She began to shiver. She crossed the sidewalk, touched the frosted parking meter. One of her brothers did that to her when she was little. Which one? Frank. Told her to lick the bottom of the ice tray. In the cold, she stood happy and clear-headed until she wanted to drink, and she went smiling into the warmth and voices and smoke.

"Where'd you go?" Wayne said.

"Outside to get straight," rubbing her hands together, drinking beer, its head gone, shaking a cigarette from her pack, her flesh recalling its alertness outside as, breathing smoke and swallowing beer and leaning on Wayne, it was lulled again. She wondered if athletes felt all the time the way she had felt outside.

"We should get some bicycles," she said.

He lowered his mouth to her ear, pushing her hair aside with his rubbing face.

"We can," his breath in her ear; she turned her groin against his leg. "It's about two thousand."

"No, *Wayne.*"

"Ssshhh. I looked at it, man."

He moved away and put a bill in her hand: a twenty.

"Jesus," she said.

"Keep cool."

"I've never—" She stopped, called McCarthy and paid for the round for Laurie and Jessie and Bobby and Mark, and tipped him a dollar. Two thousand dollars: She had never seen that much money in her life, had never had as much as one hundred dollars in her hands at one time; not of her own.

"*Last* call," McCarthy started at the other end of the bar, taking empty glasses, taking back drinks. "*Last* call."

She watched McCarthy pour her last shot and draft of the night; she faced Wayne and raised the glass of tequila: "Hi, babe."

"Hi." He licked salt from his hand.

"I been forgetting the salt," she said, and drank, looking at his eyes.

She sipped this last one, finished it and was drinking the beer when McCarthy called: "That's *it*. I'm taking the glasses in *five* minutes. You don't have to go home—"

"But you can't stay here," someone said.

"Right. Drink up."

She finished the beer and beckoned with her finger to McCarthy. When he came, she held his hands and said, "Just a quick one?"

"I can't."

"Just half a draft or a quick shot? I'll drink it while I put my coat on."

"The cops have been checking. I got to have the glasses off the bar."

"What about a roader?" Wayne said.

"Then they'll all want one."

"OK. He's right, Anna. Let go of the man."

She released his hands and he took their glasses. She put on her coat. Wayne was waving at people, calling to them. She waved: *"See* you, people. Good *night,* Jessie. Laurie. Good *night.* See you, Henry. Mark. Bye-*bye,* Mitch—"

Then she was in the falling white cold, her arm around Wayne; he drove them home, a block and a turn around the Chevrolet lot, then two blocks, while in her mind still were the light and faces and voices of the bar. She held his waist going up the dark stairs. He was breathing hard, not talking. Then he unlocked the door, she was inside, lights coming on, coat off, following Wayne to the kitchen, where he opened their one beer and took a swallow and handed it to her and pulled money from both pockets. They sat down and divided the bills into stacks of twenties and tens and fives and ones. When the beer was half gone, he left and came back from the bedroom with four Quaaludes and she said, "Mmmm," and took two from his palm and swallowed them with beer. She picked up the stack of twenties. Her legs felt weak again. She was hungry. She would make a sandwich. She put down the stack and sat looking at the money.

He was counting: "Thirty-five, forty, forty-five, fifty—" She took the ones. She wanted to start at the lowest and work up; she did not want to know how many twenties there were until the end. She counted aloud and he told her not to.

"You don't, either," she said. "All I hear is ninety-five, hundred, ninety-five, hundred—"

"OK. In our heads."

She started over. She wanted to eat and wished for a beer and lost count again. Wayne had a pencil in his hand, was writing on paper in front of him. She counted faster. She finished and picked up the twenties. She counted slowly, making a new stack on the table with the bills that she drew, one at a time, from her hand. She did not keep track of the sum of money; she knew she was too drunk. She simply counted each bill as she smacked it onto the pile. Wayne was writing again, so she counted the last twelve aloud, ending with: "And forty-*six,*" slamming it onto the fanning twenties. He wrote and drew a line and wrote again and drew another line and his pencil moved up the columns, touching each number and writing a new number at the bottom until there were four of them, and he read to her: "Two thousand and eighteen."

The Quaalude bees were in her head now and she stood and went to the living room for a cigarette in her purse, her legs wanting to go to the sink at her right, but she forced them straight through the door whose left jamb they bumped; as she reached into her purse, she heard herself humming. She had thought she was talking to Wayne, but that was in her head, she had told him. Two thousand and eighteen, we can have some music and movies now and she smiled aloud because it had come out as humming a tune she had never heard. In the kitchen, Wayne was doing something strange. He had lined up their three glasses on the counter by the sink and he was pouring milk into them; it filled two and a half, and he drank that half. Then he tore open the top of the half-gallon carton and rinsed it and swabbed it out with a paper towel. Then he put the money in it, and folded the top back, and put it in the freezer compartment and the two glasses of milk in the refrigerator. Then she was in the bedroom talking about frozen money; she saw the cigarette between her fingers as she started to undress, in the dark now; she was not aware of his turning out lights: She was in the lighted kitchen, then in the dark bedroom looking for an ashtray instead of pulling her sleeve over the cigarette and she told him about that and about a stereo and Emmylou Harris and fucking, as she found the ashtray on the floor by the bed, which was a mattress on the floor by the ashtray; that she thought about him at Sunnycorner, got horny for him; her tongue was thick, slower than her buzzing head, and the silent words backed up in the spaces between the spoken ones, so she told him something in her mind, then heard it again as her tongue caught up; her tongue in his mouth now, under the covers on the cold sheet, a swelling of joy in her breast as she opened her legs for him and the night's images came back to her: the money on the table and the faces of McCarthy and Curt and Mitch and Lou, and Wayne's hand disappearing with the money inside the carton, and Bobby and Mark and Laurie and Jessie, the empty sidewalk where she stood alone in the cold air, Lou saying: "You'd be good at it."

▪ ▪ ▪

The ringing seemed to come from inside her skull, insistent and clear through the voices of her drunken sleep: a ribbon of sound she had to climb, though she tried to sink away from it. Then her eyes were open and she turned off the alarm she did not remember setting; it was six o'clock and she was asleep again, then wakened by her alarmed heartbeat: all in what seemed a few seconds, but it was ten minutes to seven, when she had to be at work. She rose with a fast heart and a headache that made her stoop gingerly for her clothes on the floor, and shut her eyes as she put them on. She went into the kitchen: the one empty beer bottle, the ashtray, the milk-soiled glass, and her memory of him putting away the money was immediate, as if he had just done it, and she had not slept at all. She took the milk carton from the freezer. The folded money, like the bottle and ashtray and glass, seemed part of the night's drinking, something you cleaned or threw away in the morning. But she had no money and she needed aspirins and coffee and doughnuts and cigarettes; she took a cold five-dollar bill and put the carton in the freezer, looked in the bedroom for her purse and then in the kitchen again and found it in the living room, opened her wallet and saw money there. She pushed the freezer money in with it and slung the purse from her shoulder and stepped into the dim hall, shutting the door on Wayne's snoring. Outside, she blinked at sun and cold and remembered Wayne giving her twenty dollars at the bar; she crossed the street and parking lot and, with the taste of beer in her throat and tooth paste in her mouth, was in the Sunnycorner before seven.

She spent the next eight hours living the divided life of a hangover. Drinking last night had stopped time, kept her in the present until last call forced on her the end of a night, the truth of tomorrow; but once in their kitchen counting money, she was in the present again and she stayed there through twice waking, and dressing, and entering the store and relieving Eddie, the all-night clerk, at the register. So, for the first three or four hours while she worked and waited and talked, her body heavily and slowly occupied space in those brightly lit moments in the store; but in her mind were images of Wayne leaving the car and going into the drugstore and running out, and driving home through falling snow, the closed package store and the drinks and people at Timmy's and taking the Quaaludes from Wayne's palm, and counting money and making love for so drunk long; and she felt all of that and none of what she was numbly doing. It was a hangover that demanded food and coffee and cigarettes. She started the day with three aspirins and a Coke. Then she smoked and ate doughnuts and drank coffee. Sometimes from the corner of her eye she saw something move on the counter, small and gray and fast, like the shadow of a darting mouse. Her heart was fast, too, and the customers were fast and loud, while her hands were slow, and her tongue was, for it had to wait while words freed themselves from behind her eyes, where the pain was, where the aspirins had not found it. After four cups of coffee, her heart was faster and hands more shaky, and she drank another Coke. She was careful, and made no mistakes on the register; with eyes trying to close, she looked into the eyes of customers and Kermit the manager, slim and balding, in his forties; a kind man but one who, today, made her feel both scornful and ashamed, for she was certain he had not had a hangover in twenty years. Around noon, her blood slowed and her hands stopped trembling, and she was tired and lightheaded and afraid; it seemed there was always someone watching her, not only the customers and Kermit but someone above her, outside the window, in the narrow space behind her. Now there were gaps in her memory of last night: she looked at the clock so often that its hands seemed halted, and in her mind she was home after work, in bed with Wayne, shuddering away the terrors that brushed her like a curtain windblown against her back.

When she got home, he had just finished showering and shaving, and she took him to bed with lust that was as much part of her hangover as hunger and the need to smoke were; silent and hasty, she moved toward that orgasm that would bring her back to some calm mooring in the long day. Crying out, she burst into languor; slept breathing the scent of his washed flesh. But she woke alone in the twilit room and rose quickly, calling him. He came smiling from the living room and asked if she were ready to go to the mall.

▪ ▪ ▪

The indoor walk of the mall was bright and warm; coats unbuttoned, his arm over her shoulder, hers around his waist, they moved slowly among people and smells of frying meat, stopping at windows to look at shirts and coats and boots; they took egg rolls to a small pool with a fountain in its middle and sat on its low brick wall; they ate pizza alone on a bench that faced a displayed car; they had their photographs taken behind a curtain in a shop and paid the girl and left their address.

"You think she'll mail them to us?" Anna said.

"Sure."

They ate hamburgers standing at the counter, watching the old man work at the grill, then sat on a bench among potted plants to smoke. On the way to the department store, they bought fudge, and the taste of it lingered, sweet and rich in her mouth, and she wanted to go back for another piece, but they were in the store—large, with glaring white light—and as the young clerk wearing glasses and a thin mustache came to them, moving past television sets and record players, she held Wayne's arm. While the clerk and Wayne talked, she was aware of her gapped and jutting teeth, her pea jacket and old boots and jeans. She followed Wayne following the clerk; they stopped at a shelf of record players. She shifted her eyes from one to the other as they spoke; they often looked at her, and she said, "Yes. Sure." The soles of her feet ached and her calves were tired. She wanted to smoke but was afraid the clerk would forbid her. She swallowed the taste of fudge. Then she was sad. She watched Wayne and remembered him running out of the drugstore and, in the car, saying Jesus Christ, and she was ashamed that she was sad, and felt sorry for him because he was not.

Now they were moving. He was hugging her and grinning and his thigh swaggered against her hip, and they were among shelved television sets. Some of them were turned on, but to different channels, and surrounded by those faces and bodies and colliding words, she descended again into her hangover. She needed a drink, a cigarette, a small place, not all this low-ceilinged breadth and depth, where shoppers in the awful light jumped in and out of her vision. Timmy's: the corner of the bar near the door, and a slow-sipped tequila salty dog and then one more to close the spaces in her brain and the corners of her vision, stop the tingling of her gums, and the crawling tingle inside her body as though ants climbed on her veins. In her coat pocket, her hand massaged the box of cigarettes; she opened it with a thumb, stroked filters with a finger.

She wanted to cry. She watched the pictures on one set: a man and a woman in a car, talking; she knew California from television and movies, and they were driving in California: the winding road, the low brown hills, the sea. The man was talking about dope and people's names. The clerk was talking about a guarantee. Wayne told him what he liked to watch, and as she heard hockey and baseball and football and movies, she focused so hard on imagining this set in their apartment and them watching it from the couch that she felt like she had closed her eyes, though she had not. She followed them to the cash register and looked around the room for the cap and shoulders of a policeman to appear in the light that paled skin and cast no shadow. She watched Wayne count the money; she listened to the clerk's pleased voice. Then Wayne was leading her away.

"Aren't we taking them?"

He stopped, looked down at her, puzzled; then he laughed and kissed the top of her head.

"We pick them up out back."

He was leading her again.

"Where are we going now?"

"Records. Remember? Unless you want to spend a fucking fortune on a stereo and just look at it."

Standing beside him, she gazed and blinked at album covers as he flipped them forward, pulled out some, talked about them. She tried to despise his transistor radio at home, tried to feel her old longing for a stereo and records, but as she looked at each album he held in front of her, she was glutted with spending and felt more like a thief than she had last night waiting outside the drugstore, and driving home from it. Again she imagined the apartment, saw where she would put the television, the record player; she would move the chest of drawers to the living room and put them on its top, facing the couch where— She saw herself cooking. She was cooking macaroni and cheese for them to eat while they watched a movie; but she saw only the apartment now, then herself sweeping it. Wayne swept it, too, but often he either forgot or didn't see what she saw or didn't care about it. Sweeping was not hard, but it was still something to do and sometimes for days it seemed too much to do, and fluffs of dust gathered in corners and under furniture. So now she asked Wayne and he looked surprised and she was afraid he would be angry, but then he smiled and said OK. He took the records to the clerk and she watched the numbers come up on the register and the money go into the clerk's hand. Then Wayne led her past the corners and curves of washers and driers, deeper into the light of the store, where she chose a round blue vacuum cleaner.

▪ ▪ ▪

She carried it, boxed, into the apartment; behind her on the stairs, Wayne carried the stereo in two boxes that hid his face. They went quickly downstairs again. Anna was waiting. She did not know what she was waiting for, but standing on the sidewalk as Wayne's head and shoulders went into the car, she was anxious and mute. She listened to his breathing and the sound of cardboard sliding over the car seat. She wanted to speak into the air between them, the air that had risen from the floor board coming home from the mall as their talk had slowed, repeated itself, then stopped. Whenever that happened, they were about to either fight or enter a time of shy loneliness. Now, grunting, he straightened with the boxed television in his arms; she grasped the free end and walked backward up the icy walk, telling him, "Not so *fast,"* and he slowed and told her when she reached the steps and, feeling each one with her calves, she backed up them and through the door and he asked if she wanted him to go up first and she said, no, he had most of its weight, she was better off. She was breathing too fast to smell the stairway; sometimes she smelled cardboard and the television inside it, like oiled plastic; she belched and tasted hamburger, and when they reached the third floor, she was sweating. In the apartment, she took off her coat and went downstairs with him and they each carried up a boxed speaker. They brought the chest into the living room and set it down against the wall opposite the couch; she dusted its top and they put the stereo and the television on it. For a while, she sat on the couch, watching him connect wires. Then she went to the kitchen and took the vacuum cleaner from its box. She put it against the wall and leaned its pipes in the corner next to it and sat down to read the instructions. She looked at the illustrations and thought she was reading, but she was not. She was listening to Wayne in the living room: not to him, but to speakers sliding on the floor, the tapping touch of a screwdriver, and when she finished the pamphlet, she did not know what she had read. She put it in a drawer. Then, so that raising her voice would keep shyness from it, she called from the kitchen: "Can we got to Timmy's?"

"Don't you want to play with these?"

"No," she said. When he did not answer, she wished she had lied, and she felt again as she had in the department store when sorrow had enveloped her like a sudden cool breath from the television screens. She went into the living room and kneeled beside him, sitting on the floor, a speaker and wires between his legs; she nuzzled his cheek and said, "I'm sorry."

"I don't want to play with them, either. Let's go."

She got their coats and, as they were leaving, she stopped and looked back at the stereo and the television.

"Should we have bought it all in one place?" she said.

"It doesn't matter."

She hurried ahead of him down the stairs and out onto the sidewalk, then her feet slipped forward and up and he caught her against his chest. She hooked her arm in his and they crossed the street and the parking lot; she looked to her left into the Sunnycorner, two men and a woman lined at the counter and Sally punching the register. She looked fondly at the warm light in there, the colors of magazine covers on the rack, the red soft-drink refrigerator, the long shelves of bread.

"What a hangover I had. And I didn't make any mistakes."

She walked fast, each step like flight from the apartment. They went through the lot of Chevrolet pickups, walking single file between the trucks, and now if she looked back, she would not be able to see their lawn; then past the broad-windowed showroom of new cars, and she thought of their—his—old Comet. Standing on the curb, waiting for a space in traffic, she tightly gripped his arm. They trotted across the street to Timmy's door and entered the smell of beer and smoke. Faces turned from the bar, some hands lifted in a wave. It was not ten o'clock yet, the dining room was just closing, and the people at the bar stood singly; not two or three deep like last night, and the tables in the rear were empty. McCarthy was working. Anna took her place at the corner and he said, "You make it to work at seven?"

"How did you know?"

"Oh, my *God,* I've got to be at work at seven: another tequila, Johnny."

She raised a hand to her laughter, and covered it.

"I made it. I made it and tomorrow I don't work till three, and I'm going to have *two* tequila salty dogs and that's *all;* then I'm going to bed."

Wayne ordered a shot of brandy and a draft, and when McCarthy went to the middle of the bar for the beer, she asked Wayne how much was left, though she already knew, or nearly did, and when he said about 220, she was ahead of his answer, nodding but paying no attention to the words, the numbers, seeing those strange visitors in their home, staring from the top of the chest, sitting on the kitchen floor; then McCarthy brought their drinks and went away, and she found on the bar the heart enclosing their initials that she and Wayne had carved, drinking one crowded night when McCarthy either did not see them or pretended not to.

"I don't want to feel bad," she said.

"Neither me."

"Let's don't. Can we get bicycles?"

"All of one and most of the other."

"Do you want one?"

"Sure. I need to get back in shape."

"Where can we go?"

"The Schwinn place."

"I mean riding."

"All over. When it thaws. There's nice roads everywhere. I know some trails in the woods and one of them goes to a pond. A big pond."

"We can go swimming."

"Sure."

"We should have bought a canoe."

"Instead of what?"

She was watching McCarthy make a tom collins and a gimlet.

"I don't know," she said.

"I guess we bought winter sports."

"Maybe we should have got a freezer and a lot of food. You know what's in the refrigerator?"

"You said you didn't want to feel bad."

"I don't."

"So don't."

"What about you?"

"I don't want to, either. Let's have another round and hang it up."

▪ ▪ ▪

In the morning, she woke at six, not to an alarm but out of habit: her flesh alert, poised to dress and go to work, and she got up and went naked and shivering to the bathroom, then to the kitchen, where, gazing at the vacuum cleaner, she drank one of the glasses of milk. In the living room, she stood on the cold floor in front of the television and the stereo, hugging herself. She was suddenly tired, her first and false energy of the day gone, and she crept into bed, telling herself she could sleep now, she did not have to work till three, she could sleep: coaxing, as though her flesh were a small child wakened in the night. She stopped shivering, felt sleep coming upward from her legs; she breathed slowly with it, and escaped into it, away from memory of last night's striving flesh: she and Wayne, winter-pallid yet sweating in their long quiet coupled work at coming until they gave up and their fast dry breaths slowed and the Emmylou Harris album ended, the stereo clicked into the silence, a record dropped and Willie Nelson sang *Stardust*.

"I should have got some 'Ludes and Percs, too," he said.

Her hand found his on the sheet and covered it.

"I was too scared. It was bad enough waiting for the *money*. I kept waiting for somebody to come in and blow me away. Even him. If he'd had a gun, he could have. But I should have got some drugs."

"It wouldn't have mattered."

"We could have sold it."

"It wouldn't matter."

"Why?"

"There's too much to get. There's no way we could ever get it all."

"A *lot* of it, though. *Some* of it."

She rubbed the back of his hand, his knuckles, his nails. She did not know when he fell asleep. She slept two albums later, while Waylon Jennings sang. And slept now, deeply, in the morning, and woke when she heard him turning, rising, walking heavily out of the room.

She got up and made coffee and did not see him until he came into the kitchen wearing his one white shirt and one pair of blue slacks and the black shoes: he had bought them all in one store in twenty minutes of quiet anger, with money she gave him the day Wendy's hired him: he returned the money on his first payday. The toes of the shoes were scuffed now. She kept the shirt clean, some nights washing it in the sink when he came home and hanging it on a chair back near the radiator so he could wear it next day; he would not buy another one, because, he said, he hated spending money on something he didn't want.

When he left, carrying the boxes out to the dumpster, she turned last night's records over. She read the vacuum-cleaner pamphlet, joined the dull silver pipes and white hose to the squat and round blue tank and stepped on its switch. The cord was long and she did not have to change it to an outlet in another room; she wanted to remember to tell Wayne it was funny that the cord was longer than their place. She finished quickly and turned it off and could hear the records again.

She lay on the couch until the last record ended, then got the laundry bag from the bedroom and soap from the kitchen, and left. On the sidewalk, she turned around and looked up at the front of the building, old and green in the snow and against the blue glare of the sky. She scraped the car's glass and drove to the laundry: two facing rows of machines, moist warm air, gurgling rumble and whining spin of washers, resonant clicks and loud hiss of driers, and put in clothes and soap and coins. At a long table, women smoked and read magazines, and two of them talked as they shook crackling electricity from clothes they folded. Anna took a small wooden chair from the table and sat watching the round window of the machine, watched her clothes and Wayne's tossing past it, like children waving from a Ferris wheel.

Laurie Colwin

My Mistress

March 1982

Laurie Colwin (1944–1992) was a popular writer of the 1970s and 1980s whose wryly sunny urban stories and novels (*Shine On, Bright and Dangerous Object,* 1975; *Happy All the Time,* 1978) made guarded optimism seem like a reasonable approach to the world, even New York. A series of stories about the illicit lovers Francis and Billy was collected in *Another Marvelous Thing* (1986). "My Mistress," the first of them, was, she said frequently, her favorite, not only of this collection but of all the stories she ever wrote. It was Colwin's sole appearance in *Playboy*. She died suddenly of a heart attack just as her career seemed to be reaching new heights. Her last novel, *A Big Storm Knocked It Over,* appeared in 1993.

Laurie Colwin

My Mistress

My wife is precise, elegant and well dressed, but the sloppiness of my mistress knows few bounds. Apparently, I am not the sort of man who acquires a stylish mistress like the mistresses in French movies. Those women rendezvous at the café of an expensive hotel and take their cigarette cases out of alligator handbags, or they meet their lovers on bridges in the late afternoon, wearing dashing capes. My mistress greets me in a pair of worn corduroy trousers, once green and now no color at all, a gray sweater and an old shirt of her younger brother's that has a frayed collar and a pair of very old, broken shoes with tassels, the backs of which are held together with electrical tape. The first time I saw those shoes, I found them remarkable.

"What are those?" I said. "And why do you wear them?"

My mistress is a serious person, often glum, who likes to put as little inflection into a sentence as she can. She always answers a question.

"They used to be quite nice," she said. "I wore them out. Now I use them for slippers. These are my house shoes."

This person's name is Josephine Delielle, nicknamed Billy, called Josephine by her husband. I am Francis Clemens and no one but my mistress calls me Frank. The first time we went to bed, after months of longing and abstinence, my mistress turned to me, fixed me with an indifferent stare and said, "Well, well. In bed with Frank and Billy."

▪ ▪ ▪

My constant image of Billy is of her pushing her hair off her forehead with an expression of exasperation. She frowns easily, often looks puzzled and is frequently irritated. In movies, men have mistresses who soothe and pet them, who are consoling, passionate and ornamental. But I have a mistress who, while she is passionate, is mostly grumpy. Traditional things mean nothing to her. She does not flirt, cajole or wear fancy underwear. She has taken to referring to me as her "little bit of fluff" and she refers to me as *her* mistress, as in the sentence "Before you became my mistress, I led a blameless life."

But in spite of this, I am secure in her affections. I know she loves me—not that she would ever come right out and tell me. She prefers the oblique line of approach. She may say something like, "Being in love with you is making me a nervous wreck." Or, "Falling in love with you is the hobby I took up instead of knitting or wood engraving."

Here is a typical encounter. It is between two and three o'clock in the afternoon. I arrive and ring the doorbell. The Delielles, who have a lot of money, live in the duplex apartment of an old town house. Billy opens the door. There I am, an older man in my tweed coat. My hands are cold. I'd like to get them underneath her ratty sweater. She looks me up and down. "Gosh, you look sweet," she might say, or, "My, what an adorable pair of trousers."

Sometimes she gets her coat and we go for a bracing walk. Sometimes we go upstairs to her study. Billy is an economist and teaches two classes at the business school. She writes for a couple of highbrow journals. Her husband, Grey, whom she met when she worked as a securities analyst, is a Wall Street wonder boy. They are one of those dashing couples, or at least they sound like one. I am no slouch, either. For years, I was an investment banker, and now I consult from my own home. I own a rare-book store—modern English and American first editions—which is excellently run for me so that I can visit and oversee it. I, too, write for a couple of highbrow journals. We have much in common, my mistress and I, or so it looks.

Billy's study is untidy. She likes to spread her papers out. Since her surroundings mean nothing to her, her study is bare of ornament and actually cheerless.

"What have you been doing all day?" she says.

I tell her. Breakfast with my wife, Vera; newspaper reading after Vera has gone to work; an hour or so on the telephone with clients; a walk over to my shop; more telephoning; a quick sandwich; her.

"You and I ought to go out for lunch someday," she says. "One should always take one's mistress out for lunch. We could go Dutch, thereby taking both mistresses at once."

"I try to take you for lunch," I say, "but you don't like to be taken out for lunch."

"Huh," utters Billy. She stares at her bookcase as if looking for a misplaced volume, and then she may say something like, "If I gave you a couple of dollars, would you take your clothes off?"

Instead, I take her into my arms. Her words are my signal that Grey is out of town. Often he is not, and then I merely get to kiss my mistress, which makes us both dizzy. To kiss her and know that we can go forward to what Billy tonelessly refers to as "the rapturous consummation" reminds me that in relief is joy.

After kissing for a few minutes, Billy closes the study door and we practically throw ourselves at each other. After the rapturous consummation has been achieved, during which I can look upon a mistress recognizable as such to me, my mistress will turn to me and, in a voice full of the attempt to stifle emotion, say something like, "Sometimes I don't understand how I got so fond of a beat-up old person such as you."

These are the joys adulterous love brings to me.

▪ ▪ ▪

Billy is indifferent to a great many things: clothes, food, home decor. She wears neither perfume nor cologne. She uses what is used on infants: talcum powder and Ivory soap. She hates to cook and will never present me with an interesting postcoital snack. Her snacking habits are those, I have often remarked, of a late-nineteenth-century English clubman. Billy will get up all naked and disarrayed and present me with a mug of cold tea, a plate of hard wheat biscuits or a squirt of tepid soda from the siphon on her desk. As she sits under her quilt nibbling those resistant biscuits, she reminds me of a creature from another universe—the solar system that contains the alien features of her real life: her past, her marriage, why I am in her life and what she thinks of me.

I drink my soda, put on my clothes and, unless Vera is out of town, I go home to dinner. If Vera and Grey are out of town at the same time, Billy and I go out to dinner, during the course of which she either falls asleep or looks as if she is about to. Then I take her home, go home and have a large, steadying drink.

I was not entirely a stranger to adulterous love when I met Billy. I have explained this to her. In all long marriages, I expound, there are certain lapses. The look on Billy's face as I lecture is one of either amusement or contempt or both. The dinner party you are invited to as an extra man when your wife is away, I tell her. You are asked to take the extra woman, whose husband is away, home in a taxi. The divorced friend of yours and your wife's who invites you for a drink one night, and so on. These fallings into bed are the friendliest things in the world, I add. I look at my mistress.

"I see," she says. "Just like patting a dog."

My affair with Billy, as she well knows, is nothing of the sort. I call her every morning. I see her almost every afternoon. On the days she teaches, she calls me. We are as faithful as the Canada goose, more or less. She is an absolute fact of my life. When not at work, and when not with her, my thoughts rest upon the subject of her as easily as you might lay a hand on a child's head. I conduct a mental life with her when we are apart. Thinking about her is like entering a study or office, a room to which only I have access.

I, too, am part of a dashing couple. My wife is an industrial designer who has dozens of commissions and consults to everyone. Our two sons are grown up. One is a lawyer and one is a journalist. The lawyer is married to a lawyer and the journalist keeps company with a dancer. Our social life is a mixture of our friends, our children and their friends. What a lively table we must be, all of us together. So I tell my mistress. She gives me a baleful look.

"We get plenty of swell types in for meals," she says. I know this is true and I know that Billy, unlike my gregarious and party-giving wife, thinks that there is no hell more hellish than the hell of social life. She has made up a tuneless little chant, like a football cheer, to describe it. It goes:

They invited us
We invited them
They invited us
We invited them
They invited us
We invited them.

Billy and I met at a reception to celebrate the twenty-fifth anniversary of one of the journals to which we are both occasional contributors. We fell into a spirited conversation during which Billy asked me if that reception weren't the most boring thing I had ever been to. I said it wasn't, by a long shot. Billy said, "I can't stand these things where you have to stand up and be civilized. They make me itch. People either yawn, itch or drool when they get bored. Which do you do?"

I said I yawned.

"Huh," said Billy. "You don't look much like a drooler. Let's get out of here."

This particular interchange is always brought up when intentionality is discussed. Did she mean to pick me up? Did I look available? And so on. Out on the street, we revealed that while we were both married, both of our spouses were out of town on business. Having made that clear, we went out to dinner and talked shop.

After dinner, Billy said why didn't I come have a drink or a cup of tea? I did not know what to make of this invitation. I remembered that young people are more casual about these things and that a cup of tea probably meant a cup of tea. My reactions to this offer are also discussed when cause is under discussion. Did I want her to seduce me? Did I mean to seduce her? Did this mean that I, having just met her, lusted for her?

Of her house, Billy said. "We don't have good taste or bad taste. We have no taste." Her living room had no style whatsoever, but it was comfortable enough. There was a portrait of what looked like an ancestor over the fireplace.

It was not a room that revealed a thing about its occupants except solidity and a lack of decorative inspiration. Billy made herself a cup of tea and gave me a drink. We continued our conversation, and when Billy began to look sleepy, I left.

After that, we made a pass at social life. We invited them for dinner, along with some financial types, a painter and our lawyer son. At this gathering, Billy was mute, and Grey, a very clever fellow, chatted interestingly. Billy did not seem at all comfortable, but the rest of us had a fairly good time. Then they invited us, along with some financial types they knew and a music critic and his book-designer wife. At this dinner, Billy looked tired. It was clear that cooking was a strain on her. She told me later that she was the type who, when forced to cook, did every little thing, like making and straining the veal stock. From the moment she entered the kitchen, she looked longingly forward to the time when all the dishes would be clean and put away and the guests would all have gone home.

Then we invited them, but Grey had a bad cold and they had to cancel. After that, Billy and I ran into each other one day when we were both dropping off articles at the same journal and we had lunch. She said she was looking for an article of mine and two days later, after rummaging in my files, I found it. Since I was going to be in her neighborhood, I dropped it off. She wrote me a note about this article, and then I called her to discuss it further. This necessitated a lunch meeting. Then she said she was sending me a book I had said I wanted to read, and then I sent her a book, and so it went.

One evening, I stopped by to have a chat with Billy and Grey. Vera was in California and I had been out to dinner in Billy's part of town. I called her from a pay phone, and when I got there, it turned out that Grey was out of town, too. Had I been secretly hoping that this would be the case? Billy had been working in her study and without thinking about it, she led me up the stairs. I followed her, and at the door of her study, I kissed her. She kissed me right back and looked awful about it, too.

"Nothing but a kiss!" I said, rather frantically. My mistress was silent.

"A friendly kiss," I said.

My mistress gave me the sort of look that is supposed to make your blood freeze, and said, "Your friends must be very advanced. Do you kiss them all this way?"

"It won't happen again," I said. "It was all a mistake."

Billy gave me a stare so bleak and hard that I had no choice but to kiss her, and that, except for the fact that it took us a couple of months to get into bed, was the beginning of that.

That was a year ago, and it is impossible for me to figure out what is going on in Billy's life that has me into it. She once remarked that in her opinion, there is frequently too little kissing in marriage, through which frail pinprick was a microscopic dot of light thrown on the subject of her marriage, or was it? She is like a red Indian and says nothing at all, nor does she ever slip.

I, however, do slip, and I am made aware of this by the grim, sidelong glance

I am given. I once told Billy that until I met her, I had never given kissing much thought—she is an insatiable kisser for an unsentimental person—and I was rewarded for this utterance by a well-raised eyebrow and a rather frightening look of registration.

From time to time, I feel it is wise to tell Billy how well Vera and I get along.

"Swell," says Billy. "I'm thrilled for you."

"Well, it's true," I say.

"I'm sure it's true," says Billy. "I'm sure there's no reason in the world why you come and see me almost every day. It's probably just an involuntary action, like sneezing."

"But you don't understand," I say. "Vera has men friends. I have women friends. The first principle of a good marriage is freedom."

"Oh, I see," says Billy. "You sleep with your other women friends in the morning and come over here in the afternoon. What a lot of stamina you have for an older person."

One day this conversation had unexpected results. I said how well Vera and I got along, and Billy looked unadornedly hurt.

"God hates a mingy lover," she said. "Why don't you just say that you're in love with me and that it frightens you and have done with it?"

An unexpected lump rose in my throat.

"Maybe you're not in love with me," said Billy in her flattest voice. "It's nothing to me."

I said, "I am in love with you."

"Well, there you are," said Billy.

▪ ▪ ▪

My curiosity about Grey is a huge, violent dog on a very tight leash. He is four years older than Billy, a somewhat sweet-looking boy with rumpled hair who looks as if he is working out problems in higher math as you talk to him. He wears wire-rimmed glasses and his shirttail hangs out. He has the body of a young boy and the air of a genius or someone constantly preoccupied by the intense pressure of a rarefied mental life. Together he and Billy look not so much like husband and wife as like coconspirators. How often does she sleep with him? What are her feelings about him?

I begin preliminary queries by hemming and hawing. "Umm," I say, "it's, umm, it's a little hard for me to picture your life with Grey. I mean, it's hard to picture your everyday life."

"What you want to know is how often we sleep together and how much I like it," says Billy.

Well, she has me there, because that is exactly what I want to know.

"Tell you what," says my mistress. "Since you're so forthcoming about *your* life. We'll write down all about our home fronts on little slips of paper and then we'll exchange them. How's that?"

Well, she has me there, too. What we are doing in each other's lives is an unopened book.

I know how she contrasts to my wife: My wife is affable, full of conversation, loves a dinner party and is interested in clothes, food, home decor and the issues of the day. She loves to entertain, is sought out in times of crisis by her numerous friends and has a kind or original word for everyone. She is methodical, hard-working and does not fall asleep in restaurants. How I contrast to Grey is another matter, a matter about which I know nothing. I am considerably older and perhaps I appeal to some father longing in my mistress. Billy says Grey is a genius—a thrilling quality but not one that has any real relevance to life with another person. He wishes, according to his wife, that he were the conductor of a symphony orchestra, and for this reason, he is given scores, tickets and batons for his birthday. He has studied Russian and can sing Russian songs.

"He sounds so charming," I say, "that I can't imagine why you would want to know someone like me." Billy's response to this is pure silence.

Once in a while, she quotes him on the subject of the stock market. If life were not so complicated, I might very well be calling him up for tips. I hunt for signs of him on Billy—jewelry, marks, phrases. I know that he reads astronomy books for pleasure, enjoys cross-country skiing and likes to travel. Billy says she loves him, but she also says she loves several paintings in the Museum of Modern Art.

"If you love him so much," I say, taking a page from her book, "why are you hanging around with me?"

" 'Hanging around,' " Billy says in a bored monotone.

"Well?"

" 'I am large and contain multitudes,' " she says, misquoting a line from Walt Whitman.

This particular conversation took place en route to a cottage in Vermont that I had rented for a week when both Grey and Vera were going to be away for ten days.

I remember clearly with what happy anticipation I presented the idea of this cottage to her.

"Guess what," I said.

"You're pregnant," said Billy.

"I have rented a little cottage for us, in Vermont. For a week, when Grey and Vera are away on their long trips. We can go there and watch the leaves turn."

"Great," said Billy faintly. She looked away and didn't speak for some time.

"We don't have to go, Billy," I said. "I only sent the check yesterday. I can cancel it."

There appeared to be tears in my mistress' eyes.

"No," she said. "Don't do that. I'll split it with you."

"You don't seem pleased," I said.

"Pleased," said Billy. "Being pleased doesn't strike me as the appropriate response to the idea of going off to a love nest with your lover."

"What *is* the appropriate response?" I said.

"Oh," said Billy, her voice now blithe, "sorrow, guilt, craving, glee, horror, anticipation."

Well, she can run, but she can't hide. My mistress is given away from time to time by her own expressions. No matter how hard she tries to suppress the visible evidence of what she feels, she is not always successful. Her eyes turn color, becoming dark and rather smoky. This is as good as a plain declaration of love. Billy's mental life, her grumpiness, her irritability, her crotchets are like static that from time to time give way to a clear signal, just as you often hit a pure band of music on a car radio after turning the dial through a lot of chaotic squawk.

In French movies of a certain period, the lovers are seen leaving the woman's apartment or house. His car is parked on an attractive side street. She is carrying a leather valise and is wearing a silk scarf around her neck. He is carrying the wicker basket she has packed with their picnic lunch. They will have the sort of food lovers have for lunch in these movies: a roast chicken, a bottle of champagne and a cheese wrapped up in leaves. Needless to say, when Billy and I finally left to go to our love nest, no such sight presented itself to me. First of all, she met me around the corner from my garage after a number of squabbles about whose car to take. My car is bigger, so I won. I found her on an unattractive side street, which featured a rent-a-car place and an animal hospital. Second of all, she was wearing an old skirt, her old jacket and was carrying a canvas overnight bag. No lacy underwear would be withdrawn from it, I knew. My mistress buys her white-cotton undergarments at the five-and-ten-cent store. She wears an old T-shirt of Grey's to sleep in, she tells me.

For lunch we had hamburgers—no romantic rural inn or picnic spot for us—at Hud's Burger Hut on Route 22.

"We go to some swell places," Billy said.

As we drew closer to our destination, Billy began to fidget, reminding me that having her along was sometimes not unlike traveling with a small child.

In the nearest town to our love nest, we stopped and bought coffee, milk, sugar and corn flakes. Because I am a domestic animal and not a mere savage, I remembered to buy bread, butter, cheese, salami, eggs and a number of cans of tomato soup.

Billy surveyed these items with a raised eyebrow.

"This is the sort of stuff you buy when you intend to stay indoors and kick up a storm of passion," she said.

It was an off-year Election Day—Congressional and Senate races were being run. We had both voted, in fact, before taking off. Our love nest had a radio I instantly switched on to hear if there were any early returns while we gave the place a cursory glance and put the groceries away. Then we flung ourselves onto the unmade bed for which I had thoughtfully remembered to pack sheets.

When our storm of passion had subsided, my mistress stared impassively at the ceiling.

"In bed with Frank and Billy," she intoned. "It was Election Day, and Frank and Billy were once again in bed. Election returns meant nothing to them. The future of their great nation was inconsequential; so busy were they flinging themselves at each other, they could barely be expected to think for one second of any larger issue. The subjects to which these trained economists could have spoken, such as inflationary spirals or deficit budgeting, were as mere dust."

"Shut up, Billy," I said.

She did shut up. She put on my shirt and went off to the kitchen. When she returned, she had two cups of coffee and a plate of toasted-cheese sandwiches on a tray. With the exception of her dinner party, this was the first meal I had ever had at her hands.

"I'm starving," she said, getting under the covers. We polished off our snack, propped up with pillows. I asked Billy if she might like a second cup of coffee and she gave me a look of remorse and desire that made my head spin.

"Maybe you wanted to go out for dinner," she said. "You like a proper dinner." Then she burst into tears. "I'm sorry," she said. These were words I had never heard her speak before.

"Sorry?" I said. "Sorry for what?"

"I didn't ask you what you wanted to do," my mistress said. "You might have wanted to take a walk, or go for a drive, or look around the house, or make the bed."

I stared at her.

"I don't want a second cup of coffee," Billy said. "Do you?"

I got her drift and did not get out of bed. I tried to do an imitation of a man giving in to a woman, because, in fact, my thirst for her embarrassed me and I did not mind imagining that it was her thirst I was being kind enough to quench, but the forthrightness of her desire for me melted my heart.

During that week, none of my expectations came to pass. We did not, for example, have long talks about our respective marriages or our future together or apart. We did not discover what our domestic life might be like. We lived like graduate students, or mice, and not like normal people at all, but like lovers. We kept odd hours and lived off sandwiches. We stayed in bed and both were glad that it rained four days out of five. When the sun came out, we went for a walk and watched the leaves turn. From time to time, I would switch on the radio to find out what the news commentators were saying about the election results.

"Because of this historic time," Billy said, "you will never be able to forget me. It is a rule of life that care must be taken in choosing whom one will be in bed with during Great Moments in History. You are now stuck with me and this week of important Congressional elections twined in your mind forever."

▪ ▪ ▪

It was in the car on the way home that the subject of what we were doing together came up. It was twilight and we had both been rather silent.

"This is the end of the line," said Billy.

"What do you mean?" I said. "Do you mean you want to break this up?"

"No," said Billy. "It would be nice, though, wouldn't it?"

"No, it would not be nice," I said.

"I think it would," said Billy. "Then I wouldn't spend all my time wondering what we are doing together when I could be thinking about other things, like the future of the dollar."

"What do you think we are doing together?" I said.

"It's simple," said Billy. "Some people have dogs or kitty cats. You're my pet."

"Come on."

"OK, you're right. Those are only child substitutes. You're my child substitute until I can make up my mind about having a child."

At this, my blood does freeze. Whose child does she want to have?

▪ ▪ ▪

Every now and then, when overcome with tenderness—on these occasions naked, carried away and looking at each other with sweetness in our eyes—my mistress and I smile dreamily and realize that if we dwelled together for more than a week, in the real world and not in some love nest, we would soon learn to hate each other. It would never work. We both know it. She is too relentlessly dour and too fond of silence. I prefer false cheer to no cheer and I like conversation over dinner no matter what. Furthermore, we would never have proper meals, and although I cannot cook, I like to dine. I would soon resent her lack of interest in domestic arrangements and she would resent me for resenting her. Furthermore, Billy is a slob. She does not leave the towels lying on the bathroom floor, but she throws them over the shower curtain any old way, instead of folding them or hanging them properly so they can dry. It is things like this—it is actually the symbolic content of things like this—that squash out romance over a period of time.

As for Billy, she often sneers at me. She finds many of my opinions quaint. She laughs up her sleeve at me, often actually unbuttoning her cuff button (when the button is actually on the cuff) to demonstrate laughing up her sleeve. She thinks I am an old-time domestic fascist. She refers to me as "an old-style heterosexual throwback" or "old hetero" because I like to pay for dinner, open car doors and often call her at night when Grey is out of town to make sure she is safe. The day the plumber came to fix a leak in the sink, I called several times.

"He's gone," Billy said, "and he left big, greasy paw prints all over me." She found this funny, but I did not.

After a while, I believe I would be driven nuts and she would come to loathe me. My household is well run and well regulated. I like routine and I like things to go along smoothly. We employ a flawless person by the name of Mrs. Ivy Castle, who has been flawlessly running our house for some time. She is an excellent housekeeper and a marvelous cook. Our relations with her are formal.

The Delielles employ a feckless person called Mimi-Ann Browning, who comes in once a week to push the dust around. Mimi-Ann hates routine and schedules and is constantly changing the days of the people she works for. It is quite something to hear Billy on the telephone with her.

"Oh, Mimi-Ann," she will say, "please don't switch me, I beg you. I have to feed some friends of Grey's and the house is really disgusting. Please, Mimi. I'll do anything. I'll do your mother-in-law's tax return. I'll be your eternal slave. *Please*. Oh, thank you, Mimi. Thank you a million times."

Now, why, I ask myself, does my mistress never speak to me like that?

In that sad twilight on the way home from our week together, I asked myself, as I am always asking myself: Could I exist in some ugly flat with my cheerless mistress? I could not, as my mistress was the first to point out.

She said that the expression on my face at the sight of the towels thrown over the shower-curtain rod was similar to what you might find on the face of a vegetarian walking through an abattoir. She said that the small doses we got of each other made it possible for us to have a love affair but that a taste of ordinary life would do us both in. She correctly pointed out that our only real common interest was each other, since we had such vast differences of opinion on the subject of economic theory. Furthermore, we were not simply lovers, nor were we mere friends, and since we were not going to end up together, there was nothing for it.

I was silent.

"Face it," said my tireless mistress, "we have no *raison d'être*."

There was no disputing this.

I said, "If we have no *raison d'être,* Billy, then what are we to do?"

These conversations flare up like tropical storms. The climate is always right for them. It is simply a question of when they will occur.

"Well?" I said.

"I don't know," said my mistress, who generally has a snappy answer for everything.

A wave of fatherly affection and worry came over me. I said, in a voice so drenched with concern it caused my mistress to scowl like a child about to receive an injection, "Perhaps you should think about this more seriously, Billy. You and Grey are really just starting out. Vera and I have been married a long, long time. I think I am more a disruption in your life than you are in mine."

"Wanna bet?" said Billy.

"Perhaps we should see each other less," I said. "Perhaps we should part."

"OK, let's part," said Billy. "You go first." Her face was set and I entertained myself with the notion that she was trying not to burst into tears. Then she said, "What are you going to do all day after we part?"

This is not a subject to which I wanted to give much thought.

"Isn't our *raison d'être* that we're fond of each other?" I said. "I'm awfully fond of you."

"Gee, that's interesting," Billy said. "You're fond of me. I *love* you." Of course, she would not look me in the eye and say it.

"Well, I love you," I said. "I just don't quite know what to do about it."

"Whatever our status quos are," Billy said, "they are being maintained like mad."

This silenced me. Billy and I have the world right in place. Nothing flutters, changes or moves. Whatever is being preserved in our lives is safely preserved. It is quite true, as Billy, who believes in function, points out, that we are in each other's life for a reason, but neither of us will state the reason. Nevertheless, although there are some cases in which love is not a good or sufficient excuse for anything, the fact is, love is undeniable.

Yes, love is undeniable and that is the tricky point. It is one of the sobering realizations of adult life that love is often not a propellent. Thus, in those romantic movies, the tender mistress stays married to her stuffy husband—the one with the mustache and the stiff tweeds—while the lover is seen walking through the countryside with his long-suffering wife and faithful dog. It often seems that the function of romance is to give people something romantic to think about.

The question is: If it is true, as my mistress says, that she is going to stay with Grey and I am going to stay with Vera, why is it that we are together every chance we get?

There was, of course, an explanation for this and my indefatigable mistress came up with it, God bless her.

"It's an artistic impulse," she said. "It takes us out of reality and gives us a secret context all our own."

"Oh, I see," I said. "It's only art."

"Don't get in a huff," Billy said. "We're in a very unusual situation. It has to do with limited doting, restricted thrall and situational adoration."

"Oh, how interesting," I said. "Are doting, thrall and adoration things you actually feel for me?"

"Could be," said Billy. "But, actually, I was speaking for you."

▪ ▪ ▪

Every adult knows that facts must be faced. In adult life, it often seems that's all there is. Prior to our week together, the unguarded moments between us had been kept to a minimum. Now they came rather more frequently. That week together haunted us. It dogged our heels. It made us long for and dread—what an unfortunate combination!—each other.

One evening, I revealed to her how I sometimes feel as I watch her walk up the stairs to the door of her house. I feel she is walking into her real and still fairly young life. She will leave me in the dust, I think. I think of all the things that have not yet happened to her, that have not yet gone wrong, and I think of her life with Grey, which is still mostly unlived.

One afternoon, she told me how it makes her feel when she thinks of my family table—with Vera and our sons and our daughter-in-law and our daughter-in-law-to-be, of our years of shared meals, of all that lived life. Billy described this feeling as a band around her head and a hot pressure in the area of her heart. I, of course, merely get a lump in my throat. Why do these admittings take place at twilight or at dusk, in the gloomiest light, when everything looks dirty, eerie, faded or inevitable?

Our conversation comes to a dead halt, like a horse balking before a hurdle, on the issue of what we want. I have tried my best to formulate what it is I want from Billy, but I have not gotten very far. Painful consideration has brought forth this revelation: I want her not ever to stop being. This is as close as grammar or reflection will allow.

One day, the horse will jump over the hurdle and the end will come. The door will close. Perhaps Billy will do the closing. She will decide she wants a baby, or Grey will be offered a job in London, or Billy will get a job in Boston and the Delielles will move. Or perhaps Vera will come home one evening and say that she longs to live in Paris or San Francisco and the Clemenses will move. What will happen then?

Perhaps my mistress is right. A love affair is like a work of art. The large store of references, and jokes, the history of our friendship, our week together in Vermont, our numberless telephone calls, this edifice, this monument, this civilization known only to and constructed by us will be—what will it be? Billy once read to me an article in an anthropological journal about the last Coast Salish Indian to speak Wintun. All the others of his tribe were dead. That is how I would feel, deprived of Billy.

The awful day will doubtless come. It is like thinking about the inevitability of nuclear war. But as for now, I continue to ring her doorbell. Her greeting is delivered in her bored monotone. "Oh, it's you," she will say. "How sweet you look."

I will follow her up the stairs to her study and there we will hurl ourselves at each other. I will reflect, as I always do, how very bare the setting for these encounters is. Not a picture on the wall, not an ornament. Even the quilt that keeps the chill off us on the couch is faded.

In one of her snootier moments, my mistress said to me, "My furnishings are interior. I care about what I think about."

As I gather her into my arms, I cannot help imagining all that interior furniture, those hard-edged things she thinks about, whatever is behind her silence, whatever, in fact, her real story is.

She may turn to me and in a moment of tenderness say, "What a cute boy." This remark always sounds exotic to me—no one has ever addressed me this way, especially not at my age and station.

I imagine that someday she will turn to me and, with some tone in her voice I have never heard before, say, "We can't see each other anymore." We will both know the end has come. But, meanwhile, she is right close by. After a fashion, she is mine. I watch her closely to catch the look of true love that every once in a while overtakes her. She knows I am watching, and she knows the effect her look has. "A baby could take candy from you," she says.

Our feelings have edges and spines and prickles like cactus, or a porcupine. Our parting when it comes will not be simple, either. Depicted, it would look like one of those medieval beasts that has fins, fur, scales, feathers, claws, wings and horns. In a world apart from anyone else, we are Frank and Billy, with no significance to anyone but the other. Oh, the terrible privacy and loneliness of love affairs.

Under the quilt with our arms interlocked, I look into my mistress' eyes. They are dark and full of concealed feeling. If we hold each other close enough, that darkness is held at bay. The mission of the lover is, after all, to love. I can look at Billy and see clear back to the first time we met, to our hundreds of days together, to her throwing the towels over the shower-curtain rod, to each of her gestures and intonations. She is the road I have traveled to her, and I am hers.

Oh, Billy! Oh, art! Oh, memory!

Thomas McGuane

Like a Leaf

January 1983

Tom McGuane's funny, energetic novels—*The Sporting Club,* 1969; *The Bushwhacked Piano,* 1971; *Panama,* 1978 and, most recently, *Nothing but Blue Skies,* 1992—have won him a large and faithful following on and off campus. A fine essayist and nature writer, and a successful screenwriter (*Rancho Deluxe,* and the 1975 adaptation of his own *Ninety-Two in the Shade,* which he also directed), McGuane has published very few short stories. "Like a Leaf" was his first for *Playboy.* Like a number of his novels, it is set in Deadrock—read Livingston—Montana, where McGuane lives when he is not shrimping in the Gulf of Mexico or roping horses along the rodeo circuit, an occupation he claims brings in more money than writing. Born in 1939, he is originally from Michigan, but he has done his part in creating a thriving literary scene in the unlikely state of Montana.

Thomas McGuane

Like a Leaf

I'm underneath my small house in Deadrock. The real-estate people call it a starter home, however late in life you buy one. It's a modest house that gives you the feeling either that you're going places or that this won't do. This starter home is different; this one is it.

From under here, I can hear the neighbors talking. He is a newspaperman named Deke Patwell. His wife is away and he is having an affair with the lady across the street, a sweet and exciting lady I've not met yet. Frequently, he says to her, "I am going to impact on you, baby." Today, they are at one of their many turning points.

"I think I'm coming unglued," she says.

"Now, now."

"I don't follow," she says with a little heat.

"All is not easy."

"Yeah, I got that part, but when do we go someplace nice?" She has a beautiful voice, and underneath the house, I remember she is pretty. What am I doing here? I'm distributing bottle caps of arsenic for the rats that come up from the river and dispute the cats over trifles. I represent civilization in a small but real way.

Deke Patwell laughs with some wild relief. Once, I saw him at the municipal pool, watching young girls. He was wearing trunks and allergy-warning dog tags. What a guy! To me, he was like a crude foreigner or a Gaucho.

Anyway, I came down here because of the rats. Read your history: They carry black plague. Mrs. Patwell was on a Vegas excursion with the Deadrock Symphony Club.

▪ ▪ ▪

When I get back inside, the flies are orchestrating a broad, dumb movement on the windows. We never had flies like this on the ranch. We had songbirds, apple blossoms and no flies. My wife was alive then and saw to that. We didn't impact; we loved each other. She had an aneurysm let go while carding wool. She went so quietly, it was some months before I got it. She just nodded her pretty face and headed out. I sat there like a stoop. They came for her, and I just knocked around the place trying to get it. I headed for town and started seeing the doctor. Things came together: I was able to locate a place to live in, catch the series and set up housekeeping. Plus, the Gulch, everyone agrees, is Deadrock's nicest neighborhood. A traffic violator is taken right aside and lined out quick. It's a neighborhood where folks teach the dog to bring the paper to the porch, so a guy can sit back in his rocker and find out who's making hamburger of the world. I was one of this area's better cattlemen, and town life doesn't come easy. Where I once had coyotes and bears, I now have rats. Where I once had the old-time marriages of my neighbors, I now have Impact Man poking a real sweet gal who never gets taken somewheres nice.

▪ ▪ ▪

My eating became hit or miss. All I cared about was the world series after a broken season. I was high and dry, and when you're like that, you need someone or something to take you away. Death makes you different, like the colored are different. I felt I was under the spell of what had happened to me. Then someone threw a bottle onto the field in the third or fourth game of the series and almost hit the Yankee left fielder, Dave Winfield. I felt completely poisoned. I felt like a rat with a mouthful of bottle caps.

What were my wife and I discussing when she died? The Kona coast. It seems so small. Sometimes, when I think how small our topic was, I feel the weight of my hair tearing at my face. I bought a youth bed to reduce the size of the unoccupied area. The doctor says because of the shaking, I get quite a little bit less rest per hour than the normal guy.

▪ ▪ ▪

Truthfully speaking, part of me has always wanted to live in town. You hear the big milling at the switching yard; and on stormy nights, the transcontinental trucks reroute off the interstate and it's busy and kind of like a last-minute party at somebody's house. The big outfits are parked all over with their engines running and the heat shivers at the end of the stacks. The old people seem brave trying to get around on the ice: One fall and they're through, but they keep chunking, going on forward with a whole heck of a lot of grit. That fact gives me a boost.

And I love to window-shop. I go from window to window alongside people I don't know. There's never anything I want in there, but I feel good because I am excited when somebody picks out a daffy pair of shoes or a hat you wouldn't put on your dog. My wife couldn't understand this. Nature was a shrine to her. I wanted to see people more than suited her. Sit around with just anybody and make smart remarks. Sometimes, I'd pack the two of us into the hills. My wife would be in heaven. I'd want to buy a disguise and slip off to town and stare through the windows. That's the thing about heaven. It comes in all sizes and shapes.

▪ ▪ ▪

Anyone in my position feels left behind. It's normal. But you got to keep picking them up and keep on throwing them; you have got to play the combinations or quit. What I'd like is a person, a person I could enjoy until she's blue in the face. This, I believe. When the time comes, stand back from your television set.

▪ ▪ ▪

I don't know why Doc keeps an office in the kind of place he does, which is merely the downstairs of a not-so-good house. I go to him because he is never busy. He claims this saves him the cost of a receptionist.

Doc and I agree on one thing: It's all in your head. The only exception would be aspirin. Because we believe it's all in your head, we believe in immortality. Immortality is important to me, because without it, I don't get to see my wife again. Or, on the lighter side, my bird dogs and horses. That's it; that's all you need to know about the hereafter. The rest is for the professors, the regular egghead types who don't have to make the payroll.

We agree about my fling with the person. I hope to use Doc's stethoscope to hear the speeding of the person's heart. All of this has a sporting side, like hunting coyotes. When Doc and I grow old and the end is in sight, we're going to become addicted to opium. If we get our timing wrong, we'll cure ourselves with aspirin. We plan to see all the shiny cities, then *adios.* We speak of cavalry fire fights, Indian medicine, baseball and pussy.

Doc doesn't come out from behind the desk. He squints, knowing I could lie, then listens:

"My house in town is going to work fine. The attic has a swing-down ladder, and you look from a round window up there into the back yards. You can hear the radios and see people. Sometimes, couples have little shoving matches over odd things: starting the charcoal or the way the dog's been acting. I wrote some of them down in a railroad seniority book to tell you. They seem to dry up quick."

"Still window-shopping?"

"You bet."

"If you don't buy something soon, you're going to have to give that up."

"I'll think about it," I say.

"What have you been doing?"

"Not a whole heck of a lot."

"See a movie, any movie."

"I'll try."

"Take a trip."

"I can't."

"Then pack for one and don't go."

"I can do that."

"Stay out of the wind. It makes people nervous, and this is a windy town. Do what you have to do. You can always find a phone booth, but get out of that wind when it picks up. And any time you feel like falling silent, do it. Above all, don't brood about women."

"OK. Anything else?"

"Trust aspirin."

"I've been working on my mingling."

"Work on it some more."

"Doc," I say, "I've got a funny feeling about where I'm headed."

"You know anybody who doesn't?"

"So what do I do?"

"Look at the sunny side. Anyway, I better let you go. There's someone in the lobby with Blue Cross."

I go.

▪ ▪ ▪

By hauling an end table out to the porch, despite that the weather is not quite up to it, and putting a chair behind it, I make a fine place for my microwave Alfredo fettuccini. I can also watch our world with curiosity and terror. If necessary, I can speak when spoken to by sipping my ice water to keep the chalk from my mouth.

A car pulls up in front of Patwell's; Mrs. Patwell gets out with a small suitcase and goes to the house. That saves me from calling a lot of travel agents. The world belongs to me.

▪ ▪ ▪

I begin to eat the Alfredo fettuccini. Slow, spacing each mouthful. After eating about four inches of it, the lady from across the street—the Person—appears on the irregular sidewalk, gently patting each bursting tree trunk as she comes. As I am now practically a mute, I watch for visible things I can predict. And all I look for is her quick glance at Deke Patwell's house and then a turn through her chain-link gate. I love that she is pretty and carries nothing, like the Chinese ladies Doc tells me about who achieve great beauty by teetering around on feet that have been bound. I feel I am listening to the sound of a big cornfield in springtime. My heart is an urgent thud.

To my astonishment, she swings up her walk without a look. Her wantonness overpowers me. Impossible! Does she not know the Wife is home from Vegas?

I look up and down the street before lobbing the Alfredo fettuccini to a mutt. He eats in jerking movements and stares at me like I'm going to take it back. Which I'm quite capable of doing but won't. I have a taste in my mouth like the one you get in those frantic close-ins hunting coyotes. I feel like a happy crook.

Sometimes, when I told my wife I felt like this, she was touched. She said I had absolutely no secret life. The sad thing is, I probably don't.

▪ ▪ ▪

I begin sleeping in the attic. I am alone and not at full strength; so this way, I feel safer. I don't have to answer door or phone. I can see around the neighborhood better, and I have the basic timing of everybody's day down pat. For example, the lady goes to work on time every day but comes home at a different time every day. Does this suggest that she is a carefree person or that she is seeing an irregular person after work, a person to whom time means nothing or who is, perhaps, opposed to time's effects and therefore defiant about regularity? I don't know.

▪ ▪ ▪

Before I know it, I am window-shopping again. Each day, there is more in the air, more excitement among the shoppers who seem to spill off the windows into the doors of the stores. The sun is out, and I stand before the things my wife would never buy, not risqué things but things that would stand up. She seems very far away now. But when people come to my store windows, I sense a warmth that is like friendship. Any time I feel uncomfortable in front of a particular store, I move to sporting goods, where it is clear that I am OK and, besides, Doc is fixing me. My docile staring comes from the last word in tedium: guns and ammo; compound bows; fishing rods.

▪ ▪ ▪

When I say that I am OK, I mean that I am happy in the company of most people. What is wrong with me comes from my wife having unexpectedly died and from my having read the works of Ralph Waldo Emerson when my doctor and I were boning up on immortality. But I am watching the street, and something will turn up. In the concise movements of the person I'm most interested in, and in the irregularity of her returns, which she certainly despises, I sense a glow directed toward me—the kind of light in a desolate place that guides the weary traveler to his rest.

▪ ▪ ▪

Today, she walks home. She is very nearly on time. She walks so fast her pumps clatter on our broken Deadrock sidewalk. She swings her shoulder bag like a cheerful weapon and arcs into the street automatically to avoid carelessly placed sprinklers. She touches a safety match to a long filter brand as she surveys her little yard and goes in. She works, I understand, at the county assessor's office, and I certainly imagine she does a fine job for those folks. With her bounce, her cigarettes and her iffy hours, she makes just the kind of woman my wife had no use for. Hey! It takes all kinds. Human life is filled with variety, and if I have a regret in my own thus far, it is that I have not been close to that variety—that is, right up against it.

▪ ▪ ▪

I need a break and go for a daylight drive. I take the river road through the foothills north of Deadrock—a peerless jaunt—to our prison. It is an elegant old dungeon that housed many famous Western outlaws in its day. The ground it rests on was never farmed, having gone from buffalo pasture to lockup many years ago. Now it has razor wire surrounding it and a real up-to-date tower, like back East.

One man stands in blue light behind its high windows. When you see him from the country road, you think, That certainly must be the loneliest man in the world. But actually, it's not true. His name is Al Costello, and he's a good friend of mine. He's the head of a large Catholic household, and the tower is all the peace he gets.

The lonely guy is the warden, an out-of-stater, a professional imprisoned by card files: a man no one likes. He looks like Rock Hudson and he can't get a date.

Sometimes, I stop in to see Al. I go up into the tower and we look down into the yard at the goons and make specific comments about the human situation. Sometimes we knock back a beer or two. Sometimes I take a shot at one of his favorite ball clubs and sometimes he lights into mine. It's just human fellowship in kind of a funny spot.

Instead, today, I keep on cruising, out among the jack rabbits and the sagebrush, high above the running irrigation, all the way around the little burg, then back into town. I stop in front of the doughnut shop, waiting for the sun to travel the street and open the shop and herald its blazing magic up commercially zoned Deadrock. Waiting in front is a sick-looking young man muttering to himself at a high, relentless pitch of the kind we associate with Moslem fundamentalism. At eight sharp, the door opens and the Moslem and I shoot in for the counter. He seems to have lost something by coming inside, and I am riveted upon his loss. By absolute happenstance, we both order glazed. Then I add an order of jelly-filled, which I deliver, still hot, to the lady's doorstep.

■ ■ ■

I'm going to stop reading this newspaper. In one week, the following has been reported: A Deadrock man shot himself fatally in a bar demonstrating the safety of his pistol. Another man, listening to the rail, had his head run over by every car of a train that took half an hour to go by. Incidents like these make it hard for me to clearly see the spirit winging its way to heaven. And though I would like to stop reading the paper, I really know I won't. It would set a bad example for the people on the porches who have trained Spot to fetch.

■ ■ ■

"Did you get the doughnuts?" I called out that evening.

Tonight, as I fall asleep, I have a strange thought, indeed. It goes like this: Darling (my late wife), I don't know if you are watching all this or not. If you are, I have but one request: Put yourself in my shoes. That's quite an assignment, but give it the old college try for yours truly.

■ ■ ■

I know they've been talking when I see Deke Patwell give me the fishy look. I cannot imagine which exact locution she had used—probably that I was "bothering" her—but she has very evidently made of me a fly in Deke's soup. There is not a lot he can do, standing next to his warming-up sensible compact, but give me this *look* and hope that I will invest it with meaning. I decide to blow things out of proportion.

"You two should do something *nice* together!" I call out.

Deke slings his head down and bitterly studies a nail on one hand, then gets in and drives away.

▪ ▪ ▪

You think you got it bad? Says here, a man over to Arlee was jump-starting his car in the garage; he had left it in gear, and when he touched the terminals of the battery, the car shot forward and pinned him to a compressor that was running. This man was inflated to four times his normal size and was still alive, after God knows how long, when they found him. A hopeful Samaritan backed the car up and the man just blew up on the garage floor and died. As awful as that is, it adds nothing whatsoever to the basic idea. Passing in your sleep or passing as a pain-crazed human balloon on a greasy garage floor produces the same simple result year after year. The major differences lie among those who are left behind. If you're listening, please understand: I'm still trying to see why we don't all cross the line on our own or why nice people don't just help us on over. Who knows if you're even listening?

▪ ▪ ▪

"So," I cry out to the person with exaggerated innocence, illustrating how I am crazy like a fox. "So, how did you enjoy the doughnuts?"

She stops, looks, thinks. "That was you?"

"That was me."

"Why?" She is walking toward me.

"It was a little something from someone who thinks somebody should take you somewhere nice."

My foot is in the door. It feels as big as a steamboat.

"Tomorrow," she says from her beautiful face, "make it cinnamon Danish." Her eyes dance with cruel merriment. I feel she is of German extraction. She has no trace of an accent and her attire is domestic in origin. I think, What am I saying? I'm scaring myself. This is a Deadrock local with zip for morals.

I decide to leap forward in the development of things to ascertain the point at which it doesn't make sense. "We are very much in love," I say to myself. I recoil privately at this thought, knowing I am still OK if not precisely tops. I am neither a detective nor a complete stoop. I fall somewhere in between.

"Tell you what," she says with a twinkle. "I come home from work and I freshen up. Then you and me go for a stroll. How far'd you get?"

"Stroll. . . ."

"You're a good boy tonight and I let you off lightly."

Mercy. My neck prickles. She laughs in my face and heads out. I see her cross the trees at the end of the street. I see the changing flicker of different-colored cars. I see mountains beyond the city. I see her bouncing black hair even after she has gone. I say quietly, "I'm lonely; I had no idea you were not to have a long life." But I'm still in love.

▪ ▪ ▪

I call Doc. "You go to hell," I tell him. "You can put your twenty-two-fifty an hour where the sun don't shine, you dang quack."

▪ ▪ ▪

John Q. Public says, "Walk the line, boy, or pay the price." Well, John, the buck stops here. I'm going it alone.

▪ ▪ ▪

She stood me up and it's midnight.

▪ ▪ ▪

I have never felt like this. This house doesn't belong to me. It belongs to the Person, and I'm lying on her bed, viewing the furnishings. It's dark here. I can see her coming up the sidewalk. She will come alongside the house and come in through the kitchen. I am in the back room. I guess I'll say hello.

"Hello."

"Hello."

She's quite the opposite of my wife, but it's fatal if she thinks this is healthy. She's in the same blue dress and appears to view this as a clever seduction.

"It's you. Who'd have guessed? I'm going to bathe, and if you ask nice, you can help."

"I want to see."

"I know that." She laughs and goes through the door, undressing. "Just come in. You'll never get your speech right. Do I look drunk? I am a little. I suppose your plan was a neighborhood rape." Loud laugh. She hangs the last of her clothes and studies me. Then she leans against the cupboards. "Please turn the water on, kind of hot." When I turn away from the faucets, she is sitting on the side of the tub. I think I am going to fall, but I go to her and rock her in my arms so that she kind of spreads out against the white porcelain.

She looks at me and says, "The nicest thing about you is you're frightened. You're like a boy. I'm going to frighten you as much as you can stand." I undress and we get into the clear water. I look at the half of myself that is underwater; it looks like something at Sea World. Suddenly, I stand up.

"I guess I'm not doing so good. I'm not much of a rapist after all." I get out of the tub, a real stoop.

"You're making me feel great."

"That Deke has caused you to suffer."

"Oh, crap."

"It's time he took you someplace *nice.*" I'm on the muscle now.

I am drying off about a hundred miles an hour. I go into the next room and pull on my trousers. I don't even see her coming. She pushes me over on the day bed and drags my pants back off. I am so paralyzed, all I can do is say, "Please, no; please, no," as she clambers roughly atop me and takes me with almost hurtful fury, ending with a sudden dead flop. Every moment or so, she looks at me with her raging victorious eyes.

"Just don't turn me in," she says. "It would be awful for your family." She bounces up and returns to the bathroom while I dress again. There is a razor running and periodic splashes of water. Whether it is because my wife has to sit through the whole thing or that I can't bring her back, I don't know, but the whole thing makes me a different guy.

▪ ▪ ▪

She tows me outside, clattering on the steps in wooden clogs, sending forth a bright woman's cologne to savage my nerves. I see there is only one way my confused hands can regain their grasp: I burst into tears. She pops open a small flowered umbrella and uses it to conceal me from the outside world. It seems very cozy in there. She coos appropriately.

"Are you going to be OK now?" she asks. "Are you?"

I see Deke's car coming up the street. Impact Man, the one who never does anything nice for her. I dry my tears posthaste. We head down the street. We are walking together in the bright evening sky under our umbrella. This foolishness implies an intimacy that must have gone hard with Impact Man, because he arcs into his driveway and has to brake hard to keep from going through his own garage, with its barbecue, hammocks and gap-seamed, neglected canoe—things whose hopes of a future seem presently to ride on the tall, shapely legs of my companion.

I can't think of something really right for us. The only decent restaurant would seem as though we were on a date, put us face to face. We need to keep moving. I feel pretty certain we could pop up and see Al Costello, my Catholic friend in the tower. He always has the coffeepot going. So we get into my flivver and head for the prison. It makes a nice drive in a Tahiti-type sunset, and by the time I graze past staff parking to the vast space of visitors', the wonderful blue-white of the glass tower has ignited like the pilot light on a gas stove.

"I want you to meet a friend of mine," I tell the lady. "Works here. Big Catholic family. He's a grandfather in his late thirties. It looks like a lonely job and it's not."

The tower has an elevator. The gate guards know me and we sail in. The door opens in the tower.

"Hey," I say.

"What's cooking?" Al grins vacantly.

"Thought we'd pop up. Say, this is a friend of mine."

"Mighty pleased," Al says. He has the lovely manners of someone battered beyond recognition. She now is glued to the window, staring at the cons. I think she has made some friendly movements to the guys down in the yard. I glance at Al and evidently he thinks so, too.

We avert our glances, and Al says, "Can I make a spot of coffee?" I feel like a fool.

"I'm fine," she says. "Fine." She is darn well glued to that glass. "Can a person get down there?"

"Oh, a person could," says Al. I notice he is always in slow movement around the tower, always looking, in case some geek goes haywire. "Important thing, I guess, is that no one can come here unless I let them in. They screen this job good. The bad apples are long gone. It takes a family man."

"Are those desperate characters?" she asks, gazing around. I move to the window and look down at the minnowlike movement of the prisoners. This would have held zero interest for my wife.

"A few, I guess. This is your regular back-yard prison. It's just little. Plus, no celebrities. We've got the screwballs is about all we've got."

"How's the family, Al?" I dart in.

"Fine, just fine."

"Everybody healthy?"

"Oh, yeah. Andrea Elizabeth had strep, but it didn't pass to nobody in the house. Antibiotics knocked it for a loop."

"And the missus?"

"Same as ever."

"For Christ's sake," says my companion. We turn. He and I think it's us. But it's something in the yard. "Two fairies," she says through her teeth. "Can you beat that?"

After which she just stares out the window, while Al and I drink some pretty bouncy coffee with a nondairy creamer that makes shapes in it without ever really mixing. It is more or less to be polite that I drink it at all. I look over and she has her widespread hands up against the glass, like a tree frog. She is grinning very hard and I know she has made eye contact with someone down in the exercise yard. Suddenly, she turns.

"I want to get out of here."

"OK," I say brightly.

"You go downstairs," she says. "I need to talk to Al."

"OK, OK."

My heart is coated with ice. Plus, I'm mortified. But I go downstairs and wait in a green-carpeted room at the bottom of the stairs. There is a door out and a door to the yard. I think I'll wait here. I don't want to sit in the car, trying to look like I'm not abetting a jail break. I'm going downhill fast.

▪ ▪ ▪

I must be there twenty minutes when I hear the electronics of the elevator coming at me. The stainless doors open and a very disheveled Al appears with my friend. There is nothing funny or bawdy in her demeanor. Al swings by me without catching a glance and begins to open the door to the yard with a key. He has a service revolver in one hand as he does so.

"Be cool now, Al," says my friend intimately. "Or I talk."

The steel door winks and she is gone into the prison yard. "We better go back up," says Al in a doomed voice. "I'm on duty. God Almighty."

"Did I do this?" I say in the elevator.

"You better stay with me. I can't have you leaving alone." He unplugs the coffee mechanically. When I get to the bulletproof glass, I can see the prisoners migrating. There is a little of everything: old guys, stumble bums, Indians, Italians, Irishmen, all heading into the shadow of the tower. "We're just going to have to go with this one. There's no other way." He looks like Jack Benny admitting something isn't funny. He looks crummy and depleted, but he is going to draw the line. We are going to go with it. She will signal the tower, he tells me. So we wait by the glass, like a pair of sea captains' wives on their widow's walks. It goes on so long, we forget why we're waiting. We are just doing our job.

Then there is a small reverse migration of prisoners, and she—bobby pins in her teeth, checking her hair for bounce—waves up to us in the tower. We wave back in this syncopated motion, which is almost the main thing I remember: me and Al flapping away like a couple of widows.

As we ride down in the elevator again, Al says, "You take over from here." And we commence to laugh. We laugh so hard I think one of us will upchuck. Then we have to stop to get out of the elevator. We cover our mouths and laugh through our noses, tears streaming down our cheeks, while Al tries to get the door open. Our ladyfriend comes in real stern-like, though, and we stop. It is as if we'd been caught at something and she is ultrasore. She heads out the door, and Al gives me the gun.

In the car, she says with real contempt, "I guess it's your turn." Buddy, that was the wrong thing to say.

"I guess it is." I am the quiet one now.

There is a great pool on the river about a mile below the railroad bridge. It's moving, but not enough to erase the stars from its surface or the trout sailing like birds over its deep, pebbly bottom. The little home wrecker kneels at the end of the sand bar and washes herself over and over. When I am certain she feels absolutely clean, I let her have it. I roll her into the pool, where she becomes a ghost of the river trailing beautiful smoky cotton from a hole in her silly head.

It's such a relief. We never did need the social whirl. Tomorrow, we'll shop for something nice, something you can count on to stand up.

There for a while, it looked like the end.

John Gardner

Julius Caesar and the Werewolf

September 1984

Revisions of this story were piled next to the typewriter of John Gardner (1933–1982) on the day he died in a motorcycle accident in Binghamton, New York. The story was published as is, with an explanatory note suggesting the parallel between an epileptic seizure—Caesar's "falling sickness"—and the convulsions that presumably accompany the metamorphosis of a werewolf. The story helped the magazine to win the National Magazine Award for Fiction in 1985. Gardner was not only a novelist (*Grendel,* 1971; *The Sunlight Dialogues,* 1972; *Mickelsson's Ghost,* 1982), poet, and critic, but a famously charismatic teacher, whose students continue to be a strong influence on university programs and writers' workshops today. He should not be blamed for what some think of as the pervasive homogenization of these programs. Gardner's ideas about writing were displayed in three provocative books: *On Moral Fiction,* in which he took his generation of writers to task for lack of ambition and creating "bad art," and his two instruction books, *On Becoming a Novelist* and *The Art of Fiction.* No one reading them could accuse him of promoting blandness.

John Gardner

Julius Caesar and the Werewolf

As to Caesar's health, there seems to me no cause for alarm. The symptoms you mention are, indeed, visible, though perhaps a little theatricized by your informant. Caesar has always been a whirlwind of energy and for that reason subject to nervous attacks, sudden tempers, funks and so forth. When I was young, I confidently put it down to excess of blood, a condition complicated (said I) by powerful intermittent ejections of bile; but phlebotomy agitates instead of quieting him, sad to say (sad for my diagnosis), and his habitual exhilaration, lately increased, makes the bile hypothesis hogwash. I speak lightly of these former opinions of mine, but you can hardly imagine what labor I've put into the study of this man, scribbling, pondering, tabulating, while, one after another, the chickens rise to confront a new day and my candles gutter out. All to no avail, but pride's for people with good digestion. I bungle along, putting up with myself as best I can. (You'll forgive a little honest whining.) No man of science was ever presented with a puzzle more perplexing and vexatious than this Caesar, or with richer opportunity for observing the subject of his inquiry. He's interested in my work—in fact, follows it closely. He allows me to sit at his elbow or tag along wherever I please—an amusing spectacle, Caesar striding like a lion down some corridor, white toga flying, his black-robed physician leaping along like a spasm behind him on one good leg, one withered one.

In any event, at the age of fifty-five, his animal spirits have never been more vigorous. He regularly dictates to four scribes at a time—jabber, jabber, jabber, sentences crackling like lightning in a haystack, all of his letters of the greatest importance to the state. Between sentences, to distract his impatience, he reads from a book. Or so he'd have us think, and I'm gullible. It saves time, I find, and in the end makes no big difference. His baldness more annoys him, it seems to me, than all the plots of the senators. For years, as you know, he combed his straggling blond hairs straight forward, and nothing pleased him more than the people's decision to award him the crown of laurel, which he now wears everywhere except, I think, to bed. A feeble ruse and a delight to us all. The reflected light of his bald pate glows like a sun on the senate-chamber ceiling.

His nervous energy is not significantly increased, I think, from the days when I first knew him, many years ago, in Gaul. I was transferred to the legion for some disservice to the state—monumental, I'm sure, but it's been thirty-five years, and I've told the story so many times, in so many slyly self-congratulating versions, that by now I've forgotten the truth of it. I was glad of the transfer. I was a sea doctor before. I don't mind telling you, water scares the pants off me.

I remember my first days with Caesar clear as crystal. He struck me at once as singular almost to the point of freakishness. He was taller than other men, curiously black-eyed and blond-headed, like two beings in one body. But what struck me most was his speed, both physical and mental. He could outrun a deer, outthink every enemy he met—and he was, besides, very strong. We all knew why he fought so brilliantly. He was guilty of crimes so numerous, back in Rome, from theft to assault to suspicion of treason, that he couldn't afford to return there as a common citizen. (It was true of most of us, but Caesar was the worst.) By glorious victories, he could win public honors and appointments and, thus, stand above the law, or at least above its meanest kick. Whatever his reasons—this I have to give to him—no man in history, so far as it's recorded, ever fought with such effectiveness and passion or won such unshakable, blind-pig devotion from his men. He was not then the strategist he later became, killing a few left-handed and blindfolded, then persuading the rest to surrender and accept Roman citizenship. In those days, he painted the valleys red, weighed down the trees with hanging men, made the rivers run sluggish with corpses. He was always in the thick of it, like a rabid bitch, luring and slaughtering seven at a time. His body, it seems to me, runs by nature at an accelerated tempo: His sword moves much faster than a normal man's. And he's untiring. At the end of a twelve-hour day's forced march, when the whole encampment was finally asleep, he used to pace like a half-starved jaguar in his tent or sit with a small fish-oil lamp, writing verse. I wonder if he may not have some unknown substance in common with the violent little flea.

Through all his wars, Caesar fought like a man unhinged, but I give you my word, he's not crazy. He has the falling sickness, as you know. A damned nuisance but, for all the talk, nothing more. All his muscles go violent, breaking free of his will, and he has a sudden, vividly real sense of falling into the deepest abyss, a fall that seems certain never to end, and no matter what servants or friends press around him (he's dimly aware of presences, he says), there's no one, nothing, he can reach out to. From an outward point of view, he's unconscious at these times, flailing, writhing, snapping his teeth, dark eyes bulging and rolling out of sight, exuding a flood of oily tears; but from what he reports, I would say he is not unconscious but in some way transformed, as if seized for the moment by the laws of a different set of gods. (I mean, of course, "forces" or "biological constraints.")

No doubt it adds to the pressure on him that he's a creature full of pangs and contradictions. Once, in Gaul, we were surprised by an ambush. We had moved for days through dangerous, twilit forest and had come, with relief, to an area of endless yellow meadow, where the grass reached only to our knees, so that we thought we were safe. Suddenly, out of the grass all around us leaped an army of women. Caesar cried, "Save yourselves! We're not in Gaul to butcher females!" In the end, we killed them all. (I, as Caesar's physician, killed no one.) I trace Caesar's melancholy streak to that incident. He became, thereafter, moody and uneasy, praying more than necessary and sometimes pausing abruptly to glance all around him, though not a shadow had stirred. It was not the surprise of the ambush, I think. We'd been surprised before. The enemy was young and naked except for weapons and armor, and they were singularly stubborn: They gave us no choice but to kill them. I watched Caesar himself cut one in half, moving his sword more slowly than usual and staring fixedly at her face.

The melancholy streak has been darkened, in my opinion, by his years in Rome. His work load would rattle a stone Apollo—hundreds of letters to write every day, lines of suppliants stretching half a mile, each with his grievance large or small and his absurd, ancient right to spit softly into Caesar's ear—not to mention the foolish disputes brought in to him for settlement. Some starving scoundrel steals another scoundrel's newly stolen pig, the whole ramshackle slum is up in arms, and for the public good the centurions bring all parties before Caesar. Hours pass, lamps are lit, accuser and denier rant on, banging tables, giving the air fierce kicks by way of warning. Surely a man of ordinary tolerance would go mad—or go to sleep. Not our Caesar. He listens with the look of a man watching elderly people eat, then eventually points to one or the other or both disputants, which means the person's to be dragged away for hanging, and then, with oddly meticulous care, one hand over his eyes, he dictates to a scribe the details of the case and his dispensation, with all his reasonings. "Admit the next," he says, and folds his hands.

And these are mere gnats before the hurricane. He's responsible, as they say when they're giving him some medal, for the orderly operation of the largest, richest, most powerful empire the world has ever known. He must rule the senate, with all its constipated, red-nosed, wheezing factions—every bleary eye out for insult or injury, every liver-spotted hand half closed around a dagger. And he must show at least some semblance of interest in the games, escape for the bloodthirst of the citizenry. He watches the kills, man or lion or whatever, without a sign of emotion, but I'm onto him. He makes me think of my days at sea, that still, perfect weather before a plank buster.

All this work he does without a particle of help, not a single assistant except the four or five scribes who take dictation and the slave who brings him parchment, ink and fresh oil or sandals—unless one counts, as I suppose one must, Marc Antony: a loyal friend and willing drudge but, as all Rome knows, weak as parsley. (He's grown fat here in the city and even less decisive than he was on the battlefield. I've watched him trying to frame letters for Caesar, tugging his jaw over decisions Caesar would make instantly.) In short, the life of a Caesar is donkeywork and unquestionably dangerous to health. I've warned and warned him. He listens with the keenest interest, but he makes no changes. His wary glances to left and right become more frequent, more noticeable and odd. He has painful headaches, especially at executions, and now and then he sleepwalks, looking for something under benches and in every low cupboard. I find his heartbeat irregular, sometimes wildly rushing, sometimes all but turning around and walking backward, as if he were both in a frenzy and mortally bored.

Some blame the death of his daughter for all this. I'm dubious, though not beyond persuasion. That Julia was dear to his heart I don't deny. When she was well, he was off with her every afternoon he could steal from Rome's business, teaching her to ride, walking the hills with her, telling her fairy tales of gods disguised as people or people transformed into celestial constellations or, occasionally—the thing she liked best, of course—recounting his adventures. I remember how the girl used to gaze at him such times, elbows on her knees, hands on her cheeks, soft, pale hair cascading over her shoulders and down her long back—it made me think of those beautiful altar-lit statues in houses of prostitution. (I mean no offense. Old men are by nature prone to nastiness.) She was an intelligent girl, always pursing her lips and frowning, preparing to say, "Tut, tut." He taught her knots and beltwork and the nicer of the soldiers' songs, even taught her his special tricks of swordsmanship—because she nagged him to it (you know how daughters are)—and, for all I know, the subtleties of planning a campaign against India and China. I never saw a father more filled with woe than Caesar when the sickness first invaded her. He would rush up and down, far into the night (I never saw him take even a nap through all that period), and he was blistering to even the most bent-backed, senile and dangerous senators, to say nothing of whiny suppliants and his poor silent wife. His poems took an ugly turn—much talk of quicksand and maws and the like—and the bills he proposed before the senate weren't much prettier; and then there was the business with the gladiators. But when Julia died, he kissed her waxy forehead and left the room and, so far as one could see, that was that. After the great funeral so grumbled about in certain quarters, he seemed much the same man he'd seemed before, not just externally but also internally, so far as my science could reach. His blood was very dark but, for him, normal; his stools were ordinary; his seizures no more tedious than usual.

So what can have brought on this change you inquire of and find so disturbing—as do I, of course? (At my age, nothing's as terrible as might have been expected.) I have a guess I might offer, but it's so crackpot I think I'd rather sit on it. I'll narrate the circumstances that prompt it; you can draw your own conclusions.

▪ ▪ ▪

Some days ago, March first, shortly after nightfall, as I was washing out my underthings and fixing myself for bed, two messengers appeared at my door with the request—polite but very firm—that I at once get back into my clothes and go to Caesar. I naturally—after some perfunctory sniveling—obeyed. I found the great man alone in his chamber, staring out the one high window that overlooks the city. It was a fine scene, acted with great dignity, if you favor that sort of thing. He did not turn at our entrance, though only a man very deep in thought could have failed to notice the brightness of the torches as their light set fire to the wide marble floor with its inlay of gold and quartz. We waited. It was obvious that something was afoot. I was on guard. Nothing interests Caesar, I've learned, but Caesar. Full-scale invasion of the Empire's borders would not rouse in him this banked fire of restlessness—fierce playfulness, almost—except insofar as its repulsion might catch him more honor. There was a scent in the room, the smell of an animal, I thought at first, then corrected myself: a blood smell. "Show him," Caesar said quietly, still not turning.

I craned about and saw, even before my guides had inclined their torches in that direction, that on the high marble table at the far end of the room some large, wet, misshapen object had been placed, then blanketed. I knew instantly what it was, to tell the truth, and my eyes widened. They have other doctors; it was the middle of the night! I have bladder infections and prostate trouble; I can hardly move my bowels without a clyster! When the heavy brown cloth was solemnly drawn away, I saw that I'd guessed right. It was, or had once been, a tall, bronze-skinned man, a slave, probably rich and admired in whatever country he'd been dragged from. His knees were drawn up nearly to his pectorals and his head rolled out oddly, almost severed at the neck. One could guess his stature only from the length of his arms and the shiny span exposed, caked with blood, from knee to foot. One ear had been partially chewed away.

"What do you make of it?" Caesar asked. I heard him coming toward me on those dangerous, swift feet, then heard him turn, pivoting on one hissing sandal, moving back quickly toward the window. I could imagine his nervous, impatient gestures, though I did not look: gestures of a man angrily talking to himself, bullying, negotiating—rapidly opening and closing his fists or restlessly flipping his right hand, like a sailor paying out coil after coil of line.

"Dogs—" I began.

"Not dogs," he said sharply, almost before I'd spoken. I felt myself grow smaller, the sensation in my extremities shrinking toward my heart. I put on my mincing, poor-old-man expression and pulled at my beard, then reached out gingerly to move the head, examining more closely the clotted ganglia where the thorax had been torn away. Whatever had killed him had done him a kindness. He was abscessed from the thyroid to the *vena cava superior.* When I looked over at Caesar, he was back at the window, motionless again, the muscles of his arm and shoulder swollen as if clamping in rage. Beyond his head, the night had grown dark. It had been clear, earlier, with a fine, full moon; now it was heavily overcast and oppressive—no stars, no moon, only the lurid glow, here and there, of a torch. In the light of the torches the messengers held, one on each side of me, Caesar's eyes gleamed, intently watching.

"Wolves," I said, with conviction.

He turned, snapped his fingers several times in quick succession—in the high, stone room, it was like the sound of a man clapping—and almost the same instant, a centurion entered, leading a girl. Before she was through the archway, she was down on her knees, scrambling toward Caesar as if to kiss his toes and ankles before he could behead her. Obviously, she did not know his feeling of tenderness, almost piety, toward young women. At her approach Caesar turned his back to the window and raised his hands, as if to ward her off. The centurion, a young man with blue eyes, like a German's, jerked at her wrist and stopped her. Almost gently, the young man put his free hand into her hair and tipped her face up. She was perhaps sixteen, a thin girl with large, dark, flashing eyes full of fear.

Caesar said, never taking his gaze from her, "This young woman says the wolf was a man."

I considered for a moment, only for politeness. "Not possible," I said. I limped nearer to them, bending for a closer look at the girl. If she was insane, she showed none of the usual signs—depressed temples, coated tongue, anemia, inappropriate smiles and gestures. She was not a slave, like the corpse on the table—nor of his race, either. Because of her foreignness, I couldn't judge what her class was, except that she was a commoner. She rolled her eyes toward me, a plea like a dog's. It was hard to believe that her terror was entirely an effect of her audience with Caesar.

Caesar said, "The Goths have legends, doctor, about men who at certain times turn into wolves."

"Ah," I said, noncommittal.

He shifted his gaze to meet mine, little fires in his pupils. I shrank from him—visibly, no doubt. Nothing is stupider or more dangerous than toying with Caesar's intelligence. But he restrained himself. " 'Ah!' " he mimicked with awful scorn and, for an instant, smiled. He looked back at the girl, then away again at once; then he strode over to the corpse and stood with his back to me, staring down at it, or into it, as if hunting for its soul, his fists rigid on his hips to keep his fingers from drumming. "You know a good deal, old friend," he said, apparently addressing myself, not the corpse. "But possibly not everything!" He raised his right arm, making purposely awkward loops in the air with his hand, and rolled his eyes at me, grinning with what might have been malice, except that he's above that. Impersonal rage at a universe too slow for him. He said, "Perhaps, flopping up and down through the world like a great, clumsy bat, trying to spy out the secrets of the gods, you miss a few things? Some little trifle here or there?"

I said nothing, merely pressed my humble palms together. To make perfectly clear my dutiful devotion, I limped over to stand at his side, looking with him, gravely, at the body. Moving the leg—there was as yet no *rigor mortis*—I saw that the body had been partly disemboweled. The spleen was untouched in the intestinal disarray; the liver was nowhere to be seen. I could feel the girl's eyes on my back. Caesar's smile was gone now, hovering just below the surface. He had his hand on the dead man's foot, touching it as if to see if bones were broken or as if the man were a friend, a fellow warrior.

He lowered his voice. "This isn't the first," he said. "We've kept the matter quiet, but it's been happening for months." His right hand moved out like a stealthy animal, anticipating his thought. His voice grew poetic. (It was a bad idea, that laurel crown.) "A sudden black shadow, a cry out of the darkness, and in the morning—in some alley or in the middle of a field or huddled against some rotting door in the tanners' district—a corpse ripped and mauled past recognition. The victims aren't children, doctor; they're grown men, sometimes women." He frowned. The next instant, his expression became unreadable, as if he were mentally reaching back, abandoning present time, this present body. Six, maybe seven heartbeats passed; and then, just as suddenly, he was here with us again, leaning toward me, oddly smiling. "And then tonight," he said, "this treasure!" With a gesture wildly theatrical—I saw myself at the far end of the forum, at the great door where the commoners peer in—he swept his arm toward the girl. She looked, cowering, from one to the other of us, then up at the soldier.

Caesar crossed to her; I followed part way. "He was half man, half wolf; is that your story?" He bent over her, pressing his hands to his knees as he asked it. Clearly he meant to seem fatherly, but his body was all iron, the muscles of his shoulders and arms locked and huge.

After a moment, she nodded.

"He wore clothes like a man?"

Again she nodded, this time looking warily at me. She had extraordinary eyes, glistening, dark, bottomless and very large, perhaps the first symptom of a developing exophthalmic goiter.

Caesar straightened up and turned to the centurion. "And what was this young woman doing when you found her?"

"Dragging the body, sir." One side of his mouth moved, the faintest suggestion of a smile. "It appeared to us she was hiding it."

Now Caesar turned to me, his head inclined to one side, like a lawyer in court. "And why would she be doing that?"

At last the girl's terror was explicable.

▪ ▪ ▪

I admired the girl for not resisting us. She knew, no doubt—all Romans know—that torture can work wonders. Although I've never been an optimist, I like to believe it was not fear of torture that persuaded her but the certain knowledge that whatever sufferings she might put herself through, she would in the end do as we wished. She had a curious elegance for a girl of her station. Although she walked head ducked forward, as all such people do, and although her gait was odd—long strides, feet striking flat, like an Egyptian's—her face showed the composure and fixed resolve one sometimes sees on statues, perhaps some vengeful, endlessly patient Diana flanked by her hounds. Although one of the centurions in our company held the girl's elbow, there seemed no risk that she would try to run away. Caesar, wearing a dark hood and mantle now, kept even with her or sometimes moved a little ahead in his impatience. The three other centurions and I came behind, I in great discomfort, wincing massively at every right-foot lurch but, for all that, watching everything around me, especially the girl, with sharp attention. It grew darker and quieter as we descended into the slums. The sky was still overcast, so heavily blanketed one couldn't even guess in which part of the night the moon hung. Now and then, like some mysterious pain, lightning would bloom and move deep in the clouds, giving them features and shapes for a moment, and we'd hear a low rumble; then blackness would close on us deeper than before. The girl, too, seemed to mind the darkness. Every so often, as we circled downward, I would see her lift and turn her head, as if she were trying to find her bearings.

No one was about. Nothing moved except now and then a rat researching garbage or scampering along a gutter, or a chicken stirring in its coop as we passed, its spirit troubled by bad dreams. In this part of town, there were no candles, much less torches—and just as well: The whole section was a tinderbox. The buildings were three and four stories high, leaning out drunkenly over the street or against one another like beggars outside a temple, black, rotten wood that went shiny as intestines when the lightning glowed, walls patched with hides and daubs of mud, straw and rotten hay packed in tightly at the crooked foundations. The only water was the water in the streets or in the river invisible in the darkness below us, poisonously inching under bridge after bridge toward the sea. When I looked back up the hill between lightning blooms, I could no longer make out so much as an arch of Caesar's palace or the firm, white mansions of the rich—only a smoky luminosity red under the clouds. The street was airless, heavy with the smell of dead things and urine. Every door and shutter was unhealthily closed tight.

We progressed more slowly now, barely able to see one another. I cannot say what we were walking on; it was slippery and gave underfoot. I was feeling cross at Caesar's refusal to use torches; but he was the crafty old warrior, not I. Once, with a clatter I at first mistook for thunder, some large thing rushed across the street in front of us, out of darkness and in again—a man, a donkey, some rackety demon—and we all stopped. No one spoke; then Caesar laughed. We resumed our walk.

Minutes later, the girl stopped without a word. We had arrived.

The man was old. He might have been sitting there, behind his table in the dark, for centuries. It was not dark now. As soon as the hide door was tightly closed, Caesar had tipped back his hood, reached into his cloak past his heavy iron sword and brought out candles, which he gave to two centurions to light and hold; the room was far too confined for torches. The other two centurions waited outside; even so, there was not much room. The man behind the table was bearded, not like a physician but like a foreigner—a great white-silver beard that flicked out like fire in all directions. His hair was long, unkempt, his eyebrows bushy; his blurry eyes peered out as if from deep in a cave. Purple bruises fell in chevrons from just under his eyes into his mustache. If he was surprised or alarmed, he showed no sign, merely sat—stocky, firmly planted—behind his square table, staring straight ahead, not visibly breathing, like a man waiting in the underworld. The girl sat on a low stool, her back against the wall, between her father and the rest of us. She gazed at her knees in silence. Her face was like that of an actress awaiting her entrance, intensely alive, showing no expression.

The apartment, we saw as the light seeped into it, was a riddle. Although in the poorest section of the city, it held a clutter of books, and the furniture, though sparse, was elaborately carved and solid; it would bring a good price in the markets that specialize in things outlandish. Herbs hung from the rafters, only a few of them known to me. Clearly it wasn't poverty or common ignorance that had brought these people here. Something troubled my nostrils, making the hair on the back of my neck rise—not the herbs or the scent of storm in the air but something else: the six-week smell of penned animals in the hold of a ship, it came to me at last. That instant, a terrific crash of thunder struck, much nearer than the rest, making all of us, even Caesar, jump—all, that is, but the bearded old man. I heard wind sweep in, catching at the ragged edges of things, moving everything that would move.

The first indication that the old man was aware of us—or, indeed, aware of anything—came when Caesar inclined his head to me and said, "Doctor, it's close in here. Undo the window." The bearded man's mouth opened as if prepared to object—his teeth gleamed yellow—and his daughter's eyes flew wide; then both, I thought, gave way, resigned themselves. The man's beard and mustache became one again, and the flicker of life sank back out of his face. I, too, had certain small reservations. The only window in the room, its shutters now rattling and tugging, was the one behind the bearded man's right shoulder; and though he seemed not ferocious—he behaved like a man under sedation, in fact, his eyelids heavy, eyes filmed over—I did not relish the thought of moving nearer to a man who believed he could change into a wolf. Neither did I much like Caesar's expression. I remembered how once, halting his army, he'd sent three men into a mountain notch to find out whether they drew fire.

I made—cunning old fart that I am—the obvious and inevitable choice. I hobbled to the window, throwing my good leg forward and hauling in the bad one, making a great show of pitiful vulnerability, my face a heart-rending mask of profoundest apology—I unfastened the latches, threw the shutters wide and hooked them, then ran like a child playing sticks in the ring back to Caesar. To my horror, Caesar laughed. Strange to say, the bearded man, gloomier than Saturn until this moment, laughed, too. I swung around like a billy goat to give him a look. Old age, he should know, deserves respect or, at least, mercy—not really, of course; but I try to get one or the other if I can.

"He keep clear . . . werewolf," the bearded man said. His speech was slurred, his voice like the creakiest hinge in Tuscany. He tapped his finger tips together as if in slowed-down merriment. The night framed in the window behind him was as dense and black as ever but alive now, roaring and banging. Caesar and the two centurions laughed with the old man as if there were nothing strange at all in his admission that, indeed, he was a werewolf. The girl's face was red, whether with anger or shame I couldn't guess. For an instant, I was mad as a hornet, suspecting they'd set up this business as a joke on me; but gradually, my reason regained the upper hand. Take it from an old man who's seen a few things: It's always a mistake to assume that anything has been done for you personally, even evil.

The world flashed white and the loudest crash of thunder yet stopped their laughter and, very nearly, my heart. Now rain came pouring down like a waterfall, silver-gold where the candlelight reached it, a bright sheet blowing away from us, violently hissing. The girl had her hands over her ears. The werewolf smiled, uneasy, as if unsure what was making all the noise.

Now that we were all on such friendly terms, we introduced ourselves. The man's name was Vödfiet—one of those northern names that have no meaning. When he held out his leaden hand to Caesar, Caesar thoughtfully bowed and looked at it but did not touch it. I, too, looked, standing a little behind Caesar and to his left. The man's fingernails were thick yellow and carved with ridges, like old people's toenails, and stranger yet, the lines of the palm—what I could see of them—were like the scribbles of a child who has a vague sense of letters but not of words. It was from him that the animal smell came, almost intolerably rank, up close, even with the breeze from the window. I'd have given my purse to get the palps of my fingers into his cranium, especially the area—as close as I could get—of the *pallium prolectus*. Preferably after he was dead.

"Strange," Caesar said, gently stroking the sides of his mouth, head bowed, shoulders rigid, looking from the werewolf to me, then back. Caesar seemed unnaturally alert, yet completely unafraid or else indifferent—no, not indifferent: on fire, as if for some reason he thought he'd met his match. The fingers of his left hand drummed on the side of his leg. He said, with the terrible coy irony he uses on senators, "You seem not much bothered by these things you do."

The werewolf sighed, made a growllike noise, then shrugged and tipped his head, quizzical. He ran his tongue over his upper teeth, a gesture we ancients know well. We're authorities on rot. We taste it, insofar as we still taste, with every breath.

"Come, come," Caesar said, suddenly bending forward, smiling, sharp-eyed, and jerked his right hand, fingers tight, toward the werewolf's face. The man no more flinched than an ox would have done, drugged for slaughter. His heavy eyelids blinked once, slowly. Caesar said, again in a voice that seemed ironic, perhaps self-mocking, "Your *daughter* seems bothered enough!"

The werewolf looked around the room until he found her, still there on her stool. She went on staring at her knees. Thunder hit, not as close now, but loud. Her back jerked.

"And yet, you," Caesar said, his voice rising, stern—again there was that hint of self-mockery and something else: lidded violence—"that doesn't trouble you. Your daughter's self-sacrifice, her labor to protect you—"

The man raised his hands from the table, palms out, evidently struggling for concentration, and made a growling noise. Perhaps he said, "Gods." He spread one hand over his chest in the age-old sign of injured innocence, then slowly raised the hand toward the ceiling, or possibly he meant the window behind him, and with an effort splayed out the fingers. "Moon," he said, and looked at us hopefully, then saw that we didn't understand him. "Moon," he said carefully. "Cloud." His face showed frustration and confusion, like a stroke victim's, though obviously that wasn't his trouble, I thought; no muscle loss, no discernible differentiation between his left side and his right. "Full moon . . . shine . . . no, but . . ." Although his eyes were still unfocused, he smiled, eager; he'd caught my worried glance at the window. After a moment's hesitation, the werewolf lowered his hands again and folded them.

"The moon," Caesar said, and jabbed a finger at the night. "You mean you blame—"

The man shrugged, his confusion deepening, and opened his hands as if admitting that the excuse was feeble, then rested his dull eye on Caesar, tipped his head like a dog and went on waiting.

Caesar turned from him, rethinking things, and now I saw real fury rising in him at last. "The moon," he said half to himself, and looked hard at the centurion, as if checking his expression. Recklessly, he flew back to the table and slammed the top with the flat of both hands. "Wake up!" he shouted in the werewolf's face, so ferocious that the cords of his neck stood out.

The werewolf slowly blinked.

Caesar stared at him, eyes bulging, then again turned away from him and crossed the room. He clamped his hands to the sides of his face and squeezed his eyes shut—perhaps he had a headache starting up. Thunder banged away, and the rain, still falling hard, was now a steady hiss, a rattle of small rivers on the street. We could hear the two centurions outside the door flap ruefully talking. At last, Caesar half turned back to the werewolf. In the tone men use for commands, he asked, "What does it feel like, coming on?"

The werewolf said nothing for a long moment, then echoed, as if the words made no sense to him, "Feel like." He nodded slowly, as if deeply interested or secretly amused. The girl put her hands over her face.

Caesar said, turning more, raising his hand to stop whatever words might be coming, "Never mind that. What does it feel like afterward?"

Again it seemed that the creature found the question too hard. He concentrated with all his might, then looked over at his daughter for help, his expression wonderfully morose. She lowered her hands by an act of will and stared as before at her knees. After a time, the old man moistened his lips with his tongue, then tipped his head and looked at Caesar, hoping for a hint. A lightning flash behind him momentarily turned his figure dark.

Caesar bowed and shook his head, almost smiling in his impatience and frustration. "Tell me this: How many people have you killed?"

This question the werewolf did seem to grasp. He let the rain hiss and rattle for a while, then asked, "Hundreds?" He tipped his head to the other side, watching Caesar closely, then cautiously ventured a second guess. "Thousands?"

Caesar shook his head. He raised his fist, then stopped himself and changed it to a stiffly cupped hand and brought it to his mouth, sliding the finger tips up and down slowly. A pool was forming on the dirt floor, leaking in. I cleared my throat. The drift of the conversation was not what I call healthy.

The werewolf let out a sort of groan, a vocal sigh, drew back his arm and absently touched his forehead, then his beard. "Creatures," he said. The word seemed to have come to him by lucky accident. He watched hopefully; so did Caesar. At last, the werewolf groaned or sighed more deeply than before and said, "No, but . . ." Perhaps he'd suffered a stroke of some kind unknown to me. *No, but* is common, of course—often, in my experience, the only two words the victim can still command. He searched the walls, the growing pool on the floor, for language. I was sure he was more alert now, and I reached out to touch Caesar's elbow, warning him. "Man," the werewolf said; then, hopelessly, "moon!"

"Men *do* things," Caesar exploded, striking his thigh with his fist. He raised his hand to touch the hilt of his sword, not quite absently, as if grimly making sure he could get at it.

"Ax," the werewolf said. He was working his eyebrows, looking at his palely window-lit palms as if he couldn't remember having seen them before. "*Ax*!" he said. He raised his eyes to the ceiling and strained for a long time before trying again. "No, but . . . No . . . No, but . . ."

Caesar waved, dismissive, as if imagining he'd understood.

Their eyes met. The thunder was distant, the rain coming down as hard as ever.

"Ax," the werewolf said at last, softly, slowly shaking, then bowing, his head, resting his forehead on his finger tips, pausing to take a deep, slow, whistling breath through his nostrils. "Ax," he said, then something more.

The girl's voice broke out like flame. She was looking at no one. "He's saying *accident*."

Caesar started, then touched his mouth.

The werewolf breathed deeply again; the same whistling noise. "Green parks—no, but—chill-den—"

Abruptly, the girl said, shooting her burning gaze at Caesar, "He means you. You're strong; you make things safe for children." She shook her hands as if frustrated by words, like the werewolf. "But you're just lucky. Eventually, you'll die."

"The Empire will go on," Caesar broke in, as if he'd known all along what the werewolf was saying and it was not what he'd come here to talk about. "It's not Caesar's 'indomitable will.' We have laws." Suddenly, his eyes darted away, avoiding the girl's.

"Moon," the werewolf wailed.

Caesar's voice slashed at him. "*Stop* that."

It was beginning to get light out. It came to me that the old man was weeping. He laid his head to one side, obsequious. "Thank . . . gods . . . unspeakable . . . no, but . . ." His bulging forehead struggled. The candlelight was doing something queer to his glittering, tear-filled eyes, making them like windows to the underworld. He raised his voice. "No, but. No, *but!*" He gave his head a shake, then another, as if to clear it. Furtively, he brushed one eye, then the other. "Vile!" he cried out. *"No, but . . ."* His hands were trembling, as were the edges of his mouth. His voice took on pitch and intensity, the words in the extremity of his emotion becoming cloudy, more obscure than before. I had to lean close to watch his lips. I glanced at Caesar to see if he was following, then at the girl.

It was the girl's expression that made me realize my error: She was staring at the window, where the light, I saw at last, was not dawn but a parting of the thick black hood of clouds. There was no sound of rain. Moonlight came pouring through the window, sliding toward us across the room. The girl drew her feet back as if the light were alive.

I cannot say whether it was gradual or instantaneous. His beard and mouth changed; the alertness of his ears became a change in their shape and then bristling, tufted fur, and I saw distinctly that the hand swiping at his nose was a paw. All at once, the man behind the table was a wolf. A violent growl erupted all around us. He was huge, flame-eyed, already leaping, a wild beast tangled in clothes. He was still in mid-air when Caesar's sword thwunked into his head, cleaving it—a mistake, pure instinct, I saw from Caesar's face. Only the werewolf's daughter moved more quickly: She flew like a shadow past Caesar and the rest of us, running on all fours, slipped like ball lightning out the door, and vanished into the night.

▪ ▪ ▪

It's difficult to put one's finger exactly on the oddity in Caesar's behavior. One cannot call it mania in any usual sense—delusional insanity, dementia, melancholia, and so forth. Nonetheless, he's grown odd. (No real cause for alarm, I think.) You've no doubt heard of the squall of honors recently conferred on him—statues, odes, feasts, gold medals, outlandish titles: Prince of the Moon, Father of

Animals. Shepherd of Ethiopia and worse—more of them every day. They're nearly all his own inventions, insinuated into the ears of friendly senators or enemies who dare not cross him. I have it on good authority that those who hate him most are quickest to approve these absurdities, believing such inflations will ultimately make him insufferable to the people—as well they may. Indeed, the man who hungers most after his ruin has suggested that Caesar's horse be proclaimed divine. Caesar seems delighted. It cannot be put down to megalomania. At each new outrage he conceives or hears suggested, he laughs—not cynically but with childlike pleasure, as if astonished by how much foolishness the gods will put up with. (He's always busy with the gods, these days, ignoring necessities, reasoning with priests.) I did catch him once in an act of what seemed authentic lunacy. He was at the aquarium, looking down at the innumerable, flickering goldfish and carp, whispering something. I crept up on him to hear. He was saying, "Straighten up those ranks, there! Order! Order!" He shook his finger. When he turned and saw me, he looked embarrassed, then smiled, put his arm around my shoulders and walked with me. "I try to keep the Empire neat, doctor," he said. "It's not easy!" And he winked with such friendliness that, testy as I am when people touch me, I was moved. In fact, tears sprang to my eyes, I admit it. Once a man's so old he's started to piss on himself, he might as well let go with everything. Another time, I saw him hunkered down, earnestly reasoning—so it seemed—with a colony of ants. "Just playing, doctor," he said when he saw that I saw.

"Caesar, Caesar!" I moaned. He touched his lips with one finger.

The oddest thing he's come up with, of course, is his proposed war with Persia—himself, needless to say, as general. Persia, for the love of God! Even poor befuddled Mark Antony is dismayed.

"Caesar, you're not as young as you used to be," he says, and throws a woeful look over at me. He sits with interdigitated fists between his big, blocky knees. We're in Caesar's council room, the guards standing stiff as two columns, as usual, outside the door. Mark Antony grows fatter by the day. Not an interesting problem—he eats and sleeps too much. I'd prescribe exercise, raw vegetables and copulation. He has an enlarged subcutaneous cyst on the back of his neck. It must itch, but he pretends not to notice, for dignity's sake. Caesar lies on his couch as if disinterested, but his legs, crossed at the ankles, are rigid, and the pulse through his right inner jugular is visible. It's late, almost midnight. At times, he seems to be listening for something, but there's nothing to be heard. Cicadas; occasional baying of a dog.

It strikes me that, for all his flab, Mark Antony is a handsome man. His once-mighty muscles, now toneless, suggest a potential for heart disease, and there's blue under his too-smooth skin; nonetheless, one can imagine him working himself back to vigor, the dullness gradually departing from his eyes. Anything's possible. Look at me, still upright, thanks mainly to diet, though I'm farther along than he is. I frequently lose feeling in my right hand.

"If you must attack Persia," he says, "why not send me? You're needed here,

Caesar!" His eyes squirt tears, which he irritably brushes away. "Two, three years—not even you can win a war with Persia in less time than that. And all that while, Rome and all her complicated business in the hands of Mark Antony! It will be ruin, Caesar! Everyone says so!"

Caesar gazes at him. "Are you, my friend, not nobler and more honest than all the other Romans put together?"

Mark Antony looks confused, raises his hands till they're level with his shoulders, then returns them to their place between his knees, which he once more clenches. "You're needed here," he says again. "Everyone says so." For all his friends' warnings, I do not think Mark Antony grasps how thoroughly he's despised by the senate. Caesar's confidant, Caesar's right arm. But besides that—meaning no disrespect—he really would be a booby. Talk about opening the floodgates!

Caesar smiles, snatches a moth out of the air, examines the wings with great curiosity, like a man trying to read Egyptian, then gently lets it go and lies still again. After a moment, he raises his right hand, palm outward, pushing an invisible bark out to sea. "You really would like that," he says. "Away to Persia for murder and mayhem."

Mark Antony looks to me for help. What can I say?

Now suddenly, black eyes flashing, Caesar rears up on one elbow and points at Mark Antony. "*You* are Rome," he says. "*You* are the hope of humanity!"

Later, Mark Antony asks me, "Is he insane?"

"Not by any rules I understand," I say. "At any rate, there's no cause for alarm."

He moves back and forth across the room like a huge, slow mimicry of Caesar, rubbing his hands together like a man preparing to throw dice. His shadow moves, much larger than he is, on the wall. For some reason, it frightens me. Through the window I see the sharp-horned, icy-white half-moon. Most of Mark Antony's fat has gone into his buttocks.

"They'll kill him rather than leave the Empire in my hands," he says. Then, without feeling, his palms pressed together like a priest's: "After that, they'll kill me."

His clarity of vision surprises me. "Cheer up," I say. "I'm his personal physician. They'll kill me, too."

▪ ▪ ▪

Last night, the sky was alive with omens: stars exploding, falling every which way. "Something's up!" says Caesar, as tickled as if he himself had caused the discord in the heavens. His bald head glows with each star burst, then goes dark. He stood in the garden—the large one created for his daughter's tomb—till nearly sunrise, watching for more fireworks.

Mark Antony's been sent off, plainly a fool's errand, trumped up to get him out of Rome. "Don't come back," says Caesar. "Never come back until I send for you." I don't like this. Not at all, not one damn bit. My life line has changed. My stool this morning was bilious.

▪ ▪ ▪

All day, Caesar has been receiving urgent visitors, all with one message: "It would be good if tomorrow you avoided the forum." There can be no doubt that there's a plot afoot.

Late this afternoon, at the onset of twilight, I saw—I think—the werewolf's daughter. She's grown thinner, as if eaten away by disease. (Everyone, these days, looks to me eaten away by disease. My prostate's nearly plugged, and there's not a surgeon in Rome whom I'd trust to cut my fingernails.) She stood at the bottom step of the palace stairway, one shaky hand reaching out to the marble hem. She left herbs of some kind. Their use, whether for evil or good, is unknown to me. Then she fled. Later, it occurred to me that I hadn't really gotten a good look at her. Perhaps it was someone I don't know.

▪ ▪ ▪

Strange news. You'll have heard it before you get this letter. Forgive the handwriting. My poor old nerves aren't all they might be. Would that I'd never lived to see this day. My stomach will be acid for a month.

Caesar was hardly seated, had hardly gotten out the call for prayer, before they rose like a wave from every side, 60 senators with daggers. He was stabbed a dozen times before he struggled to his feet—or, rather, leaped to his feet—eyes rolling, every muscle in spasm, as if flown out of control, though it clearly wasn't that. You wouldn't have believed what strength he called up in his final moment! He dragged them from one end of the forum to the other, hurling off senators like an injured bear and shrieking, screaming his lungs out. It was as if all the power of the gods were for an instant contracted to one man. They tore his clothes from him, or possibly he did it himself for some reason. His blood came spurting from a hundred wounds, so that the whole marble floor was slippery and steaming. He fell down, stood up again, dragging his assassins; fell down, then rose to crawl on hands and knees toward the light of the high central door where, that moment, I was running for my life. His slaughtered-bull bellowings are still in my ears, strangely bright, like a flourish of trumpets or Jovian laughter.

Bob Shacochis

Easy in the Islands

February 1985

When *Playboy* first purchased a short story by Bob Shacochis ("Lord Short Shoe Wants the Monkey," July 1982), he was still a student at the Iowa Writer's Workshop. Success arrived quickly, however, and *Playboy* was soon in hot competition with other magazines for Shacochis's literate, graceful, yet very masculine stories, often set in the Caribbean islands. This one, his third in the magazine, became the title story for his first collection, which won the American Book Award for fiction in 1985. Another solid collection, *The Next New World,* appeared in 1989. Shacochis's 1993 novel, *Swimming in the Volcano,* had its genesis in a nonfiction piece (never published) for *Playboy*. Shacochis (pronounced "Sha-*coach*-is") was born in 1951, making him the second-youngest writer in this anthology, after Jay McInerney.

Bob Shacochis

Easy in the Islands

The days were small, pointless epics, long wind-ups to punches that always drifted by cartoon fashion, as if each simple task were meaningless unless immersed in more theater and threat than bad opera.

It was only Monday noon and already Tillman had been through the wringer. He had greased the trade commissioner to allow a pallet of Campbell's consommé to come ashore, fired one steel band for their hooliganism and hired another, found a carpenter he was willing to trust to repair the back veranda that was so spongy in spots that Tillman knew it was only a matter of days before a guest's foot burst through the surface into whatever terrors lived below in the tepid darkness, restocked on vitamins from the pharmacy, argued with the crayfish regulatory bureau about quotas. And argued with the inscrutable cook, a fat country woman who wore a wool watch cap and smoked hand-rolled cigars; argued with both maids, muscle-bound Lemonille and the other one, who wouldn't reveal her name; argued with the gardener, who liked to chop everything up; argued with the customs house; argued with the bartender, Jevanee. And although he had not forthrightly won any of these encounters, he had won them enough to forestall the doom that would one day descend on Rosehill Plantation.

But now the daily defeats and victories were overshadowed by a first-class doozy, a default too personal to implicate the local population. The problem was to decide what to do about his mother—Mother, who had thought life wonderful in the islands. Now she rested stiffly in the food locker, dead and coated with frost, as blue as the shallow water on the reefs, protected from the fierceness of the sun she had once loved without question or fear, a sun that was never really her enemy, no matter how it textured her skin, no matter what it revealed of her age.

In her room on Saturday, Mother had died mysteriously. As Lemonille had said when the two of them carried her out after the doctor had been there, "Mistah Tillmahn, it look so you muddah shake out she heart fah no good reason. Like she tricked by some false light, ya know."

His mother's body had been strong and brassy, her spirit itself unusually athletic for a woman only weeks away from 60. In her quick laugh was as much vitality as a girl's, and yet she had died. In bed, early in the evening, disdainful of the bars and clubs, reading a book—Colette, rediscovered on her latest Continental visit—her finger ready to turn the page. Tillman was astonished. Only after Dr. Bradley had told him that he suspected his mother had been poisoned did Tillman begin to calm down, his imperturbable self returning by degrees. Such a conclusion made no sense. The terms of life in the islands were that nothing ever made sense, unless you were a mystic or a politician or studied both with ambition. Then every stupidness seemed an act of inspiration, every cruelty part of a divine scheme. There was no dialectic here, only the obverting of all possibilities until caprice made its selection.

Bradley couldn't be sure, though. Neither he nor any of the three other sanctioned doctors on the island knew how to perform an autopsy with sufficient accuracy to assure one another or anybody else of the exact nature of death when the cause was less than obvious. Still, Bradley earned moments of miraculous credibility, as when the former minister of trade was brought into the hospital dead of a gunshot wound in his chest. To the government's relief, Bradley determined the cause of death as "heart failure," an organic demise and unembarrassing.

"I will take your permission, mahn, to cut de body open ahnd look in she stomach," Dr. B. had said to Tillman as they stood over his mother's corpse in the sunny hotel room on Sunday morning, a breeze off the ocean dancing the curtains open, billowing sunlight throughout the room and then sucking it back outside. A spray of creamy rosebuds tapped against the louvered window, an eerie beckoning in the air silenced by death.

"For God's sake, why?" Tillman had said. It sounded like the ultimate obscenity to have this fool, with his meatcutter's stubby hands, groping in his mother's abdomen.

"To determine what she eat aht de time of succumption."

"I told you what she was eating," Tillman said, exasperated. "She was eating a can of peaches with a spoon. Look here; there are still some left in the can." He shook the can angrily and syrup slopped onto his wrist. In disgust, Tillman wiped the sticky wetness on his pants, half-nauseated, associating the liquid with some oozy by-product of dissolution. "Take the peaches if you need something to cut into, but you're not taking Mother. This isn't one of your Bottom Town cadavers."

Bradley had reacted with a shrug and a patronizing twist to his smile. "Dis racial complexity—what a pity, mahn."

How often Tillman had heard this lie, so facile, from the lips of bad men. "One world," he said, biting down on the syllables as if they were a condemnation or a final sorrow.

Tillman refused to let him remove the body from Rosehill. He wrapped his mother in the mauve-chenille bedspread she had been lying on, restacked several crates of frozen chicken parts and arranged her in the walk-in freezer until he could figure out just what to do. It was easy to accept the fact that you couldn't trust a doctor in such circumstances. What was most unacceptable was that Bradley had told the police that there was a possibility the old lady had been murdered. The police, of course, were excited by this news. They had sent Inspector Cuffy over to Rosehill to inform Tillman that he was under suspicion. "You're kidding," Tillman had said.

He suggested the inspector should walk down to the beach bar the hotel maintained on the waterfront and have a drink, courtesy of the house, while he took care of two new guests who had just arrived in a taxi from the airport. "I don't believe it," the new man said in an aside to Tillman as he checked them in. "The skycaps at the airport whistled at my wife and called her a whore." His wife stood demurely by his side, looking a bit overwhelmed. Tillman could see the dark coronas of nipples under her white-muslin sun dress.

"Hey, people here are more conservative than you might think," he told the couple, and to the woman he added, "Unless you want little boys rubbing up against your leg, you shouldn't wear shorts or a bathing suit into town."

"But this is the tropics," the woman protested in an adolescent voice, looking at Tillman as if he were just being silly.

"Right," Tillman conceded, handing over the key. He escorted the couple to their room, helping with the luggage, and wished them well. Wished himself a dollar for every time their notion of paradise would be fouled by some rudeness, aggression or irrelevant accusation.

He crossed back over the veranda out onto the cobbled drive, past the derelict stone tower of the windmill, where every other Saturday the hotel sponsored a goat roast that was well attended by civil servants, Peace Corps volunteers and whatever tourists were around, down the glorious green lawn crazy with blossom, down, hot and sweaty, to the palm grove, the bamboo beach bar on its fringe, the lagoon dipping into the land like a blue pasture, Tillman walking with his hands in the pockets of his loose cotton pants, reciting a calypso and feeling, despite his troubles, elected, an aristocrat of the sensual latitudes, anointed to all the earthly privileges ordinary people dreamed about on their commuter trains fifty weeks a year. No matter that in a second-class Eden, nothing was as unprofitable as the housing of its guests. Even loss seemed less discouraging in the daily flood of sun.

Jevanee was glaring at him from behind the bar. And the inspector sat grandly on his stool, satisfied with being the big shot, bearing a smile that welcomed Tillman as if they were to be partners in future prosperity, as if the venture they were to embark on could only end profitably. He gave a little wink before he tipped his green bottle of imported beer and sank the neck between his lips.

"Dis a sad affair, mahn," he said, wagging his round head. Jevanee uncapped a second bottle and set it before the inspector, paying no attention to Tillman's presence. Tillman drew a stool up beside Cuffy and perched on it, requesting Jevanee to bring another beer, and watched with practiced patience as the bartender kicked about and finally delivered the bottle as if it were his life's savings.

"What is it with you, Jevanee? What am I doing wrong?" The bartender had come with Rosehill when he had inherited the hotel eight months ago. Somebody had trained him to be a terror.

"Mistah Trick!" Jevanee whooped. He was often too self-conscious to confront his employer head on. Nevertheless, he would not accept even the mildest reproach without an extravagant line of defense or, worse, smoldering until his tongue ignited and his hands flew threateningly, shouting in a tantrum that would go on forever with or without an audience, a man who would never be employed to his satisfaction. He turned his back on Tillman and began muttering at the whiskey bottles arrayed on the work island in the center of the oval bar.

"Mistah Trick, he say what him doin' wrong, de Devil. He say daht, he mean, 'Jevanee, why you is a chupid boy ahs blahck ahs me boot cahnt count change ahnd show yah teef nice aht de white lady?' He say daht, he mean, 'Jevanee, why you cahnt work fah free like you grahnpoppy? Why you cahnt bring you sistah here ta please me?' " Without ceasing his analysis of what the white man had meant, he marched out from the bar and into the bushes to take a leak. Tillman forced himself not to react any further to Jevanee's rage, which appeared to be taking on a decidedly historical sweep.

The inspector, who had not shown any interest in Jevanee's complaints, began to tap the long nail of his index finger on the surface of the bar. He made a show of becoming serious without wanting to deprive Tillman of his informality, his compassion, his essential sympathy, etc.—all the qualities he believed he possessed and controlled to his benefit.

"Who else, Tillmahn, but you?" he finally concluded as if it hurt him to say this. "Undah-stahnd, is only speculation."

"Who else but me?" Tillman sputtered. "Are you crazy?" The inspector frowned and Tillman immediately regretted his choice of words. Cuffy was as willfully unpredictable as almost everybody else on the island, but in a madhouse, an outsider soon learned, truth was always a prelude to disaster, the match dropped thoughtlessly onto tinder. He should have said, "Look, how can you think that?" or "Man, what will it take to end this unfortunate business?" But too late.

The inspector was pinching at his rubbery nose, no longer even considering Tillman, looking out across the harbor, the anchored sailboats bobbing like a display of various possibilities, playing the image of artful calculation for his suspect.

Tillman sighed. "Why do you think I would kill my own mother? She was my *mother.* What son could harm the woman who carried him into the world?"

The inspector pursed his lips and then relaxed them. "Well, Tillmahn, perhahps you do it to have title to dis property, true?"

The absurdity was too great even for Tillman, a connoisseur of island nonsense. "To inherit this property!" Now Tillman had to laugh, regardless of the inspector's feelings. "Cuffy, nobody wants this place. In his will, my father was excessively sorry for burdening me with Rosehill Plantation and advised I sell it at the first opportunity. My mother had absolutely no claim to Rosehill. He divorced her long ago."

Tillman paused. As far as he could tell, he was the only one in the world, besides the government, who wanted Rosehill Plantation. It had been on the market for years, not once receiving an honest offer. Its profits were marginal, its overhead crushing. But the hotel was his, so why not be there. What he had found through it was unexpected—the inexplicable sense that life on the island had a certain fullness, that it was, far beyond what he had ever experienced back home, authentic in the most elemental ways.

Cuffy had become petulant, studying him as if he were spoiled, an unappreciative child. Tillman was not intimidated. "Why should I tell you this, anyway? It has absolutely no relevance to my mother's death."

"Um-hmm, um-hmm, I see," the inspector said. "So perhahps you muddah take a lovah, a dark mahn, ahnd you become vexed wit' she fah behavin' so. You warn she to stop but she refuse. So . . ." He threw out his hands as if the rest of the scene he conceived were there before him. "Is only speculation."

Tillman was tiring fast. Inspector Cuffy had no use for what was and what wasn't; his only concern was his own role in the exercise of authority. It killed boredom, boredom amid the splendor. It created heroes and villains, wealth and poverty. No other existence offered him so much.

He discovered that he was grinding his teeth, and the muscles in his jaw ached. Jevanee had slipped back behind the bar, and every time Tillman glanced over there, Jevanee, now bold, tried to stare him down.

"My mother was an old lady," he told the inspector. "She was beyond love. She liked books and beaches, fruit, seafood and rare wines. Traveling. There was no man in her life. There never was. She was even a stranger to my father."

"You just a boy," Cuffy noted in a way that made Tillman think it was a line the inspector must use frequently. "Nobody beyond love, ya know."

"So?"

"So, nobody beyond pahssion, ahnd nobody beyond crime."

Tillman blinked. Damn, he thought, Cuffy's starting to make sense.

"Even ahn old womahn need a good roll to keep she happy," the inspector concluded.

"Oh, for Christ's sake," Tillman said, standing up. "I have to get back."

He couldn't get away before Jevanee butted in. Ignore Jevanee and life might go on. The bartender used his mouth like a gun, the words popping spitefully while he focused on whatever spirit he had summoned to witness his oppression.

"Daht ol' bony bag he call his muddah grabbin' aht every blahck boy on de beach. I see it wit' me own eyes."

"Jevanee, shut up."

"Oh, yes, massa, suh. Yes, massa." He feigned excessive servitude, wiping the bar counter, the cashbox, the bamboo supports with his shirt sleeve. The time would come when Tillman would have to face up to Jevanee's vindictiveness. He had been steaming ever since Tillman had told him not to hand out free drinks to his friends from the village. Jevanee insisted that no one but Rosehill's tourists, which were not regular, would ever patronize the beach bar if it weren't for him. Maybe he was right. Nobody was coming around anymore, except on Friday nights, when the band played. More and more, Jevanee wanted Tillman to understand that he was a dangerous man, his every move a challenge to his employer. Tillman was still trying to figure out how to fire the guy without a lot of unpleasantness.

"Don't listen to Jevanee," Tillman told the inspector. "He's pissed at me these days because of a disagreement we had over a charitable instinct of his."

"I give me bruddah a drink," Jevanee said in a self-deprecating way, as though he were the victim and Cuffy would understand. Jevanee's mood would only escalate if Tillman explained that the bartender's "bruddah" was consuming a case of Scotch on his drier visits, so he refused to debate Jevanee's claim. The inspector turned on his stool with the cold expression of a man whose duty it is to make it known that he must hurt you severely, that he may cripple you or make you weep, if you disobey him.

"Look now, you," he said, taking moral pleasure in this chastisement. "Doan you make trouble fah Mistah Tillmahn. You is lucky he give you work."

"Dis white bitch doan give me a damn t'ing," Jevanee snarled, shaking an empty beer bottle at Tillman. "I work in dis same spot a long time when he show up. Ahnd what you doin' kissin' he ahss?"

"Doan talk aht me daht way, boy, or I fuck you up. Hell goin' have a new bahtendah soon if you cahnt behave."

Jevanee tried to smile, a taut earnestness that never quite made it to his mouth. Tillman arranged chairs around the warped café tables, backing away. "OK, then, Cuffy. I'm glad we had this opportunity to straighten everything out. Stay and have another beer if you want."

Cuffy looked at his gold wrist watch. "You will be around in de aftahnoon?"

"Why?"

"I wish to view de deceased."

"Uh, can't it wait till tomorrow?" Tillman asked. "I have errands to run in town. A shipment of beef is coming in from Miami."

From his shirt pocket, Cuffy had taken a note pad and was scribbling in it. He talked without raising his head. "OK, dere's no hurry. De old womahn takin' she time goin' nowheres."

Tillman nodded, now in stride with the process, the havoc of it. "Cuffy, you're a thorough man. If anybody's going to get to the bottom of this mess, it's you."

The inspector accepted this flattery as his due, too certain of its validity to bother about the subtle mocking edge to Tillman's voice. His eyes relaxed, hooded and moist. Tillman started up the footpath through the palms, kicking a coconut ahead of him, a leaden soccer ball, turning once to check what fared in his absence and—yes—Cuffy and Jevanee had their heads together, the bartender animated, swinging his hands, the inspector with his arms crossed on his wide chest. Jevanee had too much energy today. Maybe his attitude would defuse if he were somewhere other than the bar for a while. He seemed to live there. Tillman shouted back down to them, "Jevanee, after the inspector leaves, lock everything up and take the rest of the day off."

The bartender ignored him.

▪ ▪ ▪

Tillman jogged up the perfect lawn along an avenue of floral celebration—tree-sized poinsettias, arrow ginger, bougainvillaea, oleander—a perfumer's tray of fragrance. On the knoll, graced with a millionaire's view of the channel, was the old plantation house, a stubborn remnant of colonial elegance, its whitewashed brick flaking in a way that benefited the charm of its archaic construction, the faded red of the gabled tin roof a human comfort against the green, monotonous sheets of the mountains that were its background. Farther south, the cone shell of the windmill stood like a guard tower or a last refuge. Tillman had huddled there with his guests last summer during a hurricane, the lot of them drunk and playing roundhouse bridge, the cards fluttering from the storm outside.

When he was a teenager, Tillman had flown down to the island during a summer off from Exeter to help his father build the two modern wings that flanked the manor, one-level box rooms side by side, as uninspired as any lodging on any Florida roadside. Tillman's father was a decent man, completely involved in his scheming, though his interest invariably flagged once a puzzle was solved, a challenge dispatched. The old man had worked for J. D. Root, one of the big ad agencies in New York, handling the Detroit accounts. His final act was an irony unappreciated—he perished in one of the cars he promoted, losing control on the Northway one rainy evening, going fishing up on the St. Lawrence, convinced that this time, he would hook a muskellunge. Rosehill Plantation was his most daring breakaway, but he never really had time for the place. Throughout his ownership, Rosehill lost money, and after his death the checks from the estate in New York flowed like aid from the mother country. When a lawyer's telegram reached Tillman, asking if he wanted to pursue more aggressively the sale of the plantation, he decided to dump his Lower East Side loft, where he had been mulling for two years since graduate school, sweating out the draft, and make his claim on Rosehill. Besides, Nixon had just been re-elected. The States no longer seemed like the right place to be.

Awash in perspiration, Tillman turned the corner around the east wing, his blood pressure a little jumpy, the skin on his face at the point of combustion, wondering if all the friction of a fast life could suddenly cause a person to burst into flame. Sometimes he felt as if it were happening. It wasn't very easy to find peace on the island unless you hiked up into the mountains. Whereas it was very easy to catch hell.

In the exterior courtyard behind the estate house, the new arrivals, husband and wife from Wilmington, Delaware, were inspecting one of Tillman's few unequivocal successes, the gazebo that housed his parrot aviary, in it seven of the last rainbow parrots on earth. The project was really that of the veterinarian at the ministry of agriculture, a man who hated goats and cows but spent all his spare time bird watching or digging up pre-Columbian artifacts, storing them in his living room until the far-off day a museum would be built. Together, he and Tillman had waged a public campaign on the island, the parrots' sole habitat, to prevent their extinction. A law was passed for appearances, its advantage being that it clearly defined for the bird smugglers just who needed to be paid off and who could be bypassed with impunity.

After the crusade, Tillman had decided to contact some poachers himself. They were kids, tough miniature bandits, the nest robbers. One was nine, the other eleven—Basil and Jacob, tree climbers *extraordinaire,* both as skinny as vanilla beans. They lived in a mountain village, a clump of wattle huts, one of the outposts before the vast roadless center of the island, all sharp peaks, palisades and jungle. When the hatching season had ended, Tillman and the boys trekked into the lush interior, camping overnight, Tillman's neck strained from looking up into the canopy, his ears confused by the wraithish shrieks and skraws—skra-aaa-aw!—unable to pinpoint where the sound had come from in the infinite cathedral of growth. But the kids knew their business. They were fearless, scaling to the top of the highest mahogany, indifferent to the slashing beaks of the females that refused to abandon the nest, shinnying down the trunks with the chicks held gently in their mouths, polycolored cotton balls, the fierce tiny heads lolling helplessly out from between the embrace of boyish lips.

Tillman thought he would tell his guests from Delaware the story. The woman was scrutinizing the birds rather sternly. She would cluck and whistle at them, tap the chicken-wire wall of the cage, but she did so without affection. When he finished talking, she turned to look at him, her eyes obscured behind oversized sunglasses, her mouth in a pout. Tillman guessed she was a bank teller, something that had made her very sure of herself without placing any demand on her intelligence.

"It's cruel," she said.

"It is not cruel. It's heroic. These islands have a way of forcing everything but the lowest common denominator into oblivion."

"Hero," she said sardonically. The husband looked skeptical. Light reflected off her glasses and sliced back at Tillman. He shrugged his shoulders. Perhaps he should bar Americans from Rosehill. Canadians made the better tourists. They allowed for a world outside themselves.

▪ ▪ ▪

The Land-Rover started painfully, a victim of mechanical arthritis. Soon it would take no more to the prosthetic miracle of wire, tin and hardware junk. Spare parts appeared from across the ocean as often as Halley's comet.

Onto the narrow blacktop road that circumnavigated the island, Tillman drove with reckless courage and whipping flair, showing inner strength when he refused to give way to two flat-bed lorries painted up like Easter eggs, one named Sweetfish, the other Dr. Lick, passengers clinging to everything but the wheel hubs, racing down the coastal hill side by side straight at him, Dr. Lick overtaking Sweetfish just as Tillman downshifted reluctantly to third and toed the brake pedal. Someday the lorries will spread carnage across this highway, Tillman thought. It will be a national event, the island equivalent of a 747's going down.

In the capital, a pastel city breathtaking from the heights above it but garbage-strewn and ramshackle once you were on its streets, Tillman honked his way through the crowds down along Front Street, inching his way to the docks. On the quay, three pallets of frozen steaks destined for Rosehill were sweating pink juice onto the dirty concrete. Beef from the island was as tough and stringy as rug; if a hotel wanted to serve food worthy of the name, it had to import almost everything but fish. He located the purser in one of the rum-and-Coke sheds that filled every unclaimed inch of the wharves like derelict carnival booths. There was no use complaining about the shipment's being off-loaded without anybody's being there to receive it. That was Tillman's fault—he had been too preoccupied. He signed the shipping order and then scrambled to hire a driver and boys to break down the pallets and truck the cartons out to Rosehill's freezer before the meat thawed completely.

There were other errands, less urgent—to the marketing board in search of the rare tomato, to the post office, to the stationer for a ballpoint pen, to the pharmacist, who was disappointed when Tillman bought only aspirin. Most of his regular white customers spent small fortunes on amphetamines or Quaaludes. When Tillman had finished there, he drove over to the national hospital on the edge of town. Without a death certificate from Bradley, Mother was destined to be the morbid champion of cryogenics, the queen of ice in a land where water never froze in nature.

The old colonial hospital was a structure and a system bypassed by any notion of modernity. Someone yelled at him as he entered the shadowed foyer, but it wasn't apparent who or why. The rough wooden floor boards creaked under his feet. The maze of hallways seemed to be a repository for loiterers—attendants, nurses, nuns, clerks, superfluous guards, mangled patients, talking, weeping, spending the day in rigid silence. One naked little boy asleep on the floor, hugging the wall.

He found Bradley's office and went through the door without knocking. Bradley, chief surgeon, head physician of Saint George's National People's Hospital, an agnostic operation if Tillman had ever seen one, was reading in his chair, a paperback romance, a man hovering over a fallen woman on its cover. The room smelled of sweet putrefaction and Lysol. The scent of jasmine wafted in through open, screenless windows. Tillman sat down on a wooden bench against one bare wall. Flies buzzed along the ceiling. Bradley slowly broke off from his reading, dropping his feet one by one from where they were propped on the broad window sill. His lab coat, smudged with yellow stains and laundered blood, sagged away from his middle. He recognized Tillman and smiled grudgingly.

"Mahn, I been callin' you, ya know. I examine dem peaches you muddah eat. Dey was no good. I think we solve dis big mystery."

Tillman knew this was his chance to end the affair, but he could not forgive Bradley his smugness, his careless manner, the suffering he had sown.

"You're sure? What'd you do, feed them to a chicken and the chicken died?"

"Mahn, Tillmahn, you doan have enough troubles, you must come make some wit' me? Why is daht?"

"You're telling me she died of botulism?"

"It seem so, seem so."

Tillman was incited to fury. "Botulism, doctor, causes vomiting and extreme pain. How can you not know that? My mother died a peaceful death."

Bradley turned with eyes murderous. "If it's so, de autopsy prove so. I cahnt know oddahwise."

"You're not touching her. Somebody else can do it, but not you."

"Mahn, daht's irrational."

Tillman jumped up from the bench and stood in front of the doctor's cluttered desk. "You'd be the last person on earth to touch her."

"Get out, Tillmahn."

Tillman was in no hurry to leave. "Remember Freddy Allen?" he asked.

"Who?" Then Bradley remembered and his face lost its arrogance.

"He was a friend of mine, a good one. He helped me out at Rosehill whenever I needed it."

"Tillmahn, consider I am only human."

"Yes, you are. So was Freddy until he came to you. You gave him bromides for acute appendicitis. The damn vet can diagnose better than you."

Bradley stood so fast, his eyes full of menace, that Tillman tensed to defend himself. "Get out!" he shouted, pointing his finger at Tillman. "You muddah now a permahnent guest aht Rosehill till you come to you senses. Get out!"

The doctor came around from his desk to open the office door and then kicked it shut behind him.

▪ ▪ ▪

Tillman, island hotelier, master of the business arts, student of impossibility, fond of weather that rarely oppressed, a man of contingencies and recently motherless—Tillman knew what to do. Whatever it took.

Whatever it took, Tillman told himself, back out on the streets, heedless in the late-afternoon traffic. Sometimes that meant nothing at all; sometimes the gods spared you muckery, blessed you with style, and everything was easy.

At the airport, he parked next to a single taxi out front, no one around to note this familiar island tune, the prolonged pitch of tires violently braked. Through the dark, empty airport that always reminded him of an abandoned warehouse, Tillman searched for his friend Roland, the free-lance bush pilot from Australia, maverick and proven ace. Roland leaped around the warm world in his Stearman, spraying mountainsides of bananas with chemicals that prevented leaf spot and other blights. Tillman suspected that the pilot was also part of the interisland ring sponsored by the most influential businessmen to smuggle drugs, whiskey, cigarettes, stereos—whatever contraband could be crammed surreptitiously into the fuselage of a small plane. He seemed to be able to come and go as he pleased.

Roland's plane wasn't on the tarmac, nor in the hangar. Sunset wasn't far away. Wherever Roland was, waltzing his plane through green, radical valleys, he would have to return before dark if he was coming in tonight. Tillman left a message with a mechanic in the machine shed for Roland to come find him at Rosehill.

Twilight had begun to radiate through the vegetation as he arrived back at the hotel, lifting the mélange of colors to a higher level of brilliance, as if each plant, each surface, were responding to the passage of the sun with its own interior luminosity. Inspector Cuffy was on the veranda of the west wing, laughing with Lemonille, her eyes flirtatious. They clammed up when Tillman appeared beside them.

"You haven't been waiting for me, have you?"

"Well, doan trouble youself, mahn. I been interviewin' dis pretty young lady."

Tillman looked at Lemonille, who averted her eyes shyly. "Perhahps we cahn view de body of you muddah now." Cuffy said this without the slightest conviction. Tillman understood that for the time being, the inspector was only interested in chasing Lemonille.

"I've had a hell of a day. Can I ask you to wait until tomorrow?"

"Daht strike me ahs reasonable," Cuffy said, allowing Tillman to experience his generosity.

"Besides, case solved, Cuffy," Tillman said, remembering the doctor, the hospital. "Bradley says something was wrong with the can of peaches my mother was eating when she died." ("If you want to believe such crap," Tillman added under his breath.)

"I will study daht report," the inspector said. From the way he spoke, Tillman knew the investigation would drag on for days, weeks—especially if Lemonille played hard to get.

"Mistah Till-mahn?" Lemonille buried her chin, afraid to speak now that she had drawn attention to herself. More woe, thought Tillman. More hue and cry.

"What's wrong?"

"De cook say she 'fraid wit' you dead muddah in de freezah. She say she not cookin' wit' a duppy so close by."

"All right, I'll go talk to her."

"She gone home."

"All right, I'll take care of it." He began to walk away.

"Mistah Till-mahn?" The big woman's soft and guarded voice made him stop and turn around.

"What, Lemonille?"

"De men come wit' de meat, but dey won't stock it."

Tillman inhaled nervously. "My mother again, right?"

Lemonille nodded. "Damn!" Tillman said and scuffed the dirt in frustration.

Lemonille had one last piece of news. "Jevanee in a fuss 'cause you fire him."

"I didn't fire him. I told him to take the day off."

"Oh."

"Cuffy was there. He heard me." Cuffy looked into the trees and would not support or deny this allegation.

"Oh. But Jevanee tellin' every bug in de sky you fire him. Daht mahn be fulla dread you goin' put him out since de day you poppy die."

"Well, it's not true. Tell him that when you see him."

Tillman took these developments in stride, closing the restaurant for the evening by posting a scrawled note of apology at the entrance to the modest dining hall in the manor. For an hour, he shuffled the cartons of dripping steaks from the kitchen to the freezer, stacking them around the corpse of his mother as if these walls of spoiling meat were meant to be her tomb.

Event upon event—any day in the islands could keep accumulating such events until it was overrich, festering or glorious, never to be reproduced so wonderfully. This day was really no different except that his mother had triggered some extraordinary complications that were taking him to the limit.

After showering in cold water, Tillman climbed the stairs in the main house to the sanctitude of his office, his heart feeling too dry for blood to run through it, another fire hazard. What's to be done with Mother? On a hot plate, he heated water for tea, sat with the steaming mug before the phone on his desk. Ministry offices would be closed at this hour and besides, the minister of health was no friend of his, so there was no use ringing him up.

Finally, he decided to call Dr. Layland. If Layland still were running the island's medical services, the day would have been much simpler; but Layland, a surgeon who had earned international respect for his papers on brain dysfunction in the tropics, had lost his job and his license to practice last winter when he refused to allow politics to interfere with the removal of a bullet from an opposition member's neck. Although the case was before the federation, there was little hope of reinstatement before next year's elections.

"Frankly," Layland told him, his accent bearing the vestige of an Oxford education, "your position is most unenviable, my friend. A burial certificate, likewise permission to transfer the corpse back to its native soil, must be issued by both the national police and the chief medical officer. The police, pending their own investigation of the cause of death, will not act without clearance from the C.M.O. In cases where the cause is unclear, it is unlikely that the C.M.O. will agree to such clearance, especially for an expatriate Caucasian, until an autopsy is performed."

"But Bradley said it was the peaches, a bad can of peaches." Tillman jerked his head away from the telephone. How absurd and false those words sounded.

"Unlikely, but I see what you're getting at. Any cause is better than none, in light of your problem. But you know what sort of humbug that foolish man is. And you shan't have him on your side, since you refused to have him do the autopsy."

Layland further explained that there was no alternative to removing the corpse from the walk-in freezer unless he had another to put it in or unless he committed it to the island's only morgue, in the basement of the prison at Fort Albert—again, Bradley's domain. The final solution would be to bury her at Rosehill, but even this could not be accomplished without official permits. The police would come to dig her up. Tillman asked if it were a mistake not to allow Bradley to cut open his mother.

"I'm afraid, Tillman, you must decide that for yourself," Layland answered. "But I think you must know that I am as disgusted by my erstwhile colleague as you are. Well, good luck."

Tillman pushed the phone away, rubbed his sore eyes, massaged the knots in his temples. He tilted back in his chair and almost went over backward, caught unaware by a flood of panic. Unclean paradise, he thought suddenly. What about Mother? Damn, she was dead and needed taking care of. Hard to believe. Lord, why did she come here, anyway? She probably knew she was dying and figured the only dignified place to accomplish the fact was under the roof of her only child. A mother's final strategy.

Outside on the grounds, one of the stray dogs that were always about began a rabid barking. Tillman listened more closely, the sounds of squawking audible between the gaps in the dog's racket. The protest grew louder, unmistakable. Tillman was down the stairs and out on the lawn in no time at all, running toward the aviary.

There was some light from the few bulbs strung gaily through the branches of frangipani that overhung the parking area, enough for Tillman to see what was going on, the wickedness being enacted in blue-satin shadows. In the gazebo, an angry silhouette swung a cutlass back and forth, lashing at the amorphous flutter of wings that seemed everywhere in the tall cage.

"Jevanee?" Tillman called, uncertain. The silhouette reeled violently, froze in its step and then burst through the door of the cage, yelling.

"Mahn, you cy-ahnt fire me, *I quit.*"

Tillman cringed at the vulgarity of such a dissembled *non sequitur.* All the bad television in the world, the stupid lyrics of false heroes, the latent rage of kung-fu and cowboy fantasies had entered into this man's head, and here was the result, some new breed of imperial slave and his feeble, fatuous uprising.

"I didn't fire you. I said take the day off, cool down."

"Cy-ahnt fire *me,* you bitch."

The parrots were dead. Hatred exploded through Tillman. He wanted to kill the bartender. Fuck it. He wanted to shoot him down. He sprinted back across the lawn, up on the veranda toward the main house for the gun kept locked in the supply closet behind the check-in desk. Jevanee charged after him. A guest, the woman recently arrived from Wilmington, stepped out in front of Tillman from her room that fronted the veranda. Tillman shoulder-blocked her back through the door. She sprawled on her ass and, for a second, Tillman saw on her face an expression that welcomed violence as if it were an exotic game she had paid for.

"Stay in your goddamn room and bolt the door."

Tillman felt the bad TV engulfing them, the harried scriptwriter unbalanced with drugs and spite. Jevanee's foot plunged through the rotten boards in the veranda and lodged there. An exodus of pestilence swarmed from the splintery hole into the dim light, palmetto bugs flying blindly up through an increasing cloud of smaller winged insects.

At the same time, stepping out from the darkness of a hedge of bougainvillaea that ran in bushy clumps along the veranda was Inspector Cuffy, pistol in hand. Tillman gawked at him. What was he doing around Rosehill so late? Lemonille had been encouraging him or the investigation had broadened to round-the-clock foolishness. Or, Tillman surmised, knowing it was true, Cuffy apparently knew Jevanee was going after him and had lurked on the premises until the pot boiled over. A shot whistled by Tillman's head. Jevanee had a gun, too. Tillman pitched back off the deck and flattened out in the shrubbery.

"Stop!" Cuffy shouted.

What the hell? thought Tillman. Where's Jevanee going, anyway? He was near enough to smell the heavily Scotched breath of the bartender, see his eyes, as dumb and frightened as the eyes of a wild horse. Another shot was fired off; then a flurry of them as the two men emptied their pistols at each other with no effect. Silence and awkwardness as Cuffy and Jevanee confronted each other, the action gone out of them, praying thanks for the lives they still owned. Tillman crawled away toward the main house. He couldn't care less how they finished the drama, whether they killed each other with their bare hands or retired to a rum-shop together, blaming Tillman for the sour fate of the island. There was no point in getting upset about it now, once the hate had subsided, outdone by the comics.

▪ ▪ ▪

He sat in the kitchen on the cutting table, facing the vaultlike aluminum door of the refrigerated walk-in where his mother lay, preserved in ice among more ordinary meats and perishables.

He wanted to talk to her, but even in death she seemed only another guest at the hotel, one with special requirements, nevertheless expecting courtesy and service, the proper distance kept safely between their lives. She had never kissed him on the lips, not once, but had only brushed his cheek when an occasion required some tangible sign of motherly devotion. He had never been closer to her heart than when they cried together when he was in high school and lost his first girl, less than a year before his parents divorced. She had entered his room late at night and tuned the radio loud to a big-band station and held him, the two of them together shivering on his bed. She had not written that she was coming to visit but had showed up unannounced with only hand luggage, a leather grip of novels, a variety of bathing suits, caftans and creams. Behind her she had left Paris, where the weather had begun its decline toward winter. Whatever else she had left behind in her life was as obscure and sovereign as a foreign language. He wanted to talk to her, but nothing translated.

The pilot found him there sometime in the middle of the night, Tillman forlorn, more tired than he could ever remember feeling. Roland looked worn out, too, as if he had been stuck in an engine for hours, his cutoff shorts and colorless T-shirt smudged with grease, his hiking boots unlaced; and yet, despite this general dishevelment, his self-confidence was as apparent as the gleam of his teeth. Tillman remembered him at the beach bar late one night, yelling into the face of a man dressed in a seersucker suit, "I get things done, damn you, not like *these* bloody fools," and the sweep of his arm had seemed to include the entire planet.

Tillman smiled mournfully back at him. "Roland, I need your help."

The pilot removed the mirrored sunglasses he wore at all times. "You've had a full day of it, I hear. What's on your mind, mate?"

▪ ▪ ▪

Like an unwieldy piece of lumber, his mother's frozen corpse banged to and fro in the short bed of the Land-Rover, her wrapped feet pointing up over the tail gate. With a little effort and jockeying, they fit her into the tubular chemical tank in the fuselage of the Stearman after Roland, Tillman standing by with a flashlight, unbolted two plates of sheet metal from the underbelly of the craft that concealed bay doors. "You can't smuggle bales of grass with only a nozzle and a funnel," Roland explained.

Tillman was worried that an unscheduled flight would foul up Roland's good grace with the authorities. "Man," Roland said, "I've got more connections than the friggin' P.M. And I mean of the U.K., not this bloody cow pie." He thought for a second and was less flamboyant. "I've been in trouble before, of course. Nobody, Tillman, can touch this boy from down under as long as I have me bird, you see. Let us now lift upward into the splendid atmosphere and its many bright stars."

The chemical tank smelled cloyingly of poison. With his head poked into it, Tillman gagged, maneuvering the rigid body of his mother, the limbs clunking dully against the shiny metal, until she was positioned. Roland geared the bay doors back into place. The sound of them clicking into their locks brought relief to Tillman. They tucked themselves into the tiny cockpit, Tillman behind the pilot's seat, his legs flat against the floor board, straddled as if he were riding a bobsled.

The airport shut down at dusk, the funding for runway lights never more than deadpan rhetoric during the height of the political season. Roland rested his sunglasses on the crown of his blond head as they taxied to the landward end of the strip, the mountains a cracked ridge behind them, the sea ahead down the length of pale concrete. Out there somewhere in the water, an incompatibly situated cay stuck up like a catcher's mitt for small planes whose pilots were down on their agility and nerve.

Roland switched off the lights on the instrumentation to cut all reflection in the cockpit. Transparent blackness, the gray run of concrete stretching into nearby infinity.

Roland shouted over the roar, "She's a dumpy old bird, but with no real cargo, we should have some spirited moments."

Even as Roland spoke, they were already jostling down the airstrip like an old hot rod on a rutted road, Tillman anticipating lift-off long before it actually happened. The slow climb against gravity seemed almost futile, the opaque hand of the cay suddenly materializing directly in front of them. Roland dropped a wing and slammed the rudder pedal. The Stearman veered sharply away from the hazard, then leveled off and continued mounting upward. Tillman could hear his mother thump in the fuselage.

"Bit of a thrill," Roland shouted. Tillman closed his eyes and endured the languid speed and the hard, grinding vibrations of the plane.

Roland put on his headset and talked to any ghost he could rouse. When Tillman opened his eyes again, the clouds out the windscreen had a tender pink sheen to their tops. The atmosphere tingled with blueness. The ocean was black below them, and Barbados, ten degrees off starboard, was blacker still, a solid puddle sprinkled with electricity. Along the horizon, the new day was a thin red thread unraveling westward. The beauty of it all made Tillman melancholy.

Roland floated the plane down to earth like a fat old goose that couldn't be hurried. The airport on Barbados was modern and received plenty of international traffic, so they found it awake and active at this hour. Taxiing to the small-plane tarmac, Tillman experienced a moment of claustrophobia, smelling only the acrid human sweat that cut through the mechanical fumes. He hadn't noticed it airborne, but on the ground it was unbearable.

They parked and had the Stearman serviced. In the wet, warm morning air, Tillman's spirits revived. Roland walked through customs, headed for the bar to wait for him to do his business. Two hours later, Tillman threw himself down in a chair next to the pilot and cradled his head on the sticky table, the surge of weariness through his back and neck almost making him pass out. He listened to Roland patiently suck his beer and commanded himself up to communicate the failure of the expedition.

"Bastards. They won't let me transfer her to a Stateside flight without the right paper."

"There was that chance," Roland admitted.

All along, Tillman had believed that Barbados was the answer, that people were reasonable there, that he had only to bring over the corpse of his mother, coffin her, place her on an Eastern flight to Miami connecting with Boston, have a funeral home intercept her, bury her next to her husband in the family plot on Beacon Hill. Send out death announcements to the few relatives scattered across the country, and then it would be over, back to normal. No mother, no obligations of blood. That was how she had lived, anyway.

"Just how well connected are you, Roland?"

"Barbados is a bit iffy. The people are too damn sophisticated." He left to make some phone calls but returned with his hands out, the luckless palms upturned.

"Tillman, what next?"

Tillman exhaled and fought the urge to laugh, knowing it would mount to a hysterical outpouring of wretchedness. "I just don't know. Back to the island, I guess. If you can see any other option, speak out. Please."

The pilot was unreadable behind the mirrors of his glasses. His young face had become loose and puffy since he had located Tillman at Rosehill. They settled their bar bill and left.

In the air again, the sound of the Stearman rattled Tillman so thoroughly that he felt as though the plane's engine were in his own skull. He tried to close his sleepless eyes against the killing brightness of the sun but could not stop the hypnotic flash that kept him staring below at the ocean. Halfway through the flight, Roland removed his headset and turned in his seat, letting the plane fly itself while he talked.

"Tillman," he shouted, "I didn't bolt the plates back on the fuselage."

Tillman nodded absently and made no reply.

Roland jabbed his finger, pointing at the floor. "That hand gear there by your foot opens the bay doors."

He resumed flying the plane, allowing Tillman his own thoughts. Tillman had none. He expected some inspiration or voice to break through his dizziness, but it didn't happen. After several more minutes, he tapped Roland on the shoulder.

Roland turned again, lifting his glasses so Tillman could see his full face, his strained but resolute eyes, Tillman understanding this gesture as a stripping of fear, tacit confirmation that they were two men capable of making such a decision without ruining themselves with ambiguity.

"OK, Roland, the hell with it. She never liked being in one place too long, anyway."

"Right you are, then," Roland said solemnly. "Any special spot?"

"No."

"Better this way," Roland yelled as he dropped the air speed and sank the Stearman to 1000 feet. "The thing that bothers me about burial, you see, is caseation. Your frigging body turns to cheese after a month in the dirt. How unspeakably nasty. I don't know if you've noticed, but I never eat cheese myself. Odd, isn't it?"

Tillman poked him on the shoulder again. "Knock it off."

"Sorry."

Tillman palmed the gear open. It was as easy as turning the faucet of a hose. When they felt her body dislodge and the tail bob inconsequentially, Roland banked the plane into a steep dive so they could view the interment. Tillman braced his hands against the windscreen and looked out, saw her cartwheel for a moment and then stabilize as the mauve-chenille shroud came apart like a party streamer, a sky diver's Mae West. The Stearman circled slowly around the invisible line of her descent through space.

"Too bad about your mother, mate," Roland called out finally. "My own, I don't remember much."

"I'm still young," Tillman confessed, surprising himself, the words blurting forth from his mouth unsolicited. Tears of gratitude slipped down his face from this unexpected report of the heart.

He looked down at the endless water, waves struggling and receding, the small carnation of foam marking his mother's entrance into the sea, saw her, through the medium of refraction, unwrapped from her shroud, naked and washed, crawling with pure, unlabored motion down the shafts of light and beyond their farthest reach, thawed into suppleness, small glass bubbles, the cold air of her last breath, expelled past her white lips, nuzzled by unnamed fish, a perfect swimmer, free of the air and the boundaries of the living, darkness passing through darkness, down, down, to kiss the silt of the ocean floor, to touch the bottom of the world with dead fingers.

They had watched her plummet with a sense of awe and wonderment, as boys do who have thrown an object from off a high bridge. The pilot regained altitude and they continued westward. The realization came into Tillman, a palpable weight in his chest. "I don't belong here," he said to himself, and immediately resisted the feeling, because that must have been the way she felt all her life.

Then, with the rich peaks of the island in sight, the heaviness dissipated. "It's beautiful here," he heard himself saying.

"What's that?" Roland shouted back.

"Beautiful," he repeated, and throughout Roland's clumsy landing, the jolt and thunder of the runway, "Mother, be at peace."

Bharati Mukherjee

The Middleman

April 1986

"The Middleman" was the title story for a collection that won the National Book Critics Circle Award for fiction for 1988. Bharati Mukherjee, born in Calcutta in 1940, married the Canadian writer Clark Blaise and immigrated first to Canada and then to the United States, where she currently teaches writing at Berkeley. Her fiction (*The Tiger's Daughter,* 1972; *Jasmine,* 1991) is often about the immigrant experience, feelings of strangeness and exile and not quite understanding the signals. Here she has used these feelings to power an entertaining adventure story, a nice departure for a literary writer.

Bharati Mukherjee

The Middleman

There are only two seasons in this country, the dusty and the wet. I already know the dusty and I'll get to know the wet. I've seen worse. I've seen Baghdad, Bombay, Queens—and now this moldering spread deep in Mayan country. Aztecs, Toltecs, mestizos, even some bashful whites with German accents. All that and a lot of Texans. I'll learn the ropes.

Forget the extradition order; I'm not a sinful man. I've listened to bad advice. I've placed my faith in dubious associates. My first American wife said, "In the dog eat dog, Alfred, you're a beagle." My name is Alfie Judah, of the once-illustrious Smyrna, Aleppo, Baghdad—and now Flushing, Queens—Judahs.

I intend to make it back.

This place is owned by one Clovis T. Ransome. He reached here from Waco with fifteen million dollars in petty cash hours ahead of a posse from the SEC. That doesn't buy much down here—a few thousand acres, residency papers and the right to swim with the sharks a few feet off the bottom. Me? I make a living from things that fall. The big fat belly of Clovis T. Ransome bobs above me like whale shit at high tide.

The president's name is Gutierrez. Like everyone else, he has enemies, right and left. He is on retainer from men like Ransome, from the *Contras,* maybe from the *Sandinistas* as well.

The woman's name is Maria. She came with the ranch or with the protection; no one knows.

President Gutierrez' country has definite possibilities. All day I sit by the lime-green swimming pool, sun-screened so I won't turn black, going through my routine of isometrics while Ransome's *Indios* hack away the virgin forests. Their hate is intoxicating. They hate gringos—from which my darkness exempts me—even more than Gutierrez. They hate in order to keep up their intensity. I hear a litany of Presidents' names, Hollywood names, Detroit names—Carter, *chop,* Reagan, *slash,* Buick, *thump*—bounce off the vines as machetes clear the jungle greenness. We spoke a form of Spanish in my Baghdad home. I understand more than I let on.

In this season, the air's so dry it could scratch your lungs. Bright-feathered birds screech, snakeskins glitter, as the jungle peels away. Iguanas the size of wallabies leap from behind macheted bushes. The pool is greener than the ocean waves, cloudy with chemicals that Ransome has trucked over the mountains. When toads fall in, the water blisters their skin. I've heard their cries.

Possibilities, oh, yes.

I must confess my weakness: women.

In the old Baghdad when I was young, we had the hots for blondes. We'd stroll up to the diplomatic enclaves just to look at women. Solly Nathan, cross-eyed Itzie, Naim and me. Pinkish flesh could turn our blood to boiling lust. British matrons with freckled calves, painted toenails through thin-strapped sandals, the onset of varicose veins, the brassiness of prewar bleach jobs—all of that could thrill us like cleavage. We were twelve and already visiting whores during those hot Levantine lunch hours when our French masters intoned the rules of food, rest and good digestion. We'd roll up our fried flat bread smeared with spicy potatoes, pool our change and bargain with the daughters of washerwomen while our lips and fingers still glistened with succulent grease. But the only girls cheap enough for boys our age with unspecified urgencies were swamp Arabs from Basra and black girls from Baluchistan, the broken toys discarded by our older brothers.

Thank God those European women couldn't see us. It was comforting at times just to be natives, invisible to our masters. *They* were worthy of our lust. Local girls were for amusement only, a dark place to spend some time, like a video arcade.

▪ ▪ ▪

"You chose a real bad time to come, Al," he says. He may have been born on the wrong side of Waco, but he's spent his adult life in tropical paradises, playing God. "The rains'll be here soon, a day or two at most." He makes a whooping noise and drinks Jack Daniel's from a flask.

"My options were limited." A modest provident fund I'd been maintaining for New Jersey judges had been discovered. My fresh new citizenship is always in jeopardy. My dealings can't stand too much investigation.

"Bud and I can keep you from getting bored."

Bud Wilkins should be over in his pickup any time now. Meanwhile, Ransome rubs Cutter over his face and neck. They're supposed to go deep-sea fishing today, though it looks to me as if he's dressed for the jungle. A wetted-down hand towel is tucked firmly under the back of his baseball cap. He's a Braves man. Bud ships him cassettes of all the Braves' games. There are aspects of American life I came too late for and will never understand. It isn't love of the game, he told me last week. It's love of Ted Turner.

His teams. His stations. His America's Cup, his yachts, his network.

If he could be a clone of anyone in the world, he'd choose Turner. Then he leaned close and told me his wife, Maria—once the mistress of Gutierrez himself, as if I could miss her charms or underestimate their price in a seller's market—told him she'd put out all night if he looked like Ted Turner. "Christ, Al, here I've got this setup and I gotta beg her for it!" There *are* things I can relate to, and a man in such agony is one of them. That was last week, and he was drunk and I was new on the scene. Now he snorts more J.D. and lets out a whoop.

"Wanna come fishing? Won't cost you extra, Al."

"Thanks, no," I say. "Too hot."

The only thing I like about Clovis Ransome is that he doesn't snicker when I, an Arab to some, and Indian to others, complain of the heat. Even dry heat I despise.

"Suit yourself," he says.

Why do I suspect he wants me along as a witness? I don't want any part of their schemes. Bud Wilkins got here first. He's entrenched, doing little things for many people, building up a fleet of trucks, of planes, of buses. Like Ari Onassis, he started small. That's the legitimate side. The rest of it is no secret. A man with cash and private planes can clear a fortune in Latin America. The story is, Bud was exposed as a CIA agent, forced into public life and made to go semipublic with his arms deals and transfer fees.

"I don't mind you staying back, you know. It's Bud she wants to poke."

Maria. I didn't notice Maria for the first few days of my visit. She was *here,* but in the background. And she was dark, native, and I have my prejudices. But how shall I say—is there deeper pleasure, a darker thrill than prejudice squarely faced, suppressed, fought against and then slowly, secretively surrendered to?

Now I think a single word: adultery.

On cue, Maria floats toward us out of the green shadows. She's been swimming in the ocean; her hair is wet; her big-boned, dark-skinned body is streaked with sand. The talk is, Maria was an aristocrat, a near–Miss World whom Ransome partially bought and partially seduced away from Gutierrez, so he's never sure if the president owes him one or wants to kill him. With her dark hair and smooth, dark skin, she has to be mostly Indian. In her bikini, she arouses new passion. Who wants pale, thin, pink flesh, limp, curly blonde hair, when you can have lustrous browns, purple-blacks?

Adultery and dark-eyed young women are forever entwined in my memory. It is a memory, even now, that fills me with chills and terror and terrible, terrible desire. When I was a child, one of our servants took me to his village. He wanted me to see something special from the old Iraqi culture. Otherwise, he feared, my lenient Jewish upbringing would later betray me. A young woman, possibly adulterous but certainly bold and brave and beautiful enough to excite rumors of promiscuity, was that day stoned to death. What I remember now is the breathlessness of waiting as the husband circled her, as she struggled against the rope, as the stake barely swayed to her writhing. I remember the dull *thwock* and the servant's strong fingers shaking my shoulders as the first stone struck.

I realize I am one of the very few Americans who know the sound of rocks cutting through flesh and striking bone. One of the few to count the costs of adultery.

Maria drops her beach towel onto the patio floor, close to my deck chair, and straightens the towel's edge with her toes. She has to have been a dancer before becoming Ransome's bride and before Gutierrez plucked her out of convent school to become his mistress. Only ballerinas have such blunted, misshapen toes. But she knows. To the right eyes, even her toes are desirable.

"I want to hear about New York, Alfred." She lets herself fall like a dancer onto the bright-red towel. Her husband is helping Eduardo, the houseboy, load the jeep with the day's gear, and it's him she seems to be talking to. "My husband won't let me visit the States. He absolutely won't."

"She's putting you on, Al," Ransome shouts. He's just carried a case of beer out to the jeep. "She prefers St.-Moritz."

"You ski?"

I can feel the heat rising from her, or from the towel. I can imagine as the water beads on her shoulders how cool her flesh will be for just a few more minutes.

"Do I look as though I ski?"

I don't want to get involved in domestic squabbles. The *Indios* watch us. A solemn teenager hefts his machete. We are to have an uncomplicated view of the ocean from the citadel of this patio.

"My husband is referring to the fact that I met John Travolta in St.-Moritz," she says defiantly.

"Sweets," says Ransome. The way he says it, it's a threat.

"He has a body of one long muscle, like an eel," she says.

Ransome is closer now. "Make sure Eduardo doesn't forget the crates," he says.

"OK, OK," she shouts back. "Excuse me." I watch her corkscrew to her feet. I'm so close I can hear her ligaments pop.

▪ ▪ ▪

Soon after, Bud Wilkins roars into the cleared patch that serves as the main parking lot. He backs his pickup so hard against a shade tree that a bird wheels up from its perch. Bud lines it up with an imaginary pistol and curls his fingers twice in its direction. I'm not saying he has no feeling for wildlife. He's in boots and camouflage pants, but his hair—what there is of it—is blow-dried.

He stalks my chair. "We could use you, buddy." He uncaps a beer bottle with his teeth. "You've seen some hot spots."

"He doesn't want to fish." Ransome is drinking beer, too. "We wouldn't want to leave Maria unprotected." He waits for a retort, but Bud's too much the gentleman. Ransome stares at me and winks, but he's angry. It could get ugly, wherever they're going.

They drink more beer. Finally, Eduardo comes out with the crate. He carries it bowlegged, in mincing little half-running steps. The fishing tackle, of course. The crate is dumped into Bud's pickup. He comes out with a second and a third, equally heavy, and drops them all into Bud's truck. I can guess what I'm watching. Low-grade arms transfer, rifles, ammo and maybe medicine.

"Ciao, amigo," says Bud in his heavy-duty Texan accent.

He and Ransome roar into the jungle in Ransome's jeep.

▪ ▪ ▪

"I hope you're not too hungry, Alfie." It's Maria calling from the kitchen. Alfred to Alfie before the jeep can have made it off the property.

"I'm not a big eater." What I mean to say is, I'm adaptable. What I'm hoping is, let us not waste time with food.

"Eduardo!" The houseboy, probably herniated by now, goes to her for instructions. "We just want a salad and fruit. But make it fast. I have to run into San Vincente today." That's the nearest market town. I've been there; it's not much.

She stands at the front door, about to join me on the patio, when Eduardo rushes past, broom in hand. *"¡Vaya!"* he screams.

But she is calm. "It must be behind the stove, stupid," she tells the servant. "It can't have made it out this far without us seeing it."

Eduardo wields his broom like a night stick and retreats into the kitchen. We follow. I can't see it. I can only hear desperate clawing and scraping on the tiles behind the stove.

Maria stomps the floor to scare it out. The houseboy shoves the broom handle into the dark space. I think first, being a child of the overheated deserts, giant scorpions. But there are two fugitives, not one—a pair of ocean crabs. The crabs, their shiny purple backs dotted with yellow, try to get by us to the beach, where they can hear the waves.

How do mating ocean crabs scuttle their way into Clovis T. Ransome's kitchen? I feel for them.

The broom comes down—thwack, thwack—and bashes the shells in loud, succulent cracks. *Ransome, gringo,* I hear.

He sticks his dagger into the burlap sacks of green chemicals. He rips, he cuts.

"Eduardo, it's all right. Everything's fine." She sounds stern, authoritative; the years in the presidential palace have served her well. She moves toward him, stops just short of taking his arm.

He spits out, "He kills everything." At least, that's the drift. The language of

Cervantes does not stretch around the world without a few skips in transmission. Eduardo's litany includes crabs, the chemicals, the sulphurous pool, the dead birds and snakes and lizards.

"You have my promise," Maria says. "It's going to work out. Now I want you to go to your room; I want you to rest."

We hustle him into his room, but he doesn't seem to notice his surroundings. His body has gone slack. I hear the name Santa Simona, a new saint for me. I maneuver him to the cot and keep him pinned down while Maria checks out a rusty medicine cabinet.

He looks up at me. "You drive *Doña* Maria where she goes?"

"If she wants me to, sure."

"Eduardo, go to sleep. I'm giving you something to help." She has water and a blue pill ready.

While she hovers over him, I check out his room. It's automatic with me. There are crates under the bed. There's a table covered with oilcloth. The oilcoth is cracked and grimy. A chair by the table is a catchall for clothes, shorts, even a bowl of fruits. Guavas. Eduardo could have snuck in caviar, imported cheeses, Godiva candies, but it's guavas he's chosen to stash for siesta-hour hunger pains. The walls are hung with icons of saints. Posters of stars I'd never have heard of if I hadn't been forced to drop out. Baby-faced men and women. The women are sensuous in an old-fashioned, Latin way, with curvy lips, big breasts and tiny waists. Like Maria. Quite a few are unconvincing blondes, in that brassy Latin way. The men have greater range. Some are young versions of Fernando Lamas; some are in fatigues and boots, striking Robin Hood poses. The handsomest is dressed as a guerrilla, with all the right accessories: beret, black boots, bandoleer. Maybe he'd played Ché Guevara in some B-budget Argentine melodrama.

"What's in the crates?" I ask Maria.

"I respect people's privacy," she says. "Even a servant's." She pushes me roughly toward the door. "So should you."

▪ ▪ ▪

The daylight seems too bright on the patio. The bashed shells are on the tiles. Ants have already discovered the flattened meat of ocean crabs, the blistered bodies of clumsy toads.

Maria tells me to set the table. Every day, we use a lace cloth, heavy silverware, roses in a vase. And every day, we drink champagne. Some mornings, the Ransomes start on the champagne with breakfast. Bud owns an air-taxi service and flies in cases of Épernay, caviar, any damned thing his friends desire.

She comes out with a tray. Two plates, two fluted glasses, *chèvre* cheese on a bit of glossy banana leaf, water biscuits. "I'm afraid this will have to do. Anyway, you said you weren't hungry."

I spread a biscuit and hand it to her.

"If you feel all right, I was hoping you'd drive me to San Vincente." She gestures toward Bud Wilkins' pickup truck. "I don't like to drive that thing."

"What if I don't want to?"

"You won't. Say no to me, I mean. I'm a terrific judge of character." She shrugs, and her breasts are slower than her shoulders in coming down.

"The keys are on the kitchen counter. Do you mind if I use your w.c. instead of going back upstairs? Don't worry, I don't have horrible communicable diseases." She laughs.

This may be intimacy. "How could I mind? It's your house."

"Alfie, don't pretend innocence. It's Ransome's house. This isn't *my* house."

I get the keys to Bud's pickup and wait for her by the bruised tree. I don't want to know the contents of the crates, though the stenciling says FRUITS and doubtless the top layer preserves the fiction. How easily I've been recruited, when a bystander is all I wanted to be. The Indians put down their machetes and make signs to me: *Hi, Mom, we're number one.* They must have been watching Ransome's tapes. They're all wearing Braves caps.

The road to San Vincente is rough. Deep ruts have been cut into the surface by army trucks. Whole convoys must have passed this way during the last rainy season. I don't want to know whose trucks; I don't want to know why.

Forty minutes into the trip, Maria says, "When you get to the T, take a left. I have to stop off near here to run an errand." It's a strange word for the middle of a jungle.

"Don't let it take you too long," I say. "We want to be back before hubby gets home." I'm feeling jaunty. She touches me when she talks.

"So Clovis scares you." Her hand finds its way to my shoulder.

"Shouldn't he?"

I make the left. I make it sharper than I intended. Bud Wilkins' pickup sputters up a dusty rise. A pond appears and around it shacks with vegetable gardens.

"Where are we?"

"In Santa Simona," Maria says. "I was born here, can you imagine?"

This isn't a village, it's a camp for guerrillas. I see some women here, and kids, roosters, dogs. What Santa Simona is is a rest stop for families on the run. I deny simple parallels. Ransome's ranch is just a ranch.

"You could park by the pond."

I step on the brake and glide to the rutted edge of the pond. Whole convoys must have parked here during the rainy season. The ruts hint at secrets. Now, in the dry season, what might be a lake has shrunk to a muddy pit. Ducks float on green scum.

Young men in khaki begin to close in on Bud's truck.

Maria motions to me to get out. "I bet you could use a drink." We make our way up to the shacks. The way her bottom bounces inside those cutoffs could drive a man crazy. I don't turn back, but I can hear the unloading of the truck.

So: Bud Wilkins' little shipment has been hijacked, and I'm the culprit. Some job for a middle man.

"*This* is my house, Alfie."

I should be upset. Maria has turned me into a chauffeur. You bet I could use a drink.

We pass by the first shack. There's a garage in the back where there would be the usual large cement laundry tub. Three men come at me, twirling tire irons the way night sticks are fondled by Manhattan cops. "I'm with her."

Maria laughs at me. "It's not you they want."

And I wonder, *Who* was she supposed to deliver? Bud, perhaps, if Clovis hadn't taken him out? Or Clovis himself?

We pass the second shack, and a third. Then a tall guerrilla in full battle dress floats out of nowhere and blocks our path. Maria shrieks and throws herself on him and he holds her face in his hands, and in no time they're swaying and moaning like connubial visitors at a prison farm. She has her back to me. His big hands cup and squeeze her halter top. I've seen him somewhere. Eduardo's poster.

"Hey," I try. When that doesn't work, I start to cough.

"Sorry." Maria swings around, still in his arms. "This is Al Judah. He's staying at the ranch."

The soldier is called Andreas something. He looks me over. "Yudah?" he asks Maria, frowning.

She shrugs. "You want to make something of it?"

He says something rapidly, locally, that I can't make out. She translates, "He says you need a drink," which I don't believe.

We go inside the command shack. It's a one-room affair, very clean, but dark and cluttered. I'm not sure I should sit on the narrow cot; it seems to be a catchall for the domestic details of revolution—sleeping bags, maps and charts, an empty canteen, two pairs of secondhand army boots. I need a comfortable place to deal with my traumas. There is a sofa of sorts, actually a car seat pushed tight against a wall and stabilized with bits of lumber. There are bullet holes through the fabric, and rusty stains that can only be blood. I reject the sofa. There are no tables, no chairs, no posters, no wall decorations of any kind, unless you count a crucifix. Above the cot, a sad, dark, plaster crucified Jesus recalls his time in the desert.

"Beer?" Maria doesn't wait for an answer. She walks behind a curtain and hefts a six-pack of Heineken from a noisy refrigerator. I believe I am being offered one of Bud Wilkins' unwitting contributions to the guerrilla effort. I should know it's best not to ask how Dutch beer and refrigerators and 1957 two-tone Plymouths with fins and chrome make their way to nowhere jungle clearings. Because of guys like me, in better times, that's how. There's just demand and supply running the universe.

"Take your time, Alfie." Maria is beaming so hard, it's unreal. "We'll be back soon. You'll be cool and rested in here."

Andreas manages a contemptuous wave; then, holding hands, he and Maria vault over the railing of the back porch and disappear.

She's given me beer, plenty of beer, but no church key. I look around the room. Ransome or Bud would have used his teeth. From his perch, Jesus stares at me out of huge, sad Levantine eyes. In this alien jungle, we're fellow Arabs. You should see what's happened to the old stomping grounds, *compadre*.

I test my teeth against a moist, corrugated bottle cap. It's no good. I whack the bottle cap with the heel of my hand against the metal edge of the cot. It foams and hisses. The second time, it opens. New World skill. Somewhere in the back of the shack, a parakeet begins to squawk. It's a sad, ugly sound. I go out to the back porch to give myself something to do, to maybe snoop. By the communal laundry tub, there's a cage, and inside the cage, a mean, molting bird. A kid of ten or twelve teases the bird with bits of lettuce. Its beak snaps open for the greens and scrapes the rusty sides of the bar. The kid looks defective, dull-eyed, thin but flabby.

"Gringo," he calls out to me. "Gringo, gum."

I check my pockets. No Dentyne, no Tums, just the plastic cover for spent traveler's checks. My life has changed. I don't have to worry about bad breath or gas pains turning off clients.

"Gringo, Chiclets."

The voice is husky.

I turn my palms outward. "Sorry, you're out of luck."

The kid leaps on me with moronic fury. I want to throw him down, toss him into the scummy vat of soaking clothes, but he's probably some sort of sacred mascot. "How about this pen?" It's a forty-nine-cent disposable, the perfect thing for poking a bird. I go back inside.

I am sitting in the H.Q. of the guerrilla insurgency, drinking a Heineken, nursing my indignation. A one-armed man opens the door. "Maria?" he calls. "*Prego*." Which translates, indirectly, as "The truck is unloaded and the guns are ready and should I kill this guy?" I direct him to find Andreas.

She wakes me, maybe an hour later. I sleep as I rarely have, arm across my eyes, like a Bedouin, on top of the mounds of boots and gear. She has worked her fingers around my buttons, pulls my hair, my nipples. I can't tell the degree of mockery, what spill-over of passion she may still be feeling. Andreas and the idiot boy stand framed in the bleaching light of the door, the boy's huge head pushing the bandoleer askew. Father and son, it suddenly dawns. Andreas holds the bird cage.

"They've finished," she explains. "Let's go."

Andreas lets us pass, smirking, I think, and follows us down the rutted trail to Bud's truck. He puts the bird cage in the driver's seat and, in case I miss it, points at the bird, then at me, and laughs. Very funny, I think. His boy finds it hilarious. I will *not* be mocked like this. The bird is so ill fed, so cramped and tortured and clumsy, it flutters wildly, losing more feathers merely to keep its perch.

"*Viva la revolución,* eh? A leetle gift for helping the people."

No, I think, a leetle sign to Clovis Ransome and all the pretenders to Maria's bed that we're just a bunch of scrawny blackbirds and he doesn't care who knows it. I have no feeling for revolution, only for outfitting the participants.

"Why?" I beg on the way back. The road is dark. "You hate your husband, so get a divorce. Why blow up the country?"

Maria smiles. "Clovis has nothing to do with this." She shifts her sandals on the bird cage. The bird is dizzy, flat on its back. Some of them die, just like that.

"Run off with Andreas, then."

"We were going to be married," she says. "Then Gutierrez came to my school and took me away. I was fourteen and he was minister of education. Then Clovis took me away from him. Maybe you should take me away from Clovis. I like you, and you'd like it, too, wouldn't you?"

"Don't be crazy. Try Bud Wilkins."

"Bud! Wilkins is, you say, dog meat." She smiles.

"Oh, sure," I say.

I concentrate on the road. I'm no hero; I calculate margins. I could not calculate the cost of a night with Maria, a month with Maria, though for the first time in my life, it was a cost I might have borne.

Her voice is matter-of-fact. "Clovis wanted a cut of Bud's action. But Bud refused, and that got Clovis mad. Clovis even offered money, but Bud said, 'No way.' Clovis pushed me on him, so he took, but he still didn't budge. So . . ."

"You're serious, aren't you? Oh, God."

"Of course I am serious. Now Clovis can fly in his own champagne and baseball games."

She has unbuttoned more of the halter, and I feel pressure on my chest, in my mouth, against my slacks, that I have never felt.

▪ ▪ ▪

All the lights are on in the villa when I lurch Bud's pickup into the parking lot. We can see Clovis T. Ransome, very drunk, slack-postured, trying out wicker chairs on the porch. Maria is carrying the bird cage.

He's settled on the love seat. No preliminaries, no questions. He squints at the cage. "Buying presents for Maria already, Al?" He tries to laugh.

"What's that supposed to mean?" She swings the cage in giant arcs, like a bucket of water.

"Where's Bud?" I ask.

"They jumped him, old buddy. Gang of guerrillas not more 'n half a mile down the road. Pumped twenty bullets in him. These are fierce little people, Al. I don't know how I got away." He's watching us for effect.

I suspect it helps when they're in your pay, I thought, and you give them Ted Turner caps.

"Al, grab yourself a glass if you want some Scotch. Me, I'm stinking drunk already."

He's noticed Bud's truck now. The emptiness of Bud's truck.

"That's a crazy thing to do," Maria says. "I warned you." She sets the cage down on the patio table. "Bud's no good to anyone, dead or alive. You said it yourself, he's dog meat." She slips onto the love seat beside her husband. I watch her. I can't take my eyes off her. She snakes her strong, long torso until her lips touch the cage's rusted metal. "Kiss me," she coos. "Kiss me, kiss, kiss, sweetheart."

Ransome's eyes are on her, too. "Sweets, who gave you that filthy crow?"

Maria says, "Kiss me, lover boy."

"Sweetie, I asked you who gave you that filthy crow."

I back off to the kitchen. I could use a shot of Scotch. I can feel the damp, Bombay grittiness of the air. The rains will be here, maybe tonight.

When I get back, Ransome is snoring on the love seat. Maria is standing over him, and the bird cage is on his lap. Its door is open and Clovis' fat hand is half inside. The bird pecks, it's raised blood, but Clovis is out for the night.

"Why is it," she asks, "that I don't feel pride when men kill for me?"

But she does, deep down. She wants to believe that Clovis, mad, jealous Clovis, has killed for her. I hate to think of Maria's pretty face when Clovis wakes up and remembers the munitions are gone. It's all a family plot in countries like this, revolutions fought for a schoolgirl in white with blunted toes. I, too, would kill for her.

"Kill it, Alfie, please," she says. "I can't stand it. See, Clovis tried, but his hand was too fat."

"I'll free it," I say.

"Don't be a fool—that boy broke its wings. Let it out and the crabs will kill it."

Around eleven that night, I have to carry Ransome up the stairs to the spare bedroom. He's a heavy man. I don't bother with the niceties of getting him out of his blue jeans and into his pajamas. The secrets of Clovis T. Ransome, whatever they are, are safe with me. I abandon him on top of the bedspread in his dusty cowboy boots. Maria shan't want him tonight. She's already told me so.

But she isn't waiting for me on the patio. Maybe that's just as well. Tonight, love will be hard to handle. The dirty glasses, the booze and soda bottles, the Styrofoam-lidded bowl we used for ice cubes are still on the wicker-and-glass coffee table. Eduardo doesn't seem to be around. I take the glasses into the kitchen. He must have disappeared hours ago. I've never seen the kitchen in this bad a mess. He's not in the villa. His door has swung open, but I can't hear the noises of sleeping servants in the tropics. So, Eduardo has vanished. I accept this as data. I dare not shout for Maria. If it's ever to be, it must be tonight. Tomorrow, I can tell, this cozy little hacienda will come to grief.

Someone should go from room to room and turn out the lights. But not me. I make it fast back to my room.

"You must shut doors quickly behind you in the tropics or bugs get in."

Casually, she is unbuttoning her top, untying the bottom flaps. The cutoffs have to be tugged off, around her hips. There is a rush of passion I have never known, and my fingers tremble as I tug at my belt. She is in my giant bed, propped up, and her breasts keep the sheet from falling.

"Alfie, close the door."

Her long thighs press and squeeze. She tries to hold me, to contain me, and it is a moment I would die to prolong. In a frenzy, I conjugate crabs with toads and the squawking bird, and I hear the low moans of turtles on the beach. It is a moment I fear too much, a woman I fear too much, and I yield. I begin again, immediately, this time concentrating on blankness, on burned out objects whirling in space, and she pushes against me, murmuring, "No," and pulls away.

Later, she says, "You don't understand hate, Alfie. You don't understand what hate can do." She tells stories; I moan to mount her again. "No," she says, and the stories pour out. Not just the beatings; the humiliations. Lending her out, dangling her on a leash, like a cheetah, then the beatings for what he suspects. It's the power game, I try to tell her. That's how power is played.

▪ ▪ ▪

Sometime around three, I wake to a scooter's thin roar. She has not been asleep. The rainy season must have started an hour or two before. It's like steam out there. I kneel on the pillows to look out the small bedroom windows. The parking lot is a mud slide. Uprooted shrubs, snakes, crabs, turtles are washed down to the shore.

Maria, object of my wildest ecstasy, lies inches from me. She doesn't ask what I see. The scooter's lights weave in the rain.

"Andreas," she says. "It's working out."

But it isn't Andreas who forces the door to my room. It is a tall, thin Indian with a calamitous face. The scooter's engine has been shut off and rain slaps the patio in waves.

"Americano." The Indian spits out the word. "Gringo."

Maria calmly ties her halter flaps, slowly buttons up. She says something rapidly and the Indian steps outside while she finds her cutoffs.

"Quickly," she says, and I reach for my pants. It's already cold.

When the Indian returns, I hear her say, "Jew" and "Israel." He seems to lose interest. *"Americano?"* he asks again. "Gringo?"

Two more Indians invade my room. Maria runs out to the hall and I follow to the stairs. I point upward and try out my Spanish. "Gringo is sleeping, drunk."

The revolution has convened outside Clovis' bedroom. Eduardo is there, Andreas, more Indians in Ted Turner caps, the one-armed man from Santa Simona. Andreas opens the door.

"Gringo," he calls softly. "Wake up."

I am surprised, truly astonished, at the recuperative powers of Clovis T. Ransome. Not only does he wake but he sits, boots on the floor, ignoring the intrusion. His Spanish, the first time I've heard him use it, is excellent, even respectful.

"I believe, sir, you have me at an advantage," he says. He scans the intruders, his eyes settling on me. "Button your fly, man," he says to me. He stares at Maria, up and down, his jaw working. He says, "Well, sweets? What now?"

Andreas holds a pistol against his thigh.

"Take her," Ransome says. "You want her? You got her. You want money, you got that, too. Dollars, marks, Swiss francs. Just take her, and him"—he says, pointing to me—"out of here."

"I will take your dollars, of course."

"Eduardo—" Ransome jerks his head in the direction, perhaps, of a safe. The servant seems to know where it is.

"And I will take her, of course."

"Good riddance."

"But not him. He can rot."

Eduardo and three Indians lug out a metal trunk. They throw away the pillows and start stuffing pillowcases with bundles of dollars, more pure currency than I've ever seen. They stuff the rest inside their shirts. What it must feel like, I wonder.

"Well, *Señor* Andreas, you've got the money and the woman. Now what's it to be—a little torture? A little fun with me before the sun comes up? Or what about him—I bet you'd have more fun with him. I don't scream, *Señor* Andreas, I warn you. You can kill me, but you can't break me."

I hear the safety clicking off. So does Clovis.

I know I would scream. I know I am no hero. I know none of this is worth suffering for, let alone dying for.

Andreas looks at Maria as if to say, "You decide." She holds out her hand and Andreas slips the pistol into it. This seems to amuse Clovis Ransome. He stands, presenting an enormous target. "Sweetie—" he starts, and she blasts away, and when I open my eyes, he is across the bed, sprawled in the far corner of the room.

She stands at the foot of their bed, limp and amused, like a woman disappointed in love. Smoke rises from the gun barrel, her breath condenses in little clouds and there is a halo of condensation around her hair, her neck, her arms.

When she turns, I feel it could be any of us next. Andreas holds out his hand, but she doesn't return the gun. She lines me up, low, genital level, like Bud Wilkins with a bird, then sweeps around to Andreas and smiles.

She has made love to me three times tonight. With Andreas today, doubtless more. Never has a truth been burned so deeply in me, what I owe my life to, how simple the rules of survival are. She passes the gun to Andreas, who holsters it, and they leave.

In the next few days, when I run out of food, I will walk down the muddy road to San Vincente, to the German bar with the pay phone. I'll wear Clovis' Braves cap and I'll salute the Indians. "Hi, Mom," I'll say.

"Number one," they'll answer. Bud's truck has been commandeered, along with Clovis' finer cars. Someone in the capital will be happy to know about Santa Simona, about Bud, Clovis. There must be something worth trading in the troubles I have seen.

Joseph Heller

Yossarian Survives

December 1987

According to Joseph Heller, "Yossarian Survives" is a "lost" chapter of *Catch-22* (1961), the brilliantly comic World War II novel that not only made him famous but also put an indelible new phrase for an impossible situation into the vocabulary. New York writer Heller, born in 1923, flew more than fifty combat missions during the war, and, while writing his first novel, he worked in an advertising agency, which provided the setting for his second, *Something Happened* (1974). He now lives in East Hampton, Long Island. Other novels include *Good as Gold* (1979), *God Knows* (1984), and *Picture This* (1988). Excerpts from several of the novels have appeared in *Playboy*.

Joseph Heller

Yossarian Survives

If my memory is correct, no episodes or characters were deleted when the first typed manuscript of Catch-22 *was reduced in the editing from about eight hundred pages to six hundred. My memory is not correct. Shortly after the novel was published in late 1961, a friend who had read the original deplored the omission of a series of letters from Nately to his father. Subsequently, those eight or ten pages were published in* Playboy *under the title* Love, Dad *(December 1969).*

I should state that all of the cutting had been for the sole purpose of obtaining more coherence and effectiveness for the total work.

More recently, on the twenty-fifth anniversary of the publication of the novel, two officers at the U.S. Air Force Academy doing research on the work wanted to know why I had removed an entire small chapter dealing with a physical-education instructor and with the application of calisthenics and other exercises as preparations for combat and survival.

My reactions of surprise were contradictory: I had forgotten I had written it; I was positive I had left it in. "Do you mean it's not there?" I exclaimed. "That line 'Don't just lie there while you're waiting for the ambulance. Do push-ups'?"

They assured me that the entire chapter had been excluded, that they felt it was good, still timely, and that it ought to be published.

Checking on my own, I find them correct on all points. That chapter is not in the novel; I think it ought to be published.

Here it is.

—Joseph Heller

Actually, Yossarian owed his good health to clean living—to plenty of fresh air, exercise, teamwork and good sportsmanship. It was to get away from all of them that he had gone on sick call the first time and had discovered the hospital.

At Lowry Field, where he had gone through armament school before applying for cadet training, the enlisted men were conditioned for survival in combat by a program of calisthenics that was administered six days a week by Rogoff, a conscientious physical-education instructor. Rogoff was a staff sergeant in his mid-thirties. He was a spare, wiry, obsequious man with flat bones and a face like tomato juice who was devoted to his work and always seemed to arrive several minutes late to perform it.

In reality, he always arrived several minutes early and concealed himself in some convenient hiding place nearby until everyone else had arrived, so that he could come bounding up in a hurry, as though he were a very busy man, and launch right into his exercises without any awkward preliminaries. Rogoff found conversation difficult. He would conceal himself behind a motor vehicle if one were parked in the vicinity or hide near the window in the boiler room of one of the barracks buildings or underneath the landing of the entrance to the orderly room. One afternoon, he jumped down into one of ex-Pfc. Wintergreen's holes to hide and was cracked right across the side of the head with a shovel by ex-Pfc. Wintergreen, who poured a stream of scalding abuse after him as he stumbled away in apologetic humiliation toward the men waiting for him to arrive and put them through his exercises.

Rogoff conducted his exercises from a high wooden platform between two privates on the ground he called his sergeants, who shared the same unquestioning faith in the efficacy of exercise and assisted him by performing each calisthenic up front after he himself had stopped to rest his voice, which was reedy and unpredictable to begin with. Rogoff abhorred idleness. Whenever he had nothing better to do on his platform, he strode about resolutely, clapped his hands in spasmodic outbursts of zeal and said, "Hubba, hubba." Each time he said "Hubba, hubba" to the columns of men in green fatigues on the ground before him, they would say "Hubba, hubba, hubba, hubba" right back to him and begin scuffing their feet and shaking their elbows against their sides until Rogoff made them stop by unctuously raising his hand high in an approving kind of benediction and saying, as though deeply moved, "That's the way, men. That's the way."

Hubba, hubba, he had explained, was the noise made by an eager beaver, and then he had laughed, as though at an extraordinary witticism.

Rogoff conducted them through a wide variety of obscene physical experiences. There were bending, stretching and jumping exercises, all executed in unison to a masculine, musical cadence of "One, two, three, four, one, two, three, four." The men assumed a prone position and did push-ups or assumed a supine position and did sit-ups. The men learned a lot from calisthenics. They learned the difference between prone and supine.

Rogoff named, then demonstrated, each exercise he wanted done and exercised right along with them until he had counted one, two, three, four five times, as loudly as he could, at the top of his frail voice. The two privates he had promoted to be his sergeants continued doing the same exercise after he had stopped to rest his voice and was pacing spryly about on the platform or clapping his hands with spirit.

Occasionally, he would jump down to the ground without any warning, as though the platform were on fire, and dart inside one of the two-story barracks buildings behind him to make certain that no one who was supposed to be outside doing calisthenics was inside not doing them. The men on the athletic field would still be bending, stretching or jumping when he darted back out. To bring them to a halt, he would begin bending, stretching or jumping right along with them, counting one, two, three, four twice, his voice soaring upward almost perpendicularly into another octave the first time and squeezing out the second set of numbers in an agonized, shredded falsetto that made the veins and tendons bulge out gruesomely on his neck and forehead and brought an even greater flood of color to his flat red face. Every time Rogoff brought an exercise to an end, he would say "Hubba, hubba" to them, and they would say "Hubba, hubba, hubba, hubba" right back, like the bunch of eager beavers he hoped from the bottom of his heart they would all turn out to be.

When the men were not bending, stretching, jumping or pushing up, they were taught tap dancing, because tap dancing would endow them with the rhythm and coordination necessary to do the bending, stretching, jumping and push-ups that would develop the rhythm and coordination necessary to be proficient at judo and survive in combat.

Rogoff emoted the same ardor for judo as he did for calisthenics and spent about ten minutes of each session rehearsing them in the fundamentals in slow motion. Judo was the best natural weapon an unarmed fighting man had for coping with one or more enemy soldiers in a desert or jungle, provided he was unarmed. If he had a loaded carbine or submachine gun, he would be at a distinct disadvantage, since he would have to shoot it out with them. But if he was lucky enough to be trapped by them without a gun, then he would be able to use judo.

"Judo is the best natural weapon a fighting man has," Rogoff would remind them each day from his pinnacle in his high and constricted voice, spilling the words out with haste and embarrassment, as though he could not wait to be rid of them.

The men faced one another in rows and went through the movements slowly, without making contact, since judo was so destructive a natural weapon that it could not even be practiced long enough to be learned without annihilating its students. Judo was the best natural weapon a fighting man had until the day the popular boxing champ showed up as a guest calisthenics instructor to improve their morale and introduced them to the left jab.

"The left jab," said the champ without any hesitation from Rogoff's platform, "is the best natural defensive weapon a fighting man has. And since the best defensive weapon is an offensive weapon, the left jab is also the best natural offensive weapon a fighting man has."

Rogoff's face went white as a sheet.

The champ had the men face one another in rows and counted cadence while they learned and practiced the left jab in slow motion to a dignified four-beat rhythm, without making contact.

"One, two, three, four," he counted. "One, two, jab, four. Now the other column. Remember, no contact with the left jab. Ready? Jab, two, three, four, jab, two, jab, four, one, jab, three, jab, jab, two, three, jab. That's the way. Now we'll rest a few seconds and practice it some more. You can't practice the left jab too much."

The champ had been escorted to the athletic field in his commissioned-officer's uniform by an adulating retinue of colonels and generals, who stared up at him raptly from the ground in lambent idolatry. Rogoff had been bumped aside off his platform and was completely forgotten. Even the honor of introducing the champ to the men had been denied him. An embarrassed little smile tortured his lips as he stood off by himself on the ground, ignored by everyone, including the two privates he had made his sergeants. It was one of these sergeants who asked the champ what he thought of judo.

"Judo is no good," the champ declared. "Judo is Japanese. The left jab is American. We're at war with Japan. You figure it out from there. Are there any more questions?"

There were none. It was time for the champ and his distinguished flotilla to go.

"Hubba, hubba," he said.

"Hubba, hubba, hubba, hubba," the men replied.

There was an awkward hush after the champ had gone and Rogoff had returned to his desecrated platform. Rogoff gulped in abasement, failing abysmally in his attempt to pass off with casual indifference the shattering loss of status he had just suffered.

"Men," he explained weakly in a choked and apologetic voice, "the champ is a great man and we've all got to keep in mind everything he told us. But he's been traveling around a lot in connection with the war effort, and maybe he hasn't been able to keep up to date on the latest methods of warfare. That's why he said those things he did about the left jab and about judo. For some people, I guess, the left jab is the best natural weapon a fighting man has. For others, judo is the best. We'll continue concentrating on judo here, because we have to concentrate on something and we can't concentrate on both. Once you get overseas to the jungle or desert and find yourselves attacked by one or more enemy soldiers when you're unarmed, I'll let you use the left jab if you want to instead of judo. The choice is optional. Is that fair? Now, I think we'll skip our judo session for today and go right to our game period instead. Will that be OK?"

As far as Yossarian was concerned, there was little in either the left jab or judo to justify optimism when confronted by one or more enemy soldiers in the jungle or desert. He tried to conjure up visions of regiments of Allied soldiers jabbing, judoing and tap-dancing their way through the enemy lines into Tokyo and Berlin to a stately four-beat count, and the picture was not very convincing.

Yossarian had no need of Rogoff or the champ to tell him what to do if he ever found himself cornered without a gun by two or more enemy soldiers in a jungle or desert. He knew exactly what to do: throw himself on his knees and beg for mercy. Surrender was the best natural weapon he could think of for an unarmed soldier when confronted by one or more armed enemy soldiers. It wasn't much of a weapon, but it made more sense than left jabbing, tap dancing or judoing.

And he had even less confidence in calisthenics. The whole physical-exercise program was supposed to toughen him for survival and save lives, but it couldn't have been working very well, Yossarian concluded, because there were so many lives that were being lost.

In addition to exercising, tap dancing, judo and left jabs, they played games. They played games like baseball and basketball for about an hour every day.

Baseball was a game that was called the great American pastime and was played on a square infield that was called a diamond. Baseball was a very patriotic and moral game that was played with a bat, a ball, four bases and seventeen men and Yossarian, divided up into one team of nine players and one team of eight players and Yossarian. The object of the game was to hit the ball with a bat and run around the square of bases more often than the players on the opposing team did. It all seemed kind of silly to Yossarian, since all they played for was the thrill of winning.

And all they won when they did win was the thrill of winning.

And all that winning meant was that they had run around the square of bases more times than a bunch of other people had. If there was more point to all the massive exertions involved than this, Yossarian missed it. When he raised the question with his teammates, they replied that winning proved that you were better. When he raised the question "Better at what?" it turned out that all you were better at was running around a bunch of bases. Yossarian just couldn't understand it, and Yossarian's teammates just couldn't understand Yossarian.

Once he had grown reasonably familiar with the odd game of baseball, he elected to play right field every time, since he soon observed that the right fielder was generally the player with the least amount of work.

He never left his position. When his own team was at bat, he lay down on the ground in right field with a dandelion stem in his mouth and attempted to establish rapport with the right fielder on the opposing team, who kept edging farther and farther away, until he was almost in center field, as he tried to convince himself that Yossarian was not really there in right field with a dandelion stem in his mouth, saying heretical things about baseball that he had never heard anyone say before.

Yossarian refused to take his turn at bat. In the first game, he had taken a turn at bat and hit a triple. If he hit another triple, he would just have to run around a bunch of bases again, and running was no fun.

One day, the opposing right fielder decided that baseball itself was no fun and refused to play altogether. Instead of running after a ball that had come rolling out to him between two infielders, he threw his leather baseball glove as far away from him as he could and went running in toward the pitcher's mound with his whole body quaking.

"I don't want to play anymore," he said, gesticulating wildly toward Yossarian and bursting into tears. "Unless he goes away. He makes me feel like an imbecile every time I go running after that stupid baseball."

Sometimes Yossarian would sneak away from the baseball games at the earliest opportunity, leaving his team one man short.

Yossarian enjoyed playing basketball much more than he enjoyed playing baseball.

Basketball was a game played with a very large inflated ball by nine players and Yossarian, divided up into one team of five players and one team of four players and Yossarian. It was not as patriotic as baseball, but it seemed to make a lot more sense. Basketball consisted of throwing the large inflated ball through a metal hoop horizontally fastened to a wooden backboard hung vertically high above their heads. The team that threw the ball through the hoop more often was the team that won.

All the team won, though, was the same old thrill of winning, and that didn't make so much sense. Playing basketball made a lot more sense than playing baseball, because throwing the ball through the hoop was not quite as indecorous as running around a bunch of bases and required much less teamwork.

Yossarian enjoyed playing basketball because it was so easy to stop. He was able to stop the game every time simply by throwing the ball as far away as he could every time he got his hands on it and then standing around doing nothing while somebody else ran to get it.

One day, Rogoff sprinted up to Yossarian's basketball court during the game and wanted to know why nine men were standing around doing nothing. Yossarian pointed toward the tenth man, who was chasing the ball over the horizon. He had just thrown it away.

"Well, don't just stand there while he gets it," Rogoff urged. "Do push-ups."

Finally, Yossarian had had enough, as much exercise, judo, left jabs, baseball and basketball as he could stand. Maybe it all did save lives, he concluded, but at what exorbitant cost? At the cost of reducing human life to the level of a despicable animal—of an eager beaver.

Yossarian made his decision in the morning, and when the rest of the men fell out for calisthenics in the afternoon, he took his clothes off and lay down on his bed on the second floor of his barrack.

He basked in a glow of superior accomplishment as he lay in a supine position in his undershorts and T-shirt and relaxed to the rousing, strenuous tempo of Rogoff's overburdened voice putting the others through their paces just outside the building. Suddenly, Rogoff's voice ceased and those of his two assistants took over, and Yossarian heard his footsteps race into the building and up the stairs. When Rogoff charged in from the landing on the second floor and found him in bed, Yossarian stopped smirking and began to moan. Rogoff slowed abruptly with a look of chastened solicitude and resumed his approach on tiptoe.

"Why aren't you out doing calisthenics?" he asked curiously when he stood respectfully by Yossarian's bed.

"I'm sick."

"Why don't you go on sick call if you're sick?"

"I'm too sick to go on sick call. I think it's my appendix."

"Should I phone for an ambulance?"

"No, I don't think so."

"Maybe I'd better phone for an ambulance. They'll put you in bed in the hospital and let you rest there all day long."

That prospect had not occurred to Yossarian. "Please phone for an ambulance."

"I'll do it this very minute. I'll—oh, my goodness, I forgot!"

Rogoff whirled himself around with a bleat of horror and flew at top speed down the long boards of the echoing floor to the door at the end of the barrack and out onto the tiny wooden balcony there.

Yossarian was intrigued and sat up over the foot of his bed to observe what was going on.

Rogoff jumped up and down on the small porch, clapping his hands over his head.

"One, two, three, four," he began yelling downward toward the men on the ground, his voice struggling upward dauntlessly into his tortured and perilous falsetto. "One, two, three, four. Hubba, hubba."

"Hubba, hubba, hubba, hubba," came back a sympathetic mass murmur from his invisible audience below that lasted until Rogoff raised his hand high in a formal caricature of a traffic cop and choked it off.

"That's the way, men," he shouted down to them, with a clipped nod of approbation. "Now we'll try some deep knee bends. Ready? Hands on hips . . . place!" Rogoff jammed his own hands down on his hips and, with his back and neck rigid, sank down vigorously into the first movement of a deep knee bend. "One, two, three, four, one, two, three, four."

Then Rogoff sprang up, whirled himself around again and flew back inside the building toward Yossarian and zipped right past him with a chin-up wave of encouragement and pounded down the stairs. About ten minutes later, he came pounding back up the stairs, his corrugated red face redder than a beet, zipped right past him with a chin-up wave of encouragement and flew down the full length of the building again and out onto the balcony, where he yanked the men out of their deep knee bends, hubba-hubbaed them a few seconds and flung them back into straddle jumping. He was showing signs of the heavy strain when he returned to Yossarian. His spare, ropy chest was pumping up and down convulsively in starving panic, and fat, round drops of sweat were shivering on his forehead.

"It will take—I ain't getting any air! It will take the ambulance a little while to get here," he puffed. "They have to drive from all the way across the field. I still ain't getting any air!"

"I guess I'll just have to wait," Yossarian responded bravely.

Rogoff caught his breath finally. "Don't just lie there while you're waiting for the ambulance," he advised. "Do push-ups."

"If he's strong enough to do push-ups," said one of the stretcher-bearers, when the ambulance was there, "he's strong enough to walk."

"It's the push-ups that make him strong enough to walk," Rogoff explained with professional acumen.

"I'm not strong enough to do push-ups," Yossarian said, "and I'm not strong enough to walk."

A strange, regretful silence fell over Rogoff after Yossarian had been lifted onto the stretcher and the time had come to say farewell. There was no mistaking his sincere compassion. He was genuinely sorry for Yossarian; when Yossarian realized that, he was genuinely sorry for Rogoff.

"Well," Rogoff said with a gentle wave and finally found the tactful words. "Hubba, hubba."

"Hubba, hubba to you," Yossarian answered.

▪ ▪ ▪

"Beat it," said the doctor at the hospital to Yossarian.

"Huh?" said Yossarian.

"I said, 'Beat it.' "

"Huh?"

"Stop saying 'Huh?' so much."

"Stop telling me to beat it."

"You can't tell him to beat it," a corporal there said. "There's a new order out."

"Huh?" said the doctor.

"We have to keep every abdominal complaint under observation five days, because so many of the men have been dying after we make them beat it."

"All right," grumbled the doctor. "Put him under observation five days and then throw him out."

"Don't you want to examine him first?" asked the corporal.

"No."

They took Yossarian's clothes away, gave him pajamas and put him to bed in a ward, where he was very happy when the snorers were quiet, and he began to think he might like to spend the rest of his military career there. It seemed as sensible a way to survive the war as any.

"Hubba, hubba," he said to himself.

T. Coraghessan Boyle

Modern Love

March 1988

Tom Boyle's first book of stories, *The Descent of Man* (1979), quickly attracted a following, especially on campuses. The title story details a woman's love affair with a chimpanzee, and announced to the world that T. C. Boyle had little interest in producing the ubiquitous dour realism of the literary 1980s. Inventive and prolific, he has alternated novels (*Water Music,* 1981; *East Is East,* 1991; *The Road to Wellville,* 1993) with collections of stories, all of which first appeared in magazines (*Greasy Lake,* 1985; *The River Runs Whiskey,* 1990). Boyle, who was born in 1948 in Peekskill, New York, now lives in southern California, a suitably bizarre venue, though he has nothing to do with Hollywood. He is much sought after as a performer of his own work, and "Modern Love," which satirized the "safe sex" so frequently discussed (if not practiced) in the 1980s, became a hilariously popular set piece on the reading circuit. It was his first story for *Playboy,* but others followed rapidly.

T. Coraghessan Boyle

Modern Love

There was no exchange of body fluids on the first date, and that suited both of us just fine. I picked her up at seven, took her to Mee Grop, where she meticulously separated each sliver of meat from her *phat Thai,* watched her down four bottles of Singha at three dollars per and then gently stroked her balsam-smelling hair while she snoozed through *The Terminator* at the Circle Shopping Center theater. We had a late-night drink at Rigoletto's Pizza Bar (and two slices, plain cheese), and I dropped her off. The moment we pulled up in front of her apartment, she had the door open. She turned to me with the long, elegant, mournful face of her Puritan ancestors and held out her hand.

"It's been fun," she said.

"Yes," I said, taking her hand.

She was wearing gloves.

"I'll call you," she said.

"Good," I said, giving her my richest smile. "And I'll call you."

▪ ▪ ▪

On the second date, we got acquainted.

"I can't tell you what a strain it was for me the other night," she said, staring down into her chocolate-mocha-fudge sundae. It was early afternoon, we were in Helmut's Olde Tyme Ice Cream Parlor in Mamaroneck and the sun streamed through the thick frosted windows and lighted the place like a convalescent home. The fixtures glowed behind the counter, the brass rail was buffed to a reflective sheen and everything smelled of disinfectant. We were the only people in the place.

"What do you mean?" I said, my mouth glutinous with melted marshmallow and caramel.

"I mean Thai food, the seats in the movie theater, the *ladies' room* in that place, for God's sake. . . ."

"Thai food?" I wasn't following her. I recalled the maneuver with the strips of pork and the fastidious dissection of the glass noodles. "You're a vegetarian?"

She looked away in exasperation and then gave me the full wide-eyed shock of her ice-blue eyes. "Have you seen the health-department statistics on sanitary conditions in ethnic restaurants?"

I hadn't.

Her eyebrows leaped up. She was earnest. She was lecturing. "These people are refugees. They have—well, different standards. They haven't even been inoculated." I watched her dig the tiny spoon into the recesses of the dish and part her lips for a neat, foursquare morsel of ice cream and fudge. "The illegals, anyway. And that's half of them." She swallowed with an almost imperceptible movement, a shudder, her throat dipping and rising like a gazelle's. "I got drunk from fear," she said. "Blind panic. I couldn't help thinking I'd wind up with hepatitis or dysentery or dengue fever or something."

"Dengue fever?"

"I usually bring a disposable sanitary sheet for public theaters—just think of who might have been in that seat before you, and how many times, and what sort of nasty festering little cultures of this and that there must be in all those ancient dribbles of taffy and Coke and extra-butter popcorn—but I didn't want you to think I was too extreme or anything on the first date, so I didn't. And then the *ladies' room*. . . ." She ducked her head and I nearly fell into her eyes. "I mean, after all that beer. . . . You don't think I'm overreacting, do you?"

As a matter of fact, I did. Of course I did. I liked Thai food—and *sushi* and ginger crab and greasy *souvlaki* at the corner stand, too. There was the look of the mad saint in her eye, the obsessive, the mortifier of the flesh, but I didn't care. She was lovely, wilting, clear-eyed and pure, as cool and matchless as if she'd stepped out of a Pre-Raphaelite painting, and I was in love. Besides, I tended a little that way myself. Hypochondria. Anal retentiveness. The ordered environment and alphabetized books. I was a thirty-three-year-old bachelor, I carried some scars and I read the newspapers—herpes, AIDS, the Asian clap that foiled every antibiotic in the book. I was willing to take it slow. "No," I said, "I don't think you're overreacting at all."

I paused to draw in a breath so deep it might have been a sigh. "I'm sorry," I whispered, giving her a doglike look of contrition. "I didn't know."

She reached out then and touched my hand—touched it, skin to skin—and murmured that it was all right; she'd been through worse. "If you want to know," she breathed, "I like places like this."

I glanced around. The place was still empty but for Helmut, in a blinding-white jump suit and toque, studiously polishing the tile walls. "I know what you mean," I said.

▪ ▪ ▪

We dated for a month—museums, drives in the country, French and German restaurants, ice-cream emporiums, fern bars—before we kissed. And when we kissed, after a showing of *David and Lisa* at a revival house all the way up in Rhinebeck and on a night so cold no run-of-the-mill bacterium or commonplace virus could have survived it, it was the merest brushing of the lips. She was wearing a big-shouldered coat of synthetic fur and a knit hat pulled down over her brows, and she hugged my arm as we stepped out of the theater and into the blast of the night. "God," she said, "did you see him when he screamed, 'You touched me!'? Wasn't that priceless?" Her eyes were big and she seemed weirdly excited.

"Sure," I said, "yeah, it was great," and then she pulled me close and kissed me. I felt the soft flicker of her lips against mine.

"I love you," she said, "I think."

A month of dating and one dry, fluttering kiss. At this point, you might begin to wonder about me; but really, I didn't mind. As I say, I was willing to wait—I had the patience of Sisyphus—and it was enough just to be with her. Why rush things? I thought. This is good, this is charming, like the slow, sweet unfolding of the romance in a Frank Capra movie, where sweetness and light always prevail. Sure, she had her idiosyncrasies, but who didn't? Frankly, I'd never been comfortable with the three-drinks, dinner-and-bed sort of thing, the girls who come on like they've been in prison for six years and just got out in time to put on their make-up and jump into the passenger seat of your car. Breda—that was her name, Breda Drumhill, and the very sound and syllabification of it made me melt—was different.

▪ ▪ ▪

Finally, two weeks after the trek to Rhinebeck, she invited me to her apartment. Cocktails, she said. Dinner. A quiet evening in front of the tube.

She lived in Croton, on the ground floor of a restored Victorian, half a mile from the Harmon station, where she caught the train each morning for Manhattan and her job as an editor of *Anthropology Today*. She'd held the job since graduating from Barnard six years earlier (with a double major in Rhetoric and Alien Cultures), and it suited her temperament perfectly. Field anthropologists living among the River Dayak of Borneo or the Kurds of Kurdistan would send her rough and grammatically tortured accounts of their observations and she would whip them into shape for popular consumption. Naturally, filth and exotic disease, as well as outlandish customs and revolting habits, played leading roles in her rewrites. Every other day or so, she'd call me from work and in a voice that could barely contain its joy give me the details of some new and horrific disease she'd discovered.

She met me at the door in a silk kimono that featured a plunging neckline and a pair of dragons with intertwined tails. Her hair was pinned up as if she'd just stepped out of the bath, and she smelled of Noxzema and Phisoderm. She pecked my cheek, took the bottle of Vouvray I held out in offering and led me into the front room. "Chagas' disease," she said, grinning wide to show off her perfect, outsized teeth.

"Chagas' disease?" I echoed, not quite knowing what to do with myself. The room was as spare as a monk's cell. Two chairs, a love seat and a coffee table, in glass, chrome and hard black plastic. No plants ("God knows what sort of insects might live on them—and the *dirt,* the dirt has got to be crawling with bacteria, not to mention spiders and worms and things") and no rug ("A breeding ground for fleas and ticks and chiggers").

Still grinning, she steered me to the hard-black-plastic love seat and sat down beside me, the Vouvray cradled in her lap. "South America," she whispered, her eyes leaping with excitement. "In the jungle. These bugs—assassin bugs, they're called; isn't that wild? These bugs bite you, and then, after they've sucked on you awhile, they go potty next to the wound. When you scratch, it gets into your blood stream, and anywhere from one to twenty years later, you get a disease that's like a cross between malaria and AIDS."

"And then you die," I said.

"And then you die."

Her voice had turned somber. She wasn't grinning any longer. What could I say? I patted her hand and flashed a smile. "Yum," I said, mugging for her, "what's for dinner?"

She served a cold cream-of-tofu-and-carrot soup and little lentil-paste sandwiches for an appetizer and a garlic soufflé with biologically controlled vegetables for the entree. Then it was snifters of cognac, the big-screen TV and a movie called *The Boy in the Plastic Bubble,* about a kid raised in a totally antiseptic environment because he was born without an immune system. No one could touch him. Even the slightest sneeze would have killed him. Breda sniffled through the first half hour, then pressed my hand and sobbed openly as the boy finally crawled out of the bubble, caught about thirty-seven diseases and died before the commercial break. "I've seen this movie six times now," she said, fighting to control her voice, "and it gets to me every time. What a life," she said, waving her snifter at the screen, "what a perfect life. Don't you envy him?"

I didn't envy him. I envied the jade pendant that dangled between her breasts, and I told her so.

She might have giggled or gasped or lowered her eyes, but she didn't. She gave me a long, slow look, as if she were deciding something, and then she allowed herself to blush, the color suffusing her throat in a delicious mottle of pink and white. "Give me a minute," she said mysteriously and disappeared into the bathroom.

I was electrified. This was it. Finally. After all the avowals, the pressed hands, the little jokes and routines, after all the miles driven, meals consumed, museums paced and movies watched, we were finally, naturally, gracefully going to come together in the ultimate act of intimacy and love.

I felt hot. There were beads of sweat on my forehead. I didn't know whether to stand or sit. And then the lights dimmed, and there she was at the rheostat.

She was still in her kimono, but her hair was pinned up more severely, wound in a tight coil on the crown of her head, as if she'd girded herself for battle. And she held something in her hand—a slim package wrapped in plastic. It rustled as she crossed the room.

"When you're in love, you make love," she said, easing down beside me on the rocklike settee. "It's only natural." She handed me the package. "I don't want to give you the wrong impression," she said, her voice throaty and raw, "just because I'm careful and modest and because there's so much, well, filth in the world, but I have my passionate side, too. I do. And I love you. I think."

"Yes," I said, groping for her, the package all but forgotten.

We kissed. I rubbed the back of her neck, felt something strange—an odd sag and ripple, as if her skin had suddenly turned to Saran Wrap—and then she had her hand on my chest. "Wait," she breathed, "the, the thing."

I sat up. "Thing?"

The light was dim, but I could see the blush invade her face now. She was sweet. Oh, she was sweet, my Little Em'ly, my Victorian princess. "It's Swedish," she said.

I looked down at the package in my lap. It was a clear, skinlike sheet of plastic, folded up in its transparent package like a heavy-duty garbage bag. I held it up to her huge, trembling eyes. A crazy idea darted in and out of my head. No, I thought.

"It's the newest thing," she said, the words coming in a rush, "the safest. . . . I mean, nothing could possibly—"

My face was hot. "No," I said.

"It's a condom," she said, tears starting up in her eyes. "My doctor got them for me; they're . . . they're Swedish." Her face wrinkled up and she began to cry. "It's a condom," she sobbed, crying so hard the kimono fell open and I could see the outline of the thing against the swell of her nipples, "a full-body condom."

■ ■ ■

I was offended. I admit it. It wasn't so much her obsession with germs and contagion but that she didn't trust me after all that time. I was clean. Quintessentially clean. I was a man of moderate habits and good health; I changed my underwear and socks daily—sometimes twice a day—and I worked in an office, with clean, crisp, unequivocal numbers, managing my late father's chain of shoe stores (and he died cleanly himself, of a myocardial infarction, at seventy-five). "But, Breda," I said, reaching out to console her and brushing her soft, plastic-clad breast in the process, "don't you trust me? Don't you believe me? Don't you, don't you love me?" I took her by the shoulders, lifted her head, forced her to look me in the eye. "I'm clean," I said. "Trust me."

She looked away. "Do it for me," she said in her smallest voice, "if you really love me."

In the end, I did it. I looked at her, crying, crying for me, and I looked at the thin sheet of plastic clinging to her, and I did it. She helped me into the thing, poked two holes for my nostrils, zipped the plastic zipper up the back and pulled it tight over my head. It fit like a wet suit. And the whole thing—the stroking and the tenderness and the gentle yielding—was everything I'd hoped it would be.

Almost.

▪ ▪ ▪

She called me from work the next day. I was playing with sales figures and thinking of her. "Hello," I said, practically cooing into the receiver.

"You've got to hear this—" Her voice was giddy with excitement.

"Hey," I said, cutting her off in a passionate whisper, "last night was really special."

"Oh, yes," she said, "yes, last night. It was. And I love you, I do. . . ." She paused to draw in her breath. "But listen to this: I just got a piece from a man and his wife living among the Tuareg of Nigeria—these are people who follow cattle around, picking up the dung for their cooking fires?"

I made a small noise of awareness.

"Well, they make their huts of dung, too—isn't that wild? And guess what—when times are hard, when the crops fail and the cattle can barely stand up, you know what they eat?"

"Let me guess," I said. "Dung?"

She let out a whoop. "Yes! Yes! Isn't it too much? They *eat* dung!"

I'd been saving one for her, a disease a doctor friend had told me about. "Onchocerciasis," I said. "You know it?"

There was a thrill in her voice. "Tell me."

"South America and Africa both. A fly bites you and lays its eggs in your blood stream, and when the eggs hatch, the larvae—these little white worms—migrate to your eyeballs, right underneath the membrane there, so you can see them wriggling around."

There was a silence on the other end of the line.

"Breda?"

"That's sick," she said. "That's really sick."

"But I thought . . ." I trailed off. "Sorry," I said.

"Listen," and the edge came back into her voice, "the reason I called is because I love you, I think I love you, and I want you to meet somebody."

"Sure," I said.

"I want you to meet Michael. Michael Maloney."

"Sure. Who's he?"

She hesitated, paused just a beat, as if she knew she was going too far. "My doctor," she said.

▪ ▪ ▪

You have to work at love. You have to bend, make subtle adjustments, sacrifices—love is nothing without sacrifice. I went to Dr. Maloney. Why not? I'd eaten tofu, bantered about leprosy and bilharziasis as if I were immune and made love in a bag. If it made Breda happy—if it eased the nagging fears that ate at her day and night—then it was worth it.

The doctor's office was in Scarsdale, in his home, a two-tone mock Tudor with a winding drive and oaks as old as my grandfather's Chrysler. He was a young man—late thirties, I guessed—with a red beard, a shaved head and a pair of oversized spectacles in clear plastic frames. He took me right away—the very day I called—and met me at the door himself. "Breda's told me about you," he said, leading me into the floodlit vault of his office. He looked at me appraisingly a moment, murmuring, "Yes, yes" into his beard, and then, with the aid of his nurses, Miss Archibald and Miss Slivovitz, put me through a battery of tests that would have embarrassed an astronaut.

First, there were the measurements, including digital joints, maxilla, cranium, penis and ear lobe. Next the rectal exam, the E.E.G. and the urine sample. And then the tests. Stress tests, patch tests, reflex tests, lung-capacity tests (I blew up yellow balloons till they popped, then breathed into a machine the size of a Hammond organ), X rays, sperm count and a closely printed twenty-four-page questionnaire that included sections on dream analysis, genealogy and logic and reasoning. Maloney drew blood, too, of course—to test vital organ function and exposure to disease. "We're testing for antibodies to over fifty diseases," he said, eyes dodging behind the walls of his lenses. "You'd be surprised how many people have been infected without even knowing it." I couldn't tell if he was joking or not. On the way out, he took my arm and told me he'd have the results in a week.

That week was the happiest of my life. I was with Breda every night, and over the weekend we drove up to Vermont to stay at a hygiene center her cousin had told her about. We dined by candlelight—on real food—and afterward, we donned the Saran Wrap suits and made joyous, sanitary love. I wanted more, of course—the touch of skin on skin—but I was fulfilled and I was happy. Go slow, I told myself. All things in time. One night, as we lay entwined in the big white fortress of her bed, I stripped back the hood of the plastic suit and asked her if she'd ever trust me enough to make love in the way of the centuries, raw and unprotected. She twisted free of her own wrapping and looked away, giving me that matchless patrician profile. "Yes," she said, her voice pitched low, "yes, of course. Once the results are in."

"Results?"

She turned to me, her eyes searching mine. "Don't tell me you've forgotten."

I had. Carried away, intense, passionate, brimming with love, I'd forgotten.

"Silly you," she murmured, tracing the line of my lips with a slim, plastic-clad finger. "Does the name Michael Maloney ring a bell?"

▪ ▪ ▪

And then the roof fell in.

I called and there was no answer. I tried her at work and her secretary said she was out. I left messages. She never called back. It was as if we'd never known each other, as if I were a stranger, a door-to-door salesman, a beggar on the street.

I took up a vigil in front of her house. For a solid week, I sat in my parked car and watched the door with all the fanatic devotion of a pilgrim at a shrine. Nothing. She neither came nor went. I rang the phone off the hook, interrogated her friends, haunted the elevator, the hallway and the reception room at her office. She'd disappeared.

Finally, in desperation, I called her cousin in Larchmont. I'd met her once—she was a homely, droopy-sweatered, baleful-looking girl who represented everything gone wrong in the genes that had come to such glorious fruition in Breda—and barely knew what to say to her. I'd made up a speech, something about how my mother was dying in Phoenix, the business was on the rocks, I was drinking too much and dwelling on thoughts of suicide, destruction and final judgment, and I had to talk with Breda just one more time before the end, and did she by any chance know where she was? As it turned out, I didn't need the speech. Breda answered the phone.

"Breda, it's me," I choked. "I've been going crazy looking for you."

Silence.

"Breda, what's wrong? Didn't you get my messages?"

Her voice was halting, distant. "I can't see you anymore," she said.

"Can't see me?" I was stunned, hurt, angry. "What do you mean?"

"All those feet," she said.

"Feet?" It took me a minute to realize she was talking about the shoe business. "But I don't deal with anybody's feet—I work in an office. Like you. With air conditioning and sealed windows. I haven't touched a foot since I was sixteen."

"Athlete's foot," she said. "Psoriasis. Eczema. Jungle rot."

"What is it? The physical?" My voice cracked with outrage. "Did I flunk the damn physical? Is that it?"

She wouldn't answer me.

A chill went through me. "What did he say? What did the son of a bitch say?"

There was a distant ticking over the line, the pulse of time and space, the gentle sway of Bell Telephone's hundred million miles of wire.

"Listen," I pleaded, "see me one more time, just once—that's all I ask. We'll talk it over. We could go on a picnic. In the park. We could spread a blanket and, and we could sit on opposite corners—"

"Lyme disease," she said.

"Lyme disease?"

"Spread by tick bite. They're seething in the grass. You get Bell's palsy, meningitis, the lining of your brain swells up like dough."

"Rockefeller Center, then," I said, "by the fountain."

Her voice was dead. "Pigeons," she said. "They're like flying rats."

"Helmut's. We can meet at Helmut's. Please. I love you."

"I'm sorry."

"Breda, please listen to me. We were so close—"

"Yes," she said, "we were close," and I thought of that first night in her apartment, *The Boy in the Plastic Bubble* and the Saran Wrap suit, thought of the whole dizzy spectacle of our romance till her voice came down like a hammer on the refrain, "but not that close."

Robert Coover

Lucky Pierre in the Doctor's Office

December 1989

Though several of the writers included in this collection have been, at one time or another, contributing editors to the magazine, Robert Coover is the only one to have worked in its promotion department. This was in 1960, just after he earned his graduate degree at the University of Chicago and just before he sold his first story and went off to New York to be a full-time writer. *The Origin of the Brunists* appeared in 1966 to considerable acclaim, winning the William Faulkner award for best first novel of the year. This was followed two years later by *The Universal Baseball Association, Inc., Jo Herry Waugh, Prop.* and then by several other novels, the latest being *Pinocchio in Venice,* 1991. Coover is frankly interested in experimental writing and for the past few years has led his students at Brown University in "hypertext," a kind of fluid multimedia interfacing accessible only in the computer age. Lucky Pierre, his hero here, who is the "last of the great pornographic-film icons" will eventually be the subject of a novel.

Robert Coover

Lucky Pierre in the Doctor's Office

"The doctor will see you now."

The patient, a livid mass of welts, bruises, abrasions and deep discontents, wearing only a short hospital gown tied at the back and laid out on an examining table like raw stock, is wheeled, cold and half-conscious, into the doctor's office.

"Well, well!" exclaims the doctor, exhibiting a professional jollity. "And what have we here?"

Lucky Pierre, skin-flick hero, does not answer, keeping bottled up his scripted groans. He lies darkly in his wounds, his knees and elbows turned out, as though he were coming unspooled. By contrast, the doctor, who directs this in-house segment, which for all he knows may be his last, is glowing with well-being, her silvery-blonde hair pulled back in a tight bun at the neck, her teeth sparkling, her complexion radiant, her bright uniform clean and fragrant. Cast in his misery, he is offended by such a picture of health. She picks through an array of instruments, her metallic nails clicking, selects an otoscope and a sensitometer.

"Looks like a bad case of advanced misentropy!" she chuckles, winking at her colleagues.

"Critical, doctor?"

"Fetal, I'm afraid."

Her breasts are high and pointed, her belly as flat and tight as a drumhead, her buttocks packed full and firm in the starchy white skirt. She is encircled by the glint of stainless steel and the glaze of lights, by wall charts and diplomas, by the hum of apparatus and the soft, hushing movement of nurses and production assistants. She peers under his eyelids, into his ears and nostrils, down his throat, dictating to an aide: "Signs of hypopraxia, idiodynamic delusions, hot lips and circadian decubitus. Deglutition and exteroceptors normal. More or less. There are cunt hairs between his teeth: Query cohort relationships."

"He seems so cold and lethargic, doctor. . . ."

"Yes, a consequence, perhaps, of over-cranking. . . ."

She leans down to listen to his heart, pressing her pubis against his hand: seems almost to move, to caress him. Curious, or perhaps simply because he is who he is, he turns his hand over to hold it in his palm, less numb, somehow, than the rest of him.

"Aha!" She smiles. "Feeling better?"

She peeks under his gown.

"My goodness! I guess you are!"

"A . . . terrible fall, Clara. . . ."

"Yes, I recognize the symptoms."

"No, *the* fall, I mean . . . a rupture of some kind. Permanent, I think . . . or worse!"

THE END, he means, but she just laughs and stuffs his awakening hand up her skirt.

"You're too suggestible!"

Her mound is warm and wet, thickly padded with wiry little curls. Her labia seem to reach out, grip his fingers, count them, twist his knuckles, read the palm.

"Hmm. Moderate hypopselaphesia, probably transient and cryogenetic. Ugly wart on the social finger. Diarthrodial articulation, synergetic and tender. Severe agnails, symptoms of ambivalence, but effectively excitomotory."

"Voluptafacient, doctor?" asks a nurse.

"Quite. Feels good, too. Yum! Decussate life and love lines, implying endopathic abiotrophy of the essential humors. Turn him over and let's have a reverse-angle look at his old *arrière-voussure!*"

As they pull his hand away to roll him over, her cunt sucks up his fingers . . . then—fffffpop!—lets them go. Procumbent, he feels the chill come on again. That fall: no saving jump cuts this time, no fades, no soft dissolves; they let him hit bottom and even filmed the bounce. Didn't even slow it down. Neorealism, they called it. For Clara's sake: her demand for unmediated authenticity. You can't anatomize a mock-up, as she likes to say. She wants the truth, the hard-core truth, twenty-four times a second, even if she has to create it herself. Now her assistants spread his knees and elbows out, adjust his balls for him, untie his gown. Clara smiles down at what she sees, slaps his buttocks.

"On the homely face of it, I'd have to describe it as dasygenal, wouldn't you, girls?"

"Is it . . . is it serious, doctor?" he wants to know, prepared for the worst.

"Very serious," she laughs. "It means you have a hairy ass. *Ex facie*. Relax. You may as well enjoy this."

She spreads his cheeks, sniffs about critically, squeezes a pimple, pokes a proctoscope into his rectum.

"What does it look like in there, doctor?"

"Not a pretty picture, I'm afraid. Some evidence of diathetic dysteology, as well as time-orientation compulsions, possibly due to a faulty diet. Better stick an explosimeter up there, while I take a look at his tail. What's left of it."

"An explosi—*what?"*

She probes the base of his spine, finds a raw nerve, sending him bucking off the table.

"Yowww! Damn it, Clara, take it easy! *That hurt!"*

"There it is, girls, that's where the old caudal appendage got broken off. The original hypostatic disunion; he's been looking for it ever since. Thus, the first phase of hominization: the quest motive. Which in the present instance has degenerated into a kind of sacral eschatology—you can see the open sore here—confused by the dysgnostic assumption that woman was created from that severed tail and to this day, as the doggerel goes, must serve his will and solace his posteriors still!"

The nurses hoot mockingly at that and beat his nates with stethoscopes and clipboards, artificial limbs, leather traction belts and rubber blood-pressure tubes, wagging their own tails excitedly and scratching their fleas.

"But it's true!" he protests weakly. "I remember it. . . ."

"Forget the past, dear Lucky, it's mostly waste. There is, as they rightly say, no future in it."

"But what does it matter, Clara? There's no future anyway. I'm finished. I know that. The reel's run out. . . ."

"Bullshit. Despair is a metaphor, like any other."

"I just want to sleep. . . ."

"No doubt. We all suffer these gesticidal tendencies. The lure of the fade-out. But don't worry. You're in *my* film now, dear boy, *my* care. *Experto credite*. Look: Already your ass is as red as a rose in bloom! *It* won't soon go to sleep again!"

"It's not my ass that's the problem, Clara, it's my head, my heart . . . !"

She laughs at his confusions. It's true. What does he know about anatomy? He's a complete dope.

"Rig him up for stress analysis," she says to her assistants.

His feet are bound together in ankle cuffs, and Lucky Pierre, last of the great pornographic-film icons, is hoisted upside down and hung from a gambrel stick. The gown is stripped away and he is smeared over with a photoelastic covering. Weights are suspended from his arms, neck, mustache, penis and navel, and a stereoscope is fitted to his eyes. He is subjected to a sequence of 3-D images—body parts, falling buildings, circus acts, snowstorms, genteel sodomies, worm fucking, electrocutions and the like—while the doctor studies the isochromatic patterns got by bombarding him with polarized light.

"But I've given it all I've got, Clara," he whimpers, his tongue flopping against the roof of his mouth. "I've really tried. . . ."

"I know. That's why you've been sent to me. Have faith. And don't press the chicken switch. When in doubt, exercitate! Orthopraxy saves and all that. My! Look at those gorgeous colors!"

While she watches him, he is watching the collapse of ecosystems, the gang bang of a child star, castrations and bicycle races, the fall of an airplane, the discovery of the optical printer, and as blood rushes to his head, he thinks, She's right, our bodies are full of chaos and violence; it's the way they express themselves. All actors have to understand that; the integrity of our performances depends upon it. Let it roll.

"Each color indicates the magnitude of stress at each part of the system," the doctor is explaining to her assistants, who are oohing and ahing at the sight of him all lit up like that.

"What lovely spots of blue there in his belly, doctor!"

"Yes, the hypochondrium, of course. Nearby, that ugly black spot is the liver, where much of the murder takes place, and, as is to be expected, it's the locus of least stress."

"But, oh, my, look at his testes! It's almost as though they're on fire!"

"Yes, while by contrast, observe that the penis, which is self-evidently diageotropic and so subject to additional gravitational demands, runs nevertheless—following the speeding train of received images—the whole spectrum, now black and flaccid, now crimson and aroused, now a straining, luciferous white, as though unsure of its own enthusiasms or responsibilities."

"It's rather like his head, doctor. It looks like a bowl of lit-up fruit!"

"True, but the head contains all these colors at once, like a syncretic contexture of shifting options, you might say, while his penis' dysmnesiac experience of these states is serially diachronic."

"Gosh, you're right! That sure makes it a whole lot prettier, doesn't it?"

"It's wonderful what you can learn from a silly old dick, doctor!"

"Ex pene Herculem, my dear!"

"But— *Good heavens!"*

"Yes?"

"His . . . his *heart,* doctor!"

"Mmm. You've noticed."

"It's . . . it's *green!"*

The doctor sighs, smiles, casts a long, affectionate glance at the patient.

"Yes, it . . . it almost makes you believe in love again, doesn't it?"

"Doctor!"

The doctor laughs and switches off the polarized light.

"Take him down, exuviate him, then osculate his pecker, please, and give me a coefficient of viscosity reading in centipoise."

While the doctor withdraws to her desk to fill out her examination report and feed the data into her bank of computers, her assistants unshackle him, remove the stereoscope and peel off the photoelastic sheath. One of the nurses slides a catheter down his urethra, reaches up under his scrotum and manipulates the *vas deferens* with little pumping motions and, sucking gently on the tube, draws off a small specimen of semen. He shudders: a certain tingling reminiscent of orgasm but without the spasm. Leaves him feeling suspended, weird, nervous somehow, at the edge, much as one feels when one has to sneeze but cannot, and he worries now about having come here: Is there to be an operation? Will he leave here alive? He reaches up to give himself relief, but they rap his knuckles with a steel rule.

"Don't make us strap you down, now!"

"The doctor wants it spick-and-span! She'll see you in a minute."

"Pl— *Ah-choo!* Please. . . ."

"The sample, doctor. It's pretty sticky stuff."

"Thank you. Mmm, tastes good, too. I can see why they are using it as an excipient. Pity he's been wasting so much of it."

"Come on, Clara, goddamn it! I feel all wrong! Help me get it off!"

"Are you always in such a hurry?" she asks with a smile. "We've only just begun!"

She weighs his stones on a ballocks balance, listens to them, waggles them about, beats a small electronic gong with them: hollow, echoey sound. Why does she care? Her appetite for knowledge arouses in some small part his own. It's important, he thinks, to be possessed like that. To be so eager to be alive and aware, it drives you mad. She reads the signals from the gong, runs a profilometric check on his penis, tries to bend it, slaps at it to see in which direction it bobs.

"Pubes: pterygoid. Calluses: clitoridean. Shear modular: impressive."

She nips at his glans with her teeth, stretches his prepuce, clucking her tongue ominously, separates the lips of his penis, peers down the urethra.

"Whew! That's a pretty long fall at that!" she admits.

"I told you. . . ."

"Would one of you girls dim the lights, please?"

The office darkens. Clara adjusts the aperture with a little twist at the base of his prick. Her hands are smooth and cool, good hands to be in in this crisis.

"What's important about these little things," she says, squinting, "is their power of resolution. It's a kind of optical illusion. . . ."

The nurses murmur appreciatively and take turns peeking inside while the doctor holds it open. As she touches and plays with him, he relaxes. He knows that, sooner or later, she will satisfy him, and will satisfy him as no one else can, because the inevitability of her doing so is part of the subtext that informs all her films, unscripted though she pretends them to be.

"Now, the heart of these systems," the doctor is explaining, "is the intermittent mechanism. This one uses an advanced spring-loaded, oscillating claw—if you look down in there, you'll be able to see it—which in turn is backed up by one of the most ancient of such devices, the old-fashioned dog movement, using the eccentric pin. See it wiggle there? Yes, that's it."

"Isn't it rather troublesome to have two paradoxical systems in one mechanism, doctor?"

"Perhaps. But this is the price for versatility and sufficiency."

"What's that little gaugelike device up here near the nose, doctor?"

"That's to adjust the speed. It's what makes many of your special effects possible."

She presses a little trigger under the shaft, his hips buck and slap the table and light pours through, casting a moving image on the ceiling: He, Lucky Pierre, is wallowing in heaps of unwound film up there and beautiful young starlets are cracking their maidenheads on his cock like champagne bottles.

"It's only recently," the doctor is saying, "that we have come to understand the gonads as part of the central nervous system. In the past, we tended to isolate them purely in terms of their hypothetical reproductive functions, failing to see that this anthropocentric bias ignored the communities within and the universal order without."

Her grip on his prick is firm but soothing. His hips have stopped bucking, but he still seems to be experiencing the orgasm. Not as good as most orgasms, true, but better than the frustration that went before, and he enjoys the prolonged effect. On the ceiling, dying spermatozoa are arranging themselves into astrological signals.

"We now know that no sense data—which is to say, no data at all—enter man's central nervous system without simultaneous transmission to the gonads and, at the same time, that no mental processes take place, no matter what logic circuits may have been implemented by prior environmental engineering, without gonad feedback and involvement."

He seems to remember a time when a mean girl in school stuffed his prick in an inkwell, but on the ceiling now, his teacher is showing him an apple with the laws of gravity written on it.

"And as you may have surmised from our previous stress analysis, the peculiar design factor of the gonads, perhaps because of the relative brevity of their intracommunal life cycles, is their augmented processor impact and diminished storage capacities, such that their peculiar contribution to mental activity is *projection. . . .*"

He eats the apple and falls through space at thirty-two feet per second per second, thinking, This apple tastes just like a cunt! Somewhere, he hears the sound of blades being sharpened, and the doctor's fingers have become as rigid and cold as steel.

"I assume you all know how this gadget works. You've taken these things apart . . . ?"

"Yes, but if there were snatching or excessive tension on our perforations, doctor, where would we . . . ?"

"You'd open it right here."

On the ceiling, the doctor has grown fangs and scowling brows and is stealing up on the patient with a gleaming scalpel.

"You see? We could completely dissemble it, if you like. . . ."

The doctor, grinning evilly, has slashed off the patient's genitals and is going for his heart, his head, but he pulls himself together. The doctor withdraws, cowering in a dark corner, her eyes gleaming like burning coals. Perhaps she has not yet struck the first blow. Perhaps she is naked.

"Efforts have been made to temper the impact of the gonads' signal digression and distortion through increasingly complex program designs for nonhuman cybernetic components, but, clearly, if man is to remain relevant, he must remain close to the transdimensional mainstream of life and, thus, must keep his gonads plugged into all his mental processes, and screw the consequences, to coin a phrase."

The doctor has discovered his throbbing cock. The scalpel falls from her trembling hand. Her fangs recede, her eyes glaze over with excitement. Cautiously, she approaches, her heart thumping visibly in the walls of her steaming cunt.

"That's not to say that these projections of the gonads are in themselves reliable stimuli for sound behavior—on the contrary! Barrel distortion, curvature of field, chromatic aberration, recurrent clap and flicker are only a few of the typical defects. The circle-of-confusion factor has never been satisfactorily resolved and tends to be infectious. Moreover, just as cerebral logic systems attempt to think out problems, the gonads instinctively try to fuck their way out. Thus, as you can see above, our subject somehow supposes he can neutralize what he has interpreted and projected as hostility by fucking me into quiescence or even affection. And who knows—ha, ha!—he may be right!"

Before mounting him, the hovering doctor inserts an endoscopic camera in her womb to photograph the attitude during entry and exit and shoves an extensometer up her ass to measure him through the separating membrane. Her golden body is as sleek and hard as a mannequin's—nothing sags or wobbles, not a blemish or a wrinkle—yet it's rumored she may be more than three hundred years old! The wonders of science!

"He even perceives this coitus to be initiated by me, but these projections are occluded by a veritable montage of ambivalence. Behind the mad-doctor sequence, you will discover the indifferent doctor, the heroic doctor, the incompetent doctor, the corrupt and the distracted doctor. If I adjust the focus, you will see projections that include yourselves, others of the city streets, his workplace, the decaying cosmos, his assumed past."

She does a kind of split across his body, one hand on his knee, the other pressing down on his belly.

"Does it hurt? Good. . . ."

Slowly, methodically, she lowers herself, and he feels her clitoris probe the length of his penis, feels the lips caress, suck, nibble, taste, pucker, blow, nip, feels her pubes thud softly, springily against his own.

"There is an associative rhythm to all these projections, which will become more evident as coitus proceeds, but it is clear that the projections are not any freer from the influence of the primary and secondary sense organs than our so-called rational operations are from the influence of the gonads."

He seems to see the wet red walls of her vagina, as though lit by quartz-iodine lamps, and beyond the lamps' glare, the fierce dark lens of the endoscopic camera. He wishes to perform well.

"Thus, advanced cineman's relationship with his gonads is not more remote; it is simply more complex. He has a heightened awareness of pattern, but also a heightened awareness of immediacy and randomness. Cineman is more space conscious, but he is also more time conscious. Motion is his very essence, yet no humanoid in the evolutionary scale was ever more conscious of configuration, fields, reaction formations or paradox. Kinetics is, finally, that science exclusively concerned with stasis."

He leaps and thrusts in the glistening red chamber, the insouciant pupilless eye of the camera now taunting him, infuriating him: He strives to reach it, to smash it with a head-on blow.

"He knows the circular reel and the square frame. His logic systems have led him to transcend art, his gonads have—ah!—led him beyond history. . . ."

The oozing walls flex and ripple, pushing him away, pulling him back. The extensometer is grabbing at him through the thin membrane, testing him.

"He knows he must turn away from abstractions and—foo!—fantasies toward the concrete, knows he must cope more directly with—ungh!—with disorientation and—ah! oh!—oh, this is beautiful! this is good!—with disorientation and entropy, yet he achieves this—ah! uf!—through a new respect for—*oh!*—for symbolic systems—*hah!*—and purely conceptualized—*wow!*"

Strains toward the fucking lens, can't reach it. The walls grab him. He feels himself coming gloriously apart. *"Now!"* he cries, explodes, smashes the lens with his own eruptive death. Strobes spin and crash, screams rend the deep silence, darkness falls about him, collapsing like a starry sky. Some lost part of him shudders and sinks away.

Later, he hears his own heartbeat. The wet red walls are the insides of his own eyelids. He thinks, I have been dreaming all this. I will awake in my own bed, my pajamas sticky and wet with cold come. I will walk through the sullen crowds and the blowing snow to the studio. My staff will give me a hot bath and we will make films together. But when he opens his eyes, he is still in the doctor's office. This frightens him: Something real is happening! The doctor, in her immaculate white uniform, is taking read-outs from her computers. Her assistants are dismantling and storing apparatus, preparing flow charts, admiring the splotch of dripping sperm on the ceiling high above.

"Am I . . . am I going to be all right?" he asks faintly.

The doctor comes over to him, gazes down, touches a cool hand to his forehead.

"Yes, I think so," she says.

He knows she is lying. It is serious, after all. He has made some kind of mistake. It's as though the very genre has been violated at the root, and there's nothing he can do about it.

"I want to know everything," he says, as a confession.

"You are suffering from hypotyposis compounded by severe parabologyny. I predict an episode of feverish protocunnicide, but this should be for the best, and at least an entertainment."

He sees something in her eyes he hasn't noticed before. A glint of communicative warmth behind the professional detachment. And the way she said entertainment. . . .

"Clara, I . . . I love you! What shall I do?"

"Eat more balanced meals, exercise regularly, brush your teeth at least twice a day and, for the present, go home and get under a sun lamp."

"No, I mean—"

"That's a print," she says firmly. She hands him a prescription the size of an idiot card and he is wheeled out of the office and off the screen.

Ursula K. Le Guin

Unlocking the Air

December 1990

This is Ursula K. Le Guin's second appearance in *Playboy.* In an essay about censorship she once wrote called "The Stalin in the Soul," she alluded to the first ("Nine Lives," November 1969) as follows: "After the fiction editor had accepted the story, someone else in the firm wrote me asking if they could use the letter of my first name only, saying rather touchingly, 'Many of our readers are frightened by stories by women authors.' At the time this struck me as merely funny, and I agreed. . . . Why couldn't I see that I was selling out?" The circumstances are mysterious: Joyce Engelson, Shirley Jackson, and Françoise Sagan had already been published—was it only science-fiction readers who trembled so? In any event, Le Guin's great novel of sexual ambiguity, *The Left Hand of Darkness,* had just—coincidentally—been published, and *The Dispossessed,* her first overtly political work, followed in 1974. Further political stories followed, many of them set in Orsinia, an all-purpose Eastern European country. This is one of them. It was published at the time of the collapse of the Russian behemoth, a brief, delirious moment while the world held its breath and hoped.

Ursula K. Le Guin

Unlocking the Air

This is a fairy tale. People stand in the lightly falling snow. Something is shining, trembling, making a silvery sound. Eyes are shining. Voices sing. People laugh and weep, clasp one another's hands, embrace. Something shines and trembles. They live happily ever after. The snow falls on the roofs and blows across the parks, the squares, the river.

▪ ▪ ▪

This is history. Once upon a time, a good king lived in his palace in a kingdom far away. But an evil enchantment fell upon that land. The wheat withered in the ear, the leaves dropped from the trees of the forest and nothing thrived.

▪ ▪ ▪

This is a stone. It's a paving stone of a square that slants downhill in front of an old, reddish, almost windowless fortress called the Roukh Palace. The square was paved nearly three hundred years ago, so a lot of feet have walked on this stone, bare feet and shod, children's little pads, horses' iron shoes, soldiers' boots; and wheels have gone over and over it, cart wheels, carriage wheels, car tires, tank treads. Dogs' paws every now and then. There has been dogshit on it, there has been blood, both soon washed away by water sloshed from buckets or run from hoses or dropped from the clouds.

You can't get blood from a stone, they say, nor can you give it to a stone; it takes no stain. Some of the pavement, down near that street that leads out of Roukh Square through the old Jewish quarter to the river, got dug up, once or twice, and piled into a barricade, and some of the stones even found themselves flying through the air, but not for long. They were soon put back in their place, or replaced by others. It made no difference to them. The man hit by the flying stone dropped down like a stone beside the stone that had killed him. The man shot through the brain fell down and his blood ran out on this stone, or another one maybe; it makes no difference to them. The soldiers washed his blood away with water sloshed from buckets, the buckets their horses drank from. The rain fell after a while. The snow fell. Bells rang the hours, the Christmases, the New Years. A tank stopped with its treads on this stone. You'd think that that would leave a mark, a huge heavy thing like a tank, but the stone shows nothing. Only all the feet bare and shod over the centuries have worn a quality into it, not a smoothness, exactly, but a kind of softness, like leather or like skin. Unstained, unmarked, indifferent, it does have that quality of having been worn for a long time by life. So it is a stone of power, and who sets foot on it may be transformed.

▪ ▪ ▪

This is a story. She let herself in with her key and called, "Mama? It's me, Fana!"

And her mother, in the kitchen of the apartment, called, "I'm in here," and they met and hugged in the doorway of the kitchen.

"Come on, come on!"

"Come where?"

"It's Thursday, Mama!"

"Oh," said Bruna Fabbre, retreating toward the stove, making vague protective gestures at the saucepans, the dishcloths, the spoons.

"You said."

"But it's nearly four already—"

"We can be back by six-thirty."

"I have all the papers to read for the advancement tests."

"You have to come, Mama. You do. You'll see!"

A heart of stone might resist the shining eyes, the coaxing, the bossiness. "Come on!" she said, and the mother came.

But grumbling. "This is for you," she said on the stairs.

On the bus, she said it again. "This is for you. Not me."

"What makes you think that?"

Bruna did not reply for a while, looking out the bus window at the gray city lurching by, the dead November sky behind the roofs.

"Well, you see," she said, "before Kasi, my brother Kasimir, before he was killed, that was the time that would have been for me. But I was too young. Too stupid. And then they killed Kasi."

"By mistake."

"It wasn't a mistake. They were hunting for a man who'd been getting people out across the border, and they'd missed him. So it was to . . ."

"To have something to report to the Central Office."

Bruna nodded. "He was about the age you are now," she said. The bus stopped, people climbed on, crowding the aisle. "Since then, twenty-seven years, always since then, it's been too late. For me. First too stupid, then too late. This time is for you. I missed mine."

"You'll see," Stefana said. "There's enough time to go round."

▪ ▪ ▪

This is history. Soldiers stand in a row before the reddish, almost windowless palace; their muskets are at the ready. Young men walk across the stones toward them, singing, "Beyond this darkness is the light, O Liberty, of thine eternal day!"

The soldiers fire their guns. The young men live happily ever after.

▪ ▪ ▪

This is biology.

"Where the hell is everybody?"

"It's Thursday," Stefan Fabbre said, adding, "Damn!" as the figures on the computer screen jumped and flickered. He was wearing his topcoat over sweater and scarf, since the biology laboratory was heated only by a space heater that shorted out the computer circuit if they were on at the same time. "There are programs that could do this in two seconds," he said, jabbing morosely at the keyboard.

Avelin came up and glanced at the screen. "What is it?"

"The RNA comparison count. I could do it faster on my fingers."

Avelin, a bald, spruce, pale, dark-eyed man of forty, roamed the laboratory, looked restlessly through a folder of reports. "Can't run a university with this going on," he said. "I'd have thought you'd be down there."

Fabbre entered a new set of figures and said, "Why?"

"You're an idealist."

"Am I?" Fabbre leaned back, rolled his head to get the cricks out. "I try hard not to be," he said.

"Realists are born, not made." The younger man sat down on a lab stool and stared at the scarred, stained counter. "It's coming apart," he said.

"You think so? Seriously?"

Avelin nodded. "You heard that report from Prague."

Fabbre nodded.

"Last week . . . this week . . . next year—yes. An earthquake. The stones come apart—it falls apart—there was a building, now there's not. History is made. So I don't understand why you're here, not there."

"Seriously, you don't understand?"

Avelin smiled and said, "Seriously."

"All right." Fabbre stood up and began walking up and down the long room as he spoke. He was a slight gray-haired man with youthfully intense, controlled movements. "Science or political activity, either/or: Choose. Right? Choice is responsibility, right? So I chose my responsibility responsibly. I chose science and abjured all action but the acts of science. The acts of a responsible science. Out there, they can change the rules; in here, they can't change the rules; when they try to, I resist. This is my resistance." He slapped the laboratory bench as he turned round. "I'm lecturing. I walk up and down like this when I lecture. So. Background of the choice. I'm from the northeast. Fifty-six, in the northeast, do you remember? My grandfather, my father—reprisals. So, in Sixty, I come here, to the university. Sixty-two, my best friend, my wife's brother. We were walking through a village market, talking, then he stopped, he stopped talking, they had shot him. A kind of mistake. Right? He was a musician. A realist. I felt that I owed it to him, that I owed it to them, you see, to live carefully, with responsibility, to do the best I could do. The best I could do was this," and he gestured around the laboratory. "I'm good at it. So I go on trying to be a realist. As far as possible, under the circumstances, which have less and less to do with reality. But they are only circumstances. Circumstances in which I do my work as carefully as I can."

Avelin sat on the lab stool, his head bowed. When Fabbre was done, he nodded. After a while, he said, "But I have to ask you if it's realistic to separate the circumstances, as you put it, from the work."

"About as realistic as separating the body from the mind," Fabbre said. He stretched again and reseated himself at the computer. "I want to get this series in," he said, and his hands went to the keyboard and his gaze to the notes he was copying. After five or six minutes, he started the printer and spoke without turning. "You're serious, Givan? You think it's coming apart?"

"Yes. I think the experiment is over."

The printer scraped and screeched, and they raised their voices to be heard.

"Here, you mean."

"Here and everywhere. They know it, down at Roukh Square. Go down there. You'll see. There could be such jubilation only at the death of a tyrant or the failure of a great hope."

"Or both."

"Or both," Avelin agreed.

The paper jammed in the printer, and Fabbre opened the machine to free it. His hand was shaking. Avelin, spruce and cool, hands behind his back, strolled over, looked, reached in, disengaged the corner that was jamming the feed.

"Soon," he said, "we'll have an IBM. A Mactoshin. Our hearts' desire."

"Macintosh," Fabbre said.

"Everything can be done in two seconds."

Fabbre restarted the printer and looked around. "Listen, the principles—"

Avelin's eyes shone strangely, as if full of tears; he shook his head. "So much depends on the circumstances," he said.

▪ ▪ ▪

This is a key. It locks and unlocks a door, the door to apartment 2-1 of the building at 43 Pradinestrade in the Old North Quarter of the city of Krasnoy. The apartment is enviable, having a kitchen with saucepans, dishcloths, spoons and all that is necessary, and two bedrooms, one of which is now used as a sitting room, with chairs, books, papers and all that is necessary, as well as a view from the window between other buildings of a short section of the Molsen River. The river at this moment is lead-colored and the trees above it are bare and black. The apartment is unlighted and empty. When they left, Bruna Fabbre locked the door and dropped the key, which is on a steel ring along with the key to her desk at the lyceum and the key to her sister Bendika's apartment in the Trasfiuve, into her small imitation-leather handbag, which is getting shabby at the corners, and snapped the handbag shut. Bruna's daughter Stefana has a copy of the key in her jeans pocket, tied on a bit of braided cord along with the key to the closet in her room in dormitory G of the University of Krasnoy, where she is a graduated student in the department of Orsinian and Slavic Literature, working for a degree in the field of early romantic poetry. She never locks the closet. The two women walk down Pradinestrade three blocks and wait a few minutes at the corner for the number 18 bus, which runs on Bulvard Settentre from North Krasnoy to the center of the city.

Pressed in the crowded interior of the handbag and the tight warmth of the jeans pocket, the key and its copy are inert, silent, forgotten. All a key can do is lock and unlock its door; that's all the function it has, all the meaning; it has a responsibility but no rights. I can lock or unlock. It can be found or thrown away.

▪ ▪ ▪

This is history. Once upon a time, in 1830, in 1848, in 1866, in 1918, in 1947, in 1956, stones flew. Stones flew through the air like pigeons, and hearts, too; hearts had wings. Those were the years when the stones flew, the hearts took wing, the young voices sang. The soldiers raised their muskets to the ready, the soldiers aimed their rifles, the soldiers poised their machine guns. They were young, the soldiers. They fired. The stones lay down, the pigeons fell. There's a kind of red stone called pigeon blood, a ruby. The red stones of Roukh Square were never rubies; slosh a bucket of water over them or let the rain fall and they're gray again, lead-gray, common stones. Only now and then, in certain years, they have flown, and turned to rubies.

▪ ▪ ▪

This is a bus. Nothing to do with fairy tales and not romantic; certainly realistic; though, in a way, in principle, in fact, it is highly idealistic. A city bus, crowded with people, in a city street in central Europe on a November afternoon and it's stalled. What else? Oh, dear. Oh, damn. But no, it hasn't stalled; the engine, for a wonder, hasn't broken down; it's just that it can't go any farther. Why not? Because there's a bus stopped in front of it, and another one stopped in front of that one at the cross street, and it looks like everything has stopped. Nobody on this bus has heard the word gridlock, the name of an exotic disease of the mysterious West. There aren't enough private cars in Krasnoy to bring about a gridlock even if they knew what it was. There are cars, and a lot of wheezing, idealistic buses, but all there is enough of to stop the flow of traffic in Krasnoy is people. It is a kind of equation, proved by experiments conducted over many years, perhaps not in a wholly scientific or objective spirit but nonetheless presenting a well-documented result confirmed by repetition: There are not enough people in this city to stop a tank. Even in much larger cities, it has been authoritatively demonstrated as recently as last spring that there are not enough people to stop a tank. But there are enough people in this city to stop a bus, and they are doing so. Not by throwing themselves in front of it, waving banners or singing songs about Liberty's eternal day, but merely by being in the street, getting in the way of the bus, on the supposition that the bus driver has not been trained in either homicide or suicide, and on the same supposition—upon which all cities stand or fall—that they are also getting in the way of all the other buses and all the cars and in one another's way, too, so that nobody is going much of anywhere, in a physical sense.

"We're going to have to walk from here," Stefana said, and her mother clutched her imitation-leather handbag.

"Oh, but we can't, Fana. Look at that crowd! What are they—Are they—"

"It's Thursday, ma'am," said a large, red-faced, smiling man just behind them in the aisle. Everybody was getting off the bus, pushing and talking.

"Yesterday, I got four blocks closer than this," a woman said crossly.

And the red-faced man said, "Ah, but this is Thursday."

"Fifteen thousand last time," said somebody.

And somebody else said, "Fifty, fifty thousand today!"

"We can never get near the Square. I don't think we should try," Bruna told her daughter as they squeezed into the crowd outside the bus door.

"You stay with me, don't let go and don't worry," said the student of Early Romantic Poetry, a tall, resolute young woman, and she took her mother's hand in a firm grasp. "It doesn't really matter where we get, but it would be fun if you could see the Square. Let's try. Let's go round behind the post office."

Everybody was trying to go in the same direction. Stefana and Bruna got across one street by dodging and stopping and pushing gently, then turning against the flow, they trotted down a nearly empty alley, cut across the cobbled court in back of the Central Post Office and rejoined an even thicker crowd moving slowly down a wide street and out from between the buildings. "There, there's the palace, see!" said Stefana, who could see it, being taller. "This is as far as we'll get except by osmosis." They practiced osmosis, which necessitated letting go of each other's hands and made Bruna unhappy.

"This is far enough, this is fine here," Bruna kept saying. "I can see everything. There's the roof of the palace. Nothing's going to happen, is it? I mean, will anybody speak?" It was not what she meant, but she did not want to shame her daughter with her fear, her daughter who had not been alive when the stones turned to rubies. And she spoke quietly because although there were so many people pressed and pressing into Roukh Square, they were not noisy. They talked to one another in ordinary, quiet voices. Only now and then, somebody down nearer the palace shouted out a name, and then many other voices would repeat it with a roll and crash like a wave breaking. Then they would be quiet again, murmuring vastly, like the sea between big waves.

The streetlights had come on. Roukh Square was sparsely lighted by tall, old cast-iron standards with double globes that shed a soft light high in the air. Through that serene light, which seemed to darken the sky, came drifting small, dry flecks of snow.

The flecks melted to droplets on Stefana's dark short hair and on the scarf Bruna had tied over her fair short hair to keep her ears warm.

When Stefana stopped at last, Bruna stood up as tall as she could, and because they were standing on the highest edge of the Square, in front of the old dispensary, by craning, she could see the great crowd, the faces like snowflakes, countless. She saw the evening darkening, the snow falling, and no way out, and no way home. She was lost in the forest. The palace, whose few lighted windows shone dully above the crowd, was silent. No one came out, no one went in. It was the seat of government; it held the power. It was the powerhouse, the powder magazine, the bomb. Power had been compressed, jammed into those old reddish walls, packed and forced into them over years, over centuries, till if it exploded, it would burst with horrible violence, hurling pointed shards of stone. And out here in the twilight, in the open, there was nothing but soft faces with shining eyes, soft little breasts and stomachs and thighs protected only by bits of cloth.

She looked down at her feet on the pavement. They were cold. She would have worn her boots if she had thought it was going to snow, if Fana hadn't hurried her so. She felt cold, lost, lonely to the point of tears. She set her jaw and set her lips and stood firm on her cold feet on the cold stone.

There was a sound, sparse, sparkling, faint, like the snow crystals. The crowd had gone quite silent, swept by low laughing murmurs, and through the silence ran that small, discontinuous silvery sound.

"What is that?" asked Bruna, beginning to smile. "Why are they doing that?"

▪ ▪ ▪

This is a committee meeting. Surely you don't want me to describe a committee meeting? It meets as usual on Friday at 11 in the morning in the basement of the Economics Building. At 11 on Friday night, however, it is still meeting, and there are a good many onlookers, several million, in fact, thanks to the foreigner with the camera, a television camera with a long snout, a one-eyed snout that peers and sucks up what it sees. The cameraman focuses for a long time on the tall dark-haired girl who speaks so eloquently in favor of a certain decision concerning bringing a certain man back to the capital. But the millions of onlookers will not understand her argument, which is spoken in her obscure language and is not translated for them. All they will know is how the eye snout of the camera lingered on her young face, sucking it.

▪ ▪ ▪

This is a love story. Two hours later, the cameraman was long gone, but the committee was still meeting.

"No, listen," she said, "seriously, this is the moment when the betrayal is always made. Free elections, yes; but if we don't look past that now, when will we? And who'll do it? Are we a country or a client state changing patrons?"

"You have to go one step at a time, consolidating—"

"When the dam breaks? You have to shoot the rapids! All at once!"

"It's a matter of choosing direction—"

"Exactly, direction. Not being carried senselessly by events."

"But all the events are sweeping in one direction."

"They always do. Back! You'll see!"

"Sweeping to what, to dependence on the West instead of the East, like Fana said?"

"Dependence is inevitable—realignment, but not occupation—"

"The hell it won't be occupation! Occupation by money, materialism, their markets, their values. You don't think we can hold out against them, do you? What's social justice to a color-TV set? That battle's lost before it's fought. Where do we stand?"

"Where we always stood. In an absolutely untenable position."

"He's right. Seriously, we are exactly where we always were. Nobody else is. We are. They have caught up with us, for a moment, for this moment, and so we can act. The untenable position is the center of power. Now. We can act *now.*"

"To prevent color-TVzation? How? The dam's broken! The goodies come flooding in. And we drown in them."

"Not if we establish the direction, the true direction, right now—"

"But will Rege listen to us? Why are we turning back when we should be going forward? If we—"

"We have to establish—"

"No! We have to act! Freedom can be established only in the moment of freedom—"

They were all shouting at once in their hoarse, worn-out voices. They had all been talking and listening and drinking bad coffee and living for days, for weeks, on love. Yes, on love; these are lovers' quarrels. It is for love that he pleads, it is for love that she rages. It was always for love. That's why the camera snout came poking and sucking into this dirty basement room where the lovers meet. It craves love, the sight of love; for if you can't have the real thing, you can watch it on TV, and soon you don't know the real thing from the images on the little screen where everything, as he said, can be done in two seconds. But the lovers know the difference.

▪ ▪ ▪

This is a fairy tale, and you know that in the fairy tale, after it says that they lived happily ever after, there is no after. The evil enchantment was broken; the good servant received half the kingdom as his reward; the king ruled long and well. Remember the moment when the betrayal is made, and ask no questions. Do not ask if the poisoned fields grew white again with grain. Do not ask if the leaves of the forests grew green that spring. Do not ask what the maiden received as her reward. Remember the tale of Koshchey the Deathless, whose life was in a needle, and the needle was in an egg, and the egg was in a swan, and the swan was in an eagle, and the eagle was in a wolf, and the wolf was in the palace whose walls were built of the stones of power. Enchantment within enchantment! We are a long way from the egg that holds the needle that must be broken so Koshchey the Deathless can die. And so the tale ends. Thousands and thousands of people stood on the slanting pavement before the palace. Snow sparkled in the air, and the people sang. You know the song, that old song with words like *land, love, free,* in the language you have known the longest. Its words make stone part from stone, its words prevent tanks, its words transform the world, when it is sung at the right time by the right people, after enough people have died for singing it.

A thousand doors opened in the walls of the palace. The soldiers laid down their arms and sang. The evil enchantment was broken. The good king returned to his kingdom, and the people danced for joy on the stones of the city streets.

▪ ▪ ▪

And we do not ask what happened after. But we can tell the story over, we can tell the story till we get it right.

"My daughter's on the Committee of the Student Action Council," said Stefan Fabbre to his neighbor Florens Aske as they stood in a line outside the bakery on Pradinestrade. His tone of voice was complicated.

"I know. Erreskar saw her on the television," Aske said.

"She says they've decided that bringing Rege here is the only way to provide an immediate, credible transition. They think the army will accept him."

They shuffled forward a step.

Aske, an old man with a hard brown face and narrow eyes, stuck his lips out, thinking it over.

"You were in the Rege government," Fabbre said.

Aske nodded. "Minister of education for a week," he said, and gave a bark like a sea lion—owp!—a cough or a laugh.

"Do you think he can pull it off?"

Aske pulled his grubby muffler closer round his neck and said, "Well, Rege is not stupid. But he's old. What about that scientist, that physicist fellow?"

"Rochoy. She says their idea is that Rege's brought in first, for the transition, for the symbolism, the link to Fifty-six. And if he survives, Rochoy would be the one they'd run in an election."

"The dream of the election. . . ."

They shuffled forward again. They were now in front of the bakery window, only eight or ten people from the door.

"Why do they put up the old man?" asked the old man. "These boys and girls, these young people. What the devil do they want us for again?"

"I don't know," Fabbre said. "I keep thinking they know what they're doing. She had me down there, you know, made me come to one of their meetings. She came to the lab—Come on, leave that, follow me! I did. No questions. She's in charge. All of them, twenty-two, twenty-three, they're in charge. In power. Seeking structure, order, but very definite: Violence is defeat, to them, violence is the loss of options. They're absolutely certain and completely ignorant. Like spring—like the lambs in spring. They have never done anything and they know exactly what to do."

"Stefan," said his wife, Bruna, who had been standing at his elbow for several sentences, "you're lecturing. Hello, dear. Hello, Florens, I just saw Margarita at the market, we were queuing for cabbages. I'm on my way downtown, Stefan. I'll be back, I don't know, sometime after seven, maybe."

"Again?" he said.

And Aske said, "Downtown?"

"It's Thursday," Bruna said, and bringing up the keys from her handbag, the two apartment keys and the desk key, she shook them in the air before the men's faces, making a silvery jingle; and she smiled.

"I'll come," said Stefan Fabbre.

"Owp! Owp!" went Aske. "Oh, hell, I'll come, too. Does man live by bread alone?"

"Will Margarita worry where you are?" Bruna asked as they left the bakery line and set off toward the bus stop.

"That's the problem with the women, you see," said the old man. "They worry that she'll worry. Yes. She will. And you worry about your daughter, eh?"

"Yes," Stefan said, "I do."

"No," Bruna said. "I don't. I fear her, I fear for her, I honor her. She gave me the keys." She clutched her imitation leather handbag tight between her arm and side as they walked.

▪ ▪ ▪

This is the truth. They stood on the stones in the lightly falling snow and listened to the silvery, trembling sound of thousands of keys being shaken, unlocking the air, once upon a time.

Charles Johnson

Kwoon

December 1991

Like John Updike, Charles Johnson, born in Illinois in 1948, aspired to be a cartoonist. He moved further along in that career than Updike did, having sold enough of his cartoons to publish a book, *Black Humor,* 1970. Like John Irving, Johnson is an athlete and doubtless one of the few tenured English professors (at the University of Washington in Seattle) to manage a martial-arts *kwoon* on the side. His first novel, *Faith and the Good Thing,* was published in 1974, and his first book of stories was *Sorcerer's Apprentice* in 1986. *Middle Passage,* a surprisingly funny and high-spirited novel of the slave trade, won the National Book Award in 1990. This story, which uses the *kwoon* as a backdrop, was his first for *Playboy.*

Charles Johnson

Kwoon

David Lewis' martial-arts *kwoon* was in a South Side Chicago neighborhood so rough he nearly had to fight to reach the door. Previously, it had been a dry cleaner's, then a small Thai restaurant, and although he Lysol-scrubbed the buckled linoleum floors and burned jade incense for the Buddha before each class, the studio was a blend of pungent odors, the smell of starched shirts and the tang of cinnamon pastries riding alongside the sharp smell of male sweat from nightly workouts. For five months, David had bivouacked on the back-room floor after his students left, not minding the clank of presses from the print shop next door, the noisy garage across the street or even the two-grand bank loan needed to renovate three rooms with low ceilings and leaky pipes overhead. This was his place, earned after ten years of training in San Francisco and his promotion to the hard-won title of *sifu*.

As his customers grunted through Tuesday-night warm-up exercises, then drills with Elizabeth, his senior student (she'd been a dancer and still had the elasticity of Gumby), David stood off to one side to watch, feeling the force of their *kiais* vibrate in the cavity of his chest, interrupting them only to correct a student's stance. On the whole, his students were a hopeless bunch, a Franciscan test of his patience. Some came to class on drugs; one, Wendell Miller, a retired cook trying to recapture his youth, was the obligatory senior citizen; a few were high school dropouts, orange-haired punks who played in rock bands with names like Plastic Anus. But David did not despair. He believed he was duty bound to lead them, like the Pied Piper, from Sylvester Stallone movies to a real understanding of the martial arts as a way that prepared the young, through discipline and large doses of humility, to be of use to themselves and others. Accordingly, his sheet of rules said no high school student could be promoted unless he kept a B average, and no dropouts were allowed through the door until they signed up for their G.E.D. exam; if they got straight A's, he took them to dinner. Anyone caught fighting outside his school was suspended. David had been something of a punk himself a decade earlier, pushing nose candy in Palo Alto, living on barbiturates and beer before his own teacher helped him see, to David's surprise, that in his spirit he had resources greater than anything in the world outside. The master's picture was just inside the door, so all could bow to him when they entered David's school. Spreading the style was his rationale for moving to the Midwest, but the hidden agenda, David believed, was an inward training that would make the need for conflict fall away like a chrysalis. If nothing else, he could make their workouts so tiring none of his students would have any energy left for getting into trouble.

Except, he thought, for Ed Morgan.

He was an older man, maybe forty, with a bald spot and razor burns that ran from just below his ears to his throat. This was his second night at the studio, but David realized Morgan knew the calisthenics routine and basic punching drills cold. He'd been in other schools. Any fool could see that, which meant the new student had lied on his application about having no formal training. Unlike David's regular students, who wore the traditional white Chinese T-shirt and black trousers, Morgan had changed into a butternut running suit with black stripes on the sleeves and pants legs. David had told him to buy a uniform the week before, during his brief interview. Morgan refused. And David dropped the matter, noticing that Morgan had pecs and forearms like Popeye. His triceps could have been lifted right off Marvin Hagler. He was thick as a tree, even top-heavy, in David's opinion, and he stood half a head taller than the other students. He didn't *have* a suit to fit Morgan. And Morgan moved so fluidly David caught himself frowning, a little frightened, for it was as though the properties of water and rock had come together in one creature. Then he snapped himself back, laughed at his silliness, looked at the clock—only half an hour of class remained—then clapped his hands loudly. He popped his fingers on his left hand, then his right, as his students, eager for his advice, turned to face him.

"We should do a little sparring now. Pair up with somebody your size. Elizabeth, you work with the new students."

"Sifu?"

It was Ed Morgan.

David paused, both lips pressed together.

"If you don't mind, I'd like to spar with you."

One of David's younger students, Toughie, a Filipino boy with a falcon emblazoned on his arm, elbowed his partner, who wore his hair in a stiff Mohawk, and both said, "Uh-oh." David felt his body flush hot, sweat suddenly on his palms like a sprinkling of salt water, though there was no whiff of a challenge, no disrespect in Morgan's voice. His speech, in fact, was as soft and gently syllabled as a singer's. David tried to laugh:

"You sure you want to try me?"

"Please." Morgan bowed his head, which might have seemed self-effacing had he not been so tall and still looking down at David's crown. "It would be a privilege."

Rather than spar, his students scrambled back, nearly falling over themselves to form a circle, as if to ring two gun fighters from opposite ends of town. David kept the slightest of smiles on his lips, even when his mouth tired, to give the impression of masterful indifference—he was, after all, *sifu* here, wasn't he? A little sparring would do him good. Wouldn't it? Especially with a man the size of Morgan. Loosen him up, so to speak.

He flipped his red sash behind him and stepped lower into a cat stance, his weight on his rear leg, his lead foot light and lifted slightly, ready to whip forward when Morgan moved into range.

Morgan was not so obliging. He circled left, away from David's lead leg, then did a half step of broken rhythm to confuse David's sense of distance, and then, before he could change stances, flicked a jab at David's jaw. If his students were surprised, David didn't know, for the room fell away instantly, dissolving as his adrenaline rose and his concentration closed out everything but Morgan—he always needed to get hit once before he got serious—and only he and the other existed, both in motion but pulled out of time, the moment flickerish, fibrous and strangely two-dimensional, yet all too familiar to fighters, perhaps to men falling from heights, to motorists microseconds before a head-on collision, these minutes a spinning mosaic of crescent kicks, back fists and flurry punches that, on David's side, failed. All his techniques fell short of Morgan, who, like a shadow—or Mephistopheles—simply dematerialized before they arrived.

The older man shifted from boxing to *wu*-style *ta'i chi Chuan*. From this he flowed into *pa kua,* then Korean karate: style after style, a blending of a dozen cultures and histories in one blink of an eye after another. With one move, he tore away David's sash. Then he called out each move in Mandarin as he dropped it on David, bomb after bomb, as if this were only an exhibition exercise.

On David's face, blossoms of blood opened like orchids. He knew he was being hurt; two ribs felt broken, but he wasn't sure. He thanked God for endorphins—a body's natural painkiller. He'd not touched Morgan once. Outclassed as he was, all he could do was ward him off, stay out of his way—then not even that when a fist the size of a cantaloupe crashed straight down, riving David to the floor, his ears ringing then, and legs outstretched like a doll's. He wanted to stay down forever but sprang to his feet, sweat stinging his eyes, to salvage one scrap of dignity. He found himself facing the wrong way. Morgan was behind him, his hands on his hips, his head thrown back. Two of David's students laughed.

It was Elizabeth who pressed her sweat-moistened towel under David's bloody nose. Morgan's feet came together. He wasn't even winded. "Thank you, *Sifu.*" Mockery, David thought, but his head banged too badly to be sure. The room was still behind heat waves, though sounds were coming back, and now he could distinguish one student from another. His sense of clock time returned. He said, "You're a good fighter, Ed."

Toughie whispered, "No shit, *bwana.*"

The room suddenly leaned vertiginously to David's left; he bent his knees a little to steady his balance. "But you're still a beginner in this system." Weakly, he lifted his hand, then let it fall. "Go on with class. Elizabeth, give everybody a new lesson."

"David, I think class is over now."

Over? He thought he knew what that meant. "I guess so. Bow to the master."

His students bowed to the portrait of the school's founder.

"Now to each other."

Again, they bowed, but this time to Morgan.

"Class dismissed."

Some of his students were whooping, slapping Morgan on his back as they made their way to the hallway in back to change. Elizabeth, the only female, stayed behind to let them shower and dress. Both she and the youngest student, Mark, a middle school boy with skin as smooth and pale as a girl's, looked bewildered, uncertain what this drubbing meant.

David limped back to his office, which also was his bedroom, separated from the main room only by a curtain. There, he kept equipment: free weights, a heavy bag on which he'd taped a snapshot of himself—for who else did he need to conquer?—and the rowing machine Elizabeth avoided, calling it Instant Abortion. He sat down for a few seconds at his unvarnished kneehole desk bought cheap at a Salvation Army outlet, then rolled onto the floor, wondering what he'd done wrong. Would another *sifu,* more seasoned, simply have refused to spar with a self-styled beginner?

After a few minutes, he heard them leaving, a couple of students begging Morgan to teach them, and really, this was too much to bear. David, holding his side, his head pulled in, limped back out. "Ed," he coughed, then recovered. "Can I talk to you?"

Morgan checked his watch, a diamond-studded thing that doubled as a stop watch and a thermometer, and probably even monitored his pulse. Half its cost would pay the studio's rent for a year. He dressed well, David saw. Like a retired champion, everything tailored, nothing off the rack. "I've got an appointment, *Sifu*. Maybe later, OK?"

A little dazed, David, swallowing the rest of what he wanted to say, gave a headshake. "OK."

Just before the door slammed, he heard another boy say, "Lewis ain't no fighter, man. He's a dancer." He lay down again in his office, too sore to shower, every muscle tender, strung tight as catgut, searching with the tip of his tongue for broken teeth.

As he was stuffing toilet paper into his right nostril to stop the bleeding, Elizabeth, dressed now in high boots and a baggy coat and slacks, stepped behind the curtain. She'd replaced her contacts with owl-frame glasses that made her look spinsterish. "I'm sorry—he was wrong to do that."

"You mean win?"

"It wasn't supposed to be a real fight! He tricked you. Anyone can score, like he did, if they throw out all the rules."

"Tell him that." Wincing, he rubbed his shoulder. "Do you think anybody will come back on Thursday?" She did not answer. "Do you think I should close the school?" David laughed, bleakly. "Or just leave town?"

"David, you're a good teacher. A *sifu* doesn't always have to win, does he? It's not about winning, is it?"

No sooner had she said this than the answer rose between them. Could you be a doctor whose every patient died? A credible mathematician who couldn't count? By the way the world and, more important, his students reckoned things, he was a fraud. Elizabeth hitched the strap on her workout bag, which was big enough for both of them to climb into, higher on her shoulder. "Do you want me to stick around?"

"No."

"You going to put something on that eye?"

Through the eye Morgan hadn't closed she looked flattened, like a coin, her skin flushed and her hair faintly damp after a workout, so lovely David wanted to fall against her, blend with her—disappear. Only, it would hurt now to touch or be touched. And, unlike some teachers he knew, his policy was to take whatever he felt for a student—the erotic electricity that sometimes arose—and transform it into harder teaching, more time spent on giving them their money's worth. Besides, he was always broke; his street clothes were old enough to be in elementary school: a thirty-year-old man no better educated than Toughie or Mark, who'd concentrated on shop in high school. Elizabeth was another story: a working mother, a secretary on the staff at the University of Illinois at Chicago, surrounded all day by professors who looked young enough to be graduate students. A job sweet as this, from David's level, seemed high-toned and secure. What could he offer Elizabeth? Anyway, this might be the last night he saw her, if she left with the others, and who could blame her? He studied her hair, how it fell onyx-black and abundant, like some kind of blessing over and under her collar, which forced Elizabeth into the unconscious habit of tilting her head just so and flicking it back with her fingers, a gesture of such natural grace it made his chest ache. She was so much lovelier than she knew. To his surprise, a line from *Psalms* came to him, "I will praise thee, for I am fearfully and wonderfully made." Whoever wrote that, he thought, meant it for her.

He looked away. "Go on home."

"We're having class on Thursday?"

"You paid until the end of the month, didn't you?"

"I paid for six months, remember?"

He did—she was literally the one who kept the light bill paid. "Then we'll have class."

All that night and half the next day David stayed horizontal, hating Morgan. Hating himself more. It took him hours to stop shaking. That night it rained. He fended off sleep, listening to the patter with his full attention, hoping its music might have something to tell him. Twice he belched up blood, then a paste of phlegm and hamburger pulp. Jesus, he thought, distantly, I'm sick. By nightfall, he was able to sit awhile and take a little soup, but he could not stand. Both his legs ballooned so tightly in his trousers he had to cut the cloth with scissors and peel it off like strips of bacon. Parts of his body were burning, refusing to obey him. He reached into his desk drawer for Morgan's application and saw straightaway that Ed Morgan couldn't spell. David smiled ruefully, looking for more faults. Morgan listed his address in Skokie, his occupation as a merchant marine, and provided no next of kin to call in case of emergencies.

That was all, and David for the life of him could not see that night, or the following morning, how he could face anyone in the studio again. Painfully, he remembered his promotion a year earlier. His teacher had held a ceremonial Buddhist candle, the only light in his darkened living room in a house near the Mission District barely bigger than a shed. David, kneeling, held a candle, too. "The light that was given to me," said his teacher, repeating an invocation two centuries old, "I now give to you." He touched his flame to the wick of David's candle, passing the light, and David's eyes burned with tears. For the first time in his life, he felt connected to cultures and people he'd never seen—to traditions larger than himself.

His high school instructors had dismissed him as unteachable. Were they right? David wondered. Was he made of wood too flimsy ever to amount to anything? Suddenly, he hated those teachers, as well as the ones at Elizabeth's school, but only for a time, hatred being so sharp an emotion, like the business end of a bali-song knife, he could never hang on to it for long—perhaps that was why he failed as a fighter—and soon he felt nothing, only numbness. As from a great distance, he watched himself sponge-bathe in the sink, dress himself slowly and prepare for Thursday's class, the actions previously fueled by desire, by concern over consequences, by fear of outcome, replaced now by something he could not properly name, as if a costly operation once powered by coal had reverted overnight to the water wheel.

When six o'clock came and only Mark, Wendell and Elizabeth showed, David telephoned a few students, learning from parents, roommates and live-in lovers that none were home. With Morgan, he suspected. So that's who he called next.

"Sure," said Morgan. "A couple are here. They just wanted to talk."

"They're missing class."

"I didn't ask them to come."

Quietly, David drew breath deeply just to see if he could. It hurt, so he stopped, letting his wind stay shallow, swirling at the top of his lungs. He pulled a piece of dead skin off his hand. "Are you coming back?"

"I don't see much point in that, do you?"

In the background he could hear voices, a television and beer cans being opened. "You've fought professionally, haven't you?"

"That was a long time ago—overseas. Won two, lost two, then I quit," said Morgan. "It doesn't count for much."

"Did you teach?"

"Here and there. Listen," he said, "why did you call?"

"Why did you en*roll?*"

"I've been out of training. I wanted to see how much I remembered. What do you want me to say? I won't come back, all right? What do you want from me, Lewis?"

He did not know. He felt the stillness of his studio, a similar stillness in himself, and sat quiet so long he could have been posing for a portrait. Then:

"You paid for a week in advance. I owe you another lesson."

Morgan snorted. "In what—Chinese ballet?"

"Fighting," said David. "A private lesson in *budo*. I'll keep the studio open until you get here." And then he hung up.

▪ ▪ ▪

Morgan circled the block four times before finding a parking space across from Lewis' school. Why hurry? Ten, maybe fifteen minutes he waited, watching the open door, wondering what the boy (and he was a boy to Morgan's eye) wanted. He'd known too many kids like this one. They took a few classes, promoted themselves to seventh *dan,* then opened a storefront *dojo* that was no better than a private stage, a theater for the ego, a place where they could play out fantasies of success denied them on the street, in school, in dead-end jobs. They were phony, Morgan thought, like almost everything in the modern world, which was a subject he could spend hours deriding, though he seldom did, his complaints now being tiresome even to his own ears. *Losers,* he thought, who strutted around in fancy Oriental costumes, refusing to spar or show their skill. "Too advanced for beginners," they claimed, or, "My *sensei* made me promise not to show that to anyone." Hogwash. He could see through that shit. All over America he'd seen them, and India, too, where they weren't called fakirs for nothing. And they'd made him suffer. They made him pay for the "privilege" of their teachings. In twenty years as a merchant marine, he'd been in as many schools in Europe, Japan, Korea and Hong Kong, submitting himself to the lunacy of illiterate fak(e)irs—men who claimed they could slay an opponent with their breath or *ch'i*—and simply because his hunger to learn was insatiable. So he had no rank anywhere. He could tolerate no "master's" posturing long enough to ingratiate himself into the inner circles of any school—though eighty percent of these fly-by-night *dojos* bottomed out inside a year. And, hell, he was a bilge rat, never in any port long enough to move up in rank. Still, he had killed men. It was depressingly easy. Killed them in back alleys in Tokyo with blows so crude no master would include such inelegant means among "traditional" techniques.

More hogwash, thought Morgan. He'd probably done the boy good by exposing him. His own collarbones had been broken twice, each leg three times, all but two fingers smashed, and his nose reshaped so often he couldn't remember its original contours. On wet nights, he had trouble breathing. But why complain? You couldn't make an omelet without breaking a few eggs.

And yet, Morgan thought, squinting at the door of the school, there was a side to Lewis he'd liked. At first, he had felt comfortable, as if he had at last found the *kwoon* he'd been looking for. True, Lewis had come on way too cocky when asked to spar, but what could you expect when he was hardly older than the high school kids he was teaching? And maybe teaching them well, if he was really going by that list of rules he handed out to beginners. And it wasn't so much that Lewis was a bad fighter, only that he, Morgan, was about five times better because whatever he lacked now in middle age—flexibility and youth's fast reflexes—he more than made up for in size and experience, which was a polite word for dirty tricks. Give Lewis a few more years, a little more coaching in the combat strategies Morgan could show him, and he might become a champion.

But who did he think he was fooling? Things never worked out that way. There was always too much ego in it. Something every *sifu* figured he had to protect, or save face about. A lesson in *budo?* Christ, he'd nearly killed this kid, and there he was, barking on the telephone like Saddam Hussein before the bombing started, even begging for the ground war to begin. And that was just all right, if a showdown—a duel—was what he wanted. Morgan set his jaw and stepped onto the pavement of the parking lot. However things went down, he decided, the consequences would be on Lewis—it would be *his* call.

Locking his car, then double-checking each door (this was a rough neighborhood, even by Morgan's standards), he crossed the street, carrying his workout bag under his arm, the last threads of smog-filtered twilight fading into darkness, making the door of the *kwoon* a bright portal chiseled from blocks of glass and cement. A few feet from the entrance, he heard voices. Three students had shown. Most of the class had not. The two who had visited him weren't there. He'd lectured them on his experience of strangling an assailant in Kyoto, and Toughie had gone quiet, looked edgy (fighting didn't seem like fun then) and uneasy. Finally, they left, which was fine with Morgan. He didn't want followers. Sycophants made him sick. All he wanted was a teacher he could respect.

Inside the school's foyer, he stopped, his eyes tracking the room. He never entered closed spaces too quickly or walked near corners or doorways on the street. Toward the rear, by a rack filled with halberds and single-edged broadswords, a girl about five, with piles of ebony hair and blue eyes like splinters of the sky, was reading a dog-eared copy of *The Cat in the Hat*. This would be the child of the class leader, he thought, bowing quickly at the portrait of the school's founder. But why bring her here? It cemented his contempt for this place, more a day-care center than a *kwoon*. Still, he bowed a second time to the founder. Him he respected. Where were such grand old stylists when you needed them? He did not see Lewis, or any other student until, passing the curtained office, Morgan whiffed food cooking on a hot plate and, parting the curtain slightly, he saw Wendell, who would never in this life learn to fight, stirring and seasoning a pot of couscous. He looked like that children's toy, Mr. Potato Head. Morgan wondered, Why did David Lewis encourage the man? Just to take his money? He passed on, feeling his tread shake the floor, into the narrow hall where a few hooks hung for clothing, and found Elizabeth with her left foot on a low bench, lacing the wrestling shoes she wore for working out.

"Excuse me," he said. "I'll wait until you're finished."

Their eyes caught for a moment.

"I'm done now." She kicked her bag under the bench, squeezed past Morgan by flattening herself to the wall, as if he had a disease, then spun round at the entrance and looked squarely at him. "You know something?"

"What?"

"You're wrong. Just *wrong*."

"I don't know what you're talking about."

"The hell you don't! David may not be the fighter, the killer, you are, but he *is* one of the best teachers in this system."

Morgan smirked. "Those who can't do, teach, eh?"

She burned a look of such hatred at Morgan he turned his eyes away. When he looked back, she was gone. He sighed. He'd seen that look on so many faces, yellow, black and white, after he'd punched them in. It hardly mattered anymore. Quietly, he suited up, stretched his arms wide and padded barefoot back onto the main floor, prepared to finish this, if that was what Lewis wanted, for why else would he call?

But at first he could not catch sight of the boy. The others were standing around him in a circle, chatting, oddly like chess pieces shielding an endangered king. His movements were jerky and Chaplinesque, one arm around Elizabeth, the other braced on Wendell's shoulder. Without them, he could not walk until his bruised ankles healed. He was temporarily blind in one blackened, beefed-over eye. And since he could not tie his own sash, Mark was doing it for him. None of them noticed Morgan, but in the school's weak light, he could see blue welts he'd raised like crops on Lewis' cheeks and chest. That, and something else. The hands of the others rested on Lewis' shoulder, his back, as if he belonged to them, no matter what he did or didn't do. Weak as Lewis looked now, even the old cook Wendell could blow him over, and somehow it didn't matter if he was beaten every round, or missed class, or died. The others were the *kwoon*. It wasn't his school. It was theirs. Maybe brought together by the boy, Morgan thought, but now a separate thing living beyond him. To prove the system, the teaching here, false, he would have to strike down every one of them. And still he would have touched nothing.

"Ed," Lewis said, looking over Mark's shoulder. "When we were sparring, I saw mistakes in your form, things someone better than me might take advantage of. I'd like to correct them, if you're ready."

"What things?" His head snapped back. "What mistakes?"

"I can't match your reach," said Lewis, "but someone who could, getting inside your guard, would go for your groin or knee. It's the way you stand, probably a blend of a couple of styles you learned somewhere. But they don't work together. If you do this," he added, torquing his leg slightly so that his thigh guarded his groin, "the problem is solved."

"Is that why you called me?"

"No, there's another reason."

Morgan tensed; he should have known. "You do some warm-up exercises we've never seen. I like them. I want you to lead class tonight, if that's OK, so the others can learn them, too." Then he laughed. "I think I should warm the bench tonight."

Before he could reply, Lewis limped off, leaning on Mark, who led him back to his office. The two others waited for direction from Morgan. For a moment, he shifted his weight uncertainly from his right foot to his left, pausing until his tensed shoulders relaxed and the tight fingers on his right hand, coiled into a fist, opened. Then he pivoted toward the portrait of the founder. "Bow to the master." They bowed. "Now to our teacher." They did so, bowing toward the curtained room, with Morgan, a big man, bending deepest of all.

Haruki Murakami

The Second Bakery Attack

January 1992

Japan's best-selling contemporary author was born in 1949, and there seems to be a wide generation gap between him and writers in the older Japanese tradition. He began as a translator of American writers—F. Scott Fitzgerald, Truman Capote, John Irving, Paul Theroux—and he clearly owes as much to them as to any of his countrymen. *A Wild Sheep Chase,* a surrealistic detective story with an ambiance all its own, was published in America with much fanfare in 1989, and this was followed by *Hard-Boiled Wonderland and the End of the World* in 1991. This wise little story in which an outlandish midnight caper becomes a metaphor for the surprises of love and even the most conventional marriage shows Murakami's appeal; it appeared in his 1993 collection, *The Elephant Vanishes.* For the past several years he has been living and teaching at a series of American universities.

Haruki Murakami

The Second Bakery Attack

I'm still not sure I made the right choice when I told my wife about the bakery attack. But then, it might not have been a question of right and wrong. Which is to say that wrong choices can produce right results, and vice versa. I myself have adopted the position that, in fact, *we never choose anything at all.* Things happen. Or not.

If you look at it this way, *it just so happens* that I told my wife about the bakery attack. I hadn't been planning to bring it up—I had forgotten all about it—but it wasn't one of those now-that-you-mention-it kind of things, either.

What reminded me of the bakery attack was an unbearable hunger. It hit just before two o'clock in the morning. We ate a light supper at six, crawled into bed at nine-thirty and went to sleep. For some reason, we woke up at exactly the same moment. A few minutes later, the pangs struck with the force of the tornado in *The Wizard of Oz.* These were tremendous, overpowering hunger pangs.

Our refrigerator contained not a single item that could be technically categorized as food. We had a bottle of French dressing, six cans of beer, two shriveled onions, a stick of butter and a box of refrigerator deodorizer. With only two weeks of married life behind us, we had yet to establish a precise conjugal understanding with regard to the rules of dietary behavior. Let alone anything else.

I had a job in a law firm at the time, and she was doing secretarial work at a design school. I was either twenty-eight or twenty-nine—why can't I remember the exact year we married?—and she was two years and eight months younger. Groceries were the last things on our minds.

We both felt too hungry to go back to sleep, but it hurt just to lie there. On the other hand, we were also too hungry to do anything useful. We got out of bed and drifted into the kitchen, ending up across the table from each other. What could have caused such violent hunger pangs?

We took turns opening the refrigerator door and hoping, but no matter how many times we looked inside, the contents never changed. Beer and onions and butter and dressing and deodorizer. It might have been possible to sauté the onions in the butter, but there was no chance those two shriveled onions could fill our empty stomachs. Onions are meant to be eaten with other things. They're not the kind of food you use to satisfy an appetite.

"Would madame care for French dressing sautéed in deodorizer?"

I expected her to ignore my attempt at humor, and she did. "Let's get in the car and look for an all-night restaurant," I said. "There must be one on the highway."

She rejected that suggestion. "We can't. You're not supposed to go out to eat after midnight." She was old-fashioned that way.

I breathed once and said, "I guess not."

Whenever my wife expressed such an opinion (or thesis) back then, it reverberated in my ears with the authority of a revelation. Maybe that's what happens with newlyweds, I don't know. But when she said this to me, I began to think that this was a special hunger, not one that could be satisfied through the mere expedient of taking it to an all-night restaurant on the highway.

A special kind of hunger. And what might that be? I can present it here in the form of a cinematic image.

One, I am in a little boat, floating on a quiet sea. *Two,* I look down and, in the water, I see the peak of a volcano thrusting up from the ocean floor. *Three,* the peak seems pretty close to the water's surface, but just how close, I cannot tell. *Four,* this is because the hypertransparency of the water interferes with the perception of distance.

This is a fairly accurate description of the image that arose in my mind between the time my wife said she refused to go to an all-night restaurant and I agreed with my "I guess not." Not being Sigmund Freud, I was, of course, unable to analyze with any precision what this image signified, but I knew intuitively that it was a revelation. Which is why—the almost grotesque intensity of my hunger notwithstanding—I all but automatically agreed with her thesis (or declaration).

We did the only thing we could do: opened the beer. It was a lot better than eating those onions. She didn't like beer much, so we divided the cans, two for her, four for me. While I was drinking the first one, she searched the kitchen shelves like a squirrel in November. Eventually, she turned up four butter cookies. They were leftovers, soft and soggy, but we each ate two, savoring every morsel.

It was no use. Upon this hunger of ours, as vast and boundless as the Sinai Peninsula, the butter cookies and beer left not a mark.

Time oozed through the dark like a lead weight in a fish's gut. I read the print on the aluminum beer cans. I stared at my watch. I looked at the refrigerator door. I turned the pages of yesterday's paper. I used the edge of a postcard to scrape together the cookie crumbs on the table top.

"I've never been this hungry in my whole life," she said. "I wonder if it has anything to do with being married."

"Maybe," I said. "Or maybe not."

While she hunted for more fragments of food, I leaned over the edge of my boat and looked down at the peak of the underwater volcano. The clarity of the ocean water all around the boat gave me an unsettled feeling, as if a hollow had opened somewhere behind my solar plexus—a hermetically sealed cavern that had neither entrance nor exit. Something about this weird sense of absence—this sense of the existential reality of nonexistence—resembled the paralyzing fear you might feel when you climb to the top of a steeple. This connection between hunger and acrophobia was a discovery for me.

Which is when it occurred to me that I had once before had this same kind of experience. My stomach had been just as empty then. . . . When? . . . Oh, sure, that was—

"The time of the bakery attack," I heard myself saying.

"The bakery attack? What are you talking about?"

And so it started.

▪ ▪ ▪

"I once attacked a bakery. Long time ago. Not a big bakery. Not famous. The bread was nothing special. Not bad, either. One of those ordinary little neighborhood bakeries right in the middle of a block of shops. Some old guy ran it who did everything himself. Baked in the morning, and when he sold out, he closed up for the day."

"If you were going to attack a bakery, why that one?"

"Well, there was no point in attacking a big bakery. All we wanted was bread, not money. We were attackers, not robbers."

"We? Who's we?"

"My best friend back then. Ten years ago. We were so broke we couldn't buy tooth paste. Never had enough food. We did some pretty awful things to get our hands on food. The bakery attack was one."

"I don't get it." She looked hard at me. Her eyes could have been searching for a faded star in the morning sky. "Why didn't you get a job? You could have worked after school. That would have been easier than attacking bakeries."

"We didn't want to work. We were absolutely clear on that."

"Well, you're working now, aren't you?"

I nodded and sucked some more beer. Then I rubbed my eyes. A kind of beery mud had oozed into my brain and was struggling with my hunger pangs.

"Times change. People change," I said. "Let's go back to bed. We've got to get up early."

"I'm not sleepy. I want you to tell me about the bakery attack."

"There's nothing to tell. No action. No excitement."

"Was it a success?"

I gave up on sleep and ripped open another can of beer. Once she gets interested in a story, she has to hear it all the way through. That's just the way she is.

"Well, it was kind of a success. And kind of not. We got what we wanted. But, as a holdup, it didn't work. The baker gave us the bread before we could take it from him."

"Free?"

"Not exactly, no. That's the hard part." I shook my head. "The baker was a classical-music freak, and when we got there, he was listening to an album of Wagner overtures. So he made us a deal. If we would listen to the record all the way through, we could take as much bread as we liked. I talked it over with my buddy and we figured OK. It wouldn't be work in the purest sense of the word, and it wouldn't hurt anybody. So we put our knives back into our bag, pulled up a couple of chairs and listened to the overtures to *Tannhäuser* and *The Flying Dutchman.*"

"And after that, you got your bread?"

"Right. Most of what he had in the shop. Stuffed it into our bag and took it home. Kept us fed for maybe four or five days." I took another sip. Like soundless waves from an undersea earthquake, my sleepiness gave my boat a long, slow rocking.

"Of course, we accomplished our mission. We got the bread. But you couldn't say we had committed a crime. It was more of an exchange. We listened to Wagner with him and, in return, we got our bread. Legally speaking, it was more like a commercial transaction."

"But listening to Wagner is not work," she said.

"Oh, no, absolutely not. If the baker had insisted that we wash his dishes or clean his windows or something, we would have turned him down. But he didn't. All he wanted from us was to listen to his Wagner LP from beginning to end. Nobody could have anticipated that. I mean—Wagner? It was like the baker put a curse on us. Now that I think of it, we should have refused. We should have threatened him with our knives and taken the damn bread. Then there wouldn't have been any problem."

"You had a problem?"

I rubbed my eyes again.

"Sort of. Nothing you could put your finger on. But things started to change after that. It was kind of a turning point. Like, I went back to the university, and I graduated, and I started working for the firm and studying for the bar exam, and I met you and got married. I never did anything like that again. No more bakery attacks."

"That's it?"

"Yup, that's all there was to it." I drank the last of the beer. Now all six cans were gone. Six pull-tabs lay in the ashtray, like scales from a mermaid.

Of course, it wasn't true that nothing had happened as a result of the bakery attack. There were plenty of things that you could easily have put your finger on, but I didn't want to talk about them with her.

"So, this friend of yours, what's he doing now?"

"I have no idea. Something happened, some nothing kind of thing, and we stopped hanging around together. I haven't seen him since. I don't know what he's doing."

For a while, she didn't speak. She probably sensed that I wasn't telling her the whole story. But she wasn't ready to press me on it.

"Still," she said, "that's why you two broke up, isn't it? The bakery attack was the direct cause."

"Maybe so. I guess it was more intense than either of us realized. We talked about the relationship of bread to Wagner for days after that. We kept asking ourselves if we had made the right choice. We couldn't decide. Of course, if you look at it sensibly, we *did* make the right choice. Nobody got hurt. Everybody got what he wanted. The baker—I still can't figure out why he did what he did—but, anyway, he succeeded with his Wagner propaganda. And we succeeded in stuffing our faces with bread.

"But even so, we had this feeling that we had made a terrible mistake. And somehow, this mistake has just stayed there, unresolved, casting a dark shadow on our lives. That's why I used the word curse. It's true. It was like a curse."

"Do you think you still have it?"

I took the six pull-tabs from the ashtray and arranged them into an aluminum ring the size of a bracelet.

"Who knows? I don't know. I bet the world is full of curses. It's hard to tell which curse makes any one thing go wrong."

"That's not true." She looked right at me. "You can tell, if you think about it. And unless you, yourself, personally break the curse, it'll stick with you like a toothache. It'll torture you till you die. And not just you. Me, too."

"You?"

"Well, I'm your best friend now, aren't I? Why do you think we're both so hungry? I never, ever, once in my life felt a hunger like this until I married you. Don't you think it's abnormal? Your curse is working on me, too."

I nodded. Then I broke up the ring of pull-tabs and put them into the ashtray again. I didn't know if she was right, but I did feel she was on to something.

The feeling of starvation was back, stronger than ever, and it was giving me a deep headache. Every twinge of my stomach was being transmitted to the core of my head by a clutch cable, as if my insides were equipped with all kinds of complicated machinery.

I took another look at my undersea volcano. The water was even clearer than before—much clearer. Unless you looked closely, you might not even notice it was there. It felt as though the boat were floating in mid-air, with absolutely nothing to support it. I could see every little pebble on the bottom. All I had to do was reach out and touch them.

"We've been living together for only two weeks," she said, "but all this time I've been feeling some kind of weird presence." She looked directly into my eyes and brought her hands together on the table top, her fingers interlocking. "Of course, I didn't know it was a curse until now. This explains everything. You're under a curse."

"What kind of presence?"

"Like there's this heavy, dusty curtain that hasn't been washed for years, hanging down from the ceiling."

"Maybe it's not a curse. Maybe it's just me," I said, and smiled.

She did not smile.

"No, it's not you," she said.

"OK, suppose you're right. Suppose it is a curse. What can I do about it?"

"Attack another bakery. Right away. Now. It's the only way."

"Now?"

"Yes. Now. While you're still hungry. You have to finish what you left unfinished."

"But it's the middle of the night. Would a bakery be open now?"

"We'll find one. Tokyo's a big city. There must be at least one all-night bakery."

▪ ▪ ▪

We got into my old Corolla and started drifting around the streets of Tokyo at 2:30 A.M., looking for a bakery. There we were, me clutching the steering wheel, her in the navigator's seat, the two of us scanning the street like hungry eagles in search of prey. Stretched out on the back seat, long and stiff as a dead fish, was a Remington automatic shotgun. Its shells rustled dryly in the pocket of my wife's windbreaker. We had two black ski masks in the glove compartment. Why my wife owned a shotgun, I had no idea. Or ski masks. Neither of us had ever skied. But she didn't explain and I didn't ask. Married life is weird, I felt.

Impeccably equipped, we were nevertheless unable to find an all-night bakery. I drove through the empty streets, from Yoyogi to Shinjuku, on to Yotsuya and Akasaka, Aoyama, Hiroo, Roppongi, Daikanyama and Shibuya. Late-night Tokyo had all kinds of people and shops, but no bakeries.

Twice we encountered patrol cars. One was huddled at the side of the road, trying to look inconspicuous. The other slowly overtook us and crept past, finally moving off into the distance. Both times I grew damp under the arms, but my wife's concentration never faltered. She was looking for that bakery. Every time she shifted the angle of her body, the shotgun shells in her pocket rustled like buckwheat husks in an old-fashioned pillow.

"Let's forget it," I said. "There aren't any bakeries open at this time of night. You've got to plan for this kind of thing, or else—"

"Stop the car!"

I slammed on the brakes.

"This is the place," she said.

The shops along the street had their shutters rolled down, forming dark, silent walls on either side. A barbershop sign hung in the dark like a twisted, chilling glass eye. There was a bright McDonald's hamburger sign some two hundred yards ahead, but nothing else.

"I don't see any bakery," I said.

Without a word, she opened the glove compartment and pulled out a roll of cloth-backed tape. Holding this, she stepped out of the car. I got out my side. Kneeling at the front end, she tore off a length of tape and covered the numbers on the license plate. Then she went around to the back and did the same. There was a practiced efficiency to her movements. I stood on the curb staring at her.

"We're going to take that McDonald's," she said, as coolly as if she were announcing what we would have for dinner.

"McDonald's is not a bakery," I pointed out to her.

"It's *like* a bakery," she said. "Sometimes you have to compromise. Let's go."

I drove to McDonald's and parked in the lot. She handed me the blanket-wrapped shotgun.

"I've never fired a gun in my life," I protested.

"You don't have to fire it. Just hold it. OK? Do as I say. We walk right in and as soon as they say 'Welcome to McDonald's,' we slip on our masks. Got that?"

"Sure, but—"

"Then you shove the gun in their faces and make all the workers and customers get together. Fast. I'll do the rest."

"But—"

"How many hamburgers do you think we'll need? Thirty?"

"I guess so." With a sigh, I took the shotgun and rolled back the blanket a little. The thing was as heavy as a sandbag and as black as a dark night.

"Do we really have to do this?" I asked, half to her and half to myself.

"Of course we do."

Wearing a McDonald's hat, the girl behind the counter flashed me a McDonald's smile and said, "Welcome to McDonald's." I hadn't thought that girls would work at McDonald's late at night, so the sight of her confused me for a second. But only for a second. I caught myself and pulled on the mask. Confronted with this suddenly masked duo, the girl gaped at us.

Obviously, the McDonald's hospitality manual said nothing about how to deal with a situation like this. She had been starting to form the phrase that comes after "Welcome to McDonald's," but her mouth seemed to stiffen and the words wouldn't come out. Even so, like a crescent moon in the dawn sky, the hint of a professional smile lingered at the edges of her lips.

As quickly as I could manage, I unwrapped the shotgun and aimed it in the direction of the tables, but the only customers there were a young couple—students, probably—face down on the plastic table, sound asleep. Their two heads and two strawberry-milk-shake cups were aligned on the table like an avant-garde sculpture. They slept the sleep of the dead. They didn't look likely to obstruct our operation, so I swung my shotgun back toward the counter.

All together, there were three McDonald's workers: the girl at the counter, the manager—a guy with a pale, egg-shaped face, probably in his late twenties—and a student type in the kitchen, a thin shadow of a guy with nothing on his face that you could read as an expression. They stood together behind the register, staring into the muzzle of my shotgun like tourists peering down an Incan well. No one screamed and no one made a threatening move. The gun was so heavy I had to rest the barrel on top of the cash register, my finger on the trigger.

"I'll give you the money," said the manager, his voice hoarse. "They collected it at eleven, so we don't have too much, but you can have everything. We're insured."

"Lower the front shutter and turn off the sign," said my wife.

"Wait a minute," said the manager. "I can't do that. I'll be held responsible if I close up without permission."

My wife repeated her order, slowly. He seemed torn.

"You'd better do what she says," I warned him.

He looked at the muzzle of the gun atop the register, then at my wife and then back at the gun. He finally resigned himself to the inevitable. He turned off the sign and hit a switch on an electrical panel that lowered the shutter. I kept my eye on him, worried that he might hit a burglar alarm, but, apparently, McDonald's restaurants don't have burglar alarms. Maybe it had never occurred to anybody to attack one.

The front shutter made a huge racket when it closed, like an empty bucket being smashed with a baseball bat, but the couple sleeping at the table was still out cold. Talk about a sound sleep: I hadn't seen anything like that in years.

"Thirty Big Macs. For takeout," said my wife.

"Let me just give you the money," pleaded the manager. "I'll give you more than you need. You can go buy food somewhere else. This is going to mess up my accounts and—"

"You'd better do what she says," I said again.

The three of them went into the kitchen area together and started making thirty Big Macs. The student grilled the burgers, the manager put them in buns and the girl wrapped them up. Nobody said a word.

I leaned against a big refrigerator, aiming the gun toward the griddle. The meat patties were lined up on the griddle, like brown polka dots, sizzling. The sweet smell of grilling meat burrowed into every pore of my body like a swarm of microscopic bugs, dissolving into my blood and circulating to the farthest corners, then massing together inside my hermetically sealed hunger cavern, clinging to its pink walls.

A pile of white-wrapped burgers was growing nearby. I wanted to grab one and tear into it, but I couldn't be sure that such an act would be consistent with our objective. I had to wait. In the hot kitchen area, I started sweating under my ski mask.

The McDonald's people sneaked glances at the muzzle of the shotgun. I scratched my ears with the little finger of my left hand. My ears always get itchy when I'm nervous. Jabbing my finger into an ear through the wool, I was making the gun barrel wobble up and down, which seemed to bother them. It couldn't have gone off accidentally because I had the safety on, but they didn't know that and I wasn't about to tell them.

My wife counted the finished hamburgers and put them into two small shopping bags, fifteen burgers to a bag.

"Why do you have to do this?" the girl asked me. "Why don't you just take the money and buy something you like? What's the good of eating thirty Big Macs?"

I shook my head.

My wife explained, "We're sorry, really. But there weren't any bakeries open. If there had been, we would have attacked a bakery."

That seemed to satisfy them. At least they didn't ask any more questions. Then my wife ordered two large Cokes from the girl and paid for them.

"We're stealing bread, nothing else," she said. The girl responded with a complicated head movement, sort of like nodding and sort of like shaking. She was probably trying to do both at the same time. I thought I had some idea how she felt.

My wife then pulled a ball of twine from her pocket—she came equipped—and tied the three to a post as expertly as if she were sewing on buttons. She asked if the cord hurt, or if anyone wanted to go to the toilet, but no one said a word. I wrapped the gun in the blanket, she picked up the shopping bags and out we went. The customers at the table were still asleep, like a couple of deep-sea fish. What would it have taken to rouse them from a sleep so deep?

We drove for half an hour, found an empty parking lot by a building and pulled in. There we ate hamburgers and drank our Cokes. I sent six Big Macs down to the cavern of my stomach, and she ate four. That left twenty Big Macs in the back seat. Our hunger—that hunger that had felt as if it could go on forever—vanished as the dawn was breaking. The first light of the sun dyed the building's filthy walls purple and made a gigantic SONY BETA ad tower glow with painful intensity. Soon the whine of highway-truck tires was joined by the chirping of birds. The American Armed Forces radio was playing cowboy music. We shared a cigarette. Afterward, she rested her head on my shoulder.

"Still, was it really necessary for us to do this?" I asked.

"Of course it was!" With one deep sigh, she fell asleep against me. She felt as soft and as light as a kitten.

Alone now, I leaned over the edge of my boat and looked down to the bottom of the sea. The volcano was gone. The water's calm surface reflected the blue of the sky. Little waves—like silk pajamas fluttering in a breeze—lapped against the side of the boat. There was nothing else.

I stretched out in the bottom of the boat and closed my eyes, waiting for the rising tide to carry me where I belonged.

—Translated from the Japanese by Jay Rubin

Jay McInerney

How It Ended

November 1993

Jay McInerney's *Bright Lights, Big City* (1984) was the most sensational debut novel of the 1980s, offering the hip and the wanna-bes a funny and devastatingly accurate look at the drugged-out urban club scene and a backstage glimpse of a magazine commonly believed to be *The New Yorker*. His second novel, *Ransom* (1985), was set in Japan, but it seemed clear by the end of the decade that McInerney's great strength lay in his ability to get under the skin of the yuppie generation, the people his own age (he was born in 1955) who put on neckties or pantyhose to go to work, but whose private lives can be surprisingly disorderly. Currently, he appears to be the only American writer mining this rich vein. His 1992 novel *Brightness Falls* is about these people, as is the present story.

Jay McInerney

How It Ended

I like to ask married couples how they met. It's always interesting to hear how two lives became intertwined, how of the nearly infinite number of possible conjunctions this one or that one came into being, to hear the beginning of a story in progress. As a matrimonial lawyer I deal extensively in endings and it's a relief, a sort of holiday, to visit the realm of beginnings. And I ask because I have always liked to tell my own story—our story, I should say—which I'd always felt was unique.

My name is Donald Prout, which rhymes with trout. My wife Cameron and I were in the Caribbean on vacation when we met Johnny and Jean Van Heusen. We were staying at a tiny, expensive resort in the Virgin Islands and we would see them in the dining room and later on the beach. Etiquette dictated respect for privacy but there was a countervailing, quiet camaraderie born of the feeling that one's fellow guests shared a level of good taste and financial standing. And they stood out as the only other young couple.

I'd just triumphed in a difficult case, sticking it to a rich husband, and coming out with a nice settlement despite considerable evidence that my client had been cheating on him with everything in pants for years. Of course I sympathized with the guy, but he had his own counsel, he still had inherited millions left over, and it's my job to give my client the best counsel possible. Now I was enjoying what I thought of as, for lack of a better cliché, a well-earned rest. I hadn't done much resting in twelve years, going from public high school to Amherst—where

I'd worked part-time for my tuition—to Columbia Law to a big midtown firm, where I'd knocked myself out as an associate for six years.

It is a sad fact that the ability to savor long hours of leisure is a gift which some of us have lost, or never acquired. Within an hour of waking in paradise the first morning I was restless, watching stalk-eyed land crabs skitter sideways across the sand, unwilling or unable to concentrate on the Updike I'd started on the plane. Lying on the beach in front of our cabana, I noticed the attractive young couple emerging from the water, splashing each other. She was a tall and elegant brunette. Sandy haired and lanky, he looked like a prep school boy who'd taken a semester off to go sailing. Over the next few days I couldn't help seeing them frequently. They were very affectionate, which seemed to indicate a relatively new marriage (both wore wedding bands). And they had an aura of entitlement, of being very much at home and at ease on this very pricey patch of white sand and turquoise water, so that I assumed they came from money. Also they seemed gloriously indifferent, unlike those couples who, after a few days of sun and sand and the company of the loved one begin to invite their neighbors for a daiquiri on the balcony to grope for mutual acquaintances and interests, anything to be spared the frightening monotony of each other, without distraction or relief.

The example of the Van Heusens was invigorating. Seeing them together rejuvenated the concept of matrimony for me. After all, I reasoned, we were also an attractive young couple. I thought more of us for our ostensible resemblance to them and when I overheard him tell an old gent that he'd recently graduated from law school and passed the bar I felt a rush of kinship and self-esteem, since I'd recently made partner at one of the most distinguished firms in New York.

On the evening of our fifth day we struck up a conversation at the poolside bar. I heard them speculating about a yacht out in the bay and I told them who it belonged to, having been told myself when I'd seen it in Tortolla a few days earlier. I almost expected him to recognize the name, to claim friendship with the yacht owners, but he only said, "Oh really? Nice boat."

The sun was melting into the ocean, dyeing the water red and pink and gold. We all sat, hushed, watching the spectacle. I reluctantly broke the silence to remind the waiter that I had specified a piña colada on the rocks, not frozen, my teeth being sensitive to the crushed ice. Within minutes the sun had slipped out of sight, sending up a last flare, and then we began to chat. Eventually they told us that they lived in one of those eminently respectable communities on the North Shore of Boston.

They asked if we had kids and we said no, not yet. When I said, "You?" Jean blushed and referred the question to her husband.

After a silent exchange he turned to us and said, "Jeannie's pregnant."

"We haven't really told anyone, yet," she added.

Cameron beamed at Jean and smiled encouragingly in my direction. We had been discussing this very topic, lately. I was ready; for some reason she didn't feel quite so certain. But I think we were both pleased to be the recipients of this confidence, though it was a function of our very lack of real intimacy, and of the place and time, for we learned, somewhat sadly, that this was their last night.

When I mentioned my profession, Johnny solicited my advice about firms; he was about to start job hunting when they returned. I was curious, of course, how he had come to the law so relatively late and what he had done with his twenties, but I thought it would be indiscreet to ask.

We ordered a second round of drinks and talked until it was dark. "Why don't you join us for dinner," he proposed, as we all stood on the veranda, reluctant to end the moment. And so we did. I was grateful for the company and Cameron seemed to be enlivened by the break in routine. I found Jean increasingly attractive—confident and funny—while her husband was wry and self-deprecating in a manner which suited a young man who was probably a little too rich and happy for anyone else's good. He seemed like someone who was consciously keeping his lights on dim.

As the dinner plates were cleared away, I said, "So tell me, how did you two meet?"

Cameron laughed; it was my favorite parlor game. Telling the story of meeting and courting Cameron gave me a romantic charge which I had ceased to feel in the actual day to day conduct of our marriage.

Johnny and Jean exchanged a meaningful look, seeming to consult about whether to reveal a great secret. He laughed through his nose and then she began to laugh; within moments they were both in a state of high hilarity. Of course, we'd had several Planter's Punches and two bottles of wine with dinner and none of us except for Jean was legally sober. Cameron in particular seemed to me to be getting a little sloppy, particularly so in contrast to abstinent Jean, and when she reached again for the wine bottle I tried to catch her eye but she was bestowing her bright, blurred attention on the other couple. Finally Johnny Van Heusen said to his wife, "How we met. God. You want to tackle this one?"

She shook her head. "You try, babe."

"Do you smoke a cigar, Don?" He produced two metal tubes from his pocket. Though I am not a big fan of cigars, I occasionally smoke one with a client or a partner and I took one now. He handed me a cutter and lit us up, then leaned back and stroked his sandy bangs away from his eyes and released a spume of smoke.

"Maybe it's not such an unusual story," he proposed. Jean laughed skeptically.

"You sure you don't mind, honey?" he asked her.

She considered, shrugged her shoulders, then shook her head. "It's up to you."

"Well, I think this story begins when I got thrown out of Bowdoin," he said. "Not to put too fine a point on it, I was dealing pot. Well, pot and a little coke, actually." He stopped to check our reaction.

I, for one, tried to keep an open, inviting demeanor, eager to encourage him. I wouldn't say I was shocked—not yet—but I was certainly surprised.

"I got caught," he continued. "By agreeing to pack my old kit bag and go away forever I escaped prosecution. My parents weren't too pleased about the whole thing, but unfortunately for them, virtually that week I'd come into a little bit of Gramps' filthy lucre and there wasn't much they could do about it. I was tired of school anyway—it's funny, I enjoyed it when I finally went back a few years ago to get my B.A. and then do law school but at the time it was wasted on me. Or I was wasted on it. Wasted in general. I'd wake up in the morning and fire up the old bong and then huff up a few lines to get through geology seminar."

He inhaled on his stogie and shook his head ruefully at the memory of this youthful excess. He did not seem particularly ashamed, but rather bemused, as if he were describing the behavior of an incorrigible cousin.

"Well, I went sailing for about a year—spent some time in these waters, actually, these are some of the best sailing waters in the world—and then I drifted back to Boston. I'd run through most of my capital and I didn't feel ready to hit the books again and somehow I just kind of naturally got back in touch with the people who had been supplying me when I was dealing at Bowdoin. I still had a boat, a little thirty-six footer. And I got back in the trade. It was different then—this was more than ten years ago, before the Colombians really moved in and took over stateside distribution. Everything was more relaxed. We were gentleman outlaws, adrenaline junkies, sail bums, freaks with an entrepreneurial jones."

He frowned slightly, as if hearing the faint note of self-justification, of self-delusion, of sheer datedness. I'd largely avoided the drug culture of the seventies, but even I could remember when drugs were viewed as the sacraments of a vague, joyous liberation theology or later, as a slightly risky form of recreation. But in this era the romance of drug dealing was a hard sell, and Johnny seemed to realize it.

"Well, that's how we saw it then," he amended. "Let's just say that we were less ruthless and less financially motivated than the people who eventually took over the business."

Wanting to discourage his sudden attack of scruples, I waved to the waiter for another bottle of wine.

"Anyway, I did quite well. Initially I was very hands on, rendezvousing with mother ships out in the water beyond Nantucket, bringing in small loads in a hollow keel. Eventually my partner Derek and I moved up the food chain. We were making money so fast we had a hard time thinking of ways to make it legit. I mean, you can't just keep hiding it under your mattress. First we were buying cars and boats in cash and then we bought a bar in Cambridge to run some of our earnings through. We were actually paying taxes on drug money just so we could have some legitimate income. We always used to say we'd get out before it got too crazy, once we'd really put aside a big stash, but there was so much more cash to be made, and craziness is like anything else, you get into it one step at a time and no single step really feels like it's taking you over the cliff. Until you go right over the edge and down and then it's too late. You're smoking reefer in high school and then you're doing lines and then you're selling a little and then you're buying an AK 47 and then you're bringing a hundred kilos into Boston harbor."

I wasn't about to interrupt to question this logic, say that some of us never even thought of dealing drugs, let alone buying firearms. I filled his wineglass, nicely concealing my skepticism, secretly pleased to hear this golden boy revealing his baser metal. But I have to say I was intrigued.

"This goes on for two, three years. I wish I could say it wasn't fun but it was. The danger, the secrecy, the money. . . ." He puffed on his cigar and looked out over the water. "So anyway we set up one of the bigger deals of our lives, and our buyer's been turned. He's facing fifteen to life on his own so he delivers us up on a platter. A very exciting moment. We're in a warehouse in the Back Bay and suddenly there are twenty narcs pointing thirty-eights on us."

"And one of them was Jean," Cameron proposed.

I shot her a look but she didn't turn to catch it.

"For the sake of our new friends here I wish I had been," Jean said. She looked at her husband and touched his wrist and at that moment I found her extraordinarily attractive. "I think you're boring these nice people."

"Not at all," I protested, directing my reassurance at the storyteller's wife. I was genuinely sorry for her sake that she was a part of this sordid tale. She turned and smiled at me, as I'd hoped she would, and for a moment I forgot about the story altogether as I conjured up a sudden vision of the future—slipping from the cabana for a walk that night, unable to sleep . . . and encountering her out at the edge of the long beach, talking, claiming insomnia, then confessing that we had been thinking of each other, a long kiss and a slow recline to the soft sand.

"You must think . . ." She smiled helplessly. "I don't know what you must think. John's never really told anyone about all of this before. You're probably shocked."

"Please, go on," said Cameron. "We're dying to hear the rest. Aren't we, Don?"

I nodded, a little annoyed at this aggressive use of the marital pronoun. Her voice seemed loud and grating and she was wearing a gaudy print top which I hated, which seemed all the gaudier beside Jeannie's elegant but sexy navy halter.

Johnny said, "Long story short—I hire Carson Baxter to defend me. And piece by piece he gets virtually every shred of evidence thrown out. Makes it disappear right before the jury's very eyes. Then he sneers at the rest. I mean, the man is the greatest performer I've ever seen . . ."

"He's brilliant," I murmured. Carson Baxter was one of the finest defense attorneys in the country. Although I did not always share his political views—he specialized in left-wing causes—I admired his adherence to his principles and his legal scholarship. He was actually a hero of mine. I don't know why, but I was surprised to hear his name in this context.

"So I walked," Johnny concluded.

"You were acquitted?" I asked.

"Absolutely." He puffed contentedly on his cigar. "Of course, you would think that would be the end of the story and the end of my illicit but highly profitable career. Unfortunately not. Of course, I told myself and everyone else I'd go straight. But after six months the memory of prison and the bust had faded and a golden opportunity practically fell into my lap, a chance for one last big score. The retirement run. That's the one you should never make—the last one. Always a mistake. Remember, never do a farewell gig. Always stop one run before the final one." He laughed.

"That waiter is asleep on his feet," Jean said soberly. "Like the waiter in that Hemingway story. He's silently poxing you, Johnny Van Heusen, with a special voodoo curse for long-winded white boys, because he wants to reset the table and go back to the cute little turquoise-and-pink staff quarters and make love to his wife the chubby laundress who is waiting for him all naked on her fresh white linen."

"I wonder how the waiter and the laundress met," said Johnny cheerfully, standing up and stretching. "That's probably the best story."

Cameron, my beloved wife, said, "Probably they met when the waiter comforted her after Don yelled at her about a stain on his linen shirt."

Johnny looked at his watch. "My goodness, ten thirty already, way past official Virgin Islands bedtime."

"But you can't go to bed yet," Cameron said. "You haven't even met your wife."

"Oh, right. So anyway, later I met Jean and we fell in love and got married and lived happily ever after."

"No fair," Cameron shrieked.

"I'd be curious to hear your observations about Baxter," I said quietly.

"The hell with Carson Baxter," Cameron said. When she was drinking her voice took on a more pronounced nasal quality as it rose in volume. "I want to hear the love story."

"Let's at least take a walk on the beach," Jean suggested, standing up.

So we rolled out to the beach and dawdled along the water's edge as Johnny resumed the tale.

"Well, Derek and I went down to the Keys and picked up a boat, a Hatteras 62 with a false bottom. Had a kid in the Coast Guard on our payroll and another in Customs and they were going to talk us through the coastal net on our return. For show we load up the boat with a lot of big game fishing gear, big Nakamichi rods and reels. And we stow the real payload—the automatic weapons with night scopes and the cash. The guns were part of the deal, thirty of them, enough for a small army. The Colombians were always looking for armament and we picked these up cheap from an Israeli in Miami who had to leave town quick. It was a night like this, a warm winter starry Caribbean night, when the rudder broke about a hundred miles off Cuba. We started to drift and by morning we were picked up by a Cuban naval vessel. Well, you can imagine how they reacted when they found the guns and the cash. I mean, think about it, an American boat loaded with guns and cash and high-grade electronics. We tried to explain that we were just drug dealers, but they weren't buying it."

We had come to the edge of the sandy beach; further on, a rocky ledge rose up from the gently lapping water of the cove. Johnny knelt down and scooped up a handful of fine silvery sand. Cameron sat down beside him. I remained standing, looking up at the powdery spray of stars above us, feeling in my intoxicated state that I exercised some important measure of autonomy by refusing to sit just because Johnny was sitting. By this time I simply did not approve of him and I did not quite approve of the fact that this self-confessed drug runner had just passed the bar and was about to enter the practice of law. And I suppose I did not approve of his happiness, of the fact that he was obviously rich and had a beautiful and charming wife.

"That was the worst time of my life," he said softly, the jauntiness receding. Jean, who had been standing beside him, knelt down and put a hand on his shoulder. Suddenly he smiled and patted her arm. "But hey—at least I learned Spanish, right?"

Cameron chuckled appreciatively at this.

"After six months in a Cuban prison me and Derek and the captain were sentenced to death as American spies. I hadn't even seen either of them the whole time, they kept us apart hoping to break us. And they would have broken us, except that we couldn't tell them what they wanted to hear because we were just a couple of dumb drug runners and not CIA. Jesus, God," he muttered.

I sat down on the sand, finally, drawing my knees up against my chest, watching Jean's sympathetic face as if the sordid ordeal of the husband would be more real, reflected there. I didn't feel sorry for him—he'd gotten himself into this mess. But I could see she knew at least some of the story that he was eliding for us and that it pained her and I felt sorry for her.

"Anyway, we were treated better than some of the Cuban dissidents because they always had to consider the possibility of using us for barter or propaganda. A few weeks before we're supposed to be shot, I manage to get a message to Baxter who uses his left-wing contacts to fly down to Cuba and get an audience with fucking Castro. This is when it's illegal to even go to Cuba. And Baxter has his files with him, and—here's the beauty of it—he uses the same evidence which he discredited in Boston to convince Castro and his defense ministry that we are honest-to-God drug dealers as opposed to dirty Yankee spies. And they finally release us into Baxter's custody. Well, we fly back to Miami and . . ." He paused, looked around at his audience. ". . . the Feds are waiting for us on the tarmac. A welcoming committee of sweating G-men in cheap suits. They arrest all of us for coming from Cuba. But of course the feds are aware of our story—they've been monitoring this for the better part of a year. Out of the fucking frittata pan . . ."

"The sarten, actually," Jean corrected impishly.

"Yeah, yeah." He stuck his tongue out at her and resumed. "I mean, I thought I was going to lose it right there on the runway, after almost seven months in a cell without a window, thinking I was free and then—"

Cameron blurted, "God, you must have been . . . I mean—"

"I was. So now the federal boys contact Havana and ask for the evidence which led to our acquittal as spies so that they can use it for a smuggling rap."

I heard the sounds of a thousand insects and the lapping of water on the beach a few feet away as he paused and smiled.

"And the Cubans say, basically—Fuck You, Yankee pigs. And we all walk. And lord, it was sweet."

To my amazement, Cameron began to applaud. I realized that she was drunk.

"We still haven't heard about Jean," I noted, wanting to challenge him in some way. As if I suspected, and was about to prove, Your Honor, that they had in fact never actually met at all.

Jean shared with her husband a conspiratorial smile which deflated and saddened me, reminding me that they were indeed together. Turning to me, she said, "My name is Jean Carson Baxter."

I'm not a complete idiot. "Baxter's daughter?" I asked.

She nodded.

Cameron broke out laughing. "That's great," she said. "I love it."

"How did your father feel about it?" I said, sending a weak point.

Jeannie's smile disappeared. She picked up a handful of sand and threw it out over the water. "Not too good. Apparently it's one thing to defend a drug dealer, prove his innocence and take his money. But it's quite another thing when he falls in love with your precious daughter."

"Jeannie used to come to my trial to watch her father perform. And that, to answer your question finally, is how we met. In court. Exchanging steamy looks, then steamy notes, across a stuffy courtroom." Pulling Jean close against his shoulder he said, "God, you looked good."

"Right," she said. "Anything without a Y chromosome would have looked good to you after three months in custody."

"We started seeing each other secretly, after I was acquitted. Carson didn't know when he flew to Cuba. He didn't have any idea until we walked out of the courthouse in Miami and Jean threw her arms around me, and except for a few scream-and-threat fests, he hasn't really spoken to us since that day." He paused. "He did send me a bill, though."

Jean said, "The really funny thing is that Johnny was so impressed with my dad that he decided to go to law school."

Cameron laughed. At least one of us found this funny. My response was much more complicated and in fact it took me a long time to sort it out.

"What a great story," Cameron said.

I wanted to slap her, tell her to shut the hell up.

"So what about you guys?" said Jean, sitting on the moonlit sand with her arm around her husband. "What's your wildly romantic story? Tell us about how you two met."

Cameron turned to me eagerly, smiling with anticipation. "Tell them, Don."

I stared out into the bay at a light on the yacht we'd all admired earlier and I thought about the boy who'd been polishing brass on deck when we'd walked up the deck on Tortolla, a shirtless teenager with limp white hair and a tiny gold ring through his nostril who'd told us the name of his employer, the owner, before he turned back to his task, bobbing his head and humming, looking forward, I imagined, to a night on the town.

I turned back to my wife, sitting beside me on the cold sand.

"You tell them," I said.

Plume Dutton

THE FINEST IN SHORT FICTION

(0452)

☐ **HAUNTED *Tales of the Grotesque.* by Joyce Carol Oates.** This collection of sixteen tales—ranging from classic ghost stories to portrayals of chilling psychological terror—raises the genre to the level of fine literature. It is complex, multilayered, and gripping fiction that is very scary indeed. (273749—$10.95)

☐ **PLAYBOY STORIES *The Best of Forty Years of Short Fiction.* Edited by Alice K. Turner.** The very best short story from each of *Playboy*'s forty years—with a special bonus from 1971, when tales by Nobel Prize winner Gabriel Garcia Marquez and Vladimir Nobokov demanded to be included—are gathered in this superlative anthology. The result is an enthralling array and rich variety of literary genius, by such names as Joyce Carol Oates, Nadine Gordimer, Isaac Bashevis Singer, James Jones and many more. (271177—$13.95)

☐ **BODIES OF WATER by Michelle Cliff.** These short stories tell of oppression and liberation, prejudice and compassion, and are colored by the vivid imagery and emotive, spare language of this remarkable author. Many of the characters and incidents within these stories are linked, connecting images of water and travel, yet catalogs a separate incident from the layered geography and history of America. "Passions seethe below the surface . . . lean, controlled, full of meticulous images."—*San Diego Tribune* (273757—$9.95)

☐ **THE COLLECTED STORIES by Reynolds Price.** Marked by grace and intensity, and often filled with autobiographical detail, the author's exquisitely crafted stories impart a deep understanding of the joy, agony, and, above all, the goodness of life. "Eminently worth reading."—*San Francisco Chronicle* (272181—$12.95)

Prices slightly higher in Canada.

Visa and Mastercard holders can order Plume, Meridian, and Dutton books by calling **1-800-253-6476**.

They are also available at your local bookstore. Allow 4-6 weeks for delivery.
This offer is subject to change without notice.

PL34W

Dutton ⓟ Plume

ON THE LITERARY SCENE

☐ **CONCEIVED WITH MALICE** ***Literature as Revenge in the Lives and Works of Virginia and Leonard Woolf, D.H. Lawrence, Djuna Barnes, and Henry Miller.*** **by Louise De Salvo.** Full of enticing literary gossip, the author vividly describes how these great literary figures each perceived an attack on the self—and struck back through their art, creating lasting monuments to their deepest hurts and darkest obsessions. (938990—$24.95)

☐ **THE SEED AND THE VISION** ***On the Writing and Appreciation of Children's Books.*** **by Eleanor Cameron.** The National Book Award-winning author is back with another superb collection of essays about the transforming power of children's fiction and the sources of its inspiration. Involving, provocative, and informative, it illuminates the maturity and complexity of what we call "children's literature." (271835—$14.95)

☐ **THE READING GROUP BOOK** ***The Complete Guide to Starting and Sustaining A Reading Group, with Annotated Lists of 250 Titles for Provocative Discussion.*** **by David Laskin and Holly Hughes.** This lively, down-to-earth book is a complete guide to reading groups—from getting one going to sparkling lively discussions to revitalizing a long-established group. This one-stop handbook covers the history of reading groups, how to attract those who love good books and good conversation, even what food to serve. (272017—$9.95)

Prices slightly higher in Canada.

Visa and Mastercard holders can order Plume, Meridian, and Dutton books by calling **1-800-253-6476**.

They are also available at your local bookstore. Allow 4-6 weeks for delivery. This offer is subject to change without notice.

PL228

PLUME

SENSATIONAL SHORT STORY COLLECTIONS

☐ **BLESS ME, FATHER *Stories of Catholic Childhood.* Edited by Amber Coverdale Sumrall and Patrice Vecchione.** The 54 stories, poems, and memoirs in this marvelous collection take a nostalgic, sometimes skeptical look at Catholic childhood and the lifelong struggles posed by faith. A wide range of feelings about being Catholic is expressed by a host of literary figures such as Michael Dorris, Mary Daly, Gary Soto, Lucille Clifton, as well as dozens of others. (271541—$11.95)

☐ **CATHOLIC GIRLS edited by Amber Coverdale Sumrall and Patrice Vecchione.** The Catholic experience is explored with humor, sensitivity, and passion in this remarkable collection of stories, poems, and memoirs. (268427—$11.00)

☐ **THE LONELINESS OF THE LONG-DISTANCE RUNNER by Alan Sillitoe.** The classic collection of short fiction from "one of the best English writers of our day."—*The New York Times* (269083—$8.95)

☐ **BILLIE DYER AND OTHER STORIES by William Maxwell.** Through seven wonderfully moving stories, William Maxwell revisits his native town of Lincoln, Illinois, in the early 1900s and considers some of its inhabitants who have remained haunting figures to him. "A wonderfully persuasive fictional world . . . surveyed gravely and wisely, with sympathy, humor, and compassion." —Wallace Stegner, *Washington Post Book World* (269504—$8.00)

Prices slightly higher in Canada.

Visa and Mastercard holders can order Plume, Meridian, and Dutton books by calling **1-800-253-6476**.

They are also available at your local bookstore. Allow 4-6 weeks for delivery.
This offer is subject to change without notice.

PL217

Plume **Meridian** (0452)

UNIQUE COLLECTIONS

☐ **NEW AMERICAN SHORT STORIES** ***The Writers Select Their Own Favorites*** **edited by Gloria Norris.** This unique anthology brings together twenty of today's most distinguished practitioners of the short story, including Alice Adams, T. Coraghessan Boyle, John Updike and many others—each of whom has selected a favorite from his or her recent work. It is a rich panorama of the best in contemporary fiction. (258790—$9.95)

☐ **THE MERIDIAN ANTHOLOGY OF RESTORATION AND EIGHTEENTH-CENTURY PLAYS BY WOMEN. Edited by Katharine M. Rogers.** The women represented in this groundbreaking anthology—the only collection of Restoration and eighteenth-century plays devoted exclusively to women—had but one thing in common: the desire to ignore convention and write for the stage. These women legitimized the profession for their sex. (011108—$14.95)

☐ **THE MERIDIAN ANTHOLOGY OF EARLY AMERICAN WOMEN WRITERS** ***From Anne Bradstreet to Louisa May Alcott, 1650–1865*** **edited by Katherine M. Rogers.** Encompassing a wide spectrum of experience and expression, this outstanding collection celebrates the rich heritage of literary creativity among early American women. (010756—$15.00)

☐ **THE MERIDIAN ANTHOLOGY OF EARLY WOMEN WRITERS** ***British Literary Women From Aphra Behn to Maria Edgeworth 1660–1800*** **edited by Katharine M. Rogers and William McCarthy.** Here are nineteen stunning pre-nineteenth-century female literary talents never before collected in a single volume. Their stories bring to light the rich heritage of early literary creativity among women. (008484—$14.95)

Prices slightly higher in Canada.

Visa and Mastercard holders can order Plume, Meridian, and Dutton books by calling **1-800-253-6476**.

They are also available at your local bookstore. Allow 4-6 weeks for delivery. This offer is subject to change without notice.

PL 131